TRIPLE CROWN

DICK FRANCIS

B
BERKLEY BOOKS, NEW YORK

THE BERKLEY PUBLISHING GROUP
Published by the Penguin Group
Penguin Group (USA) Inc.
375 Hudson Street, New York, New York 10014, USA
Penguin Group (Canada), 90 Eglinton Avenue East, Suite 700, Toronto, Ontario M4P 2Y3, Canada
(a division of Pearson Penguin Canada Inc.)
Penguin Books Ltd., 80 Strand, London WC2R 0RL, England
Penguin Group Ireland, 25 St. Stephen's Green, Dublin 2, Ireland (a division of Penguin Books Ltd.)
Penguin Group (Australia), 250 Camberwell Road, Camberwell, Victoria 3124, Australia
(a division of Pearson Australia Group Pty. Ltd.)
Penguin Books India Pvt. Ltd., 11 Community Centre, Panchsheel Park, New Delhi—110 017, India
Penguin Group (NZ), Cnr. Airborne and Rosedale Roads, Albany, Auckland 1310, New Zealand
(a division of Pearson New Zealand Ltd.)
Penguin Books (South Africa) (Pty.) Ltd., 24 Sturdee Avenue, Rosebank, Johannesburg 2196, South Africa

Penguin Books Ltd., Registered Offices: 80 Strand, London WC2R 0RL, England

The book is an original publication of The Berkley Publishing Group.
Published by arrangement with HarperCollins Publishers, Inc.

This is a work of fiction. Names, characters, places, and incidents either are the product of the author's imagination or are used fictitiously, and any resemblance to actual persons, living or dead, business establishments, events, or locales is entirely coincidental.

PRINTING HISTORY
Berkley trade paperback edition / September 2005

Library of Congress Cataloging-in-Publication Data

Francis, Dick.
    Triple crown / Dick Francis.—Berkley trade pbk. ed.
        p. cm.
    Contents: Dead cert—Nerve—For kicks.
    ISBN 0-425-20670-X
    1. Detective and mystery stories, English. 2. Horse racing—Fiction. I. Title.

PR6056.R27A6 2005
823'.914—dc22   2005045339

PRINTED IN THE UNITED STATES OF AMERICA

10 9 8 7 6 5 4 3 2 1

CONTENTS

DEAD CERT

CHAPTER 1

THE MINGLED SMELLS of hot horse and cold river mist filled my nostrils. I could hear only the swish and thud of galloping hooves and the occasional sharp click of horseshoes striking against each other. Behind me, strung out, rode a group of men dressed like myself in white silk breeches and harlequin jerseys, and in front, his body vividly red and green against the pale curtain of fog, one solitary rider steadied his horse to jump the birch fence stretching blackly across his path.

All, in fact, was going as expected. Bill Davidson was about to win his ninety-seventh steeplechase. Admiral, his chestnut horse, was amply proving he was still the best hunter 'chaser in the kingdom, and I, as often before, had been admiring their combined back view of several minutes.

Ahead of me the powerful chestnut hindquarters bunched, tensed, sprang: Admiral cleared the fence with the effortlessness of the really great performer. And he'd gained another two lengths, I saw, as I followed him over. We were down at the far end of Maidenhead racecourse with more than half a mile to go to the winning post. I hadn't a hope of catching him.

The February fog was getting denser. It was now impossible to see much farther than from one fence to the next, and the silent surrounding whiteness seemed to shut us, an isolated string of riders, into a private lonely limbo. Speed was the only reality. Winning post, crowds, stands and stewards, left behind in the mist, lay again invisibly ahead, but on the long deserted mile and a half circuit it was quite difficult to believe they were really there.

It was an eerie, severed world in which anything might happen. And something did.

We rounded the first part of the bend at the bottom of the racecourse and straightened to jump the next fence. Bill was a good ten lengths in front of me and the other horses, and hadn't exerted himself. He seldom needed to.

The attendant at the next fence strolled across the course from the outside to the inside, patting the top of the birch as he went, and ducked under the rails. Bill glanced back over his shoulder and I saw the flash of his teeth as he smiled with satisfaction to see me so far behind. Then he turned his head towards the fence and measured his distance.

Admiral met the fence perfectly. He rose to it as if flight were not only for birds.

And he fell.

Aghast, I saw the flurry of chestnut legs threshing the air as the horse pitched over in a somersault. I had a glimpse of Bill's bright-clad figure hurtling head downwards from the highest point of his trajectory, and I heard the crash of Admiral landing upside down after him.

Automatically I swerved over to the right and kicked my horse into the fence. In mid-air, as I crossed it, I looked down at Bill. He lay loosely on the ground with one arm outstretched. His eyes were shut. Admiral had fallen solidly, back downwards, across Bill's unprotected abdomen, and he was rolling backward and forward in a frantic effort to stand up again.

I had a brief impression that something lay beneath them. Something incongruous, which ought not to be there. But I was going too fast to see properly.

As my horse pressed on away from the fence, I felt as sick as if I'd been kicked in the stomach myself. There had been a quality about that fall which put it straight into the killing class.

I looked over my shoulder. Admiral succeeded in getting to his feet and cantered off loose, and the attendant stepped forward and bent over Bill, who still lay motionless on the ground. I turned back to attend to the race. I had been left in front and I ought to stay there. At the side of the course a black-suited, white-sashed First-Aid man was running towards and past me. He had been standing at the fence I was now approaching, and was on his way to help Bill.

I booted my horse into the next three fences, but my heart was no longer in it, and when I emerged as the winner into the full view of the crowded stands, the mixed gasp and groan which greeted me seemed an apt enough welcome. I passed the winning post, patted my mount's neck, and looked at the stands. Most heads were still turned towards the last fence, searching in the impenetrable mist for Admiral, the odds-on certainty who had lost his first race in two years.

Even the pleasant middle-aged woman whose horse I was riding met me with the question, "What happened to Admiral?"

"He fell," I said.

"How lucky," said Mrs. Mervyn, laughing happily.

She took hold of the bridle and led her horse into the winner's unsaddling enclosure. I slid off and undid the girth buckles with fingers clumsy from shock. She patted the horse and chattered on about how delighted she was to have won, and how unexpected it was, and how fortunate that Admiral had tripped up for a change, though a great pity in another way, of course.

I nodded and smiled at her and didn't answer, because what I would have said would have been savage and unkind. Let her enjoy her win, I thought. They come seldom enough. And Bill might, after all, be all right.

I tugged the saddle off the horse and, leaving a beaming Mrs. Mervyn receiving congratulations from all around, pressed through the crowd into the weighing room. I sat on the scales, was passed as correct, walked into the changing room, and put my gear down on the bench.

Clem, the racecourse valet who looked after my stuff, came over. He was a small elderly man, very spry, and tidy, with a weatherbeaten face and wrists whose tendons stood out like tight strung cords.

He picked up my saddle and ran his hand caressingly over the leather. It was a habit he had grown into, I imagine, from long years of caring for fine-grained skins. He stroked a saddle as another man would a pretty girl's cheek, savouring the suppleness, the bloom.

"Well done, sir," he said; but he didn't look overjoyed.

I didn't want to be congratulated. I said abruptly, "Admiral should have won."

"Did he fall?" asked Clem anxiously.

"Yes," I said. I couldn't understand it, thinking about it.

"Is Major Davidson all right, sir?" asked Clem. He valeted Bill too and, I knew, looked upon him as a sort of minor god.

"I don't know," I said. But the hard saddle-tree had hit him plumb in the belly with the weight of a big horse falling at thirty miles an hour behind it. What chance has he got, poor beggar, I thought.

I shrugged my arms into my sheepskin coat and went along to the First-Aid room. Bill's wife, Scilla, was standing outside the door there, pale and shaking and doing her best not to be frightened. Her small neat figure was dressed gaily in scarlet, and a mink hat sat provocatively on top of her cloudy dark curls. They were clothes for success, not sorrow.

"Alan," she said, with relief, when she saw me. "The doctor's looking at him and asked me to wait here. What do you think? Is he bad?" She was pleading, and I hadn't much comfort to give her. I put my arm round her shoulders.

She asked me if I had seen Bill fall, and I told her he had dived onto his head and might be slightly concussed.

The door opened, and a tall slim well-groomed man came out. The doctor. "Are you Mrs. Davidson?" he said to Scilla. She nodded.

"I'm afraid your husband will have to go along to the hospital," he said. "It wouldn't be sensible to send him home without an X-ray." He smiled reassuringly, and I felt some of the tension go out of Scilla's body.

"Can I go in and see him?" she said.

The doctor hesitated. "Yes," he said finally, "but he's almost unconscious. He had a bit of a bang on the head. Don't try to wake him."

When I started to follow Scilla into the First-Aid room the doctor put his hand on my arm to stop me.

"You're Mr. York, aren't you?" he asked. He had given me a regulation check after an easy fall I'd had the day before.

"Yes."

"Do you know these people well?"

"Yes. I live with them most of the time."

The doctor closed his lips tight, thinking. Then he said, "It's not good. The concussion's not much, but he's bleeding internally, possibly from a ruptured spleen. I've telephoned the hospital to take him in as an emergency case as soon as we can get him there."

As he spoke, one of the racecourse ambulances backed up towards us. The men jumped out, opened the rear doors, took out a big stretcher and carried it into the First-Aid room. The doctor went in after them. Soon they all reappeared with Bill on the stretcher. Scilla followed, the anxiety plain on her face, deep and well-founded.

Bill's firm brown humourous face now lolled flaccid, bluish-white, and covered with fine beads of sweat. He was gasping slightly through his open mouth, and his hands were restlessly pulling at the blanket which covered him. He was still wearing his green and red checked racing colours, the most ominous sign of all.

Scilla said to me, "I'm going with him in the ambulance. Can you come?"

"I've a ride in the last race," I said. "I'll come along to the hospital straight after that. Don't worry, he'll be all right." But I didn't believe it, and nor did she.

After they had gone I walked along beside the weighing room building and down through the car park until I came to the bank of the river. Swollen from recently melted snow, the Thames was flowing fast, sandy brown and grey with froths of white. The water swirled out of the mist a hundred yards to my right, churned round the bend where I stood, and disappeared again into the fog. Troubled, confused, not seeing a clear course ahead. Just like me.

For there was something wrong about Bill's accident.

Back in Bulawayo where I got my schooling, the mathematics master spent hours (too many, I thought in my youth) teaching us to draw correct inferences from a few known facts. But deduction was his hobby as well as his job, and occasionally we had been able to sidetrack him from problems of geometry or algebra to those of Sherlock Holmes. He produced class after class of boys keenly observant of well-worn toe-caps on charwomen and vicars and calluses on the finger tips of harpists; and the mathematics standard of the school was exceptionally high.

Now, thousands of miles and seven years away from the sun-baked schoolroom, standing in an English fog and growing very cold, I remembered my master and took out my facts, and had a look at them.

Known facts . . . Admiral, a superb jumper, had fallen abruptly in full flight for no apparent reason. The racecourse attendant had walked across the course behind the fence as Bill and I rode towards it, but this was not at all unusual. And as I had cleared the fence, and while I was looking down at Bill, somewhere on the edge of my vision there had been a dull damp gleam from something grey and metallic. I thought about these things for a long time.

The inference was there all right, but unbelievable. I had to find out if it was the correct one.

I went back into the weighing room to collect my kit and weigh out for the last race, but as I packed the flat lead pieces into my weight cloth to bring my weight up to that set by the handicapper, the loudspeakers were turned on and it was announced that owing to the thickening fog the last race had been abandoned.

There was a rush then in the changing room and the tea and fruitcake disappeared at a quickened tempo. It was a long time since breakfast, and I stuffed a couple of beef sandwiches into my mouth while I changed. I arranged with Clem for my kit to go to Plumpton, where I was due to ride four days later, and set off on an uninviting walk. I wanted to have a close look at the place where Bill had fallen.

It is a long way on foot from the stands to the far end of Maidenhead race-course, and by the time I got there my shoes, socks, and trouser legs were wet through from the long sodden grass. It was very cold, very foggy. There was no one about.

I reached the fence, the harmless, softish, easy-to-jump fence, made of black birch twigs standing upright. Three feet thick at the bottom slanting to half that size at the top, four feet six inches tall, about ten yards wide. Ordinary, easy.

I looked carefully along the landing side of the fence. There was nothing unusual. Round I went to the takeoff side. Nothing. I poked around the wing which guides the horses into the fence, the one on the inside of the course, the side Bill had been when he fell. Still nothing.

It was down underneath the wing on the outside of the course that I found what I was looking for. There it lay in the long grass, half hidden, beaded with drops of mist, coiled and deadly.

Wire.

There was a good deal of it, a pale silver grey, wound into a ring about a foot across, and weighted down with a piece of wood. One end of it led up the main side post of the wing and was fastened round it two feet above the level of the top of the birch. Fastened, I saw, very securely indeed. I could not untwist it with my fingers.

I went back to the inside wing and had a look at the post. Two feet above the fence there was a groove in the wood. This post had once been painted white, and the mark showed clearly.

It was clear to me that only one person could have fixed the wire in place. The attendant. The man whom I myself had seen walk across from one side of the course to the other. The man, I thought bitterly, whom I had left to *help* Bill.

In a three mile 'chase at Maidenhead one rode twice round the course. On the first circuit there had been no trouble at this fence. Nine horses had jumped it safely, with Admiral lying third and biding his time, and me riding alongside telling Bill I didn't think much of the English climate.

Second time around, Admiral was lengths out in front. As soon as the attendant had seen him land over the fence before this one, he must have walked over holding the free end of wire and wound it round the opposite post so that it stretched there taut in the air, almost invisible, two feet above the birch. At that height it would catch the high-leaping Admiral straight across the shoulders.

The callousness of it awoke a slow deep anger which, though I did not then know it, was to remain with me as a spur for many weeks to come.

Whether the horse had snapped the wire when he hit it, or pulled it off the post, I could not be sure. But as I could find no separate pieces, and the coil by the outer wing was all one length, I thought it likely that the falling horse had jerked the less secure end down with him. None of the seven horses following me had been brought down. Like me, they must have jumped clear over the remains of the trap.

Unless the attendant was a lunatic, which could by no means be ruled out, it was a deliberate attack on a particular horse and rider. Bill on Admiral had normally reached the front by this stage in a race, often having opened up a lead of twenty lengths, and his red and green colours, even on a misty day, were easy to see.

At this point, greatly disturbed, I began the walk back. It was already growing dark. I had been longer at the fence than I had realised, and when I at length reached the weighing room, intending to tell the Clerk of the Course about the wire, I found everyone except the caretaker had gone.

The caretaker, who was old and bad-tempered and incessantly sucked his teeth, told me he did not know where the Clerk of the Course could be found. He said the racecourse manager had driven off towards the town five minutes earlier. He did not know where the manager had been going, nor when he would be back; and with a grumbling tale that he had five separate stoves besides the central boiler to see to, and that the fog was bad for his bronchitis, the caretaker shuffled purposefully off towards the dim murky bulk of the grandstand.

Undecided, I watched him go. I ought, I knew, to tell someone in authority about the wire. But who? The Stewards who had been at the meeting were all on their way home, creeping wearily through the fog, unreachable. The manager had gone; the Clerk of the Course's office, I discovered, was locked. It would take me a long time to locate any of them, persuade them to return to the racecourse and get them to drive down the course over the rough ground in the dark; and after that there would be discussion, repetition, statements. It would be hours before I could get away.

Meanwhile Bill was fighting for his life in Maidenhead hospital, and I wanted profoundly to know if he were winning. Scilla faced racking hours of anxiety and I had promised to be with her as soon as I could. Already I had delayed too long. The wire, fog-bound and firmly twisted round the post, would keep until tomorrow, I thought; but Bill might not.

Bill's Jaguar was alone in the cark park. I climbed in, switched on the side lights and the fog lights, and drove off. I turned left at the gates, went gingerly along the road for two miles, turning left again over the river, twisted through Maidenhead's one-way streets, and finally arrived at the hospital.

There was no sign of Scilla in the brightly lit busy hall. I asked the porter.

"Mrs. Davidson? Husband a jockey? That's right, she's down there in the waiting rooom. Fourth door on the left."

I found her. Her dark eyes looked enormous, shadowed with grey smudges beneath them. All other colour had gone from her sad strained face, and she had taken off her frivolous hat.

"How is he?" I asked.

"I don't know. They just tell me not to worry." She was very close to tears.

I sat down beside her and held her hand.

"You're a comfort, Alan," she said.

Presently the door opened and a fair young doctor came in, stethoscope dangling.

"Mrs. Davidson, I think . . ." He paused. "I think you should come and sit with your husband."

"How is he?"

"Not . . . very well. We are doing all we can." Turning to me he said, "Are you a relative?"

"A friend. I am going to drive Mrs. Davidson home."

"I see," he said. "Will you wait, or come back for her? Later this evening." There was meaning in his careful voice, his neutral words. I looked closely into his face, and I knew that Bill was dying.

"I'll wait."

"Good."

I waited for four hours, getting to know intimately the pattern of the curtains and the cracks in the brown linoleum. Mostly, I thought about wire.

At last a nurse came, serious, young, pretty.

"I am so sorry . . . Major Davidson is dead."

Mrs. Davidson would like me to go and see him, she said, if I would follow her. She took me down the long corridors, and into a white room, not very big, where Scilla sat beside the single bed.

Scilla looked up at me. She couldn't speak.

Bill lay there, grey and quiet, finished. The best friend a man could wish for.

CHAPTER 2

EARLY NEXT MORNING I drove Scilla, worn out from the vigil she had insisted on keeping all night beside Bill's body, and heavily drugged now with sedatives, home to the Cotswolds. The children came out and met her on the doorstep, their three faces solemn and round-eyed. Behind them stood Joan, the briskly competent girl who looked after them, and to whom I had telephoned the news the evening before.

There on the step Scilla sat down and wept. The children knelt and sat beside her, putting their arms round her, doing their best to comfort a grief they could only dimly understand.

Presently Scilla went upstairs to bed. I drew the curtains for her and tucked her in, and kissed her cheek. She was exhausted and very sleepy, and I hoped it would be many hours before she woke again.

I went along to my own room and changed my clothes. Downstairs I found Joan putting coffee, bacon and eggs, and hot rolls for me on the kitchen table. I gave the children the chocolate bars I had bought for them the previous morning (how very long ago it seemed) and they sat with me, munching, while I ate my breakfast. Joan poured herself some coffee.

"Alan?" said William. He was five, the youngest, and he would never go on speaking until you said "Yes?" to show you were listening.

"Yes?" I said.

"What happened to Daddy?"

So I told them about it, all of it except the wire.

They were unusually silent for a while. Then Henry, just eight, asked calmly, "Is he going to be buried or burnt?"

Before I could answer, he and his elder sister, Polly, launched into a heated and astonishingly well-informed discussion about the respective merits of burial and cremation. I was horrified, but relieved, too, and Joan, catching my eye, was hard put to it not to laugh.

The innocent toughness of their conversation started me on my way back to Maidenhead in a more cheerful frame of mind. I put Bill's big car in the garage and set off in my own little dark blue Lotus. The fog had completely gone, but I drove slowly (for me), working out what was best to do.

First I called at the hospital. I collected Bill's clothes, signed forms, made arrangements. There was to be a routine post mortem examination the next day.

It was Sunday. I drove to the racecourse, but the gates were locked. Back in the town the Clerk of the Course's office was shut and empty. I telephoned his home, but there was no answer.

After some hesitation I rang up the Senior Steward of the National Hunt Committee, going straight to the top steeplechase authority. Sir Creswell Stampe's butler said he would see if Sir Creswell was available. I said it was very important that I should speak with him. Presently he came on the line.

"I certainly hope what you have to say *is* very important, Mr. York. I am in the middle of luncheon with my guests."

"Have you heard, sir, that Major Davidson died yesterday evening?"

"Yes. I'm very sorry about it, very sorry indeed." He waited. I took a deep breath.

"His fall wasn't an accident," I said.

"What do you mean?"

"Major Davidson's horse was brought down by wire," I said.

I told him about my search in the fence, and what I had found there.

"You have let Mr. Dace know about this?" he asked. Mr. Dace was the Clerk of the Course.

I explained that I had been unable to find him.

"So you rang me. I see." He paused. "Well, Mr. York, if you are right, this is too serious to be dealt with entirely by the National Hunt Committee. I think you should inform the police in Maidenhead without delay. Let me know this evening, without fail, what is happening. I will try to get in touch with Mr. Dace."

I put down the receiver. The buck had been passed, I thought. I could imagine the Stampe roast beef congealing on the plate while Sir Creswell set the wires humming.

The police station in the deserted Sunday street was dark, dusty-looking, and uninviting. I went in. There were three desks behind the counter, and at one of them sat a young constable reading a newspaper of the juicier sort. Keeping up with his crime, I reflected.

"Can I help you, sir?" he said, getting up.

"Is there anyone else here?" I asked. "I mean, someone senior? It's about a . . . a death."

"Just a minute, sir." He went out of a door at the back, and returned to say, "Will you come in here, please?"

He stood aside to let me into a little inner office, and shut the door behind me.

The man who rose to his feet was small for a policeman, thickset, dark, and in his late thirties. He looked more of a fighter than a thinker, but I found later that his brain matched his physique. His desk was littered with papers and heavy-looking law books. The gas fire had made a comfortable warm fug, and his ashtray was overflowing. He, too, was spending.his Sunday afternoon reading up crime.

"Good afternoon. I am Inspector Lodge," he said. He gestured to a chair facing his desk, asking me to sit down. He sat down again himself, and began to shape his papers into neat piles.

"You have come about a death?" My own words, repeated, sounded foolish, but his tone was matter-of-fact.

"It's about a Major Davidson . . ." I began.

"Oh yes. We had a report. He died in the hospital last night after a fall at the races." He waited politely for me to go on.

"That fall was engineered," I said bluntly.

Inspector Lodge looked at me steadily, then drew a sheet of paper out of a drawer, unscrewed his fountain pen, and wrote, I could see, the date and the time. A methodical man.

"I think we had better start at the beginning," he said. "What is your name?"

"Alan York."

"Age?"

"Twenty-four."

"Address?"

I gave Davidsons' address, explaining whose it was, and that I lived there a good deal.

"Where is your own home?"

"In Southern Rhodesia," I said. "On a cattle station near a village called Induna, about fifteen miles from Bulawayo."

"And are you a professional jockey?"

"No, an amateur. I work in London three days or so a week."

"Occupation?"

"I represent my father in his London office."

"And your father's business?"

"The Bailey York Trading Company."

"What do you trade on?" asked Lodge.

"Copper, lead, cattle. Anything and everything. We're transporters mainly," I said.

He wrote it all down, in quick distinctive script.

"Now then," he put down the pen, "what is it all about?"

"I don't know what it's about," I said, "but this is what happened." I told him the whole thing. He listened without interrupting, then he said, "What made you even begin to suspect that this was not a normal fall?"

"Admiral is the safest jumper there is. He's sure-footed, like a cat. He doesn't make mistakes."

But I could see from his politely surprised expression that he knew little, if anything, about steeplechasing, and thought that one horse was as likely to fall as another.

I tried again. "Admiral is brilliant over fences. He would never fall like that, going into an easy fence in his own time, not being pressed. He took off perfectly. I saw him. That fall was unnatural. It looked to me as though something had been used to bring him down. I thought it might be wire, and I went back to look, and it was. That's all."

"Hm. Was the horse likely to win?" asked Lodge.

"Certain," I said.

"And who did win?"

"I did," I said.

Lodge paused, and bit the end of his pen.

"How do the racecourse attendants get their jobs?" he asked.

"I don't really know. They are casual staff, taken on for the meeting, I think," I said.

"Why would a racecourse attendant wish to harm Major Davidson?" He said this naively, and I looked at him sharply.

"Do you think I have made it all up?" I asked.

"No." He sighed. "I suppose I don't. Perhaps I should have said, how difficult would it be for someone who wished to harm Major Davidson to get taken on as a racecourse attendant?"

"Easy," I said.

"We'll have to find out." He reflected. "It's a very chancy way to murder a man."

"Whoever planned it can't have meant to kill him," I said flatly.

"Why not?"

"Because it was so unlikely that he would die. I should think it was simply meant to stop him winning."

"Why was such a fall unlikely to result in death?" said Lodge. "It sounds highly dangerous to me."

I said: "It could have been meant to injure him, I suppose. Usually, when a horse is going fast and hits a fence hard when you're not expecting it, you get catapulted out of the saddle. You fly through the air and hit the ground way out in front of where your horse falls. That may do a lot of damage, but it doesn't often kill. But Bill Davidson wasn't flung off forwards. His toe may have stuck in his stirrup, though that's not very likely. Perhaps the wire caught round his leg and pulled him back. Anyway, he fell straight down and his horse crashed on top of him. Even then it was sheer bad luck that the saddle tree hit him in the stomach. You couldn't even hope to kill a man like that on purpose."

"I see. You seem to have given it some thought."

"Yes." The pattern of the hospital waiting room curtains, the brown linoleum, came back into my mind in association.

"Can you think of anyone who might wish to hurt Major Davidson?" asked Lodge.

"No," I said. "He was very well liked."

Lodge got up and stretched. "We'll go and have a look at your wire," he said. He put his head out into the big office. "Wright, go and see if Hawkins is there, and tell him I want a car if there's one available."

There was a car. Hawkins (I presumed) drove, I sat in the back with Lodge. The main gates of the racecourse were still locked, but there were ways and means, I found. A police key opened another, inconspicuous, gate in the wooden fence.

"In case of fire," said Lodge, seeing my sideways look.

There was no one about in the racecourse buildings: the manager was out. Hawkins drove over the course into the centre and headed down towards the farthest fence. We bumped a good deal on the uneven ground. The car drew up just short of the inside wing, and Lodge and I climbed out.

I led the way past the fence to the outer wing.

"The wire is over here," I said.

But I was wrong.

There was the post, the wing, the long grass, the birch fence. And no coil of wire.

"Are you sure this is the right fence?" said Lodge.

"Yes," I said. We stood looking at the course set out in front of us. We were at the very far end, the stands a blurred massive block in the distance. The fence by which we stood was alone on a short straight between two curves, and the nearest fence to us was three hundred yards to the left, round a shallow bend.

"You jump that fence," I said, pointing away to it. "Then there's quite a long run, as you can see, to this one." I patted the fence beside us. "Then twenty yards after we land over this one there is that sharpish left turn into the straight. The next fence is some way up the straight, to allow the horses to balance themselves properly after coming round the bend, before they have to jump. It's a good course."

"You couldn't have made a mistake in the mist?"

"No. This is the fence," I said.

Lodge sighed. "Well, we'll take a closer look."

But all there was to be seen was a shallow groove on the once white inner post, and a deeper groove on the outer post, where the wire had bitten into the wood. Both grooves needed looking for and would ordinarily have been unnoticed. Both were at the same level, six feet, six inches from the ground.

"Very inconclusive indeed," said Lodge.

We went back to Maidenhead in silence. Glum and feeling foolish, I knew now that even though I could reach no one in authority, I should have found someone, anyone, even the caretaker, the day before, to go back to the fence with me, after I had found the wire, to see it in its place. A witness who had seen wire fastened to a fence, even though it would have been dark and foggy, even though perhaps he could not swear at which fence he had seen it, would definitely have been better than no witness at all. I tried to console myself with the possibility that the attendant had been returning to the fence with his wire clippers at the same time that I was walking back to the stands, and that even if I had returned at once with a witness, it would already have been too late.

From Maidenhead police station I called Sir Creswell Stampe. I had parted him this time, he said, from his toasted muffins. The news that the wire had disappeared didn't please him, either.

"You should have got someone else to see it at once. Photographed it. Removed it. We can't proceed without evidence. I can't think why you didn't have sense enough to act more quickly, either. You have been very irresponsible, Mr. York." And with these few kind words he put down his receiver.

Depressed, I drove home.

I put my head quietly round Scilla's door. Her room was dark, but I could hear her even breathing. She was still sound asleep.

Downstairs, Joan and the children were sitting on the floor in front of the welcoming log fire playing poker. I had introduced them to the game one rainy day when the children were tired of snap and rummy and had been behaving very badly, quarrelling and shouting and raising tempers all round. Poker, the hitherto mysterious game of the cowboys in Westerns, had worked a miracle.

Henry developed in a few weeks into the sort of player you wouldn't sit down with twice without careful thought. His razor-sharp mathematical mind knew the odds to a fraction against any particular card turning up; his visual memory was formidable; and his air of slight bewilderment, calculated to be misleading, led many an unsuspecting adult straight into his traps. I admired Henry. He could out-bluff an angel.

Polly played well enough for me to be sure she would never lose continually in ordinary company, and even William knew a running flush from a full house.

They had been at it for some time. Henry's pile of poker chips was, as usual, three times as big as anyone else's.

Polly said, "Henry won all the chips a little while ago, so we had to share them out and start all over again."

Henry grinned. Cards were an open book to him and he couldn't help reading.

I took ten of Henry's chips and sat in with them. Joan dealt. She gave me a pair of fives and I drew another one. Henry discarded and drew two cards only, and looked satisfied.

The others threw in during the first two rounds. Then I boldly advanced two more chips to join the two on the table. "Raise you two, Henry," I said.

Henry glanced at me to make sure I was looking at him, then made a great show of indecision, drumming his fingers on the table and sighing. Knowing his habit of bluffing, I suspected he had a whopper of a hand and was scheming how to get me to disgorge the largest possible number of chips.

"Raise you one," he said at last.

I was just about to put another two chips firmly out, but I stopped and said, "Oh no you don't, Henry. Not this time," and I threw in my hand. I pushed the four chips across to him. "This time you get four, and no more."

"What did you have, Alan?" Polly turned my cards over, showing the three fives.

Henry grinned. He made no attempt to stop Polly looking at his cards, too. He had a pair of kings. Just one pair.

"Got you that time, Alan," he said happily.

William and Polly groaned heavily.

We played until I had won back my reputation and a respectable number of Henry's chips. Then it was the children's bedtime, and I went up to see Scilla.

She was awake, lying in the dark.

"Come in, Alan."

I went over and switched on the bedside lamp. The first shock was over. She looked calm, peaceful.

"Hungry?" I asked. She had not eaten since lunch the day before.

"Do you know, Alan, I am," she said as if surprised.

I went downstairs and with Joan rustled up some supper. I carried the tray up and ate with Scilla. Sitting propped up with pillows, alone in the big bed, she began to tell me about how she had met Bill, the things they had done together, the fun they had had. Her eyes shone with remembered happiness. She talked for a long time, all about Bill, and I did not stop her until her lips began to tremble. Then I told her about Henry and his pair of kings, and she smiled and grew calm again.

I wanted very much to ask her whether Bill had been in any trouble or had been threatened in any way during the last few weeks, but it wasn't the right time to do it. So I got her to take another of the sedatives the hospital had given me for her, turned off her light, and said good night.

As I undressed in my own room the tiredness hit me. I had been awake for over forty hours, few of which could be called restful. I flopped into bed.

It was one of those times when the act of falling asleep is a conscious, delicious luxury.

Half an hour later Joan shook me awake again. She was in her dressing-gown.

"Alan, wake up for goodness sake. I've been knocking on your door for ages."

"What's the matter?"

"You're wanted on the telephone. Personal call," she said.

"Oh no," I groaned. It felt like the middle of the night. I looked at my watch. Eleven o'clock.

I staggered downstairs, eyes bleary with sleep.

"Hello?"

"Mr. Alan York?"

"Yes."

"Hold on, please." Some clicks on the line. I yawned.

"Mr. York? I have a message for you from Inspector Lodge, Maidenhead police. He would like you to come here to the police station tomorrow afternoon, at four o'clock."

"I'll be there," I said. I rang off, went back to bed, and slept and slept.

LODGE WAS WAITING for me. He rose, shook hands, pointed to a chair. I sat down. The desk was clear now of everything except a neat, quarto-sized folder placed squarely in front of him. Slightly behind me, at a small table in the corner, sat a constable in uniform, pencil in hand, shorthand notebook at the ready.

"I have some statements here," Lodge tapped the file, "which I will tell you about. Then I have some questions to ask." He opened the file and took out two sheets of paper clipped together.

"This is a statement from Mr. J. L. Dace, Clerk of the Course of Maidenhead racecourse. In it he says nine of the attendants, the men who stand by to make temporary repairs to the fences during the races, are regularly employed in that capacity. Three of them were new this meeting."

Lodge laid down this statement, and took out the next.

"This is a statement from George Watkins, one of the regular attendants. He says they draw lots among themselves to decide which fence each of them shall stand by. There are two at some fences. On Friday they drew lots as usual, but on Saturday one of the new men volunteered to go down to the farthest fence. None of them likes having to go right down there, Watkins says, because it is too far to walk back between races to 'have a bit' on a horse. So they were glad enough to let the stranger take that fence, and they drew lots for the rest."

"What did this attendant look like?" I asked.

"You saw him yourself," said Lodge.

"No, not really," I said. "All he was to me was a man. I didn't look at him. There's at least one attendant at every fence. I wouldn't know any of them again."

"Watkins says he thinks he'd know the man again, but he can't describe him. Ordinary, he says. Not tall, not short. Middle-aged, he thinks. Wore a cap, old grey suit, loose mackintosh."

"They all do," I said gloomily.

Lodge said, "He gave his name as Thomas Cook. Said he was out of work, had a job to go to next week and was filling in time. Very plausible, nothing odd about him at all, Watkins says. He spoke like a Londoner though, not with a Berkshire accent."

Lodge laid the paper down and took out another.

"This is a statement from John Russell of the St. John Ambulance Brigade. He says he was standing beside the first fence in the straight watching the horses go round the bottom of the course. Because of the mist he says he could see only three fences: the one he was standing beside, the next fence up the straight, and the farthest fence, where Major Davidson fell. The fence before that, which was opposite him on the far side of the course, was an indistinct blur.

"He saw Major Davidson race out of the mist after he had jumped that fence. Then he saw him fall at the next. Major Davidson did not reappear, though his horse got up and galloped off riderless. Russell began to walk towards the fence where he had seen Major Davidson fall; then when you, Mr. York, passed him looking over your shoulder, he began to run. He found Major Davidson lying on the ground."

"Did he see the wire?" I asked eagerly.

"No. I asked him if he had seen anything at all unusual. I didn't mention wire specifically. He said there was nothing."

"Didn't he see the attendant roll up the wire while he was running towards him?"

"I asked him if he could see either Major Davidson or the attendants as he ran towards them. He says that owing to the sharp bend and the rails round it he could not see them until he was quite close. I gather he ran round the course instead of cutting across the corner through the long rough grass because it was too wet."

"I see," I said despondently. "And what was the attendant doing when he got there?"

"Standing beside Major Davidson looking down at him. He says the attendant looked frightened. This surprised Russell, because although he was knocked out Major Davidson did not appear to him to be badly injured. He waved his white flag, the next First-Aid man saw it and waved his, and the message was thus relayed through the fog all the way up the course to the ambulance."

"What did the attendant do then?"

"Nothing particular. He stayed beside the fence after the ambulance had taken Major Davidson away, and Russell says he was there until the abandonment of the last race was announced."

Clutching at straws, I said, "Did he go back with the other attendants and collect his pay?"

Lodge looked at me with interest. "No," he said, "he didn't."

He took out another paper.

"This is a statement from Peter Smith, head travelling lad for the Gregory stables, where Admiral is trained. He says that after Admiral got loose at Maidenhead he tried to jump a blackthorn hedge. He stuck in it and was caught beside it, scared and bleeding. There are cuts and scratches all over the horse's shoulders, chest, and forelegs." He looked up. "If the wire left any mark on him at all, it is impossible to distinguish it now."

"You have been thorough," I said, "and quick."

"Yes. We were lucky, for once, to find everyone we wanted without delay."

There was only one paper left. Lodge picked it up, spoke slowly.

"This is the report of the post mortem of Major Davidson. Cause of death was multiple internal injuries. Liver and spleen were both ruptured."

He sat back in his chair and looked at his hands.

"Now, Mr. York, I have been directed to ask you some questions which . . ." his dark eyes came up to mine suddenly, ". . . which I do not think you will like. Just answer them." His half smile was friendly.

"Fire away," I said.

"Are you in love with Mrs. Davidson?"

I sat up straight, surprised.

"No," I said.

"But you live with her?"

"I live with the whole family," I said.

"Why?"

"I have no home in England. When I first got to know Bill Davidson he asked me to his house for a weekend. I liked it there, and I suppose they liked me. Anyway, they asked me often. Gradually the weekends got longer and longer, until Bill and Scilla suggested I should make their house my head-quarters. I spend a night or two every week in London."

"How long have you lived at the Davidsons'?" asked Lodge.

"About seven months."

"Were your relations with Major Davidson friendly?"

"Yes, very."

"And with Mrs. Davidson?"

"Yes."

"But you do not love her?"

"I am extremely fond of her. As an elder sister," I said, sitting tight on my anger. "She is ten years older than I am."

Lodge's expression said quite plainly that age had nothing to do with it. I was aware, just then, that the constable in the corner was writing down my replies.

I relaxed. I said, tranquilly, "She was very much in love with her hus-band, and he with her."

Lodge's mouth twitched at the corners. He looked, of all things, amused. Then he began again.

"I understand," he said, "that Major Davidson was the leading amateur steeplechase jockey in this country?"

"Yes."

"And you yourself finished second to him, a year ago, after your first sea-son's racing in England?"

I stared at him. I said, "For someone who hardly knew steeplechasing ex-isted twenty-four hours ago, you've wasted no time."

"Were you second to Major Davidson on the amateur riders' list last year? And were you not likely to be second to him again? Is it not also likely that now, in his absence, you will head the list?"

"Yes, yes, and I hope so," I said. The accusation was as plain as could be, but I was not going to rush unasked into protestations of my innocence. I waited. If he wanted the suggestion made that I had sought to injure or kill Bill in order to acquire either his wife or his racing prestige, or both, Lodge would have to make it himself.

But he didn't. A full minute ticked by, during which I sat still. Finally Lodge grinned.

"Well, I think that's all, then, Mr. York. The information you gave us yesterday and your answers today will be typed together as one statement, and I shall be glad if you will read and sign it."

The policeman with the notebook stood up and walked into the outer office. Lodge said, "The coroner's inquest on Major Davidson is to be held on Thursday. You will be needed as a witness; and Mrs. Davidson, too, for evidence of identification. We'll be getting in touch with her."

He asked me questions about steeplechasing, ordinary conversational questions, until the statement was ready. I read it carefully and signed it. It was accurate and perfectly fair. I could imagine these pages joining the others in Lodge's tidy file. How fat would it grow before he found the accidental murderer of Bill Davidson?

If he ever did.

He stood up and held out his hand, and I shook it. I liked him. I wondered who had "directed" him to find out if I might have arranged the crime I had myself reported.

CHAPTER 3

I RODE AT Plumpton two days later.

The police had been very discreet in their enquiries, and Sir Creswell also, for there was no speculation in the weighing room about Bill's death. The grapevine was silent.

I plunged into the bustle of a normal racing day, the minor frustration of a lot of jockeys changing in a smallish space, the unprintable jokes, the laughter, the cluster of cold half-undressed men round the red-hot coke stove.

Clem gave me my clean breeches, some pants, a thin fawn under-jersey, a fresh white stock for my neck, and a pair of nylon stockings. I stripped and put on the racing things. On top of the nylon stockings (laddered, as always) my soft, light, close-fitting racing boots slid on easily. Clem handed me my racing colours, the thick woolen sweater of coffee and cream checks, and the brown satin cap. He tied my stock for me. I pulled on the jersey, and slid the cap onto my crash helmet, ready to put on later.

Clem said, "Only the one ride today, sir?" He pulled two thick rubber bands from his large apron pocket and slipped them over my wrists. They were to anchor the sleeves of my jersey and prevent the wind blowing them up my arms.

"Yes," I said. "So far, anyway." I was always hopeful.

"Will you be wanting to borrow a light saddle? The weight's near your limit, I should think."

"No," I said, "I'd rather use my own saddle if I can. I'll get on the trial scales with that first, and see how much over-weight I am."

"Right you are, sir."

I went over with Clem, picked up my six pound racing saddle with its girths and stirrup leathers wound round it, and weighed myself with it, my crash helmet perched temporarily and insecurely on the back of my head. The total came to ten stone, nine pounds, which was four pounds more than the handicapper thought my horse deserved.

Clem took back the saddle, and I put my helmet on the bench again.

"I think I'll carry the overweight, Clem," I said.

"Right." He turned off to attend to someone else.

I could have got down to the proper weight—just—by using a three pound "postage stamp" saddle and changing into silk colours and "paper" boots. But as I was riding my own horse I could please myself, and he was an angular animal whose ribs would probably have been rubbed raw by too small a saddle.

He, Forlorn Hope, my newest acquisition, was a strongly built brown gelding only five years old. He looked as though he would develop into a 'chaser in a year or two, but meanwhile I was riding him in novice hurdle races to give him some sorely needed experience.

His unreliability as a jumper had made Scilla, the evening before, beg me not to ride him at Plumpton, a course full of snares for the unwary.

Unbearably strung up, and facing her loss for the first time without the help of drugs, she was angry and pleading by turns.

"Don't, Alan. Not a novice hurdle at Plumpton. You know your wretched Forlorn Hope isn't safe. You haven't got to do it, so why do you?"

"I like it."

"There never was a horse more aptly named," she said, miserably.

"He'll learn," I said. "But not if I don't give him the opportunity."

"Put someone else up. Please."

"There isn't any point in my having a horse if I don't ride it myself. That's really why I came to England at all, to race. You know that."

"You'll be killed, like Bill." She began to cry, helplessly, worn out. I tried to reason with her.

"No, I won't. If Bill had been killed in a motor crash you wouldn't expect me to stop driving a car. Steeplechasing's just as safe and unsafe as motoring." I paused, but she went on crying. "There are thousands more people killed on the roads than on the race-track," I said.

At this outrageous statement she recovered enough to point out acidly the difference in the number of people engaged in the two pursuits.

"Very few people are killed by steeplechasing," I tried again.

"Bill was . . ."

"Only about one year, out of hundreds," I went on.

"Bill was the second since Christmas."

"Yes." I looked at her warily. There were still tears in her eyes.

"Scilla, was Bill in any sort of trouble recently?"

"Why ever do you ask?" She was astounded by my question.

"Was he?"

"Of course not."

"Not worried about anything?" I persisted.

"No. Did he seem worried to you?"

"No," I said. It was quite true. Until the moment of his fall Bill had been the same as I had always known him, cheerful, poised, reliable. He had had, and enjoyed, a pretty wife, three attractive children, a grey stone manor house, a considerable fortune, and the best hunter 'chaser in England. A happy man. And rack my memory as I would, I could not recall the slightest ruffling of the pattern.

"Then why do you ask?" said Scilla, again.

I told her as gradually, as gently as I could, that Bill's fall had not been an ordinary accident. I told her about the wire and about Lodge's investigations.

She sat like stone, absolutely stunned.

"Oh no," she said. "Oh, no. Oh, no."

As I stood now outside the weighing room at Plumpton I could still see her stricken face. She had raised no more objections to my racing. What I had told her had driven every other thought out of her head.

A firm hand came down on my shoulder. I knew it well. It belonged to Pete Gregory, racehorse trainer, a burly man nearly six feet tall, running to fat, growing bald, but in his day, I had been told, the toughest man ever to put his foot in a racing stirrup.

"Hello, Alan me lad. I'm glad to see you're here. I've already declared you for your horse in the second race."

"How is he?" I asked.

"All right. A bit thin, still." Forlorn Hope had only been in his stable for a month. "I should give him an 'easy,' coming up the hill the first time, or he'll blow up before the finish. He needs more time before we can hope for much."

"O.K.," I said.

"Come out and see what the going is like," said Pete. "I want to talk to you." He hitched the strap of his binoculars higher on his shoulder.

We walked down through the gate onto the course and dug our heels experimentally into the turf. They sank in an inch.

"Not bad, considering all the snow that melted into it a fortnight ago," I said.

"Nice and soft for you to fall on," said Pete with elementary humour.

We went up the rise to the nearest hurdle. The landing side had a little too much give in it, but we knew the ground at the other end of the course was better drained. It was all right.

Pete said abruptly, "Did you see Admiral fall at Maidenhead?" He had been in Ireland buying a horse when it happened and had only just returned.

"Yes. I was about ten lengths behind him," I said, looking down the course, concentrating on the hurdle track.

"Well?"

"Well, what?" I said.

"What happened? Why did he fall?" There was some sort of urgency in his voice, more than one would expect, even in the circumstances. I looked at him. His eyes were grey, unsmiling, intent. Moved by an instinct I didn't understand, I retreated into vagueness.

"He just fell," I said. "When I went over the fence he was on the ground with Bill underneath him."

"Did Admiral meet the fence all wrong, then?" he probed.

"Not as far as I could see. He must have hit the top of it." This was near enough to the truth.

"There wasn't . . . anything else?" Pete's eyes were fierce, as if they would look into my brain.

"What do you mean?" I avoided the direct answer.

"Nothing." His anxious expression relaxed. "If you didn't see anything . . ." We began to walk back. It troubled me that I hadn't told Pete the truth. He had been too searching, too aware. I was certain he was not the man to risk destroying a great horse like Admiral, let alone a friend, but why was he so relieved now he believed I had noticed nothing?

I had just decided to ask him to explain his attitude, and to tell him what had really happened, when he began to speak.

"Have you got a ride in the Amateur 'Chase, Alan?" He was back to normal, bluff and smiling.

"No, I haven't," I said. "Pete, look . . ."

But he interrupted, "I had a horse arrive in my yard five or six days ago, with an engagement in today's Amateur 'Chase. A chestnut. Good sort of animal. I should say. He seems to be fit enough—he's come from a small stable in the West country—and his new owner is very keen to run him. I tried to ring you this morning about it, but you'd already left."

"What's his name?" I asked, for all this preamble of Pete's was, I knew, his way of cajoling me into something I might not be too delighted to do.

"Heavens Above."

"Never heard of him. What's he done?" I asked.

"Well, not much. He's young, of course . . ."

I interrupted. "What *exactly* has he done?"

Pete sighed and gave in. "He's only had two runs, both down in Devon last autumn. He didn't fall, but—er—he got rid of his jockey both times. But he jumped well enough over my schooling fences this morning. I don't think you'd have any difficulty in getting him round safely, and that's the main thing at this stage."

"Pete, I don't like to say no, but . . ." I began.

"His owner is so hoping you'll ride him. It's her first horse, and it's running for the first time in her brand new colours. I brought her to the races with me. She's very excited. I said I'd ask you . . ."

"I don't think . . ." I tried again.

"Well at least meet her," said Pete.

"If I meet her, you know it'll be far more difficult for me to refuse to ride her horse."

Pete didn't deny it.

I went on, "I suppose she's another of your dear old ladies about to go into a nursing home from which she is unlikely to return, and wants a final thrill before she meets her fate?"

This was the sad tale which Pete had used not long before to inveigle me onto a bad horse against my better judgement. And I often saw the old lady at the races afterwards. The nursing home and her fate were still presumably awaiting her.

"This one is not," said Pete, "a dear old lady."

We came to a stop in the paddock, and Pete looked around him and beckoned to someone. Out of the corner of my eye I saw a woman begin to walk towards us. It was already, without unforgivable rudeness, too late to escape. I had time for one heartfelt oath in Pete's ear before I turned to be introduced to the new owner of the jockey-depositing Heavens Above.

"Miss Ellery-Penn, Alan York," said Pete.

I was lost before she spoke a word. The first thing I said was, "I'll be glad to ride your horse."

Pete was laughing openly at me.

She was beautiful. She had clear features, wonderful skin, smiling grey eyes, dark glossy hair falling almost to her shoulders. And she was used to the effect she had on men: but how could she help it?

Pete said, "Right, then I'll declare you for the amateurs'—it's the fourth race. I'll give the colours to Clem." He went off towards the weighing room.

"I am so glad you agreed to ride my horse," the girl said. Her voice was low-pitched and unhurried. "He's a birthday present. Rather a problem one, don't you think? My Uncle George, who is a dear fellow but just the slightest bit off the beat, *advertised* in *The Times* for a racehorse. My aunt says he received fifty replies and bought this horse without seeing it because he liked the name. He said it would be more amusing for me to have a horse for my birthday than the conventional string of pearls."

"Your Uncle George sounds fascinating," I said.

"But just a little devastating to live with." She had a trick of lifting the last two or three words in a sentence so that they sounded like a question. As if she had added "Don't you agree?" to her remark.

"Do you in fact live with him?" I asked.

"Oh, yes. Parents divorced in the murky past. Scattered to the four winds, and all that."

"I'm sorry."

"Waste no sympathy. I can't remember either of them. They abandoned me on Uncle George's doorstep, figuratively speaking, at the tender age of two."

"Uncle George has done a good job," I said, looking at her with the frankest admiration.

She accepted this without gaucherie, almost as a matter of course.

"Aunt Deb, actually. She is faintly more on the ball than Uncle George. Absolute pets, the pair of them."

"Are they here today?" I asked.

"No, they aren't," said Miss Ellery-Penn. "Uncle George remarked that having given me a passport into a new world peopled entirely by brave and charming young men, it would defeat the object if my path were cluttered up with elderly relatives."

"I am getting fonder of Uncle George every minute," I said.

Miss Ellery-Penn gave me a heavenly smile which held no promises of any sort.

"Have you seen my horse? Isn't he a duck?" she said.

"I haven't seen him. I'm afraid I didn't know he existed until five minutes ago. How did Uncle George happen to send him to Pete Gregory? Did he pick the stable with a pin?"

She laughed. "No, I don't think so. He had the stable all planned. He said I could get a Major Davidson to ride for me if the horse went to Mr. Gregory's." She reflected, wrinkling her brow. "He was quite upset on Monday when he read in the paper that Major Davidson had been killed."

"Did he know him?" I asked idly, watching the delicious curves at the corner of her red mouth.

"No, I'm sure he didn't know him personally. Probably he knew his father. He seems to know most people's fathers. He just said 'Good God, Davidson's dead' in a shocked sort of way and went on eating his toast. But he didn't hear me or Aunt Deb until we had asked him four times for the marmalade!"

"And that was all?"

"Yes. Why do you ask?" said Miss Ellery-Penn, curiously.

"Oh, nothing special," I said. "Bill Davidson and I were good friends."

She nodded. "I see." She dismissed the subject. "Now what do I have to do in my new role as racehorse owner? I don't particularly want to make a frightful boob on my first day. Any comments and instructions from you will be welcome, Mr. York."

"My name is Alan," I said.

She gave me an appraising look. It told me plainer than words that although she was young she was already experienced at fending off unwelcome attentions and not being rushed into relationships she was not prepared for.

But finally she smiled, and said, "Mine is Kate." She bestowed her name like a gift; I was pleased to receive it.

"How much do you know about racing?" I asked.

"Not a thing. Never set foot on the Turf before today." She gave the capital letter its full value, ironically.

"Do you ride, yourself?"

"Positively not."

"Perhaps your Uncle George is fond of horses? Perhaps he hunts?" I suggested.

"Uncle George is the most un-addicted man to horses I have ever met. He says one end kicks and the other bites, and as for hunting, he says that he has cosier things to do than chase bushy-tailed vermin in the gravest discomfort over water-logged countryside in the depths of winter."

I laughed. "Perhaps he bets. Off the course?" I asked.

"Uncle George has been known to ask, on Cup Final day, what has won the Derby."

"Then why Heavens Above?"

"Wider horizons for me, Uncle George says. My education has been along the well-tramped lines of boarding school, finishing school, and an over-chaperoned tour of Europe. I needed to get the smell of museums out of my nose, Uncle George said."

"So he gave you a racehorse for your twenty-first birthday," I stated matter-of-factly.

"Yes," she said: then she looked at me sharply. I grinned. I had jumped her defences, that time.

"There's nothing special for you to do as an owner," I said, "except go along to those stalls over there," I pointed, "before the fourth race, to see your horse being saddled up. Then you'll go into the parade ring with Pete, and stand around making intelligent remarks about the weather until I arrive and mount and go out for the race."

"What do I do if he wins?"

"Do you expect him to win?" I asked. I was not sure how much she really knew about her horse.

"Mr. Gregory says he won't."

I was relieved. I did not want her to be disappointed.

"We'll all know much more about him after the race. But if he should come in the first three, he will be unsaddled down there opposite the weighing room. Otherwise, you'll find us up here on the grass."

It was nearly time for the first race. I took the delectable Miss Ellery-Penn on to the stands and fulfilled Uncle George's design by introducing to her several brave and charming young men. I unfortunately realized that by the time I came back from riding in the novice hurdle, I should probably be an "also-ran" in the race for Miss Ellery-Penn's attentions.

I watched her captivating a group of my friends. She was a vivid, vital person. It seemed to me that she had an inexhaustible inner fire battened down tight under hatches, and only the warmth from it was allowed to escape into the amused, slow voice. Kate was going to be potently attractive even in middle age, I thought inconsequently, and it crossed my mind that had Scilla possessed this springing vitality instead of her retiring, serene passiveness, Inspector Lodge's implications might not have been very far off the mark.

After we had watched the first race I left Kate deciding which of her new acquaintances should have the honour of taking her to coffee, and went off to weigh out for the novice hurdle. Looking back, I saw her setting off to the refreshment room with a trail of admirers, rather like a comet with a tail. A flashing, bewitching comet.

For the first time in my life I regretted that I was going to ride in a race.

CHAPTER 4

IN THE CHANGING room Sandy Mason stood with his hands on his hips and laid about him with his tongue. His red hair curled strongly, his legs, firmly planted with the feet apart, were as rigid as posts. From the top to toe he vibrated with life. He was a stocky man in his thirties, on the short side, very strong, with dark brown eyes fringed disconcertingly by pale, reddish lashes.

As a jockey, a professional, he was not among the top dozen, but he had had a good deal of success, mainly owing to his fighting spirit. Nothing ever frightened him. He would thrust his sometimes unwilling mounts into the smallest openings, even occasionally into openings which did not exist until he made them by sheer force. His aggressiveness in races had got him into hot water more than once with the Stewards, but he was not particularly unpopular with the other jockeys, owing to his irrepressible, infectious cheerfulness.

His sense of humour was as vigorous as the rest of him, and if I thought privately that some of his jokes were too unkindly practical or too revoltingly obscene, I appeared to be in a minority.

"Which of you sods has half-inched my balancing pole?" he roared in a voice which carried splendidly above the busy chatter to every corner of the room. To this enquiry into the whereabouts of his whip, he received no reply.

"Why don't you lot get up off your fannies and see if you're hatching it," he said to three or four jockeys who were sitting on a bench pulling on their boots. They looked up appreciatively and waited for the rest of the tirade. Sandy kept up a flow of invective without repeating himself until one of the valets produced the missing whip.

"Where did you find it?" demanded Sandy. "Who had it? I'll twist his bloody arm."

"It was on the floor under the bench, in your own place."

Sandy was never embarrassed by his mistakes. He roared with laughter and took the whip. "I'll forgive you all this time, then." He went out into the weighing room carrying his saddle and whacking the air with his whip as if to make sure it was as pliable as usual. He always used it a good deal in the course of a race.

As he passed me where I stood just inside the changing room door, his eyes lifted to mine with one of the darting, laughing glances which made him likeable in spite of his faults. I turned and watched him go over and sit on the scales, parking the whip on the table beside him. He said something I couldn't hear, and both the Clerk of the Scales and the Judge, who was sitting there learning the colours so that he could distinguish them at the finish, laughed as they checked him against their lists and passed him for the race.

There had been rumours, a while back, that Sandy had "stopped" a few horses and had been rewarded handsomely by bookmakers for the service. But nothing had been proved, and the official enquiry had lasted barely an hour. Those who had felt the rough edge of Sandy's practical jokes believed him capable of anything. Everyone else pointed out that stopping a horse was entirely out of character for one who had been in trouble for trying too ruthlessly to win.

Watching the free and easy way he handled the two racing officials, I could understand that in face of that friendly, open manner, the Stewards at the enquiry must have found it impossible, in the absence of solidly convincing evidence, to believe him guilty. The general opinion among the jockeys was that Sandy had "strangled" a couple at one stage, but not during the past few months.

"Stopping" a horse can be done by missing the start, setting off some lengths behind, and staying at the back. Then the crooked jockey can ride a fairly honest finish from the second last fence, when he is closely under the eyes of the crowd, secure in the knowledge that he has left his horse far too much to do and cannot possibly win. It is rare enough, because a jockey seen to do it regularly soon finds himself unemployed.

During my one and a half season's racing I had seen it happen only twice. It was the same man both times, a fair, round-faced youth called Joe Nantwich. On the second occasion, about two months ago, he had been lucky to escape with his licence, for he had been foolish enough to try it in a race where one of the jockeys was David Stampe, the tale-bearing younger son of the Senior Steward.

Joe, and, I was sure, Sandy, too, had both gone to the lengths of deliberately holding back horses which, without their interference, would have been certain to win. They had, in fact, been guilty of criminal fraud. But was I so very much better, I wondered, as I tied on my helmet and took my saddle over to the scales. For I proposed to take Forlorn Hope sensibly over the hurdles, concentrating on getting round the course, and I had no intention of riding him all out in the faint possibility that he might finish in the first three. He was not properly fit, and too hard a race would do him great harm. Of course, if by some unforeseen circumstances, such as a lot of falls among the other horses, I found myself placed with a winning chance, I intended to seize it. There is a world of difference between "stopping" and "not trying hard, but willing to win" but the result for disgruntled backers is the same. They lose their money.

I took my saddle out to the saddling boxes, where Pete was already waiting with Forlorn Hope. He saddled up, and Rupert, the tiny stable lad, led the horse out into the parade ring. Pete and I strolled in after him, discussing the other horses in the race. There was no sign of Kate.

When the time came I mounted and rode out on to the course. The familiar excitement was in my blood again. Not Bill's death nor Scilla's mourning, nor the thought of Kate making progress with someone else, could affect the gripping happiness I always felt when cantering down to the starting gate. The speed of racing, the quick decisions, the risks, these were what I badly needed to counteract the safeties of civilisation. One can be too secure. Adventure is good for the soul, especially for someone like me, whose father stopped counting after the fourth million.

And my father, with an understanding based on his own much wilder youth, had given me unconditionally a fast car and three good horses and turned me loose in a country five thousand miles from home. He said however, as he despatched me with his blessing, that he thought steeplechasing was rather mild for one who had been taken crocodile hunting on the Zambezi every year since he was ten. My father's annual month away from his trading empire usually meant for us a dash across the veldt and a plunge into the primeval forest, sometimes equipped with the absolute minimum of kit and no one but ourselves to carry it. And I, for whom the deep jungle was a familiar playground, found the challenge I needed in a tamed land, on friendly animals, in a sport hemmed all about with rules and regulations. It was very odd, when one came to consider it.

The starter called the roll to make sure everyone had arrived, while we circled round and checked the tightness of the girths. I found Joe Nantwich guiding his horse along beside me. He was wearing his usual unpleasant expression, half petulance, half swank.

"Are you going back to the Davidsons' after the races, Alan?" he asked. He always spoke to me with a familiarity I slightly resented, though I tried not to.

"Yes," I said. Then I thought of Kate. "I may not go at once, though."

"Will you give me a lift as far as Epsom?"

"I don't go that way," I said, very politely.

"But you go through Dorking. I could get a bus on from there if you don't want to go to Epsom. I came with someone who is going on to Kent, so I've got to find some transport home." He was persistent, and although I thought he could easily find someone going directly to Epsom if he tried hard enough, I agreed in the end to take him.

We lined up for the start. Joe was on one side of me and Sandy on the other, and from the looks they gave each other across me, there was no love lost between them. Sandy's smile was a nasty one: Joe's round baby face puckered up like a child trying not to cry. I imagined that Sandy had been puncturing Joe's inflated ego with one of those famous practical jokes, such as filling the feet of his racing boots with jam.

Then we were off, and I gave all my attention to getting Forlorn Hope round as neatly, quickly, and safely as I could. He was still very green and inclined to waver as he met the clattering hurdles, but the basic spring was there. He was going so well that for over half the race I lay in third place, staying slightly towards the outside, to give him a clear view of the obstacles. The last quarter mile coming up the hill was too much for him, though, and we finished sixth. I was satisfied, and Scilla would be reassured.

Sandy Mason finished ahead of me. Then Joe Nantwich's horse galloped past loose, reins dangling, and looking back to the far end of the course, I saw the tiny figure of Joe himself trudging back to the stands. No doubt I would be hearing a stride by stride account of the calamity all the way to Dorking.

I unsaddled; went back to the weighing room, changed into Kate's brand new colours, got Clem to pack me a weight cloth with ten pounds of flat lead pieces, the weight I needed for the Amateur 'Chase and went out to see what had become of Miss Ellery-Penn.

She was leaning on the parade ring rails, looking alternately at the horses and (with too much approval, I thought) at Dane Hillman, one of the brave and charming young men I had introduced to her.

"Mr. Hillman has been telling me," said Kate, "that that poor looking bag of bones over there—the one with his head down by his knees and those floppy ears—is the fastest horse in the race. Am I to believe it, or is the mickey being gently taken?"

"No mickey," I said. "That's the best horse. Not on looks, I grant you, but he's a certainty today, in this company."

Dane said, "Horses who go along with their heads down like that are nearly always good jumpers. They look where they're going."

"But I like this gorgeous creature coming round now," said Kate, looking at a bay with an arched neck and high head carriage. Most of his body was covered by a rug to keep out the February cold, but at the back his glossy rump swelled roundly.

"He's much too fat," said Dane. "He probably ate his head off during the snow and hasn't had enough exercise since. He'll blow up when he's asked to do anything."

Kate sighed. "Horses appear to be as full of paradoxes as G. K. Chesterton. The duds look good, and the good look duds."

"Not always," said Dane and I together.

"I shall be glad," said Dane, "to give you a prolonged course in racehorse recognition, Miss Ellery-Penn."

"I am a slow learner, Mr. Hillman."

"All the better," said Dane, cheerfully.

"Aren't you riding today, Dane?" I asked hopefully.

"In the last two, my lad. Don't worry, I shall be able to look after Miss Ellery-Penn for you while you ride her horse." He grinned.

"Are you a jockey too, Mr. Hillman?" asked Kate in a surprised voice.

"Yes," said Dane, and left it at that. He was the rising star of the profession, clearly heading straight to the top. Pete Gregory had first claim on him, which, apart from natural affinity, brought us together a good deal. Strangers often mistook us for each other. We were the same age, both dark, both of middle height and medium build. On horseback the difference was greater; he was a better jockey than I would ever be.

"I thought all jockeys were instantly recognisable as having come straight from Lilliput," said Kate, "but you two are quite a decent size." She had to look up to both of us, although she was tall enough herself.

We laughed. I said, "Steeplechasing jockeys are nearly all a decent size. It's easier to stick on over big fences if you have long legs to grip with."

"Several of the Flat chaps are as tall as us, too," said Dane. "But they are very skinny, of course."

"All my illusions are being shattered," said Kate.

Dane said, "I like your new horse, Alan. He'll make a good 'chaser next year."

"Are you riding your own horses today, too?" Kate asked Dane.

"No, I'm not. I haven't any," said Dane. "I'm a professional, so I'm not allowed to own racehorses."

"A professional?" Kate's eyebrows went up. She had clearly taken in the superlative tailoring of the suit under the short camel overcoat, the pleasant voice, the gentle manners. Another illusion was being shattered, I was amused to see.

"Yes. I ride for my life," said Dane, smiling. "Unlike Alan, I haven't a stinking rich father. But I get paid for doing what I like best in the world. It's a very satisfactory state of affairs."

Kate looked carefully from one to the other of us. "Perhaps in time I shall understand what makes you want to risk your elegant necks," she said.

"When you find out, please tell us," said Dane. "It's still a mystery to me."

We wandered back to the stands and watched the third race. The poor-looking horse won in a canter by twenty lengths. Kate's fancy was tailed-off after a mile and refused at the third last fence.

"Don't imagine that we always know what's going to win," said Dane. "Jockeys are bad tipsters. But that one was a cert, a dead cert."

A dead cert. The casual, everyday racing expression jabbed in my mind like a needle. Bill Davidson's attacker had relied on Admiral's being a certainty.

A dead cert. Dead . . .

KATE'S HORSE, FOR a pig in a poke, was not as bad as I feared. At the second fence he put in a short one and screwed in mid-air. I came clear out of the saddle and landed back in it more by luck than judgement. This was obviously the trick which had rid Heavens Above of his former jockey, who now had all my sympathy. He did it again at the third open ditch, but the rest of our journey was uneventful. The horse even found an unsuspected turn of foot up the hill and, passing several tired animals, ran on into fourth place.

Kate was delighted.

"Bless Uncle George for a brainwave," she said. "I've never had such a happy day in my life."

"I thought you were coming off at the second, Alan," said Pete Gregory, as I undid the girth buckles.

"So did I," I said, feelingly. "It was sheer luck I didn't."

Pete watched the way Heavens Above was breathing: the ribs were moving in and out a good deal, but not labouring. He said, "He's remarkably fit, considering everything. I think we'll win a race or two with him before the end of the season."

"Can't we all go and celebrate with the odd magnum?" asked Kate. Her eyes were shining with excitement.

Pete laughed. "Wait till you have a winner, for the magnum," he said. "I'd like to have drunk a more modest toast to the future with you, though, but I've a runner in the next. Alan will take you, no doubt." He looked at me sideways, very amused still at my complete surrender to the charm of Miss Ellery-Penn.

"Will you wait for me, Kate?" I asked. "I have to go and weigh in now, because we were fourth. I'll change and be out as quickly as I can."

"I'll come down outside the weighing room," promised Kate, nodding.

I weighed in, gave my saddle to Clem, washed and changed back into ordinary clothes. Kate was waiting outside the weighing room, looking at a group of girls standing near her chatting.

"Who are they?" asked Kate. "They have been here all the time I have, just doing nothing."

"Jockeys' wives, mostly," I said, grinning. "Waiting outside the weighing room is their chief occupation."

"And jockeys' girlfriends too, I suppose," said Kate, wryly.

"Yes," I said. "And I've just found out how nice it is to know there is someone waiting for you outside."

We went round to the bar, and settled for cups of coffee.

"Uncle George will be shattered to hear we drank to Heavens Above so non-alcoholically," said Kate. "Don't grain and grapes figure in your life?"

"Oh, yes, of course. But I've never got used to them at three o'clock in the afternoon. How about you?"

"Champers for breakfast is my passion," said Kate, with smiling eyes.

I asked her then if she would spend the evening with me, but she said she could not. Aunt Deb, it appeared, was having a dinner party, and Uncle George would be agog to hear how the birthday present had got on.

"Tomorrow, then?"

Kate hesitated and looked down at her glass. "I'm . . . er . . . going out with Dane, tomorrow."

"Blast him," I said, exploding.

Kate positively giggled.

"Friday?" I suggested.

"That would be lovely," said Kate.

We went up on to the stands and watched Dane win the fifth race by a short head. Kate cheered him home uninhibitedly.

CHAPTER 5

A BATTLE WAS raging in the car park. I walked out of the gate to go home after the last race, and came to a dead stop. In the open space between the gate and the first rank of parked cars, at least twenty men were fighting, and fighting to hurt. Even at first glance there was a vicious quality about the strictly non-Queensberry type blows.

It was astounding. Scuffles between two or three men are common on racecourses, but a clash of this size and seriousness had to be caused by more than a disagreement over a bet.

I looked closer. There was no doubt about it. Some of the men were wearing brass knuckles. A length of bicycle chain swung briefly in the air. The two men nearest to me were lying on the ground, almost motionless, but rigid with exertion, as if locked in some strange native ritual. The fingers of one were clamped round the wrist of the other, whose hand held a knife with a sharp three-inch blade. Not long enough to be readily lethal, it was designed to rip and disfigure.

There seemed to be two fairly equally matched sides fighting each other, but one could not distinguish which was which. The man with the knife, who was slowly getting the worst of it, I saw to be little more than a boy, but most of the men were in their full strength. The only older-looking fighter was on his knees in the centre with his arms folded over his head, while the fight raged on around him.

They fought in uncanny silence. Only their heavy breathing and a few grunts were to be heard. The semicircle of open-mouthed homeward-bound racegoers watching them was growing larger, but no one felt inclined to walk into the mêlée and try to stop it.

I found one of the newspaper sellers at my elbow.

"What's it all about?" I asked. Nothing much to do with racing escapes the newsboys.

"It's the taxi-drivers," he said. "There's two rival gangs of 'em, one lot from London and one lot from Brighton. There's usually trouble when they meet."

"Why?"

"Couldn't tell you, Mr. York. But this isn't the first time they've been at it."

I looked back at the struggling mob. One or two of them still had peaked caps on. Some pairs were rolling about on the ground, some were straining and heaving against the sides of the taxis. There were two rows of taxis parked there. All the drivers were fighting.

The fists and what they held in the way of ironmongery were doing a lot of damage. Two of the men were bent over, clasping their bellies in agony. There was blood on nearly all their faces, and the clothes of some of them had been torn off to the skin.

They fought on with appalling fury, taking no notice at all of the swelling crowd around them.

"They'll kill each other," said a girl standing next to me, watching the scene in a mixture of horror and fascination.

I glanced up over her head at the man standing on the other side of her, a big man well over six feet tall, with a deeply tanned skin. He was watching the fight with grim disapproval, his strong profile bleak, his eyes narrowed. I could not remember his name, though I had a feeling I ought to know it.

The crowd was growing uneasy, and began looking round for the police. The girl's remark was not idle. Any of the men might die, if they were unlucky, from the murderous chopping, gouging, and slogging, which showed no signs of abating.

The fight had caused a traffic jam in the car park. A policeman came, took a look, and disappeared fast for reinforcements. He returned with four constables on foot and one on horseback, all armed with truncheons. They plunged into the battle, but it took them several minutes to stop it.

More police arrived. The taxi-drivers were dragged and herded into two groups. Both lots appeared to be equally battered, and neither side seemed to have won. The battlefield was strewn with caps and torn pieces of coats and shirts. Two shoes, one brown, one black, lay on their sides ten feet apart. Patches of blood stained the ground. The police began making a small pile of collected weapons.

The main excitement over, people began drifting away. The little knot of prospective customers for the taxis moved across to ask a policeman how long the drivers would be detained. The tall sunburned man who had been standing near me went over to join them.

One of the racing journalists paused beside me, scribbling busily in his notebook.

"Who is that very big man over there, John?" I asked him. He looked up and focused his eyes. He said, "His name's Tudor, I think. Owns a couple of horses. A newly arrived tycoon type. I don't know much about him. He doesn't look too pleased about the transport situation."

Tudor, in fact, looked heavily angry, his lower jaw jutting forward obstinately. I was still sure there was something about this man which I ought to remember, but I did not know what. He was not having any success with the policeman, who was shaking his head. The taxis remained empty and driverless.

"What's it all about?" I asked the journalist.

"Gang warfare, my spies tell me," he said cheerfully.

Five of the taxi-drivers were now lying flat out on the cold damp ground. One of them groaned steadily.

The journalist said, "Hospital and police station in about equal proportions, I should say. What a story!"

The man who was groaning rolled over and vomited.

"I'm going back to phone this lot through to the office," said the journalist. "Are you off home now?"

"I'm waiting for that wretched Joe Nantwich," I said. "I promised him a lift to Dorking, but I haven't seen a sign of him since the fourth race. It would be just like him to get a lift right home with someone else and forget to let me know."

"The last I saw of him, he was having a few unfriendly words with Sandy in the gents, and getting the worst of it."

"Those two really hate each other," I said.

"Do you know why?"

"No idea. Have you?" I asked.

"No," said the journalist. He smiled good-bye and went back into the racecourse towards the telephone.

Two ambulances drove up to collect the injured drivers. A policeman climbed into the back of each ambulance with them, and another sat in front beside the driver. With full loads the ambulances trundled slowly up the road to the main gates.

The remaining drivers began to shiver as the heat of the battle died out of them and the raw February afternoon took over. They were stiff and bruised, but unrepentant. A man in one group stepped forward, gave the other group a sneer, and spat, insultingly, on the ground in their direction. His shirt was in ribbons and his face was swelling in lumps. The muscles of his forearm would have done credit to a blacksmith, and silky dark hair grew low on his forehead in a widow's peak. A dangerous-looking man. A policeman touched his arm to bring him back into the group and he jumped round and snarled at him. Two more policemen began to close in, and the dark-haired man subsided angrily.

I was just giving Joe up when he came out of the gate and hailed me with no apology for his lateness. But I was not the only person to notice his arrival.

The tall dark Mr. Tudor strode towards us.

"Nantwich, be so good as to give me a lift into Brighton, will you?" he said, authoritatively. "As you can see, the taxis are out of action, and I have an important appointment in Brighton in twenty minutes."

Joe looked at the taxi-drivers with vague eyes.

"What's happened?" he said.

"Never mind that now," said Tudor impatiently. "Where is your car?"

Joe looked at him blankly. His brain seemed to be working at half speed. He said, "Oh—er—it isn't here, sir. I've got a lift."

"With you?" said Tudor to me. I nodded. Joe, typically, had not introduced us.

"I'll be obliged if you will take me into Brighton," said Tudor, briskly. "I'll pay you the regular taxi fare."

He was forceful and in a hurry. It would have been difficult to refuse to do him a favour so small to me, so clearly important for him.

"I'll take you for nothing," I said, "but you'll find it a bit of a squeeze. I have a two-seater sports car."

"If it's too small for all of us, Nantwich can stay here and you can come back for him," said Tudor in a firm voice. Joe showed no surprise, but I thought that the dark Mr. Tudor was too practised at consulting no one's convenience but his own.

We skirted the groups of battered taxi-drivers, and threaded our way to my car. Tudor got in. He was so large that it was hopeless to try to wedge Joe in as well.

"I'll come back for you, Joe," I said, stifling my irritation. "Wait for me up on the main road."

I climbed into the car, nosed slowly out of the car park, up the racecourse road, and turned out towards Brighton. There was too much traffic for the Lotus to show off the power of the purring Climax engine, and going along at a steady forty gave me time to concentrate on my puzzling passenger.

Glancing down as I changed gear, I saw his hand resting on his knee, the fingers spread and tense. And suddenly I knew where I had seen him before. It was his hand, darkly tanned, with the faint bluish tint under the fingernails, that I knew.

He had been standing in the bar at Sandown with his back towards me and his hand resting flat on the counter beside him, next to his glass. He had been talking to Bill; and I had waited there, behind him, not wanting to interrupt their conversation. Then Tudor finished his drink and left, and I had talked with Bill.

Now I glanced at his face.

"It's a great shame about Bill Davidson," I said.

The brown hand jumped slightly on his knee. He turned his head and looked at me while I drove.

"Yes, indeed it is." He spoke slowly. "I had been hoping he would ride a horse for me at Cheltenham."

"A great horseman," I said.

"Yes indeed."

"I was just behind him when he fell," I said, and on an impulse added, "There are a great many questions to be asked about it."

I felt Tudor's huge body shift beside me. I knew he was still looking at me, and I found his presence overpowering. "I suppose so," he said. He hesitated, but added nothing more. He looked at his watch.

"Take me to the Pavilion Plaza Hotel, if you please. I have to attend a business meeting there," he said.

"Is it near the Pavilion?" I asked.

"Fairly. I will direct you when we get there." His tone relegated me to the status of chauffeur.

We drove for some miles in silence. My passanger sat apparently deep in thought. When we reached Brighton he told me the way to the hotel.

"Thank you," he said, without warmth, as he lifted his bulk clumsily out of the low-slung car. He had an air of accepting considerable favours as merely his due, even when done him by complete strangers. He took two steps away from the car, then turned back and said, "What is your name?"

"Alan York," I said. "Good afternoon." I drove off without waiting for an answer. I could be brusque, too. Glancing in the mirror I saw him standing on the pavement looking after me.

I went back to the racecourse.

Joe was waiting for me, sitting on the bank at the side of the road. He had some difficulty opening the car door, and he stumbled into his seat, muttering. He lurched over against me, and I discovered that Joe Nantwich was drunk.

The daylight was almost gone. I turned on the lights. I could think of pleasanter things to do than drive the twisty roads to Dorking with Joe breathing alcohol all over me. I sighed, and let in the clutch.

Joe was nursing a grievance. He would be. Everything which went wrong for Joe was someone else's fault, according to him. Barely twenty, he was a chronic grumbler. It was hard to know which was worse to put up with, his grousing or his bragging, and that he was treated with tolerance by the other jockeys said much for their good nature. Joe's saving grace was his undoubted ability as a jockey, but he had put that to bad use already by his "stopping" activities, and now he was threatening it altogether by getting drunk in the middle of the afternoon.

"I would have won that race," he whined.

"You're a fool, Joe," I said.

"No, honestly, Alan, I would have won that race. I had him placed just right. I had the others beat, I had 'em stone cold. Just right." He made sawing motions with his hands.

"You're a fool to drink so much at the races," I said.

"Eh?" He couldn't focus.

"Drink," I said. "You've had too much to drink."

"No, no, no, no . . ." The words came dribbling out, as if once he had started to speak it was too much effort to stop.

"Owners won't put you on their horses if they see you getting drunk," I said, feeling it was no business of mine, after all.

"I can win any race, drunk or not," said Joe.

"Not many owners would believe it."

"They know I'm good."

"So you are, but you won't be if you go on like this," I said.

"I can drink and I can ride and I can ride and I can drink. If I want to." He belched.

I let it pass. What Joe needed was a firm hand applied ten years ago. He looked all set now on the road to ruin and he wasn't going to thank anyone for directions off it.

He was whining again. "That bloody Mason."

I didn't say anything. He tried again.

"That bloody Sandy, he tipped me off. He bloody well tipped me off over the bloody rails. I'd have won that race as easy as kiss your hand and he knew it and tipped me off the bloody rails."

"Don't be silly, Joe."

"You can't say I wouldn't have won the race," said Joe argumentatively.

"And I can't say you would have won it," I said. "You fell at least a mile from home."

"I didn't fall. I'm telling you, aren't I? Sandy bloody Mason tipped me off over the rails."

"How?" I asked idly, concentrating on the road.

"He squeezed me against the rails. I shouted to him to give me more room. And do you know what he did? Do you know? He laughed. He bloody well laughed. Then he tipped me over. He stuck his knee into me and gave a heave and off I went over the bloody rails." His whining voice finished on a definite sob.

I looked at him. Two tears were rolling down his round cheeks. They glistened in the light from the dashboard, and fell with a tiny flash on to the furry collar of his sheepskin coat.

"Sandy wouldn't do a thing like that," I said mildly.

"Oh yes he would. He told me he'd get even with me. He said I'd be sorry. But I couldn't help it, Alan, I really couldn't." Two more tears rolled down.

I was out of my depth. I had no idea what he was talking about; but it began to look as though Sandy, if he had unseated him, had had his reasons.

Joe went on talking. "You're always decent to me, Alan, you're not like the others. You're my friend . . ." He put his hand heavily on my arm, pawing, leaning over towards me and giving me the benefit of the full force of his alcoholic breath. The delicate steering of the Lotus reacted to his sudden weight on my arm with a violent swerve towards the curb.

I shook him off. "For God's sake sit up, Joe, or you'll have us in the ditch," I said.

But he was too immersed in his own troubles to hear me. He pulled my arm again. There was a lay-by just ahead. I slowed, turned into it, and stopped the car.

"If you won't sit up and leave me alone you can get out and walk," I said, trying to get through to him with a rough tone.

But he was still on his own track, and weeping noisily now.

"You don't know what it's like to be in trouble," he sobbed.

I resigned myself to listen. The quicker he got his resentments off his chest, I thought, the quicker he would relax and go to sleep.

"What trouble?" I said. I was not in the least interested.

"Alan, I'll tell you because you're a pal, a decent pal." He put his hand on my knee. I pushed it off.

Amid a fresh burst of tears Joe blurted, "I was supposed to stop a horse and I didn't, and Sandy lost a lot of money and said he'd get even with me and he's been following me around saying that for days and days and I knew he'd do something awful and he has." He paused for breath. "Lucky for me I hit a soft patch or I might have broken my neck. It wasn't funny. And that bloody Sandy," he choked on the name, "was laughing. I'll make him laugh on the other side of his bloody face."

This last sentence made me smile. Joe with his baby face, strong of body perhaps, but weak of character, was no match for the tough, forceful Sandy, more than ten years older and incalculably more self-assured. Joe's bragging, like his whining, sprang from feelings of insecurity. But the beginning of his outburst was something different.

"What horse did you not stop?" I asked. "And how did Sandy know you were supposed to be going to stop one?"

For a second I thought caution would silence him, but after the smallest hesitation he babbled on. The drink was still at the flood. So were the tears.

From the self-pitying, hiccuping, half incoherent voice I learned a sorry enough story. Shorn of blasphemy and reduced to essentials, it was this. Joe had been paid well for stopping horses on several occasions, two of which I had seen myself. But when David Stampe had told his father the Senior Steward about the last one, and Joe had nearly lost his licence, it gave him a steadying shock. The next time he was asked to stop a horse he said he would, but in the event, from understandable nerves, he had not done it thoroughly enough early in the race, and at the finish was faced with the plain knowledge that if he lost the race he would lose his licence as well. He won. This had happened ten days ago.

I was puzzled. "Is Sandy the only person who has harmed you?"

"He tipped me over the rails . . ." He was ready to start all over again.

I interrupted. "It wasn't Sandy, surely, who was paying you not to win?"

"No. I don't think so. I don't know," he snivelled.

"Do you mean you don't know who was paying you? Ever?"

"A man rang up and told me when he wanted me to stop one, and afterwards I got a packet full of money through the post."

"How many times have you done it?" I asked.

"Ten," said Joe, "all in the last six months." I stared at him.

"Often it was easy," said Joe defensively. "The ——s wouldn't have won anyway, even if I'd helped them."

"How much did you get for it?"

"A hundred. Twice it was two-fifty." Joe's tongue was still running away with him, and I believed him. It was big money, and anyone prepared to pay on that scale would surely want considerable revenge when Joe won against orders. But Sandy? I couldn't believe it.

"What did Sandy say to you after you won?" I asked.

Joe was still crying. "He said he'd backed the horse I beat and that he'd get even with me," said Joe. And it seemed that Sandy had done that.

"You didn't get your parcel of money, I suppose?"

"No," said Joe, sniffing.

"Haven't you any idea where they come from?" I asked.

"Some had London postmarks," said Joe. "I didn't take much notice." Too eager to count the contents to look closely at the wrappings, no doubt.

"Well," I said, "surely now that Sandy has had his little revenge, you are in the clear? Can't you possibly stop crying about it? It's all over. What are you in such a state about?"

For answer Joe took a paper from his jacket pocket and gave it to me.

"You might as well know it all. I don't know what to do. Help me, Alan. I'm frightened."

In the light from the dashboard I could see that this was true. And Joe was beginning to sober up.

I unfolded the paper and switched on the lights inside the car. It was a single sheet of thin, ordinary typing paper. In simple capital letters, written with a ball-point pen, were five words: BOLINGBROKE. YOU WILL BE PUNISHED.

"Bolingbroke is the horse you were supposed to stop and didn't?"

"Yes." The tears no longer welled in his eyes.

"When did you get this?" I asked.

"I found it in my pocket, today, when I put my jacket on after I'd changed. Just before the fifth race. It wasn't there when I took it off."

"And you spent the rest of the afternoon in the bar, in a blue funk, I suppose," I said.

"Yes . . . and I went back there while you took Mr. Tudor to Brighton. I didn't think anything was going to happen to me because of Bolingbroke, and I've been frightened ever since he won. And just as I was thinking it was all right Sandy pushed me over the rails and then I found this letter in my pocket. It isn't fair." The self-pity still whined in his voice.

I gave him back the paper.

"What am I to do?" said Joe.

I couldn't tell him, because I didn't know. He had got himself into a thorough mess, and he had good reason to be afraid. People who manipulated horses and jockeys to that extent were certain to play rough. The time lag of ten days between Bolingbroke's win and the arrival of the note could mean, I thought, that there was a cat-and-mouse, rather than a straightforward mentality at work. Which was little comfort to offer Joe.

Apart from some convulsive hiccups and sniffs, Joe seemed to have recovered from his tears, and the worst of the drunkenness was over. I switched off the inside lights, started the car up, and pulled back on to the road. As I had hoped, Joe soon went to sleep. He snored loudly.

Approaching Dorking, I woke him up. I had some questions to ask.

"Joe, who is that Mr. Tudor I took to Brighton? He knows you."

"He owns Bolingbroke," said Joe. "I often ride for him."

I was surprised. "Was he pleased when Bolingbroke won?" I asked.

"I suppose so. He wasn't there. He sent me ten-percent afterwards, though, and a letter thanking me. The usual thing."

"He hasn't been in racing long, has he?" I asked.

"Popped up about the same time you did," said Joe, with a distinct return to his old brash manner. "Both of you arrived with dark sun-tans in the middle of winter."

I had come by air from the burning African summer to the icy reception of October in England but after eighteen months my skin was as pale as an Englishman's. Tudor's, on the other hand, remained dark.

Joe was sniggering. "You know why Mr. Clifford bloody Tudor lives at Brighton? It gives him an excuse to be sunburnt all the year round. Touch of the old tar, really."

After that I had no compunction in turning Joe out at the bus stop for Epsom. Unloading his troubles onto me seemed, for the present at least, to have restored his ego.

I drove back to the Cotswolds. At first I thought about Sandy Mason and wondered how he had got wind of Joe's intention to stop Bolingbroke.

But the last hour of the journey I thought about Kate.

CHAPTER 6

SCILLA WAS LYING asleep on the sofa with a rug over her legs and a half-full glass on a low table beside her. I picked up the glass and sniffed. Brandy. She usually drank gin and Campari. Brandy was for bad days only.

She opened her eyes. "Alan, I'm so glad you're back. What time is it?"

"Half past nine," I said.

"You must be starving," she said, pushing off the rug. "Why ever didn't you wake me? Dinner was ready hours ago."

"I've only just got here, and Joan is cooking now, so relax," I said.

We went in to eat. I sat in my usual place. Bill's chair, opposite Scilla, was empty. I made a mental note to move it back against the wall.

Halfway through the steaks, Scilla said, breaking a long silence, "Two policemen came to see me today."

"Did they? About the inquest tomorrow?"

"No, it was about Bill." She pushed her plate away. "They asked me if he was in any trouble, as you did. They asked me the same questions in different ways for over half an hour. One of them suggested that if I was as fond of my husband as I said I was and on excellent terms with him, I ought to know if something was wrong in his life. They were rather nasty, really."

She was not looking at me. She kept her eyes down, regarding her half-eaten, congealing steak, and there was a slight embarrassment in her manner, which was unusual.

"I can imagine," I said, realising what was the matter. "They asked you, I suppose, to explain your relationship with me, and why I was still living in your house?"

She glanced up in surprise and evident relief. "Yes, they did. I didn't know how to tell you. It seems so ordinary to me that you should be here, yet I couldn't seem to make them understand that."

"I'll go tomorrow, Scilla," I said. "I'm not letting you in for any more gossip. If the police can think that you were cheating on Bill with me, so can the village and the county. I've been exceedingly thoughtless, and I'm very very sorry." For I, too, had found it quite natural to stay in Bill's house after his death.

"You will certainly not go tomorrow on my account, Alan," said Scilla with more resolution than I would have given her credit for. "I need you here. I shall do nothing but cry all the time if I don't have you to talk to, especially in the evenings. I can get through the days, with the children and the house to think about. But the nights . . ." And in her suddenly ravaged face I could read all the tearing, savage pain of a loss four days old.

"I don't care what anyone says," she said through starting tears, "I need you here. Please, please, don't go away."

"I'll stay," I said. "Don't worry. I'll stay as long as you want me to. But you must promise to tell me when you are ready for me to go."

She dried her eyes and raised a smile. "When I begin to worry about my reputation, you mean? I promise."

I had driven the better part of three hundred miles besides riding in two races, and I was tired. We went to our beds early, Scilla promising to take her sleeping pills.

But at two o'clock in the morning she opened my bedroom door. I woke at once. She came over and switched on my bedside light, and sat down on my bed.

She looked ridiculously young and defenceless. She was wearing a pale blue knee-length chiffon nightdress which flowed transparently about her slender body and fell like mist over the small round breasts.

I propped myself up on my elbow and ran my fingers through my hair.

"I can't sleep," she said.

"Did you take the pills?" I asked.

But I could answer my own question. Her eyes looked drugged, and in her right mind she would not have come into my room so revealingly undressed.

"Yes, I took them. They've made me a bit groggy, but I'm still awake. I took an extra one." Her voice was slurred and dopey. "Will you talk for a bit?" she said. "Then perhaps I'll feel more sleepy. When I'm on my own I just lie and think about Bill . . . Tell me more about Plumpton . . . You said you rode another horse. Tell me about it. Please . . ."

So I sat up in bed and wrapped my eiderdown round her shoulders, and told her about Kate's birthday present and Uncle George, thinking how often I had told Polly and Henry and William bedside stories to send them to sleep. But after a while I saw she was not listening, and presently the slow heavy tears were falling from her bent head onto her hands.

"You must think me a terrible fool to cry so much," she said, "but I just can't help it." She lay down weakly beside me, her head on my pillow. She took hold of my hand and closed her eyes. I looked down at her sweet, pretty face with the tears trickling past her ears into her cloudy dark hair, and gently kissed her forehead. Her body shook with two heavy sobs. I lay down and slid my arm under her neck. She turned towards me and clung to me, holding me fiercely, sobbing slowly with her deep terrible grief.

And at last, gradually, the sleeping pills did their job. She relaxed, breathing audibly, her hand twisted into the jacket of my pyjamas. She was lying half on top of my bedclothes, and the February night was cold. I tugged the sheet and blankets gently from underneath her with my free hand and spread them over her, and pulled the eiderdown up over our shoulders. I switched off the light and lay in the dark, gently cradling her until her breath grew soft and she was soundly asleep.

I smiled to think of Inspector Lodge's face if he could have seen us. And I reflected that I should not have been content to be so passive a bedfellow had I held Kate in my arms instead.

During the night Scilla twisted uneasily several times, murmuring jumbled words that made no sense, seeming to be calmed each time by my hand stroking her hair. Towards morning she was quiet. I got up, wrapped her in the eiderdown, and carried her back to her own bed. I knew that if she woke in my room, with the drugs worn off, she would be unnecessarily ashamed and upset.

She was still sleeping peacefully when I left her.

A FEW HOURS later, after a hurried breakfast, I drove her to Maidenhead to attend the inquest. She slept most of the way and did not refer to what had happened in the night. I was not sure she even remembered.

Lodge must have been waiting for us, for he met us as soon as we went in. He was carrying a sheaf of papers, and looked businesslike and solid. I introduced him to Scilla, and his eyes sharpened appreciatively at the sight of her pale prettiness. But what he said was a surprise.

"I'd like to apologise," he began, "for the rather unpleasant suggestions which have been put to you and Mr. York about each other." He turned to me. "We are now satisfied that you were in no way responsible for Major Davidson's death."

"That's big of you," I said lightly, but I was glad to hear it.

Lodge went on, "You can say what you like to the Coroner about the wire, of course, but I'd better warn you that he won't be too enthusiastic. He hates anything fancy, and you've no evidence. Don't worry if you don't agree with his verdict—I think it's sure to be accidental death—because inquests can always be reopened, if need be."

In view of this I was not disturbed when the Coroner, a heavily moustached man of fifty, listened keenly enough to my account of Bill's fall, but dealt a little brusquely with my wire theory. Lodge testified that he had accompanied me to the racecourse to look for the wire I had reported, but that there had been none there.

The man who had been riding directly behind me when Bill fell was also called. He was an amateur rider who lived in Yorkshire, and he had had to come a long way. He said, with an apologetic glance for me, that he had seen nothing suspicious at the fence, and that in his opinion it was a normal fall. Unexpected maybe, but not mysterious. He radiated common sense.

Had Mr. York, the Coroner enquired in a doubtful voice, mentioned the possible existence of wire to anyone at all on the day of the race? Mr. York had not.

The Coroner, summing up medical, police, and all other evidence, found that Major Davidson had died of injuries resulting from his horse having fallen in a steeplechase. He was not convinced, he said, that the fall was anything but an accident.

Owing to a mistake about the time, the local paper had failed to send a representative to the inquest, and from lack of detailed reporting the proceedings rated only small paragraphs in the evening and morning papers. The word "wire" was not mentioned. This omission did not worry me one way or the other, but Scilla was relieved. She said she could not yet stand questions from inquisitive friends, let alone reporters.

Bill's funeral was held quietly in the village on Friday morning, attended only by his family and close friends. Bearing one corner of his coffin on my shoulder and bidding my private good-byes, I knew for sure that I would not be satisfied until his death was avenged. I didn't know how it was to be done, and, strangely enough, I didn't feel any urgency about it. But in time, I promised him, in time, I'll do it.

Scilla's sister had come to the funeral and was to stay with her for two or three days; so, missing lunch out of deference to the light weight I was committed to ride at on the following day, I drove up to London to spend some long overdue hours in the office, arranging the details of insurance and customs duty on a series of shipments of copper.

The office staff were experts. My job was to discuss with Hughes, my second in command, the day-to-day affairs of the company, to make decisions and agree to plans made by Hughes, and to sign my name to endless documents and letters. It seldom took me more than three days a week. On Sunday it was my weekly task to write to my father. I had a feeling he skipped the filial introduction and the accounts of my racing, and fastened his sharp brain only on my report of the week's trade and my assessment of the future.

Those Sunday reports had been part of my life for ten years. School homework could wait, my father used to say. It was more important for me to know every detail about the kingdom I was to inherit; and to this end he made me study continually the papers he brought home from his office.

By the time I left school I could appraise at a glance the significance of fluctuations in the world prices of raw materials, even if I had no idea when Charles I was beheaded.

On Friday evening I waited impatiently for Kate to join me for dinner. Unwrapped from the heavy overcoat and woolly boots she had worn at Plumpton, she was more ravishing than ever. She wore a glowing red dress, simple and devastating, and her dark hair fell smoothly to her shoulders. She seemed to be alight from within with her own brand of effervescence. The evening was fun and, to me at least, entirely satisfactory. We ate, we danced, we talked.

While we swayed lazily round the floor to some dreamy slow-tempo music, Kate introduced the only solemn note of the evening.

"I saw a bit about your friend's inquest in this morning's paper," she said.

I brushed my lips against her hair. It smelled sweet. "Accidental death," I murmured vaguely. "I don't think."

"Hm?" Kate looked up.

"I'll tell you about it one day, when I know the whole story," I said, enjoying the taut line of her neck as she tilted her face up to mine. It was strange, I thought, that it was possible to feel two strong emotions at once. Pleasure in surrendering to the seduction of the music with a dancing Kate balanced in my arms, and a tugging sympathy for Scilla trying to come to terms with her loneliness eighty miles away in the windy Cotswold hills.

"Tell me now," said Kate with interest. "If it wasn't accidental death, what was it?"

I hesitated. I didn't want too much reality pushing the evening's magic sideways.

"Come on, come on," she urged, smiling. "You can't stop there. I'll die of suspense."

So I told her about the wire. It shocked her enough to stop her dancing, and we stood flat-footed in the middle of the floor with the other couples flowing round and bumping into us.

"Dear heavens," she said, "how . . . how wicked."

She wanted me to explain why the inquest verdict had been what it was, and after I told her that with the wire gone there was no evidence of anything else, she said, "I can't bear to think of anyone getting away with so disgusting a trick."

"Nor can I," I said, "and they won't, I promise you, if I can help it."

"That's good," she said seriously. She began to sway again to the music, and I took her in my arms and we drifted back into the dance. We didn't mention Bill again.

It seemed to me for long periods that evening as if my feet were not in proper contact with the floor, and the most extraordinary tremors constantly shook my knees. Kate seemed to notice nothing: she was friendly, funny, brimming over with gaiety, and utterly unsentimental.

When at length I helped her into the chauffeur-driven car which Uncle George had sent up from Sussex to take her home, I had discovered how painful it is to love. I was excited, keyed up. And also anxious; for I was sure that she did not feel as intensely about me as I about her.

I already knew I wanted to marry Kate. The thought that she might not have me was a bitter one.

THE NEXT DAY I went to Kempton Park races. Outside the weighing room I ran into Dane. We talked about the going, the weather, Pete's latest plans for us, and the horses. Usual jockey stuff. Then Dane said, "You took Kate out last night?"

"Yes."

"Where did you go?"

"The River Club," I said. "Where did you take her?"

"Didn't she tell you?" asked Dane.

"She said to ask you."

"River Club," said Dane.

"Damn it," I said. But I had to laugh.

"Honours even," said Dane.

"Did she ask you down to stay with Uncle George?" I asked suspiciously.

"I'm going today, after the races," said Dane, smiling. "And you?"

"Next Saturday," I said gloomily. "You know, Dane, she's teasing us abominably."

"I can stand it," said Dane. He tapped me on the shoulder. "Don't look so miserable, it may never happen."

"That's what I'm afraid of," I sighed. He laughed and went into the weighing room.

It was an uneventful afternoon. I rode my big black mare in a novice 'chase and Dane beat me by two lengths. At the end of the day we walked out to the car park together.

"How is Mrs. Davidson bearing up?" Dane asked.

"Fairly well, considering the bottom has dropped out of her world."

"Jockeys' wives' nightmare come true."

"Yes," I said.

"It makes you pause a bit, before you ask a girl to put up with that sort of constant worry," said Dane, thoughtfully.

"Kate?" I asked. He looked round sharply and grinned.

"I suppose so. Do you mind?"

"Yes," I said, keeping my voice light. "I mind very much."

We came to his car first, and he put his race glasses and hat on the seat. His suitcase was in the back.

"So long, mate," he said. "I'll keep you posted."

I watched him drive off, answered his wave. I seldom felt envious of anybody, but at that moment I envied Dane sorely.

I climbed into the Lotus and pointed its low blue nose towards home.

It was on the road through Maidenhead Thicket that I saw the horse-box. It was parked in a lay-by on the near side, with tools scattered on the ground round it and the bonnet up. It was facing me as I approached, as if it had broken down on its way into Maidenhead. A man was walking a horse up and down in front of it.

The driver, standing by the bonnet scratching his head, saw me coming and gestured to me to stop. I pulled up beside him. He walked round to talk to me through the window, a middle-aged man, unremarkable, wearing a leather jacket.

"Do you know anything about engines, sir?" he asked.

"Not as much as you, I should think," I said, smiling. He had grease on his hands. If a horse-box driver couldn't find the fault in his own motor, it would be a long job for whoever did. "I'll take you back into Maidenhead, though, if you like. There's bound to be someone there who can help you."

"That's extremely kind of you, sir," he said, civilly. "Thank you very much. But—er—I'm in a bit of a difficulty." He looked into the car and saw my binoculars on the seat beside me. His face lightened up. "You don't possibly know anything about horses, sir?"

"A bit, yes," I said.

"Well, it's like this, sir. I've got these two horses going to the London docks. They're being exported. Well, that one's all right." He pointed to the horse walking up and down. "But the other one, he don't seem so good.

Sweating hard, he's been, the last hour or so, and biting at his stomach. He keeps trying to lie down. Looks ill. The lad's in there with him now, and he's proper worried, I can tell you."

"It sounds as though it might be colic," I said. "If it is, he ought to be walking round, too. It's the only way to get him better. It's essential to keep them on the move when they've got colic."

The driver looked troubled. "It's a lot to ask, sir," he said, tentatively, "but would you have a look at him? Motors are my fancy, not horses, except to back 'em. And these lads are not too bright. I don't want a rocket from the boss for not looking after things properly."

"All right," I said, "I'll have a look. But I'm not a vet you know, by a long way."

He smiled in a relieved fashion. "Thank you, sir. Anyway, you'll know if I've got to get a vet at once or not, I should think."

I parked the car in the lay-by behind the horse-box. The door at the back of the horse-box opened and a hand, the stable lad's, I supposed, reached out to help me up. He took me by the wrist.

He didn't leave go.

There were three men waiting for me inside the horse-box. And no horse, sick or otherwise. After a flurried ten seconds during which my eyes were still unused to the dim light, I ended up standing with my back to the end post of one of the partition walls.

The horse-box was divided into three stalls with two partition walls between them, and there was a space across the whole width of the box at the back, usually occupied by lads travelling with their horses.

Two of the men held my arms. They stood one each side of the partition and slightly behind me, and they had an uncomfortable leverage on my shoulders. The post of the partition was padded with matting, as it always is in racehorse boxes, to save the horses hurting themselves while they travel. The matting tickled my neck.

The driver stepped up into the box and shut the door. His manner, still incredibly deferential, held a hint of triumph. It was entitled to. He had set a neat trap.

"Very sorry to have to do this, sir," he said politely. It was macabre.

"If it's money you want," I said, "you're going to be unlucky. I don't bet much and I didn't have a good day at the races today. I'm afraid you've gone to a lot of trouble for a measly eight quid."

"We don't want your money, sir," he said. "Though as you're offering it we might as well take it, at that." And still smiling pleasantly he put his hand inside my jacket and took my wallet out of the inside pocket.

I kicked his shin as hard as I could, but was hampered because of my position against the post. As soon as they felt me move the two men behind me jerked my arms painfully backwards.

"I shouldn't do that, sir, if I was you," said the friendly driver, rubbing his leg. He opened my wallet and took out the money, which he folded carefully and stowed inside his leather coat. He peered at the other things in the wallet, then stepped towards me, and put it back in my pocket. He was smiling faintly.

I stood still.

"That's better," he said, approvingly.

"What's all this about?" I asked. I had some idea that they intended to ransom me to my distant millionaire parent. Along the lines of "Cable us ten thousand pounds or we post your son back to you in small pieces." That would mean that they knew all along who I was, and had not just stopped any random motorist in a likely looking car to rob him.

"Surely you know, sir?" said the driver.

"I've no idea."

"I was asked to give you a message, Mr. York."

So he did know who I was. And he had not this minute discovered it from my wallet, which contained only money, stamps, and a cheque book in plain view. One or two things with my name on were in a flapped pocket, but he had not looked there.

"What makes you think my name is York?" I asked, trying a shot at outraged surprise. It was no good.

"Mr. Alan York, sir, was scheduled to drive along this road on his way from Kempton Park to the Cotswolds at approximately five fifteen p.m. on Saturday, February 27th, in a dark blue Lotus Elite, licence number KAB 890. I must thank you, sir, for making it easy for me to intercept you. You could go a month on the road without seeing another car like yours. I'd have had a job flagging you down if you'd been driving, say, a Ford or an Austin." His tone was still conversational.

"Get on with the message, I'm listening," I said.

"Deeds speak louder than words," said the driver mildly.

He came close and unbuttoned my jacket, looking at me steadily with wide eyes, daring me to kick him. I didn't move. He untied my tie, opened the neck of my shirt. We looked into each other's eyes. I hoped mine were as expressionless as his. I let my arms go slack in the grip of the two men behind me, and felt them relax their hold slightly.

The driver stepped back and looked towards the fourth man, who had been leaning against the horse-box wall, silently. "He's all yours, Sonny. Deliver the message," he said.

Sonny was young, with sideboards. But I didn't look at his face, particularly. I looked at his hands.

He had a knife. The hilt lay in his palm, and his fingers were lightly curled round it, not gripping. The way a professional holds a knife.

There was nothing of the driver's mock deference in Sonny's manner. He was enjoying his work. He stood squarely in front of me and put the point of his short blade on my breastbone. It scarcely pricked, so light was his touch.

Oh bloody hell, I thought. My father would not be at all pleased to receive ransom messages reinforced by pleas from me for my own safety. I would never be able to live it down. And I was sure that this little melodrama was intended to soften me up into a suitably frightened state of mind. I sagged against the post, as if to shrink away from the knife. Sonny's grim mouth smiled thinly in a sneer.

Using the post as a springboard I thrust forwards and sideways as strongly as I knew how, bringing my knee up hard into Sonny's groin and tearing my arms out of the slackened grasp of the men behind me.

I leaped for the door and got it open. In the small area of the horse-box I had no chance, but I thought that if only I could get out into the thicket I might be able to deal with them. I had learned a nasty trick or two about fighting from my cousin, who lived in Kenya and had taken lessons from the Mau Mau.

But I didn't make it.

I tried to swing out with the door, but it was stiff and slow. The driver grabbed my ankle. I shook his hand off, but the vital second had gone. The two men who had held me clutched at my clothes. Through the open door I glimpsed the man who had been leading the horse up and down. He was looking enquiringly at the horse-box. I had forgotten about him.

I lashed out furiously with feet, fists, and elbows, but they were too much for me. I ended up where I began, against the matting-padded post with my arms pulled backwards. This time the two men were none too gentle. They slammed me back against the post hard and put their weight on my arms. I felt the wrench in my shoulders and down my chest to my stomach. I shut my teeth.

Sonny, clutching his abdomen, was half sitting, half kneeling in the corner. He watched with satisfaction.

"That hurt the bastard, Peaky," he said. "Do it again."

Peaky and his mate did it again.

Sonny laughed. Not a nice laugh.

A little more pressure and I should have some torn ligaments and a dislocated shoulder. There didn't seem to be much I could do about it.

The driver shut the horse-box door and picked the knife up from the floor, where it had fallen. He was not looking quite so calm as before. My fist had connected with his nose and blood was trickling out of it. But his temper was intact.

"Stop it. Stop it, Peaky," he said. "The boss said we weren't to hurt him. He made quite a point of it. You wouldn't want the boss to know you disobeyed him, would you?" There was a threat in his voice.

The tension on my arms slowly relaxed. Sonny's smile turned to a sullen scowl. It appeared I had the boss to thank for something, even if not much.

"Now, Mr. York," said the driver reproachfully, wiping his nose on a blue handkerchief, "all that was quite unnecessary. We only want to give you a message."

"I don't like listening with knives sticking into me," I said.

The driver sighed. "Yes, sir, I can see that was a mistake. It was meant for you to understand that the warning is serious, see. Take no notice of it, and you'll find you're in real trouble. I'm telling you, real trouble."

"What warning?" I said, mystified.

"You're to lay off asking questions about Major Davidson," he said.

"What?" I goggled at him. It was so unexpected. "I haven't been asking questions about Major Davidson," I said weakly.

"I don't know about that, I'm sure," said the driver, mopping away, "but that's the message, and you'd do well to take heed of it, sir. I'm telling you for your own good. The boss don't like people poking into his affairs."

"Who is the boss?" I asked.

"Now, sir, you know better than to ask questions like that. Sonny, go and tell Bert we've finished here. We'll load up the horse."

Sonny stood up with a groan and went over to the door, his hand still pressed to his groin. He yelled something out of the window.

"Stand still, Mr. York, and you'll come to no harm," said the driver, his politeness unimpaired. He mopped, and looked at his handkerchief to see if his nose was still bleeding. It was. I took his advice, and stood still. He opened the door and climbed down out of the horse-box. A little time passed during which Sonny and I exchanged glares and nobody said anything.

Then there was the noise of bolts and clips being undone, and the side of the horse-box which formed the ramp was lowered to the ground. The fifth man, Bert, led the horse up the ramp and fastened him into the nearest stall. The driver raised the ramp again and fastened it.

I used the brief period while what was left of the daylight flooded into the box, to twist my head round as far as I could and take a clear look at Peaky. I saw what I expected, but it only increased my bewilderment.

The driver climbed into the cab, shut the door, and started the engine.

Bert said, "Take him over to the door." I needed no urging.

The horse-box began to move. Bert opened the door. Peaky and his pal let go of my arms and Bert gave me a push. I hit the ground just as the accelerating horse-box pulled out of the lay-by onto the deserted road. It was as well I had had a good deal of practice at falling off horses. Instinctively, I landed on my shoulder and rolled.

I sat on the ground and looked after the speeding horse-box. The number plate was mostly obscured by thick dust, but I had time to see the registration letters. They were APX.

The Lotus still stood in the lay-by. I picked myself up, dusted the worst off my suit, and walked over to it. I intended to follow the horse-box and see where it went. But the thorough driver had seen to it that I should not. The car would not start. Opening the bonnet to see how much damage had been done, I found that three of the four sparking plugs had been taken out. They lay in a neat row on the battery. It took me ten minutes to replace them, because my hands were trembling.

By then I had no hope of catching the horse-box or of finding anyone who had noticed its direction. I got back into the car and fastened the neck of my suit. My tie was missing altogether.

I took out the A.A. book and looked up the registration letters PX. For what it was worth, the horse-box was originally registered in West Sussex. If the number plate were genuine, it might be possible to discover the present owner. For a quarter of an hour I sat and thought. Then I started the car, turned it, and drove back into Maidenhead.

The town was bright with lights, though nearly all the shops were shut. The door of the police station was open wide. I went in and asked for Inspector Lodge.

"He isn't in yet," said the policeman at the enquiry desk, glancing up at the clock. It was ten past six. "He'll be here any minute, if you care to wait, sir."

"He isn't in yet? Do you mean he is just starting work for the day?"

"Yes, sir. He's on late turn. Busy evening here, Saturdays." He grinned. "Dance halls, pubs, and car crashes." I smiled back, sat down on the bench and waited. After five minutes Lodge came in quickly, peeling off his coat.

"Evening, Small, what's new?" he said to the policeman at the enquiry desk.

"Gentleman here to see you, sir," said Small, gesturing to me. "He's only been waiting a few minutes."

Lodge turned round. I stood up. "Good evening," I said.

"Good evening, Mr. York." Lodge gave me a piercing look but showed no surprise at seeing me. His eyes fell to the neck of my shirt, and his eyebrows rose a fraction. But he said only, "What can I do for you?"

"Are you very busy?" I asked. "If you have time, I would like to tell you . . . how I lost my tie." In mid-sentence I flunked saying baldly that I had been man-handled. As it was, Small looked at me curiously, clearly thinking me mad to come into a police station to tell an inspector how I lost my tie.

But Lodge, whose perception was acute, said, "Come into my office, Mr. York." He led the way. He hung up his hat and coat on pegs and lit the gas fire, but its glowing bars couldn't make a cosy place of the austere, square, filing-cabineted little room.

Lodge sat behind his tidy desk, and I, as before, faced him. He offered me a cigarette and gave me a light. As the smoke went comfortingly down into my lungs, I was wondering where to begin.

I said, "Have you got any further with the Major Davidson business since the day before yesterday?"

"No, I'm afraid not. It no longer has any sort of priority with us. Yesterday we discussed it in conference and consulted your Senior Steward, Sir Creswell Stampe. In view of the verdict at the inquest, your story is considered, on the whole, to be the product of a youthful and overheated imagination. No one but you saw any wire. The grooves on the posts of the fence may or may not have been caused by wire, but there is no indication *when* they were made. I understand it is fairly common practice for groundsmen to raise a wire across a fence so that members of the riding public shall not try to jump it and make holes in the birch." He paused, then went on, "Sir Creswell says the view of the National Hunt Committee, several of whom he has talked to on the telephone, is that you made a mistake. If you saw any wire, they contend, it must have belonged to the groundsman."

"Have they asked him?" I said.

Lodge sighed. "The head guardsman says he didn't leave any wire on the course, but one of his staff is old and vague, and can't be sure that he didn't."

We looked at each other in glum silence.

"And what do you think, yourself?" I asked finally.

Lodge said, "I believe you saw the wire and that Major Davidson was brought down by it. There is one fact which I personally consider significant enough to justify this belief. It is that the attendant who gave his name as Thomas Cook did not collect the pay due to him for two days' work. In my experience there has to be a very good reason for a workman to ignore his pay packet." He smiled sardonically.

"I could give you another fact to prove that Major Davidson's fall was no accident," I said, "but you'll have to take my word for it again. No evidence."

"Go on."

"Someone has been to great pains to tell me not to ask awkward questions about it." I told him about the events in and around the horse-box, and added, "And how's that for the product of a youthful and overheated imagination?"

"When did all this happen?" asked Lodge.

"About an hour ago."

"And what were you doing between then and the time you arrived here?"

"Thinking," I said, stubbing out my cigarette.

"Oh," said Lodge. "Well, have you given any thought to the improbabilities in your story? My chief isn't going to like them when I make my report."

"Don't make it then," I said, smiling. "But I suppose the most glaring improbability is that five men, a horse, and a horse-box should all be employed to give a warning which might much more easily have been sent by post."

"That certainly indicates an organisation of unusual size," said Lodge, with a touch of irony.

"There are at least ten of them," I said. "One or two are probably in hospital, though."

Lodge sat up straighter.

"What do you mean. How do you know?"

"The five men who stopped me today are all taxi-drivers. Either from London or Brighton, but I don't know which. I saw them at Plumpton races three days ago, fighting a pitched battle against a rival gang."

"What?" Lodge exclaimed. Then he said, "Yes, I saw a paragraph about it in a newspaper. Do you recognise them positively?"

"Yes," I said. "Sonny had his knife out at Plumpton, too, but he was pinned down by a big heavy man, and didn't get much chance to use it. But I saw his face quite clearly. Peaky you couldn't mistake, with that dark widow's peak growing down his forehead. The other three were all rounded up into the same group at Plumpton. I was waiting to give someone a lift, and I had a long time to look at the taxi-drivers after the fight was over. Bert, the man with the horse, had a black eye today, and the man who held my right arm, whose name I don't know, he had some sticking plaster on his forehead. But why were they all free? The last I saw them, they were bound for the cells, I thought, for disturbing the peace."

"They may be out on bail, or else they were let off with a fine. I don't know, without seeing a report," said Lodge. "Now why, in your opinion, were so many sent to warn you?"

"Rather flattering, sending five, when you come to think of it," I grinned. "Perhaps the taxi business is in the doldrums and they hadn't anything else to do. Or else it was, as the driver said, to ram the point home."

"Which brings me," said Lodge, "to another improbability. Why, if you were faced with a knife at your chest, did you throw yourself forward? Wasn't that asking for trouble?"

"I wouldn't have been so keen if he'd held the point a bit higher up; but it was against my breastbone. You'd need a hamamer to get a knife through that. I reckoned that I'd knock it out of Sonny's hand rather than into me, and that's what happened."

"Didn't it cut you at all?"

"Not much," I said.

"Let's see," said Lodge, getting up and coming round the desk.

I opened my shirt again. Between the second and third buttons there was a shallow cut an inch or so long in the skin over my breastbone. Some blood had clotted on the cut and there was a dried rusty trail down my chest where a few drops had run. My shirt was spotted here and there. Nothing. I hadn't felt it much.

Lodge sat down again. I buttoned my shirt.

"Now," he said, picking up his pen and biting the end of it. "What questions have you been asking about Major Davidson, and of whom have you asked them?"

"That is really what is most surprising about the whole affair," I said. "I've hardly asked anything of anybody. And I certainly haven't had any useful answers."

"But you must have touched a nerve somewhere," said Lodge. He took a sheet of paper out of the drawer. "Tell me the names of everyone with whom you have discussed the wire."

"With you," I said promptly. "And with Mrs. Davidson. And everyone at the inquest heard me say I'd found it."

"But I noticed that the inquest wasn't properly reported in the papers. There was no mention of wire in the press," he said. "And anyone seeing you at the inquest wouldn't have got the impression that you were hell-bent on unravelling the mystery. You took the verdict very calmly and not at all as if you disagreed with it."

"Thanks to your warning me in advance what to expect," I said.

Lodge's list looked short and unsatisfactory on the large sheet of paper.

"Anyone else?" he said.

"Oh . . . a friend . . . a Miss Ellery-Penn. I told her last night."

"Girl friend?" he asked bluntly. He wrote her down.

"Yes," I said.

"Anyone else?"

"No."

"Why not?" he asked, pushing the paper away.

"I reckoned you and Sir Creswell needed a clear field. I thought I might mess things up for you if I asked too many questions. Put people on their guard, ready with their answers—that sort of thing. But it seems, from what you've said about dropping your enquiries, that I might as well have gone ahead." I spoke a little bitterly.

Lodge looked at me carefully. "You resent being considered youthful and hot-headed," he said.

"Twenty-four isn't young," I said. "I seem to remember England once had a Prime Minister of that age. He didn't do so badly."

"That's irrelevant, and you know it," he said.

I grinned.

Lodge said, "What do you propose to do now?"

"Go home," I said, looking at my watch.

"No, I meant about Major Davidson?"

"Ask as many questions as I can think of," I said promptly.

"In spite of the warning?"

"Because of it," I said. "The very fact that five men were sent to warn me off means that there is a good deal to find out. Bill Davidson was a good friend, you know. I can't tamely let whoever caused his death get away with it." I thought a moment. "First, I'll find out who owns the taxis which Peaky and Co. drive."

"Well, unofficially, I wish you luck," said Lodge. "But be careful."

"Sure," I said, standing up.

Lodge came to the street door of the police station and shook hands. "Let me know how you get on," he said.

"Yes, I will."

He raised his hand in a friendly gesture, and went in. I resumed my interrupted journey to the Cotswolds. My wrenched shoulders were aching abominably, but as long as I concentrated on Bill's accident I could forget them.

It struck me that both the accident and the affair of the horse-box should give some clue to the mind which had hatched them. It was reasonable to assume it was the same mind. Both events were elaborate, where some simpler plan would have been effective, and the word "devious" drifted into my thoughts and I dredged around in my memory chasing its echo. Finally I traced it to Joe Nantwich and the threatening letter that had reached him ten days late, but decided that Joe's troubles had nothing to do with Bill's.

Both the attack on Bill and the warning to me had been, I was certain, more violent in the event than in the plan. Bill had died partly by bad luck; and I would have been less roughly handled had I not tried to escape. I came to the conclusion that I was looking for someone with a fanciful imagination, someone prepared to be brutal up to a point, and whose little squibs, because of their complicated nature, were apt to go off with bigger bangs than were intended.

And it was comforting to realize that my adversary was not a man of superhuman intelligence. He could make mistakes. His biggest so far, I thought, was to go to great lengths to deliver an unnecessary warning whose sole effect was to stir me to greater action.

FOR TWO DAYS I did nothing. There was no harm in giving the impression that the warning was being taken to heart.

I played poker with the children and lost to Henry because half my mind was occupied with his father's affairs.

Henry said, "You aren't thinking what you're doing, Alan," in a mock sorrowful tone as he rooked me of ten chips with two pairs.

"I expect he's in love," said Polly, turning on me an assessing female eye. There was that, too.

"Pooh," said Henry. He dealt the cards.

"What's in love?" said William, who was playing tiddly-winks with his chips, to Henry's annoyance.

"Soppy stuff," said Henry. "Kissing, and all that slush."

"Mummy's in love with me," said William, a cuddly child.

"Don't be silly," said Polly loftily, from her eleven years. "In love means weddings and brides and confetti and things."

"Well, Alan," said Henry, in a scornful voice, "you'd better get out of love quick or you won't have any chips left."

William picked up his hand. His eyes and mouth opened wide. This meant he had at least two aces. They were the only cards he ever raised on. I saw Henry give him a flick of a glance, then look back at his own hand. He discarded three, and took three more, and at his turn, he pushed away his cards. I turned them over. Two queens and two tens. Henry was a realist. He knew when to give in. And William, bouncing up and down with excitement, won only four chips with three aces and a pair of fives.

Not for the first time I wondered at the quirks of heredity. Bill had been a friendly, genuine man of many solid virtues. Scilla, matching him, was compassionate and loving. Neither was at all intellectually gifted; yet they had endowed their elder son with a piercing, exceptional intelligence.

And how could I guess, as I cut the cards for Polly and helped William straighten up his leaning tower of chips, that Henry already held in his sharp eight-year-old brain the key to the puzzle of his father's death.

He didn't know it himself.

CHAPTER 7

THE CHELTENHAM NATIONAL Hunt Festival meeting started on Tuesday, March 2nd.

Three days of superlative racing lay ahead, and the finest 'chasers in the world crowded into the racecourse stables. Ferries from Ireland brought them across by boat and plane load; dark horses from the bogs whose supernatural turn of foot was foretold in thick mysterious brogue, and golden geldings who had already taken prizes and cups galore across the Irish Sea.

Horse-boxes from Scotland, from Kent, from Devon, from everywhere, converged on Gloucestershire. Inside, they carried Grand National winners, champion hurdlers, all-conquering handicappers, splendid hunters: the aristocrats among jumpers.

With four big races in the three days reserved for them alone, every amateur jockey in the country who could beg, borrow, or buy a mount hurried to the course. A ride at Cheltenham was an honour: a win at Cheltenham an experience never to be forgotten. The amateur jockeys embraced the Festival with passionate fervour.

But one amateur jockey, Alan York, felt none of this passionate fervour as he drove into the car park. I could not explain it to myself, but for once the hum of the gathering crowd, the expectant faces, the sunshine of the cold invogorating March morning, even the prospect of riding three good horses at the meeting, stirred me not at all.

Outside the main gate I sought out the newspaper seller I had spoken to at Plumpton. He was a short, tubby little Cockney with a large moustache and a cheerful temperament. He saw me coming, and held out a paper.

"Morning Mr. York," he said. "Do you fancy your horse today?"

"You might have a bit on," I said, "but not your shirt. There's the Irishman to be reckoned with."

"You'll do him, all right."

"Well, I hope so." I waited while he sold a newspaper to an elderly man with enormous race glasses. Then I said, "Do you remember the taxi-drivers fighting at Plumpton?"

"Couldn't hardly forget it, could I?" He beamed.

"You told me one lot came from London and one from Brighton."

"Yes, that's right."

"Which lot were which?" I said. He looked mystified I said, "Which lot came from London and which came from Brighton?"

"Oh, I see." He sold a paper to two middle-aged ladies wearing thick tweeds and ribbed woolen stockings, and gave them change. Then he turned back to me.

"Which lot was which, like? Hm. I see 'em often enough, you know, but they ain't a friendly lot. They don't talk to you. Not like the private chauffeurs, see? I'd know the Brighton lot if I could see 'em, though. Know 'em by sight, see?" He broke off to yell "Midday Special" at the top of his lungs, and as a result sold three more papers. I waited patiently.

"How do you recognize them?" I asked.

"By their faces, 'course." He thought it a foolish question.

"Yes, but which faces? Can you describe them?"

"Oh, I see. There's all sorts."

"Can't you describe just one of them?" I asked.

He narrowed his eyes, thinking, and tugged his moustache. "One of 'em. Well, there's one nasty-looking chap with sort of slitty eyes. I wouldn't like a ride in his taxi. You'd know him by his hair, I reckon. It grows nearly down to his eyebrows. Rum-looking cove. What do you want him for?"

"I don't want him," I said. "I just want to know where he comes from."

"Brighton, that's it." He beamed at me. "There's another one I see sometimes, too. A young ted with sideboards, always cleaning his nails with a knife."

"Thanks a lot," I said. I gave him a pound note and his beam grew wider. He tucked it into an inside pocket.

"Best of luck, sir," he said. I left him, with "Midday Special" ringing in my ears, and went in to the weighing room, pondering on the information that my captors with the horse-box came from Brighton. Whoever had sent them could not have imagined that I had seen them before, and could find them again.

Preoccupied, I suddenly realised that Pete Gregory was talking to me. "Had a puncture on the way, but they've got here safely, that's the main thing. Are you listening, Alan?"

"Yes, Pete. Sorry. I was thinking."

"Glad to hear you can," said Pete with a fat laugh. Tough and shrewd though he was, his sense of humour had never grown up. Schoolboy insults passed as the highest form of wit for him; but one got used to it.

"How is Palindrome?" I asked. My best horse.

"He's fine. I was just telling you, they had a puncture . . ." He broke off, exasperated. He hated having to repeat things. "Oh well . . . do you want to go over to the stables and have a look at him?"

"Yes, please," I said.

We walked down to the stables. Pete had to come with me because of the tight security rules. Even owners could not visit their horses without the trainer to vouch for them, and stable boys had passes with their photographs on, to show at the stable gate. It was all designed to prevent the doping or "nobbling" of horses.

In his box I patted my beautiful 'chaser, an eight-year-old bay with black points, and gave him a lump of sugar. Pete clicked his tongue disapprovingly and said, "Not before the race," like a nanny who had caught her charge being given sweets before lunch. I grinned. Pete had a phobia on the subject.

"Sugar will give him more energy," I said, giving Palindrome another lump and making a fuss of him. "He looks well."

"He ought to win if you judge it right," said Pete. "Keep your eyes on that Irishman, Barney. He'll try to slip you all with a sudden burst as you go into the water so that he can start up the hill six lengths in front. I've seen him do it time and again. He gets everyone else chasing him like mad up the hill using up all the reserves they need for the finish. Now, either you burst with him, and go up the hill at his pace and no faster, or, if you lose him, take it easy up the hill and pile on the pressure when you're coming down again. Clear?"

"As glass," I said. Whatever one might think of Pete's jokes, his advice on how to ride races was invaluable, and I owed a great deal to it.

I gave Palindrome a final pat, and we went out into the yard. Owing to the security system, it was the quietest place on the racecourse.

"Pete, was Bill in any trouble, do you know?" I said, plunging in abruptly.

He finished shutting the door of Palindrome's box, and turned round slowly, and stood looking at me vaguely for so long that I began to wonder if he had heard my question.

But at last he said, "That's a big word, trouble. Something happened . . ."

"What?" I said, as he lapsed into silence again.

But instead of answering, he said, "Why should you think there was any . . . trouble?"

I told him about the wire. He listened with a calm, unsurprised expression, but his grey eyes were bleak.

He said, "Why haven't we all heard about it before?"

"I told Sir Creswell Stampe and the police a week ago," I said, "but with the wire gone they've nothing tangible to go on, and they're dropping it."

"But you're not?" said Pete. "Can't say I blame you. I can't help you much, though. There's only one thing . . . Bill told me he'd had a telephone call which made him laugh. But I didn't listen properly to what he said— I was thinking about my horses, you know how it is. It was something about Admiral falling. He thought it was a huge joke and I didn't go into it with him to find out what I'd missed. I didn't think it was important. When Bill was killed I did wonder if there could possibly be anything odd about it, but I asked you, and you said you hadn't noticed anything . . ." His voice trailed off.

"Yes, I'm sorry," I said. Then I asked, "How long before his accident did Bill tell you about the telephone call?"

"The last time I spoke to him," Pete said. "It was on the Friday morning, just before I flew to Ireland. I rang him to say that all was ready for Admiral's race at Maidenhead the next day."

We began to walk back to the weighing room. On an impulse I said, "Pete, do you ever use the Brighton taxis?" He lived and trained on the Sussex Downs.

"Not often," he said. "Why?"

"There are one or two taxi-drivers there I'd like to have a few words with," I said, not adding that I'd prefer to have the words with them one at a time in a deserted back alley.

"There are several taxi lines in Brighton, as far as I know," he said. "If you want to find one particular driver, why don't you try the railway station? That's where I've usually taken a taxi from. They line up there in droves for the London trains." His attention drifted off as an Irish horse passed us on its way into the paddock for the first race.

"That's Connemara Pal or I'm a Dutchman," said Pete enviously. "I took one of my owners over and tried to buy him, last August, but they wanted eight thousand for him. He was tucked away in a broken down hut behind some pig-styes, so my owner wouldn't pay that price. And now look at him. He won the Leopardstown novice 'chase on Boxing Day by twenty lengths and wouldn't have blown a candle out afterwards. Best young horse we'll see this year." Pete's mind was firmly back in its familiar groove, and we talked about the Irish raid until we were back in the weighing room.

I sought out Clem, who was very busy, and checked with him that my kit was all right, and that he knew the weight I was due to carry on Palindrome.

Kate had told me she was not coming to Cheltenham, so I went in search of the next best thing: news of her.

Dane's peg and section of bench were in the smaller of the two changing rooms, and he was sitting only one place away from the roaring stove, a sure sign of his rise in the jockeys' world. Champions get the warmest places by unwritten right. Beginners shiver beside the draughty doors.

He was clad in his shirt and pants, and was pulling on his nylon stockings. There was a hole in each foot and both his big toes were sticking comically out of them. He had long narrow feet, and long, narrow delicately strong hands to match.

"It's all very well for you to laugh," said Dane, pulling the tops of the stockings over his knees. "They don't seem to make nylons for size eleven shoes . . ."

"Get Walter to get you some stretching ones," I suggested. "Have you a busy day?"

"Three, including the Champion Hurdle," said Dane. "Pete has entered half the stable here." He grinned at me. "I might just find time to tell you about the Penn household, though, if that's what you're after. Shall I start with Uncle George, or Aunt Deb, or . . ." He broke off to pull on his silk breeches and his riding boots. His valet, Walter, gave him his under-jersey and some particularly vile pink and orange colours. Whoever had chosen them had paid no regard to their effect against a manly complexion. "Or do you want to hear about Kate?" finished Dane, covering up the sickening jersey with a windproof jacket.

The changing room was filling up, packed with the extra Irish jockeys who had come over for the meeting and were in high spirits and robust voice. Dane and I went out into the crowded weighing room, where at least one could hear oneself speak.

"Uncle George," he said, "is a gem. And I'm not going to spoil him for you by telling you about him. Aunt Deb is the Honourable Mrs. Penn to you and me, mate, and Aunt Deb to Kate alone. She has a chilly sort of charm that lets you know she would be downright rude if she were not so well bred. She disapproved of me, for a start. I think she disapproves on principle of everything to do with racing, including Heavens Above and Uncle George's idea of a birthday present."

"Go on," I urged, anxious for him to come to the most interesting part of the chronicle before someone else buttonholed him.

"Ah yes. Kate. Gorgeous, heavenly Kate. Strictly, you know, her name is Kate Ellery, not Penn at all. Uncle George added the hyphen and the Penn to her name when he took her in. He said it would be easier for her to have the same surname as him—save a lot of explanations. I suppose it does," said Dane, musingly, knowing full well how he was tantalising me. He relented, and grinned. "She sent you her love."

I felt a warm glow inside. The Cheltenham Festival meeting suddenly seemed not a bad place to be, after all.

"Thanks," I said, trying not to smile fatuously and scarcely succeeding. Dane looked at me speculatively; but I changed the subject back to racing, and presently I asked him if he had ever heard Bill Davidson spoken of in connection with any sort of odd happenings.

"No, I never did," he said positively. I told him about the wire. His reaction was typical.

"Poor Bill," he said with anger. "Poor old Bill. What a bloody shame."

"So if you hear anything which might have even the faintest significance . . ."

"I'll pass it on to you," he promised.

At that moment Joe Nantwich walked straight into Dane as if he hadn't seen him. He stopped without apology, took a step back, and then went on his way to the changing room. His eyes were wide, unfocused, staring.

"He's drunk," said Dane, incredulously. "His breath smells like a distillery."

"He has his troubles," I said.

"He'll have more still before the afternoon's much older. Just wait till one of the Stewards catches that alcoholic blast."

Joe reappeared at our side. It was true that one could smell his approach a good yard away. Without preamble he spoke directly to me.

"I've had another one." He took a paper out of his pocket. It had been screwed up and straightened out again, so that it was wrinkled in a hundred fine lines, but its ball-pointed message was still abundantly clear.

"BOLINGBROKE. THIS WEEK," it said.

"When did you get it?" I asked.

"It was here when I arrived, waiting for me in the letter rack."

"You've tanked up pretty quickly, then," I said.

"I'm not drunk," said Joe indignantly. "I only had a couple of quick ones in the bar opposite the weighing room."

Dane and I raised our eyebrows in unison. The bar opposite the weighing room had no front wall, and anyone drinking there was in full view of every trainer, owner, and Steward who walked out of the weighing room. There might be a surer way for a jockey to commit professional suicide than to have "a couple of quick ones" at that bar before the first race, but I couldn't think of it off-hand. Joe hiccuped.

"Double quick ones, I imagine," said Dane with a smile, taking the paper out of my hand and reading it. "What does it mean, 'Bolingbroke. This week'? Why are you so steamed up about it?"

Joe snatched the paper away and stuffed it back into his pocket. He seemed for the first time to be aware that Dane was listening.

"It's none of your business," he said rudely.

I felt a great impulse to assure him it was none of mine, either. But he turned back to me and said, "What shall I do?" in a voice full of whining self-pity.

"Are you riding today?" I asked.

"I'm in the fourth and the last. Those bloody amateurs have got two races all to themselves today. A bit thick, isn't it, leaving us only four races to earn our living in? Why don't the fat-arsed gentlemen riders stick to the point-to-points where they belong? That's all they're—well fit for," he added, alliteratively.

There was a small silence. Dane laughed. Joe was after all not too drunk to realise he was riding his hobby horse in front of the wrong man. He said weakly, in his smarmiest voice, "Well, Alan, of course I didn't mean you personally."

"If you still want my advice, in view of your opinion of amateur jockeys," I said, keeping a straight face, "you should drink three cups of strong black coffee and stay out of sight as long as you can."

"I mean, what shall I do about this note?" Joe had a thicker skin than a coach-hide cabin trunk.

"Pay it no attention at all," I said. "I should think that whoever wrote it is playing with you. Perhaps he knows you like to drown your sorrows in whisky and is relying on you to destroy yourself without his having to do anything but send you frightening letters. A neat, bloodless, and effective revenge."

The sullen pout on Joe's babyish face slowly changed into a mulish determination which was only slightly less repellent.

"No one's going to do that to me," he said, with an aggressiveness which I guessed would diminish with the alcohol level in his blood. He weaved off out of the weighing room door, presumably in search of black coffee. Before Dane could ask me what was going on, he received a hearty slap on the back from Sandy Mason, who was staring after Joe with dislike.

"What's up with that stupid little clot?" he asked, but he didn't wait for an answer. He said, "Look, Dane, be a pal and gen me up on this horse of Gregory's. I'm riding in the first. I've never seen it before, as far as I know. It seems the owner likes my red hair or something." Sandy's infectious laugh made several people look round with answering smiles.

"Sure," said Dane. They launched into a technical discussion and I turned away from them. But Dane touched my arm.

He said, "Is it all right for me to tell people, say Sandy for instance, about the wire and Bill?"

"Yes, do. You might strike oil with someone I wouldn't have thought of asking about it. But be careful." I thought of telling him about the warning in the horse-box, but it was a long story and it seemed enough to say, "Remember that you're stirring up people who can kill, even if by mistake."

He looked startled. "Yes, you're right. I'll be careful."

We turned back to Sandy together.

"What are you two so solemn about? Has someone swiped that luscious brunette you're both so keen on?" he said.

"It's about Bill Davidson," said Dane, disregarding this.

"What about him?"

"The fall that killed him was caused by some wire being strung across the top of the fence. Alan saw it."

Sandy looked aghast. "Alan saw it," he repeated, and then, as the full meaning of what Dane had said sank in, "but that's murder."

I pointed out the reasons for supposing the murder had not been intended. Sandy's brown eyes stared at me unwinkingly until I had finished.

"I guess you're right," he said. "What are you going to do about it?"

"He's trying to find out what is behind it all," said Dane. "We thought you might be able to help. Have you heard anything that might explain it? People tell you things, you know." '

Sandy ran his strong brown hands through his unruly red hair, and rubbed the nape of his neck. This brain massage produced no great thoughts, however. "Yes, but mostly they tell me about their girl friends or their bets or such like. Not Major Davidson though. We weren't exactly on a bosom pals basis, because he thought I strangled a horse belonging to a friend of his. Well," said Sandy with an engaging grin, "maybe I did, at that. Anyway, we had words, as they say, a few months ago."

"See if your bookmaker friends have heard any whispers, then," said Dane. "They usually have their ears usefully to the ground."

"O.K.," said Sandy. "I'll pass the news along and see what happens. Now come on, we haven't much time before the first and I wanted to know what this sod of a horse is going to do." And as Dane hesitated, he said, "Come on, you don't have to wrap it up. Gregory only asks me to ride for him when it's such a stinker that he daren't ask any sensible man to get up on it."

"It's a mare," said Dane, "with a beastly habit of galloping into the bottoms of fences as if they weren't there. She usually ends up in the open ditch."

"Well thanks," said Sandy, apparently undaunted by this news. "I'll tan her hide for her and she'll soon change her ways. See you later, then." He went into the changing room.

Dane looked after him. "The horse isn't foaled that could frighten that blighter Sandy," he said with admiration.

"Nothing wrong with his nerve," I agreed. "But why ever is Pete running an animal like that here, of all places?"

"The owner fancies having a runner at Cheltenham. You know how it is. Snob value, and so on," he said indulgently.

We were being jostled continually, as we talked, by the throng of trainers and owners. We went outside. Dane was immediately appropriated by a pair of racing journalists who wanted his views on his mount in the Gold Cup, two days distant.

The afternoon wore on. The racing began. With the fine sunny day and the holiday mood of the crowd, the excitement was almost crackling in the air.

Sandy got the mare over the first open ditch but disappeared into the next. He came back with a broad smile, cursing hard.

Joe reappeared after the second race, looking less drunk but more frightened. I avoided him shamelessly.

Dane, riding like a demon, won the Champion Hurdle by a head. Pete, patting his horse and sharing with the owner the congratulations of the great crowd round the unsaddling enclosure, was so delighted he could hardly speak. Large and red-faced, he stood there with his hat pushed back showing his baldness, trying to look as if this sort of thing happened every day, when it was in fact the most important winner he had trained.

He was so overcome that he forgot, as we stood some time later in the parade ring before the amateur's race, to make his customary joke about Palindrome going backwards as well as forwards. And when I, following his advice to the letter, stuck like a shadow to the Irishman when he tried to slip the field, lay a scant length behind him all the way to the last fence, and passed him with a satisfying spurt fifty yards from the winning post, Pete said his day was complete.

I could have hugged him, I was so elated. Although I had won several races back in Rhodesia and about thirty since I had been in England, this was my first win at Cheltenham. I felt as high as if I had already drunk the champagne which waited unopened in the changing room, the customary crateful of celebration for Champion Hurdle day. Palindrome was, in my eyes, the most beautiful, most intelligent, most perfect horse in the world. I walked on air to the scales to weigh in, and changed into my ordinary clothes, and had still not returned to earth when I went outside again. The gloom I had arrived in seemed a thousand years ago. I was so happy I could have turned cartwheels like a child. Such total, unqualified fulfillment comes rarely enough and unexpectedly. I wished that my father were there to share it.

The problem of Bill had receded like a dot in the distance, and it was only because I had earlier planned to do it that I directed my airy steps down to the horse-box parking ground.

It was packed. About twenty horses ran in each race that day, and almost every horse-box available must have been pressed into service to bring them. I sauntered along the rows, humming lightheartedly, looking at the number plates with half an eye and less attention.

And there it was.

APX 708.

My happiness burst like a bubble.

There was no doubt it was the same horse-box. Regulation wooden

Jennings design. Elderly, with dull and battered varnish. No name or owner or trainer painted anywhere on the doors or bodywork.

There was no one in the driver's cab. I walked round to the back, opened the door, and climbed in.

The horse-box was empty except for a bucket, a hay net, and a rug, the normal traveling kit for racehorses. The floor was strewn with straw, whereas three days earlier it had been swept clean.

The rug, I thought, might give me a clue as to where the box had come from. Most trainers and some owners have their initials embroidered or sewn in tape in large letters on the corners of their horse rugs. If there were initials on this one, it would be easy.

I picked it up. It was pale fawn with a dark brown binding. I found the initials. I stood there as if turned to stone. Plainly in view, embroidered in dark brown silk, where the letters A. Y.

It was my own rug.

PETE, WHEN I ran him to earth, looked in no mood to answer any questions needing much thought. He leaned back against the weighing room wall with a glass of champagne in one hand and a cigar in the other, surrounded by a pack of friends similarly equipped. From their rosy smiling faces I gathered the celebration had already been going on for some time.

Dane thrust a glass into my hand.

"Where have you been? Well done on Palindrome. Have some bubbly. The owner's paying, God bless him." His eyes were alight with that fantastic, top-of-the-world elation that I had lately felt myself. It began to creep back into me, too. It was, after all, a great day. Mysteries could wait.

I drank a sip of champagne and said, "Well done yourself, you old son-of-a-gun. And here's to the Gold Cup."

"No such luck," said Dane. "I haven't much chance in that." And from his laughing face I gathered he didn't care, either. We emptied our glasses. "I'll get another bottle," he said, diving into the noisy, crowded changing room.

Looking around I saw Joe Nantwich backed up into a nearby corner by the enormous Mr. Tudor. The big man was doing the talking, forcefully, his dark face almost merging with the shadows. Joe, still dressed in racing colours, listened very unhappily.

Dane came back with the bubbles fizzing out of a newly opened bottle and filled our glasses. He followed my gaze.

"I don't know whether Joe was sober or not, but didn't he make a hash of the last race?" he said.

"I didn't see it."

"Brother, you sure missed something. He didn't try a yard. His horse damned nearly stopped altogether at the hurdle over on the far side, and it was second favourite, too. What you see now," he gestured with the bottle, "is, I should think, our Joe getting the well-deserved sack."

"That man owns Bolingbroke," I said.

"Yes, that's right. Same colours. What a fool Joe is. Owners with five or six goodish horses don't grow on bushes any more."

Clifford Tudor had nearly done. As he turned away from Joe in our direction we heard the tail end of his remarks.

". . . think you can make a fool of me and get away with it. The Stewards can warn you off altogether, as far as I'm concerned."

He strode past us, giving me a nod of recognition, which surprised me, and went out.

Joe leaned against the wall for support. His face was pallid and sweating. He looked ill. He took a few unsteady steps towards us and spoke without caution, as if he had forgotten that Stewards and members of the National Hunt Committee might easily overhear.

"I had a phone call this morning. The same voice as always. He just said, 'Don't win the sixth race' and rang off before I could say anything. And then that note saying 'Bolingbroke. This week.' . . . I don't understand it. And I didn't win the race and now that bloody wog says he'll get another jockey . . . and the Stewards have started an enquiry about my riding . . . and I feel sick."

"Have some champagne," said Dane, encouragingly.

"Don't be so bloody helpful," said Joe, clutching his stomach and departing towards the changing room.

"What the hell's going on?" said Dane.

"I don't know," I said, perplexed and more interested in Joe's troubles than I had been before. The phone call was inconsistent, I thought, with the notes. One ordered business as usual, the other promised revenge. "I wonder if Joe always tells the truth," I said.

"Highly unlikely," said Dane, dismissing it.

One of the Stewards came and reminded us that even after the Champion Hurdle, drinking in the weighing room itself was frowned on, and would we please drift along into the changing room. Dane did that, but I finished my drink and went outside.

Pete, still attended by a posse of friends, had decided that it was time to go home. The friends were unwilling. The racecourse bars, they were saying, were still open.

I walked purposefully up to Pete, and he made me his excuse for breaking away. We went towards the gates.

"Whew, what a day!" said Pete, mopping his brow with a white handkerchief and throwing away the stub of his cigar.

"A wonderful day," I agreed, looking at him carefully.

"You can take that anxious look off your face, Alan, my lad. I'm as sober as a judge and I'm driving myself home."

"Good. In that case you'll have no difficulty in answering one small question for me?"

"Shoot."

"In what horse-box did Palindrome come to Cheltenham?" I said.

"Eh? I hired one. I had five runners here today. The hurdler, the mare, and the black gelding came in my own box. I had to hire one for Palindrome and the novice Dane rode in the first."

"Where did you hire it from?"

"What's the matter?" asked Pete. "I know it's a bit old, and it had a puncture on the way, as I told you, but it didn't do him any harm. Can't have done, or he wouldn't have won."

"No, it's nothing like that," I said. "I just want to know where the horse-box comes from."

"It's not worth buying. If that's what you're after. Too old by half."

"Pete, I don't want to buy it. Just tell me where it comes from."

"The firm I usually hire a box from, Littlepeths of Steyning." He frowned. "Wait a minute. At first they said all their boxes were booked up, then they said they could get me a box if I didn't mind an old one."

"Who drove it here?" I asked

"Oh, one of their usual drivers. He was swearing a bit at having to drive such an old hen coop. He said the firm had got two good horse-boxes out of action in Cheltenham week and he took a poor view of the administration."

"Do you know him well?"

"Not exactly well. He often drives the hired boxes, that's all. He's always grousing about something. Now, what is all this in aid of?"

"It may have something to do with Bill's death," I said, "but I'm not sure what. Can you find out where the box really comes from? Ask the hire firm? And don't mention me, if you don't mind."

"Is it important?" asked Pete.

"Yes, it is."

"I'll ring 'em tomorrow morning, then," he said.

AS SOON AS he saw me the next day, Pete said, "I asked about that horse-box. It belongs to a farmer near Steyning. I've got his name and address here." He tucked two fingers into his breast pocket, brought out a slip of paper, and gave it to me. "The farmer uses the box to take his hunters around, and his children's show jumpers in the summer. He sometimes lets the hire firm use it, if he's not needing it. Is that what you wanted?"

"Yes, thank you very much," I said. I put the paper in my wallet.

By the end of the Festival meeting, I had repeated the story of the wire to at least ten more people, in the hope that someone might know why it had been put there. The tale spread fast round the racecourse.

I told fat Lew Panake, the well-dressed bookmaker who took my occasional bets. He promised to "sound out the boys" and let me know.

I told Calvin Bone, a professional punter, whose nose for the smell of dirty work was as unerring as a bloodhound's.

I told a sly little tout who made his living passing on stray pieces of information to anyone who would pay for them.

I told the newspaper seller, who tugged his moustache and ignored a customer.

I told a racing journalist who could scent a doping scandal five furlongs away.

I told an army friend of Bill's; I told Clem in the weighing room; I told Pete Gregory's head traveling lad.

From all this busy sowing of the wind I learned absolutely nothing. And I would still, I supposed, have to reap the whirlwind.

CHAPTER 8

ON SATURDAY MORNING as I sat with Scilla and the children and Joan round the large kitchen table having a solidly domestic breakfast, the telephone rang.

Scilla went to answer it, but came back saying, "It's for you, Alan. He wouldn't give his name."

I went into the drawing-room and picked up the receiver. The March sun streamed through the windows onto a big bowl of red and yellow striped crocuses which stood on the telephone table. I said, "Alan York speaking."

"Mr. York, I gave you a warning a week ago today. You have chosen to ignore it."

I felt the hairs rising on my neck. My scalp itched. It was a soft voice with a husky, whispering note to it, not savage or forceful, but almost mildly conversational.

I didn't answer. The voice said, "Mr. York? Are you still there?"

"Yes."

"Mr. York, I am not a violent man. Indeed, I dislike violence. I go out of my way to avoid it, Mr. York. But sometimes it is thrust upon me, sometimes it is the only way to achieve results. Do you understand me, Mr. York?"

"Yes," I said.

"If I were a violent man, Mr. York, I would have sent you a rougher warning last week. And I'm giving you another chance, to show you how reluctant I am to harm you. Just mind your own business and stop asking foolish questions. That's all. Just stop asking questions, and nothing will happen to you." There was a pause, then the soft voice went on, with a shade, a first tinge of menace, "Of course, if I find that violence is absolutely necessary, I always get someone else to apply it. So that I don't have to watch. So that it is not too painful to me. You do understand me, I hope, Mr. York?"

"Yes," I said again. I thought of Sonny, his vicious grin, and his knife.

"Good, then that's all. I do so hope you will be sensible. Good morning, Mr. York." There was a click as he broke the connection.

I jiggled the telephone rest to recall the operator. When she answered I asked if she could tell me where the call had come from.

"One moment, please," she said. She suffered from enlarged adenoids. She came back. "It was routed through London," she said, "but I can't trace it beyond there. So sorry."

"Never mind. Thank you very much," I said.

"Pleasure, I'm sure," said the adenoids.

I put down the receiver and went back to my breakfast.

"Who was that?" asked Henry, spreading marmalade thickly on his toast.

"Man about a dog," I said.

"Or in other words," said Polly, "ask no questions and you'll be told no thumping lies."

Henry made a face at her and bit deeply into his toast. The marmalade oozed out of one corner of his mouth. He licked it.

"Henry always wants to know who's ringing up," said William.

"Yes, darling," said Scilla absently, rubbing some egg off his jersey. "I wish you would lean over your plate when you eat, William." She kissed the top of his blond head.

I passed my cup to Joan for more coffee.

Henry said, "Will you take us out to tea in Cheltenham, Alan? Can we have some of those squelchy cream things like last time, and ice-cream sodas with straws, and some peanuts for coming home?"

"Oh, yes," said William, blissfully.

"I'd love to," I said, "but I can't today. We'll do it next week, perhaps." The day of my visit to Kate's house had come at last. I was to stay there for two nights, and I planned to put in a day at the office on Monday.

Seeing the children's disappointed faces I explained, "Today I'm going to stay with a friend. I won't be back until Monday evening."

"What a bore," said Henry.

THE LOTUS ATE up the miles between the Cotswolds and Sussex with the deep purr of a contented cat. I covered the fifty miles of good road from Cirencester to Newbury in fifty-three minutes, not because I was in a great hurry, but out of sheer pleasure in driving my car at the speed it was designed for. And I was going towards Kate. Eventually.

Newbury slowed me to a crawl, to a halt. Then I zipped briefly down the Basingstoke road, past the American air base at Greenham Common, and from the twisty village of Kingsclere onwards drove at a sedate pace which seldom rose over sixty.

Kate lived about four miles from Burgess Hill, in Sussex.

I arrived in Burgess Hill at twenty past one, found my way to the railway station, and parked in a corner, tucked away behind a large shooting brake. I went into the station and bought a return ticket to Brighton. I didn't care to reconnoitre in Brighton by car: the Lotus had already identified me into one mess, and I hesitated to show my hand by taking it where it could be spotted by a cruising taxi driven by Peaky, Sonny, Bert, or the rest.

The journey took sixteen minutes. On the train I asked myself, for at least the hundredth time, what chance remark of mine had landed me in the horse-box hornet's nest. Whom had I alarmed by not only revealing that I knew about the wire, but more especially by saying that I intended to find out who had put it there? I could think of only two possible answers; and one of them I didn't like a bit.

I remembered saying to Clifford Tudor on the way from Plumpton to Brighton that a lot of questions would have to be answered about Bill's death; which was as good as telling him straight out that I knew the fall hadn't been an accident, and that I meant to do something about it.

And I had made the same thing quite clear to Kate. To Kate. To Kate. To Kate. The wheels of the train took up the refrain and mocked me.

Well, I hadn't sworn her to secrecy, and I hadn't seen any need to. She could have passed on what I had said to the whole of England, for all I knew. But she hadn't had much time. It had been after midnight when she left me in London, and the horse-box had been waiting for me seventeen hours later.

The train slowed into Brighton station. I walked up the platform and through the gate in a cluster of fellow passengers, but hung back as we came through the booking hall and out towards the forecourt. There were about twelve taxis parked there, their drivers standing outside them, surveying the outpouring passengers for custom. I looked at all the drivers carefully, face by face.

They were all strangers. None of them had been at Plumpton.

Not unduly discouraged, I found a convenient corner with a clear view of arriving taxis and settled myself to wait, resolutely ignoring the cold draught blowing down my neck. Taxis came up and went like busy bees, bringing passengers, taking them away. The trains from London attracted them like honey.

Gradually a pattern emerged. There were four distinct groups of them. One group had a broad green line painted down the wings, with the name Green Band on the doors. A second group had yellow shields on the doors, with small letters in black on the shields. A third group were bright cobalt blue all over. Into the fourth group I put the indeterminate taxis which did not belong to the other lines.

I waited for nearly two hours, growing stiffer and stiffer, and receiving more and more curious looks from the station staff. I looked at my watch. The last train I could catch and still arrive at Kate's at the right time was due to leave in six minutes. I had begun to straighten up and massage my cold neck, ready to go and board it, when at last my patience was rewarded.

Empty taxis began to arrive and form a waiting line, which I now knew meant that another London train was due. The drivers got out of their cars and clustered in little groups, talking. Three dusty black taxis arrived in minor convoy and pulled up at the end of the line. They had faded yellow shields painted on the doors. The drivers got out.

One of them was the polite driver of the horse-box. A sensible, solid citizen, he looked. Middle-aged, unremarkable, calm. I did not know the others.

I had three minutes left. The black letters were tantalisingly small on the yellow shields. I couldn't get close enough to read them without the polite driver seeing me, and I had no time to wait until he had gone. I went over to the ticket office, hovered impatiently while a woman argued about half fares for her teenage child, and asked a simple question.

"What is the name of the taxis with yellow shields on the doors?" The young man in the office gave me an uninterested glance.

"Marconicars, sir. Radio cabs, they are."

"Thank you," I said, and sprinted for the platform.

KATE LIVED IN a superbly proportioned Queen Anne house which generations of gothic-ruin-minded Victorians had left miraculously unspoilt. Its graceful symmetry, its creamy gravelled drive, its tidy lawns already mown in early spring, its air of solid serenity, all spoke of a social and financial security of such long standing that it was to be taken entirely for granted.

Inside, the house was charming, with just a saving touch of shabbiness about the furnishings, as if, though rich, the inhabitants saw no need to be either ostentatious or extravagant.

Kate met me at the door and took my arm, and walked me across the hall.

"Aunt Deb is waiting to give you tea," she said. "Tea is a bit of a ritual with Aunt Deb. You will be in her good graces for being punctual, thank goodness. She is very Edwardian, you'll find. The times have moved without her in many ways." She sounded anxious and apologetic, which meant to me that she loved her aunt protectively, and wished me to make allowances. I squeezed her arm reassuringly, and said, "Don't worry."

Kate opened one of the white panelled doors and we went into the drawing-room. It was a pleasant room, wood panelled and painted white, with a dark plum-coloured carpet, good Persian rugs, and flower-patterned curtains. On a sofa at right angles to a glowing log fire sat a woman of about seventy. Beside her stood a low round table bearing a tray with Crown Derby cups and saucers and a Georgian silver teapot and cream jug. A dark brown dachshund lay asleep at her feet.

Kate walked across the room and said with some formality, "Aunt Deb, may I introduce Alan York?"

Aunt Deb extended to me her hand, palm downwards. I shook it, feeling that in her younger days it would have been kissed.

"I am delighted to meet you, Mr. York," said Aunt Deb. And I saw exactly what Dane meant about her chilly, well-bred manner. She had no warmth, no genuine welcome in her voice. She was still, for all her years, or even perhaps because of them, exceedingly good-looking. Straight eyebrows, perfect nose, clearly outlined mouth. Grey hair cut and dressed by a first-class man. A slim, firm body, straight back, elegant legs crossed at the ankles. A fine silk shirt under a casual tweed suit, hand-made shoes of soft leather. She had everything. Everything except the inner fire which would make Kate at that age worth six of Aunt Deb.

She poured me some tea, and Kate handed it to me. There were pâté sandwiches and a home-made Madeira cake, and although tea was usually a meal I avoided if possible, I found my jinks in Brighton and no lunch had made me hungry. I ate and drank, and Aunt Deb talked.

"Kate tells me you are a jockey, Mr. York." She said it as if it were as dubious as a criminal record. "Of course I am sure you must find it very amusing, but when I was a gel it was not considered an acceptable occupation in acquaintances. But this is Kate's home, and she may ask whoever she likes here, as she knows."

I said mildly, "Surely Aubrey Hastings and Geoffrey Bennett were both jockeys and acceptable when you were—er—younger?"

She raised her eyebrows, surprised. "But they were gentlemen," she said.

I looked at Kate. She had stuffed the back of her hand against her mouth, but her eyes were laughing.

"Yes," I said to Aunt Deb, with a straight face. "That makes a difference, of course."

"You may realise then," she said, looking at me a little less frigidly, "that I do not altogether approve of my niece's new interests. It is one thing to own a racehorse, but quite another to make personal friends of the jockeys one employs to ride it. I am very fond of my niece. I do not wish her to make an undesirable . . . alliance. She is perhaps too young, and has led too sheltered a life, to understand what is acceptable and what is not. But I am sure you do, Mr. York?"

Kate, blushing painfully, said, "Aunt Deb!" This was apparently worse than she was prepared for.

"I understand you very well, Mrs. Penn," I said, politely.

"Good," she said. "In that case, I hope you will have an enjoyable stay with us. May I give you some more tea?"

Having firmly pointed out to me my place and having received what she took to be my acknowledgement of it, she was prepared to be a gracious hostess. She had the calm authority of one whose wishes had been law from the nursery. She began to talk pleasantly enough about the weather and her garden, and how the sunshine was bringing on the daffodils.

Then the door opened, and a man came in. I stood up.

Kate said, "Uncle George, this is Alan York."

He looked ten years younger than his wife. He had thick well-groomed grey hair and a scrubbed pink complexion with a fresh-from-the-bathroom moistness about it, and when he shook hands his palm was soft and moist also.

Aunt Deb said, without disapproval in her voice, "George, Mr. York is one of Kate's jockey friends."

He nodded. "Yes, Kate told me you were coming. Glad to have you here."

He watched Aunt Deb pour him a cup of tea, and took it from her, giving her a smile of remarkable fondness.

He was too fat for his height, but it was not a bloated-belly fatness. It was spread all over him as though he were padded. The total effect was of a jolly rotundity. He had a vaguely good-natured expression so often found on fat people, a certain bland, almost foolish, looseness of the facial muscles. And yet his fat-lidded eyes, appraising me over the rim of the teacup as he drank, were shrewd and unsmiling. He reminded me of so many businessmen I had met in my work, the slap-you-on-the-back, come-and-play-golf men who would ladle out the Krug '49 and caviar with one hand while they tried to take over your contracts with the other.

He put down his cup and smiled, and the impression faded.

"I am very interested to meet you, Mr. York," he said, sitting down and gesturing to me to do the same. He looked me over carefully, inch by inch, while he asked me what I thought of Heavens Above. We discussed the horse's possibilities with Kate, which meant that I did most of the talking, as Kate knew little more than she had at Plumpton, and Uncle George's total information about racing seemed to be confined to Midday Sun's having won the Derby in 1937.

"He remembers it because of 'Mad Dogs and Englishmen'," said Kate. "He hums it all the time. I don't think he knows the name of a single other horse."

"Oh, yes I do," protested Uncle George. "Bucephalus, Pegasus, and Black Bess."

I laughed. "Then why did you give a racehorse to your niece?" I asked.

Uncle George opened his mouth and shut it again. He blinked. Then he said, "I thought she should meet more people. She has no young company here with us, and I believe we may have given her too sheltered an upbringing."

Aunt Deb, who had been bored into silence by the subject of horses, returned to the conversation at this point.

"Nonsense," she said briskly. "She has been brought up as I was, which is the right way. Gels are given too much freedom nowadays, with the result that they lose their heads and elope with fortune hunters or men-about-town of unsavoury background. Gels need strictness and guidance if they are to behave as ladies, and make suitable, well-connected marriages."

She at least had the grace to avoid looking directly at me while she spoke. She leaned over and patted the sleeping dachshund instead.

Uncle George changed the subject with an almost audible jolt, and asked me where I lived.

"Southern Rhodesia," I said.

"Indeed?" said Aunt Deb. "How interesting. Do your parents plan to settle there permanently?" It was a delicate, practised, social probe.

"They were both born there," I answered.

"And will they be coming to visit you in England?" asked Uncle George.

"My mother died when I was ten. My father might come some time if he is not too busy."

"Too busy doing what?" asked Uncle George interestedly.

"He's a trader," I said, giving my usual usefully non-commital answer to this question. "Trader" could cover anything from a rag-and-bone man to what he actually was, the head of the biggest general trading concern in the Federation. Both Uncle George and Aunt Deb looked unsatisfied by this reply, but I did not add to it. It would have embarrassed and angered Aunt Deb to have had my pedigree and prospects laid out before her after her little lecture on jockeys, and in any case for Dane's sake I could not do it. He had faced Aunt Deb's social snobbery without any of the defences I could muster if I wanted to, and I certainly felt myself no better man than he.

I made instead a remark admiring an arrangement of rose prints on the white panelled walls, which pleased Aunt Deb but brought forth a sardonic glance from Uncle George.

"We keep our ancestors in the dining-room," he said.

Kate stood up. "I'll show Alan where he's sleeping, and so on," she said.

"Did you come by car?" Uncle George asked. I nodded. He said to Kate, "Then ask Culbertson to put Mr. York's car in the garage, will you, my dear?"

"Yes, Uncle George," said Kate, smiling at him.

As we crossed the hall again for me to fetch my suitcase from the car, Kate said, "Uncle George's chauffeur's name is not really Culbertson. It's Higgins, or something like that. Uncle George began to call him Culbertson because he plays bridge, and soon we all did it. Culbertson seems quite resigned to it now. Trust Uncle George," said Kate, laughing, "to have a chauffeur who plays bridge."

"Does Uncle George play bridge?"

"No, he doesn't like cards, or games of any sort. He says there are too many rules to them. He says he doesn't like learning rules and can't be bothered to keep them. I should think bridge with all those conventions would drive him dotty. Aunt Deb can play quite respectably, but she doesn't make a thing of it."

I lifted my suitcase out of the car, and we turned back.

Kate said, "Why didn't you tell Aunt Deb you were an amateur rider and rich, and so on?"

"Why didn't you?" I asked. "Before I came."

She was taken aback. "I . . . I . . . because." She could not bring out the truthful answer, so I said it for her.

"Because of Dane?"

"Yes, because of Dane." She looked uncomfortable.

"That's quite all right by me," I said lightly. "And I like you for it." I kissed her cheek, and she laughed and turned away from me, and ran up the stairs in relief.

A**FTER LUNCHEON—AUNT** Deb gave the word three syllables—on Sunday I was given permission to take Kate out for a drive.

In the morning Aunt Deb had been to church with Kate and me in attendance. The church was a mile distant from the house, and Culbertson drove us there in a well-polished Daimler. I, by Aunt Deb's decree, sat beside him. She and Kate went in the back.

While we stood in the drive waiting for Aunt Deb to come out of the house, Kate explained that Uncle George never went to church.

"He spends most of his time in his study. That's the little room next to the breakfast room," she said. "He talks to all his friends on the telephone for hours, and he's writing a treatise or a monograph or something about Red Indians, I think, and he only comes out for meals and things like that."

"Rather dull for your Aunt," I said, admiring the way the March sunlight lay along the perfect line of her jaw and lit red glints in her dark eyelashes.

"Oh, he takes her up to Town once a week. She has her hair done, and he looks things up in the library of the British Museum. Then they have a jolly lunch at the Ritz or somewhere stuffy like that, and go to a matinee or an exhibition in the afternoon. A thoroughly debauched programme," said Kate, with a dazzling smile.

After lunch, Uncle George invited me into his study to see what he called his "trophies." These were a collection of objects belonging to various primitive or barbaric peoples, and, as far as I could judge, would have done credit to any small museum.

Ranks of weapons, together with some jewellery, pots, and ritual objects were labelled and mounted on shelves inside glass cases which lined three walls of the room. Among others, there were pieces from Central Africa and the Polynesian Islands, from the Viking age of Norway and from the Maoris of New Zealand. Uncle George's interest covered the globe.

"I study one people at a time," he explained. "It gives me something to do since I retired, and I find it enthralling. Did you know that in the Fiji Islands the men used to fatten women like cattle and eat them?"

His eyes gleamed, and I had a suspicion that part of the pleasure he derived from primitive peoples lay in contemplation of their primitive violences. Perhaps he needed a mental antidote to those lunches at the Ritz, and the matinees.

I said, "Which people are you studying now? Kate said something about Red Indians . . . ?"

He seemed pleased that I was taking an interest in his hobby.

"Yes, I am doing a survey of all the ancient peoples of the Americas, and the North American Indians were my last subject. Their case is over here."

He showed me over to one corner. The collection of feathers, beads, knives, and arrows looked almost ridiculously like those in Western films, but I had no doubt that these were genuine. And in the centre hung a hank of black hair with a withered lump of matter dangling from it, and underneath was gummed the laconic label, "Scalp."

I turned round, and surprised Uncle George watching me with a look of secret enjoyment. He let his gaze slide past me to the case.

"Oh, yes," he said. "The scalp's a real one. It's only about a hundred years old."

"Interesting," I said noncommittally.

"I spent a year on the North American Indians because there are so many different tribes," he went on. "But I've moved on to Central America now. Next I'll do the South Americans, the Incas and the Fuegians and so on. I'm not a scholar, of course, and I don't do any field work, but I do write articles sometimes for various publications. At the moment I am engaged on a series about Indians for the *Boys' Stupendous Weekly*." His fat cheeks shook as he laughed silently at what appeared to be an immense private joke. Then he straightened his lips and the pink folds of flesh grew still, and he began to drift back towards the door.

I followed him, and paused by his big, carved, black oak desk which stood squarely in front of the window. On it, besides two telephones and a silver pen tray, lay several cardboard folders with pale blue stick-on labels marked Arapaho, Cherokee, Sioux, Navajo, and Mohawk.

Separated from these was another folder marked Mayas, and I idly stretched out my hand to open it, because I had never heard of such a tribe. Uncle George's plump fingers came down firmly on the folder, holding it shut.

"I have only just started on this nation," he said apologetically. "And there's nothing worth looking at yet."

"I've never heard of that tribe," I said.

"They were Central American Indians, not North," he said pleasantly. "They were astronomers and mathematicians, you know. Very civilised. I am finding them fascinating. They discovered that rubber bounced, and they made balls of it long before it was known in Europe. At the moment I am looking into their wars. I am trying to find out what they did with their prisoners of war. Several of their frescoes show prisoners begging for mercy." He paused, his eyes fixed on me, assessing me. "Would you like to help me correlate the references I have so far collected?" he said.

"Well . . . er . . . er . . ." I began.

Uncle George's jowls shook again. "I didn't suppose you would," he said. "You'd rather take Kate for a drive, no doubt."

As I had been wondering how Aunt Deb would react to a similar suggestion, this was a gift. So three o'clock found Kate and me walking round to the big garage behind the house, with Aunt Deb's grudging consent to our being absent at tea-time.

"You remember me telling you, a week ago, while we were dancing, about the way Bill Davidson died?" I said casually, while I helped Kate open the garage doors.

"How could I forget?"

"Did you by any chance mention it to anyone the next morning? There wasn't any reason why you shouldn't . . . but I'd like very much to know if you did."

She wrinkled her nose. "I can't really remember, but I don't think so. Only Aunt Deb and Uncle George, of course, at breakfast. I can't think of anyone else. I didn't think there was any secret about it, though." Her voice rose at the end into a question.

"There wasn't," I said, reassuring, fastening back the door.

"What did Uncle George do before he retired and took up anthropology?"

"Retired?" she said. "Oh, that's only one of his jokes. He retired when he was about thirty, I think, as soon as he inherited a whacking great private income from his father. For decades he and Aunt Deb used to set off round the world every three years or so, collecting all those gruesome relics he was showing you in the study. What did you think of them?"

I couldn't help a look of distaste, and she laughed and said, "That's what I think, too, but I'd never let him suspect it. He's so devoted to them all."

The garage was a converted barn. There was plenty of room for the four cars standing in it in a row. The Daimler, a new cream coloured convertible, my Lotus, and after a gap, the social outcast, an old black eight-horse-power saloon. All of them, including mine, were spotless. Culbertson was conscientious.

"We use that old car for shopping in the village and so on," said Kate. "This gorgeous cream job is mine. Uncle George gave it to me a year ago when I came home from Switzerland. Isn't it absolutely rapturous?" She stroked it with love.

"Can we go out in yours, instead of mine?" I asked. "I would like that very much, if you wouldn't mind."

She was pleased. She let down the roof and tied a blue silk scarf over her head, and drove us out of the garage into the sunlight, down the drive, and onto the road towards the village.

"Where shall we go?" she said.

"I'd like to go to Steyning," I said.

"That's an odd sort of place to choose," she said. "How about the sea?"

"I want to call on a farmer in Washington, near Steyning, to ask him about his horse-box," I said. And I told her how some men in a horse-box had rather forcefully told me not to ask questions about Bill's death.

"It was a horse-box belonging to this farmer at Washington," I finished. "I want to ask him who hired it from him last Saturday."

"Good heavens," said Kate. "What a lark." And she drove a little faster. I sat sideways and enjoyed the sight of her. The beautiful profile, the blue scarf whipped by the wind, with one escaping wisp of hair blowing on her forehead, the cherry-red curving mouth. She could twist your heart.

It was ten miles to Washington. We went into the village and stopped, and I asked some children on their way home from Sunday school where farmer Lawson lived.

"Up by there," said the tallest girl, pointing.

"Up by there" turned out to be a prosperous workmanlike farm with a yellow old farmhouse and a large new Dutch barn rising behind it. Kate drove into the yard and stopped, and we walked round through a garden gate to the front of the house. Sunday afternoon was not a good time to call on a farmer, who was probably enjoying his one carefree nap of the week, but it couldn't be helped.

We rang the door bell, and after a long pause the door opened. A young-ish good-looking man holding a newspaper looked at us enquiringly.

"Could I speak to Mr. Lawson, please?" I said.

"I'm Lawson," he said. He yawned.

"This is your farm?" I asked.

"Yes. What can I do for you?" He yawned agin.

I said I understood he had a horse-box for hire. He rubbed his nose with his thumb while he looked us over. Then he said, "It's very old, and it de-pends when you want it."

"Could we see it, do you think?" I asked.

"Yes," he said. "Hang on, a moment." He went indoors and we heard his voice calling out and a girl's voice answering him. Then he came back with-out the newspaper.

"It's round here," he said, leading the way. The horse-box stood out in the open, sheltered only by the hay piled in the Dutch barn. APX 708. My old friend.

I told Lawson then that I didn't really want to hire his box, but I wanted to know who had hired it eight days ago. And because he thought this ques-tion decidedly queer and was showing signs of hustling us off at once, I told him why I wanted to know.

"It can't have been my box," he said at once.

"It was," I said.

"I didn't hire it to anyone, eight days ago. It was standing right here all day."

"It was in Maidenhead," I said, obstinately.

He looked at me for a full half minute. Then he said, "If you are right, it was taken without me knowing about it. I and my family were all away last week-end. We were in London."

"How many people would know you were away?" I asked.

He laughed. "About twelve million, I should think. We were on one of those family quiz shows on television on Friday night. My wife, my eldest son, my daughter, and I. The younger boy wasn't allowed on because he's only ten. He was furious about it. My wife said on the programme that we were all going to the Zoo on Saturday and to the Tower of London on Sunday, and we weren't going home until Monday."

I sighed. "And how soon before you went up to the quiz show did you know about it?"

"A couple of weeks. It was all in the local papers, that we were going. I was a bit annoyed about it, really. It doesn't do to let every tramp in the neighborhood know you'll be away. Of course, there are my cowmen about, but it's not the same."

"Could you ask them if they saw anyone borrow your box?"

"I suppose I could. It's almost milking time, they'll be in soon. But I can't help thinking you've mistaken the number plate."

"Have you a middleweight thoroughbred bay hunter, then," I said, "with a white star on his forehead, one lop ear, and a straggly tail?"

His scepticism vanished abruptly. "Yes, I have," he said. "He's in the stable over there."

He went and had a look at him. It was the horse Bert had been leading up and down, all right.

"Surely your men would have missed him when they went to give him his evening feed?" I said.

"My brother—he lives a mile away—borrows him whenever he wants. The men would just assume he'd got him. I'll ask the cowmen."

"Will you ask them at the same time if they found a necktie in the box?" I said. "I lost one there, and I'm rather attached to it. I'd give ten bob to have it back."

"I'll ask them," said Lawson. "Come into the house while you wait." He took us through the back door, along a stone-flagged hall into a comfortably battered sitting-room, and left us. The voices of his wife and children and clatter of teacups could be heard in the distance. A half-finished jig-saw puzzle was scattered on a table; some toy railway lines snaked round the floor.

At length Lawson came back. "I'm very sorry," he said, "the cowmen thought my brother had the horse and one of them noticed the box had gone. They said they didn't find your tie, either. They're as blind as bats unless it's something of theirs that's missing."

I thanked him all the same for his trouble, and he asked me to let him know, if I found out, who had taken his box.

Kate and I drove off towards the sea.

She said, "Not a very productive bit of sleuthing, do you think? Anyone in the world could have borrowed the horse-box."

"It must have been someone who knew it was there," I pointed out. "I expect it was because it was so available that they got the idea of using it at all. If they hadn't known it would be easy to borrow, they'd have delivered their message some other way. I dare say one of those cowmen knows more than he's telling. Probably took a quiet tenner to turn a blind eye, and threw in the horse for local colour. Naturally he wouldn't confess it in a hurry to Lawson this afternoon."

"Well, never mind," said Kate lightheartedly. "Perhaps it's just as well Farmer Lawson had nothing to do with it. It would have been rather shattering if he had turned out to be the head of the gang. You would probably have been bopped behind the ear with a gun butt and dumped in a bag of cement out at sea and I would have been tied up on the railway lines in the path of oncoming diesels."

I laughed. "If I'd thought he could have possibly been the leader of the gang I wouldn't have taken you there."

She glanced at me. "You be careful," she said, "or you'll grow into a cossetting old dear like Uncle George. He's never let Aunt Deb within arm's length of discomfort, let alone danger. I think that's why she's so out of touch with modern life."

"You don't think danger should be avoided, then?" I asked.

"Of course not. I mean, if there's something you've got to do, then to hell with the danger." She gave an airy wave with her right hand to illustrate this carefree point of view, and a car's horn sounded vigourously just behind us. A man swept past glaring at Kate for her unintentional signal. She laughed.

She swung the car down to the sea in Worthing, and drove eastwards along the coast road. The smell of salt and seaweed was strong and refreshing. We passed the acres of new bungalows outside Worthing, the docks and the power stations of Shoreham, Southwick, and Portslade, the sedate façades of Hove, and came at length to the long promenade at Brighton. Kate turned deftly into a square in the town, and stopped the car.

"Let's go down by the sea," she said. "I love it."

We walked across the road, down some steps, and staggered across the bank of shingle on to the sand. Kate took her shoes off and poured out a stream of little stones. The sun shone warmly and the tide was out. We walked slowly along the beach for about a mile, jumping over the break-waters, and then turned and went back. It was a heavenly afternoon.

As we strolled hand in hand up the road towards Kate's car, I saw for the first time that she had parked it only a hundred yards from the Pavilion Plaza Hotel, where I had driven Clifford Tudor from Plumpton ten days earlier.

And talk of the devil, I thought. There he was. The big man was standing on the steps of the hotel, talking to the uniformed doorman. Even at a distance there was no mistaking that size, that dark skin, that important carriage of the head. I watched him idly.

Just before we arrived at Kate's car a taxi came up from behind us, passed us, and drew up outside the Pavilion Plaza. It was a black taxi with a yellow shield on the door, and this time it was close enough for me to read the name: Marconicars. I looked quickly at the driver and saw his profile as he went past. He had a large nose and a receding chin, and I had never seen him before.

Clifford Tudor said a few last words to the doorman, strode across the pavement, and got straight into the taxi without pausing to tell the driver where he wanted to go. The taxi drove off without delay.

"What are you staring at?" said Kate, as we stood beside her car.

"Nothing much," I said. "I'll tell you about it if you'd like some tea in the Pavilion Plaza Hotel."

"That's a dull dump," she said. "Aunt Deb approves of it."

"More sleuthing," I said.

"All right, then. Got your magnifying glass and bloodhound handy?"

We went into the hotel. Kate said she would go and tidy her hair. While she was gone I asked the young girl in the reception desk if she knew where I could find Clifford Tudor. She fluttered her eyelashes at me and I grinned encouragingly back.

"You've just missed him, I'm afraid," she said. "He's gone back to his flat."

"Does he come here often?" I asked.

She looked at me in surprise. "I thought you knew. He's on the board of governors. One of the chief shareholders. In fact," she added with remarkable frankness, "he very nearly owns this place and has more say in running it than the manager." It was clear from her voice and manner that she thoroughly approved of Mr. Tudor.

"Has he got a car?" I asked.

This was a very odd question, but she prattled on without hesitation. "Yes, he's got a lovely big car with a long bonnet and lots of chromium. Real classy. But he doesn't use it, of course. Mostly it's taxis for him. Why, just this minute I rang for one of those radio cabs for him. Real useful, they are. You just ring their office and they radio a message to the taxi that's nearest here and in no time at all it's pulling up outside. All the guests use them . . ."

"Mavis!"

The talkative girl stopped dead and looked round guiltily. A severe girl in her late twenties had come into the reception desk.

"Thank you for relieving me, Mavis. You may go now," she said.

Mavis gave me a flirting smile and disappeared.

"Now, sir, can I help you?" She was polite enough, but not the type to gossip about her employers.

"Er—can we have afternoon tea here?" I asked.

She glanced at the clock. "It's a little late for tea, but go along into the lounge and the waiter will attend to you."

Kate eyed the resulting fishpaste sandwiches with disfavour. "This is one of the hazards of detecting, I suppose," she said, taking a tentative bite. "What did you find out about what?"

I said I was not altogether sure, but that I was interested in anything that had even the remotest connection with the yellow shield taxis or with Bill Davidson, and Clifford Tudor was connected in the most commonplace way with both.

"Nothing in it, I shouldn't think," said Kate, finishing the sandwich but refusing another.

I sighed. "I don't think so, either," I said.

"What next, then?"

"If I could find out who owns the yellow shield taxis . . ."

"Let's ring them up and ask," said Kate, standing up. She led the way to the telephone and looked up the number in the directory.

"I'll do it," she said. "I'll say I have a complaint to make and I want to write directly to the owner about it."

She got through to the taxi office and gave a tremendous performance, demanding the names and addresses of the owners, managers, and the company's solicitors. Finally, she put down the receiver and looked at me disgustedly.

"They wouldn't tell me a single thing," she said. "He was a really patient man, I must say. He didn't get ruffled when I was really quite rude to him. But all he would say was, 'Please write to us with the details of your complaint and we will look into it fully.' He said it was not the company's policy to disclose the names of its owners and he had no authority to do it. He wouldn't budge an inch."

"Never mind. It was a darned good try. I didn't really think they would tell you. But it gives me an idea . . ."

I rang up the Maidenhead police station and asked for Inspector Lodge. He was off duty, I was told. Would I care to leave a message? I would.

I said, "This is Alan York speaking. Will you please ask Inspector Lodge if he can find out who owns or controls the Marconicar radio taxi cabs in Brighton? He will know what it is about."

The voice in Maidenhead said he would give Inspector Lodge the message, but could not undertake to confirm that Inspector Lodge would institute the requested enquiries. Nice official jargon. I thanked him and rang off.

Kate was standing close to me in the telephone box. She was wearing a delicate flowery scent, so faint that it was little more than a quiver in the air. I kissed her, gently. Her lips were soft and dry and sweet. She put her hands on my shoulders, and looked into my eyes, and smiled. I kissed her again.

A man opened the door of the telephone box. He laughed when he saw us. "I'm so sorry . . . I want to telephone . . ." We stepped out of the box in confusion.

I looked at my watch. It was nearly half-past six.

"What time does Aunt Deb expect us back?" I asked.

"Dinner is at eight. We've got until then," said Kate. "Let's walk through the Lanes and look at the antique shops."

We went slowly down the back pathways of Brighton, pausing before each brightly lit window to admire the contents. And stopping, too, in one or two corners in the growing dusk, to continue where we had left off in the telephone box. Kate's kisses were sweet and virginal. She was unpractised in love, and though her body trembled once or twice in my arms, there was no passion, no hunger in her response.

At the end of the Lanes, while we were discussing whether to go any further, some lights were suddenly switched on behind us. We turned round. The licensee of the Blue Duck was opening his doors for the evening. It looked a cozy place.

"How about a snifter before we go back?" I suggested.

"Lovely," said Kate. And in this casual inconsequential way we made the most decisive move in our afternoon's sleuthing.

We went into the Blue Duck.

CHAPTER 9

THE BAR WAS covered with a big sheet of gleaming copper. The beer handles shone. The glasses sparkled. It was a clean, friendly little room with warm lighting and original oils of fishing villages round the walls.

Kate and I leaned on the bar and discussed sherries with the innkeeper. He was a military-looking man of about fifty with a bristly moustache waxed at the ends. I put him down as a retired sergeant-major. But he knew his stuff, and the sherry he recommended to us was excellent. We were his first customers, and we stood chatting to him. He had the friendly manner of all good innkeepers, but underlying this I saw a definite wariness. It was like the nostril cocked for danger in a springbok, uneasy, even when all appeared safe. But I didn't pay much attention, for his troubles, I thought erroneously, had nothing to do with me.

Another man and a girl came in, and Kate and I turned to take our drinks over to one of the small scattered tables. As we did so she stumbled, knocked her glass against the edge of the bar and broke it. A jagged edge cut her hand, and it began to bleed freely.

The innkeeper called his wife, a thin, small woman with bleached hair. She saw the blood welling out of Kate's hand, and exclaimed with concern, "Come and put it under the cold tap. That'll stop the bleeding. Mind you don't get it on your nice coat."

She opened a hatch in the bar to let us through, and led us into her kitchen, which was as spotless as the bar. On a table at one side were slices of bread, butter, cooked meats, and chopped salads. We had interrupted the innkeeper's wife in making sandwiches for the evening's customers. She went across to the sink, turned on the tap, and beckoned to Kate to put her hand in the running water. I stood just inside the kitchen door looking round me.

"I'm sorry to be giving you all this trouble," said Kate, as the blood dripped into the sink. "It really isn't a very bad cut. There just seems to be an awful lot of gore coming out of it."

"It's no trouble at all, dear," said the innkeeper's wife. "I'll find you a bandage." She opened a dresser drawer to look for one, giving Kate a reassuring smile.

I started to walk over from the doorway to take a closer look at the damage. Instantly there was a deadly menacing snarl, and a black Alsatian dog emerged from a box beside the refrigerator. His yellow eyes were fixed on me, his mouth was slightly open with the top lip drawn back, and the razor-sharp teeth were parted. There was a collar round his neck, but he was not chained up. Another snarl rumbled deep in his throat.

I stood stock still in the center of the kitchen.

The innkeeper's wife took a heavy stick from beside the dresser and went over to the dog. She seemed flustered.

"Lie down, Prince. Lie down." She pointed with the stick to the box. The dog, after a second's hesitation, stepped back into it and sat erect, still looking at me with the utmost hostility. I didn't move.

"I'm very sorry, sir. He doesn't like strange men. He's a very good guard dog, you see. He won't hurt you now, not while I'm here." And she laid the stick on the dresser, and went over to Kate with cotton wool, disinfectant, and a bandage.

I took a step towards Kate. Muscles rippled along the dog's back, but he stayed in his box. I finished the journey to the sink. The bleeding had almost stopped, and, as Kate said, it was not a bad cut. The innkeeper's wife dabbed it with cotton wool soaked in disinfectant, dried it, and wound on a length of white gauze bandage.

I leaned against the draining board, looking at the dog and the heavy stick, and remembering the underlying edginess of the innkeeper. They added up to just one thing.

Protection.

Protection against what? Protection against Protection, said my brain, dutifully, in a refrain. Someone had been trying the protection racket on my host. Pay up or we smash up your pub . . . or you . . . or your wife. But this particular innkeeper, whether or not I was right about his sergeant-major past, looked tough enough to defy that sort of bullying. The collectors of Protection had been met, or were to be met, by an authentically lethal Alsatian. They were likely to need protection themselves.

The innkeeper put his head round the door.

"All right?" he said.

"It's fine, thank you very much," said Kate.

"I've been admiring your dog," I said.

The innkeeper took a step into the room. Prince turned his head away from me for the first time and looked at his master.

"He's a fine fellow," he agreed.

Suddenly out of nowhere there floated into my mind a peach of an idea. There could not, after all, be too many gangs in Brighton, and I had wondered several times why a taxi line should employ thugs and fight pitched battles. So I said, with a regrettable lack of caution, "Marconicars."

The innkeeper's professionally friendly smile vanished, and he suddenly looked at me with appalling, vivid hate. He picked the heavy stick off the dresser and raised it to hit me. The dog was out of his box in one fluid stride, crouching ready to spring, with his ears flat and his teeth bared. I had struck oil with a vengeance.

Kate came to the rescue. She stepped to my side and said, without the slightest trace of alarm, "For heaven's sake don't hit him too hard because Aunt Deb is expecting us for roast lamb and the odd potato within half an hour or so and she is very strict about us being back on the dot."

This surprising drivel made the innkeeper hesitate long enough for me to say, "I don't belong to the Marconicars. I'm against them. Do be a good chap and put that stick down, and tell Prince his fangs are not required."

The innkeeper lowered the stick, but he left Prince where he was, on guard four feet in front of me.

Kate said to me, "Whatever have we walked into?" The bandage was trailing from her hand, and the blood was beginning to ooze through. She wound up the rest of the bandage unconcernedly and tucked in the end.

"Protection, I think?" I said to the innkeeper. "It was a just a wild guess, about the taxis. I'd worked out why you need such an effective guard dog, and I've been thinking about taxi-drivers for days. The two things just clicked, that's all."

"Some of the Marconicar taxi-drivers beat him up a bit a week ago," said

Kate conversationally to the innkeeper's wife. "So you can't expect him to be quite sane on the subject."

The innkeeper gave us both a long look. Then he went to his dog and put his hand round its neck and fondled it under its chin. The wicked yellow eyes closed, the lips relaxed over the sharp teeth, and the dog leaned against his master's leg in devotion. The innkeeper patted its rump, and sent it back to its box.

"A good dog, Prince," he said, with a touch of irony. "Well, now, we can't leave the bar unattended Sue, dear, will you look after the customers while I talk to these young people?"

"There's the sandwiches not made yet," protested Sue.

"I'll do them," said Kate, cheerfully. "And let's hope I don't bleed into them too much." She picked up a knife and began to butter the slices of bread. The innkeeper and his wife looked less able to deal with Kate than with the taxi-drivers; but after hesitating a moment, the wife went out to the bar.

"Now, sir," said the innkeeper.

I outlined for him the story of Bill's death and my close contact with the taxi-drivers in the horse-box. I said, "If I can find out who's at the back of Marconicars, I'll probably have the man who arranged Major Davidson's accident."

"Yes, I see that," he said. "I hope you have more luck than I've had. Trying to find out who owns Marconicars is like running head on into a brick wall. Dead end. I'll tell you all I can, though. The more people sniping at them, the sooner they'll be liquidated." He leaned over and picked up two sandwiches. He gave one to me, and bit into the other.

"Don't forget to leave room for the roast lamb," said Kate, seeing me eating. She looked at her watch. "Oh, dear, we'll be terribly late for dinner and I hate to make Aunt Deb cross." But she went on placidly with her buttering.

"I bought the Blue Duck eighteen months ago," said the innkeeper. "When I got out into civvy street."

"Sergeant-major?" I murmured.

"Regimental," he said, with justifiable pride. "Thomkins, my name is. Well, I bought the Blue Duck with my savings and my retirement pay, and dead cheap it was, too. Too cheap. I should have known there'd be a catch. We hadn't been here more than three weeks, and taking good money, too, when this chap comes in one night and says as bold as brass that if we didn't pay up like the last landlord it'd be just too bad for us. And he picked up six glasses off the bar and smashed them. He said he wanted fifty quid a week. Well, I ask you, fifty quid! No wonder the last landlord wanted to get out. I was told afterwards he'd been trying to sell the place for months, but all the locals found out they would be buying trouble and left it alone for some muggins like me straight out of the army and still wet behind the ears to come along and jump in with my big feet."

Innkeeper Thomkins chewed on his sandwich while he thought.

"Well, then, I told him to eff off. And he came back the next night with about five others and smashed the place to bits. They knocked me out with one of my own bottles and locked my wife in the heads. Then they smashed all the bottles in the bar and all the glasses, and all the chairs. When I came round I was lying on the floor in the mess, and they were standing over me in a ring. They said that was just a taste. If I didn't cough up the fifty quid a week they'd be back to smash every bottle in the storeroom and all the wine in the cellar. After that, they said, it would be my wife."

His face was furious, as he relived it.

"What happened?" I asked.

"Well, my God, after the Germans and the Japs I wasn't giving in meekly to some little runts at the English seaside. I paid up for a couple of months to give myself a bit of breathing space, but fifty quid takes a bit of finding, on top of overheads and taxes. It's a good little business, see, but at that rate I wasn't going to be left with much more than my pension. It wasn't on."

"Did you tell the police?" I asked.

A curious look of shame came into Thomkins' face. "No," he said hesitantly, "not then I didn't. I didn't know then where the men had come from, see, and they'd threatened God knows what if I went to the police. Anyway, it's not good army tactics to reengage an enemy who has defeated you once, unless you've got reinforcements. That's when I started to think about a dog. And I did go to the police later," he finished, a little defensively.

"Surely the police can close the Marconicar taxi line if it's being used for systematic crime," I said.

"Well, you'd think so," he said, "but it isn't like that. It's a real taxi service, you know. A big one. Most of the drivers are on the up and up and don't even know what's going on. I told a couple of them once that they were a front for the protection racket and they refused to believe me. The crooked ones look so plausible, see? Just like the others. They drive a taxi up to your door at closing time, say, all innocent like, and walk in and ask quietly for the money, and as like as not they'll pick up a customer in the pub and drive him home for the normal fare as respectable as you please."

"Couldn't you have a policeman in plainclothes sitting at the bar ready to arrest the taxi-driver when he came to collect the money?" suggested Kate.

The innkeeper said bitterly, "It wouldn't do no good, miss. It isn't only that they come in on different days at different times, so that a copper might have to wait a fortnight to catch one, but there aren't any grounds for arrest. They've got an I.O.U. with my signature on it for fifty pounds, and if there was any trouble with the police, all they'd have to do would be show it, and they couldn't be touched. The police'll help all right if you can give them something they can use in court, but when it's just one man's word against another, they can't do much."

"A pity you signed the I.O.U." I sighed.

"I didn't," he said, indignantly, "but it looks like my signature, even to me. I tried to grab it once, but the chap who showed it to me said it wouldn't matter if I tore it up, they'd soon make out another one. They must have had my signature on a letter or something, and copied it. Easy enough to do."

"You do pay them, then," I said, rather disappointed.

"Not on your nellie, I don't," said the innkeeper, his moustache bristling. "I haven't paid them a sou for a year or more. Not since I got Prince. He chewed four of them up in a month, and that discouraged them, I can tell you. But they're still around all the time. Sue and I daren't go out much, and we always go together and take Prince with us. I've had burglar alarm bells put on all the doors and windows and they go off with an awful clatter if anyone tries to break in while we're out or asleep. It's no way to live, sir. It's getting on Sue's nerves."

"What a dismal story," said Kate, licking chutney off her fingers. "Surely you can't go on like that for ever?"

"Oh, no, miss, we're beating them now. It isn't only us, see, that they got money from. They had a regular round. Ten or eleven pubs like ours—free houses. And a lot of little shops, tobacconists, souvenir shops, that sort of thing, and six or seven little cafés. None of the big places. They only pick on businesses run by the people who own them, like us. When I cottoned to that I went round to every place I thought they might be putting the screws on and asked the owners straight out if they were paying protection. It took me weeks, it's such a big area. The ones that were paying were all dead scared, of course, and wouldn't talk, but I knew who they were, just by the way they clammed up. I told them we ought to stop paying and fight. But a lot of them have kids and they wouldn't risk it, and you can't blame them."

"What did you do?" asked Kate, enthralled.

"I got Prince. A year old, he was then. I'd done a bit of dog handling in the army, and I trained Prince to be a proper fighter."

"You did, indeed," I said, looking at the dog who now lay peacefully in his box with his chin on his paws.

"I took him round and showed him to some of the other victims of the protection racket," Thomkins went on, "and told them that if they'd get dogs, too, we'd chase off the taxi-drivers. Some of them didn't realise the taxis were mixed up in it. They were too scared to open their eyes. Anyway, in the end a lot of them did get dogs and I helped to train them, but it's difficult, the dog's only got to obey one master, see, and I had to get them to obey someone else, not me. Still, they weren't too bad. Not as good as Prince, of course."

"Of course," said Kate.

The innkeeper looked at her suspiciously, but she was demurely piling sandwiches onto a plate.

"Go on," I said.

"In the end I got some of the people with children to join in, too. They bought Alsatians or bullterriers, and we arranged a system for taking all the kiddies to school by car. Those regular walks to school laid them wide open to trouble, see? I hired a judo expert and his car to do nothing but ferry the children and their mothers about. We all club together to pay him. He's expensive, of course, but nothing approaching the protection money."

"How splendid," said Kate warmly.

"We're beating them all right, but it isn't all plain sailing yet. They smashed up the Cockleshell Café a fortnight ago, just round the corner from here. But we've got a system to deal with that, too, now. Several of us went round to help clear up the mess, and we all put something into the hat to pay for new tables and chairs. They've got an Alsatian bitch at the café, and she'd come into season and they'd locked her in a bedroom. I ask you! Dogs are best," said the innkeeper, seriously.

Kate gave a snort of delight.

"Have the taxi-drivers attacked any of you personally, or has it always been your property?" I asked.

"Apart from being hit on the head with my own bottle, you mean?" The innkeeper pulled up his sleeve and showed us one end of a scar on his forearm. "That's about seven inches long. Three of them jumped me one evening when I went out to post a letter. It was just after Prince had sent one of their fellows off, and silly like, I went out without him. It was only a step to the pillar box, see? A mistake though. They made a mess of me, but I got a good look at them. They told me I'd get the same again if I went to the police. But I rang the boys in blue right up, and told them the lot. It was a blond young brute who slashed my arm and my evidence got him six months," he said with satisfaction. "After that I was careful not to move a step without Prince, and they've never got near enough to have another go at me."

"How about the other victims?" I asked.

"Same as me," he said. "Three or four of them were beaten up and slashed with knives. After I'd got them dogs I persuaded some of them to tell the police. They'd had the worst of it by then, I thought, but they were still scared of giving evidence in court. The gang have never actually killed anyone, as far as I know. It wouldn't be sense, any how, would it? A man can't pay up if he's dead."

"No," I said, thoughtfully. "I suppose he can't. They might reckon that one death would bring everyone else to heel, though."

"You needn't think I haven't that in my mind all the time," he said somberly. "But there's a deal of difference between six months for assault and a life sentence or a hanging, and I expect that's what has stopped 'em. This isn't Chicago after all, though you'd wonder sometimes."

I said, "I suppose if they can't get money from their old victims, the gang try 'protecting' people who don't know about your systems and your dogs . . ."

The innkeeper interrupted, "We've got a system for that, too. We put an advertisement in the Brighton paper every week telling anyone who has been threatened with protection to write to a box number and they will get help. It works a treat, I can tell you."

Kate and I looked at him with genuine admiration.

"They should have made you a general," I said, "not a sergeant-major."

"I've planned a few incidents in my time," he said modestly. "Those young lieutenants in the war, straight out of civvy street and rushed through an officer course, they were glad enough now and then for a suggestion from a regular." He stirred, "Well, how about a drink now?"

But Kate and I thanked him and excused ourselves, as it was already eight o'clock. Thomkins and I promised to let each other know how we fared in battle, and we parted on the best of terms. But I didn't attempt to pat Prince.

Aunt Deb sat in the drawing-room tapping her foot. Kate apologised very prettily for our lateness, and Aunt Deb thawed. She and Kate were clearly deeply attached to each other.

During dinner it was to Uncle George that Kate addressed most of the account of our afternoon's adventures. She told him amusingly and lightly about the wandering horse-box and made a rude joke about the Pavilion Plaza's paste sandwiches, which drew mild reproof from Aunt Deb to the effect that the Pavilion Plaza was the most hospitable of the Brighton hotels. I gave a fleeting thought to the flighty Mavis, whom I had suspected, perhaps unjustly, of dispensing her own brand of hospitality on the upper floors.

"And then we had a drink in a darling little pub called the Blue Duck," said Kate, leaving out the telephone box and our walk through the Lanes. "I cut my hand there—" she held it out complete with bandage, "—but not very badly of course, and we went into the kitchen to wash the blood off, and that's what made us late. They had the most terrifying Alsatian there that I'd ever seen in my life. He snarled a couple of times at Alan and made him shiver in his shoes like a jelly . . ." she paused to eat a mouthful of roast lamb.

"Do you not care for dogs, Mr. York?" said Aunt Deb, with a touch of disdain. She was devoted to her dachshund.

"It depends," I said.

Kate said, "You don't exactly fall in love with Prince. I expect they call him Prince because he's black. The Black Prince. Anyway, he's useful if any dog is. If I told you two dears what the man who keeps the Blue Duck told Alan and me about the skullduggery that goes on in respectable little old Brighton, you wouldn't sleep sound in your beds."

"Then please don't tell us, Kate dear," said Aunt Deb. "I have enough trouble with insomnia as it is."

I looked at Uncle George to see how he liked being deprived of the end of the story, and saw him push his half-filled plate away with a gesture of revulsion, as if he were suddenly about to vomit.

He noticed I was watching, and with a wry smile said, "Indigestion, I'm afraid. Another of the boring nuisances of old age. We're a couple of old crocks now, you know."

He tried to raise a chuckle, but it was a poor affair. There was a tinge of grey in the pink cheeks, and fine beads of sweat had appeared on the already moist-looking skin. Something was deeply wrong in Uncle George's world.

Aunt Deb looked very concerned about it, and as sheltering her from unpleasant realities was for him so old and ingrained a habit, he made a great effort to rally his resources. He took a sip of water and blotted his mouth on his napkin, and I saw the tremor in his chubby hands. But there was steel in the man under all that fat, and he cleared his throat and spoke normally enough.

He said, "It quite slipped my mind, Kate my dear, but while you were out Gregory rang up to talk to you about Heavens Above. I asked him how the horse was doing and he said it had something wrong with its leg and won't be able to run on Thursday at Bristol as you planned."

Kate looked disappointed. "Is he lame?" she asked.

Uncle George said, "I could swear Gregory said the horse had thrown out a splint. He hadn't broken any bones though, had he? Most peculiar." He was mystified, and so, I saw, was Kate.

"Horse's leg bones sometimes grow knobs all of a sudden, and that is what a splint is," I said. "The leg is hot and tender while the splint is forming, but it usually lasts only two or three weeks. Heavens Above will be sound again after that."

"What a pest," said Kate. "I was so looking forward to Thursday. Will you be going to Bristol, Alan, now that my horse isn't running?"

"Yes," I said. "I'm riding Palindrome there. Do try and come, Kate, it would be lovely to see you." I spoke enthusiastically, which made Aunt Deb straight her back and bend on me a look of renewed disapproval.

"It is not good for a young gel's reputation for her to be seen too often in the company of jockeys," she said.

AT ELEVEN O'CLOCK, when Uncle George had locked the study door on his collection of trophies, and when Aunt Deb had swallowed her nightly quota of sleeping pills, Kate and I went out of the house to put her car away in the garage. We had left it in the drive in our haste before dinner.

The lights of the house, muted by curtains, took the blackness out of the night, so that I could still see Kate's face as she walked beside me.

I opened the car door for her, but she paused before stepping in.

"They're getting old," she said, in a sad voice, "and I don't know what I'd do without them."

"They'll live for years yet," I said.

"I hope so . . . Aunt Deb looks very tired sometimes, and Uncle George used to have so much more bounce. I think he's worried about something now . . . and I'm afraid it's Aunt Deb's heart, though they haven't said . . . They'd never tell me if there was anything wrong with them." She shivered.

I put my arms round her and kissed her. She smiled.

"You're a kind person, Alan."

I didn't feel kind. I wanted to throw her in the car and drive off with her at once to some wild and lonely hollow on the Downs for a purpose of which the cave men would thoroughly have approved. It was an effort for me to hold her lightly, and yet essential.

"I love you, Kate," I said, and I controlled even my breathing.

"No," she said. "Don't say it. Please don't say it." She traced my eyebrows with her finger. The dim light was reflected in her eyes as she looked at me, her body leaning gently against mine, her head held back.

"Why not?"

"Because I don't know . . . I'm not sure . . . I've liked you kissing me and I like being with you. But love is so big a word. It's too important. I'm . . . I'm not . . . ready . . ."

And there it was. Kate the beautiful, the brave, the friendly, was also Kate the unawakened. She was not aware yet of the fire that I perceived in her at every turn. It had been battened down from childhood by her Edwardian aunt, and how to release it without shocking her was a puzzle.

"Love is easy to learn," I said. "It's like taking a risk. You set your mind on it and refuse to be afraid, and in no time you feel terrifically exhilarated and all your inhibitions fly out of the window."

"And you're left holding the baby," said Kate, keeping her feet on the ground.

"We could get married first," I said, smiling at her.

"No. Dear Alan. No. Not yet." Then she said, almost in a whisper, "I'm so sorry."

She got into the car and drove slowly round to the barn garage. I followed behind the car and helped her shut the big garage doors, and walked back with her to the house. On the doorstep she paused and squeezed my hand, and gave me a soft, brief, sisterly kiss.

I didn't want it.

I didn't feel at all like a brother.

CHAPTER 10

ON TUESDAY IT began to rain, cold slanting rain which lashed at the opening daffodils and covered the flowers with splashed up mud. The children went to school in shining black capes with sou'westers pulled down to their eyes and gum boots up to their knees. All that could be seen of William was his cherubic mouth with milk stains at the corners.

Scilla and I spent the day sorting out Bill's clothes and personal belongings. She was far more composed than I would have expected, and seemed to have won through to an acceptance that he was gone and that life must be lived without him. Neither of us had mentioned, since it happened, the night she had spent in my bed, and I had become convinced that when she woke the next morning she had no memory of it. Grief and drugs had played tricks with her mind.

We sorted Bill's things into piles. The biggest section was to be saved for Henry and William, and into this pile Scilla put not only cuff links and studs and two gold watches, but dinner jackets and a morning suit and grey top hat. I teased her about it.

"It isn't silly," she said. "Henry will be needing them in ten years, if not before. He'll be very glad to have them." And she added a hacking jacket and two new white silk shirts.

"We might just as well put everything back into the cupboards and wait for Henry and William to grow," I said.

"That's not a bad idea," said Scilla, bequeathing to the little boys their father's best riding breeches and his warmly lined white mackintosh.

We finished the clothes, went downstairs to the cosy study, and turned our attention to Bill's papers. His desk was full of them. He clearly hated to throw away old bills and letters, and in the bottom drawer we found a bundle of letters that Scilla had written to him before their marriage. She sat on the window seat reading them nostalgically while I sorted out the rest.

Bill had been methodical. The bills were clipped together in chronolog-
ical order, and the letters were in boxes and files. There were some miscellaneous collections in the pigeon holes, and a pile of old, empty, used envelopes
with day-to-day notes on the backs. They were reminders to himself, mostly,
with messages like "Tell Simpson to mend fence in five acre field," and
"Polly's birthday Tuesday." I looked through them quickly, hovering them
over the heap bound for the wastepaper basket.

I stopped suddenly. On one of them, in Bill's loopy sprawling handwriting, was the name Clifford Tudor, and underneath, a telephone number and
an address in Brighton.

"Do you know anyone called Clifford Tudor?" I asked Scilla.

"Never heard of him," she said without looking up.

If Tudor had asked Bill to ride for him, as he had told me when I drove
him from Plumpton to Brighton, it was perfectly natural for Bill to have his
name and address. I turned the envelope over. It had come from a local trades-
man, whose name was printed on the top left hand corner, and the postmark
was date-stamped January, which meant that Bill had only recently acquired
Tudor's address.

I put the envelope in my pocket and went on sorting. After the old envelopes I started on the pigeon holes. There were old photographs and some
pages the children had drawn and written on with straggly letters in their
babyhood, address books, luggage labels, a birthday card, school reports, and
various notebooks of different shapes and sizes.

"You'd better look through these, Scilla," I said.

"You look," she said, glancing up from her letters with a smile. "You can
tell me what's what, and I'll look at them presently."

Bill had had no secrets. The notebooks mainly contained his day-to-day
expenses, jotted down to help his accountant at the annual reckoning. They
went back some years. I found the latest, and leafed through it.

School fees, hay for the horses, a new garden hose, a repair to the Jaguar's
head-lamp in Bristol, a present for Scilla, a bet on Admiral, a donation to
charity. And that was the end. After that came the blank pages which were
not going to be filled up.

I looked again at the last entries. A bet on Admiral. Ten pounds to win,
Bill had written. And the date was the day of his death. Whatever had been
said to Bill about Admiral's falling, he had taken it as a joke and had backed
himself to win in spite of it. I would dearly have liked to know what the

"joke" had been. He had told Pete, whose mind was with the horses. He had not told Scilla, nor any of his friends as far as I could find out. Possibly he had thought it so unimportant that after he spoke to Pete it had wholly slipped his mind.

I stacked up the notebooks and began on the last pigeon hole full of oddments. Among them were fifteen or twenty of the betting tickets issued by bookmakers at race meetings. As evidence of bets lost, they are usually torn up or thrown away by disappointed punters, not carefully preserved in a tidy desk.

"Why did Bill keep these betting tickets?" I asked Scilla.

"Henry had a craze for them not long ago, don't you remember?" she said. "And after it wore off Bill still brought some home for him. I think he kept them in case William wanted to play bookmakers in his turn."

I did remember. I had backed a lot of horses for half-pennies with Henry the bookmaker, the little shark. They never won.

The extra tickets Bill had saved for him were from several different bookmakers. It was part of Bill's pleasure at the races to walk among the bookmakers' stands in Tattersall's and put his actual cash on at the best odds, instead of betting on credit with a bookmaker on the rails.

"Do you want to keep them for William still?" I asked.

"May as well," said Scilla.

I put them back in the desk, and finished the job. It was late in the afternoon. We went into the drawing-room, stoked up the fire, and settled into armchairs.

She said, "Alan, I want to give you something which belonged to Bill. Now, don't say anything until I've finished. I've been wondering what you'd like best, and I'm sure I've chosen right."

She looked from me to the fire and held her hands out to warm them.

She said, "You are to have Admiral."

"No." I was definite.

"Why not?" She looked up, sounding disappointed.

"Dearest Scilla, it's far too much," I said. "I thought you meant something like a cigarette case, a keepsake. You can't possibly give me Admiral. He's worth thousands. You must sell him, or run him in your name if you want to keep him, but you can't give him to me. It wouldn't be fair to you or the children for me to have him."

"He might be worth thousands if I sold him—but I couldn't sell him, you know. I couldn't bear to do that. He meant so much to Bill. How could I sell him as soon as Bill's back was turned? And if I keep him and run him, I'll have to pay the bills, which might not be easy for a while with death duties hanging over me. If I give him to you, he's in hands Bill would approve of, and you can pay for his keep. I've thought it all out, so you're not to argue. Admiral is yours."

She meant it.

"Then let me lease him from you," I said.

"No, he's a gift. From Bill to you, if you like."

And on those terms I gave in, and thanked her as best I could.

THE FOLLOWING MORNING, early, I drove to Pete Gregory's stables in Sussex to jump my green young Forlorn Hope over the schooling hurdles. A drizzling rain was falling as I arrived, and only because I had come so far did we bother to take the horses out. It was not a very satisfactory session, with Forlorn Hope slipping on the wet grass as we approached the first hurdle and not taking on the others with any spirit after that.

We gave it up and went down to Pete's house. I told him Admiral was to be mine and that I would be riding him.

He said, "He's in the Foxhunters' at Liverpool, did you know?"

"So he is!" I exclaimed delightedly. I had not yet ridden round the Grand National course, and the sudden prospect of doing it a fortnight later was exciting.

"You want to have a go?"

"Yes, indeed," I said.

We talked over the plans for my other horses, Pete telling me Palindrome was in fine fettle after his Cheltenham race and a certainty for the following day at Bristol. We went out to look at him and the others, and I inspected the splint which Heavens Above was throwing out. His leg was tender, but it would right itself in time.

When I left Pete's I went back to Brighton, parking the Lotus and taking a train as before. I walked out of Brighton station with a brief glance at the three taxis standing there (no yellow shields) and walked briskly in the direction of the headquarters of the Marconicars as listed in the telephone directory.

I had no particular plan, but I was sure the core of the mystery was in Brighton, and if I wanted to discover it, I would have to dig around on the spot. My feelers on the racecourse had still brought me nothing but a husky warning on the telephone.

The Marconicars offices were on the ground floor of a converted Regency terrace house. I went straight into the narrow hall.

The stairs rose on the right, and on the left were two doors, with a third, marked Private, facing me at the far end of the passage. A neat board on the door nearest the entrance said, "Enquiries." I went in.

It had once been an elegant room and even the office equipment could not entirely spoil its proportions. There were two girls sitting at desks with typewriters in front of them, and through the half-open folded dividing doors I could see into an inner office where a third girl sat in front of a switchboard. She was speaking into a microphone.

"Yes, madam, a taxi will call for you in three minutes," she said. "Thank you." She had a pleasant high voice of excellent carrying quality.

The two girls in the outer office looked at me expectantly. They wore tight sweaters and large quantities of mascara. I spoke to the one nearest the door.

"Er . . . I'm enquiring about booking some taxis . . . for a wedding. My sister's," I added, improvising and inventing the sister I never had. "Is that possible?"

"Oh, yes, I think so," she said. "I'll ask the manager. He usually deals with big bookings."

I said, "I'm only asking for an estimate . . . on behalf of my sister. She has asked me to try all the firms, to find out which will be most—er—reasonable. I can't give you a definite booking until I've consulted her again."

"I see," she said. "Well, I'll ask Mr. Fielder to see you." She went out, down the passage, and through the door marked Private.

While I waited I grinned at the other girl, who patted her hair, and I listened to the girl at the switchboard.

"Just a minute, sir. I'll see if there's a taxi in your area," she was saying. She flipped a switch and said, "Come in, any car in Hove two. Come in, any car in Hove two."

There was a silence and then a man's voice said out of the radio receiving set, "It looks as though there's no one in Hove two, Marigold. I could get there in five minutes. I've just dropped a fare in Langbury Place."

"Right, Jim." She gave him the address, flipped the switch again, and spoke into the telephone. "A taxi will be with you in five minutes, sir. I am sorry for the delay, we have no cars available who can reach you faster than that. Thank you, sir." As soon as she had finished speaking the telephone rang again. She said, "Marconicars. Can I help you?"

Down the hall came the clip clop of high heels on linoleum, and the girl came back from Mr. Fielder. She said, "The manager can see you now, sir."

"Thank you," I said. I went down the hall and through the open door at the end.

The man who rose to greet me and shake hands was a heavy, well-tailored, urbane man in his middle forties. He wore spectacles with heavy black frames, had smooth black hair and hard blue eyes. He seemed a man of too strong a personality to be sitting in the back office of a taxi firm, too high-powered an executive for the range of his job.

I felt my heart jump absurdly, and I had a moment's panic in which I feared he knew who I was and what I was trying to do. But his gaze was calm and businesslike, and he said only, "I understand you wish to make a block booking for a wedding."

"Yes," I said, and launched into fictitious details. He made notes, added up some figures, wrote out an estimate, and held it out to me. I took it. His writing was strong and black. It fitted him.

"Thank you," I said. "I'll give this to my sister, and let you know."

As I went out of his door and shut it behind me, I looked back at him. He was sitting behind his desk staring at me through his glasses with un-winking blue eyes. I could read nothing in his face.

I went back into the front office and said, "I've got the estimate I wanted. Thank you for your help." I turned to go, and had a second thought. "By the way, do you know where I can find Mr. Clifford Tudor?" I asked.

The girls, showing no surprise at my enquiry, said they did not know.

"Marigold might find out for you," said one of them. "I'll ask her."

Marigold, finishing her call, agreed to help. She pressed the switch. "All cars. Did anyone pick up Mr. Tudor today? Come in please."

A man's voice said, "I took him to the station this morning, Marigold. He caught the London train."

"Thanks, Mike," said Marigold.

"She knows all their voices," said one of the girls, admiringly. "They never have to tell her the number of their car."

"Do you all know Mr. Tudor well?" I asked.

"Never seen him," said one girl, and the others shook their heads in agreement.

"He's one of our regulars. He takes a car whenever he wants one, and we book it here. The driver tells Marigold where he's taking him. Mr. Tudor has a monthly account, and we make it up and send it to him."

"Suppose the driver takes Mr. Tudor from place to place and fails to report it to Marigold?" I asked conversationally.

"He wouldn't be so silly. The drivers get commission on regulars. Instead of tips, do you see? We put ten per cent on the bills to save the regulars having to tip the drivers every five minutes."

"A good idea," I said. "Do you have many regulars?"

"Dozens," said one of the girls. "But Mr. Tudor is about our best client."

"And how many taxis are there?" I asked.

"Thirty-one. Some of them will be in the garage for servicing, of course, and sometimes in the winter we only have half of them on the road. There's a lot of competition from the other firms."

"Who actually owns the Marconicars?" I asked casually.

They said they didn't know and couldn't care less.

"Not Mr. Fielder?" I asked.

"Oh, no," said Marigold. "I don't think so. There's a Chairman, I believe, but we've never seen him. Mr. Fielder can't be all that high-up, because he sometimes takes over from me in the evenings and at week-ends. Though another girl comes in to relieve me on my days off, of course."

They suddenly all seemed to realise that this had nothing to do with my sister's wedding. It was time to go, and I went.

I stood outside on the pavement wondering what to do next. There was a café opposite, across the broad street, and it was nearly lunch-time. I went over and into the café, which smelled of cabbage, and because I had arrived before the rush there was a table free by the window. Through the caste net curtains of the Olde Oake Café I had a clear view of the Marconicar office. For what it was worth.

A stout girl with wispy hair pushed a typed menu card in front of me. I looked at it, depressed. English home cooking at its very plainest. Tomato soup, choice of fried cod, sausages in batter, or steak and kidney pie, with suet pudding and custard to follow. It was all designed with no regard for an amateur rider's weight. I asked for coffee. The girl said firmly I couldn't have coffee by itself at lunch-time, they needed the tables. I offered to pay for the full lunch if I could just have the coffee, and to this she agreed, clearly thinking me highly eccentric.

The coffee, when it came, was surprisingly strong and good. I was getting the first of the brew, I reflected, idly watching the Marconicar front door. No one interesting went in or out.

On the storey above the Marconicars a big red neon sign flashed on and off, showing little more than a flicker in the daylight. I glaned up at it. Across the full width of the narrow building was the name L. C. PERTH. The taxi office had "Marconicars" written in bright yellow on black along the top of its big window, and looking up I saw that the top storey was decorated with a large blue board bearing in white letters the information "Jenkins, Wholesale Hats."

The total effect was colourful indeed, but hardly what the Regency architect had had in mind. I had a mental picture of him turning in his grave so often that he made knots in his winding sheet, and I suppose I smiled, for a voice suddenly said, "Vandalism, isn't it?"

A middle-aged woman had sat down at my table, unnoticed by me as I gazed out of the window. She had a mournful horsey face with no make-up, a hideous brown hat which added years to her age, and an earnest look in her eyes. The café was filling up, and I could no longer have a table to myself.

"It's startling, certainly," I agreed.

"It ought not to be allowed. All these old houses in this district have been carved up and turned into offices, and it's really disgraceful how they look now. I belong to the Architectural Preservation Group," she confided solemnly, "and we're getting out a petition to stop people desecrating beautiful buildings with horrible advertisements."

"Are you having success?" I asked.

She looked depressed. "Not very much, I'm afraid. People just don't seem to care as they should. Would you believe it, half the people in Brighton don't know what a Regency house looks like, when they're surrounded by them all the time? Look at that row over there, with all those boards and signs. And that neon," her voice quivered with emotion, "is the last straw. It's only been there a few months. We've petitioned to make them take it down, but they won't."

"That's very discouraging," I said, watching the Marconicar door. The two typists came out and went chattering up the road, followed by two more girls whom I supposed to have come down from the upper floors.

My table companion chatted on between spoonfuls of tomato soup. "We can't get any satisfaction from Perth's at all because no one in authority there will meet us, and the men in the office say they can't take the sign down because it doesn't belong to them, but they won't tell us who it does belong to so that we can petition him in person." I found I sympathised with Perth's invisible ruler in his disinclination to meet the Architectural Preservation Group on the warpath. "It was bad enough before, when they had their name just painted on the windows, but neon . . ." Words failed her, at last.

Marigold left for lunch. Four men followed her. No one arrived.

I drank my coffee, parted from the middle-aged lady without regret, and gave it up for the day. I took the train back to my car and drove up to London. After a long afternoon in the office, I started for home at the tail end of the rush-hour traffic. In the hold-ups at crossings and roundabouts I began, as a change from Bill's mystery, to tackle Joe Nantwich's.

I pondered his "stopping" activities, his feud with Sandy Mason, his disgrace with Tudor, his obscure threatening notes. I thought about the internal workings of the weighing room, where only valets, jockeys, and officials are allowed in the changing rooms, and trainers and owners are confined to the weighing room itself, while the press and the public may not enter at all.

If the "Bolingbroke. This week" note was to be believed, Joe would already have received his punishment, because "this week" was already last week. Yet I came to the conclusion that I would see him alive and well at Bristol on the following day, even if not in the best of spirits. For, by the time I reached home, I knew I could tell him who had written the notes, though I wasn't sure I was going to.

Sleep produces the answers to puzzles in the most amazing way. I went to bed on Wednesday night thinking I had spent a more or less fruitless morning in Brighton. But I woke on Thursday morning with a name in my mind and the knowledge that I had seen it before, and where. I went downstairs in my dressing-gown to Bill's desk, and took out the betting tickets he had saved for Henry. I shuffled through them, and found what I wanted. Three of them bore the name L. C. PERTH.

I turned them over. On their backs Bill had penciled the name of a horse, the amount of his bet, and the date. He was always methodical. I took all the tickets up to my room, and looked up the races in the form book. I remembered many casual snatches of conversation. And a lot of things became clear to me.

But not enough, not enough.

CHAPTER 11

IT POURED WITH rain at Bristol, a cold, steady unrelenting wetness which took most of the pleasure out of racing.

Kate sent a message that she was not coming because of the weather, which sounded unlike her, and I wondered what sort of pressure Aunt Deb had used to keep her at home.

The main gossip in the weighing room concerned Joe Nantwich. The Stewards had held an enquiry into his behavior during the last race on Champion Hurdle day, and had, in the official phrase, "severely cautioned him as to his future riding." It was generally considered that he was very lucky indeed to have got off so lightly, in view of his past record.

Joe himself was almost as cocky as ever. From a distance his round pink face showed no traces of the fear or drunkenness which had made a sudden mess of him at Cheltenham. Yet I was told that he had spent the preceding Friday and Saturday and most of Sunday in the Turkish baths, scared out of his wits. He had drunk himself silly and sweated it off alternately during the whole of that time, confiding to the attendants in tears that he was safe with them, and refusing to get dressed and go home.

The authority for this story, and one who gave it its full flavour, was Sandy, who had happened, he said, to go into the Turkish baths on Sunday morning to lose a few pounds for Monday's racing.

I found Joe reading the notices. He was whistling through his teeth.

"Well, Joe," I said, "what makes you so cheerful?"

"Everything." He smirked. At close quarters I could see the fine lines round his mouth and the slightly bloodshot eyes, but his experiences had left no other signs of strain. "I didn't get suspended by the Stewards. And I got paid for losing that race."

"You what?" I exclaimed.

"I got paid. You know, I told you. The packet of money. It came this morning. A hundred quid." I stared at him. "Well, I did what I was told, didn't it?" he said aggrievedly.

"I suppose you did," I agreed, weakly.

"And another thing, those threatening notes. I fooled them you know. I stayed in the Turkish baths all over the week-end, and they couldn't harm me there. I got off scot free," said Joe, triumphantly, as if "this week" could not be altered to "next week." He did not realise either that he had already taken his punishment, that there are other agonies than physical ones. He had suffered a week of acute anxiety, followed by three days of paralysing fear, and he thought he had got off scot free.

"I'm glad you think so," I said, mildly. "Joe, answer me a question. The man who rings you up to tell you what horse not to win on, what does his voice sound like?"

"You couldn't tell who it is, not by listening to him. It might be anybody. It's a soft voice, and soft of fuzzy. Almost a whisper, sometimes, as if he were afraid of being overheard. But what does it matter?" said Joe. "As long as he delivers the lolly he can croak like a frog for all I care."

"Do you mean you'll stop another horse, if he asks you to?" I said.

"I might do. Or I might not," said Joe, belatedly deciding that he had been speaking much too freely. With a sly, sidelong look at me he edged away into the changing room. His resilience was fantastic.

Pete and Dane were discussing the day's plans not far away, and I went over to them. Pete was cursing the weather and saying it would play merry hell with the going, but that Palindrome, all the same, should be able to act on it.

"Go to the front at halfway, and nothing else will be able to come to you. They're a poor lot. As far as I can see, you're a dead cert."

"That's good," I said, automatically, and then remembered with a mental wince that Admiral had been a dead cert at Maidenhead.

Dane asked me if I had enjoyed my stay with Kate and did not look too overjoyed by my enthusiastic answer.

"Curses on your head, pal, if you have cut me out with Kate." He said it in a mock ferocious voice, but I had an uncomfortable feeling that he meant it. Could a friendship survive between two men who were in love with the same girl? Suddenly at that moment, I didn't know; for I saw in Dane's familiar handsome face a passing flash of enmity. It was as disconcerting as a rock turning to quicksand. And I went rather thoughtfully into the changing room to find Sandy.

He was standing by the window, gazing through the curtain of rain which streamed down the glass. He had changed into colours for the first race, and was looking out towards the parade ring, where two miserable-looking horses were being led round by dripping, mackintoshed stable lads.

"We'll need windscreen wipers on our goggles in this little lot," he remarked, with unabashed good spirits. "Anyone for a mud bath? Blimey, it's enough to discourage ducks."

"How did you enjoy your Turkish bath on Sunday?" I asked, smiling.

"Oh, you heard about that, did you?"

"I think everyone has heard about it," I said.

"Good. Serve the little bastard right," said Sandy, grinning hugely.

"How did you know where to find him?" I asked.

"Asked his mother . . ." Sandy broke off in the middle of the word, and his eyes widened.

"Yes," I said. "You sent him those threatening Bolingbroke notes."

"And what," said Sandy, with good humour, "makes you think so?"

"You like practical jokes, and you dislike Joe," I said. "The first note he received was put into his jacket while it hung in the changing room at Plumpton, so it had to be a jockey or a valet or an official who did it. It couldn't have been a bookmaker or a trainer or an owner or any member of the public. So I began to think that perhaps the person who planted the note in Joe's pocket was not the person who was paying him to stop horses. That person has, strangely enough, exacted no revenge at all. But I asked myself who else would be interested in tormenting Joe, and I came to you. You knew before the race that Joe was not supposed to win on Bolingbroke. When he won you told him you'd lost a lot of money, and you'd get even with him. And I guess you have. You even tracked him down to enjoy seeing him suffer."

"Revenge is sweet, and all that. Well, it's a fair cop," said Sandy. "Though how you know such a lot beats me."

"Joe told me most of it," I said.

"What a blabbermouth. That tongue of Joe's will get him into a right mess one of these days."

"Yes, it will," I said, thinking of the incautious way Joe had spoken of his "stopping" and its rewards.

"Did you tell him I had sent him those notes?" asked Sandy, with his first show of anxiety.

"No, I didn't. It would only stir up more trouble," I said.

"Thanks for that, anyway."

"And in reward for that small service, Sandy," I said, "will you tell me how you knew in advance that Bolingbroke was not supposed to win?"

He grinned widely, rocking gently on his heels, but he didn't answer.

"Go on," I said. "It isn't much to ask, and it might even give me a lead to that other mystery, about Bill Davidson."

Sandy shook his head. "It won't help you any," he said. "Joe told me himself."

"What?" I exclaimed.

"He told me himself. In the washroom when we were changing before the race. You know how he can't help swanking? He wanted to show off, and I was handy, and besides, he knew I'd stopped a horse or two in my time."

"What did he say?" I asked.

"He said if I wanted a lesson in how to choke a horse I'd better watch him on Bolingbroke. Well, a nod's as good as wink to Sandy Mason. I got a punter to put fifty quid on Leica, which I reckoned was bound to win with Bolingbroke not trying. And look what happened. The little sod lost his nerve and beat Leica by two lengths. I could have throttled him. Fifty quid's a ruddy fortune, mate, as far as I'm concerned."

"Why did you wait as long as ten days before you gave him that first note?" I asked.

"I didn't think of it until then," he said, frankly. "But it was a damn good revenge, wasn't it? He nearly got his licence suspended at Cheltenham, and he sweated his guts out for three days at the week-end, all in the screaming heeby-jeebies worked up by yours truly." Sandy beamed. "You should have seen him in the Turkish baths. A sodden, whining, clutching wreck. In tears, and begging me to keep him safe. Me! What a laugh. I was nearly sick, trying not to laugh. A cracking good revenge, that was."

"And you put him over the rails at Plumpton, too," I said.

"I never did," said Sandy, indignantly. "Did he tell you that? He's a bloody liar. He fell off, I saw him. I've a good mind to frighten him again." His red hair bristled and his brown eyes sparkled. Then he relaxed. "Oh, well . . . I'll think of something, sometime. There's no rush. I'll make his life uncomfortable—ants in his pants, worms in his boots, that sort of thing. Harmless," and Sandy began to laugh. Then he said, "As you're such a roaring success as a private eye, how are you getting on with that other business?"

"Not fast enough," I said. "But I know a lot more than I did at this time last week, so I haven't lost hope. You haven't heard anything useful?" He shook his head.

"Not a squeak anywhere. You're not giving it up, then?"

"No," I said.

"Well, the best of British luck," said Sandy, grinning.

An official poked his head round the door. "Jockeys out, please," he said. It was nearly time for the first race.

Sandy put his helmet on and tied the strings. Then he took out his false teeth, the two centre incisors off the upper jaw, wrapped them in a handkerchief and tucked them into the pocket of the coat hanging on his peg. He, like most jockeys, never rode races wearing false teeth, for fear of losing them, or even swallowing them if he fell. He gave me a gap-toothed grin, sketched a farewell salute, and dived out into the rain.

It was still raining an hour later when I went out to ride Palindrome. Pete was waiting for me in the parade ring, the water dripping off the brim of his hat in a steady stream.

"Isn't this a God-awful day?" he said. "I'm glad it's you that's got to strip off and get soaked, and not me. I had a bellyful when I was riding. I hope you're good at swimming."

"Why?" I asked, mystified.

"If you are, you'll know how to keep your eyes open under water." I suspected another of Pete's rather feeble jokes, but he was serious. He pointed to the goggles slung round my neck. "You won't need those, for a start. With all the mud that's being kicked up today, they'd be covered before you'd gone a furlong."

"I'll leave them down, then," I said.

"Take them off. They'll only get in your way," he said.

So I took them off, and as I turned my head to ease the elastic over the back of my helmet, I caught a glimpse of a man walking along outside the parade ring. There were few people standing about owing to the rain, and I had a clear view of him.

It was Bert, the man in charge of the horse in the layby on Maidenhead Thicket. One of the Marconicar drivers.

He was not looking at me, but the sight of him was as unpleasant as an electric shock. He was a long way from base. He might have travelled the hundred and forty miles solely to enjoy an afternoon's racing in the rain. Or he might not.

I looked at Palindrome, plodding slowly round the parade ring in his waterproof rug.

A dead cert.

I shivered.

I knew I had made some progress towards my quarry, the man who had caused Bill's death, even though he himself was as unknown to me as ever. I had disregarded his two emphatic warnings and I feared I had left a broad enough trail for him to be well aware of my pursuit. Bert would not be at Bristol alone, I thought, and I could guess that a third deterrent message was on its way.

There are times when one could do without an intuition, and this was one of them. Palindrome, the dead cert. What had been done once would be tried again, and somewhere out on the rain-swept racecourse another strand of wire could be waiting. For no logical reason, I was certain of it.

It was too late to withdraw from the race. Palindrome was an odds-on favourite, and clearly in the best of health; he showed no lameness, no broken blood vessels, none of the permitted excuses for a last minute cancellation. And if I myself were suddenly taken ill and couldn't ride, another jockey would be quickly found to take my place. I couldn't send someone out in my colours to take a fall designed for me.

If I refused point-blank, without explanation, to let Palindrome run in the race, my permit to ride would be withdrawn, and that would be the end of my steeplechasing.

If I said to the Stewards, "Someone is going to bring Palindrome down with wire," they might possibly send an official round the course to inspect the fences: but he wouldn't find anything. I was quite sure that if a wire were rigged, it would be, as in Bill's case, a last minute job.

If I rode in the race, but kept Palindrome reined in behind other horses the whole way, the wire might not be rigged at all. But my heart sank as I regarded the faces of the jockeys who had already ridden, and remembered in what state they had come back from their previous races. Mud was splashed on their faces like thick khaki chicken-pox, and their jerseys were soaked and muddied to such an extent that their colors were almost unrecognizable from a few steps away, let alone the distance from one fence to the next. My own coffee and cream colours would be particularly indistinct. A man waiting with wire would not be able to tell for certain which horse was in front, but he would expect me and act accordingly.

I looked at the other jockeys in the parade ring, now reluctantly taking off their raincoats and mounting their horses. There were about ten of them. They were men who had taught me a lot, and accepted me as one of themselves, and given me a companionship I enjoyed almost as much as the racing itself. If I let one of them crash in my place, I couldn't face them again.

It was no good. I'd have to ride Palindrome out in front and hope for the best. I remembered Kate saying, "If there's something you've got to do, then to hell with the danger."

To hell with the danger. After all, I could fall any day, without the aid of wire. If I fell today, with it, that would be just too bad. But it couldn't be helped. And I might be wrong; there might be no wire at all.

Pete said, "What's the matter? You look as if you'd seen a ghost."

"I'm all right," I said, taking off my coat. Palindrome was standing beside me, and I patted him, admiring his splendid intelligent head. My chief worry from then on was that he, at least, should come out of the next ten minutes unscathed.

I swung up on to his back and looked down at Pete, and said, "If . . . if Palindrome falls in this race, please will you ring up Inspector Lodge at Maidenhead police station, and tell him about it?"

"What on earth . . . ?"

"Promise," I said.

"All right. But I don't understand. You could tell him yourself, if you want to, and anyway, you won't fall."

"No, perhaps not," I said.

"I'll meet you in the winner's enclosure," he said, slapping Palindrome's rump as we moved off.

The rain was blowing into our faces as we lined up for the start in front of the stands, with two circuits of the course to complete. The tapes went up, and we were off.

Two or three horses jumped the first fence ahead of me, but after that I took Palindrome to the front, and stayed there. He was at his best, galloping and jumping with the smooth flow of a top class 'chaser. On any other day, the feel of this power beneath me would have pleased me beyond words. As it was, I scarcely noticed it.

Remembering Bill's fall, I was watching for an attendant to walk across behind a fence as the horses approached it. He would be uncoiling the wire, raising it, fixing it . . . I planned when I saw that to try to persuade Palindrome to take off too soon before the fence, so that he would hit the wire solidly with his chest when he was already past the height of his spread. That way, I hoped he might break or pull down the wire and still stay on his feet; and if we fell, it should not be in a shattering somersault like Admiral's. But it is easier to plan than to do, and I doubted whether a natural jumper like Palindrome *could* be persuaded to take off one short stride too soon.

We completed the first circuit without incident, squelching on the sodden turf. About a mile from home, on the far side of the course, I heard hoof-beats close behind, and looked over my shoulder. Most of the field were bunched up some way back, but two of them were chasing me with determination and they were almost up to Palindrome's quarters.

I shook him up and he responded immediately, and we widened the gap from our pursuers to about five lengths.

No attendant walked across the course.

I didn't see any wire.

But Palindrome hit it, just the same.

It wouldn't have been too bad a fall but for the horses behind me. I felt the heavy jerk on Palindrome's legs as we rose over the last fence on the far side of the course, and I shot off like a bullet, hitting the ground with my shoulder several yards ahead. Before I had stopped rolling the other horses were jumping the fence. They would have avoided a man on the ground if they possibly could, but in this case, I was told afterwards, they had to swerve round Palindrome, who was struggling to get up, and found me straight in their path.

The galloping hooves thudded into my body. One of the horses kicked my head and my helmet split so drastically that it fell off. There were six seconds of bludgeoning, battering chaos, in which I could neither think nor move, but only feel.

When it was all over I lay on the wet ground, limp and growing numb, unable to get up, unable even to stir. I was lying on my back with my feet towards the fence. The rain fell on my face and trickled through my hair, and the drops felt so heavy on my eyelids that opening them was like lifting a weight. Through a slit, from under my rain-beaded lashes, I could see a man at the fence.

He wasn't coming to help me. He was very quickly coiling up a length of wire, starting on the outside of the course and working inwards. When he reached the inner post he put his hand in his raincoat pocket, drew out a tool, and clipped the wire where it was fastened eighteen inches above the fence. This time, he had not forgotten his wire cutters. He finished his job, hooked the coil over his arm, and turned toward me.

I knew him.

He was the driver of the horse-box.

The colour was going out of everything. The world looked grey to me, like an under-exposed film. The green grass was grey, the box driver's face was grey . . .

Then I saw that there was another man at the fence, and he was walking towards me. I knew him, too, and he was not a taxi-driver. I was so glad to find I had some help against the box driver that I could have wept with relief. I tried to tell him to look at the wire, so that this time there should be a witness. But the words could get no farther than my brain. My throat and tongue refused to form them.

He came over and stood beside me, and stooped down. I tried to smile and say hello, but not a muscle twitched. He straightened up.

He said, over his shoulder, to the box driver, "He's been knocked out." He turned back to me.

He said, "You nosey bastard," and he kicked me. I heard the ribs crack, and I felt the hot stab in my side. "Perhaps that'll teach you to mind your own business." He kicked me again. My grey world grew darker. I was nearly unconscious, but even in that dire moment some part of my mind went on working, and I knew why the attendant had not walked across with the wire. He had not needed to. He and his accomplice had stood on opposite sides of the course and had raised it between them.

I saw the foot drawn back a third time. It seemed hours, in my disjointed brain, until it came towards my eyes, growing bigger and bigger until it was all that I could see.

He kicked my face, and I went out like a light.

CHAPTER 12

HEARING CAME BACK first. It came back suddenly, as if someone had pressed a switch. At one moment no messages of any sort were getting through the swirling, distorted dreams which seemed to have been going on inside my head for a very long time, and in the next I was lying in still blackness, with every sound sharp and distinct in my ears.

A woman's voice said, "He's still unconscious."

I wanted to tell her it was not true, but could not.

The sounds went on, swishing, rustling, clattering, the murmur of distant voices, the thump and rattle of water in pipes of ancient plumbing. I listened, but without much interest.

After a while I knew I was lying on my back. My limbs, when I became aware of them, were as heavy as lead and ached persistently, and ton weights rested on my eyelids.

I wondered where I was. Then I wondered who I was. I could remember nothing at all. This seemed too much to deal with, so I went to sleep.

The next time I woke up the weights were gone from my eyes. I opened them, and found I was lying in a dim light in a room whose fuzzy lines slowly grew clear. There was a washbasin in one corner, a table with a white cloth on it, an easy chair with wooden arms, a window to my right, a door straight ahead. A bare, functional room.

The door opened and a nurse came in. She looked at me in pleased surprise and smiled. She had nice teeth.

"Hello there," she said. "So you've come back at last. How do you feel?"

"Fine," I said, but it came out as a whisper, and in any case it wasn't strictly true.

"Are you comfortable?" she asked, holding my wrist for the pulse.

"No," I said, giving up the pretence.

"I'll go and tell Dr. Mitcham you've woken up, and I expect he will come and see you. Will you be all right for a few minutes?" She wrote something on a board which lay on the table, gave me another bright smile, and swished out of the door.

So I was in hospital. But I still had no idea what had happened. Had I, I wondered, been run over by a steam roller? Or a herd of elephants?

Dr. Mitcham, when he came, would solve only half the mystery.

"Why am I here?" I asked, in a croaky whisper.

"You fell off a horse," he said.

"Who am I?"

At this question he tapped his teeth with the end of his pencil and looked at me steadily for some seconds. He was a blunt-featured young man with fluffy, already receding, fair hair, and bright intelligent pale blue eyes.

"I'd rather you remember that for yourself. You will, soon, I'm sure. Don't worry about it. Don't worry about anything. Just relax, and your memory will come back. Not all at once, don't expect that, but little by little you'll remember everything, except perhaps the fall itself."

"What is wrong with me, exactly?" I asked.

"Concussion is what has affected your memory. As to the rest of you," he surveyed me from head to foot, "you have a broken collar-bone, four cracked ribs, and multiple contusions."

"Nothing serious, thank goodness," I croaked.

He opened his mouth and gasped, and then began to laugh. He said, "No, nothing serious. You lot are all the same. Quite mad."

"What lot?" I said.

"Never mind, you'll remember soon," he said. "Just go to sleep for a while, if you can, and you'll probably understand a great deal more when you wake up."

I took his advice, closed my eyes and drifted to sleep. I dreamed of a husky voice which came from the centre of a bowl of red and yellow crocuses, whispering menacing things until I wanted to scream and run away, and then I realised it was my own voice whispering, and the crocuses faded into a vision of deep green forests with scarlet birds darting in the shadows. Then I thought I was very high up, looking to the ground, and I was leaning farther and farther forward until I fell, and this time what I said made perfect sense.

"I fell out of the tree." I knew it had happened in my boyhood.

There was an exclamation beside me. I opened my eyes. At the foot of the bed stood Dr. Mitcham.

"What tree?" he said.

"In the forest," I said. "I hit my head, and when I woke my father was kneeling beside me."

There was an exclamation again at my right hand. I rolled my head over to look.

He sat there, sunburnt, fit, distinguished, and at forty-six looking still a young man.

"Hi, there," I said.

"Do you know who this is?" asked Dr. Mitcham.

"My father."

"And what is your name?"

"Alan York," I said at once, and my memory bounded back. I could remember everything up to the morning I was going to Bristol races. I remembered setting off, but what happened after that was still a blank.

"How did you get here?" I asked my father.

"I flew over. Mrs. Davidson rang me up to tell me you had a fall and were in hospital. I thought I'd better take a look."

"How long . . ." I began slowly.

"How long were you unconscious?" said Dr. Mitcham. "This is Sunday morning. Two and a half days. Not too bad, considering the crack you had. I kept your crash-helmet for you to see." He opened a locker and took out the shell which had undoubtedly saved my life. It was nearly in two pieces.

"I'll need a new one," I said.

"Quite mad. You're all quite mad," said Dr. Mitcham.

This time I knew what he meant. I grinned, but it was a lopsided affair, because I discovered that half my face was swollen as well as stiff and sore. I began to put up my left hand to explore the damage, but I changed my mind before I had raised it six inches, owing to the sudden pain which the movement caused in my shoulder. In spite of the tight bandages which arched my shoulders backward, I heard and felt the broken ends of collar-bone grate together.

As if they had been waiting for a signal, every dull separate ache in my battered body sprang to vicious, throbbing life. I drew in a deep breath, and the broken ribs sharply rebelled against it. It was a bad moment.

I shut my eyes. My father said anxiously, "Is he all right?" and Dr. Mitcham answered, "Yes, don't worry. I rather think his breakages have caught up with him. I'll give him something to ease it, shortly."

"I'll be out of bed tomorrow," I said. "I've been bruised before, and I've broken my collarbone before. It doesn't last long." But I added ruefully to myself that *while* it lasted it was highly unpleasant.

"You will certainly not get up tomorrow," said Dr. Mitcham's voice. "You'll stay where you are for a week, to give that concussion a chance."

"I can't stay in bed for a week," I protested. "I shouldn't have the strength of a flea when I got up, and I'm going to ride Admiral at Liverpool."

"When is that?" asked Dr. Mitcham suspiciously.

"March twenty-fourth," I said.

There was a short silence while they worked it out.

"That's only a week on Thursday," said my father.

"You can put it right out of your head," said Dr. Mitcham severely.

"Promise me," said my father.

I opened my eyes and looked at him, and when I saw the anxiety in his face I understood for the first time in my life how much I meant to him. I was his only child, and for ten years, after my mother died, he had reared me himself, not delegating the job to a succession of housekeepers, boarding schools, and tutors as many a rich man would have done, but spending time playing with me and teaching me, and making sure I learned in my teens how to live happily and usefully under the burden of extreme wealth. He himself had taught me how to face all kinds of danger, yet I realised that it must seem to him that if I insisted on taking my first tilt at Liverpool when I was precariously unfit, I was risking more than I had any right to do.

"I promise," I said. "I won't ride at Liverpool this month. But I'm going on racing afterwards."

"All right. It's a deal." He relaxed, smiling, and stood up. "I'll come again this afternoon."

"Where are you staying? Where are we now?" I asked.

"This is Bristol Hospital, and I'm staying with Mrs. Davidson," he said.

I said, "Did I get this lot at Bristol races? With Palindrome?" My father nodded. "How is he? Was he hurt? What sort of fall did he have?"

"No, he wasn't hurt," he said. "He's back in Gregory's stables. No one saw how or why he fell because it was raining so hard. Pete said you had a premonition you were going to fall, and he asked me to tell you he had done what you wanted."

"I don't remember anything about it, and I don't know what it was I wanted him to do." I sighed. "It's very irritating."

Dr. Mitcham and my father went away and left me puzzling over the gap in my memory. I had an illusive feeling that I had known for a few seconds a fact of paramount significance, but grope as I would my conscious life ended on the road to Bristol races and began again in Bristol Hospital.

The rest of the day passed slowly and miserably, with each small movement I made setting up a chorus of protest in every crushed muscle and nerve. I had been kicked by horses before, but never in so many places all at once, and I knew, though I couldn't see it, that my skin must be covered with large angry crimson patches which had spread and were turning black and finally yellow as the blood underneath congealed and dispersed. My face, I knew, must be giving the same rainbow performance, and I undoubtedly had two lovely black eyes.

The pills Dr. Mitcham had sent via the nurse with pretty teeth made less difference than I would have liked, so I lay with my eyes shut and pretended I was floating on the sea in the sunshine, with my grating bones and throbbing head cushioned by a gentle swell. I filled in the scene with seagulls and white clouds and children splashing in the shallows, and it worked well each time until I moved again.

Late in the evening my headache grew worse and I slid in and out of weird troubled dreams in which I imagined that my limbs had been torn off by heavy weights, and I woke soaked in sweat to wiggle my toes and fingers in an agony of fear that they were missing. But no sooner had the feel of them against the sheets sent relief flooding over me than I was drifting away into the same nightmare all over again. The cycle of short awakenings and long dreams went on and on, until I was no longer sure what was real and what was not.

So shattering was the night passed in this fashion that when Dr. Mitcham came into my room in the morning I implored him to show me that my hands and feet were in fact still attached to me. Without a word he stripped back the bedclothes, grasped my feet firmly, and lifted them a few inches so that I could see them. I raised my hands and looked at them, and laced my fingertips together on my stomach; and felt a complete idiot to have been so terrified over nothing.

"There's no need to be embarrassed," said Mitcham. "You can't expect your brain to be in perfect working order when you've been unconscious for so long. I promise you that you have no injuries you don't know about. No internal damage, no bits missing. You'll be as good as new in three weeks." His steady pale blue eyes were reliable. "Only," he added, "you'll have a scar on your face. We stitched up a cut over your left cheekbone."

As I had not been exactly handsome before, this news did not disturb me. I thanked him for his forbearance, and he pulled the sheet and blankets over me again. His blunt face suddenly lit up with a mischievous smile, and he said, "Yesterday *you* told *me* there was nothing seriously wrong with you and you'd be out of bed today, if I remember correctly."

"Blast you," I said weakly. "I'll be out of bed tomorrow."

IN THE END it was Thursday before I made it on to my feet, and I went home to Scilla's on Saturday morning feeling more tottery than I cared to admit, but in good spirits nevertheless. My father, who was still there but planning to leave early the next week, came to fetch me.

Scilla and Polly clicked their tongues and made sympathetic remarks as I levered myself out of the Jaguar at one quarter my usual speed and walked carefully up the front steps. But young Henry, giving me a sweeping, comprehensive glance which took in my black and yellow face and the long newly healed cut across one cheek, greeted me with, "And how's the horrible monster from outer space?"

"Go and boil your head," I said, and Henry grinned delightedly.

At seven o'clock in the evening, just after the children had gone upstairs to bed, Kate rang up. Scilla and my father decided to bring some wine up from the cellar, and left me alone in the drawing-room to talk to her.

"How are the cracks?" she asked.

"Knitting nicely," I said. "Thank you for your letter, and for the flowers."

"The flowers were Uncle George's idea," she said. "I said it was too much like a funeral, sending you flowers, and he thought that was so funny that he nearly choked. It didn't seem all that funny to me, actually, when I knew from Mrs. Davidson that it very nearly was your funeral."

"It was nowhere near that," I said. "Scilla was exaggerating. And whether it was your idea or Uncle George's, thank you anyway for the flowers."

"Lilies, I expect I should have sent, not tulips," Kate teased.

"You can send me lilies next time," I said, taking pleasure in hearing her slow attractive voice.

"Good heavens, is there going to be a next time?"

"Bound to be," I said cheerfully.

"Well all right," said Kate, "I'll place a standing order with Interflora, for lilies."

"I love you, Kate," I said.

"I must say," she said happily, "it's nice hearing people say that."

"People? Who else has said it? And when?" I asked, fearing the worst.

"Well," she said, after a tiny pause, "Dane, as a matter of fact."

"Oh."

"Don't be so jealous," she said. "And Dane's just as bad as you. He glowers like a thunderstorm if he hears your name. You're both being childish."

"Yes, ma'am," I said. "When will I see you again?"

We fixed a luncheon date in London, and before she rang off I told her again that I loved her. I was about to put down my own receiver, when I heard the most unexpected sound on the telephone.

A giggle. A quickly suppressed, but definite giggle.

I knew she had disconnected; but I said into the dead mouthpiece in front of me, "Hang on a minute, Kate, I—er—want to read you something . . . in the paper. Just a minute while I get it." I put my receiver down on the table, went carefully out of the drawing-room, up the stairs, and into Scilla's bedroom.

There stood the culprits, grouped in a guilty huddle round the extension telephone. Henry, with the receiver pressed to his ear; Polly, her head close against his; and William, looking earnestly up at them with his mouth open. They were all in pyjamas and dressing-gowns.

"And just what do you think you're doing?" I asked, with a severe expression.

"Oh golly," said Henry, dropping the receiver on to the bed as if it were suddenly too hot to hold.

"Alan!" said Polly, blushing deeply.

"How long have you been listening?" I demanded.

"Actually, right from the beginning," said Polly shamefacedly.

"Henry always listens," said William, proud of his brother.

"Shut up," said Henry.

"You little beasts," I said.

William looked hurt. He said again, "But Henry always listens. He listens to everyone. He's checking up, and that's good, isn't it? Henry checks up all the time, don't you, Henry?"

"Shut up, William," said Henry, getting red and furious.

"So Henry checks up, does he?" I said, frowning crossly at him. Henry stared back, caught out, but apparently unrepentant.

I advanced towards them, but the homily on the sacredness of privacy that I was about to deliver suddenly flew out of my mind. I stopped and thought.

"Henry, how long have you been listening to people on the telephone?" I asked mildly.

He looked at me warily. Finally he said, "Quite some time."

"Days? Weeks? Months?"

"Ages," said Polly, taking heart again as I no longer seemed angry with them.

"Did you ever listen to your father?" I asked.

"Yes, often," said Henry.

I paused, studying this tough, intelligent little boy. He was only eight, but if he knew the answers to what I was going to ask him, he would understand their significance and be appalled by his knowledge all his life. But I pressed on.

"Did you by any chance ever hear him talking to a man with a voice like this?" I asked. Then I made my voice husky and whispering, and said, "Am I speaking to Major Davidson?"

"Yes," said Henry without hesitation.

"When was that?" I asked, trying to show nothing of the excitement I felt I was sure now that he had listened in to the telephone call which Bill had mentioned as a joke to Pete, who had not taken in what he said.

"It was that voice the last time I listened to Daddy," said Henry, matter-of-factly.

"Do you remember what the voice said?" I forced myself to speak slowly, gently.

"Oh, yes, it was a joke. It was two days before he was killed," said Henry, without distress. "Just when we were going to bed, like now. The phone rang and I scooted in here and listened as usual. That man with the funny voice was saying, 'Are you going to ride Admiral on Saturday, Major Davidson?' and Daddy said he was." Henry paused. I waited, willing him to remember.

He screwed up his eyes in concentration and went on. "Then the man with the funny voice said, 'You are not to win on Admiral, Major Davidson.' Daddy just laughed, and the man said, 'I'll pay you five hundred pounds if you promise not to win.' And Daddy said, 'Go to hell' and I nearly snorted because he was always telling me not to say that. Then the whispery man said he didn't want Daddy to win, and that Admiral would fall if Daddy didn't agree not to win, and Daddy said, 'You must be mad.' And then he put down the telephone, and I ran back to my room in case he should come up and find me listening."

"Did you say anything to your father about it?" I asked.

"No," said Henry frankly. "That's the big snag about listening. You have to be awfully careful not to know too much."

"Yes, I can see that," I said, trying not to smile.

Then I saw the flicker in Henry's eyes as the meaning of what he had heard grew clearer to him. He said jerkily, "It wasn't a joke after all, was it?"

"No, it wasn't," I said.

"But that man didn't make Admiral fall, did he? He couldn't . . . could he? Could he?" said Henry desperately, wanting me to reassure him. His eyes were stretched wide open, and he was beginning to realise that he had listened to the man who had caused his father's death. Although he would have to know one day about the strand of wire, I didn't think I ought to tell him at that moment.

"I don't really know. I don't expect so," I lied calmly. But Henry's eyes stared blindly at me as if he were looking at some inward horror.

"What's the matter?" said Polly. "I don't understand why Henry is so upset. Just because someone told Daddy they didn't want him to win is no reason for Henry to go off in a fit."

"Does he always remember so clearly what people say?" I asked Polly. "It's a month ago, now, since your father died."

"I expect Daddy and that man said a lot of things that Henry has forgotten," said Polly judiciously, "but he doesn't make things up." And I knew this was true. He was a truthful child.

He said stonily, "I don't see how he could have done it."

I was glad at least that Henry was dealing with his revelation practically and not emotionally. Perhaps I had not done him too much harm, after all, in making him understand what he had heard and disregarded.

"Come along to bed and don't worry about it, Henry," I said, holding out my hand to him. He took it, and uncharacteristically held on to it all the way along the landing and into his bedroom.

CHAPTER 13

WHILE I WAS dressing myself at tortoise pace the following morning the front door bell rang downstairs, and presently Joan came up to say that an Inspector Lodge would like to see me, please.

"Tell him I'll be down as soon as possible," I said, struggling to get my shirt on over the thick bracing bandage round my shoulders. I did up most of the buttons, but decided I didn't need a tie.

The strapping round my ribs felt tight and itched horribly, my head ached, large areas of flesh were black still and tender, I had slept badly, and I was altogether in a foul mood. The three aspirins I had swallowed in place of breakfast had not come up to scratch.

I picked up my socks, tried to bend to put them on with my one useful arm, found how far away my feet had become, and flung them across the room in a temper. The day before, in the hospital, the nurse with nice teeth had helped me to dress. Today perverseness stopped me asking my father to come and do it for me.

The sight of my smudgy, yellow, unshaven face in the looking-glass made matters no better. Henry's "horrible monster from outer space" was not so far off the mark. I longed to scratch the livid scar on my cheek, to relieve its irritation.

I plugged in my electric razor and took off the worst, brushed my hair sketchily, thrust my bare feet into slippers, put one arm into my hacking jacket and swung it over the other shoulder, and shuffled gingerly downstairs.

Lodge's face when he saw me was a picture.

"If you laugh at me I'll knock your block off. Next week," I said.

"I'm not laughing," said Lodge, his nostrils twitching madly as he tried to keep a straight face.

"It's not funny," I said emphatically.

"No."

I scowled at him.

My father said, glancing at me from behind his Sunday newspaper in the depths of an armchair by the fire, "You sound to me as if you need a stiff brandy."

"It's only half past ten," I said crossly.

"Emergencies can happen at any time of the day," said my father, standing up, "and this would appear to be a grave one." He opened the corner cupboard where Scilla kept a few bottles and glasses, poured out a third of a tumbler full of brandy, and splashed some soda into it. I complained that it was too strong, too early, and unnecessary.

My father handed me the glass. "Drink it and shut up," he said.

Furious, I took a large mouthful. It was strong and fiery, and bit into my throat. I rolled the second mouthful round my teeth so that the scarcely diluted spirit tingled on my gums, and when I swallowed I could feel it slide warmly down to my empty stomach.

"Did you have any breakfast?" asked my father.

"No," I said.

I took another, smaller gulp. The brandy worked fast. My bad temper began draining away, and in a minute or two I felt reasonably sane. Lodge and my father were looking at me intently as though I were a laboratory animal responding to an experiment.

"Oh very well then," I admitted grudgingly, "I feel better." I took a cigarette from the silver box on the table and lit it, and noticed the sun was shining.

"Good." My father sat down again.

It appeared that he and Lodge had introduced themselves while they waited for me, and Lodge had told him, among other things, about my adventures in the horse-box outside Maidenhead, a detail I had omitted from my letters. This I considered to be treachery of the basest sort, and said so and I told them how Kate and I had tracked down the horse-box, and that that particular line of enquiry was a dead end.

I took my cigarette and glass across the room and sat on the window seat in the sun. Scilla was in the garden, cutting flowers. I waved to her.

Lodge, dressed today not in uniform, but in grey flannels, fine wool shirt, and sports jacket, opened his briefcase, which lay on the table, and pulled out some papers. He sat down beside the table and spread them out.

He said, "Mr. Gregory rang me up at the station on the morning after your fall at Bristol to tell me about it."

"Why on earth did he do that?" I asked.

"You asked him to," said Lodge. He hesitated, and went on, "I understand from your father that your memory is affected."

"Yes. Most bits of that day at Bristol have come back now, but I still can't remember going out of the weighing room to ride Palindrome, or the race or the fall, or anything." My last mental picture was of Sandy walking out into the rain. "Why did I ask Pete to tell you I fell?"

"You asked him before the race. You apparently thought you were likely to fall. So, unofficially, I checked up on that crash of yours." He smiled suddenly. "You've accounted for all my free time lately, and today is really my day off. Why I bother with you I really don't know!" But I guessed that he was as addicted to detecting as an alcoholic to drink. He couldn't help doing it.

He went on, "I went down to Gregory's stables and took a look at Palindrome. He had a distinct narrow wound across his front of those two pads of flesh . . ."

"Chest," I murmured.

". . . Chest, then, and I'll give you one guess at what cut him."

"Oh, no," I said, guessing, but not believing it.

"I checked up on the attendants at the fences," he said. "One of them was new and unknown to the others. He gave his name as Thomas Butler and an address which doesn't exist, and he volunteered to stand at the farthest fence from the stands, where you fell. His offer was readily accepted because of the rain and the distance of the fence from the bookmakers. The same story as at Maidenhead. Except that this time Butler collected his earnings in the normal way. Then I got the Clerk of the Course to let me inspect the fence, and I found a groove on each post six feet, six inches from the ground."

There was a short silence.

"Well, well, well," I said blankly. "It looks as though I was luckier than Bill."

"I wish you could remember something about it . . . anything. What made you suspect you would fall?" asked Lodge.

"I don't know."

"It was something that happened while you were in the parade ring waiting to mount." He leaned forward, his dark eyes fixed intently on my face, willing my sluggish memory to come to life. But I remembered nothing, and

I still felt weary from head to foot. Concentration was altogether too much of an effort.

I looked out into the peaceful spring garden. Scilla held an armful of forsythia, golden yellow against her blue dress.

"I can't remember," I said flatly. "Perhaps it'll come back when my head stops aching."

Lodge sighed and sat back in his hard chair.

"I suppose," he said, a little bitterly, "that you do at least remember sending me a message from Brighton, asking me to do your investigating for you?"

"Yes, I do," I said. "How did you get on?"

"Not very well. No one seems to know who actually owns the Marconicar taxi line. It was taken over just after the war by a businessman named Clifford Tudor . . ."

"What?" I said in astonishment.

"Clifford Tudor, respectable Brighton resident, British subject. Do you know him?"

"Yes," I said. "He owns several racehorses."

Lodge sorted out a paper from his briefcase. "Clifford Tudor born Khroupista Thasos, in Trikkala, Greece. Naturalised nineteen thirty-nine, when he was twenty-five. He started life as a cook, but owing to natural business ability, he acquired his own restaurant that same year. He sold it for a large profit after the war, went to Brighton, and bought for next to nothing an old taxi business that had wilted from wartime restrictions and lack of petrol. Four years ago he sold the taxis, again at a profit, and put his money into the Pavillion Plaza Hotel. He is unmarried."

I leaned my head back against the window and waited for these details to mean something significant, but all that happened was that my inability to think increased.

Lodge went on. "The taxi line was bought from Tudor by nominees, and that's where the fog begins. There have been so many transfers of ownership from company to company mostly, through nominees who can't be traced, that no one can discover who is the actual present owner. All business matters are settled by a Mr. Fielder, the manager. He says he consults with a person he calls 'the Chairman' by telephone, but that 'the Chairman' rings him up every morning, and never the other way round. He says the Chairman's name is Claud Thiveridge, but he doesn't know his address or telephone number."

"It sounds very fishy to me," said my father.

"It is," said Lodge. "There is no Claud Thiveridge on the electoral register, or in any other official list, including the telephone accounts department, in the whole of Kent, Surrey, or Sussex. The operators in the telephone exchange are sure the office doesn't receive a long distance call regularly every morning, yet the morning call has been standard office routine for the last four years. As this means that the call must be a local one, it seems fairly certain that Claud Thiveridge is not the gentleman's real name."

He rubbled the palm of his hand round the back of his neck and looked at me steadily. "You know a lot more than you've told me, amnesia or not," he said. "Spill the beans, there's a good chap."

"You haven't told me what the Brighton police think of the Marconicars," I said.

Lodge hesitated. "Well, they were a little touchy on the subject, I would say. It seems they have had several complaints, but not much evidence that will stand up in court. What I have just told you is the result of their enquiries over the last few years."

"They would not seem," said my father dryly, "to have made spectacular progress. Come on, Alan, tell us what's going on."

Lodge turned his head towards him in surprise. My father smiled.

"My son is Sherlock Holmes reincarnated, didn't you know?" he said. "After he went to England I had to employ a detective to do the work he used to do in connection with frauds and swindles. As one of my head clerks put it, Mr. Alan has an unerring instinct for smelling out crooks."

"Mr. Alan's unerring instinct is no longer functioning," I said gloomily. Clouds were building up near the sun, and Scilla's back disappeared through the macrocarpa hedge by the kitchen door.

"Don't be infuriating, Alan," said my father. "Elucidate."

"Oh, all right." I stubbed out my cigarette, began to scratch my cheek, and dragged my fingers away from the scar with a strong effort of will. It went on itching.

"There's a lot I don't know," I said, "but the general gist appears to be this. The Marconicars have been in the protection racket for the last four years, intimidating small concerns like cafés and free house pubs. About a year ago, owing to the strongmindedness of one particular publican, mine host of the Blue Duck, business in the protection line began to get unexpectedly rough for the protectors. He set Alsatians on them, in fact." I told my fascinated father and an aghast Lodge what Kate and I had learned in the Blue Duck's kitchen, carefully watched by the yellow-eyed Prince.

"Ex-Regimental Sergeant-Major Thomkins made such serious inroads into the illicit profits of Marconicars," I continued, "that as a racket it was more or less defunct. The legitimate side hadn't been doing too well during the winter, either, according to the typists who work in the office. There are too many taxis in Brighton for the number of fares at this time of year, I should think. Anyway, it seems to me that the Marconicar boss—the Chairman, your mysterious Claud Thiveridge—set about mending his fortunes by branching out into another form of crime. He bought, I think, the shaky bookmaking business on the floor above the Marconicars, in the same building."

I could almost smell the cabbage in the Olde Oake Café as I remembered it. "An earnest lady told me the bookmakers had been taken over by a new firm about six months ago, but that its name was still the same. L. C. PERTH, written in neon. She was very wrought up about them sticking such a garish sign on an architectural gem, and she and her old buildings society, whose name I forget, had tried to reason with the new owners to take down what they had just put up. Only they couldn't find out who the new owner was. It's too much of a coincidence to have two businesses, both shady, one above the other, both with invisible and untraceable owners. They must be owned by the same person."

"It doesn't follow, and I don't see the point," said my father.

"You will in a minute," I said. "Bill died because he wouldn't stop his horse winning a race. I know his death wasn't necessarily intended, but force was used against him. He was told not to win by a husky-voiced man on the telephone. Henry, Bill's elder son—he's eight—" I explained to Lodge, "has a habit of listening on the extension upstairs, and he heard every word. Two days before Bill died, Henry says, the voice offered him five hundred pounds to stop his horse winning, and when Bill laughed at this, the voice told him he wouldn't win because his horse would fall."

I paused, but neither Lodge nor my father said anything. Swallowing the last of the brandy, I went on. "There is a jockey called Joe Nantwich who during the last six months, ever since L. C. Perth changed hands, has regularly accepted a hundred pounds, sometimes more, to stop a horse winning. Joe gets his instructions by telephone from a husky-voiced man he has never met."

Lodge stirred on his hard, self-chosen chair.

I went on. "I, as you know, was set upon by the Marconicar drivers, and a few days later the man with the husky voice rang me up and told me to take heed of the warning I had been given in the horse-box. One doesn't have to be Sherlock Holmes to see that the crooked racing and the Marconicar protection racket were being run by the same man." I stopped.

"Finish it off, then," said my father impatiently.

"The only person who would offer a jockey a large sum to lose a race is a crooked bookmaker. If he *knows* a well-fancied horse is not going to win, he can accept any amount of money on that horse without risk."

"Enlarge," said Lodge.

"Normally bookmakers try to balance their books so that whichever horse wins they come out on the winning side," I said. "If too many people want to back one horse, they accept the bets, but they back the horse themselves with another bookmaker; then if that horse wins, they collect their winnings from the second bookmaker, and put it out to their customers. It's a universal system known as 'laying off.' Now suppose you were a crooked bookmaker and Joe Nantwich is to ride a fancied horse. You tip Joe the wink to lose. Then however much is betted with you on that horse, you do no laying off, because you know you won't have to pay out."

"I would have thought that a hundred pounds would have been more than it was worth," said Lodge, "since bookmakers normally make a profit anyway."

"Your friend wasn't satisfied with the legitimate gains from the taxis," my father pointed out.

I sighed, and shifted my stiff shoulders against the frame of the window.

"There's a bit more to it, of course," I said. "If a bookmaker knows he hasn't got to pay out on a certain horse, he can offer better odds on it. Not enough to be suspicious, but just enough to attract a lot of extra custom. A point better than anyone else would go to—say eleven to four, when the next best offer was five to two. The money would roll in, don't you think?"

I stood up and went towards the door, saying, "I'll show you something."

The stairs seemed steeper than usual. I went up to my room and fetched the racing form book and the little bunch of bookmakers' tickets, and shuffled back to the drawing-room. I laid the tickets out on the table in front of Lodge, and my father came over to have a look.

"These," I explained, "are some tickets Bill kept for his children to play with. Three of them, as you see, were issued by L. C. Perth, and all the others are from different firms, no two alike. Bill was a methodical man. On the backs of all the tickets he wrote the date, the details of his bet, and the name of the horse he'd put his money on. He used to search around in Tattersall's for the best odds and bet in cash, instead of betting on credit with Tote Investors or one of the bookmakers on the rails—those," I added for Lodge's benefit, as I could see the question forming on his lips, "are bookmakers who stand along the railing between Tattersall's and the Club enclosures, writing down bets made by Club members and other people known to them. They send out weekly accounts, win or lose. Bill didn't bet in large amounts, and he thought credit betting wasn't exciting enough."

Lodge turned over the three Perth tickets.

Bill's loopy writing was clear and unmistakable. I picked up the first ticket, and read aloud, "'Peripatetic. November 7th. Ten pounds staked at eleven to ten.' So he stood to win eleven pounds for his money." I opened the detailed form book and turned to November 7.

"Peripatetic," I said, "lost the two mile hurdle at Sandown that day by four lengths. He was riden by Joe Nantwich. The starting price was eleven to ten on—that is, you have to stake eleven pounds to win ten—and had earlier been as low as eleven to eight on. L. C. Perth must have done a roaring trade at eleven to ten against."

I picked up the second card and read, "'Sackbut. October 10th. Five pounds staked at six to one.'" I opened the form book for that day. "Sackbut was unplaced at Newbury and Joe Nantwich rode it. The best price generally offered was five to one, and the starting price was seven to two."

I put the Sackbut ticket back on the table, and read the third card where it lay. "'Malabar. December 2nd. Eight pounds staked at fifteen to eight.'" I laid the form book beside it, opened at December 2nd. "Malabar finished fourth at Birmingham. Joe Nantwich rode him. The starting price was six to four."

Lodge and my father silently checked the book with the ticket.

"I looked up all the other cards as well," I said. "Of course, as Bill still had the tickets, all the horses lost, but on only one of them did he get better odds than you'd expect. Joe didn't ride it, and I don't think it's significant, because it was an outsider at a hundred to six."

"I wish the racing fraternity would use only whole numbers and halves," said Lodge plaintively.

"Haven't you heard," I asked, "about the keen gambler who taught his baby son to count? One, six-to-four, two . . ."

Lodge laughed, his dark eyes crinkling at the corners. "I'll have to write down these figures on the Perth tickets alongside the form book information,

and get it straightened out in my mind," he said, unscrewing his pen and settling to the task.

My father sat down beside him and watched the tell-tale list grow. I went
back to the window seat and waited.

Presently Lodge said, "I can see why your father misses you as a fraud
spotter." He put his pen back in his pocket.

I smiled and said, "If you want to read a really blatant fraud, you should
look up the Irish racing in that form book. It's fantastic."

"Not today. This is quite enough to be going on with," said Lodge, rubbing his hand over his face and pinching his nose between thumb and forefinger.

"All that remains, as far as I'm concerned, is for you to tell us who is organising the whole thing," said my father with a touch of mockery, which
from long understanding I interpreted as approval.

"That, dear Pa, I fear I cannot do," I said.

But Lodge said seriously, "Could it be anyone you know on the racecourse?
It must be someone connected with racing. How about Perth, the bookmaker?"

"It could be. I don't know him. His name won't actually be Perth of
course. That name was sold with the business. I'll have a bet on with him
next time I go racing and see what happens," I said.

"You will do no such thing," said my father emphatically, and I felt too
listless to argue.

"How about a jockey, or a trainer, or an owner?" asked Lodge.

"You'd better include the Stewards and the National Hunt Committee,"
I said, ironically. "They were almost the first to know I had discovered the
wire and was looking into it. The man we are after knew very early on that I
was inquisitive. I didn't tell many people I suspected more than an accident,
or ask many pointed questions, before that affair in the horse-box."

"People you know . . ." said Lodge, musingly. "How about Gregory?"

"No," I said.

"Why not? He lives near Brighton, near enough for the Marconicar
morning telephone call."

"He wouldn't risk hurting Bill or Admiral," I said.

"How can you be sure?" asked Lodge. "People aren't always what they
seem, and murderers are often fond of animals, until they get in the way. One
chap I saw at the assizes lately killed a nightwatchman and showed no remorse

at all. But when evidence was given that the nightwatchman's dog had had his head bashed in, too, the accused burst into tears and said he was sorry."

"Pathetic," I said. "But no dice. It isn't Pete."

"Faith or evidence?" persisted Lodge.

"Faith," I said grudgingly, because I was quite sure.

"Jockeys?" suggested Lodge, leaving it.

"None of them strikes me as being the type we're looking for," I said, "and I think you're overlooking the fact that racing came second on the programme and may even have been adopted solely because a shaky bookmaking business existed on the floor above the Marconicars. I mean, that in itself may have turned the boss of Marconicars towards racing."

"You may be right," admitted Lodge.

My father said, "It's just possible that the man who originally owned Marconicars decided to launch out into crime, and faked a sale to cover his tracks."

"Clifford Tudor, nee Thasos, do you mean?" asked Lodge with interest. My father nodded, and Lodge said to me, "How about it?"

"Tudor pops up all over the place," I said. "He knew Bill, and Bill had his address noted down on a scrap of paper." I put my hand into my jacket pocket. The old envelope was still there. I drew it out and looked at it again. "Tudor told me he had asked Bill to ride a horse for him."

"When did he tell you that?" asked Lodge.

"I gave him a lift from Plumpton races into Brighton, four days after Bill died. We talked about him on the way."

"Anything else?" asked Lodge.

"Well . . . Tudor's horses have been ridden—up until lately—by our corrupted friend Joe Nantwich. It was on Tudor's horse Bolingbroke that Joe won once when he had been instructed to lose . . . but at Cheltenham he threw away a race on a horse of Tudor's, and Tudor was very angry about it."

"Camouflage," suggested my father.

But I rested my aching head against the window, and said, "I don't think Tudor can possibly be the crook we're looking for."

"Why not?" asked Lodge. "He has the organising ability, he lives in Brighton, he owned the taxis, he employs Joe Nantwich, and he knew Major Davidson. He seems the best proposition so far."

"No," I said tiredly. "The best lead we've had is the taxis. If I hadn't recognised that the men who stopped me in the horse-box were also taxi-drivers, I'd never have found out anything at all. Whoever put them on to me can't possibly have imagined I would know them, or he wouldn't have done it. But if there's one person who knew I would recognise them, it's Clifford Tudor. He was standing near me while the taxi-drivers fought, and he knew I'd had time to look at them after the police had herded them into two groups."

"I don't rule him out altogether, even so," said Lodge, gathering his papers together and putting them back into his briefcase. "Criminals often make the stupidest mistakes."

I said, "If we ever do find your Claud Thiveridge, I think he will turn out to be someone I've never met and never heard of. A complete stranger. It's far more likely."

I wanted to believe it.

I did not want to have to face another possibility, one that I shied away from so uncomfortably that I could not bring myself even to lay it open for Lodge's inspection.

Who, besides Tudor, knew before the horse-box incident that I wanted Bill's death avenged? Kate. And to whom had she passed this on? To Uncle George. Uncle George, who I suspected, housed a lean and hungry soul in his fat body, behind his fatuous expression.

Uncle George, out of the blue, had bought a horse for his niece. Why? To widen her interests, he had said. But through her, I thought, he would learn much of what went on at the races.

And Uncle George had sent Heavens Above to be trained in the stable which housed Bill's horse. Was it a coincidence . . . or the beginning of a scheme which Bill's unexpected death had cut short?

It was nebulous, unconvincing. It was based only on supposition, not on facts, and bolstered only by memory of the shock on Uncle George's face when Kate told him we had been to the Blue Duck—shock which he had called indigestion. And perhaps it had been indigestion, after all.

And all those primitive weapons in his study, the ritual objects and the scalp . . . were they the playthings of a man who relished violence? Or who loathed it? Or did both at the same time?

Scilla came into the drawing-room, carrying a copper bowl filled with forsythia and daffodils. She put it on the low table near me, and the spring sun suddenly shone on the golden flowers, so that they seemed like a burst of light, reflecting their colour upwards onto her face as she bent over them, tweaking them into order.

She gave me a sharp glance, and turned round to the others.

"Alan looks very tired," she said. "What have you been doing?"

"Talking," I said, smiling at her.

"You'll find yourself back in the hospital if you're not careful," she scolded mildly, and without pausing offered mid-morning coffee to Lodge and my father.

I was glad for the interruption, because I had not wished to discuss with them what was to be done next in pursuit of Mr. Claud Thiveridge. Every small advance I had made in his direction had brought its retribution, it was true; yet in each of his parries I had found a clue. My faulty memory was still cheating me of the information I had paid for with the drubbing at Bristol, but it did not deter me from wanting to see the busines through.

I would get closer to Thiveridge. He would hit out again, and in doing it show me the next step towards him, like the flash of a gunshot in the dark revealing the hiding place of a sniper.

CHAPTER 14

JOE NANTWICH FOUND the sniper first.

Eight days after Lodge's visit I drove down to West Sussex races, having put in a short morning at the office. My bruises had faded and gone; the ribs and collar-bone were mended and in perfect working order, and even my stubborn headache was losing its grip. I whistled my way into the changing room and presented to Clem my brand new crash-helmet, bought that morning from Bates of Jermyn Street for three guineas.

The weighing room was empty, and distant oohs and ahs proclaimed that the first race was in progress. Clem, who was tidying up the changing room after the tornado of getting a large number of jockeys out of their ordinary clothes, into racing colours, past the scales and out to the parade ring, greeted me warmly and shook hands.

"Glad to see you back, sir," he said, taking the helmet. With a ball-point pen he wrote my name on a piece of adhesive tape and stuck it on to the shiny shell. "Let's hope you won't be needing another new one of these in a hurry." He pressed his thumb firmly on to the adhesive tape.

"I'm starting again tomorrow, Clem," I said. "Can you bring my gear? Big saddle. There's no weight problem, I'm riding Admiral."

"Top flipping weight," said Clem, resignedly. "And a lot of lead, which Admiral isn't used to. Major Davidson hardly ever needed any." Clem gave me an assessing sideways look and added, "You've lost three or four pounds, I shouldn't wonder."

"All the better," I said cheerfully, turning to the door.

"Oh, just a minute, sir," said Clem. "Joe Nantwich asked me to let you know, if you came, that he has something to tell you."

"Oh, yes?" I said.

"He was asking for you on Saturday at Liverpool, but I told him you'd probably be coming here, as Mr. Gregory mentioned last week that you'd be riding Admiral tomorrow," said Clem, absent-mindedly picking up a saddle and smoothing his hand over the leather.

"Did Joe say what it was he wanted to tell me?" I asked.

"Yes, he wants to show you a bit of brown wrapping paper with something written on it. He said you'd be interested to see it, though I can't think why—the word I saw looked like something to do with chickens. He had the paper out in the changing room at Liverpool, and folded it up flat on the bench into a neat shape, and tucked it into the inside pocket of his jacket. Giggling over it, he was. He'd had a drink or two I reckon, but then most people had, it was after the National. He said what was written on the paper was double dutch to him, but it might be a clue, you never knew. I asked him a clue to what? But he wouldn't say, and anyway, I was too busy to bother with him much."

"I'll see him, and find out what it's all about," I said. "Has he still got the paper with him, do you know?"

"Yes, he has. He patted his pocket just now when he asked me if you were here, and I heard the paper crackle."

"Thanks, Clem," I said.

I went outside. The race was over, the winner was being led towards the unsaddling enclosure in front of the weighing room, and down from the stands streamed the hundreds of chattering racegoers. I stood near the weighing-room door, waiting for Joe and catching up with the latest gossip. Liverpool, I learned, had been disappointing, fabulous, bloody, a dead loss and the tops, according to who told it. I had not been there. I had been too busy getting intensive treatment on my shoulder muscles to help my strength back.

Sandy clapped me soundly on the back as he passed, remarking that it was "Bloody good to see your old physog on the horizon again, even if you do look like an understudy for Scarface." He went on, "Have you seen Joe? The little drip's been squealing for you."

"So I hear," I said. "I'm waiting for him now."

A couple of press men asked me my riding plans, and made note about Admiral for their morning edition. Sir Creswell Stampe noticed my existence with a nod of his distinguished head and the characteristic puffing up on his top lip which passed with him for a smile.

My content at being back in my favourite environment was somewhat marred by the sight of Dane strolling across the grass, talking intently to a slender, heart-catchingly beautiful girl at his side. Her face was turned intimately towards his, and she was laughing. It was Kate.

When they saw me they quickened their steps and approached me smiling, a striking pair evenly matched in grave and dark good looks.

Kate, who had got used to my battered face over lunch some days earlier, greeted me with a brisk "Hi, there," from which all undertones of love and longing were regrettably absent. She put her hand on my arm and asked me to walk down the course with her and Dane to watch the next race from beside the water jump.

I glanced at Dane. His smile was faint, and his dark eyes looked at me inscrutably, without welcome. My own muscles had tensed uncontrollably when I saw him and Kate together; so now I knew exactly how he felt about me.

It was as much unease over the low ebb of our friendship as desire to chase Claud Thiveridge which made me say, "I can't come at this instant. I must find Joe Nantwich first. How about later on . . . if you'd like to walk down again?"

"All right, Alan," she said. "Or maybe we could have tea together?" She turned away with Dane and said, "See you later," over her shoulder with a mischievous grin, in which I read her mockery of the jealousy she could arouse in me.

Watching them go, I forgot to look out for Joe, and went in to search for him through the weighing and changing rooms again. He wasn't there.

Pete towered over me as I returned to my post outside the door and greeted me like a long-lost friend. His hat tipped back on his big head, his broad shoulders spreading apart the lapels of his coat, he gazed with good humour at my face, and said, "They've made a good job of sewing you up, you know. You were a very gory sight indeed last time I saw you. I suppose you still can't remember what happened?"

"No," I said, regretfully. "Sometimes I think . . . but I can't get hold of it . . ."

"Perhaps it's just as well," he said comfortingly, hitching the strap of his race glasses higher on to his shoulder and preparing to go into the weighing room.

"Pete," I said, "have you seen Joe anywhere? I think he's been asking for me."

"Yes," he said. "He was looking for you at Liverpool, too. He was very keen to show you something, an address I think, written on some brown paper."

"Did you see it?" I asked.

"Yes, as a matter of fact I did, but he annoys me and I didn't pay much attention. Chichester, I think the place was."

"Do you know where Joe is now?" I asked. "I've been waiting for him for some time, but there isn't a sign of him."

Pete's thin lips showed contempt. "Yes, I saw the little brute going into the bar, about ten minutes ago."

"Already!" I exclaimed.

"Drunken little sod," he said dispassionately. "I wouldn't put him up on one of my horses if he was the last jockey on earth."

"Which bar?" I pressed.

"Eh? Oh, the one at the back of Tattersall's, next to the Tote. He and another man went in with that dark fellow he rides for . . . Tudor, isn't that his name?"

I gaped at him. "But Tudor finished with Joe at Cheltenham . . . and very emphatically, too."

Pete shrugged. "Tudor went into the bar with Joe and the other chap a few steps behind him. Maybe it was only coincidence."

"Thanks, anyway," I said.

It was only a hundred yards round one corner to the bar where Joe had gone. It was a long wooden hut backing onto the high fence which divided the racecourse from the road. I wasted no time, but nonetheless when I stepped into the building and threaded my way through the overcoated, beer-drinking customers, I found that Joe was no longer there. Nor was Clifford Tudor.

I went outside again. The time for the second race was drawing near, and long impatient queues waited at the Tote next door to the bar, eyes flickering between racecards and wrist watches, money clutched ready in hopeful hands. The customers from the bar poured out, hurrying past me. Men were running across the grass towards the stands, coattails flapping. Bells rang loudly in the Tote building, and the queues squirmed with the compulsion to push their money through the little windows before the shutters came down.

I hovered indecisively. There was no sign of Joe in all this activity, and I decided to go up to the jockeys' box in the stands and look for him there. I put my head into the bar for a final check, but it was now empty except for three ageing young ladies mopping up the beer-slopped counter.

It was only because I was moving so slowly that I found Joe at all.

Owing to the curve of the road behind them, the Tote and bar buildings did not stand in a perfectly straight line. The gap between the two was narrow at the front, barely eighteen inches across; but it widened farther back until, by the high fence itself, the Tote and bar walls were four or five feet apart.

I glanced into this narrow area as I passed. And there was Joe. Only I did not know it was Joe until I got close to him.

At first I saw only a man lying on the ground in the corner made by the boundary fence and the end wall of the Tote, and thinking he might be ill, or faint, or even plain drunk, went in to see if he needed help.

He lay in shadow, but something about his shape and ragdoll relaxedness struck me with shocking recognition as I took the five or six strides across to him.

He was alive, but only just. Bright red frothy blood trickled from his nose and the corner of his mouth, and a pool of it lay under his cheek on the weedy gravel. His round young face still wore, incredibly, a look of sulky petulance, as if he did not realise that what had happened to him was more than a temporary inconvenience.

Joe had a knife in his body. Its thick black handle protruded incongruously from his yellow and white checked shirt, slanting downwards from underneath his breastbone. A small patch of blood stained the cloth round it, a mild enough indication of the damage the blade was doing inside.

His eyes were open, but vague and already glazing.

I said, urgently, "Joe!"

His eyes came round to mine and I saw them sharpen into focus and recognise me. A muscle moved in his cheek and his lips opened. He made a great effort to speak.

The scarlet blood suddenly spilled in a gush from his nostrils and welled up in a sticky, bottomless pool in his open mouth. He gave a single choking sound that was almost indecently faint, and over his immature face spread a look of profound astonishment. Then his flesh blanched and his eyes rolled up, and Joe was gone. For several seconds after he died his expression said clearly, "It's not fair." The skin settled in this crisis into the lines most accustomed to it in life.

Fighting nausea at the sweet smell of his blood, I shut the eyes with my fingers, and sat back on my heels, looking at him helplessly.

I knew it was useless, but after a moment or two I opened his coat and felt in his pockets for the brown paper he had wanted to show me. It was not there, and his death would not have made sense if it had been. The brown paper was, I thought, the wrapping from Joe's last payment for stopping a horse. It had to be. With something about it which he thought would disclose who had sent it. A postmark? An address? Something to do with chickens, Clem had said; and Pete said it was Chichester. Neither of these held any significance at all for me. According to Clem it meant nothing to Joe either, and he was simply going to show it to me because he had said he would.

He had always been too talkative for his own good. Not quick or quiet. Prudently and privately he could have telephoned to tell me his discovery as soon as he made it. But instead he had flourished the paper at Liverpool. Someone had taken drastic steps to make sure he did not show it to me.

"Poor, silly blabbermouth," I said softly, to his still body.

I got to my feet, and went back to the narrow entrance of the little area. There was no one about. The voice of the commentator boomed over the loudspeakers that the horses were approaching the second open ditch, which meant that the race was already half over and that I would have to hurry.

I ran the last fifty yards to the Clerk of the Course's office and thrust open the door. A nondescript, grey-haired man in glasses, sitting at a desk, looked

up, startled, his pen in mid-air and the paper he was writing on pressed under the palm of his hand. He was the Clerk of the Course's secretary.

"Mr. Rollo isn't here?" I asked unnecessarily, glancing round the otherwise empty office.

"He's watching the race. Can I help you?" A dry voice, a dry manner. Not
the sort of man one would choose to announce a murder to. But it had to be
done. Suppressing all urgency from my voice I told him plainly and quietly
that Joe Nantwich was lying dead between the Tote and the bar with a knife
through his lungs. I suggested that he send for a canvas screen to put across
the gap between the two buildings, as when the crowds began to stream
towards the bar and the playing-out Tote windows after the race, someone
would be certain to see him. The ground round his body would be well trod-
den over. Clues, if there were any, would be lost.

The eyes behind the spectacles grew round and disbelieving.

"It's not a joke," I said desperately. "The race is nearly over. Tell the police then. I'll find a screen." He still did not move. I could have shaken him,
but I could not spare the time. "Hurry," I urged. But his hand had still not
gone out to his telephone when I shut the door.

The ambulance room was attached to the end of the weighing-room
building. I went in in a hurry, to find two motherly St. John's nurses drinking tea. I spoke to the younger one, a middle-aged soul of ample proportions.

"Put that down and come with me quickly," I said, hoping she would not
argue. I picked up a stretcher which was standing against the wall, and as she
put her cup down slowly, I added, "Bring a blanket. There's a man hurt.
Please hurry."

The call to duty got my nurse moving without demur, and picking up a
blanket she followed me across the paddock, though at under half speed.

The commentator's voice rose slightly as he described the race from the
last fence, and crisply into the silence when the cheers died away came another voice announcing the winner. I reached the gap by the Tote building as
he spoke the names of the second and third horses.

The final stalwart punters began to drift back towards the bar. I looked
in at Joe. He had not been disturbed.

I set the stretcher up on end on its handles, to make a sort of screen across
the gap. The nurse came up to me, breathing audibly. I took the blanket from
her and hung it over the stretcher so that no one could see into the area at all.

"Listen," I said, trying to speak slowly. "There is a man between these two buildings. He is dead, not hurt. He has been killed with a knife. I am going to make sure that the police are coming, and I want you to stand here holding the stretcher up like this. Don't let anyone past you until I come back with a policeman. Do you understand?"

She did not answer. She twisted the stretcher a little so that she could peer through the gap. She took a long look. Then, drawing up her considerable bosom and with the light of battle in her eyes, she said firmly, "No one shall go in, I'll see to that."

I hurried back to the Clerk of the Course's office. Mr. Rollo was there himself this time, and after I had told him what had happened things at last began to move.

It is always difficult to find a place to be alone at the races. After I had taken a policeman along to where Joe lay, and seen the routine bustle begin, I needed a pause to think. I had had an idea while I crouched beside Joe's body, but it was not one to be acted upon headlong.

People thronged everywhere in the paddock and the racecourse buildings, and to get away from them I walked out on to the course and over the rough grass in the centre until the stands were some way behind. Distance, I hoped, would give me a sense of proportion as well as solitude.

I thought about Bill and Scilla, and also about what I owed to my father, now back in Rhodesia. I thought about the terrorised pub-keepers in Brighton and the bloody face of Joe Nantwich.

It was no use pretending that Joe's murder had not made a great deal of difference to the situation, for until now I had blithely pursued Mr. Claud Thiveridge in the belief that though he might arrange for people to be beaten up, he did not purposely kill. Now the boundary was crossed. The next killing would come easier, and the next easier still. The plucky, dog-owning rebels against protection were in greater danger than before, and I was probably responsible.

Joe had shown his brown paper to several people, and no one, including apparently himself, had immediately seen the meaning of what was written on it. Yet he had been killed before he could show it to me. To me, then, the words would have told their tale. Perhaps to me alone.

I watched the rising wind blowing the grass in flattening ripples across the course, and heard the distant voices of the bookmakers as they shouted the odds for the next race.

The question to be answered was simple. Was I, or was I not, going on with the chase. I'm no hero. I did not want to end up dead. And there was no doubt that the idea I had had beside Joe's body was as safe as a stick of dynamite in a bonfire.

The horses for the third race came out and cantered down to the start. Idly I watched them. The race was run, the horses returned to the paddock: and still I stood in the centre of the course, dithering on top of my mental fence.

At last I walked back to the paddock. The jockeys were alrady out in the parade ring for the fourth race, and as I reached the weighing room one of the racecourse officials grabbed my arm, saying the police had been looking everywhere for me. They wanted me to make a statement, he said, and I would find them in the Clerk of the Course's office.

I went along there, and opened the door.

Mr. Rollo, spare and short, leaned against the window wearing a worried frown. His grey-haired bespectacled secretary still sat at his desk, his mouth slightly open as if even yet he had not grasped the reality of what had happened.

The police inspector, who introduced himself as Wakefield, had established himself at Mr. Rollo's table, and was attended by three constables, one of them armed with shorthand notebook and pencil. The racecourse doctor was sitting on a chair by the wall, and a man I did not know stood near him.

Wakefield was displeased with me for what he called my irresponsibility in disappearing for over half an hour at such a time. Big and thick, he dominated the room. Authority exuded from his short upspringing grey hair, his narrow eyes, his strong stubby fingers. A policeman to put the fear of God into evildoers. His baleful glare suggested that at the moment I should be included in this category.

"If you're quite ready, Mr. York," he began sarcastically, "we'll take your statement."

I looked round the crowded little office, and said, "I prefer to make my statement to you alone."

The inspector growled and erupted and argued; but finally everyone left except Wakefield, myself, and the notebook constable, to whom I agreed as a compromise. I told Wakefield exactly what had happened. The whole truth, and nothing but the truth.

Then I went back to the weighing room, and to every one of the dozens who clustered round asking for an eyewitness account, I said I had found Joe alive. Yes, I agreed steadily, he had spoken to me before he died. What did he say? Well, it was only two or three words, and I preferred not to discuss it at present, if they did not mind. I added that I had not actually mentioned it to the police yet, but of course I would if I thought it would be important. And I put on a puzzled, thoughtful expression, hoping I looked as if I had a key in my hand and was on the point of finding the right lock to put it in.

I took Kate to tea, and Pete, catching sight of us, came over to join us. To them, too, I told the same story, feeling ashamed, but not caring to risk their broadcasting the truth, that Joe had died without uttering a syllable.

Shortly before the sixth race I left the meeting. The last thing I saw, as I glanced back from the gate, was Wakefield and Cliffor Tudor standing outside the door of the Clerk of the Course's office, shaking hands. Tudor, who had been with Joe so soon before his death, had apparently been "assisting the police with their investigations." Satisfactorily, it seemed.

I went through the car park to the Lotus, started up, and drove out towards the west, and along the straight secondary roads of the South Downs I opened up the engine and sent the little car along at over a hundred. No Marconicars, I thought with satisfaction, could compete with that. But to make quite certain I was not being followed I stopped once at a vantage point on top of a rise, and studied the road behind me with raceglasses. It was deserted. There was nothing on my tail.

About thirty miles from the racecourse I stopped at an undistinguished roadhouse and booked a room for the night. I insisted also on a lock-up garage for the car. It was too far from Brighton to be within the normal reach of the Marconicars, but I was taking no chances. I wanted to be invisible. It is one thing to stick your neck out; but quite another to go to sleep in full view of the axe.

After a dull dinner I went to my room and wrote a letter to my father. A difficult one. I told him about Joe's death, and that I was trying to use it to entice Mr. Thiveridge out of his lair. I asked him, as lightly as I could, to forgive me. I am, I wrote, only hunting another crocodile.

I finished the letter, sealed it, went early to bed, and lay awake for a long time before I slept.

On the way back to the racecourse in the morning I stopped at a post office and air-mailed my letter. I also acquired four shillings' worth of pennies, which I stacked into a paper-wrapped roll. I took the spare pair of socks out of my overnight case and slid the roll of pennies down into the foot of one of them, knotting them there securely. I swung my little cosh experimentally on to the palm of my hand. It was heavy enough, I thought, to knock a man out. I put it in my trouser pocket and finished the journey to the course.

I asked a constable on duty in the paddock where I could find Inspector Wakefield if I wanted him. The constable said that Wakefield was at the station, he thought, and was not coming to the course that afternoon, although he had been there in the morning. I thanked him, and went into the weighing room, and asked several people in a loud voice to tell me if they saw Inspector Wakefield about, as I wanted to have a word with him about what Joe had said to me before he died.

The awareness of danger, though I had brought it on myself, had a noticeable effect on my nerves. The wrought-up, quickened pulse of a race was unduly magnified, so that I could hear my own heart beating. Every noise seemed louder, every chance remark more significant, every light brighter. But I was not so much afraid as excited.

I was careful only about what I turned my back to, having no intention of being attacked from behind. It was more likely, I thought, that someone would try to cajole me into an out of the way place as they must have done with Joe, because most of the racecourse was too public for murder.

A knife in the ribs seemed what I should be most wary of. Effective in Joe's case, it had the advantages—to its wielder—of being silent and accurate. Moreover the weapon was left with the body, so that there was no subsequent difficulty in getting rid of it. The black handle protruding from Joe had the familiar knobbed shape of the sort of French steel cooking knife on sale in any hardware shop. Too common to be a clue of any kind, I suspected, and easy to replace with another to stick into the guts of a second victim. If anyone tried that I intended to be ready. My fingers closed comfortably on the pennies in my pocket.

I hoped to be able to deliver an attacker (unconscious from a four-shilling bump behind the ear) to Inspector Wakefield, to be charged with attempted murder. I had great faith that Wakefield's bulldog personality would shake information out of the toughest criminal in those circumstances, and that with reasonable luck a firm clue to Thiveridge's identity might disclose itself. It was too much to hope that Thiveridge would appear himself. I believed his husky avowal to me on the telephone that he hated personal violence and ordered others to do his dirty work for him, out of his squeamish sight.

I changed, and weighed on the trial scales, and chatted, and went about my ordinary business, and waited.

Nothing happened.

No one asked me to step into dim corners to discuss private business. No one showed any particular interest in what Joe was supposed to have told me before he died. Naturally his murder was still the chief topic of conversation, but it lost ground as the day wore on, and the living horses became more interesting to the inmates of the weighing room than the dead jockey.

Admiral was to run in the fifth race. By the time the fourth was over my nerves had calmed down and my tense readiness had evaporated. I had expected action before this. I had been at the meeting for nearly three hours, a man with essential information inviting to have his mouth permanently shut, and no move had been made against me.

It crossed my mind, not for the first time, that cause and effect in the Thiveridge organisation never followed closely on each other. Joe's death happened two whole days after he showed his brown paper at Liverpool. The warning to me on the telephone was delivered two days after I had spread at Cheltenham the news of the wire which had killed Bill. The horse-box affair had taken at least a day to arrange. The Bristol wire was rigged to bring me down two days after my excursion into the Marconicar office.

I had begun to suspect that the whole organisation was still geared to the telephone call Thiveridge made every morning to Fielder, and that Fielder had no other way of getting urgent messages to his "Chairman," or of receiving instructions from him. Presumably Thiveridge still felt the delay in his news service was a lesser evil than providing an address or telephone number at which he could be reached and perhaps discovered.

Depressed, I was coming to believe that my carefully acted lies had not at all reached the ears for which they were meant, and felt that offering myself as bait to a predator who did not know he should be hunting me was a bit idiotic.

Trying to shake off this deflation, I went out to the parade ring to join Pete and mount Admiral. Bill's horse, now mine, looked as splendid as ever. With his intelligent head, deep chest, straight hocks, and good bone below the knee, he was a perfect example of what a top class steeplechaser should be.

"Even though he hasn't been on a racecourse since that ghastly day at Maidenhead, he's at the top of his form," said Pete, admiring him beside me. "You can't lose the race, so go along quietly for a while, getting used to him. You'll find he has plenty in reserve. You'll never get to the bottom of him. Bill used to take him to the front early on, as you know, but you don't need to. He's got a terrific turn of foot from the last."

"I'll do as you say," I said.

Pete gave me a leg-up. "Admiral's odds-on, again," he said. "If you make a mess of this race the crowd'll murder you. So will I." He grinned.

"I'll try to stay alive," I said, grinning back cheerfully.

Admiral was as superb to ride as he looked. He put himself right before every fence, making his spring at exactly the right moment and needing no help from the saddle. He had the low, flowing galloping stride of the really fast mover, and from the first fence onward I found racing on his back an almost ecstatic pleasure. Following Pete's advice I went round the whole course without forcing the pace, but riding into the last fence alongside two others, I gave Admiral a kick in the ribs and shook up the reins. He took off from just inside the wings and landed as far out on the other side, gaining two lengths in the air and shedding the other two horses like dead leaves. We came home alone, easy winners, to warm cheers from the stands.

In the winner's unsaddling enclosure, where I dismounted and undid the girths, Admiral behaved as if he had only been out for an exercise gallop, his belly hardly moving as he breathed. I patted his glossy chestnut neck, noticed that he was hardly sweating at all, and asked Pete, "What on earth can he do if he really tries?"

"The National, no less," said Pete, rocking back on his heels, and tipping his hat off his face, as he collected his due congratulations from all around.

I grinned, pulled the saddle off over my arm, and went into the weighing room to weigh-in and change. The familiar joy of winning flushed through my limbs, as warming as a hot bath, and I could have done handsprings down the changing room if I hadn't known it was the horse to whom all credit was due, not the jockey.

Pete called to me to hurry up and we'd have a celebration drink together, so I changed quickly and went outside to join him. He steered me towards the bar next to the Tote building, and we stopped at the gap, looking in to where Joe had died. There was a shoulder-high wooden fence across the entrance now, to keep sensation seekers out. A rusty brown stain on the gravel was all that was left of Joe.

"A terrible thing, that," Pete said, as we stepped into the bar. "What did he say to you before he died?"

"I'll tell you sometime," I said idly. "But just now I'm more interested in where Admiral runs next." And over our drinks we talked solely about horses.

Returning to the weighing room we found two men in belted raincoats waiting for us near the door. They wore trilby hats and large shoes, and gave off that indefinable aura of solid menace which characterises many plain-clothes policemen.

One of them put his hand inside his coat, drew out a folded warrant and flipped it in my direction.

"Mr. York?"

"Yes."

"Inspector Wakefield's compliments, and will you come down to the po-lice station to help his enquiries, please." The "please" he tacked on as an afterthought.

"Very well," I said, and asked Pete to see Clem about my kit.

"Sure," he said.

I walked with the two men across to the gate and through the car park.

"I'll get my car and follow you to the station," I said.

"There's a police car waiting for us in the road, sir," said the larger of the two. "Inspector Wakefield did say to bring you in it, and if you don't mind, sir, I'd rather do as the Inspector says."

I grinned. If Inspector Wakefield were my boss I'd do as he said, too. "All right," I agreed.

Ahead of us the sleek black Wolseley was parked outside the gate, with a uniformed driver standing beside it and another man in a peaked cap in the front passenger's seat.

Away towards my right, in front of the ranks of parked horse-boxes, sev-eral of the runners from Admiral's race were being led up and down to get the stiffness out of their limbs before they were loaded up for the journey home. Admiral was among them, with Victor, his lad, walking proudly at his head.

I was telling the man on my right, the smaller of the two, that there was my horse and wasn't he a beauty, when I got a shock which knocked the breath out of me as thoroughly as a kick in the stomach.

To cover myself I dropped my race glasses on to the turf and bent slowly to pick them up, my escort stopping a pace ahead of me to wait. I grasped the strap and slung it over my shoulder, straightening and looking back at the same time to where we had come from. Forty yards of grass separated us from the last row of cars. There was no one about except some distant people go-ing home. I looked at my watch. The last race was just about to begin.

I turned round unhurriedly, letting my eyes travel blankly past the man

on my right and on towards Admiral, now going away from me. As usual after a race, he was belted into a rug to avoid cooling down too quickly, and he
still wore his bridle. Victor would change that for a head collar when he put
him in the horse-box.

Victor's great drawback was his slow wits. Endowed with an instinctive
feeling for horses and an inborn skill in looking after them, he had never risen
above "doing his two" in forty years of stable life, and never would. I would
have to do without much help from him.

"Victor," I shouted, and when he turned round I signalled to him to
bring Admiral over.

"I just want to make sure the horse's legs are all right," I explained to the
two men. They nodded and waited beside me, the larger one shifting from
foot to foot.

I did not dare to take a third look, and in any case I knew I was not mistaken.

*The man on my right was wearing the tie I had lost in the horse-box on Maiden-
head Thicket.*

It was made from a piece of silk which had been specially woven and
given to me on my twenty-first birthday by a textile manufacturer who
wanted to do business with my father. I had two other ties like it, and a scarf,
and the pattern of small red and gold steamships interlaced with the letter Y
on a dark green background was unique.

How likely was it that a junior C.I.D. officer should have come honestly
by my tie, I asked myself urgently. Farmer Lawson had not found it, and none
of his men admitted to having seen it. It was too much of a coincidence to be
innocent that it should reappear round the throat of a man who was asking
me to step into a car and go for a ride with him.

Here was the attack I had been waiting for, and I had damn nearly
walked meekly into the trap. Getting out of it, when it was so nearly sprung,
was not going to be easy. The "police" car was parked across the gateway
barely twenty paces ahead, with the driver standing by the bonnet and looking in our direction. The menacing aura of my two tough escorts now revealed itself to be something a great deal more sinister than a manner
assumed to deal with crooks. One of them, perhaps, had killed Joe.

If I gave the slightest sign of doubting them, I was sure the three of them
would hustle me into the car and drive off in a cloud of dust, leaving only
Victor to report doubtfully what he had seen. And that, as far as I was

concerned, would be that. It was to be one of those rides from which the passenger did not return.

My plan to present Wakefield with an attempted murder was no good. One, I could have managed. But not three, and another sitting in the car.

When Victor was within fifteen paces of me I let the strap of my race glasses slip from my shoulder, down my arm and into my hand. Abruptly, with all my strenth, I swung the glasses like a scythe round the legs of the larger man and overbalanced him, tripped the smaller man with the one elementary judo throw I knew, and sprinted for Admiral.

The five seconds it took them to recover from the unexpected assault were enough. As they started after me with set faces I leaped on to Admiral's back, picked up the reins which lay loosely on his neck, and turned him round sharply out of Victor's grasp.

The third man was running towards me from the car. I kicked Admiral into a canter in two strides, swerving round the advancing chauffeur, and set him toward the hedge which formed the boundary of the car park. He cleared it powerfully, landing on the grass verge of the road a few yards in front of the black car. The fourth man had the door open and was scrambling out. I looked back quickly.

Victor was standing stock-still with his mouth open. The three men were all running towards the gate with purposeful strides. They had nearly reached it. I had barely time to hope they were not carrying guns, since I presented a large and close target, when I saw the sun glint on something bright in the hand of the man who was wearing my tie. It hardly seemed the moment to stop and discover whether the glint came from a black-handled chef's knife: but I nearly found out the hard way, because he drew back his arm and threw it at me. I flung myself flat on the horse's neck and it missed, and I heard it clatter on to the road beyond.

I urged Admiral straight across the road, ignoring the squeal of brakes from a speeding lorry, and jumped him into the field opposite. The land sloped upwards, so that when I reined in about halfway up it and turned round to see what was happening, the road and the car park were spread out below like a map.

The men were making no attempt to follow. They had moved the Wolseley away from the gate and were now drawing to a halt some yards farther along on the verge. It looked as if all four were inside the car.

Victor still stood in the car park, scratching his head as he looked up towards me. I could imagine his bewilderment. I wondered how long it would be before he went to tell Pete what had happened.

Once the last race was over the car park would be buzzing with people, and cars would pour out of the now unobstructed gateway. I thought that then I would be able to return safely to the racecourse without being abducted.

At this point another black car drew up behind the Wolseley, and then another, and several others, until a line of eight or more stretched along the side of the road. There was something rather horribly familiar about the newcomers.

They were Marconicars.

CHAPTER 15

ALL THE DRIVERS climbed out of the taxis and walked along towards the Wolseley. With its low expensive lines and its efficient-looking aerial on top, it still looked every inch a police car, but the reinforcements it had called up dispelled any last doubts it was possible to have about the nature of the "C.I.D. officers."

The men stood in a dark group on the road, and I sat on Admiral halfway up the field watching them. They seemed to be in no hurry, but having seen their armoury of bicycle chains, knives, and assorted knuckledusters when they fought the London gang at Plumpton, and with Joe's fate constantly in mind, I had no doubt what would happen if I let them catch me.

I was in a good position. They could not drive the taxis up the field because there was no gate into it from the road, nor could they hope to reach me on foot, and I was still confident that when the race crowd flocked out I could evade the enemy and return to the course.

Two things quickly happened to change the picture.

First, the men began looking and pointed towards the side of the field I was in. Turning my head to the right I saw a car driving downhill on the farther side of the hedge, and realised that there was a road there. Twisting round, I now took note for the first time that a large house with out-buildings and gardens spread extensively across the skyline.

Three of the taxis detached themselves from the line and drove round into the road on my right, stopping at intervals along it. I now had taxi-drivers to the right and ahead, and the big house at my back, but I was still not unduly dismayed.

Then yet another Marconicar came dashing up and stopped with a jerk in front of the Wolseley. A stocky man swung open the door and raised himself out of the driver's seat. He strode across the road to the hedge, and stood there pointed up at me with his arm extended. I was still wondering why when I heard the low whine of a bullet passing at the level of my feet. There was no sound of a shot.

As I turned Admiral to gallop off across the field, a bullet hit the ground with a phut in front of me. Either the range was too far for accurate shooting with a gun fitted with a silencer, or . . . I began to sweat . . . the marksman was aiming deliberately low, not at me but at Admiral.

It was only an eight or ten acre field, nothing like big enough for safety. I used precious moments to pull the horse up and take a look at the ragged sprawling hedge on the far side of the field. It was threaded halfway up with barbed wire. Over my shoulder I could see the man with the gun running along the road parallel to the course I had just taken. He would soon be within range again.

I took Admiral back a little way, faced him towards the hedge and urged him to jump. He cleared the whole thing, wire and all, without bending so much as a twig. We landed in another field, this time occupied by a herd of cows but again small and much too open to the road. Also, I discovered, trotting along the top boundary, that barbed wire had been laid lavishly in three strong strands all round it. All pastures have a gate, however, and I came to it in the farthest corner. I opened it, guided Admiral through into the next field, and shut it behind me.

This field was fenced with posts and wire only, and it was the extent of the barbed wire which decided me then to put as much space as I could between me and my pursuers in the shortest possible time. If I let the taxi-drivers follow me slowly from field to field I might find myself in a corner that even Admiral could not jump out of.

I was glad the sun was shining, for at least I could tell in which direction I was going. Since I was already headed towards the east, and because it seemed sensible to have a definite destination to aim for, I decided to take Admiral back to his own stable in Pete's yard.

I reckoned I had about twelve miles to cover, and I racked my brains to remember what the country was like in between. I knew the patchwork farmland which I was then grappling with gave way at some point ahead to Forestry Commission plantations. Then there would be a short distance of bare downland before I reached the hollow and the small village where Pete trained. Of the roads which crossed this area I had but the vaguest idea, and on any of them I could be spotted by a cruising Marconicar.

With this thought uncomfortably in mind, I found another by-road ahead. I let myself out onto it through a gate, and was trotting down it, looking for an opening in the neglected growth on the other side, when a squat black car swept round a distant bend and sped uphill towards me. Without giving Admiral a good chance to sight himself I turned him sharply towards the overgrown hedge and kicked his ribs.

It was too high for him, and too unexpected, but he did his best. He leaped straight into the tangle of sagging wire and beech saplings, crashed his way heavily through, and scrambled up almost from his knees on to the higher ground of the next field. It had been ploughed and planted with mangolds and made heavy going, but I urged him into a canter, hearing behind me the screech of brakes forcefully applied. A glance showed me the driver thrusting through the hole Admiral had made, but he did not try to chase me and I realised thankfully that he was not the man with the gun.

All the same, he had his radio. My whereabouts would be known to all the Marconicars within a minute.

I put another field between us and the taxi before pulling up and dismounting to see what damage Admiral had done himself. To my relief there were only a few scratches and one jagged cut on his stifle from which a thread of blood was trickling. I left it to congeal.

Patting his neck and marvelling at how he retained his calm sensible nature in very upsetting circumstances, I grasped the leather roller he wore round his middle, and sprang up again on to his back. The rug he was wearing now gaped in a right-angled tear on one side, but I decided not to take it off as it gave more purchase for my legs than riding him completely bare-back.

Three or four fields farther on the arable land began to give way to bracken, and ahead lay the large enclosures of the Forestry Commission.

The trees, mostly conifers, were being grown in large orderly expanses with rough tracks between each section. These acted both as convenient road-ways for the foresters and as breaks in case of fire. They occurred about one in each half-mile, and were crossed at intervals by tracks leading in the opposite direction.

I wanted to set a course towards the southeast, but by consulting my watch and the sun in conjunction, found that the tracks ran from almost due north to south, and from east to west. Fretting at the extra mileage this was going to cost me, I steered Admiral into an eastbound track, took the next turning right to the south, then the next left to the east, and so on, crab-wise across the forest.

The sections of trees were of varying ages and stages of growth, and turning again to the south, I found the area of my left was planted with trees only two feet high. This did not specially alarm me until I saw, a hundred yards to my left, a red and white motor coach speeding along apparently through the middle of the plantation.

I pulled Admiral up. Looking carefully I could see the posts and the high wire fence which formed the boundary between the little trees and the road beyond. If I turned east at the next track according to schedule, I would be facing straight down to the road.

The far side of the road looked similar to the section I was in: regular rows of conifers, put there by careful design.

At some point, I knew, I would have to cross a road of some sort. If I retreated back into the part of the forest I had crossed and took no risks, I would have to stay there all night. All the same, I thought, as I cantered Admiral along the southbound track and turned into the east one, I could have wished for more cover just at that moment.

Ahead of me the wire gates to the road were open, but before going through them I stopped and took a look at the other side of the road. Not all the plantations were surrounded by high mesh wire like the one I was in, and opposite only three strands of plain wire threaded through concrete posts barred the way.

The road had to be crossed quickly because where I was I felt as sheltered as a cock pheasant on a snow field. The heads in all the passing cars turned curiously towards me. But I saw nothing which looked like a Marconicar, and waiting only for a gap in the traffic, I clicked my tongue and set Admiral towards the wire fence opposite. His hooves clattered loudly on the tarmac, drummed on the firm verge, and he lifted into the air like a bird. There was no track straight ahead, only some fairly sparsely growing tall pines, and as Admiral landed I reined him in to a gentle trot before beginning to thread a way through them.

Coming eventually to another track I checked again with my watch and the sun to make sure it was still running from east to west, which it was, and set off along it at a good pace. The going underfoot was perfect, dry and springy with loam and pine needles, and Admiral, though he had completed a three mile race and covered several miles of an unorthodox cross-country course, showed no signs of flagging.

We made two more turns and the sky began to cloud over, dulling the brilliant spring afternoon, but it was not the fading of beauty which bothered me so much as the fact that you cannot use a wrist watch as a compass unless the sun is shining. I would have to be careful not to get lost.

Just ahead, to my right, a small grass-grown hill rose sharply to its little rounded summit, the conifer forest flowing round its edges like sea round a rock. I had now left the bigger trees and was cantering through sections of young feathery pines only slightly taller than the top of my head, and I could see the hill quite clearly. A man, a black distant silhouetted man, was standing on the top, waving his arms.

I did not connect him with myself at all because I thought I had slipped my pursuers, so that what happened next had the full shock of a totally unexpected disaster.

From a track to the right, which I had not yet reached and could not see, a sleek black shape rolled out across my path and stopped, blocking the whole width of the track. It was the Wolseley.

The young pines on each side of me were too thick and low growing to be penetrated. I flung a look over my shoulder. A squat black Marconicar was bumping up the track behind me.

I was so close to the Wolseley that I could see one of the men looking out of the rear window with a gloating grin on his face, and I decided then that even if I broke Admiral's neck and my own in trying to escape, it would be a great deal better than tamely giving in.

There was scarcely a pause between the arrival of the Wolseley and my legs squeezing tight into Admiral's sides.

I had no reason to suppose he would do it. A horse can dare just so much

and no more. He had had a hard day already. He might be the best hunter-
'chaser in England, but . . . The thoughts flickered through my brain in a second
and were gone. I concentrated wholly, desperately, on getting Admiral to jump.

He scarcely faltered. He put in a short stride and a long one, gathered the
immense power of his hindquarters beneath him, and thrust himself into
the air. Undeterred even by the opening doors and the threatening shouts of
the men scrambling out of the Wolseley, he jumped clear over its gleaming
black bonnet. He did not even scratch the paint.

I nearly came off when we landed. Admiral stumbled, and I slipped off
the rug onto his shoulder, clinging literally for dear life to the leather roller
with one hand and Admiral's plaited mane with the other. The reins hung
down, swaying perilously near his galloping feet, and I was afraid he would
put his foot through them and trip. I still had one leg half across his rump,
and, bumping heavily against his side, I hauled myself inch by inch on to his
back. A warning twinge in my shoulder told me my newly mended collar-
bone could not be relied upon for too much of this, but leaning along his
neck and holding on with all my strength, I reached the reins, gathered them
up, and finally succeeded in reducing Admiral to a less headlong pace.

When I got my breath back I looked to see if the Wolseley was following, but it was so far behind that I was not sure whether it was moving or not.
I could not spare time to stop and find out.

I realised that I had underestimated the Marconicars, and that it was only
thanks to Admiral's splendid courage that I was still free. They had had an
advantage in knowing the lie of the land, and had used the little hill as a
spotting point. I suspected that its summit commanded quite a large area,
and that as soon as I had entered the younger pines I had been seen.

I was forced to admit that they had guessed which direction I would take
and had circled round in front of me. And that being so, they probably knew
I had been making for Pete's stable. If I went on I should find them in my way
again, with perhaps as little warning and less chance of escape.

I had left the hill behind me, and turned right again on the next track,
seeing in the distance a section of taller trees. The horse cantered along tire-
lessly, but he could not keep it up forever. I had to reach shelter as quickly as
I could, out of sight of the man still standing on the hilltop, and out of the
danger of being ambushed on another of the straight and suddenly uninviting tracks. Once we were hidden in the big trees, I promised Admiral, he
should have a rest.

The light was dim under the tall pines. They had been allowed to grow close together to encourage their bare trunks to height, and the crowns of foliage far above were matted together like a roof, shutting out most of the daylight. I was glad for the obscurity. I slowed Admiral to a walk and dismounted as we entered the trees, and we went quietly and deeply into them. It was like walking through a forest of telegraph poles. Which of course, I thought fleetingly, perhaps they were destined to be.

The forest felt like home, even though it was different from those I was schooled in. It was very quiet, very dark. No birds at all. No animals. The horse and I went steadily on, silent on the thick pine needles, relying on instinct to keep us on a straight course.

I did not find our situation particularly encouraging. Whichever way I went in this extensive plantation I would have to come to a road in the end, and within three or four square miles the Marconicars knew exactly where I was. They had only to stand round the forest like hounds waiting for the fox to break cover, then it would be view tally-ho over the radio intercoms and the hunt would be on again.

There was a track ahead. A narrow one. I tied the reins round a tree and went forward alone. Standing still on the edge of the track and giving, I hoped, a good imitation of a tree trunk in my tweed suit, I slowly turned my head both ways. The daylight was much stronger on the track owing to the gap in the trees overhead, and I could see quite clearly for several hundred yards. There was no one in sight.

I went back for Admiral, made a final check, and led him across the track. There was no alarm. We walked steadily on. Admiral had begun to sweat long ago and had worked up a lather after our dash away from the Wolseley, damping large patches of the rug. Now that he was cooling down it was not good for him to keep it on, but I hadn't a dry one to give him. I decided that a damp rug was better than no rug, and trudged on.

Eventually I began to hear the hum of traffic and the occasional toot of a horn, and as soon as I could see the road in the distance, I tied Admiral to a tree and went on alone again.

The end of the plantation was marked by a fence made of only two strands of stout wire, looking as if it were designed mainly to prevent picnickers driving their cars farther in than the verge. I chose a tree as near to the fence as I could get, dropped down on to my belly behind it, and wriggled forward until I could look along the road. There was only sporadic traffic on it.

On the far side of the road there were no plantations, and no fence either. It was unorganised woodland, a mixture of trees, rhododendrons and briars. Perfect cover, if I could reach it.

A heavy lorry ground past five feet from my nose, emitting a choking cloud of diesel fumes. I put my face down into the pine needles and coughed. Two saloon cars sped by in the other direction, one trying to pass the other, followed by a single-decker country bus full of carefree people taking home their Tuesday afternoon's shopping. A pair of schoolgirls in green uniform cycled past without noticing me, and when their high twittering voices had faded into the distance and the road was empty, I put my hands under my chest to heave myself up and go back for Admiral.

At that moment two Marconicars came into sight round a bend. I dropped my face down again and lay absolutely still. They drove past my head slowly, and though I did not look at them, I guessed they must be staring keenly into the forest. I hoped wholeheartedly that I had left Admiral far enough back to be invisible, and that he would not make a noise.

The Marconicars swerved across the road and pulled up on the opposite verge barely twenty-five yards away. The drivers got out of the taxis and slammed the doors. I risked a glance at them. They were lighting cigarettes, leaning casually against the taxis, and chatting. I could hear the mumble of their voices, but not what they were saying.

They had not seen me, or Admiral. Yet. But they seemed to be in no hurry to move on. I glanced at my watch. It was six o'clock. An hour and a half since I had jumped off the racecourse. More important, there was only one hour of full daylight left. When it grew dark my mobility on Admiral would end and we should have to spend the night in the forest, as I could not get him to jump a fence if he could not see it.

There was a sudden clattering noise from one of the taxis. A driver put his hand through the window and brought out a hand microphone attached to a cord. He spoke into it distinctly, and this time I could make out what he said.

"Yeah, we got the road covered. No, he ain't crossed it yet." There was some more clattering on the taxi radio, and the driver answered, "Yeah, I'm sure. I'll let you know the second we see him." He put the microphone back in the taxi.

I began to get the glimmerings of an idea of how to use the manhunt I had caused.

But first things first, I thought; and slowly I started to slither backwards through the trees, pressing close to the ground and keeping my face down. I had left Admiral a good way inside the forest, and I was now certain that the taxi-drivers could not see him. It was uncomfortable travelling on my stomach, but I knew if I stood up the drivers would see me moving among the bare tree trunks. When finally I got to my feet my suit was a filthy peat brown, clogged with prickling pine needles. I brushed off the dirt as best I could, went over to Admiral, and untied his reins.

Out in the daylight on the road I could still catch glimpses, between the tree trunks, of the two taxis and their drivers, but knowing that they could not see me, I set off towards the west, keeping parallel with the road and at some distance from it. It was, I judged, a little more than a quarter of a mile before I saw another Marconicar parked at the side of the road. I turned back and, as I went along, began to collect an armful of small dead branches. About halfway between the parked taxis, where they were all out of my sight, I took Admiral right up to the wire fence to give him a look at it. Although extremely simple in construction, it was difficult to see in the shade of the trees. I set the dead branches up on end in a row to make it appear more solid; then jumped on to Admiral's back, and, taking him back a few paces, faced him towards the fence and waited for a heavy vehicle to come along. In still air the sound of hooves on tarmacadam would carry clearly, and I did not want the taxi-drivers round the nearby bends to hear me crossing the road. The longer they believed I was still in the pine forest, the better. But how long the taxis would *remain* parked I did not know, and the palms of my hands grew damp with tension.

A motor bike sped past, and I stayed still with an effort; but then, obligingly, a big van loaded with empty milk bottles came rattling round the bend on my right. It could not have been better. As it went past me I trotted Admiral forward. He made nothing of the dead-wood patch of fence, popped over on to the grass verge, took three loping strides over the tarmac, and in an instant was safely in the scrub on the far side. The milk lorry rattled out of sight.

I pulled up behind the first big rhododendron, dismounted, and peered round it.

I had not been a second too soon. One of the Marconicars was rolling slowly along in the wake of the milk lorry, and the driver's head was turned towards the forest I had left.

If one driver believed me still there, they all did. I walked Admiral away from the road until it was safe to mount, then jumped on to his back and broke him into a slow trot. The ground now was unevenly moulded into little hillocks and hollows and overgrown with brambles, small conifers and the brown remains of last year's bracken, so I let the horse pick his own footing to a great extent while I worked out what I was going to do. After a little way he slowed to a walk and I left him to it, because if his limbs felt as heavy and tired as mine he was entitled to crawl.

As nearly as I could judge I travelled west, back the way I had come. If there is one thing you can be sure of in England, it is that a straight line in any direction will bring you to a road without much delay, and I had covered perhaps a mile when I came to the next one. Without going too close I followed it to the north.

I was hunting a prey myself, now. A taxi, detached from the herd.

Admiral was picking his way silently across a bare patch of leaf-moulded earth when I suddenly heard the now familiar clatter of a Marconicar radio, and the answering voice of its driver. I pulled up in two strides, dismounted, and tied Admiral to a nearby young tree. Then I climbed up into the branches.

Some way ahead I saw a white four-fingered signpost, and beside it stood a Marconicar, of which only the roof and the top half of the windows were visible. The rest was hidden from me by the rhododendrons, trees, and undergrowth which crowded the ground ahead. My old friend the pine forest rose in a dark green blur away to the right.

I climbed down from the tree and felt in my pocket for the roll of pennies. I also found two lumps of sugar, which I fed to Admiral. He blew down his nostrils and nuzzled my hand, and I patted his neck gently and blessed Scilla for giving him to me.

With so much good cover it was easy enough to approach the cross-roads without being seen, but when, from the inside of an old rhododendron I at length had a clear view of the taxi, the driver was not in it. He was a youngish sallow-faced man in a bright blue suit, and he was standing bareheaded in the middle of the cross-roads with his feet well apart, jingling some coins in his pocket. He inspected all four directions, saw nothing, and yawned.

The radio clattered again, but the driver took no notice. I had intended to creep up to his taxi and knock him out before he could broadcast that I was there; but now I waited, and cursed him, and he stood still and blew his nose.

Suddenly he began to walk purposefully in my direction.

For an instant I thought he had seen me, but he had not. He wheeled round a large patch of brambles close in front of me, turned his back towards my hiding place, and began to relieve himself. It seemed hardly fair to attack a man at such a moment, and I know I was smiling as I stepped out of the rhododendron, but it was an opportunity not to be missed. I took three quick steps and swung, and the sock-wrapped roll of pennies connected solidly with the back of his head. He collapsed without a sound.

I put my wrists under his shoulders and dragged him back to where I had left Admiral. Working as quickly as I could I ripped all the brown binding off the edge of the horse rug and tested it for strength. It seemed strong enough. Fishing my penknife out of my trouser pocket I cut the binding into four pieces and tied together the driver's ankles and knees with two of them. Then I dragged him closer to the tree and tied his wrists behind him. The fourth piece of binding knotted him securely to the trunk.

I patted his pockets. His only weapon was a spiked metal knuckleduster, which I transferred to my own jacket. He began to wake up. His gaze wandered fuzzily from me to Admiral and back again, and then his mouth opened with a gasp as he realised who I was.

He was not a big man in stature, nor, I now discovered, in courage. The sight of the horse looming so close above him seemed to worry him more than his trussed condition or the bump on the head.

"He'll tread on me," he yelled, fright drawing back his lips to show a nicotine-stained set of cheap artificial teeth.

"He's very particular what he walks on," I said.

"Take him away. Take him away," he shouted. Admiral began to move restlessly at the noise.

"Be quiet and he won't harm you," I said sharply to the driver, but he took no notice and shouted again. I stuffed my handkerchief unceremoniously into his mouth until his eyes bulged.

"Now shut up," I said. "If you keep quiet he won't harm you. If you screech you'll frighten him and he might lash out at you. Do you understand?"

He nodded. I took out the handkerchief, and he began to swear vindictively, but fairly quietly.

I soothed Admiral and lengthened his tether so that he could get his head down to a patch of grass. He began munching peacefully.

"What is your name?" I asked the taxi-driver.

He spat and said nothing.

I asked him again, and he said, "What the ruddy hell has it go to do with you?"

I needed particularly to know his name and I was in a hurry.

With no feelings of compunction I took hold of Admiral's reins and turned him round so that the driver had a good close view of a massive pair of hind-quarters. My captive's new-found truculence vanished in a flash. He opened his mouth to yell.

"Don't," I said. "Remember he'll kick you if you make a noise. Now, what is your name?"

"John Smith."

"Try again," I said, backing Admiral a pace nearer.

The taxi-driver gave in completely, his mouth trembling and sweat breaking out on his forehead.

"Blake." He stumbled on the word.

"First name?"

"Corny. It's a nickname, sort of." His eyes flickered fearfully between me and Admiral's hind legs.

I asked him several questions about the working of the radio, keeping the horse handy. When I had learned all I wanted I untied the reins from the tree and fastened them to a sapling a few feet away, so that when it grew dark the horse would not accidentally tread on the taxi-driver.

Before leaving them I gave Blake a final warning. "Don't start yelling for help. For one thing there's no one to hear you, and for another, you'll upset the horse. He's a thoroughbred, which means nervous, from your point of view. If you frighten him by yelling he's strong enough to break his reins and lash out at you. Shut up and he'll stay tied up. Get it?" I knew if Admiral broke his reins he would not stop to attack the man, but luckily, Blake did not. He nodded, his body sagging with fear and frustration.

"I won't forget you're here," I said. "You won't have to stay here all night. Not that I care about you, but the horse needs to be in a stable."

Admiral had his head down to the grass. I gave his rump a pat, made sure the knots were still tight on the demoralised driver, and picked my way quickly through the bushes to the taxi.

The signpost was important, for I would have to come back and find it in the dark in miles of haphazard woodland. I wrote down all the names and mileages on all of its four arms, just to make sure. Then I got into the taxi and sat in the driver's seat.

Inside the taxi one could hear the radio as a voice and not as a clatter. The receiver was permanently tuned in so that each driver could hear all messages and replies going from taxis to base and base to taxis.

A man was sying, "Sid, here. No sign of him. I've got a good mile and a half of the road in view from up here, nearly the whole side of that wood he's in. I'll swear he hasn't got across here. The traffic's too thick for him to do it quickly. I'm sure to see him if he tries it." Sid's voice came out of the radio small and tinny, like a voice on the telephone, and he spoke casually, as if he were looking for a lost dog.

While he spoke I started the engine, sorted out the gears, and drove off along the road going south. The daylight was just beginning to fade. Half an hour of twilight, I calculated, and perhaps another ten minutes of dusk. I put my foot down on the accelerator.

There was a short silence on the radio. Then someone said, "He has got to be found before dark."

Even though I had been half-hoping, half-expecting it, the husky timbreless whisper made me jerk in my seat. I gripped the steering wheel tightly and the muscles round my eyes contracted. The voice was so close it seemed suddenly as if the danger it spelled for me were close as well, and I had to reassure myself by looking out sideways at the deserted heartland, and backwards in the driving mirror at the empty road astern.

"We're doing our best, sir," said a quiet voice, respectfully. "I've been driving up and down this ruddy road for nearly an hour. Two miles up and two miles back. All the parked cars in my section are still in position."

"How many of you have guns?" said the whisper.

"Four altogether, sir. We could do with more, to be sure of him."

There was a pause. Then the husky voice said, "I have one here, but you haven't time to come in for it. You'll have to manage with what you've got."

"Yes, sir."

"Pay attention, all drivers. Aim for the horse. Shoot the horse. The man is not to be found with bullets in him. Do you understand?"

There was a chorus of assent.

"Fletcher, repeat your orders."

The polite taxi-driver said, "As soon as we spot him either in the trees or breaking cover, we shoot, aiming for the horse. Call up all drivers, chase and catch the man. We are to . . . er . . . restrain him as necessary, place him in one of the taxis, and wait for your instructions."

Halfway through this recital of plans for my disposal, I recognised his voice. The polite tone, in the first instance, gave him away. I had heard it on the Maidenhead road, luring me with its false respectability into a waiting trap: he was the driver of the horse-box. Fletcher. I made a note of it.

Suddenly, as if someone had pressed a switch, a light flooded into my brain and I remembered the fence at Bristol. I remembered the pouring rain on my face and the greyness of everything, and now clearly I remembered the horse-box driver cutting the wire down from the fence, rolling it up, and hanging it over his arm.

There was something else, too—but before I could pin it down I came to a halt sign at a main road. I turned left from my empty by-road into a stream of traffic, and began to look for a signpost which would tell me how far away I was from Brighton. After half a mile I found one. Eleven miles. Say, twenty minutes to my destination.

I thought back to the Bristol fence, but the shade had come down again in my memory, and now I was not even sure that any gaps in it remained. My fingers wandered of their own accord to the scar on my cheek and traced along it gently, but it was a gesture I had caught myself in once or twice before, and I attached no importance to it. Besides the immediate future needed all my thought.

All the way to Brighton I listened to the husky voice. Its tone grew both more urgent and more violent. I found it weird at first to eavesdrop on a manhunt of which I was myself the quarry, but after a few minutes I got used to it and paid it less and less attention, and this could have been a catastrophic mistake.

"Have you anything to report, twenty-three?" said the husky whisper. There was no reply on the radio. I was only half aware of it. More sharply the voice said, "Twenty-three. Blake, have you anything to report?"

I came back to the present with a jerk. I picked up the microphone, clicked over the switch, and said "No" in as bored and nasal a tone as I could muster.

"Answer more quickly next time," said the husky voice severely. He was apparently checking that all the outlying taxis were still in position, for he went on to ask three more drivers whether they had anything to report. I thanked heaven, as I switched off the microphone, that I had not had to impersonate Blake's voice for more than one second, for any attempt at conversation would have found me out. As it was, I listened more intently than before to the exchanges on the radio.

The whispering voice began to acquire tone and characteristics as I became more familiar with it, until it formed a pattern of phrasing and emphasis which tantalised me at first because I could not remember its origin.

Then I knew. I knew for sure, at last.

You can start on a plan that you think touches the limit of what you can do; and then you have to do much, much more. Once more into the breach . . . only the breach had got bigger. Stiffen the sinews, summon up the blood . . . and bend up every spirit to his full height. There was no one like Bill Shakespeare for bounding things in a nutshell.

I drove into the outskirts of Brighton very thoughtfully indeed.

CHAPTER 16

A TAXI-DRIVER ASKING the way to the main police station would be enough to arouse suspicion in a moron. I parked the taxi in a side street and hurried round the corner to ask directions in the nearest shop.

It was a tobacconist's, and busy, so I buttonholed one of the customers, an elderly man with watery eyes and a cloth cap. He told me the way quite clearly, though with frequent sniffs.

"You in trouble, mate?" he enquired inquisitively, eyeing my dirty, dishevelled appearance as I thanked him.

"Lost my dog," I said, smiling, pulling out the most unexciting reason I could think of for wanting the police.

The watery-eyed man lost interest. I walked quickly back to the taxi and found two small boys listening open-mouthed to the radio. I got into the taxi, winked at them, and said, "It's a thrilling story on children's hour, isn't it?" Their faces cleared and they grinned.

I drove off. The husky voice was saying, ". . . at all costs. I don't care how you do it. He must not get away. If you can't catch him alive you must kill him. No bullets, though."

"It would be more certain if you would let us shoot him, sir," said the polite voice of Fletcher.

Real children's hour stuff. I smiled a little sourly.

Following the watery-eyed man's instructions I found the police station without trouble. Lights shone inside it as I drove past. The daylight was going quickly.

I circled the police station until I found a quiet side turning a hundred yards away. There I stopped, close to the curb. I turned on the side-lights and shut the windows. The radio was still chattering, and the man with the husky voice could no longer keep his fury in control. For a last moment I listened to him conceding, now that time was running out, to Fletcher's plea that they should be allowed to shoot me on sight. Then with a grimace I got out of the taxi, shut the door, and walked away from it.

The Marconicars office, I reckoned, was not more than half a mile off. I half-walked, half-ran towards it, looking, as I went, for a telephone. The street lamps were suddenly turned on, the bulbs glowing palely in the fading light.

The red telephone box outside a sub-post office was lit up inside, too, and although my reason told me I was in no danger, instinct would have made me stay in darkness. The whispering voice had done my nerves no good.

Though I knew I was still out of sight of the Marconicar office, I went into the telephone box with a conscious effort. I asked enquiries for the number of the Maidenhead police station, and without delay was put through to the desk sergeant. Inspector Lodge, he told me, had left an hour earlier, but after some urging he parted with Lodge's home number. I thanked him and rang off.

Fumbling with haste, I fed more coins into the machine and gave the operator the new number. It rang and rang. My heart sank, for if I couldn't get hold of Lodge quickly I did not stand nearly so good a chance of cleaning up the Marconicars the way I wanted. But at last a voice answered. A woman's.

"Inspector Lodge? Just a minute, I'll see if I can find him."

A pause. And, finally, Lodge's voice.

"Mr. York?"

I explained briefly what had happened. I said, "I've left the taxi in Melton Close, a hundred yards back from the police station here. I want you to ring the Brighton police and get them to send someone responsible to fetch it in. Tell them to listen carefully to the radio in the taxi. Our friend with the husky voice is speaking on it, inciting all the drivers to kill me. That should settle the Marconicars once and for all, I should think. One of the drivers out looking for me is called Fletcher. He's the one who drove the horse-box at

Maidenhead, and he also rigged that wire for me at Bristol. I've remembered about it. It's likely he did the same for Bill Davidson, don't you think?"

"Yes, I do. Where are you now?" asked Lodge.

"In a 'phone box," I said.

"Well, go back to the taxi and wait there while I telephone the Brighton police. I don't really understand why you didn't go straight to them and explain it at first hand yourself."

"I thought it would have more weight, coming from you. And anyway . . ." I broke off, realising just in time that I could not tell Lodge what I was going to do next. I said instead, "Don't tell the Brighton police to expect me back at the taxi. I've a few 'phone calls to make . . . er . . . I must tell Scilla I'll be late, and things like that. But you won't waste any time, will you? Mr. Claud Thiveridge won't go on talking forever, especially after it gets dark."

"I'll ring at once," promised Lodge, disconnecting. I put down the receiver and pushed out into the street.

I went on my way, totting up the time I could count on before Lodge sent the Brighton police to the Marconicar office. He had to ring them up and give them a fairly lengthy account of what was going on. Then they had to find the taxi, listen to the radio, and make a shorthand record of what they heard, to be used as proof a court would accept that the whole organisation was illegal. Very shortly after that they would come chasing round to apprehend the owner of the voice. Ten minutes altogether perhaps, if they hustled; perhaps a quarter of an hour.

When the Marconicar office was in sight I stayed close to the buildings so that I should not be seen from the Marconicar window. The street was nearly empty, and across the road the Olde Oake Café had closed its doors for the night. Through the glass I could see the plump waitress tiredly piling the old oak chairs onto the old oak tables.

A small black car was parked by the curb ahead. I glanced at it curiously, and then with sudden recognition. I stopped. I purposely had not told Lodge whose face I had attached to the husky voice, though I knew I ought to have done. The sight of his car, parked flagrantly barely twenty yards from the Marconicar door, gave me a chance to square things with my conscience. I lifted the bonnet, unclipped the distributor lid, and took off the rocker arm, which I put in my pocket. Whatever happened now, there would be no quick getaway for Mr. Thiveridge.

There were no lights in the Marconicar office, nor in any of the floors above. The neon sign, L. C. Perth, was flashing steadily on and off at two second intervals, wasting its message on the empty road. The only gambler in sight, I reflected, was myself.

Reaching the Marconicar window I bent double below the sill and edged past as close to the wall as I could press. The street door was closed, but opened readily at a touch. I stepped very quietly into the hall, leaving the door open behind me. The silence in the house was tensely oppressive, and for a cowardly instant I was tempted to go out into the street again and wait like a sensible citizen for the police.

Stepping cautiously I went down the hall and pressed my ear to the door of Fielder's room. I could hear nothing. I opened the door gently and looked in. The room was tidy and empty. Next I tried the door on my left, which led into the back office where Marigold by day presided over her radio switchboard.

Through the thick door I could hear nothing, but when I opened it an inch a faint hum reached my ears. There was no one in the office. I went quietly in.

The hum was coming from the radio equipment. A small red brightly glowing circle in the control panel indicated that it was switched on, and through a crack in the casing the tiny light of a valve shone blue-white. The microphone lay casually on its side on its ledge.

For a sickening moment I thought that my bird had flown during the time it had taken me to ring Lodge and travel the half mile from the taxi; then I remembered the car outside, and at the same time, looking for wires leading out of the radio, saw a narrow plastic-covered cable running up the far wall and into the ceiling.

Praying that the stairs in the old house would not creak, I went up them lightly and quickly, and pressed my ear to the panels of the door of the main office of L. C. Perth. There were some large painted capital letters beside my nose. I squinted across at them while I listened. They said PLEASE ENTER.

Owing to the solidity of the regency door I could hear only a fierce hissing sound, but by this time the whisper was so familiar to me that an inch of mahogany could not disguise it.

He was there.

The hair on the back of my neck began to itch.

I judged it must have been seven or eight minutes since I spoke to Lodge.

As I had to give the Brighton police time to find the taxi and record something of what they would hear on its radio, I could not risk interrupting the husky voice too soon. But neither did I intend to hover where I was until the police arrived. I made myself count one hundred slowly, and it seemed the longest three minutes of my life. Then I rubbed the palm of my hand on my trousers, and gingerly took hold of the ornate glass doorknob.

It turned silently and I eased the door open a few inches. It made no noise at all. I could see straight into the unlit room.

He was sitting at a desk with his back turned squarely towards me, and he seemed to be looking out into the street. The neon sign flashed off and on outside the window, illuminating the whole of the room and lighting up his dusky outline with a red glow. Red reflections winked on chromium ashtrays and slid along the metal edges of filing cabinets. A row of black telephones, ranked like an army on a long desk, threw curious angular shadows on the wall.

At close quarters the husky whisper lost some of its disembodied menace, even though what it was saying was now almost hysterically violent.

The open door can have stirred no current of air, for the man at the desk went on talking into his microphone, completely unaware that I was standing behind him.

"Kill him," he said. "Kill him. He's in that wood somewhere. He's an animal. Hunt him. Turn your cars towards the wood and put the headlight on. You'd better start beating through the trees. Fletcher, organise it. I want York dead, and quickly. Shoot him down. Smash him."

The man paused and drew in so sharp a breath that it gagged in his throat. His hand stretched out for a glass of water, and he drank.

Fletcher's voice came tinnily into the room through an extension loudspeaker on the desk. "We haven't seen a sign of him since he went into the wood. I think he might have got past us."

The man at the desk shook with fury. He began to whisper again with a rough burring rasp.

"If he escapes, you'll pay for it. You'll pay, I tell you. I want him dead. I want him smashed. You can do what you like with him. Use those chains to good purpose, and the spiked knuckles. Tear him to pieces. If he lives it will be the end for all of us, remember that." The whisper rose in tone to a thin sound like a strangled shriek. "Rip his guts out . . . smash . . . destroy . . ."

He went on for some time elaborating on the way I should be killed, until it was clear that his mind was very nearly unhinged.

Abruptly I had heard enough. I opened the door wide, and put my hand on the light switch, and pressed it down. The room was suddenly brilliantly flooded with light.

The man at the desk whirled round and gaped at me.

"Good evening, Uncle George," I said softly.

CHAPTER 17

HIS EYES SCORCHED with hate. The vacuous expression was torn away, the hidden personality now out in the open and as mean and savage as any crocodile. He was still Kate's amusing Uncle George in corpulent outline and country-gentleman tweeds, the Uncle George who had written for boys' magazines and taken his wife to matinees, but the face was the one which had had a knife stuck into Joe Nantwich and had urged a bloodthirsty mob to tear me to bits.

His hand snaked out across the desk and came up with a gun. It was a heavy, old-fashioned pistol, cumbersome, but deadly enough, and it was pointing straight at my chest. I resolutely looked at Uncle George's eyes, and not at the black hole in the barrel. I took a step towards him.

Then it came, the instant on which I had gambled my safety.

Uncle George hesitated.

I saw the flicker, the drawing back. For all his sin, for all the horror he had spread into the lives of others, he had never himself committed an act of violence. When he had delivered his threatening warning to me on the telephone on the very morning that I went to stay in his house, he had told me that he hated even to watch violence; and in spite of, or perhaps because of, his vicarious pleasure in the brutalities of primitive nations, I believed him. He was the sort of man, I thought, who liked to contemplate atrocities he could never inflict himself. And now, in spite of the fury he felt against me, he couldn't immediately, face to face, shoot me down.

I gave him no time to screw himself up. One fast stride and I had my hand on his wrist. He was trying to stand up. Too late he found the power to kill and squeezed the trigger, but the bullet smashed harmlessly into the wall. I bent his arm outwards with force, and twisted the gun out of his grasp. His muscles were soft and without strength, and he didn't know how to fight.

I flung him back hard into his chair, knocking the wind out of him, and then I reached over and switched off his microphone. I wasn't anxious that either the police or the taxi drivers should overheard what I was going to say.

There was a crackle as I brushed against his coat. I pulled it open. A folded piece of brown paper protruded from an inner pocket, and I tugged it out and spread it open on the desk. He was gasping for breath and didn't try to stop me. I read what was on it.

Joe's address.

I turned it over. In one corner on the other side, scribbled carelessly as if someone were not sure of the spelling and had used the nearest piece of paper to try them out on, were the words:

Chitchen Itza
Chitchen Itsa
Chitsen

Not chickens, not Chichester. Chichen Itza. I had the vaguest memory of having heard it before. It was the name of an emperor I thought; and it meant nothing to me, nothing. Yet Joe had died for it.

I left the paper on the desk, and hoped that the police would find it useful.

The hysteria had drained out of Uncle George. He looked suddenly ill and old, now that his day was done. I could summon no compassion for him, all the same: but then it was not regard for Kate's uncle that had brought me into the Marconicar office, but love for Kate herself.

"The police will be here in less than a minute," I said, speaking slowly and distinctly. He shifted in his seat and made a sharp helpless gesture with his pudgy hands. I went on, "They have been listening in to what you have been saying on the radio."

Uncle George's eyes widened. "Twenty-three," he said, with a remnant of anger. "Twenty-three hasn't answered my last few calls."

I nodded. I said, "You will be charged with incitement to murder. Gaol for life, at least." I paused. "Think," I said with emphasis. "Think of your wife. You did it all for her, didn't you, so that she could go on living in the luxury she was used to?" I was guessing, but I felt sure it was true, and he didn't deny it.

"You have shielded her from reality too long," I said. "What will it do to her, if you are arrested and tried, and maybe hanged?"

Or to Kate either, I added hopelessly to myself.

Uncle George listened and stared at me, and slowly his gaze fell to the pistol I still held in my hand.

"It's quicker," I said.

There was a short silence.

Very faintly in the distance I heard an alarm bell. Uncle George heard it too. He looked up. He hated me still, but he had come to the end of the line, and he knew it.

"The police," I said. The bell grew perceptibly louder.

I took the three steps across the door, turned, and tossed the gun back into Uncle George's lap. As his stubby fingers fumbled and clutched it I went through the door, closed it, and ran down the stairs. The front door was still open. I hurried through that and pulled it shut behind me. The police alarm bells were no longer ringing.

In the shadow of the building, I slipped along into the dark porch of the next-door house, and I was only just in time. Two police cars slowed, crawled, and halted in front of the Marconicar building.

Over at the Olde Oake Café the lights were out. The plump waitress had gone home.

There had been no sound from upstairs. I shivered, struck by the horrifying thought that Uncle George, having already screwed himself once to pull the trigger, might just possibly shoot a policeman instead of himself. With the gun I had so thoughtfully given back to him.

As the doors of the police cars slammed open and the black figures poured out I took the first step towards them to warn them that their quarry was armed. But Uncle George's devotion to Aunt Deb's interests remained steadfast after all. I thought that the single crashing shot in the room behind the neon sign was the best thing he had ever done for her sake.

I WAITED FOR a few minutes in my dark doorway, and while I stood there a small crowd began to collect on the pavement, drawn by the noise of the shots and the presence of the police cars. I slipped unhurriedly among them, and after a little while walked quietly away.

Round two or three turnings I found a telephone box and stepped inside, feeling in my pocket for coins. The calls to Lodge had taken all my small change, and for a moment I looked blankly at the threepenny piece and two halfpennies which were all I could dredge from my trouser pocket. Then I remembered my cosh. I untied the sock, tipped some of the pennies out on to my hand, pushed four of them into the slot, and asked the operator for Pete's number.

He answered at the second ring.

He said, "Thank God you've rung. Where the hell have you been?"

"Touring Sussex."

"And where's Admiral?"

"Well . . . I left him tied to a tree somewhere in the heathland," I said.

Pete began to sputter, but I interrupted him.

"Can you send the horse-box to collect him? Get the driver to come down to Brighton and pick me up on the sea-front, near the main pier. And Pete . . . have you got a decent map of Sussex?"

"A map? Are you mad? Don't you know where you left him? Have you really just tied the best hunter's 'chaser in the country to a tree and forgotten where?" He sounded exasperated.

"I'll find him easily if you send a map. Don't be too long, will you? I'll tell you all about it later. It's a bit complicated."

I put down the receiver, and after some thought, rang up the Blue Duck. Ex-Regimental Sergeant-Major Thomkins answered the 'phone himself.

"The enemy is routed, sergeant-major," I said. "The Marconicars are out of business."

"A lot of people will be thankful to hear it," said the strong deep voice, with a good deal of warmth.

I went on, "However, the mopping up operations are still in progress. Would you be interested in taking charge of a prisoner and delivering him to the police?"

"I would indeed," he said.

"Meet me down at the main pier, then, at the double, and I'll gen you up."

"I'm on my way," said the sergeant-major.

He joined me by the sea wall soon after I got there myself. It was quite dark by then, and the lights along the front barely lit the ghostly grey lines of the breaking waves.

We had not long to wait for the horse-box, and when it came, Pete himself poked his big bald head out of the passenger seat and called to me. He, I and the sergeant-major got into the back and sat on a couple of straw bales, and as we swayed to the movement of the box on its way west I told them all that had happened since the day Bill died at Maidenhead. All, that is, up to my last conversation with Lodge. Of my visit to the Marconicar office and the true identity of Claud Thiveridge, I said nothing. I didn't know how English law viewed the crime of inciting to suicide, and for various reasons had decided to tell no one about it.

Parts of the story Pete already knew, and part Thomkins knew, but I had to go over the whole thing for them both to get it clear from first to last.

The horse-box driver had been given my note of the all-important signpost, and by comparing it with the map Pete had brought, he drove us back to it in remarkably short time.

Both Admiral and Corny Blake were still attached to their various trees, and we led one and frog-marched the other into the horse-box. Admiral was overjoyed to see us, but Blake's emotions seemed slightly mixed, especially when he recognised Thomkins. It appeared that it was Blake who had bashed the sergeant-major on the head with one of his own bottles.

With a grin I fished Blake's brass knuckleduster out of my pocket and handed it to Thomkins. "The prisoner's armoury," I said.

Thomkins tossed the wicked-looking weapon in his hand and tried it on for size, and Blake gave one agonised look at it and rolled off his bale of straw in a dead faint.

"We had better get round by West Sussex racecourse, if you don't mind," I said. "My car is still in the car park there; I hope."

It was there, all alone in the big field, the rising moon glinting on its low dark shape. I stepped down into the road, shook hands with Thomkins and Pete, wished them luck, and watched the red tail lights of the horse-box until they disappeared into the darkness.

Then I went over and started my car, turned my back firmly on what was doubtless my duty—the answering of interminable questions in Brighton police station—and with a purring roar set off for the Cotswolds.

Driven by an irresistible curiosity, I made a detour along the coast to Portsmouth, taking a chance that the public library would still be open there; and it was. In the reference department I hefted out a volume of an encyclopedia and looked up Chichen Itza. The first spelling on the paper was the right one.

Chichen Itza, I found, was not an emperor, it was a capital city. It was the ancient Yucatan capital of the Mayas, an Indian nation who had flourished in Central America fifteen hundred years ago.

I stared at the page until the words faded into a blur.

What happened next was partly, I suppose, delayed reaction from the abysmal fear I felt when I looked into the barrel of Uncle George's gun; and partly it was hunger and a wave of deathly tiredness, and the sudden letting up of the stresses of the past weeks. My hands, my whole body began to shake. I braced my foot against the leg of the table I was sitting at and gripped the big book hard to stop it. It went on for minutes, until I could have cried with weakness, but gradually the spasm lessened, and the tension went out of my muscles, and I was just plain cold.

Chichen Itza. I stood up stiffly and closed the book and put it back on the shelf, and went soberly out to the car. I had set a better trap than I knew, pretending to be on the point of understanding what Joe might have said before he died.

I remembered clearly the study lined with glass cases. I could see the heavy carved oak desk, the folders devoted to Indian tribes, and the one separate folder clearly marked "Mayas." Uncle George had told me too much about the Mayas; and he'd known that Chichen Itza would lead me conclusively to him.

CHAPTER 18

WHAT I HAD not managed to do for Kate by loving her, I had done by tearing her world apart.

She stood in front of me, rigidly controlling herself, with a look of such acrid unrelenting hatred that I tasted my misery literally as a bitterness in the mouth. The banked fires were burning fiercely at last. There was a new depth and maturity in her face, as if in two weeks she had become wholly a woman. It made her more desirable than ever.

The inquest and enquiry into the life and death of George Penn had been adjourned twice, and had just ended; and police, witnesses, and Kate and I were standing in the hall of the Brighton court building, preparing to leave.

The verdict of temporary insanity was merciful, but there had been no hiding from news-scenting journalists the extent of Uncle George's criminal activities, and L. C. Perth and Marconicars had been front-page news, on and off, for a fortnight.

My getting Uncle George to kill himself had been no help after all to Aunt Deb. It had been impossible to keep the truth from her, and shock and distress had brought on a series of heart attacks, of which the fourth was fatal. But for Kate, though she knew nothing about it, it was still the best thing. She had had to face the knowledge of his guilt, but not his trial and punishment.

But my letters of condolence had been unanswered. My telephone calls had regularly found her "out." And now I saw why. She blamed me alone for the sorrows which had come to her.

"I loathe you," she said implacably. "You nauseate me. You wormed your way into our house and accepted everything we gave you . . ." I thought of those gentle kisses, and so, from the extra flash in her eyes, did Kate . . . "and all you have done in return is to hound a poor old man to his death, and kill a defenceless old woman as a result. I have no Uncle and no Aunt. I have no one anywhere at all. I have no one." She spoke in anguish. "Why did you do it? Why couldn't you leave them alone? Why did you have to destroy my home? You know how much I loved them. I can't bear to look at you, I loathe you so much . . ."

I swallowed, and tried to work some saliva into my dry mouth. I said, "Do you remember the children who had to be driven to school by a judo expert to keep them safe?"

But Kate stared blackly back as if she hadn't heard. "You are the most beastly person I have ever known, and although you have made it impossible for me to forget you, I shall never think of you without . . . without . . ." Her throat moved convulsively as if she were going to be sick. She turned away abruptly and walked unsteadily out through the big main door into the street.

The flash of camera bulbs met her and caught her unawares, and I saw her throw up her arm in a forlorn attempt to hide her face. The vulnerability and the loneliness in the droop of her shoulders cried out for comfort, and I who most wanted to give it, was the only person she wouldn't accept it from. I watched her walk quickly through the questioning newspapermen and get into the hired car which was waiting for her.

It drove off. I stared after it, numbly.

Presently I became aware that Lodge was standing at my elbow and had been talking for some seconds. I hadn't heard a word he said, and he appeared to be waiting for a reply.

"I beg your pardon," I said. "What did you say?"

Lodge glanced out through the door where Kate had gone and sighed. "It wasn't very important. Look, she'll see things more reasonably in a little while, when she begins to think straight again. I heard a good deal of what she said . . . but you aren't to blame because her uncle took to crime."

"If I had known . . ." I stopped, on the verge of adding the give-away words "for sure": "If I had known that George Penn was Claud Thiveridge, I would have done things differently."

"Things worked out well for the Penns, I think," said Lodge. "A quick end has its mercies."

His tone was loaded with meaning, and I knew that he half guessed what part I had played in Uncle George's death. He had several times earlier remarked that my disapperance from Brighton at the moment of success was out of character, and had shown polite scepticism over my excuse that I was growing anxious about my horse. He had mentioned pointedly that the Brighton police, listening in the Marconicar taxi to Uncle George's ravings, had heard a faint murmur (indistinguishable) in the background, a single shot, and nothing more. They had not been able to account for this, apart from later finding the microphone switched off and a bullet in the wall, had come to the conclusion that Uncle George had been testing the old pistol to see if it were in working order. The shot had, however, brought them in haste to the Marconicar building, where they had arrived just in time to hear him shoot himself.

"You may be right," I said noncommittally to Lodge. His eyelids flickered, and he smiled and changed the subject.

"The Marconicar drivers come up in court again this week. You'll be there to give evidence, I suppose," he said.

"Yes," I agreed, not liking the prospect.

All the drivers who had been looking for me had been alarmed by the shot and the silence on their radios. Some had begun to drive back to Brighton, some had made for London, and one or two had left their taxis and started out on foot. But all had quickly been rounded up, as following the rather vague directions I had phoned to Lodge, the police had begun making road blocks round them while they were still listening to Uncle George. Now the drivers faced charges ranging from intimidation and grievous bodily harm to murder itself.

Records discovered in Uncle George's study, inside a folder marked with gory humour "Notes on Human Sacrifices," made it clear that Joe Nantwich had indeed been knifed by the man who had been wearing my tie.

And Uncle George's motives were now clear, too. Keeping up old standards of luxury had been too much for his income after the war, and instead of making Aunt Deb face reality, or facing it himself, he had gradually spent most of his capital. With almost the last of it he had bought Marconicars and launched into crime. He had directed everything through Fielder and had apparently never seen with his own eyes the brutal results of his orders. I doubted whether his misdeeds had seemed either more or less real to him than the primitive barbarities he spent his time studying.

The police had found neat lists, in files going back four years, of the money he had collected from the little terrorised businesses; and occasionally against the name of a café or a shop or a pub, Lodge told me, was written the single word, "Persuaded."

The racing record was shorter and contained lists of sums of money which the police did not know the purpose of; but one sheet headed "Joe Nantwich" was clear enough. It was a list of dates and amounts, of which the smallest was one hundred pounds. And underneath was drawn a thick line, with the words: "Account closed" printed in Uncle George's neat handwriting.

With Kate gone, the press men had drifted away. Their fun was over.

"Are you ready to go?" I asked Lodge. I had picked him up in Maidenhead on my way down. He nodded, and we went out to my car.

I drive fastest when I'm happy. That day I had no trouble at all in keeping within the speed limit through all the twisty Sussex villages, and Lodge endured my gloomy silence without comment half the way back to Maidenhead.

Finally he said, "Miss Ellery-Penn was very useful to her uncle. Everything you did in pursuing him went straight back to him through her. No wonder he was so well informed about your movements."

I had lived with this thought for a long time now; but hearing someone else speak it aloud had a most extraordinary effect. A tingle ran up my spine and set my brain suddenly alive, as if an alarm bell were ringing in my subconscious.

We were running through scrub and heathland. I slowed, swung the car off the road on to the peaty verge, and stopped. Lodge looked at me questioningly.

"What you said. I want to think," I said.

He waited a while in silence, and then said, "What's worrying you? The case is over. There are no more mysteries."

I shook my head. "There's someone else," I said.

"What do you mean?"

"There's someone else we don't know about. Someone in Uncle George's confidence." In spite of everything, I still thought of him as Uncle George.

Lodge said, "Fielder, the manager, was rounded up. So were all the L. C. Perth operators, though they have been freed again. Only two of the clerks had any idea of what was going on, one who went to the race tracks and one in the office. They received their instructions through Fielder about which horses to accept unlimited money on."

"Joe was stopping horses for months before Uncle George gave Heavens Above to Kate, and she had never been racing before that. Someone else who goes racing must have been working for Uncle George," I said with conviction.

"Penn would need only the morning paper and a form book for choosing a horse to stop. He wouldn't need to go to the races himself. He didn't need an accomplice at the races apart from his bookmaker—Perth. You're imagining things."

"Uncle George didn't know enough about horses," I said.

"So he made out," said Lodge skeptically.

"Kate told me that for as long as she remembers he was a dead loss on the subject. He started the Marconicar Protection racket only four years ago, and the racing racket less than a year go. Before that he had no reason to pretend. Therefore his ignorance of horses was genuine."

"I'll give you that," he said, "but I don't see that it proves anything."

"He *must* have had a contact on the racecourse. How else did he manage to pick on the one jockey who could most easily be corrupted?" I said.

"Perhaps he tried several, until he found a taker," suggested Lodge.

"No. Everyone would have talked about it, if he had."

"He tried Major Davidson," said Lodge. "That looks like a very bad mistake from your mythical adviser."

"Yes," I conceded. I changed to another tack. "There have been one or two things which have been relayed recently to Uncle George which Kate herself didn't know. How do you explain that?"

"What things?"

"Joe's bit of brown wrapping paper, for instance. He told everyone in the weighing room at Liverpool about it. Kate wasn't at the meeting. But two days later, on Uncle George's instructions, Joe was killed and the paper taken away from him."

Lodge pondered. "Someone might have rung her up on the Sunday and mentioned it in passing."

I thought fleetingly of Dane. I said, "Even then, it was surely not interesting enough for her to have told Uncle George."

"You never know," he said.

I started up and drove on in silence for some miles. I was loath to produce for his scepticism the most deep rooted of my reasons for believing an enemy still existed: the near-certainty that in the concussed gap in my memory I already knew who it was.

When at last I tentatively told him this, he treated it more seriously than I had expected. And after some minutes of thought he pierced and appalled me by saying, "Perhaps your subconscious won't let you remember who this enemy of yours is *because you like him*."

I DROPPED LODGE at Maidenhead and went on to the Cotswolds.

Entering the old stone house with the children noisily tumbling through the hall on their way to tea was like stepping into a sane world again. Scilla was coming down the stairs with her arms full of Polly's summer dresses: I went over and met her on the bottom step and kissed her cheek.

"Joan and I will have to lengthen all these," she said, nodding at the dresses. "Polly's growing at a rate of knots."

I followed her into the drawing-room and we sat down on the hearthrug in front of a newly lit fire.

"Is it all over?" asked Scilla, pushing the dresses off her lap onto the floor.

"Yes, I think so." Too much was all over.

I told her about the inquest and the verdict. I said, "It was only because of Bill that George Penn was ever found out. Bill didn't die for nothing."

She didn't answer for a long time, and I saw the yellow flames glinting on the unshed tears in her eyes. Then she sniffed and shook her head as if to free herself from the past, and said, "Let's go and have tea with the children."

Polly wanted me to mend a puncture on her bicycle. Henry said he'd worked out some gambits in chess and would I play against him after tea. William gave me a sticky kiss and pressed an aged fruit drop into my palm as a present. I was home again.

CHAPTER 19

THE ALMOST UNBEARABLE belief that I had lost Kate grew very little easier as the days passed. I couldn't get her out of my mind. When I woke in the morning the ache rushed in to spoil the day: when I slept I dreamed continually that she was running away down a long dark tunnel. I thought it unlikely I would ever see her again, and tried to make myself be sensible about it.

Then, a week after the inquest on Uncle George, I went to ride at Banbury races, and Kate was there. She was dressed in dark navy blue and there were big grey hollows round her eyes. Her face was pale and calm, and her expression didn't change when she saw me. She was waiting outside the weighing room, and spoke to me as soon as I drew near.

"Alan, I think I should apologise for what I said to you the other day." The words were clearly an effort.

"It's all right," I said.

"No . . . it's not. I thought about what you said . . . about those children going to school with the judo expert . . . and I realise Uncle George had got to be stopped." She paused. "It was not your fault Aunt Deb died. I'm sorry I said it was." She let out a breath as if she had performed an intolerable duty.

"Did you come all the way here especially to say that?" I asked.

"Yes. It has been worrying me that I was so unjust."

"My dear precious Kate," I said, the gloom of the past week beginning to vanish like morning mist, "I would have given anything for it not to have been Uncle George, believe me." I looked at her closely. "You look very hungry. Have you had anything to eat today?"

"No," she said, in a small voice.

"You must have some lunch," I said, and giving her no chance to refuse, took her arm and walked her briskly to the luncheon-room. There I watched her eat, pecking at first but soon with ravenous appetite, until some colour came back into her cheeks and a faint echo of her old gaiety to her manner.

She was well into her second helping of hot game pie when she said in a friendly tone. "I wish you'd eat something, too."

I said, "I'm riding."

"Yes I know, I saw in the paper. Forlorn Hope, isn't it?" she asked between forkfuls.

"Yes," I said.

"You will be careful, won't you? He's not a very good jumper, Pete says."

I looked at her with delighted astonishment, and she blushed deeply.

"Kate!" I said.

"Well . . . I thought you'd never forgive me for being so abysmally beastly. I've spent the most vile week of my life regretting every word I said. But at least it brought me to my senses about you. I tried to tell myself I'd be delighted never to see you again and instead I got more and more miserable. I . . . I didn't think you'd come back for a second dose, after the way you looked at Brighton. So I thought if I wanted you to know I was sorry I'd have to come and tell you, and then I could see . . . how you reacted."

"How did you expect me to react?"

"I thought you'd be rather toffee-nosed and cool, and I wouldn't have blamed you." She stuffed an inelegant amount of pie-crust into her mouth.

"Will you marry me, then, Kate?" I asked.

She said, "Yes" indistinctly with her mouth full and went on uninterruptedly cutting up her food. I waited patiently while she finished the pie and made good time with a stack of cheese and biscuits.

"When did you eat last?" I asked, as she eventually put down her napkin.

"Can't remember." She looked across at me with a new joy in her face and the old sadness beneath it, and I knew from that and from her remark about Forlorn Hope—the first concern she had ever shown for my safety—that she had indeed grown up.

I said, "I want to kiss you."

"Racecourses were not designed for the convenience of newly affianced lovers," she said. "How about a horse-box?"

"We've only got ten minutes," I said. "I'm riding in the second race."

We borrowed Pete's horse-box without more ado. I took her in my arms, and found this time on Kate's lips a satisfactorily unsisterly response.

The ten minutes fled in a second, and the races wouldn't wait. We walked back, and I went into the weighing room and changed into colours, leaving Kate, who looked a bit dazed and said she felt it, sitting on a bench in the sun.

It was the first time I had been racing since Uncle George's inquest. I glanced uneasily round the changing room at the well-known faces, refusing to believe that any was the go-between who had brought death to Joe. Perhaps Lodge was right, and I didn't want to find out. I had liked Uncle George himself, once. Did I shrink from seeing the façade stripped from another friend to reveal the crocodile underneath?

Clem handed me my lead packed weight cloth. I looked at his patient wrinkled face, and thought "Not you, not you."

It was a sort of treachery to reflect that Clem heard all that went on and that no event of any significance ever escaped his ears. "The oracle," some of the lads called him.

A hearty thump on the back cut off my speculations.

"Wotcher, me old cock sparrow, how's the sleuthing business?" bellowed Sandy, pausing and balancing his saddle on one knee while he looped up the girths. "How's Sherlock these days?"

"Retired," I said, grinning.

"No, really? After such grade A results?"

"I'll stick to steeplechasing, I think. It's less risky."

Sandy's friendly gaze strayed to the scar on my cheek.

"You're welcome to your little illusions, chum," he said. "You'll change your mind when you've broken as many bones as I have." He wound the girths round the saddle, tucked in the buckles, and with his helmet pushed far back on his head and his cheerful voice drawing heads round like a magnet, made his way out to the scales.

From across the changing room I had a good view of Dane's back solidly and deliberately turned towards me. Talking to someone by the gate, he had unfortunately seen Kate and me returning from the horse-box parking ground. He had had a good look at our radiant faces before we knew he was there, and he didn't need to have things spelled out for him. He had congratulated Kate in two clipped sentences, but to me he had still not spoken a word.

I went past his unyielding back and out to the paddock. He followed. Pete trained both the horses we were riding, and we both had to join him.

Pete jumped in with both feet.

"Alan, Kate's told me your news. Well done."

He received a fierce glower from Dane, and hastily began to assess the race. He was talking about Dane's mount, and my attention wandered.

There, ten yards away, stood the craggy Clifford Tudor, opulently rolling a cigar round his mouth and laying down the law to his trainer and jockey. Odd, I thought, how often I had come across that man. I watched him make heavy chopping motions with his dark hands to emphasise his points, and caught the young jockey, Joe's substitute, wrinkling his forehead in acute anxiety.

My gaze slid beyond him to where Sir Creswell Stampe was superintending the raising of his unamiable son David into the saddle, before going to take his judicial position in the Stewards' box. Beyond him again were other groups of owners and trainers planning their plans, hoping their hopes, giving their jockeys instructions (and counter-instructions) and calculating their last-minute bets.

So many people I knew. So many people I liked. Which of them . . . which of them was not what he seemed?

Pete gave me a leg up on to Forlorn Hope's narrow back, and I waved to Kate, who was standing by the parade ring rails, and cantered down towards the start.

On the way Dane came past briskly, turning his head in my direction as he drew level. With cold eyes he said, "Blast you," giving both words equal punch, and shook up his horse to get away from me and give me no chance to reply. I let him go. Either he would get over it or he wouldn't; and in either case there wasn't much I could do about it.

There were eleven runners in the race. We circled round while the starter's assistant tightened girths and the starter himself called the roll. Sandy asked his permission to dismount in order to straighten his saddle, which had slipped forwards on the way down to the gate. The starter nodded, looking at his wrist watch and telling Sandy not to be too long. This particular starter hated to start his races late and grew fidgety over every minor delay.

Sandy unbuckled the girths, pulled his saddle straight, and tightened it up again. I was watching him instead of concentrating wholly on Forlorn Hope, so that what happened was entirely my own fault.

An attendant flapped open under my horse's nose the white flag which it was his job to wave aloft, to signal to the stands that the horses were about to start. My green young hurdler took fright, reared up like a circus horse, twised sideways, and threw me off. I hit the ground almost flat on my back, winding myself, and I saw Forlorn Hope kick up his heels and depart at a smart pace up the course.

For a few seconds I lay there trying to get my breath back, and Sandy walked over with his hand outstretched to help me up, laughing and making some rude remark about my sudden descent.

The most extraordinary dizziness suddenly swept over me, and my senses began to play fantastic tricks. Lying in the spring sun, I felt rain on my face. Winded but unhurt, my body was momentarily invaded by shocking pain. In my whirling brain it seemed as if past and present had become confused, and that two completely different events were somehow happened at the same time.

I stared up at Sandy's face. There was the familiar wide gap-toothed grin, the false incisors removed for safety; there were the laughing brown eyes with the reddish lashes and the bold devil-may-care expression. The sunshine bathed his face in light. And what I saw as well was the same face looming towards me in pouring rain, with cruel eyes and a grim mouth. I heard a voice say, "You nosey bastard, perhaps that'll teach you to mind your own business"; and I threw up my hand to shield my cheek against the kick which was coming . . .

My sight cleared and steadied, and Sandy and I were looking straight into each other's eyes as if a battle were being fought there. He dropped the hand outstretched to help me, and the friendliness went out of his face with the completeness of an actor shielding a role when the play is over.

I found my palm was still pressed against my cheek. I let it drop away, but the gesture had told its tale. I had remembered what had happened by the fence at Bristol, and Sandy knew it.

Strength returned to my limbs, and I stood up. The starter consulting his watch in barely concealed annoyance, asked if I was all right. I replied that I was, and apologised for holding up the race. Some way down the course someone had caught Forlorn Hope, and as I watched he was turned to be led back to the starting gate.

Sandy, showing no haste to remount, stood his ground in front of me.

"You can't prove a thing," he said, characteristically taking the bull by the horns. "No one can connect me with Penn."

"Fletcher," I said at once.

"He'll keep his mouth shut," said Sandy, with conviction. "He's my cousin."

Uncle George's racing venture, I now saw, had not been inspired solely by the availability of a shaky bookmaking business. The existence of an easily recruited ally on the racecourse might have been the very factor which decided him, in the first place, to buy L. C. Perth.

I mentally reviewed the rest of the gang.

"How about Fielder?" I suggested after a short pause.

"I'm the voice on the phone to him. A voice called Smith. He doesn't know me from Adam," said Sandy.

Temporarily, I gave up. I said, "What did you do it for?"

"Money. What else?" he said scornfully, clearling thinking the question foolish.

"Why didn't you stop the horses yourself? Why let Joe collect the big fat fees for losing?"

Sandy seemed perfectly willing to explain. "I did stop a couple myself. The Stewards had me in over the second one, and I got off by the skin of my bloody teeth. I saw the red light, mate. I tipped the boss to try that little bastard Joe instead. Let him lose his licence, not me, I told him. But mind you, I was on to a bloody good percentage every time he strangled one."

"Which made you all the more angry when he won against orders on Bolingbroke," I said.

"That's right."

"Then Joe didn't tell you in the washroom he was going to pull Bolingbroke. You knew already."

"Proper little Sherlock," mocked Sandy.

"And you did put him over the rails at Plumpton, I suppose?"

"He bloody well deserved it. He lost me fifty quid on Leica as well as my bonus from the boss."

"Did he deserve to die, as well?" I asked bitterly.

The man leading Forlorn Hope back was now only a hundred yards away.

"The stupid little sod couldn't keep his mouth shut," said Sandy violently. "Waving that brown paper at Liverpool and yelling for you. I saw what was written on it, and told Fielder, that's all. I didn't know what it meant, but it was a ton to a tanner the boss wouldn't like it. Joe was asking for it."

"And after he'd got it, you rang Fielder and told him the job had been bungled, and Joe had lived long enough to talk to me?"

"Yes," said Sandy morosely. "I heard you telling every bloody body in the weighing room."

I couldn't resist it. I said, "I was lying. Joe died without saying a word."

As the full significance of this slowly dawned on him, his jaw dropped, and I saw him waver in some secret inner place as if an axe had hacked into the roots of his colossal self-confidence. He turned on his heel, strode across to where the starter's assistant held the horse, and swung abruptly into the saddle.

I went to meet Forlorn Hope, thanked the man who had brought him back, and remounted. The starter's patience had run out.

"Get into line, please," he said, and the circling horses began to straighten out across the course. I came up from behind and took a place alongside Sandy. I had one more question to ask.

"Tell me," I said, "why on earth did you get Penn to try to bribe Major Davidson? You must have known he wouldn't have stopped Admiral winning for all the money in the world."

"It was the boss's idea, not mine," said Sandy roughly. "I warned Fielder to tell him it wouldn't work, but the boss knew bee-all about horses and was pigheaded besides. Fielder said he wouldn't listen, because he thought if he fixed a cert it would be worth a fortune. He made a pocket out of it, all right. He thought up the wire himself. And I'd be a ruddy sight better off if the wire had killed you, too," he added, with a spurt of venom.

The starter's hand swept down on the lever. The tape flew up, and, five minutes later, the horses bounded forward towards the first hurdle.

I don't know exactly when Sandy decided to put me over the rails. Perhaps the thought of all the money he would not be getting overwhelmed him, and perhaps I had brought it on myself by recalling that he had done it to Joe when Joe, as he saw it, had cheated him.

In any case, as we approached the second hurdle, he swerved his horse toward me. We were both in the group just behind the leaders, and I was on the inside, with the rails on my left.

I glanced at Sandy's face. His slitted eyes were concentrated on the jump ahead, but with every stride his horse drew nearer to mine. He wasn't leaving me much room, I thought.

Only just in time did I realise that he intended to leave me no room at all. He was aiming to crowd my horse so closely that I would be thrust into the six foot high wing leading up to the hurdles. A crash through the wings, I had been told, was one of the most dangerous of all falls. The time had clearly come for rapid evasive action if I were not to find this out for myself.

I literally hauled on the reins. Forlorn Hope lost impetus dramatically, and as soon as the quarters of Sandy's horse were past his shoulder I pulled his head unceremoniously to the right. It was only just in time. The hurdles were beneath his feet before he had time to see them, and he knocked one flat with his forelegs. The horse following us, going faster, bumped hard into the back of him, and the jockey yelled at me to mind what I was doing.

Forlorn Hope was too much of a novice to stand this sort of thing, and I decided that if I were not to ruin his nerve for good, I would have to keep out of Sandy's way for the rest of the race.

But Sandy was not content with that. Along the straight in front of the stands he gradually worked himself back to my side. He was a better jockey than I and his horse was more experienced. When I tried to go faster, he kept pace, and when I slowed down, he slowed too. I could not shake him off. In front of the crowds, apart from keeping pace with me, he rode fairly enough; but round the next bend lay the long curved leg out into the comparatively deserted country, and what he might do there I hated to think.

I did consider pulling up and dropping out of the race altogether, but that seemed an even more ignominious defeat than being put over the rails.

As the field swept round the bend in a bunch, Sandy tried again. He closed his horse tight up against mine and very slightly behind. On my left I was jammed against Dane. He glanced across and shouted, "Get over, Sandy. Give me some room."

Sandy did not answer. Instead I felt his knee slide along under my thigh until it was pressing fiercely on my hamstrings. Then he gave a sudden violent jerk forwards and upwards with his whole leg.

My foot flew out of the stirrup and I lost my balance completely. I swayed wildly over to the left, my head tipping down beside my horse's neck, my fingers clutching frantically at his mane. I looked down and saw the blur of hooves pounding tight-packed round the bend, and I struggled to prevent myself slipping off among them. But all my weight was too far forward, and the jolt of the horse's galloping stride tended to tip me farther forward still. I knew that in a few seconds I would be off.

It was Dane who saved me. He put his hand on my side and literally pushed me back into my saddle.

"Thanks," I gasped, feeling with my right foot for the dangling stirrup.

Not far round the bend lay the next flight of hurdles, and I fought to get myself and the horse properly balanced before we met it. As we came round the bend the sun had shone straight into our faces, but swinging out towards the country it lay on our right. Glancing to see if Sandy was still beside me I caught the sunshine full in the eyes and was for a second dazzled. He was there. He appeared to me as a black silhouette against the sun.

I remembered then that on such bright days on this course the sun shone straight into the eyes of the crowds on the stands also, and that it was difficult for them to distinguish what was happening on the far side of the course. Whatever Sandy did, he could be fairly sure the Stewards would not be able to see.

I gained a yard or two on Sandy and Dane at the next hurdle, but over my shoulder I could hear Sandy clicking with his tongue to hurry his horse, and in a few more strides he was beside me again. His shadow lay across my horse's withers.

Suddenly he swung his arm; and had I not been so acutely ready he would have had me. He swung his right arm around his body in a chop at my face, slashing with his riding whip. I ducked in a reflex, without actually seeing the whip at all. The heavy blow landed across my helmet just above the peak, and knocked it clean off my head. It bounced away on the turf.

I felt, rather than saw, Sandy draw back his arm for another try. I slipped my own whip and the reins into my left hand, and when he struck, threw up my right. More by luck than design my fingers fastened on the stick and I gripped and twisted and pulled with the strength of desperation.

I had him half out of his saddle and I almost exulted, but at the vital moment he let go of his stick and regained his balance. Rebounding, his horse swerved away from me, leaving a gap, and I looked hopefully over my shoulder for one of the other runners to come up between us. But most of them had gone on in front, and there was no one close. I threw Sandy's stick away.

The next hurdle lay ahead. I kept well away from the rails and tried to steady Forlorn Hope so that he should have a fair chance at it, but I was all too aware that Sandy was beginning to close on me again with a burst of extra speed.

My horse jumped the hurdle in reasonable style. Sandy kicked his horse into a tremendous leap, and as he landed he pulled straight across in front of me.

Forlorn Hope crashed into the rails.

By some miracle he did not fall. He bounced off, staggered, faltered, and galloped on. My leg, which had been crushed just below the knee between his body and the rails, was completely numb. I looked down at it, it appeared to be doing its job all right, even though I no longer seemed to be connected to it. My silk breeches were ripped open across the knee, and in my new extremely expensive made-to-measure racing boots flapped a large triangular tear.

Illogically, this made me very angry.

Sandy was some lengths ahead and had not so far managed to pull back again. Dane came up on my right, and I was glad to see him there.

He yelled, "What the hell's going on? What the blazes does Sandy think he's playing at?"

"He's not playing," I shouted. "He wants to get me off."

"Why?" yelled Dane.

"He was working for George Penn. He was making a lot of money. Now he isn't. He blames me," I shouted in snatches, the wind picking the words out of my mouth and blowing them back over my shoulder.

"With reason," shouted Dane.

"Yes," I agreed. I glanced at him, but now it was he who was outlined against the sun, and I could not see his expression clearly. If he felt badly enough about Kate to carry on where Sandy had for the moment left off, I should have no chance at all. He could ride rings round me, and Sandy, too.

We raced in silence towards the next hurdle, the last on the far side. Sandy was gradually slowing to wait for me.

Then Dane said, "Alan?"

"Yes?" I shouted back.

"Do you want to give Sandy some of his own medicine?"

"Yes." I suddenly had no reservations. It was a terrible thing to do, and if the Stewards saw me I'd lose my permit; but I had taken just about enough from Uncle George's assorted strong-arm boys.

Dane shouted, "I'll go up on his outside. You come outside me. Then I'll get away and leave him between you and the rails. O.K.?"

I nodded. I tried to foresee the future. If I unseated Sandy he would not dare to complain to the Stewards; and I, as he said, could give no tangible evidence against him to the police. There could be an uneasy truce between us. And fall for fall, the score would be equal.

"Come on, then," Dane shouted.

He kicked his horse and began to take his place on Sandy's right. I pulled away from the rails and urged Forlorn Hope to the outside. There was nearly a mile to go to the finish, and as no one had yet begun to put on the pressure the field was still fairly closely bunched just ahead of us. There was no one behind. After the hurdle lay the long oval bend leading round into the straight. If either Sandy or I were to get the other off, it would have to be done on the bend; once we were round into the straight the Stewards would have too clear a view of our behavior.

Dane jumped the hurdle alongside Sandy with me not far behind. As soon as I was level with them both, Dane shook up his horse and sped clear away from us, leaving me, as he had promised, with Sandy between me and the rails.

I swung Forlorn Hope over roughly on to Sandy's horse, bumping him against the rails. Sandy yelled and lashed out with his fist. I hit his arm sharply with my stick.

I had got to unseat him without hurting his horse. I was being unfair enough already to the owner in trying to lose him the race by dislodging his jockey: if I could not do it without damaging the horse I must not do it at all.

Shifting the reins into my right hand, I planted my left abruptly on Sandy's body just behind his armpit, and shoved. But I was too far away to get enough force behind it. He swayed in the saddle, but kept his balance. He began to swear at me.

We were on the crown of the bend. It had to be now or never. I pushed Sandy's horse harder against the rails. He yelled again. His leg, I knew, must be being crushed, pounded, even torn by the white-painted wood. With my own leg numb from the same treatment, I had no sympathy for him. Then his foot crashed into one of the uprights with an audible snap.

He screamed.

I gritted my teeth, shot my arm, and pushed him with all my might. I knew if he had not gone then I would not have had the resolution to try again. But he began to topple, slowly, it seemed, at first, and then with an accelerating rush, as if he had been sucked away by a slipstream.

I caught a final glimpse of his face, eyes staring widely, mouth twisted with agony, as he fell into the long grass on the other side of the rails. Then I was round the bend into the straight, bruised, tattered and helmetless, but still on board.

Sandy's loose horse, relieved of his weight, spurted forward through the other runners.

Dane saw him, and turned round in his saddle and grinned at me, and jerked up his thumb.

NERVE

CHAPTER 1

ART MATHEWS SHOT himself, loudly and messily, in the center of the parade ring at Dunstable races.

I was standing only six feet away from him, but he did it so quickly that had it been only six inches I would not have had time to stop him.

He had walked out of the changing room ahead of me, his narrow shoulders hunched inside the khaki jerkin he had put on over his racing colors, and his head down on his chest as if he were deep in thought. I noticed him stumble slightly down the two steps from the weighing room to the path; and when someone spoke to him on the short walk to the parade ring, he gave absolutely no sign of having heard. But it was just another walk from the weighing room to the parade ring, just another race like a hundred others. There was nothing to suggest that when he had stood talking for two or three minutes with the owner and the trainer of the horse he was due to ride, he would take off his jerkin, produce from under it as he dropped it to the ground a large automatic pistol, place the barrel against his temple, and squeeze the trigger.

Unhesitating. No pause for a final weighing up. No good-bys. The casualness of his movement was as shocking as its effect.

He hadn't even shut his eyes, and they were still open as he fell forward to the ground, his face hitting the grass with an audible thud and his helmet rolling off. The bullet had passed straight through his skull, and the exit wound lay open to the sky, a tangled, bloody mess of skin and hair and brain, with splinters of bone sticking out.

The crack of the gunshot echoed round the paddock, amplified by the high back wall of the stands. Heads turned searchingly and the busy buzz and hum of conversation from the three-deep railside racegoers grew hushed and finally silent as they took in the appalling, unbelievable, indisputable fact that what remained of Art Mathews lay face downward on the bright green turf.

Mr. John Brewar, the owner of Art's prospective mount, stood with his middle-aged mouth stretched open in a soundless oval, his eyes glazed with surprise. His plump, well-preserved wife toppled to the ground in the graceless sprawl of a genuine faint, and Corin Kellar, the trainer for whom both Art and I had been about to ride, went down on one knee and shook Art by the shoulder, as if he could still awaken one whose head was half blown away.

The sun shone brightly. The blue and orange silk on Art's back gleamed: his white breeches were spotless, and his racing boots had been polished into a clean, soft shine. I thought inconsequentially that he would have been glad that—from the neck down at least—he looked as immaculate as ever.

The two Stewards hurried over and stood stock-still, staring at Art's head. Horror dragged down their jaws and narrowed their eyes. It was part of their responsibility at a meeting to stand in the parade ring while the horses were led round before each race, so that they should be both witnesses and adjudicators if anything irregular should occur. Nothing as irregular as a public suicide of a topnotch steeplechase jockey had ever, I imagined, required their attention before.

The elder of them, Lord Tirrold, a tall, thin man with an executive mind, bent over Art for a closer inspection. I saw the muscles bunch along his jaw, and he looked up at me across Art's body and said quietly, "Finn . . . fetch a rug."

I walked twenty steps down the parade ring to where one of the horses due to run in the race stood in a little group with his owner, trainer and jockey. Without a word the trainer took the rug off the horse and held it out to me.

"Mathews?" he said incredulously.

I nodded unhappily and thanked him for the rug, and went back with it.

The other Steward, a sour-tempered hulk named Ballerton, was, I was meanly pleased to see, losing his cherished dignity by vomiting up his lunch.

Mr. Brewar pulled down his unconscious wife's rucked-up skirt and began anxiously to feel her pulse. Corin Kellar kept passing his hand over his face from forehead to chin, still down on one knee beside his jockey. His face was colorless, his hand shaking. He was taking it badly.

I handed one end of the rug to Lord Tirrold and we opened it out and spread it gently over the dead man. Lord Tirrold stood for a moment looking down at the motionless brown shape, then glanced round at the little silent groups of people who had runners in the race. He went over and spoke to one or two, and presently the stable lads led all the horses out from the parade ring and back to the saddling boxes.

I stood looking down at Corin Kellar and his distress, which I thought he thoroughly deserved. I wondered how it felt to know one had driven a man to kill himself.

There was a click, and a voice announced over the loudspeaker system that owing to a serious accident in the parade ring the last two races would be abandoned. Tomorrow's meeting would be held as planned, it said, and would everyone please go home. As far as the growing crowd of racegoers round the ring was concerned, this might never have been said, for they remained glued to the rails with all eyes on the concealing rug. Nothing rivets human attention as hungrily as a bloody disaster, I thought tolerantly, picking up Art's helmet and whip from the grass.

Poor Art. Poor badgered, beleaguered Art, rubbing out his misery with a scrap of lead.

I turned away from his body and walked thoughtfully back to the weighing room.

While we changed back from riding kit into our normal clothes, the atmosphere down our end of the changing room was one of irreverence covering shock. Art, occupying by general consent the position of elder statesman among jockeys, though he was not actually at thirty-five by any means the eldest, had been much deferred to and respected. Distant in manner sometimes, withdrawn even, but an honest man and a good jockey. His one noticeable weakness, at which we usually smiled indulgently, was his conviction that a lost race was always due to some deficiency in his horse or its training and never to a mistake on his part. We all knew perfectly well that Art was no exception to the rule that every jockey misjudges things once in a while, but he would never admit a fault, and he could put up a persuasive defense every time if called to account.

"Thank the Lord," said Tick-Tock Ingersoll, stripping off his blue-and-black checked jersey, "that Art was considerate enough to let us all weigh out for the race before bumping himself off." Tick-Tock's face emerged from the woolly folds with a wide grin, which faded comically when no one laughed.

"Well," he said, dropping his jersey absent-mindedly in a heap on the floor. "If he'd done it an hour ago we'd all have been ten quid out of pocket."

He was right. Our fees for each race were technically earned once we had sat on the scales and been checked out as carrying the correct weight, and they would be automatically paid whether we ran the race or not.

"In that case," said Peter Cloony, "we should put half of it into a fund for his widow." He was a small, quiet young man prone to overemotional, quickly roused and quickly spent bouts of pity both for others and for himself.

"Not ruddy likely," said Tick-Tock, who disliked him openly. "Ten quid's ten quid to me, and Mrs. Art's rolling in it. And snooty with it. Catch me giving her the time of day, you'll be lucky."

"It's a mark of respect," said Peter obstinately, looking round at us with rather damp large eyes and carefully refraining from returning young Tick-Tock's belligerent glare.

I sympathized with Tick-Tock. I needed the money, too. Besides, Mrs. Art had treated me, along with all the other rank-and-file jockeys, with her own particular arctic brand of coolness. Giving her a fiver in Art's memory wouldn't thaw her. Pale, straw-haired, light-eyed, she was the original ice maiden, I thought.

"Mrs. Art doesn't need our money," I said. "Remember how she bought herself a mink coat last winter and used it as a hedge against all of us who didn't measure up to her standards? She hardly knows two of us by name. Let's just buy Art a wreath, and perhaps a useful memorial, something he would have appreciated, like some hot showers in the washroom here."

Tick-Tock's angular young face registered delight. Peter Cloony bent on me a look of sorrowful reproof. But from the others came nods of agreement.

Grant Oldfield said violently, "He probably shot himself because that whey-faced bitch short-changed him in bed."

There was a curious little silence. A year ago, I reflected, a year ago we might have laughed. But a year ago Grant Oldfield would have said the same thing amusingly and perhaps vulgarly, but not with this ugly, unsmiling venom.

I was aware, we all were, that he didn't know or care a jot about the private practices of Art's marriage; but in the past months Grant had seemed more and more to be consumed by some inner rage, and lately he could scarcely make the most commonplace remark without in some way giving vent to it. It was caused, we thought, by the fact that he was going down the ladder again without ever having got to the top. He had always been ambitious and ruthless in character, and had developed a riding style to match. But at the vital point when he had attracted public attention with a string of successes and had begun to ride regularly for James Axminster, one of the very top trainers, something had happened to spoil it. He had lost the Axminster job, and other trainers booked him less and less. The race we had not run was his only engagement that day.

Grant was a dark, hairy, thickset man of thirty, with high cheekbones and a wide-nostriled nose bent permanently out of shape. I endured a great deal more of his company than I would have liked because my peg in the changing room at nearly all racecourses was next to his, since both our kits were looked after by the same racecourse valet. He borrowed my things freely without asking first or thanking afterward and, if he had broken something, denied he had used it. When I first met him I had been amused by his pawky humor but two years later, by the day Art died, I was heartily sick of his thunderous moods, his roughness, and his vile temper.

Once or twice in the six weeks since the new season had begun I had found him standing with his head thrust forward looking round him in bewilderment, like a bull played out by a matador. A bull exhausted by fighting a piece of cloth, a bull baffled and broken, all his magnificent strength wasted on something he could not pin down with his horns. At such times I could pity Grant all right, but at all others I kept out of his way as much as I could.

Peter Cloony, paying him no attention as usual, indicated the peg on which Art's everyday clothes hung, and said, "What do you think we had better do with these?"

We all looked at them, the well-cut tweed suit neatly arranged on a hanger, with the small grip which contained his folded shirt and underclothes standing on the bench beneath. His almost obsessive tidiness was so familiar to us that it aroused no comment, but now that he was dead I was struck afresh by it. All the others hung up their jackets by the loop at the back of the neck, hooked their braces onto the pegs, and piled their other clothes into the tops of their trousers. Only Art had insisted on a hanger, and had provided his valet with one to bring for him.

Before we had got any further than an obscene suggestion from Grant, a racecourse official threaded his way down the changing room, spotted me, and shouted, "Finn, the Stewards want you."

"Now?" I said, standing in shirt and underpants.

"At once." He grinned.

"All right." I finished dressing quickly, brushed my hair, walked through the weighing room, and knocked on the Stewards' door. They said to come in, and in I went.

All three Stewards were there, also the clerk of the course and Corin Kellar. They were sitting in uncomfortable-looking, straight-backed chairs around a large, oblong table.

Lord Tirrold said, "Come along in and close the door."

I did as he said.

He went on: "I know you were near Mathews when he . . . er . . . shot himself. Did you actually see him do it? I mean, did you see him take the pistol out and aim it, or did you look at him when you heard the shot?"

"I saw him take out the pistol and aim it, sir," I said.

"Very well. In that case the police may wish to take a statement from you; please do not leave the weighing-room building until they have seen you. We are waiting now for the inspector to come back from the first-aid room."

He nodded to dismiss me, but when I had my hand on the doorknob he said, "Finn . . . do you know of any reason why Mathews should have wished to end his life?"

I hesitated a fraction too long before I turned round, so that a plain "No" would have been unconvincing. I looked at Corin Kellar, who was busy studying his fingernails.

"Mr. Kellar might know," I said noncommittally.

The Stewards exchanged glances. Mr. Ballerton, still pallid from his bout of sickness by Art's body, made a push-away gesture with his hand, and said, "You're not asking us to believe that Mathews killed himself merely because Kellar was dissatisfied with his riding?" He turned to the other Stewards. "Really," he added forcefully, "if these jockeys get so big for their boots that they can't take a little well-earned criticism, it is time they looked about for other employment. But to suggest that Mathews killed himself because of a few hard words is irresponsible mischief."

At that point I remembered that Ballerton himself owned a horse which Corin Kellar trained. "Dissatisfied with his riding"—the colorless phrase he had used to describe the recent series of acrimonious post-race arguments between Art and the trainer suddenly seemed to me a deliberate attempt at oiling troubled waters. You know why Art killed himself, I thought: you helped to cause it, and you won't admit it.

I shifted my gaze back to Lord Tirrold and found him regarding me with speculation.

"That will be all, Finn," he said.

"Yes, sir," I said.

I went out and this time they did not call me back, but before I had

crossed the weighing room the door opened again and shut and I heard
Corin's voice behind me.

"Rob."

I turned round and waited for him.

"Thanks very much," he said sarcastically, "for tossing that little bomb
into my lap."

"You had told them already," I said.

"Yes, and just as well."

He still looked shocked, his thin face deeply lined with worry. He was an
exceptionally clever trainer, but a nervous, undependable man who offered
you lifelong friendship one day and cut you dead the next. Just then, it appeared, he needed assurance.

He said, "Surely you and the other jockeys don't believe Art killed himself because . . . er . . . I had decided to employ him less? He must have had
another reason."

"Today was supposed to be his last as your jockey in any case, wasn't it?"
I said.

He hesitated and then nodded, surprised at my knowing what had not
been published. I didn't tell him that I had bumped into Art in the car park
the evening before, and that Art, bitterly dispairing and smarting from a cor-
roding sense of injustice, had lowered the customary guard on his tongue
enough to tell me that his job with Kellar was finished.

I said only, "He killed himself because you gave him the sack, and he did
it in front of you to cause you the maximum amount of remorse. And that, if
you want my opinion, is that."

"But people don't kill themselves because they've lost their jobs," he
said, with a tinge of exasperation.

"Not if they're normal, no," I agreed.

"Every jockey knows he'll have to retire sometime. And Art was getting
too old . . . he must have been mad."

"Yes, I suppose so," I said.

I left him standing there, trying to convince himself that he was in no
way responsible for Art's death.

Back in the changing room the discussion on what to do with Art's
clothes had been ended by his valet's taking charge of them, and Grant Oldfield, I was glad to find, had finished dressing and gone home. Most of the

other jockeys had gone also, and the valets were busy tidying up the chaos they had left behind, sorting dirty white breeches into kit bags, and piling helmets, boots, whips and other gear into large wicker hampers. It had been a dry sunny day and for once there was no mud to wash off.

As I watched the quick, neat way they flipped the things into the baskets, ready to take the dirty ones home, clean them and return them laundered and polished on the following day, I reflected that possibly they did deserve the very large fees we had to pay them for the service. I knew I would loathe, after a day of traveling and of dressing jockeys, to have to face those hampers and bags when I reached home; take out the grubby piles and set to work. Ugh.

I had often seen Art paying his valet, counting through a wad of notes. At the height of the season it always amounted to over twenty pounds each week. My own valet, Young Mike (in his middle forties), twitched my helmet up from the bench and smiled at me as he went by. He earned more than most of the dozen or so jockeys he regularly looked after, and decidedly more than I did. But all the same . . . ugh!

Tick-Tock, whistling the latest hit tune between his teeth, sat on the bench and pulled on a pair of very fancy yellow socks. On top of those went smooth, slim-toed shoes reaching up to the anklebone. He shook down the slender legs of his dark tweed trousers (no turnups) and feeling my gaze upon him looked up and grinned at me across the room.

He said, "Look your fill on the 'Tailor and Cutter's dream boy.'"

"My father in his time," I said blandly, "was a Twelve Best Dressed man."

"My grandfather had vicuna linings in his raincoats."

"My mother," I said, dredging for it, "was a Pucci shirt."

"Mine," he said carefully, "cooks in hers."

At this infantile exchange we regarded each other with high good humor. Five minutes of Tick-Tock's company were as cheering as rum punch in a snowstorm, and some of his happy-go-lucky enjoyment of living always rubbed off onto the next man. Let Art die of shame, let the murk spread in Grant Oldfield's soul; surely nothing could be really wrong in the racing world, I thought, while young Ingersoll ticked so gaily.

He waved his hand at me, adjusted his Tyrolean trilby, said, "See you tomorrow," and was gone.

But all the same there *was* something wrong in the racing world. Very wrong. I didn't know what; I could see only the symptoms, and see them all the more clearly, perhaps, since I had been only two years in the game. Between trainers and jockeys there seemed to be an all-round edginess, sudden outbursts of rancor, and an ebbing and flowing undercurrent of resentment and distrust. There was more to it, I thought, than the usual jungle beneath the surface of any fiercely competitive business, more to it than the equivalent of gray-flannel-suit maneuvering in the world of jodhpurs and hacking jackets; but Tick-Tock, to whom alone I had in any way suggested my misgivings, had brushed the whole thing aside.

"You must be on the wrong wavelength, pal," he said. "Look around you. Those are smiles you can see, boy. Smiles. It's an okay life by me."

The last few pieces of kit were disappearing into the hampers and some of the lids were already down. I drank a second cup of sugarless tea, lukewarm, and eyed the moist-looking pieces of fruit cake. As usual it took a good deal of resolution not to eat one. Being constantly hungry was the one thing I did not enjoy about race riding, and September was always a bad time of the year, with the remains of the summer's fat still having to be starved off. I sighed, averted my eyes from the cake, and tried to console myself that in another month my appetite would have shrunk back to its winter level.

Young Mike shouted down the room from the doorway through which he had been staggering with a hamper, "Rob, there's a copper here to see you."

I put down the cup and went out into the weighing room. A middle-aged, undistinguished-looking policeman in a peaked cap was waiting for me with a notebook in his hand.

"Robert Finn?" he asked.

"Yes," I said.

"I understand from Lord Tirrold that you saw Arthur Mathews put the pistol against his temple and pull the trigger?"

"Yes," I agreed.

He made a note; then he said, "It's a very straightforward case of suicide. There won't be any need for more than one witness at the inquest, apart from the doctor, and that will probably be Mr. Kellar. I don't think we will need to trouble you any further." He smiled briefly, shut the notebook, and put it in his pocket.

"That's all?" I asked rather blankly.

"Yes, that's all. When a man kills himself as publicly as this there's no question of accident or homicide. The only thing for the coroner to decide is the wording of his verdict."

"Unsound mind and so on?" I said.

"Yes," he said. "Thank you for waiting, though it was your Steward's idea, not mine. Good afternoon, then." He nodded at me, turned, and walked across toward the Stewards' room.

I collected my hat and binoculars and walked down to the racecourse station. The train was already waiting and full, and the only seat I could find was in a compartment packed with bookmakers' clerks playing cards on a suitcase balanced across their knees. They invited me to join them, and between Luton and St. Pancras I fear I repaid their kindness by winning from them the cost of the journey.

CHAPTER 2

THE FLAT IN Kensington was empty. There were a few letters from the day's second post in the wire basket on the inner side of the door, and I fished them out and walked through into the sitting room, sorting out the two which were addressed to me.

As usual, the place looked as if it had lately received the attentions of a minor tornado. My mother's grand piano lay inches deep in piano scores, several of which had cascaded to the floor. Two music stands leaned at a drunken angle against the wall with a violin bow hooked onto one of them. The violin itself was propped up in an armchair, with its case open on the floor beside it. A cello and another music stand rested side by side like lovers along the length of the sofa. An oboe and two clarinets lay on a table beside another untidy pile of music, and round the room and on all the bedroom chairs, which filled most of the floor space, lay a profusion of white silk handkerchiefs, rosin, coffee cups and batons.

Running a practiced eye over the chaos I diagnosed the recent presence of my parents, two uncles and a cousin. As they never traveled far without their instruments, it was safe to predict that the whole circus was within walking distance and would return in a very short while. I had, I was thankful to realize, struck the interval.

I threaded a path to the window and looked out. No sign of returning Finns. The flat was at the top of a house two or three streets back from Hyde Park, and across the rooftops I could see the evening sunlight striking on the green dome of the Albert Hall. The Royal Institute of Music, where one of my uncles taught, rose in a solid dark mass beside it. The large airy apartment, which was the headquarters of the Finn family, was held by my father to be an economy, as it was within walking distance of where so many of them from time to time worked.

I was the odd one out. The talents with which both my parents' families had been lavishly endowed had not descended to me. This had become painfully clear to them when at the age of four I had failed to distinguish between the notes of an oboe and a cor anglais. To the uninitiated there may not seem to be much difference, but my father happened to be an oboist of international reputation, against whom other oboists were measured. Also, high musical talent, if it exists, is apparent in a child from an extremely early age, earlier than any other form of inborn ability, and at three years (when Mozart began composing), concertos and symphonies made less impression on me than the noise of the men emptying the dustbins.

By the time I was five my shattered parents had reluctantly faced the fact that the child they had bred by mistake (I had caused an important American tour to be canceled) was unmusical. Unmusical, that is, in their pure sense. I was not tone-deaf and soaring flights of melody had drawn from me childish tears, but I never had, and still have not, their complete understanding, intellectual, emotional, technical and spiritual, of the effect of putting certain sounds in certain orders.

My mother never being one to do things by halves, I had henceforth been shuffled off from London between school terms to a succession of long holidays on farms, ostensibly for my health, but in reality, I knew later, to free my parents for the complicated and lengthy concert tours in which they were engaged. I grew up into a sort of truce with them, in which it was tacitly agreed that as they had not intended to have a child in the first place, and as he had proved to be less than a (musical) credit to them in the second, the less we saw of each other the better.

They disapproved of my venture into jockeyship for no other reason than that racing had nothing to do with music. It was no use my pointing out that the one thing I had learned on the various holiday farms was how to ride (for

I was enough my father's son for farming itself to bore me stiff), and that my present occupation was directly due to their actions in the past. To what they did not want to hear my acute-eared parents were sublimely deaf.

There was still no sign of them down in the street, nor of the uncle who lived with us who played the cello, nor of the visiting uncle and cousin, violin and clarinet.

I opened my two letters. The first informed me that my income tax returns were overdue. I slit the second envelope with a smiling and complacent anticipation of enjoyment, which just shows how often life can get up and slap you when you least expect it. In a familiar childish hand the letter said:

> Dearest Rob,
>
> I am afraid this may come as a surprise to you, but I am getting married. He is Sir Morton Henge, who you may have heard of, and he is very sweet and kind and no cracks from you about him being old enough to be my father, etc. I don't think I had better ask you to the reception, do you? Morton doesn't know about you and you will be a great dear not to let on to anybody about us, if you don't mind. I shall never forget you, dearest Rob, and all the sweet times we had together. Thank you for everything, and good-by.
>
> Your loving Paulina

Sir Morton Henge, middle-aged widower and canning tycoon. Well, well. I wondered sardonically how his serious-minded son, whom I knew slightly, would enjoy the prospect of a cuddly twenty-year-old model girl for a stepmother. But being in a lopsided way able to laugh at Paulina's catch made it no less of a blow.

In the eighteen months since I had first met her she had progressed from mousy-haired obscurity to a blonde blossoming on the cover of at least one glossy magazine a week. In the past month her radiant eyes had smiled at me (and eight million other men) from a cigarette advertisement in every underground station in London. I had known that it was inevitable that one day she would forsake me if she struck gold in her profession, and our whole relationship had from the start been based on that assumption; but a future without her happy inanity and her generous lovemaking seemed all of a sudden more bleak than I had expected.

I went through to my bedroom and, putting down Paulina's letter on the chest of drawers, caught sight of myself in the oval mirror on the wall above it. That is the face, I thought, that she had been pleased to see beside her on her pillow, but which was no match for a title and a canning fortune. Looking objectively at my reflection I noted the black hair, black eyebrows and lashes, brown eyes . . . not a distinguished face, nor handsome; too thin perhaps. Not bad, not good. Just a face.

I turned away and looked around the little sloping-ceilinged room, which had been converted for me from a lumber room when I came home from my travels. There was very little in it: a bed, the chest of drawers, an armchair, and a bedside table with a lamp on it. One picture, an impressionist sketch of racing horses, hung on the wall facing my bed. There were no other ornaments, few books, no clutter. In six years of wandering round the world I had become so used to living with a minimum of possessions that, although I had now occupied this little room on and off for two years, I had amassed nothing to put into it.

A clothes cupboard had been built for me across one end of the room. I opened the door and tried to look at its contents as Paulina must have looked, the twice she had been there. One good dark-gray suit, one evening jacket with black trousers, one hacking jacket, two pairs of gray slacks, and a pair of jodhpurs. I took off the suit I was wearing and hung it at the end of the meager row, a tweed mixture of browns. They were enough for me, those clothes. They covered every situation. Sir Morton Henge probably counted his suits in dozens and had a manservant to look after them. I shrugged my shoulders. There was no profit in this melancholy stocktaking. Paulina was gone, and that was that.

Picking up a pair of black sneakers I shut the cupboard door and changed into jeans and an old checked shirt. That done, I contemplated the desert of time between then and the next day's racing. The trouble with me was that steeplechasing had got into my blood like a drug addiction, so that all the normal pleasures of life, and even Paulina herself, had become merely ways of passing as quickly as possible the hours away from it.

My stomach gave an extra twist, which I would like to have believed was due to romantic desolation at my blasted love life but which I knew very well was only the result of not having eaten for twenty-three hours. Admitting wryly that being jettisoned had not spoiled my appetite, I made for the kitchen. Before I reached it, however, the front door of the flat banged open and in trooped my parents, uncles and cousin.

"Hello, darling," said my mother, presenting a smooth sweet-smelling cheek for a kiss. It was her usual greeting to everyone from impresarios to back-row chorus singers, and when applied to me still utterly lacked any maternal quality. She was not a motherly person in any way. Tall, slender, and immensely chic in a style that looked casual but was the result of much thought and expenditure, she was becoming more and more a "presence" as she approached fifty. As a woman I knew her to be passionate and temperamental; as an artist to be a first-class interpretive vehicle for the genius of Haydn, whose piano concertos she poured out with magical, meticulous, ecstatic precision. I had seen hardened music critics leave her performances with tears in their eyes. So I had never expected a broad motherly bosom to comfort my childish woes, nor a sock-darning, cake-making mum to come home to.

My father, who treated me always with polite friendliness, said as a form of greeting, "Did you have a good day?" He always asked. I usually answered briefly yes or no, knowing that he was not really interested.

I said, "I saw a man kill himself. No, it wasn't a good day."

Five heads swiveled toward me.

My mother said, "Darling, what do you mean?"

"A jockey shot himself at the races. He was only six feet away from me. It was a mess." All five of them stood looking at me with their mouths open. I wished I hadn't told them, for it seemed even more horrible in memory than it had at the time.

But they were unaffected. The cello uncle shut his mouth with a snap, shrugged, and went on into the sitting room, saying over his shoulder, "Well, if you will go in for these peculiar pursuits . . ."

My mother followed him with her eyes. There was a bass twang as he picked up his instrument from the sofa, and as if drawn by an irresistible magnet the others drifted after him. Only my cousin stayed long enough to spare Art a thought, then he too went back to his clarinet.

I listened to them returning and setting up the music stands. They began to play a jigging piece for strings and woodwind that I particularly disliked. The flat was suddenly intolerable. I went out and down into the street and began to walk.

There was only one place to go if I wanted a certain kind of peace, and I didn't care to go there too often for fear of wearing out my welcome. But it was a full month since I had seen my cousin Joanna, and I needed some more of her company. Need. That was the only word for it.

She opened the door with her usual air of good-humored invitation.

"Well, hello," she said, smiling. I followed her into the big converted mews garage which served her as sitting room, bedroom and rehearsal room all in one. Half of the roof was a sloping skylight, through which the remains of the evening sun still shone. The size and comparative bareness of the room gave it unusual acoustic qualities; if one spoke ordinarily, it was like any other room; if one sang, as Joanna did, there was a satisfying illusion of distance and some good amplification from the concrete walls.

Joanna's voice was deep and clear and resonant. When she liked, in singing dramatic passages, she could color it with the suggestion of graininess, a very effective hint of a crack in the bell. She could have made a fortune as a blues singer; but having been born a true classical Finn, so commercial a use of her talent was out of the question. Instead she preferred songs which to me were unmelodic and unrewarding, though she seemed to be amassing a fair-sized reputation with them among people who enjoyed that sort of thing.

She had greeted me in a pair of jeans as old as my own and a black sweater streaked here and there with paint. On an easel stood a half-finished portrait of a man, with some brushes and paints on a table beside it.

"I'm trying my hand at oils," she said, picking up a brush and making a tentative dab at the picture, "but it's not going very well, damn it."

"Stick to charcoal, then," I said. She had drawn with flowing lines the racing horses which hung in my bedroom, short on anatomy, but full of life and movement.

"I'll finish this, at least," she said.

I stood and watched her. She squeezed out some carmine.

Without looking at me she said, "What's the matter?"

I didn't answer. She paused with her brushes in the air and turned and regarded me calmly for some seconds.

"There's some steak in the kitchen," she said.

A mind reader, my cousin Joanna. I grinned at her and went out into the long narrow lean-to where she both took her bath and did her cooking. It was rump steak, thick and dark. I grilled it with a couple of tomatoes and made some French dressing for a lettuce I found already prepared in a wooden bowl. When the steak was done I divided it onto two plates and took the whole lot back to Joanna. It smelled wonderful.

She put down her brush and came to eat, wiping her hands on the seat of her pants.

"I'll say one thing for you, Rob, you cook a mean steak," she said, after her first mouthful.

"Thanks for nothing," I said, with my mouth full.

We ate every scrap. I finished first, and sat back and watched her. She had a fascinating face, full of strength and character, with straight dark eyebrows and, that night, no lipstick. She had tucked her short wavy hair in a no-nonsense style behind her ears, but on top it still curled forward onto her forehead in an untidy fringe.

My cousin Joanna was the reason I was still a bachelor, if one can be said to need a reason at twenty-six years of age. She was three months older than I, which had given her an advantage over me all our lives, and this was a pity, since I had been in love with her from the cradle. I had several times asked her to marry me, but she always said no. First cousins, she explained firmly, were too closely related. Besides which, she added, I didn't stir her blood.

Two other men, however, had done that for her. Both were musicians. And each of them in his turn in a most friendly way had told me how greatly having Joanna for a lover had deepened their appreciation of living, given new impetus to their musical inspiration, opened new vistas, and so on and so on. They were both rather intense brooding men with undeniably hand-some faces, and I didn't like hearing what they had to say. On the first occa-sion, when I was eighteen, I departed in speed and grief to foreign lands, and somehow had not returned for six years. On the second occasion I went straight to a wild party, got thoroughly drunk for the first and only time in my life, and woke up in Paulina's bed. Both adventures had turned out to be satisfying and educational. But they had not cured me of Joanna.

She pushed away her empty plate and said, "Now, what's the matter?"

I told her about Art. She listened seriously and when I had finished she said, "The poor man. And his poor wife . . . Why did he do it, do you know?"

"I think it was because he lost his job," I said. "Art was such a perfec-tionist in everything. He was too proud . . . He would never admit he had done anything wrong in a race . . . And I think he simply couldn't face everyone's knowing he'd been given the sack. But the odd thing is, Joanna, that he looked as good as ever to me. I know he was thirty-five, but that's not really old for a jockey, and although it was obvious that he and Corin Kellar, the trainer who retained him, were always having rows when their horses didn't win, he hadn't lost any of his style. Someone else would have employed him, even if not one of the top stables like Corin's."

"And there you have it, I should think," she said. "Death was preferable to decline."

"Yes, it looks like it."

"I hope that when your time comes to retire you will do it less drastically," she said. I smiled, and she added, "And just what will you do when you retire?"

"Retire? I have only just started," I said.

"And in fourteen years' time you'll be a second-rate, battered, bitter forty, too old to make anything of your life and with nothing to live on but horsy memories that no one wants to listen to." She sounded quite annoyed at the prospect.

"You, on the other hand," I said, "will be a fat, middle-aged, contralto's understudy, scared stiff of losing your looks and aware that those precious vocal cords are growing less flexible every year."

She laughed. "How gloomy. But I see your point. From now on I'll try not to disapprove of your job because it lacks a future."

"But you'll go on disapproving for other reasons?"

"Certainly. It's basically frivolous, unproductive, escapist, and it encourages people to waste time and money on inessentials."

"Like music," I said.

She glared at me. "For that you shall do the washing up," she said, getting to her feet and putting the plates together.

While I did my penance for the worst heresy possible in the Finn family, she went back to her portrait, but it was nearly dusk, and when I brought in a peace offering of some freshly made coffee she gave it up for the day.

"Is your television set working?" I asked, handing her a cup.

"Yes, I think so."

"Do you mind if we have it on for a quarter of an hour?"

"Who's playing?" she asked automatically.

I sighed. "No one. It's a racing program."

"Oh, very well. If you must." But she smiled.

I switched it on, and we saw the end of a variety show. I enjoyed the songs of the last performer, a vivacious blonde, but Joanna, technique minded, said her breath control creaked. A batch of advertisements followed, and then the fluttering, urgent opening bars of "The Galloping Major," accompanied by speeded-up, superimposed views of horses racing, announced the weekly fifteen minutes of *Turf Talk*.

The well-known, good-looking face of Maurice Kemp-Lore came on the screen, smiling and casual. He began in his easy charming way to introduce his guest of the evening, a prominent bookmaker, and his topic of the evening, the mathematics involved in making a book.

"But first," he said, "I would like a pay a tribute to the steeplechase jockey, Art Mathews, who died today by his own hand at Dunstable races. Many of you have watched him ride . . . I expect nearly all of you have seen televised races in which he has appeared . . . and you will feel with me a great sense of shock that such a long and successful career should end in a tragedy of this sort. Although never actually champion jockey, Art was acknowledged to be one of the six best steeplechase riders in the country, and his upright incorruptible character has been a splendid example to young jockeys just starting in the game."

Joanna lifted an eyebrow at me, and Maurice Kemp-Lore, neatly finishing off Art's glowing obituary, reintroduced the bookmaker, who gave a clear and fascinating demonstration of how to come out on the winning side. His talk, illustrated with films and animated charts, described the minute-by-minute decisions made daily in a big London starting price office, and was well up to the high standard of all the Kemp-Lore programs.

Kemp-Lore thanked him and rounded off the quarter of an hour with a review of the following week's racing, not tipping particular animals to win but giving snippets of information about people and horses on the basis that there would be more interest in the outcome of a race if the public already knew something of the background of the contestants. His anecdotes were always interesting or amusing, and I had heard him called the despair of racing journalists since he so often beat them to a good story.

He said finally, "See you all next week at the same time," and "The Galloping Major" faded him out.

I switched off the set. Joanna said, "Do you watch that every week?"

"Yes, if I can," I said. "It's a racing must. It's so full of things one ought not to miss, and quite often his guest is someone I've met."

"Mr. Kemp-Lore knows his onions, then?" she said.

"He does indeed," I said. "He was brought up to it. His father rode a

Grand National winner back in the thirties and is now a big noise on the National Hunt Committee; which," I went on, seeing her blank look, "is the ruling body of steeplechasing."

"Oh. And has Mr. Kemp-Lore ridden any Grand National winners himself?" she asked.

"No," I said. "I don't think he rides much at all. Horses give him asthma, or something like that. I'm not sure. I only know him by sight. He is often at the races but I have never spoken to him."

Joanna's interest in racing, never very strong, subsided entirely at this point, and for an hour or so we gossiped amicably and aimlessly about how the world wagged.

The doorbell rang. She went to answer it and came back followed by the man whose portrait she was attempting, the second of her two blood stirrers, still stirring away. He put his arm possessively round her waist and kissed her. He nodded to me.

"How did the concert go?" she asked. He played a first violin in the London Symphony Orchestra.

"So-so," he said. "The Mozart B Flat went all right, except that some fool in the audience started clapping after the slow movement and ruined the transition to the allegro."

My cousin made sympathetic noises. I stood up. I did not enjoy seeing them so cozily together.

"Going?" asked Joanna, detaching herself.

"Yes."

"Good night, Rob," he said, yawning. He took off his black tie and loosened the neck of his shirt.

I said politely, "Good night, Brian." And may you rot, I thought.

Joanna came with me to the door and opened it, and I stepped out into the dark cobbled mews and turned to say good-by. She was silhouetted against the warm light in the studio room where Brian, I could see, was sitting and taking off his shoes.

I said flatly, "Thank you for the steak . . . and the television."

"Come again," she said.

"Yes. Well, good night."

"Good night," she said, and then in an afterthought added, "How is Paulina?"

"She is going to marry," I said, "Sir Morton Henge."

I am not sure what I expected in the way of sympathy, but I should have
known.

Joanna laughed.

CHAPTER 3

TWO WEEKS AFTER Art died I stayed a night in Peter Cloony's house.
It was the first Cheltenham meeting of the season, and having no car, I
went down as usual on the race train, carrying some overnight things in a
small suitcase. I had been engaged for two races at the meeting, one on each
day, and I intended to find a back-street pub whose charges would make the
smallest possible dent in my pocket. But Peter, seeing the case, asked me if I
was fixed up for the night, and offered me a bed. It was kind of him, for we
were not particularly close friends, and I thanked him and accepted.

From my point of view it was an unexciting day. My one ride, a novice
hurdler revoltingly called Neddikins, had no chance of winning. His past
form was a sorry record of falls and unfinished races. Tailed-off and pulled-up
figured largely. I wondered why on earth the owner bothered with the
wretched animal, but at the same time rehearsed in advance some complimentary things to say about it. I had long ago discovered that owners hated
to be told their horses were useless and often would not again employ a
jockey who spoke too much unpalatable truth. It was wiser not to answer the
typical question, "What do you think we should do with beautiful Neddikins next?" with an unequivocal "Shoot it."

By working hard from start to finish I managed to wake Neddikins up
slightly, so that although we finished plainly last, we were not exactly tailed-
off. A triumph, I considered it, to have got round at all, and to my surprise
this was also the opinion of his trainer, who clapped me on the shoulder and
offered me another novice hurdler on the following day.

Neddikins was the first horse I rode for James Axminster, and I knew I
had been asked because he had not wanted to risk injury to his usual jockey.
A good many rides of that sort came my way, but I was glad to have them. I

reckoned if I could gain enough experience on bad horses when nothing much was expected of me, it would stand me in good stead if ever I found myself on better ones.

At the end of the afternoon I joined Peter and we drove off in his sedate family sedan. He lived in a small village, scarcely more than a hamlet, in a hollow in the Cotswold Hills about twenty miles from Cheltenham. We turned off the main road onto a narrow secondary road bordered on each side by thick hedges. It seemed to stretch interminably across bare farmland, but eventually, turning a corner, it came to the edge of the plateau and one could see a whole village spread out in the small valley below.

Peter pointed. "That bungalow down there is where I live. The one with the white windows."

I followed his finger. I had time to see a neatly fenced little garden round a new-looking house before a curve in the road hid it from view. We slid down the hill, rounded several blind corners with a good deal of necessary horn blowing, and at the beginning of the village curled into an even smaller lane and drew up outside Peter's home. It was modern, brick built, and freshly attractive, with neatly edged flower beds and shaved squares of lawn.

Peter's wife opened the white front door and came down the path to meet us. She was, I saw, very soon to have a child. She herself looked hardly old enough to have left school. She spoke shyly.

"Do come in," she said, shaking my hand. "Peter telephoned to say you were coming, and everything is ready."

I followed her into the bungalow. It was extremely neat and clean and smelled of furniture polish. All the floors were covered with mottled soft-blue linoleum, with a few terra-cotta rugs scattered about. Peter's wife, she told me during the evening, had made the rugs herself.

In the sitting room there was only a sofa, a television set, and a dining table with four chairs. The bareness of the room was to some extent disguised by one wall being almost completely covered in photographs. They had been framed by Peter himself and were edged in passe-partout in several different bright colors, so that the effect was gay and cheerful. Peter showed them to me while his wife cooked the dinner.

They were clearly devoted to each other. It showed in every glance, every word, every touch. They seemed very well matched; good-natured, quickly moved to sympathy, sensitive, and with not a vestige of a sense of humor between them.

"How long have you two been married?" I asked, biting into a wedge of cheese.

Peter said, "Nine months," and his wife blushed beguilingly.

We cleared away the dishes and washed them, and spent the evening watching television and talking about racing. When we went to bed they apologized for the state of my bedroom.

"We haven't furnished it properly yet," said Peter's wife, looking at me with anxious eyes.

"I'll be very comfortable indeed," I said. "You are so kind to have had me at all." She smiled happily.

The bedroom contained a bed and a chair only. There was the blue linoleum on the floor, with a terra-cotta rug. A small mirror on the wall, some thin rust-colored curtains at the window, and a hook and two hangers on the back of the door to serve as a wardrobe. I slept well.

In the morning, after breakfast, Peter did a lot of household jobs while his wife showed me round the small garden. She seemed to know every flower and growing vegetable individually. The plants were cherished as thoroughly as the house.

"Peter does most of my housework just now," she said, looking fondly back at the house. "The baby is due in six days. He says I mustn't strain myself."

"He is a most considerate husband," I said.

"The best in the world," she said fervently.

It was because Peter insisted at the last minute on driving down to the village shop to fetch a loaf of bread to save his wife the walk that we started out for Cheltenham later than we had intended.

We wound up the twisty hill too fast for prudence, but nothing luckily was on its way down. At least, it seemed to be lucky until we had streaked across the farmland and were slowing down to approach the turn into the main road. That was when we first saw the tank carrier. It was slewed across the road diagonally, completely blocking the way.

Peter's urgent tooting on the horn produced one soldier, who ambled over to the car and spoke soothingly.

"I'm very sorry, sir, but we were looking for the road to Timberley."

"You turned too soon. It's the next road on the right," said Peter impatiently.

"Yes, I know," said the soldier. "We realized we had turned too soon, and my mate tried to back out again, but he made a right mess of it, and we've hit the hedge on the other side. As a matter of fact," he said casually, "we're ruddy well stuck. My mate's just hitched a lorry to go and ring up our HQ about it."

We both got out of the car to have a look, but it was true. The great unwieldy trailer tank carrier was solidly jammed across the mouth of the narrow lane, and the driver was gone.

Pale and grim, Peter climbed back into his seat with me beside him. He had to reverse for a quarter of a mile before we came to a gateway he could turn the car in; then we backtracked down the long bend-ridden hill, raced through the village and out onto the road on the far side. It led south, away from Cheltenham, and we had to make a long detour to get back to the right direction. Altogether the tank carrier added at least twelve miles to our journey.

Several times Peter said, "I'll be late," in a despairing tone of voice. He was, I knew, due to ride in the first race, and the trainer for whom he rode liked him to report to him in the weighing room an hour earlier. Trainers had to state the name of the jockey who would be riding their horse at least three quarters of an hour before the event; if they took a chance and declared a jockey who had not arrived, and then he did not arrive at all, however good the reason, the trainer was in trouble with the Stewards. Peter rode for a man who never took this risk. If his jockey was not there an hour before the race, he found a substitute; and since Peter was his jockey, the rule was a good one, because he was by nature a last-minute rusher who left no time margin for things to go wrong.

We reached the racecourse just forty-three minutes before the first race. Peter sprinted from the car park, but he had some way to go and we both knew that he wouldn't do it. As I followed him more slowly and walked across the big expanse of tarmac toward the weighing room I heard the click of the loudspeakers being turned on, and the announcer began to recite the runners and riders of the first race. P. Cloony was not among them.

I found him in the changing room, sitting on the bench with his head in his hands.

"He didn't wait," he said miserably. "He didn't wait. I knew he wouldn't. I knew it. He's put Ingersoll up instead."

I looked across the room to where Tick-Tock was pulling his boots up over his nylon stockings. He already wore the scarlet jersey which should have been Peter's. He caught my eye and grimaced and shook his head in sympathy; but it was not his fault he had been given the ride, and he had no need to be too apologetic.

The worst of it was that Tick-Tock won. I was standing beside Peter on the jockeys' stand when the scarlet colors skated past the winning post, and he made a choking sound as if he were about to burst into tears. He managed not to, but there was a certain dampness about his eyes and his face changed to a bloodless, grayish white.

"Never mind," I said awkwardly, embarrassed for him. "It's not the end of the world."

It had been unfortunate that we had arrived so late, but the trainer he rode for was a reasonable man, if impatient, and there was no question of his not engaging him in the future. Peter did in fact ride for him again that same afternoon, but the horse ran less well than was expected, and pulled up lame. My last glimpse of him showed a face still dragged down in lines of disappointment, and he was boring everyone in the weighing room by harping on the tank carrier over and over again.

For myself, things went slightly better. The novice chaser fell at the water jump, but went down slowly and I suffered nothing but grass stains on my breeches.

The young hurdler I was to ride for James Axminster in the last race on the card had as vile a reputation as his stablemate of the previous day and I had made completing the race my sole target. But for some reason the wayward animal and I got on very well together from the start, and to my surprise, an emotion shared by every single person present, we came over the last hurdle in second place and passed the leading horse on the uphill stretch to the winning post. The odds-on favorite finished fourth. It was my second win of the season, and my first ever at Cheltenham: and it was greeted with dead silence.

I found myself trying to explain it away to James Axminster in the winners' unsaddling enclosure.

"I'm very sorry, sir," I said. "I couldn't help it." I knew he hadn't a penny on it, and the owner had not even bothered to come to see the horse run.

He looked at me broodingly without answering, and I thought that there was one trainer who would not employ me again in a hurry. Sometimes it is as bad to win unexpectedly as to lose on a certainty.

I unbuckled the girths, pulled the saddle off over my arm, and stood waiting for the storm to break.

"Well, go along and weigh in," he said abruptly. "And when you're dressed I want to talk to you."

When I came out of the changing room he was standing just inside the weighing-room door talking to Lord Tirrold, whose horses he trained. They stopped talking and turned toward me as I went over to them, but I could not see their expressions clearly as they had their backs to the light.

James Axminster said, "What stable do you ride for most?"

I said, "I ride mainly for farmers who train their own horses. I haven't a steady job with a public trainer, but I have ridden for several when they have asked me. Mr. Kellar has put me up a few times." And that, I thought a little wryly, is the true picture of the smallness of the impression I had made in the racing world.

"I have heard one or two trainers say," said Lord Tirrold, speaking directly to Axminster, "that for their really bad horses they can always get Finn."

Axminster grinned back at him. "Just what I did today, and look at the result! How am I going to convince the owner it was as much a surprise to me as it will be to him when he hears about it? I've told him often that the horse is pretty useless." He turned to me. "You have made me look a proper fool, you know."

"I'm sorry, sir," I said again, and meant it.

"Don't look so glum about it. I'll give you another chance; several, in fact. There's a slow old plug you can ride for me on Saturday, if you're not booked already for that race, and two or three others next week. After that . . . we'll see."

"Thank you," I said dazedly. "Thank you very much."

It was as if he had thrust a gold brick into my hands when I had expected a scorpion: if I acquitted myself at all well on his horses, he might use me regularly as a second-string jockey. That would be, for me, a giant step up.

He smiled a warm, almost mischievous smile, which crinkled the skin round his eyes, and said, "Geranium in the handicap chase at Hereford on Saturday, then. Are you free?"

"Yes," I said.

"And you can do the weight? Ten stone?"

"Yes," I said. I'd need to lose another three pounds in the two days, but starvation had never seemed so attractive.

"Very well. I'll see you there."

"Yes, sir," I said.

He and Lord Tirrold turned away and went out of the weighing room

together, and I heard them laugh. I watched them go, the thin angular Lord
Tirrold and the even taller trainer, a pair who had between them won almost
every important event in the National Hunt calendar.

James Axminster was a big man in every sense. Six-foot-four and solidly
bulky, he moved and spoke and made decisions with easy assurance. He had
a big face with a prominent nose and a square-looking heavy lower jaw.
When he smiled his lower teeth showed in front of the upper ones, and they
were good strong teeth, evenly set and unusually white.

His stable was one of the six largest in the country: his jockey, Pip
Pankhurst, had been champion for the past two seasons; and his horses, about
sixty of them, included some of the best alive. To have been offered a toehold
in this setup was almost as frightening as it was miraculous. If I messed up
this chance, I thought, I might as well follow Art into oblivion.

I spent most of the next day running round Hyde Park in three sweaters
and a wind cheater and resisting the temptation to drink pints of water to replace what I had sweated off. Some of the other jockeys used dehydrating
pills to rid their bodies of fluid (which weighs more than fat and is easier to
shift), but I had found, the only time I took some, that they left me feeling almost too weak to ride.

At about six o'clock I boiled three eggs and ate them without salt or
bread, and then removed myself hurriedly, for my mother was entertaining
some friends at dinner, and the girl who came to cook for us on these occasions was beginning to fill the kitchen with demoralizingly savory smells. I
decided to go to the pictures to take my mind off my stomach; but it wasn't
a great success as I chose the film somewhat carelessly and found myself
watching three men staggering on their parched way through a blazing
desert sharing out their rations into ever-dwindling morsels.

After that I went to the Turkish baths on Jermyn Street and spent the
whole night there, sweating gently all evening and again when I woke in the
morning. Then I went back to the flat and ate three more boiled eggs, which
I no longer cared for very much, and at last made my way to Hereford.

The needle quivered when I sat on the scales with the lightest possible
saddle and thin boots. It swung up over the ten-stone mark and pendulumed
down and finally settled a hairsbreadth on the right side.

"Ten stone," said the clerk of the scales in a surprised voice. "What have
you been doing? Sandpapering it off?"

"More or less." I grinned.

In the parade ring James Axminster looked at the number boards where the weights the horses carried were recorded, if they differed from those printed in the race cards. He turned back to me.

"No overweight?" he asked.

"No, sir," I said matter-of-factly, as if it were the easiest thing in the world.

"Hm." He beckoned the lad who was leading round the slow old plug I was to ride and said, "You'll have to kick this old mare along a bit. She's lazy. A good jumper, but that's about all."

I was used to kicking lazy horses. I kicked and the mare jumped: and we finished third.

"Hm," said Axminster again as I unbuckled the girths. I took my saddle and weighed in—half a pound lighter—and changed into the colors of the other horse I had been engaged to ride that afternoon, and when I walked out into the weighing room, Axminster was waiting for me. He had a paper in his hand. He gave it to me without a word.

It was a list of five horses running in various races during the following week. Against each horse's name he had put the weight it had to carry and the race it was to run in. I read through them.

"Well?" he said. "Can you ride them?"

"I can ride four of them," I said. "But I'm already booked for that novice chase on Wednesday."

"Is it important? Can you get off?" he asked.

I would dearly have liked to say yes. The paper I held was an invitation to my personal paradise, and there was always the chance that if I refused one of his mounts, the man who got it might corner all the future ones.

"I . . . no," I said, "I ought not to. It's for the farmer who gave me my first few rides . . ."

Axminster smiled faintly, the lower teeth showing in front. "Very well. Ride the other four."

I said, "Thank you, sir. I'd be glad to." He turned away, and I folded up the precious list and put it in my pocket.

My other ride later that afternoon was for Corin Kellar. Since Art's death he had employed several different jockeys and moaned to them about the inconvenience of not having a first-class man always on call. As it was his treatment of Art that had driven a first-class man to leave him in the most drastic possible way, Tick-Tock and I considered him a case for psychiatry; but both of us were glad enough to ride his horses, and Tick-Tock had ridden more of them than anyone else.

"If Corin asks you," I said as we collected our saddles and helmets ready to weigh out for the race, "will you accept Art's job?"

"If he asks me, yes," said Tick-Tock. "He won't harass *me* into the here-after." He looked up slantwise from under his rakishly tilted eyebrows, the thin-lipped, wide mouth stretched in a carefree grin. A vivid, almost aggressive sanity molded the angular planes of his face, and for a moment he seemed to me more than ever to have been born too soon. He was what I pictured twenty-first-century man should be—intensely alive, curiously innocent, with no taint of apathy or anger or greed. He made me feel old. He was nineteen.

We went out together to the parade ring.

"Paste on a toothy leer," he said. "The eye of the world has swiveled our way."

I glanced up. From its drafty platform a television camera swung its square snout toward us as it followed the progress of a gray horse round the ring. It tracked briefly over us and moved on.

"I'd forgotten we were on the air," I said indifferently.

"Oh, yes," said Tick-Tock, "and the great man himself is here somewhere too, the one and only M. Kemp-Lore no less. Puff pastry, that man is."

"How do you mean?" I asked.

"A quick riser. And full of hot air. But rich, man, and tasty. A good crisp flavor, nice and crunchy."

I laughed. We joined Corin and he began to give us both our instructions for the race. Tick-Tock's mount was a good one, but I was as usual riding a horse of whom little was expected, and quite rightly, as it turned out. We trailed in a long way behind, and I saw from the numbers going up in the frame that Corin's other horse had won.

Corin and Tick-Tock and the horse's owner were conducting a mutual admiration session in the winner's enclosure when I walked back to the weighing room with my saddle, but Corin caught me by the arm as I went past and asked me to come straight out again, when I had dumped my saddle and helmet, to tell him how the horse had run.

When I rejoined him he was talking to a man who had his back toward me. I hovered, not wanting to interrupt, but Corin saw me and beckoned, and I walked across to them. The man turned round. He was in his early thirties,

I judged. Of average height and slim build, with good features and light hair. It never ceases to be disconcerting, meeting for the first time in the flesh a man whose face is as familiar to you as a brother's. It was Maurice Kemp-Lore.

Television is unflattering to everybody. It fattens the body and flattens the personality, so that to sparkle from the small screen an entertainer must be positively incandescent in real life, and Kemp-Lore was no exception. The charm which came over gradually in his program was instantly compelling when one met him. Intensely blue eyes looked at me from a firm, sun-tanned face; his handshake was quick and strong; his smile, infectious and warm, indicated his delight in meeting me. But it was a professional delight, and even as I responded to him I recognized that the effect he had on me was calculated. His stock in trade. All good interviewers know how to give people confidence so that they expand and flower, and Kemp-Lore was a master of his art. Dull men had shone as wits on his program, taciturn men chattered, bigoted men thought again.

"I see you were last in the race," he said. "Bad luck."

"Bad horse," said Corin, put into smiling good humor by his presence.

"I've been waiting for some time to do a program on—if you'll forgive me—an unsuccessful jockey." His smile took the sting out of his words. "Or at least, a jockey who is not yet successful. Perhaps that would be a fairer way of putting it?" His blue eyes twinkled. "Would you consider coming on my program and telling viewers what sort of life you lead? I have in mind your financial position, your reliance on chance rides, insecurity—that sort of thing. Just to give the public the reverse side of the coin. They know all about big retainers, and fat presents, and jockeys who win important races. I want to show them how a jockey who seldom wins even unimportant races manages to live. A jockey on the fringe." He smiled his warm smile. "Will you do it?"

"Yes," I said, "certainly. But I'm not really typical. I—"

He interrupted me. "Don't tell me anything now," he said. "I know enough about your career to find you suitable for what I have in mind, but I always prefer not to know the answers to my specific questions until we are actually on the air. It makes the whole thing more spontaneous. I have found that if I rehearse with my subject what we are going to say, the program comes over stiffly and unconvincingly. Instead, I will send you a list of the sort of questions I will be asking, and you can think out your replies. Okay?"

"Yes," I said. "All right."

"Good. Next Friday then. The program goes out at nine o'clock. Get to the studios by seven-thirty, will you? That gives time for seeing to lighting, makeup, and so on, and perhaps for a drink beforehand. Here is a card that will tell you how to get there." He produced a card, which had UNIVERSAL TELECAST printed in large capitals on one side and a simplified map of Willesden on the other.

"Oh, and by the way, there will be a fee, of course, and your expenses." He smiled sympathetically, letting me know that he knew that that was good news.

"Thank you." I smiled back. "I'll be there."

He spoke a word to Corin and strolled away. I turned to Corin and caught on his face, as he watched the retreating figure of Kemp-Lore, the same expression that I saw so often on hangers-on round my parents. The smug, fawning smirk which meant I am on speaking terms with a famous person, clever me. It would have been more impressive, I thought, if like most other trainers he had taken knowing the illustrious Kemp-Lore entirely for granted.

"I know Maurice quite well," said Corin aloud, in a self-satisfied voice. "He asked my advice about whether you'd be any good as his—er—unsuccessful jockey, and I told him to go ahead."

"Thanks," I said, as he waited for it.

"Yes, a grand fellow, Maurice. Good family, you know. His father won the National—an amateur, of course—and his sister is the best lady point-to-point rider there has been for years. Poor old Maurice, though, he hardly rides at all. Doesn't even hunt. Horses give him the most ghastly asthma, you know. He's very cut up about it. Still, he'd never have taken to broadcasting if he'd been able to race, so perhaps it's all for the best."

"I dare say," I said. I was still in lightweight silk colors and breeches and the afternoon was growing cool. I dragged the conversation back to the horse I had just come last on, got the postmortem over, and eventually went back to the weighing room to change.

The jockeys had already gone out for the last race, but several others were standing about in various stages of undress, gossiping and putting on their street clothes. As I went down the room I saw Grant Oldfield standing by my peg, holding a paper in his hand, and on drawing nearer I was annoyed to find that it was the list of horses James Axminster had given me. Grant had been going through my pockets.

My protest was never uttered. Without a word, without any warning, Grant swung his fist and punched me heavily on the nose.

CHAPTER 4

THE AMOUNT OF blood which resulted would have done credit to a
clinicful of donors. It splashed in a scarlet stain down the front of my pale-
green silk shirt and made big uneven blotches on the white breeches. There
were large spots of it on the bench and on the floor and it was all over my
hands where I had tried to wipe it out of my mouth.

"For God's sake, lay him down on his back," said one of the valets, hurrying over. His advice was almost unnecessary, since I was already lying
down, mostly on the floor but half propped up by the leg of the bench. It was
where that one blow, catching me off balance, had felled me.

Grant stood at my feet, looking down as if surprised to have caused so
much mess. I could have laughed if I had not been so busy swallowing what
seemed like cupfuls of my own blood.

Young Mike thrust a saddle under my shoulders and pushed my head
backward over it. A second later he was piling a cold, wet towel across the
bridge of my nose; and gradually the breath-clogging bleeding lessened and
stopped.

"You'd better stay there for a bit," said Mike. "I'll go and get one of the
first-aid men to see to you."

"Don't bother," I said. "Please don't bother, it's all right now."

He came back irresolutely from the door and stood by my head. He
looked upside down to me, as my eyes were level with his ankles.

"What the hell did you do that for?" he said to Grant.

I wanted to hear his answer too, but Grant did not reply. He scowled
down at me, then turned on his heel and pushed his way out of the changing
room against the incoming tide of the jockeys returning from the last race.
The list of Axminster horses fluttered to the floor in his wake. Mike picked it
up and put it into my outstretched hand.

Tick-Tock dumped his saddle on the bench, tipped back his helmet, and
put his hands on his hips.

"What have we here? A bloodbath?" he said.

"Nosebleed," I said.

"You don't say."

The others began crowding round and I decided I'd been lying down long enough. I lifted the towel off my face and stood up gingerly. All was well. The fountains had dried up.

"Grant socked him," said one of the jockeys who had been there all the time. "Why?"

"Ask me another," I said. "Or ask Grant."

"You ought to report it to the Stewards."

"It's not worth it," I said.

I cleaned myself up and changed, and walked down to the station with Tick-Tock.

"You must know why he hit you," he said. "Or was it merely target practice?"

I handed him Axminster's list. He read it and gave it back.

"Yes, I see. Hatred, envy and jealousy. You're stepping into the shoes he couldn't fill himself. He had his chance there, and he muffed it."

"What happened?" I asked. "Why did Axminster drop him?"

"I don't honestly know," Tick-Tock said. "You'd better ask Grant and find out what mistakes not to make." He grinned. "Your nose looks like a vulgar seaside postcard."

"It's good enough for the goggle box," I said. I told him about Maurice Kemp-Lore's invitation.

"My dear sir," he said, sweeping off his Tyrolean hat and making me a mocking bow, "I am impressed."

"You're a fool," I said, grinning.

"Thank God."

We went our ways, Tick-Tock to his digs in Berkshire and I to Kensington. The flat was empty, the usual state of affairs on Saturday evenings, a busy night for concerts. I took half the ice cubes from the refrigerator, wrapped them in a plastic bag and a tea towel, and lay down on the bed with the ice bag balanced on my forehead. My nose felt like a jelly. Grant's fist had had the power of severe mental disturbance behind it.

I shut my eyes and thought about them, Grant and Art; two disintegrated people. One had been driven to violence against himself, and the other had turned violent against the world. Poor things, I thought rather too complacently, they were not stable enough to deal with whatever had under-mined them: and I remembered that easy pity, later on.

On the following Wednesday Peter Cloony came to the races bubbling over with happiness. The baby was a boy, his wife was fine, everything was rosy. He slapped us all on the back and told us we didn't know what we were missing. The horse he rode that afternoon started favorite and ran badly, but it didn't dampen his spirits.

The next day he was due to ride in the first race, and he was late. We knew before he arrived that he had missed his chance, because five minutes before the deadline for declaring jockeys his trainer had sent an official into the changing room to find out if he was there, and he wasn't.

I was standing outside the weighing room when Peter finally came, forty minutes before the first race. He was running over the grass, anxiety clear on his face even from a distance. His trainer detached himself from the group of people he had been talking to and intercepted him. Fragments of angry remarks floated across to me.

"Is this your idea of an hour before the first? . . . I've had to get another jockey . . . very stupid of you . . . second time in a week . . . irresponsible . . . not the way to go on if you want to keep your job with me." He stalked away.

Peter brushed past me, white, trembling, and looking sick, and when I went back into the changing room a short time later he was sitting on a bench with his head in his hands.

"What happened this time?" I asked. "Is your wife all right? And the baby?" I thought he must have been so busy attending to them that he had forgotten to watch the clock.

"They're fine," he said miserably. "My mother-in-law is staying with us to look after them. I wasn't late setting out . . . only five minutes or so . . . but"—he stood up and gazed at me with his large, moist-looking eyes—"you'll never believe it, but there was something else stuck across the lane, and I had to go miles round again, even farther than last time . . ." His voice trailed off as I looked at him in disbelief.

"Not another tank carrier?" I asked incredulously.

"No, a car. An old car, one of those heavy old Jaguars. It had its nose in the hedge and one front wheel in the ditch, and it was jammed tight, right across the lane."

"You couldn't have helped its driver push it straight again?" I asked.

"There wasn't any driver. No one at all. And the car doors were locked, and the hand brake was full on, and he'd left the thing in gear. The stinking bastard." Peter seldom used such strong language. "Another man had driven up the hill behind me and we both tried to shift the Jag, but it was absolutely hopeless. We had to reverse again for miles, and he had to go first, and he wouldn't hurry a yard . . . he had a new car and he was afraid of scratching it."

"It's very bad luck," I said inadequately.

"Bad luck!" he repeated explosively, apparently near to tears. "It's more than bad luck, it's—it's awful. I can't afford . . . I need the money." He stopped talking and swallowed several times, and sniffed. "We've got a big mortgage to pay off," he said, "and I didn't know babies could cost so much. And my wife had to stop working, which we hadn't reckoned on . . . we didn't mean to have a baby so soon."

I remember vividly the new little bungalow with its cheap blue linoleum, its homemade terra-cotta rugs, its bare, bare furnishings. And he had a car to run and now a child to keep. I saw that the loss of a ten-guinea riding fee was a calamity.

He had not been booked for any other ride that afternoon, and he spent the whole day mooching about the weighing room so as to be under the eye of any trainers looking hurriedly for a jockey. He wore a desperate, hunted look all the time, and I knew that that alone would have discouraged me had I been a trainer. He left, unemployed and disconsolate, just before the fifth race, having done himself no good at all in the eyes of every trainer at the meeting.

I watched him trailing off to the car park as I walked down from the weighing room to the parade ring for my one and only ride of the day, and I felt a surge of irritation against him. Why couldn't he pretend a little, make light of his misfortune, shrug it off? And why above all didn't he leave himself a margin for error on his journeys, when unprompt arrivals cost him so much? A punctured tire, a windscreen shattered by a flying stone, anything might make him late. It didn't have to be as unforeseeable as a tank carrier or a locked Jaguar wedged immovably across his path. And what a dismal coincidence, I reflected, that it should have happened twice in a week.

James Axminster smiled his disconcerting, heavy-jawed smile in the parade ring and introduced me to the owner of the horse I was to ride. He shook hands and we made the usual desultory pre-race conversation. The middle-aged handicap hurdler plodding sleepily round the ring was the third Axminster horse I had ridden during the week, and I had already grown to appreciate the sleekness and slickness of his organization. His horses were well schooled and beautifully turned out, and there was nothing makeshift or second best in any of his equipment. Success and prosperity spoke from every brightly initialed horse rug, every top quality bridle, every brush, bandage and bucket that came to the meetings.

In the two earlier races that week I had been riding the stable's second string while Pip Pankhurst took his usual place on the better horses. Thursday's handicap hurdle, however, was all my own because Pip could not do the weight.

"Anything under 10 stone 6, and it's yours," he told me cheerfully, when he found I was riding some of his stable's horses. "Anything under 10.6 is hardly worth riding, anyway."

By eating and drinking very little I had managed to keep my riding weight down to 10 stone for a whole week. This meant a body weight of 9 stone 8, which was a strain at my height, but with Pip in that ungrudging frame of mind it was well worth it.

James Axminster said, "At the fourth hurdle, you want to be somewhere in the middle. About three from home, providing they're not too strung out, you want to lie about fourth. He takes some time to get into top gear, so start him moving going into the second last. Keep him going, try to come up to the leader at the last and see how much you can gain in the air there. This horse is a great jumper, but has no finishing speed. Very one-paced. See what you can do, anyway."

He had not given me such detailed instructions before, and it was the first time he had mentioned anything about what to do at the last obstacle. I felt a deep quiver of excitement in my stomach. At last I was about to ride a horse whose trainer would not be thoroughly surprised if he won.

I followed my instructions to the letter, and coming into the last hurdle level with two other horses I kicked my old mount with all the determination I could muster. He responded with a zipping leap which sped him clean past the other horses in mid-air and landed us a good two lengths clear of them. I heard the clatter of the hurdles as the others rapped them, and basely hoped they had made stumbling, time-wasting landings. It was true that the old hurdler could not quicken. I got him balanced and ran him straight to the winning post, using my whip hardly at all and concentrating mainly on sitting still and not disturbing him. He held on gamely, and still had half a length in hand when we passed the post. It was a gorgeous moment.

"Well done," said Axminster matter-of-factly. Winners were nothing out of the ordinary to him. I unbuckled the girths and slid the saddle off over my arm, and patted the hurdler's sweating neck.

The owner was delighted. "Well done, well done," he said to the horse, Axminster and me indiscriminately. "I never thought he'd pull it off, James, even though I took your advice and backed him."

I looked quickly at Axminster. His piercingly blue eyes regarded me quizz-ically.

"Do you want the job?" he asked. "Second to Pip, regular?"

I nodded and dragged in a deep breath, and said, "Yes." It sounded like a croak.

The hurdler's owner laughed. "It's Finn's lucky week. John Ballerton tells me Maurice is interviewing him on his television program tomorrow evening."

"Really?" Axminster said. "I'll try and watch it."

I went to weigh in and change, and when I came out Axminster gave me another list of horses, four of them, which he wanted me to ride the follow-ing week.

"From now on," he said, "I don't want you to accept any rides without finding out first if I need you. All right?"

"Yes, sir," I said, trying not to show too much of the idiotic delight I was feeling. But he knew. He was too old a hand not to. His eyes glimmered with understanding and friendliness and promise.

I TELEPHONED JOANNA. "How about dinner? I want to celebrate."

"What?" she asked economically.

"A winner. A new job. All's right with the world," I said.

"You sound as if you've been celebrating already."

"No," I said. "Any drunkenness you can hear in my voice is due to being hit on the head by good luck."

She laughed. "All right then. Where?"

"Hennibert's," I said. It was a small restaurant on St. James's Street with a standard of cooking to match its address, and prices to match both.

"Oh, yes," said Joanna. "Shall I come in my golden coach?"

"I mean it," I said. "I've earned forty pounds this week. I want to spend some of it. And besides, I'm hungry."

"You won't get a table," she said.

"It's booked."

"I'm sold," she said. "I'll be there at eight."

She came in a taxi, a compliment to me as she was a girl who liked walking. She wore a dress I had not seen before, a slender straight affair made of firm, deep-blue material, which moved with a faint shimmer when the light fell on it. Her springy dark hair curved neatly down onto the nape of her neck, and the slanting outward tapering lines she had drawn on her eyelids made her black eyes look bigger and deep-set and mysterious. Every male head turned to look at her as we walked down the room; yet she was not pretty, not eye-catchingly glamorous, not even notably well dressed. She looked . . . I surprised myself with the word . . . intelligent.

We ate avocados with French dressing and beef Stroganoff with spinach, and late-crop strawberries and cream, and a mushroom and bacon and prune savory. For me, after so many bird-sized meals, it was a feast. We took a long time eating and drank a bottle of wine, and sat over our coffee talking with the ease of a friendship that stretched back to childhood. Most of the time, after so much practice, I could keep my more uncousinly feelings for Joanna well concealed from her, and it was necessary to conceal them because I knew from past experience that if I even approached the subject of love she would begin to fidget and avoid my eyes, and would very soon find a good reason for leaving. If I wanted to enjoy her company, it had to be on her terms.

She seemed genuinely pleased about the James Axminster job. Even though racing didn't interest her, she saw clearly what it meant to me.

"It's like the day the musical director of the Handel Society picked me out of the choir to sing my first recitative. I felt like a pouter pigeon and so full of air that I thought I would need guy ropes to keep my feet on the ground."

"Heady stuff," I agreed. My first elation had settled down to a warm cozy glow of satisfaction. I did not remember ever having felt so content.

I told her about the television program.

"Tomorrow?" she said. "Good, I think I'll be free to watch you. You don't do things by halves, do you?"

I grinned. "This is just the start," I said. I almost believed it.

We walked all the way back to Joanna's studio. It was a clear crisp night, with the stars blazing coldly in the black sky. Depth upon depth of infinity. We stopped in the dark mews outside Joanna's door and looked up.

"They put things into proportion, don't they?" she said.

"Yes." I wondered what it was that she needed to see in proportion. I looked at her. It was a mistake. The uptilted face with starlight reflected in the shadowy eyes, the dark hair tousled again by our walk, the strong line of throat, the jut of breasts close to my arm, they swept me ruthlessly into the turmoil I had been suppressing all evening.

"Thank you for coming," I said abruptly. "Good night, Joanna."

She said, surprised, "Wouldn't you like some more coffee . . . or something?"

Or something. Yes.

I said, "I couldn't eat or drink another thing. Anyway . . . there's Brian . . ."

"Brian's in Manchester, on tour," she said. But it was a statement of fact, not an invitation.

"Oh. Well, all the same, I think I'd better get some sleep," I said.

"All right, then." She was undisturbed. "A lovely dinner, Rob. Thank you." She put her hand for a moment on my shoulder in a friendly fashion and smiled good night. She put the key in her door and opened it and waved briefly to me as I turned and started back down the mews. She shut her door. I swore violently, aloud. It wasn't much relief. I looked up at the sky. The stars went on whizzing round in their courses, uncaring and cold.

CHAPTER 5

THEY GAVE ME what in the Finn family was known as F.I.P. treatment at the Universal Telecast Studios. Fairly Important Person. It meant being met by someone well enough up in the hierarchy of the organization for it to be clear that trouble was being taken, but not so high that he needed to be supported by lieutenants.

My mother was a connoisseur of all the shades between V.I.P. and F.I.P. and invariably noticed every detail of the pains or lack of them taken to make her feel comfortable. Her awareness had rubbed off on to me at a very early age and the whole gambit caused me a lot of quiet amusement when I grew up. Years of being a U.I.P. (Unimportant Person) had only sharpened my appreciation.

I went through the swinging glass doors into the large echoing entrance

hall and asked the girl at the reception desk where I should go. She smiled
kindly. Would I sit down, she said, gesturing to a nearby sofa. I sat. She spoke
into the telephone: "Mr. Finn is here, Gordon."

Within ten seconds a burly young man with freckles and a rising-young-
executive, navy-blue, pin-striped suit advanced briskly from one of the corridors.

"Mr. Finn?" he said expansively, holding out a hand protruding from a
snowy gold-linked shirt cuff.

"Yes," I said, standing up and shaking hands.

"Glad to have you here. I am Gordon Kildare, Associate Producer. Maurice is up in the studio running over the last-minute details, so I suggest we
go along and have a drink and a sandwich first." He led the way down the
corridor he had come from and we turned in through an open door into a
small, impersonal reception room. On the table stood bottles and glasses and
four plates of fat, freshly cut and appetizing-looking sandwiches.

"What will you have?" he asked hospitably, his hands hovering over the
bottles.

"Nothing, thank you," I said.

He was not put out. "Perhaps afterward, then?" He poured some whiskey
into a glass, added soda and raised it to me, smiling. "Good luck," he said. "Is
this your first time on television?"

I nodded.

"The great thing is to be natural." He picked up a sandwich with a pink
filling and took a squelchy bite.

The door opened and two more men came in. Introduced to me as Dan
something and Paul something, they were a shade less carefully dressed than
Gordon Kildare, to whom they deferred. They too dug into the sandwiches
and filled their glasses, and wished me luck and told me to be natural.

Maurice Kemp-Lore strode briskly in with a couple of sports-jacketed assistants in tow.

"My dear chap," he greeted me, shaking me warmly by the hand. "Glad
to see you're here in good time. Has Gordon been looking after you? That's
right. Now, what are you drinking?"

"Nothing just now," I said.

"Oh? Oh, well, never mind. Perhaps afterward? You got the list of questions all right?"

I nodded.

"Have you thought out some answers?"

"Yes," I said.

"Good, good. That's fine," he said.

Gordon handed him a well-filled glass and offered him the sandwiches. The assistants helped themselves. It dawned on me that the refreshments provided for the entertainment of visitors probably served all of them as their main evening meal.

Kemp-Lore looked at his watch. "Our other guest is cutting it rather fine." As he spoke the telephone rang. Gordon answered it, listened briefly, said, "He's here, Maurice," and opened the door.

Kemp-Lore went out first, followed by Gordon and either Dan or Paul, who looked very much alike. It was a more impressive welcoming committee than had been accorded me; I smiled to think of what my mother would have said.

A sports-jacketed assistant offered me sandwiches.

"No?" he said. "Oh, well, a lot of people feel like that beforehand. You'll be very hungry afterward." He put two sandwiches carefully together and stretched open his mouth to bite them.

The voice of Kemp-Lore could be heard coming back along the corridor talking with someone who spoke in a harsh voice with a nasal twang. I wondered idly who the other guest would be and whether I knew him. At the doorway Kemp-Lore stood respectfully back to let his guest precede him into the room. My spirits sank. Paunch and horn rims well to the fore, Mr. John Ballerton allowed himself to be ushered in.

Kemp-Lore introduced all the television men to him.

"And Rob Finn, of course, you know?" he said.

Ballerton nodded coldly in my direction without meeting my eyes. Evidently it still rankled with him that I had seen him sicking up beside Art's body. Perhaps he knew that I had not kept it a secret from the other jockeys.

"It's time we went up to the studio, I think," Kemp-Lore said, looking inquiringly at Gordon, who nodded.

We all filed out into the corridor, and as I passed the table I noticed the sandwich plates now held nothing but crumbs and a few straggly pieces of cress.

The smallish studio held a chaotic-looking tangle of cameras trailing their thick cables over the floor. At one side there was a shallow carpet-covered platform on which stood three low chairs and a coffee table. A tray with three cups, cream jug and sugar bowl shared the table with three empty balloon brandy glasses, a silver cigarette box, and two large glass ashtrays.

Kemp-Lore took Ballerton and me toward this arrangement.

"We want to look as informal as possible," he said pleasantly. "As if we had just had dinner and were talking over coffee and brandy and cigars."

He asked Ballerton to sit in the left-hand chair and me in the right, and then took his place between us. Set in front and slightly to one side stood a monitor set with a blank screen; and in a semicircle a battery of cameras converged their menacing black lenses in our direction.

Gordon and his assistants spent some time checking their lights, which dazed us with a dazzling intensity for a few moments, and then tested for sound while the three of us made stilted conversation over the empty cups. When he was satisfied, Gordon came over to us.

"You all need makeup," he said. "Maurice, you'll see to yours as usual? Then Mr. Ballerton and Mr. Finn, I'll show you where to go. If you will follow me?"

He led us to a small room off one corner of the studio. There were two girls there in pink coveralls and bright smiles.

"It won't take long," they said, smoothing colored cream into our skins. "Just a little darkener under the eyes . . . that's right. Now powder . . ." They patted the powder on with pads of cotton wool, carefully flicking off the excess. "That's all."

I looked in the mirror. The makeup softened and blurred both the outlines of the face and the texture of the skin. I didn't much care for it.

"You'd look ill on television without it," the girls assured us. "You need makeup to look natural and healthy."

Ballerton frowned and complained as one of them powdered the bald patch on his head. The girl insisted politely. "It'll shine too much otherwise, you see," she said, and went on patting his head with the cotton wool.

He caught me grinning at him and it clearly made him furious, raising a dark flush under the sun-tone makeup. There was no question of his ever sharing a rueful joke at his own expense, and I should have known it. I sighed to myself. This made twice that I had seen him at what he considered a disadvantage, and though I had not meant at all to antagonize him, it seemed that I had made a thorough job of it.

We went back into the studio and Kemp-Lore beckoned to us to take our place in the chairs on the platform.

"I'll just run through the order of the program," he said, "so that you will know what to expect. After the introductory music I am going to talk to you first, John, along the lines we discussed. After that, Rob will tell us what his sort of life entails. We have some film of a race you rode in, Rob, which we are using as an illustration, and I plan to fit that in fairly near the beginning of our talk. It will be thrown onto that screen over there." He pointed.

"For the last few minutes, John will have a chance to comment on what you have said and we might have a final word or two from you. We'll see how it goes. Now, the great thing is to talk naturally. I've explained that too much rehearsal spoils the spontaneity of a program like this, but it means that a lot of the success of the next quarter of an hour depends on you. I'm sure you will both do splendidly." He finished his pep talk with a cheerful grin, and I did in fact feel confidence flowing into me from him.

One of the sports-jacketed assistants stepped onto the shallow platform with a coffeepot in one hand and a brandy bottle in the other. He poured hot black coffee into the three cups, and put the pot down on the tray. Then he uncorked the brandy and wetted the bottom of the balloon glasses.

"No expense spared," he said cheerfully. He produced three cigars from the breast pocket of the sports jacket and offered them to us. Ballerton accepted one and sniffed it and rolled it between his fingers, curving his bad-tempered mouth into what passed with him for a smile.

"Two minutes," shouted a voice.

The spotlights flashed on, dazzling as before, blacking out everything in the studio. For a moment the monitor set showed a close-up of the coffee cups: then it went dark and the next picture on it was an animated cartoon advertising petrol. It was tuned now to what was actually being transmitted.

"Thirty seconds. Quiet please. Quiet please," Gordon said.

A hush fell over the whole area. I glanced at the monitor set in front of us. It was busy with a silent advertisement for soap flakes. Dimly seen beyond the lights, Gordon stood with his hand raised. There was dead silence. Steam rose gently from the three coffee cups. Everyone waited. Kemp-Lore beside me arranged his features in the well-known smile, looking straight ahead at the round black lens of the camera. The smile stayed in position for ten seconds without wavering.

On the monitor set the superimposed horses galloped and faded. Gordon's hand swept down briskly. The camera in front of Kemp-Lore developed a shining red eye and he began to speak, pleasantly, intimately, straight into a million sitting rooms.

"Good evening . . . tonight I am going to introduce you to two people who are both deeply involved with National Hunt racing, but who look at it, so to speak, from opposite poles. First, here is Mr. John Ballerton . . ." He gave him a good build-up but overdid the importance. There were about forty-nine other members of the National Hunt Committee (including Kemp-Lore's own father) all at least as active and devoted as the fat man now basking in praise.

Skillfully guided by Kemp-Lore, he talked about his duties as one of the three Stewards at a race meeting. It involved, he said, hearing both sides if there was an objection to a winner and awarding the race justly to the more deserving, and, yes, summoning jockeys and trainers for minor infringements of the rules and fining them a fiver or a tenner a time.

I watched him on the monitor set. I had to admit he looked a solid, sober, responsible citizen with right on his side. The aggressive horn rims gave him, on the screen, a definite air of authority; also for the occasion his habitually sour expression had given way to a rather persuasive geniality. No one watching the performance Kemp-Lore coaxed out of him would have suspected him to be the bigoted, pompous bully we knew on the racecourse. I understood at last how he had come to be voted on to the National Hunt Committee.

Before I expected it, Kemp-Lore was turning round to me. I swallowed convulsively. He smiled at the camera.

"And now," he said with the air of one producing a treat, "here is Rob Finn. This is a young steeplechase jockey just scratching the surface of his career. Few of you will have heard of him. He has won no big races, nor ridden any well-known horses, and that is why I have invited him here tonight to meet you, to give us all a glimpse of what it is like to try to break into a highly competitive sport."

The red light was burning on the camera pointing at me. I smiled at it faintly. My tongue stuck to the roof of my mouth.

"First," he went on, "here is a piece of film which shows Finn in action. He is the rider with the white cap, fourth from last."

We watched on the monitor set. I was all too easy to pick out. It was one of the first races I ever rode in, and my inexperience showed sorely. During the few seconds the film lasted the white cap lost two places, and as an illustration of an unsuccessful jockey it could not have been bettered.

The film faded out and Kemp-Lore said, smiling, "How did you set about starting to be a jockey, once you had decided on it?"

I said, "I knew three farmers who owned and trained their own horses, and I asked them to let me try my hand in a race."

"And did they?"

"Yes, in the end," I agreed. I could have added, "After I had promised to return the riding fees and not even ask for expenses"; but the method I had used to persuade the string of farmers to give me rides was strictly against the rules.

"Usually," Kemp-Lore said, turning toward the camera, which immediately glowed with its red eye, "jumping jockeys either start as amateur steeplechase riders or as apprentices on the flat, but I understand that you did neither of these things, Rob?"

"No," I said. "I started too old to be an apprentice and I couldn't be an amateur because I had earned my living riding horses."

"As a stable lad?" He put it in the form of a question but from his intonation he clearly expected me to say yes. It was, after all, by far the commonest background of jockeys riding as few races as I had been doing.

"No," I said.

He was waiting for me to go on, his eyebrows a fraction raised in a tinge of surprise mingled with what looked like the beginning of apprehension. Well, I thought in amusement, you wouldn't listen when I said I was hardly typical, so if my answers are not what you expect, it's entirely your own fault.

I said, "I was away from England for some years, wandering round the world, you know. Mainly in Australia and South America. Most of the time I got jobs as a stockman, but I spent a year in New South Wales working as a hand in a traveling rodeo. Ten seconds on the bucking bronc; that sort of thing." I grinned.

"Oh." The eyebrows rose another fraction, and there was a perceptible pause before he said, "How very interesting." He sounded as if he meant it. He went on: "I wish we had more time to hear about your experiences, but I want to give viewers a picture of the economics of a jockey in your position . . . trying to make a living on a race or two a week. Now, your fee is ten guineas a time, that's right? . . ."

He took me at some length through my finances, which didn't sound too good when dissected into traveling expenses, valets' fees, replacement of kit and so on. It emerged quite clearly that my net income over the past two years was less than I could have earned driving a delivery van, and that my future prospects were not demonstrably much better. I could almost feel the thought clicking into the viewers' heads that I was a fool.

Kemp-Lore turned deferentially to Ballerton. "John, have you any comment to make on what we have been hearing from Rob?"

A trace of purely malicious pleasure crept into Ballerton's man-of-authority smile.

"All these young jockeys complain too much," he stated in his harsh voice, ignoring the fact that I had not complained at all. "If they aren't very good at their job they shouldn't expect to be highly paid. Racehorse owners don't want to waste their money and their horses' chances by putting up jockeys in whom they have no confidence. I speak as an owner myself, of course."

"Eh . . . of course," said Kemp-Lore. "But surely every jockey has to make a start? And there must always be large numbers of jockeys who never quite reach the top grade, but who have a living to make, and families to support."

"They'd be better off in a factory, earning a fair wage on a production line," said Ballerton, with heavy, reasonable-sounding humor. "If they can't endure the fact that they are unsuccessful without sniveling about how poor they are, they ought to get out of racing altogether. Not many of them do," he added with an unkind chuckle, "because they like wearing those bright silks. People turn to look at them as they go by, and it flatters their little egos."

There was a gasp somewhere out in the dark studio at this ungentlemanly blow below the belt, and I saw out of the corner of my eye that the red spot on the camera pointing at me was glowing. What expression it had initially caught on my face I did not know, but I raised a smile for Mr. Ballerton then, as sweet and cheerful and forgiving a smile as ever turned the other cheek. It was made easier by the certain knowledge that wearing bright shirts was if anything an embarrassment to me, not a gratification.

Kemp-Lore's head switched to me. "And what do you say to that, Rob?"

I spoke truthfully, vehemently, and straight from the heart. "Give me a horse and a race to ride it in, and I don't care if I wear silks or . . . or . . . pajamas. I don't care if there's anyone watching or not. I don't care if I don't earn much money, or if I break my bones, or if I have to starve to keep my weight down. All I care about is racing . . . racing . . . and winning, if I can."

There was a small silence.

"I can't explain it," I said.

Both of them were staring at me. John Ballerton looked as if a squashed wasp had revived and stung him, and his earlier animosity settled and deepened into a scowl. And Kemp-Lore? There was an expression in his face that I could not read at all. There were only a few empty seconds before he turned smoothly back to his camera and slid the familiar smile into place, but I felt irrationally that something important had taken place in them. I found it oddly disturbing not to have the slightest clue to what it was.

Kemp-Lore launched into his usual review of the following week's racing, and was very soon closing the program with the customary words: "See you all next week at the same time."

The image on the monitor faded on Kemp-Lore's smile and changed to another soap advertisement. The hot spotlight flicked off and my eyes began to get used to not being dazzled.

Gordon strode up beaming. "A very good program. It came over well. Just what they like, an argument with an edge to it. Well done, well done, Mr. Ballerton, Mr. Finn. Splendid." He shook us both by the hand.

Kemp-Lore stood up and stretched and grinned around at us all. "Well, John. Well, Rob. Thank you both very much." He bent down, picked up my brandy glass and handed it to me. "Drink it," he said, "you deserve it." He smiled warmly. He crackled with released tension.

I smiled back and drank the brandy, and reflected again how superlative he was at his job. By encouraging Ballerton to needle me he had drawn from me, for the ears of a few million strangers, a more soul-baring statement than I would ever have made privately to a close friend.

A good deal of backslapping followed, and more plates of sandwiches were dealt with downstairs in the reception room before I left the television building and went back to Kensington. In view of the approval which had been generously, if undeservedly, heaped upon Ballerton and me after the show, I wondered why it was that I felt more apprehensive than I had before it started.

CHAPTER 6

THREE WEEKS AND a day after the broadcast, Pip Pankhurst broke his leg. His horse, falling with him and on him at the last hurdle of the second race on a dreary, drizzly mid-November Saturday afternoon, made a thorough job of putting the champion jockey out of action for the bulk of the steeplechasing season.

The first-aid men beside the hurdle were slow to move him into the ambulance for the good reason that a sharp arrow of shinbone was sticking out at a crazy angle through a tear in the thin leather racing boot; and they finally managed to lift him onto a stretcher, one of them told me later, only because Pip slid off into a dead faint.

From the stands I saw only the white flag waving, the ambulance creeping down over the bumpy ground, and the flat, ominously unmoving figure of Pip on the ground. It would be untrue to say that I went down the stairs to the weighing room with a calm heart. However sincere my pity for his plight might be, the faint chance that I might take his place in the following race was playing hop, skip, and jump with my pulse.

It was the big race of the day, the big race of the week, a three-mile chase with a substantial prize put up by a firm of brewers. It had attracted a good number of top horses and had been well discussed on the sports pages of all the day's papers. Pip's mount, which belonged to Lord Tirrold, was the rising star of the Axminster stable; a stringy six-year-old brown gelding with nothing much to recommend him at first sight; but intelligent, fast, and a battler. He had all the qualities of a world beater, and his best years lay ahead. At present he was still reckoned "promising." He was called Template.

Stifling hope is a hopeless business. As I went into the weighing room I saw James Axminster talking to Pip's close friend, another leading jockey. The jockey shook his head, and across the room I watched his lips say, "No, I can't."

Axminster turned slowly round looking at faces. I stood still and waited. Gradually his head came round and he saw me. He looked at me steadily, pondering, unsmiling. Then his eyes went past me and focused on someone to my left. He came to a decision and walked briskly past me.

Well, what did I expect? I had ridden for him for only four weeks. Three winners. A dozen also-rans. During the past fortnight I had taken digs in the village near his stable and ridden out at exercise on his horses every morning; but I was still the new boy, the unknown, unsuccessful jockey of the television program. I began to walk disconsolately over to the changing-room door.

"Rob," he said in my ear. "Lord Tirrold says you can ride his horse. You'd better tell Pip's valet; he has the colors."

I half turned toward him. They stood together, the two tall men, looking at me appraisingly, knowing they were giving me the chance of a lifetime, but not sure that I was up to it.

"Yes, sir," I said, and went on into the changing room, queerly steadied by having believed that I had been passed over.

I rode better than I had ever done before, but that was probably because Template was the best horse I had ever ridden. He was smooth and steely, and his rocketing spring over the first fence had me gasping; but I was ready for it at the second, and exulted in it at the third; and by the fourth I knew I had entered a new dimension of racing.

Neither Axminster nor Lord Tirrold had given me any orders in the paddock on how to shape the race. They had been too concerned about Pip, whom they had just briefly visited. The sight of his shattered leg had left them upset and preoccupied.

Axminster said only, "Do the best you can, Rob," and Lord Tirrold, unusually tactless for so diplomatic a man, said gloomily, "I put a hundred on Template this morning. Oh, well, it's too late to cancel it, I suppose." Then seeing my rueful amusement he added, "I beg your pardon, Rob. I'm sure you'll do splendidly." But he did not sound convinced.

As the pattern of the race shifted and changed, I concentrated solely on keeping Template lying about fourth position in the field of twelve runners. To be farther back meant leaving him a lot to do at the end, and to be farther forward meant that one could not see how well or how badly everyone else was going. Template jumped himself into third place at the second-last fence, and was still not under pressure. Coming toward the last I brought him to the outside, to give him a clear view, and urged him on. His stride immediately quickened. He took off so far in front of the fence that for a heartbreaking second I was sure he would land squarely on top of it, but I had underestimated his power. He landed yards out on the far side, collecting himself without faltering and surging ahead toward the winning post.

One of the two horses close in front had been passed in mid-air over the fence. There remained only a chestnut to be beaten. Only. Only the favorite, the choice of the critics, the public and the press. No disgrace, I fleetingly thought, to be beaten only by him.

I dug my knees into Template's sides and gave him two taps with the whip down his shoulder. He needed only this signal, I found, to put every ounce into getting to the front. He stretched his neck out and flattened his stride, and I knelt on his withers and squeezed him and moved with his rhythm, and kept my whip still for fear of disturbing him. He put his head in front of the chestnut's five strides from the winning post, and kept it there.

I was almost too exhausted to unbuckle the saddle. There was a cheer as we went into the unsaddling enclosure, and a lot of smiling faces, and some complimentary things were said, but I felt too weak and breathless to enjoy them. No race had ever before taken so much out of me. Nor given me so much, either.

Surprisingly Lord Tirrold and Axminster were almost subdued.

"That was all right, then," said Axminster, the lower teeth glimmering in a smile.

"He's a wonderful horse," I said fervently.

"Yes," said Lord Tirrold, "he is." He patted the dark sweating neck.

Axminster said, "Don't hang about then, Rob. Go and weigh in. You haven't any time to waste. You're riding in the next race. And the one after."

I stared at him.

"Well, what did you expect?" he said. "Pip's obviously going to be unfit for months. I took you on to ride second to him, and you will stand in for him until he comes back."

TICK-TOCK SAID, "SOME people would climb out of a septic tank smelling of lavender."

He was waiting for me to change at the end of the afternoon.

"Six weeks ago you were scrounging rides. Then you get yourself on television as a failure and make it obvious you aren't one. Sunday newspapers write columns about you and your version of the creed gets a splash in the *Times* as well. Now you do the understudy-into-star routine, and all that jazz. And properly, too. Three winners in one afternoon. What a nerve."

I grinned at him. "What goes up must come down. You can pick up the pieces later on."

I tied my tie and brushed my hair, and looked in the mirror at the fatuous smile I could not remove from my face. Days like this don't happen very often, I thought.

"Let's go and see Pip," I said abruptly, turning round.

"Okay," he agreed.

We asked the first-aid men where Pip had been taken, and as they were leaving in any case they gave us a lift to the hospital in the ambulance. It was not until they told us that we realized how seriously the leg was broken.

We saw Pip for only a few moments. He lay in a cubicle in the Casualty Department, a cradle over his leg and blankets up to his chin. A brisk nurse told us he was going to the operating theater within minutes, and not to disturb the patient, as he had been given his premed. "But you can say hello," she said, "as you've come."

Hello was just about all we did say. Pip looked terribly pale and his eyes were fuzzy, but he said weakly, "Who won the big race?"

"Template," I said, almost apologetically.

"You?"

I nodded. He smiled faintly. "You'll ride the lot now, then?"

"I'll keep them warm for you," I said. "You won't be long."

"Three bloody months." He shut his eyes. "Three bloody months."

The nurse came back with a stretcher trolley and two khaki-overalled porters, and asked us to leave. We waited outside in the hall, and saw them trundle Pip off toward the open lift.

"He'll be four months at least, with a leg like that," said Tick-Tock. "He might just be ready for Cheltenham in March. Just in time to take back all the horses and do you out of a chance in the Champion Hurdle and the Gold Cup."

"It can't be helped," I said. "It's only fair. And anything can happen before then."

I THINK AXMINSTER had trouble persuading some of his owners that I was capable of taking Pip's place, because I didn't ride all of the stable's horses, not at first. But gradually as the weeks went by and I seemed to make no unforgivable bloomers, fewer and fewer other jockeys were engaged. I became used to seeing my name continually in the number boards, to riding three or four races a day, to going back to my digs contentedly tired in body and mind, and waking the next morning with energy and eagerness. In some ways, I even became used to winning. It was no longer a rarity for me to be led into the first's enclosure, or to talk to delighted owners, or to see my picture in the sporting papers.

I began earning a good deal of money, but I spent very little of it. There was always the knowledge, hovering in the background, that my prosperity was temporary. Pip's leg was mending.

Tick-Tock and I decided, however, to share the cost of buying a car. It was a secondhand cream-colored Mini-Cooper, which did forty miles to the gallon on a long run and could shift along at a steady seventy on the flat, and a friend of Tick-Tock's, who kept a garage had recommended it to him as a bargain.

"All we want now are some leopard-skin seat covers and a couple of blondes in the back," said Tick-Tock, as we dusted the small vehicle parked outside my digs, "and we'll look like one of those 'gracious living' advertisements in the *Tatler*." He lifted up the bonnet and took at least his tenth look at the engine. "A beautiful job of design," he said fondly.

Gracious living, good design or not, the little car smoothed our paths considerably, and within a fortnight I could not imagine how we had ever managed without it. Tick-Tock kept it where he lived, seven miles away, near the stable he rode for, and came to collect me whenever Axminster himself was not taking me to meetings in his own car. Race trains came and went without any further support from either of us, as we whizzed homeward through the black December afternoons in our cozy box on wheels.

While the gods heaped good fortune on my head, others fared badly.

Grant had offered neither explanation nor apology for hitting me on the nose. He had not, in fact, spoken one word to me since that day, but as at the same time he had also stopped borrowing my kit, I was not sure that I minded. He withdrew more and more into himself. The inner volcano of violence showed itself only in the stiffness of his body and the tightness of his lips, which seemed always to be compressed in fury. He loathed to be touched, even accidentally, and would swing round threateningly if anyone bumped into him in the changing room. With my peg at most meetings still next to his, I had knocked into him several times. For however hard I tried, it was impossible in those cramped quarters not to, and the glare he gave me each time was frankly murderous.

It was not only to me that he had stopped speaking. He no longer said much at all. The trainers and owners who still employed him could get him neither to discuss a race beforehand nor explain what had happened afterward. He listened to his orders in silence and left the trainer to draw his own conclusions through his race glasses about how the horse had run. When he did speak, his remarks were laden with such a burden of obscenity that even the hardened inmates of the changing room shifted uncomfortably.

Oddly enough Grant's riding skill had not degenerated with his character. He rode the same rough, tough race as always; but he had, we knew, begun to let out his anger onto his mounts, and twice during November he was called before the Stewards for "excessive use of the whip." The horses in question had each come in from their races with raw red weals on their flanks.

The Oldfield volcano erupted, as far as I was concerned, one cold afternoon in the jockeys and trainers' car park at Warwick. I was late leaving the meeting as I had won the last race and been taken off to the bar afterward by the elated owner, one of my farmer friends. Tick-Tock had gone to a different meeting, and I had the car. By the time I got there the park was empty except for the Mini-Cooper and another car standing almost next to it, and two or three cars farther on down the row.

I went toward the Mini still smiling to myself with the pleasure of this latest win, and I did not see Grant until I was quite close to him. I was approaching the cars from behind, with Grant's on the right of mine. His near hind wheel lay on the grass, surrounded by a collection of implements spilling out of a holdall tool bag. A jack held up the bare axle of his black saloon and he was kneeling beside it with the spare wheel in his hand.

He saw me coming and he saw me smiling, and he thought I was laughing at him for having a puncture. I could actually see the uncontrollable fury rise in his face. He got to his feet and stood rigid, his thickset body hunched with belligerence, the strong shoulders bunching under his coat, his arms hanging down. Then he bent forward and from among the mess of tools picked up a tire lever. He swished it through the air, his eyes on me.

"I'll help you with your puncture, if you like," I said mildly.

For an answer he took a step sideways, swung his arm in a sort of backward chop, and smashed the tire lever through the back window of the Mini-Cooper. The glass crashed and tinkled into the car, leaving only a fringe of jagged peaks round the frame.

Tick-Tock and I had had the car barely three weeks. My own anger rose quick and hot and I took a step toward Grant to save my most precious possession from further damage. He turned to face me squarely and lifted the tire lever again.

"Put it down," I said reasonably, standing still. We were now about four feet apart. He told me to do something which is biologically impossible.

"Don't be an ass, Grant," I said. "Put that thing down and let's get on with changing your tire."

"You . . ." he said, "you took my job."

"No," I said. It was pointless to add more, not least because if he was going to try to hit me I wanted to have all my concentration focused on what he was doing, not on what I was saying.

His eyes were red-rimmed above the high cheekbones. The big nostrils flared open like black pits. With his wild face, his bursting anger, and the upheld quivering tire lever, he was a pretty frightening sight.

He slashed forward and downward at my head.

I think that at that moment he must have been truly insane, for had the blow connected he would surely have killed me, and he couldn't have hoped to get away with it with his car standing there with the wheel off. He was beyond thought.

I saw his arm go up a fraction before it came down, and it gave me time to duck sideways. The lever whistled past my right ear. His arm returned in a backhand, again aiming at my head. I ducked again underneath it, and this time, as his arm swung wide and his body lay open to me, I stepped close and hit him hard with my fist just below his breastbone. He grunted as the wind rushed out of his lungs, and the arm with the tire lever dropped, and his head came forward. I took a half pace to the right and hit him on the side of the neck with the edge of my hand.

He went down on his hands and knees, and then weakly sprawled on the grass. I took the tire lever from his slack fingers and put it with all the other tools into the holdall, and shut the whole thing into the boot of his car.

It was getting very cold and the early dusk was turning colors to black and gray. I squatted beside Grant. He was hovering on the edge of consciousness, breathing heavily and moaning slightly.

I said conversationally, close to his ear, "Grant, why did you get the sack from Axminster?"

He mumbled something I could not hear. I repeated my question. He said nothing. I sighed and stood up. It had been only a faint chance, after all.

Then he said distinctly, "He said I passed on the message."

"What message?"

"Passed on the message," he said, less clearly.

I bent down and asked him again, "What message?" His lips moved but he said nothing more.

I decided that in spite of everything I could not just drive off and leave him lying there in the cold. I took out the tools again, and sorting out the brace, put the spare wheel on and tightened up the nuts. Then I pumped up the tire, let the jack down and slung it with the punctured wheel into the boot on top of the tools.

Grant was still not properly conscious. I knew I hadn't hit him hard enough to account for such a long semiwaking state, and it occurred to me that perhaps his disturbed brain was finding this a helpful way to dodge reality. I bent down and shook his shoulder and called his name. He opened his eyes. For a split second it seemed as though the old Grant smiled out of them,

and then the resentment and bitterness flooded back as he remembered what
had happened. I helped him sit up, and propped him against his car. He
looked desperately tired, utterly worn out.

"O God," he said. "O God." It sounded like a true prayer, and it came from
lips, which usually blasphemed without thought.

"If you went to see a psychiatrist," I said gently, "you could get some help."

He didn't answer; but neither did he resist when I helped him into the
passenger seat of the Mini-Cooper. He was in no state to drive his own car,
and there was no one else about to look after him. I asked him where he lived,
and he told me. His car was safe enough where it was, and I remarked that he
could fetch it on the following day. He made no reply.

Luckily he lived only thirty miles away, and I drew up where he told me,
outside a semidetached, featureless house on the outskirts of a small country
town. There were no lights in the windows.

"Isn't your wife in?" I asked.

"She left me," he said absently. Then his jaw tensed and he said. "Mind
your own——business." He jerked the door open, climbed out and slammed
it noisily. He shouted, "Take your bloody do-gooding off and——it. I don't
want your help, you——"

He appeared to be back to his usual frame of mind, which was a pity, but
there didn't seem to be any point in staying to hear more so I let in the clutch
and drove off: but I had gone only half a mile down the road when I reluctantly
came to the conclusion that he shouldn't be left alone in an empty house.

I was at that point in the center of the little town, whose brightly lit shops
were closing their doors for the day, and I stopped and asked an elderly woman
with a shopping basket where I could find a doctor. She directed me to a large
house in a quiet side street, and I parked outside and rang the doorbell.

A pretty girl appeared and said, "Surgery at six," and began to close the
door again.

"If the doctor is in, please let me speak to him," I said quickly, "it's not a
case for the surgery."

"Well, all right," she said and went away. Children's voices sounded noisily somewhere in the house. Presently a youngish, chubby, capable-looking
man appeared, munching at a piece of cream-filled cake and wearing the resigned, inquiring expression of a doctor called to duty during his free time.

"Are you by any chance Grant Oldfield's doctor?" I asked. If he wasn't, I
thought, he could tell me where else to go.

But he said at once, "Yes, I am. Has he had another fall?"

"Not exactly," I said, "but could you please come and take a look at him?"

"Now?"

"Yes, please," I said. "He . . . er . . . he was knocked out at the races."

"Half a mo," he said and went back into the house, reappearing with his medical bag and another piece of cake. "Can you run me down there? Save me getting my car out again for those few yards."

We went out to the Mini-Cooper and as soon as he sat in it he made a remark about the broken back window, not unreasonably, since gusts of December wind blowing through it were freezing our necks. I told him that Grant had smashed it, and explained how I had come to bring him home.

He listened in silence, licking the cream as it oozed out of the sides of the cake. Then he said, "Why did he attack you?"

"He seems to believe I took his job."

"And did you?"

"No," I said. "He lost it months before it was offered to me."

"Are you a jockey too, then?" he asked, looking at me curiously, and I nodded and told him my name. He said his was Parnell. I started the car and drove the few hundred yards back to Grant's house. It was still in complete darkness.

"I left him here not ten minutes ago," I said as we went up the path to the front door. The small front garden was ragged and uncared for, with rotting dead leaves and mournful grass-grown flower beds dimly visible in the light from the street lamp. We rang the bell. It sounded shrilly in the house, but produced no other results. We rang again. The doctor finished his cake and licked his fingers.

There was a faint rustle in the darkness of the patch of garden. The doctor unclipped from his breast pocket the pen-shaped torch he normally used for peering into eyes and down throats, and directed its tiny beam round the bordering privet hedge. It revealed first some pathetic rosebushes choked with last summer's unmown grass; but in the corner where the hedge dividing the garden from the next-door one met the hedge bordering the road, the pinpoint of light steadied on the hunched shape of a man.

We went over to him. He was sitting on the ground, huddling back into the hedge, with his knees drawn up to his chin and his head resting on his folded arms.

"Come along, old chap," said the doctor encouragingly, and half helped, half pulled him to his feet. He felt in Grant's pockets, found a bunch of keys, and handed them to me. I went over and unlocked the front door and turned on the lights in the hall. The doctor guided Grant through the hall and into the first room we came to, which happened to be a dining room. Everything in it was covered with a thick layer of dust.

Grant collapsed in a heap on a dining-room chair and laid his head down on the dirty table. The doctor examined him, feeling his pulse, lifting up his eyelid and running both hands round the thick neck and the base of the skull. Grant moved irritably when Parnell's fingers touched the place where I had hit him and he said crossly, "Go away, go away."

Parnell stepped back a pace and sucked his teeth.

"There's nothing physically wrong with him as far as I can see, except for what is going to be a stiff neck. We'd better get him into bed and I'll give him something to keep him quiet, and in the morning I'll arrange for him to see someone who can sort out his troubles for him. You'd better give me a ring during the evening if there's any change in his condition."

"I?" I said. "I'm not staying here all evening . . ."

"Oh, yes, I think so, don't you?" he said cheerfully, his eyes shining sardonically in his round face. "Who else? All night too, if you don't mind. After all, you hit him."

"Yes, but," I protested, "that's not what's the matter with him."

"Never mind. You cared enough to bring him home and to fetch me. Be a good chap and finish the job. I do really think someone ought to stay here all night . . . someone strong enough to deal with him in a crisis. It's not a job for elderly female relatives, even if we could rake one up so late in the day."

Put like that, it was difficult to refuse. We took Grant upstairs, balancing his thickset body between us as he stumbled up the treads. His bedroom was filthy. Dirty tangled sheets and blankets were piled in heaps on the unmade bed, dust lay thick on every surface, and soiled clothes were scattered over the floor and hung sordidly over chairs. The whole room smelled of sour sweat.

"We'd better put him somewhere else," I said, switching on lights and opening all the other doors on the small landing. One door led into a bathroom whose squalor defied description. Another opened onto a linen cupboard which still contained a few sheets in a neat pile, and the last revealed an empty bedroom with bright pink rosebuds on the walls. Grant stood blinking on the landing while I fetched some sheets and made up the bed for him. There were no clean pajamas. Dr. Parnell undressed Grant as far as his underpants and socks and made him get into the fresh bed. Then he went downstairs and returned with a glass of water, wearing so disgusted an expression that I knew without being told what state the kitchen must be in.

Opening his case, he shook two capsules onto his hand and told Grant to swallow them, which he docilely did. Grant at this time seemed to be sleepwalking; he was only a shell, his personality a blank. It was disturbing but, on the other hand, it made the business of putting him to bed much easier than it might have been.

Parnell looked at his watch. "I'm late for surgery," he said as Grant lay back on his pillow and shut his eyes. "Those pills ought to keep him quiet for a bit. Give him two more when he wakes up." He handed me a small bottle. "You know where to find me if you want me," he added with a callous grin. "Have a good night."

I spent a miserable evening and dined off a pint of milk I found on the back doorstep. Nothing else in the stinking kitchen was any longer edible. There were no books and no radio, and to pass the hours I made an effort to clean up some of the mess, but what that dreadful house really needed was a breezy spring day, lashings of disinfectant, and an army of strong-minded charwomen.

Several times I went softly in to see how Grant was doing, but he slept peacefully, flat on his back, until midnight. I found him then with his eyes open, but when I went close to him there was no recognition in them. He was still in a withdrawn blank state and he obediently, without a word, swallowed the capsules when I offered them to him. I waited until his eyes had closed again, then I locked his door and went downstairs and eventually fell uneasily asleep myself, wrapped in a traveling rug on a too-short sofa. There was no sound from Grant all night, and when I went up to him at six in the morning he was still sleeping quietly.

Dr. Parnell at least had the decency to release me at an early hour, arriving with a middle-aged male nurse at 7:30 in the freezing dawn. He had also brought a basket packed by his wife, containing eggs, bacon, bread, milk and coffee, and from his medical bag he produced a powerful battery razor.

"All modern conveniences," he said cheerfully, his round face beaming.

So I went back to the races washed, shaved and fed, but, thinking of the husk of a man I left behind me, not in a happy frame of mind.

CHAPTER 7

"THE TROUBLE IS, there's such a shortage of jockeys just now," said James Axminster.

We were on our way to Sandown, discussing whom he should engage to ride for him in the following week when he would be sending horses to two different places on the same day.

"You'd almost think there was a hoodoo on the whole tribe," he said, expertly swinging his large car between a wobbly girl cyclist and an oncoming furniture van. "Art shot himself, Pip's broken his leg, Grant's had a breakdown. Two or three others are out with more ordinary things like busted collarbones, and at least four quite useful chaps took that wretched Ballerton's misguided advice and are now churning out car bodies on assembly lines. There's Peter Cloony . . . but I've heard he's very unreliable and might not turn up in time; and Danny Higgs bets too much, they say, and Ingersoll doesn't always try, so I've been told . . ."

He slowed down while a mother pushed a perambulator and three small children untidily across the road in front of us, and went on talking. "Every time I think I've found a good up-and-coming jockey I seem to hear something to his disadvantage. With you, it was that film, the one they showed on that television program. It was shocking, wasn't it? I watched it and thought, My God, what have I done, asking this clod to ride for me, how ever will I explain it away to the owners?" He grinned. "I was on the point of ringing them all up and assuring them you'd not be on their horses after all. Luckily for you I remembered the way you had already ridden for me and I watched the rest of the program first, and when it had finished I had changed my mind. I had even begun to think I had perhaps struck oil in annexing you. Nothing that has happened since," he glanced at me sideways, smiling, "has led me to alter that opinion."

I smiled back. In the weeks since Pip broke his leg I had come to know him well, and liked him better with every day that passed. Not only was he a superb craftsman at his job and a tireless worker, but he was reliable in other ways. He was never moody; one did not have to approach him circumspectly every time to see if he was in a good or a bad humor because he was always the same, neither boisterous nor irritable, just reasonable and receptive. He said directly what he thought, so that one never had to search for innuendoes or suspect hidden sarcasm, and it made any relationship with him stable and free from worry. He was, on the other hand, in many ways thoroughly selfish. Unless it was a strictly business matter, his own comfort and convenience came first, second and third, and he would do a favor for someone else only if it caused him absolutely no personal sacrifice of time or effort. Even this was often a blessing to his stable lads, since it was typical of him, if the occasion arose, to give them a generous traveling allowance out of his own pocket to visit their homes, rather than go five miles out of his way to drop them on their doorsteps.

He had seemed from the first to be as satisfied with my company as I was with his, and had quite soon told me to drop the "sir" and stick to "James." Later the same week as he drove us back from the Birmingham races, we passed some brightly lit posters advertising a concert which was to be held there that evening.

"Conductor, Sir Trelawny Finn," he read aloud, the enormous lettering catching his eye. "No relation, I suppose," he said jokingly.

"Well, yes, as a matter of fact, he's my uncle," I said.

There was dead silence. Then he said, "And Caspar Finn?"

"My father." A pause.

"Anyone else?"

"Dame Olivia Cottin is my mother," I said matter-of-factly.

"Good God!" he said explosively.

I grinned.

"You keep it very quiet," he said.

"It's really the other way round," I said cheerfully. "They like to keep me quiet. A jockey in the family is a disgrace to them, you see. It embarrasses them. They don't like the connection to be noticed."

"All the same," he said thoughtfully, "it explains quite a lot about you that I had begun to wonder about. Where you got that air of confidence from . . . and why you've said so little about yourself."

I said, smiling, "I'd be very glad . . . James . . . if you'd not let my parentage loose in the weighing room, as a favor to them."

He had said he would not, and he had kept his word, but he had accepted me more firmly as a friend from then on. So when he ran through the reported shortcomings of Peter Cloony, Danny Higgs and Tick-Tock, it was with some confidence that I said, "You seem to have heard a great many rumors. Do you know all these things for a fact?"

"For a fact?" he repeated, surprised. "Well, Peter Cloony definitely missed two races a few weeks back because he was late. That's a fact."

I told him about Peter's atrocious luck in twice finding a vehicle stuck across the mouth of the narrow lane from his village to the main road. "As far as I know," I said, "he hasn't been late since then. His reputation for lateness seems to be built mainly on those two days."

"I've heard several times that he can't be trusted to turn up," said James obstinately.

"Who from?" I asked curiously.

"Oh, I don't know. Corin Kellar, for one. And of course Johnson, who employs him. Ballerton too, though it's against my better judgment to pay too much attention to what he says. It's common knowledge though."

"How about Danny Higgs, then?" I said. Danny was an irrepressible Cockney, tiny in size but ferociously brave.

"He bets too heavily," James said positively.

"Who says so?" I asked. I knew Danny broke the regulations by backing horses, but from what he said in the changing room, it was only in amounts of five or ten pounds, which would cause few trainers to look askance at him.

"Who says? I . . . er . . . Corin," he finished lamely. "Corin, come to think of it, has told me so several times. He says he never puts him up because of it."

"And Tick-Tock?" I said. "Who says Ingersoll doesn't always try?"

He didn't answer at once. Then he said, "Why shouldn't I believe what Corin says? He has no ax to grind. He's an excellent trainer, but he depends as we all do on securing good jockeys. He certainly wouldn't deny himself the use of people like Cloony and Higgs if he didn't have a good reason."

I thought for a few moments, and then said, "I know it's really none of my business, but would you mind very much telling me why you dropped Grant Oldfield? He told me himself that it was something to do with a message, but he wouldn't explain what." I refrained from mentioning that he had been semiconscious at the time.

"A message? Oh, yes, he passed on the message, I couldn't have that."

I still looked mystified. Axminster squeezed through the traffic lights on the amber and glanced sideways at me.

"The message," he said impatiently, "you know, the news. He was passing on the news. If we had a fancied runner, he would tip off a professional backer. The owner of the horse didn't get good odds to his money because the professional was there before him and spoiled the market. Three of my owners were very angry about it—no fun for them having to take two or three to one when they had expected sixes or sevens. So Grant had to go. It was a pity; he was a strong jockey, just what I needed."

"How did you discover that it was Grant passing on the information?"

"Maurice Kemp-Lore found out while he was working on one of those programs of his. Something to do with how professional backers work, I think it was, and he found out about Grant more or less by accident. He told me very apologetically, and just said it would be wiser not to let Grant know too much. But you can't work properly with a jockey and keep secrets from him, it's a hopeless setup."

"What did Grant say when you sacked him?" I asked.

"He denied the whole thing very indignantly. But of course he would. No jockey would ever confess to selling information if he wanted another trainer to take him on."

"Did you talk to the professional backer in question?" I asked.

"Yes, I did, as a matter of fact," he said. "I didn't want to believe it, you see. But it was open and shut. I had to press him a bit, because it didn't reflect well on him, but Lubbock, the professional, did admit that Grant had been tipping off over the telephone, and that he had been paying him ever since he had started to ride for me."

It seemed conclusive enough, but I had an elusive feeling that I had missed something somewhere.

I changed the subject. "Going back to Art," I said, "why was he always having rows with Corin?"

"I don't really know," James said reflectively. "I heard Corin say once or twice that Art didn't ride to orders. Perhaps it was that." He neatly passed two slow lorries on a traffic circle, and glanced at me again. "What are you getting at?"

"It seems to me sometimes that there is too much of a pattern," I said. "Too many jockeys are affected by rumors. You said yourself that there seems to be a hoodoo on the whole tribe."

"I didn't mean it seriously," he protested. "You're imagining things. And as for rumors, what rumor made Art kill himself, or broke Pip's leg, or made Grant sell information? Rumor didn't make Cloony late either."

"Danny Higgs doesn't bet heavily," I said, feeling I was fighting a rearguard action, "and Ingersoll rides as honestly as anyone."

"You can't know about Higgs," he pointed out; "and Ingersoll, let me remind you, was called in before the Stewards last week for easing his mount out of third place. John Ballerton owned the horse and he was very annoyed about it, he told me so himself."

I sighed. Tick-Tock's version was that, since Corin had told him not to overwork the horse, which was not fully fit, he had decided that he ought not to drive the horse too hard just for the sake of finishing third. Better to save the horse's energy for winning next time, he had thought, adopting a view commonly held and acted on by at least half the jockeys and trainers engaged in the sport; but owners and members of the public who had backed the horse for a place were liable to disagree. After the inquiry, changing with the wind as usual, Corin had been heard condemning Tick-Tock for his action.

"I may be quite wrong about it all," I said slowly, "I hope so. Only . . ."

"Only?" he prompted as I paused.

"Only," I finished lightly, "if you ever hear any rumors about me, will you remember what I think . . . and make utterly sure they're true before you believe them?"

"All right," he said, humoring me. "I think it's nonsense, but all right, I'll agree to that." He drove in silence for a while, and then said with an impatient shake of his big head, "No one stands to gain anything by trying to ruin jockeys. It's nonsense. Pointless."

"I know," I said. "Pointless."

We changed the subject.

CHRISTMAS CAME, AND during the week before it, when there was no racing, I spent several days in Kensington. My parents greeted me with their usual friendly detachment and left me to my own devices. They were both preoccupied with crowded Christmas schedules, and my mother also spent each morning working at her piano on a new concerto, which was to have its first performance in the new year. She started daily at seven punctually, and played, with short interruptions for coffee and thought, until twelve-thirty. I awoke as so often during my life to the sound of warming-up chromatics and wrist-loosening arpeggios, and lay lazily in bed listening to her pick her way phrase by phrase through a dissonant modern score, repeating and repeating each section until she was satisfied she knew it, until the notes flowed easily in their intended order.

I could picture her exactly, dressed for work in a cashmere sweater and ski pants, sitting upright on her special stool, with her head thrust forward as if to hear more from the piano than the notes themselves. She was digging the bones out of the piece, and I knew better than to interrupt her. Digging the bones, the essence, the composer's ultimate intention: and when she had these things firmly in her mind she would begin the process of clothing them with her own interpretation, sharpening the contrasts of mood and tone, until the finished conception emerged clear and shining and memorable.

My mother might not have been a comforting refuge in my childhood nor take much loving interest in me now that I was a man, but she had by her example shown me many qualities to admire and value. Professionalism, for instance; a tough-minded singleness of purpose; a refusal to be content with a low standard when a higher one could be achieved merely by working. I had become self-reliant young and thoroughly as a result of her rejection of motherhood, and because I saw the grind behind the gloss of her public performances I grew up not expecting life's plums to be tossed into my lap without any effort from me. What mother could teach her son more?

Joanna's time was tangled inextricably with several performances in different places of the Christmas Oratorio. I managed to hook her only for one chilly morning's walk in the Park, which was not a success from my point of view since Handel easily shoved me into second place for her attention. She hummed bits of the Oratorio continuously from the Albert Gate to the Serpentine, and from the Serpentine to Bayswater Road. There I put her into a taxi and gave her a Christmasy lunch at the Savoy, where she appeared to restrain herself with difficulty from bursting into full song, as the acoustics in the entrance hall appealed to her. I couldn't decide whether or not she was being irritating on purpose, and if she was, why.

She was definitely a great deal less serene than usual, and there was a sort of brittleness in her manner, which I didn't like and couldn't understand, until we were halfway through some excellent mince pies it belatedly occurred to me that she might be unhappy. Unhappiness was not a state I had seen her in before, so I couldn't be sure. I waited until the coffee came, and then said casually, "What's up, Joanna?"

She looked at me, then she looked round the room, then at me again, then at her coffee.

Finally she said, "Brian wants me to marry him."

It wasn't what I expected, and it hurt. I found myself looking down at my own coffee; black and bitter, very appropriate, I thought.

"I don't know what to do," she said. "I was content as we were. Now I'm unsettled. Brian keeps talking about 'living in sin' and 'regularizing the position.' He goes to church a lot now, and he can't reconcile our relationship with his religion. I never thought of it as sinful, just as enjoyable and fruitful and . . . and comfortable. He is talking about buying a house and settling down, and sees me as the complete housewife, cleaning, mending, cooking, and so on. I'm not that sort of person. The thought appalls me. If I marry him, I know I'll be miserable . . ." Her voice trailed off.

"And if you don't marry him?" I asked.

"I'll be miserable then, too, because he refuses to go on as we are. We're not easy together any more. We nearly have rows. He says it's irresponsible and childish not to want to marry at my age, and I say I'll gladly marry him if we live as we do now, with him coming and going from the studio when he likes, and me free to work and come and go as I please too. But he doesn't want that. He wants to be respectable and conventional and . . . and stuffy." The last word came out explosively, steeped in contempt. There was a pause while she stirred her coffee vigorously. There was no sugar in it. I watched the nervous gesture, the long strong fingers with the pink varnished nails gripping the spoon too hard.

"How much do you love him?" I asked painfully.

"I don't know," she said unhappily. "I don't know any more what love is." She looked straight across the little table. "If it means that I want to spend my life attending to his creature comforts, then I don't love him. If it means being happy in bed, then I do."

She saw the movement in my face, and she said abruptly, "Oh, hell, Rob, I'm sorry. It's so long since you said anything . . . I thought you didn't still—"

"Never mind," I said. "It can't be helped."

"What . . . what do you think I should do?" she said after a pause, still fiddling with the coffee spoon.

"It's quite clear," I said positively, "that you should not marry Brian if you can't bear the prospect of the life he intends to lead. It wouldn't work for either of you."

"So?" she said in a small voice.

But I shook my head. The rest she would have to resolve for herself. No advice I could give her would be unbiased, and she must have known it.

She left presently to go to a rehearsal, and I paid the bill and wandered out into the festive streets. I bought some presents for my family on the way, walking slowly back to the flat. The sort of marriage which Joanna had offered Brian, and which he spurned, was what I most wanted in the world. Why, I wondered disconsolately, was life so ruddy unfair.

ON BOXING DAY Template won the King Chase, one of the ten top races of the year. It put him conclusively into the star class, and it didn't do me any harm either.

The race had been televised, and afterward, as was his custom, Maurice Kemp-Lore interviewed me as the winning jockey before the camera. Toward the end of the brief talk he invited me to say hello directly to Pip, who, he explained to viewers, was watching at home. I had seen Pip only a week or two earlier and had discussed big-race tactics with him, but I obligingly greeted him and said I hoped his leg was mending well. Kemp-Lore smilingly added, "We all wish you a speedy recovery, Pip," and the interview was over.

On the following day the sporting press was complimentary about the race, and a number of trainers I had not yet ridden for offered me mounts. I began to feel at last as though I were being accepted as a jockey in my own right, and not principally as a substitute for Pip. It even seemed likely that when Pip returned to his job I would not fade back into the wilderness, for two of the new trainers said they would put me up on their horses as often as I was free.

I had, of course, my share of falls during this period, for however fortunate I was I couldn't beat the law of averages: but no damage was done except for a few bruises here and there, and none of them was bad enough to stop me from riding.

The worst fall from the spectators' point of view happened one Saturday afternoon in January, when the hurdler I was riding tripped over the flight of hurdles nearest to the grandstand and flung me off onto my head. I woke up dizzily as the first-aid men lifted me into the ambulance on a stretcher, and for a moment or two could not remember where I was.

James's face, looming over me as they carried me into the first-aid room, brought me back to earth with a click, and I asked him if his horse was all right.

"Yes," he said. "How about you?"

"Nothing broken," I assured him, having explored my limbs rather drunkenly during the short trip back in the ambulance.

"He rolled on you," he said.

"I'm not surprised." I grinned up at him. "I feel a bit squashed, come to think of it."

I lay for a while on a bed in the first-aid room, but there was nothing wrong with me that a good sleep wouldn't cure, and at the end of the afternoon I went back to Berkshire with James as expected.

"Are you all right?" he asked once, on the way.

"Yes," I said cheerfully. "Fine." Actually I felt dizzy now and then, and also shivery and unsettled, but concealing one's true state of health from trainers was an occupational habit, and I knew I would be fit again to ride on Monday.

The only person who was openly annoyed at the run of good luck I had had was John Ballerton, and I had caught him several times in the parade ring staring tight-lipped at me, with a patent and most unstewardly animosity.

Since the day of our joint broadcast we had exchanged the fewest possible words, but I had heard from Corin, who repeated it to me with sly relish, that Ballerton had said loudly to him and Maurice Kemp-Lore in the members' bar at Kempton. "Finn isn't worth all the fuss that's being made of him. He'll come down just as quickly as he's gone up, you'll see. And I for one won't weep about it."

In view of this it was astonishing that on the day after my fall I should be offered a ride on one of his horses. At first I refused to take Corin seriously. His telephone call woke me on Sunday morning, and I was inclined to think the concussion had returned.

"If it were a choice between me and a sack of potatoes," I said sleepily, "he'd choose the potatoes."

"No, seriously, Rob, he wants you to ride Shantytown at Dunstable tomorrow." Corin's voice held no trace of humor. "I must say, I don't really understand why, as he's been so set against you before. But he was quite definite on the telephone, not five minutes ago. Perhaps it's an olive branch."

And perhaps not, I thought. My first instinct was to refuse to ride the horse, but I couldn't think of a reasonable excuse, as Corin had found out I was free for the race before he told me whose the horse was. A point-blank excuse-less refusal was, while possible, a senseless course. It would give Ballerton a genuine grievance against me, and if he sincerely wanted to smooth over his hostility, which I doubted, I should only deepen it by spurning his offer.

Shantytown was no Template. Far, far from it. His uncertain temper and unreliable jumping were described to me in unreassuring terms by Tick-Tock on the way to Dunstable the following morning.

"A right one," he said, putting his foot down on the Mini-Cooper's ac-celerator. "A knacker's delight. Dog meat on the hoof."

"His form's not bad," I protested mildly, having looked it up the previ-ous day.

"Hmph. Any time he's won or been placed it's because he's dragged his jockey's arms out of the sockets by a blast-off start and kept right on going. Hang on and hope, that's how to ride him when he's in that mood. His mouth is as hard as Gibraltar. In fact I cannot," finished Tick-Tock with satiric formal-ity, "I cannot instantly recall any horse who is less receptive of his jockey's ideas."

There was no bitterness in his voice, but we were both aware that a few weeks ago riding Shantytown would have been his doubtful pleasure, not mine. Since his parade before the Stewards for not pushing his horse all out into third place, he had been ignored by Corin Kellar. It was the sort of in-justice typical of Corin, to sack a man who ran into trouble looking after his interests, and it had done nothing to lay the unfair rumor that Tick-Tock was a habitual nontrier.

Apart from abruptly lessening the number of races he rode in, the rumor had had little effect on Tick-Tock himself. He shrugged his shoulders, and with a determined look on his angular young face stated, "They'll change their minds again in time. I'll mash every horse I ride into a pulp. I'll do my nut on every hopeless hack. No one henceforth will see me finish eighth when by bashing the beast I could be sixth."

I had smiled to hear these fighting words from one whose chief asset was his lightness of touch, but was relieved, too, that he was intact in spirits. No suicides, no mental breakdowns for him.

Shantytown, when it came to the race, was not what I had been led to ex-pect. The damp raw January afternoon had drawn only a small crowd of stal-warts to watch a second-class program at a minor meeting, and as I watched the big chestnut plod around the parade ring I thought how well he matched the circumstances. Uninspiring.

But far from pulling my arms out of their sockets Shantytown seemed to me to be in danger of falling asleep. The start caught him flat-footed, so little interest was he taking in it, and I had to boot him into the first fence. He rose to it fairly well, but was slow in his recovery, and it was the same at every jump. It was puzzling, after what Tick-Tock had said, but horses do have their off days for no discernible reason, and I could only suppose that this was one of them.

We trailed round the entire three miles in the rear of the field, and finished ingloriously last. All my efforts to get him to quicken up the straight met with no response. Shantytown hadn't taken hold of his bit from the beginning, and at the end he seemed to be dead beat.

A hostile reception met us on our return, John Ballerton, with whom I had exchanged coldly polite "Good afternoons" in the parade ring before the race, now glowered like a July thunderstorm. Corin, standing on one leg and wearing an anxious, placatory expression, was obviously going to use me as the scapegoat for the horse's failure, to save his face as its trainer. That was always one of the hazards to be run in riding Corin's horses.

"What the hell do you think you were doing?" Ballerton said aggressively, as I slid off to the ground and began to unbuckle the saddle girths.

"I'm sorry, sir," I said. "He wouldn't go any faster."

"Don't talk such bloody rubbish," he said, "he always goes faster than that. I've never seen a more disgusting display of incompetence. You couldn't ride in a cart with a pig net over it. If you ask me, the horse wasn't given a chance. You missed the start and couldn't be bothered to make it up."

"I did say," said Corin to me reproachfully, "not to let him run away with you, and to keep tucked in behind for the first two miles. But I do think you carried my orders a bit too far—"

"A bit too far!" interrupted Ballerton furiously. "Were you afraid to let him go, or something? If you can't manage to ride a decent race on a horse which pulls, why the hell do you try to? Why not say straight out that you can't? Save us all a lot of time and money."

I said, "The horse didn't pull. There was no life in him."

"Kellar," Ballerton was nearly shouting, "is my horse a puller, or is he not?"

"He is," said Corin, not meeting my eyes.

"And you told me he was fit. On his toes."

"Yes," said Corin. "I thought he'd win."

They looked at me accusingly. Corin must have known that the horse had run listlessly because he had seen the race with experienced eyes, but he was not going to admit it. If I had to ride often for Corin, I thought wryly, I would soon have as many rows with him as Art had had.

Ballerton narrowed his eyes and said to me, "I asked you to ride Shanty-town against my better judgment and only because Maurice Kemp-Lore insisted I had been misjudging you and that you were really a reliable man who would ride a genuine race. Well, I'm going to tell him he is wrong. Very wrong. You'll never ride another horse of mine, I promise you that."

He turned on his heel and stalked off, followed by Corin. My chief feeling, as I went back to the weighing room, was of irritation that I hadn't relied on instinct and refused to ride for him in the first place.

By the end of the afternoon the puzzlement I had felt over Shantytown's dead running had changed to a vague uneasiness, for neither of the other two horses I rode afterward did anything like as well as had been expected. Both were well backed, and both finished nearly last, and although their owners were a great deal nicer about it than Ballerton had been, their disappointment was obvious.

On the following day, still at Dunstable, the run of flops continued. I had been booked for three horses, and they all ran badly. I spent the whole depressing afternoon apologetically explaining to owner after owner that I had not been able to make their horses go faster. The third horse, in fact, went so badly that I had to pull him up halfway round. He was a slow jumper on the best of days, but on that particular one he took so long putting himself right and so long starting off again when he landed that the rest of the field was a whole fence ahead by the time we had gone a mile. It was hopeless. When I reined him in he slowed from a reluctant gallop to a walk in a couple of strides, sure sign of a very tired horse. I thought, as he was trained by a farmer-owner who might not know better, that he must have been given too stiff a training gallop on the previous day, but the farmer said he was sure he had not.

Runs of bad luck are commoner in racing than good ones, and the fact that six of my mounts in a row had made a showing far below their usual capabilities would not have attracted much notice had it not been for John Ballerton.

I changed into street clothes after the fifth race and strolled out of the weighing room to find him standing close by with a small circle of cronies. All the heads turned toward me with that sideways assessing look which meant they had been talking about me, and Ballerton said something forceful to them, of which the word "disgrace" floated across clearly.

Jockeys being as accustomed as politicians to abuse, I gave no sign of having heard what had obviously been intended for my ears, and walked casually off to the stands to watch the last race: but I did wonder how long and how maliciously Ballerton would hold Shantytown's failure against me and what effect his complaints would have on the number of horses I was asked to ride. He was not a man to keep his grudges to himself, and as a National Hunt Committee member he was not without influence either.

Up on the stands Maurice Kemp-Lore came across to talk to me. We had met briefly on racecourses several times now and were on superficially friendly terms, but in spite of his charm, or perhaps because it sometimes seemed too polished, I felt his friendship came strictly into the professional, "might be useful" category. I did not believe that he liked me for my own sake.

He smiled vividly, the charm turned on to full wattage, his slim figure radiating health and confidence and his blue eyes achieving the near impossible of twinkling on a gray January afternoon. I smiled back automatically: one couldn't help it. All his impressive success stemmed from the instantaneous, irresistible feeling of well-being he inspired in whomever he talked to, and there was no one from the Senior Steward down who did not enjoy his company, even if, like me, one suspected his unfailing motive was the gathering of material for his program.

"What bad luck, Rob," he said cheerfully. "I hear the good word I put in for you with John Ballerton has gone awry."

"You can say that again," I agreed. "But thanks for trying, anyway."

The blue eyes glimmered. "Anything to help," he said.

I could hear distinctly a faint high-pitched wheeze as he drew a breath into his lungs, and I realized it was the first time I had encountered him in an asthmatic attack. I was vaguely sorry for him.

The horses for the sixth race cantered past, going down to the start.

"Are James's plans fixed for the Midwinter Cup?" he asked casually, his eyes on the horses. I smiled. But he had his job to do, I supposed, and there was no harm in telling him.

"Template runs, all being well," I said.

"And you ride him?"

"Yes," I agreed.

"How is Pip getting along?" he asked, wheezing quietly.

"They think his leg is mending well, but he is still in plaster," I said. "It comes off next week, I believe, and he might be ready for Cheltenham, but of course he won't be fit for the Midwinter."

The race in question was a richly endowed new event at Ascot, introduced to provide a high spot in mid-February, and nicely timed to give three full weeks for recovery and returning before the Cheltenham Gold Cup. It lay almost a month ahead, on that day at Dunstable, and I was looking forward to it particularly as it seemed possible that it would be my last chance on Template. Pip would do his very best to be fit to ride him in the Gold Cup, and so would I have done in his place.

"What chance do you give Template in the Midwinter?" Maurice asked, watching the start through his race glasses.

"Oh, I hope he'll win," I said, grinning. "You can quote me."

"I probably will," he agreed, grinning back. We watched the race together, and such was the effect of his personality that I left Dunstable quite cheerfully, the dismal two days' results temporarily forgotten.

CHAPTER 8

IT WAS A false security. My charmed run of good luck had ended with a vengeance, and Dunstable proved to be only the fringe of the whirlpool. During the next two weeks I rode seventeen horses. Fifteen of them finished in the rear of the field, and in only two cases was this a fair result.

I couldn't understand it. As far as I knew there was no difference in my riding, and it was unbelievable that my mounts should all lose their form simultaneously. I began to worry about it, and that didn't help, as I could feel my confidence oozing away as each disturbing and embarrassing day passed.

There was one gray mare I particularly liked riding because of the speed of her reactions: she often seemed to know what I intended to do a split second before I gave her signals, rather as if she had sized up the situation as I had and was already taking independent action. She was sweet tempered and

silken mouthed, and jumped magnificently. I liked her owner too, a short jolly
farmer with a thick Norfolk accent, and while we watched her walk round the
parade ring before her race he commiserated with me on my bad luck and said,
"Never mind, lad. The mare will put you right. She'll not fail you. You'll do
all right on her, never fear."

I went out smiling to the race because I too believed I would do all right
on her. But that week she might have been another horse. Same color, same
size, same pretty head. But no zip. It was like driving a car with four flat tires.

The jolly farmer looked less jolly and more pensive when I brought
her back.

"She's not been last ever before, lad," he said reproachfully.

We looked her over, but there was nothing wrong with her that we could
see, and she wasn't even blowing very hard.

"I could get her heart tested, I suppose," the farmer said doubtfully. "Are
you sure you gave her her head, lad?"

"Yes," I said. "But she had no enthusiasm at all today."

The farmer shook his head, doleful and puzzled.

One of the horses I rode belonged to a tall sharp-faced woman who knew
a great deal about racing and had no sympathy with bunglers. She laid straight
into me with her tongue after I had eased her ultraexpensive new gelding
from last into second-last place only feet from the winning post.

"I suppose you realize," she said in a loud, hard voice, unashamedly listened to by a large group of racegoers, "that in the last five minutes you had
succeeded both in halving the value of my horse and in making me look a fool
for having paid a fortune for him."

I apologized. I suggested possibly that her animal needed a little time.

"Time?" she repeated angrily. "For what? For you to wake up? You speak
as if it were my judgment that is at fault, not yours. You lay far too far out of
your ground. You should have taken closer order from the beginning." Her
acid lecture went on and on and on and I looked at the fine head of her glossy
high-bred black gelding and admitted to myself that he was probably a great
deal better than he had appeared.

One Wednesday was the big day for a ten-year-old schoolboy with sparkly
brown eyes and a conspiratorial grin. His wealthy, eccentric grandmother,
having discovered that there was no minimum age laid down for racehorse
owners, had given Hugo a colossal chestnut steeplechaser twice his height,
and was considerate enough to foot the training bills as well.

I had become firm friends with Hugo. Knowing that I saw his horse most mornings at James's, he used to send me tiny parcels containing lumps of sugar filched from the dining table at his prep school, which I conscientiously passed on to their intended destination: and I used to write back to Hugo, giving him quite detailed accounts of how his giant pet was progressing.

On that Wednesday Hugo had not only begged a day off from school to see his horse run, but had brought three friends with him. The four of them stood with me and James in the parade ring, Hugo's mother being the rare sort who liked her son to enjoy his limelight alone. As I had walked down from the weighing room she had smiled broadly to me from her station on the rails.

The four little boys were earnest and excited, and James and I had great fun with them before the race, treating them with seriousness and as man to man, which they obviously appreciated. This time, I promised myself, this time, for Hugo, I will win. I must.

But the big chestnut jumped very clumsily that day. On the far side of nearly every fence he ducked his head, and once, to prevent myself being hauled over in a somersault, I had to stretch forward down his neck with one hand only, letting go of the reins entirely with the other. The free arm, swinging up sideways, helped to bring my weight far enough back to keep me in the saddle, but the gesture known as "calling a cab" was not going to earn me any bonus points with James, who had denounced it often as the style of "bad, tired, scared or unfit amateurs."

Hugo's little face was pink when I dismounted, and the three friends glumly shuffled their feet behind him. With them as witnesses there would be no chance of Hugo's smoothing over the disaster with the rest of his schoolmates.

"I'm very sorry, Hugo," I said sincerely, apologizing for everything— myself, the horse, the race, and the miserliness of fate.

He answered with a stoicism which would have been a lesson to many of his seniors. "I expect it was an off day," he said kindly. "And anyway, some-one always has to be last. That's what Daddy said when I came bottom in history." He looked at the chestnut forgivingly, and said to me, "I expect he's keen really, don't you?"

"Yes," I agreed. "Keen, very."

"Well," said Hugo, turning bravely to the friends, "that's that, then. We might as well have tea."

Failures like these were too numerous to escape anyone's attention, but as the days passed I noticed a change in the way people spoke to me. One or two,

and Corin in particular, showed something like contempt. Others looked uncomfortable, others sympathetic, others pitying. Heads turned toward me
wherever I went, and I could almost feel the wave of gossip I left in my wake.
I didn't know exactly what they were saying, so I asked Tick-Tock.

"Pay no attention," he said. "Ride a couple of winners and they'll be throwing the laurel wreaths again, and backpedaling on everything they're saying
now. It's bad-patchville, chum, that's all."

And that was all I could get out of him.

One Thursday evening James Axminster telephoned to my digs and asked
me to go up to his house. I walked up in the dark, rather miserably wondering
whether he, like two other trainers that day, was going to find an excuse for putting someone else up on his horses. I couldn't blame him. Owners could make
it impossible for him to continue with a jockey so thoroughly in the doldrums.

James called me into his office, a square room joining his house to the stable yard. Its walls were covered with racing photographs, bookshelves, a long
row of racing colors on clothes hangers, and filing cabinets. A huge rolltop desk
stood in front of the window, which looked out onto the yard. There were three
broken-springed armchairs with faded chintz covers, a decrepit Turkish carpet
on the floor, and a red-hot coal fire in the grate. I had spent a good many hours
there in the past three months, discussing past performances and future plans.

James waited for me and stood aside to let me go in first. He followed me
in and shut the door, and faced me almost aggressively across the familiar room.

"I hear," he said without preamble, "that you have lost your nerve."

The room was very still. The fire crackled slightly. A horse in a nearby
loose box banged the floor with his hoof. I stared at James, and he stared
straight back, gravely.

I didn't answer. The silence lengthened. It was not a surprise. I had
guessed what was being said about me when Tick-Tock had refused to tell me
what it was.

"No one is to blame for losing his nerve," James said noncommittally. "But
a trainer cannot continue to employ someone to whom it has happened."

I still said nothing.

He waited for a few seconds, and then went on: "You have been showing
the classic symptoms . . . trailing round nearly last, pulling up for no clear
reason, never going fast enough to keep warm, and calling a cab. Keeping at
the back out of trouble, that's what you've been doing."

I thought about it, rather numbly.

"A few weeks ago," he said, "I promised you that if I heard any rumors about you I would make sure they were true before I believed them. Do you remember?"

I nodded.

"I heard this rumor last Saturday," he said. "Several people sympathized with me because my jockey had lost his nerve. I didn't believe it. I have watched you closely ever since."

I waited dumbly for the ax. During the week I had been last five times out of seven.

He walked abruptly over to an armchair by the fire and sat down heavily.

Irritably he said, "Oh, sit down, Rob. Don't just stand there like a stricken ox, saying nothing."

I sat down and looked at the fire.

"I expected you to deny it," he said in a tired voice. "Is it true, then?"

"No," I said.

"Is that all you've got to say? It isn't enough. What has happened to you? You owe me an explanation."

I owed him much more than an explanation.

"I can't explain," I said despairingly. "Every horse I've ridden in the past three weeks seems to have had its feet dipped in treacle. The difference is in the horses . . . I am the same." It sounded futile and incredible, even to me.

"You have certainly lost your touch," he said slowly. "Perhaps Ballerton is right—"

"Ballerton?" I said sharply.

"He's always said you were not as good as you were made out to be, and that I'd pushed you on too fast . . . given you a top job when you weren't ready for it. Today he has been going round smugly saying, 'I told you so.' He can't leave the subject alone, he's so pleased."

"I'm sorry, James," I said.

"Are you ill, or something?" he asked exasperatedly.

"No," I said.

"They say the fall you had three weeks ago was what frightened you—the day you got knocked out and your horse rolled on you. But you were all right going home, weren't you? I remember you being a bit sore, but you didn't seem in the least scared of falling again."

"I didn't give that fall another thought," I said.

"Then why, Rob, why?"

But I shook my head. I didn't know why.

He stood up and opened a cupboard which contained bottles and glasses, poured out two whiskies, and handed one to me.

"I can't convince myself yet that you've lost your nerve," he said. "Remembering the way you rode Template on Boxing Day, only a month ago, it seems impossible. No one could change as fundamentally in so short a time. Before I took you on, wasn't it your stock in trade to ride all the rough and dangerous horses that trainers didn't want to risk their best jockeys on? That's why I first engaged you, I remember it clearly. And all those years you spent in wherever it was as a stockman, and that spell in a rodeo . . . you aren't the sort of man to lose his nerve suddenly and for nothing, and especially not when you're in the middle of a most spectacularly successful season."

I smiled for almost the first time that day, realizing how deeply I wanted him not to lose faith in me.

I said, "I feel as if I'm fighting a fog. I tried everything I knew today to get those horses to go faster, but they were all half dead. Or I was. I don't know . . . it's a pretty ghastly mess."

"I'm afraid it is," he said gloomily. "And I'm having owner trouble about it, as you can imagine. All the original doubters are doubting again. I can't reassure them . . . it's like a Stock Exchange crash: catching. And you're the bad stock that's being jettisoned."

"What rides can I still expect?" I said.

He sighed. "I don't exactly know. You can have all the Broome runners because he's on a cruise in the Mediterranean and won't hear the rumors for a while. And my two as well; they both run next week. For the rest, we'll have to wait and see."

I could hardly bring myself to say it, but I had to know.

"How about Template?" I asked.

He looked at me steadily. "I haven't heard from George Tirrold," he said. "I think he will agree that he can't chuck you out after you've won so many races for him. He is not easily stampeded, there's that to hope for, and it was he who drew my attention to you in the first place. Unless something worse happens," he finished judiciously, "I think you can still count on riding Template in the Midwinter a week on Saturday. But if you bring him in last in that . . . it will be the end."

I stood up and drained the whisky.

"I'll win that race," I said; "whatever the cost, I'll win it."

. . .

WE WENT SILENTLY together to the races the following day, but when we arrived I discovered that two of my three prospective mounts were mine no longer. I had been, in the expressive phrase, jocked off. The owners, the trainer in question brusquely explained, thought they would have no chance of winning if they put me up as planned. Very sorry and all that, he said, but no dice.

I stood on the stands and watched both the horses run well: one of them won, and the other finished a close third. I ignored as best I could the speculative, sideways glances from all the other jockeys, trainers and press men standing near me. If they wanted to see how I was taking it, that was their affair: just as it was mine if I wanted to conceal from them the inescapable bitterness of these two results.

I went out to ride James's runner in the fourth race absolutely determined to win. The horse was capable of it on his day, and I knew him to be a competent jumper and a willing battler in a close finish.

We came last.

All the way round I could barely keep him in touch with the rest of the field. In the end he cantered slowly past the winning post with his head down in tiredness, and mine down too, in defeat and humiliation. I felt ill.

It was an effort to go back and face the music. I felt more like driving the Mini-Cooper at top speed into a nice solid tree.

The freckle-faced lad who looked after the horse deliberately did not glance at me when he took hold of the reins in the paddock. He usually greeted me with a beaming smile. I slid off the horse. The owner and James stood there, their faces blank. No one said anything. There was nothing to say. Finally, without a word, the owner shrugged his shoulders and turned on his heel, and walked off.

I took my saddle off the horse and the lad led him away.

James said, "It can't go on, Rob."

I knew it.

He said, "I'm sorry. I'm very sorry. I'll have to get someone else to ride my horses tomorrow."

I nodded.

He gave me a searching look in which puzzlement and doubt were tinged for the first time with pity. I found it unbearable.

"I think I'll go to Kensington tonight after the races," I said, trying to speak evenly. "Instead of coming back with you."

"Very well," he said, obviously relieved at not having to face an embarrassing return journey. "I really am sorry, Rob."

"Yes," I said. "I know."

I took my saddle back to the weighing room, acutely aware of the glances
that followed me. The conversation in the changing room died into an embarrassed silence when I walked in. I went over to my peg, put the saddle on
the bench, and began to take off my colors. I looked at the circle of faces
turned toward me, reading on some curiosity, on some hostility, on some
sympathy, and on one or two pleasure. No contempt; they would leave that
to people who didn't ride, to the people who didn't know at first hand how
formidable a big fence can look to a jockey on a bad horse. In the changing
room there was too much consciousness in their minds of "there but for the
grace of God go I" for them to feel contempt.

They began to talk again, but not much to me. I guessed they didn't
know what to say. Nor did I.

I felt neither more nor less courageous than I had done all my life. It was
surely impossible, I thought confusedly, to be subconsciously afraid, to keep
out of trouble, and yet think one was as willing as ever to accept risks. Three
weeks earlier I would have laughed at the idea. But the shattering fact remained that none of the twenty-eight horses I had ridden since I had been
knocked out in that fall had made any show at all. They were trained by several different trainers and owned by different owners; all they had had in
common was me. There were too many of them for it to be coincidence, especially as those I had been removed from had done well.

Round and round in a jumble went the profitless thoughts, the hopeless sta-
tistics, the feeling that the sky had fallen. I put on my street clothes and brushed
my hair, and was surprised to see in the mirror that I looked the same as usual.

I went to the steps outside the weighing room and heard the normal
chatter, which my presence had muffled in the changing room, break out
cheerfully again as soon as I was gone. No one outside seemed very anxious to
talk to me, either; no one, that is, except a weedy little ferret of a man, who
worked, I knew, for one of the minor sporting papers.

He was standing with John Ballerton, but when he caught sight of me he
came directly over.

"Oh, Finn," he said, taking a notebook and pencil out of his pocket and
looking at me with a sly, malicious smile. "May I have a list of the horses you
are riding tomorrow? And next week?"

I looked across at Ballerton. There was a smirk of triumph on his heavy face. I took a great grip on my rising temper and spoke mildly to the reporter.

"Ask Mr. Axminster," I said. He looked disappointed, but he didn't know how close he had come to feeling my fist in his face. I had just enough sense to know that letting fly at him would be the worst thing I could do.

I strode away from him, seething with rage; but the day was not done with me even yet. Corin, crossing my path purposefully, stopped me and said, "I suppose you've seen this?" He held out a copy of the paper for which the ferrety little man wrote.

"No," I said. "And I don't want to."

Corin smiled thinly, enjoying himself. "I think you ought to sue them. Everyone thinks so. You'll have to sue them when you've read it. You can't ignore it, or everyone will think—"

"Everyone can think what they damn well please," I said roughly, trying to walk on.

"Read it," insisted Corin, thrusting the paper in front of my eyes. "Everyone else has."

It needed only half a glance to see the headline. There was no missing it. In bold type it said: NERVE LOST.

Against my will I began to read:

Nerve, depending on how it takes you, is either fear overcome by an effort of will, or a total lack of imagination. If you ride steeplechasing it doesn't matter which sort you have, as long as you have one of them.

Does anyone understand why one man is brave and another is not? Or why a person can be brave at one time and cowardly at another?

Maybe it is all a matter of hormones! Maybe a bang on the head can destroy the chemical makeup which produces courage. Who knows? Who knows?

The crumbling of a jumping jockey's nerve is a pathetic sight, as every recent racegoer will realize. But while one may extend sympathy to a man for a state which he cannot help, one must at the same time ask whether he is doing the right thing if he continues to seek and accept rides in races.

The public deserves a fair run for its money. If a jockey can't give it to them because he is afraid of hurting himself, he is taking fees under false pretenses.

But it is only a matter of time, of course, before owners and trainers withdraw their custom from such a man, and by forcing him into retirement protect the betting public from wasting any more of its money.

And a good thing too!

I gave the paper back to Corin and tried to lessen the clamped tension of my jaw muscles.

"I can't sue them," I said. "They don't mention my name."

He didn't look surprised, and I realized sharply that he had known it all along. He had wanted only the pleasure of watching me read, and there was still about his eyes a remnant of a very nasty smile.

"What did I ever do to you, Corin," I asked, "to make you feel the way you do?"

He looked taken aback, and said weakly, "Er . . . nothing . . ."

"Then I'm sorry for you," I said stonily. "I'm sorry for your spiteful, mean, cowardly little soul."

"Cowardly!" he exclaimed, stung and flushing. "Who are you to call anyone else cowardly? That's a laugh, that really is. Just wait till they hear this. Just wait till I tell—"

But I didn't wait. I had had far, far more than enough. I went back to Kensington in as deep and terrible a mood of despair as I ever hope to have to live through.

There was no one in the flat, and for once it was spotlessly tidy. The family, I concluded, was away. The kitchen confirmed it. There was no food or milk in the refrigerator, no bread in the bin, no fruit in the basket.

Back in the silent sitting room I took a nearly full whisky bottle out of the cupboard and lay down full length on the sofa. I uncorked the bottle and took two large gulps. The neat spirit bit into my gums and scorched down to my empty stomach. I put the cork in the bottle and the bottle on the floor beside me. What is the point of getting drunk, I thought. I'd only feel worse in the morning. I could stay drunk for several days perhaps, but it wouldn't do any good in the end. Nothing would do any good. Everything was finished. Everything was busted and gone.

I spent a long time looking at my hands. Hands. The touch they had for horses had earned me my living all my adult life. They looked the same as always. They were the same, I thought desperately. Nerves and muscles, strength and sensitivity, nothing was changed. But the memory of the last twenty-eight horses I had ridden denied it: heavy, cumbersome and unresponsive.

I knew no other skill but riding, nor had ever wanted any. I felt more than whole on horseback: I felt extended. Four extra limbs and a second brain. More speed, more strength, more courage . . . I winced at the word . . . and quicker reactions. A saddle was to me as the sea to a fish, natural and easy. Home. And a racing saddle? I drew in a breath, shivering. For a racing saddle, I thought bleakly, I am not sufficient.

It wasn't enough, after all, to *want* to race as well as anybody; one had to have the talent and the staying power as well, and I was face to face with the conviction that I was not good enough, that I was never going to be good enough to take firm hold of the position which had been so nearly in my grasp. I had thought myself capable of seizing the incredible opportunity I had been given. The mess I had made of it, the weak degrading retreat from the brink of success, was tearing to shreds all I had known or believed about myself.

I picked up the whisky bottle and held it on my chest. It was all the company I had, and it offered sleep at least. But I suppose old habits cling hard: I held the bottle to my chest like a life jacket to a drowning man and I knew I wouldn't pull the cork out again. Not for a while. Not that night, anyway.

And what of the future? I could return during the next week and race on one or two of James's horses, if he would still let me, and perhaps even on Template in the Midwinter. But I no longer either expected or hoped to do well, and I could feel myself shrink at the prospect of going back to a racecourse to face all those stares and insults again. Better to start a new life at once, perhaps. But a new life doing what?

It couldn't be the old life. Being a stockman might have suited me at twenty, but it was not what I would want at thirty, nor at forty, nor at fifty. And whatever I did, wherever I went now, I would drag around with me the knowledge that I had totally failed at what I had tried hardest to do.

After a long time I stood up and put the bottle back in the cupboard.

It was then a good twenty-six hours since I had eaten, and despite everything, my stomach was beginning its squeezing routine. On a second inspection the kitchen revealed only some assorted tins of escargots, cheese straws, and marrons glacés; so I went out and along the streets until I came to a decent-looking pub where I was sure I was not known by sight. I didn't want to have to talk.

I ordered ham sandwiches and a glass of beer, but when the food came the thick new white bread stuck tastelessly in my mouth and my throat kept closing convulsively against all attempts to swallow. This can't go on, I thought. I've got to eat. If I can't get drunk and I can't have Joanna and I can't . . . I can't be a jockey any more . . . at least I can eat now as much as I like, without worrying about gaining a pound or two . . . but after ten minutes' trying I had swallowed only two mouthfuls, and I couldn't manage another bite.

The fact that it was Friday had meant nothing to me all evening, and the approach of nine o'clock went unnoticed. But just when I had pushed away the sandwiches and was eyeing the beer with the beginnings of nausea, someone turned up the volume of the television set, which stood at one end of the bar, and the opening bars of "The Galloping Major" suddenly blared out across the tinkling glasses and the buzzing voices. A large bunch of devotees who had settled themselves with full pint pots in front of the set made shooshing noises to those nearest to them, and by the time Maurice Kemp-Lore's tidy features materialized there was a more or less attentive audience to receive him. My little glass-topped table was as far as it could be from the door. So it was more because leaving meant weaving my way through the sprawling silent crowd, than from a positive desire to watch, that I stayed where I was.

"Good evening," Maurice said, the spellbinding smile in place. "This evening we are going to talk about handicapping, and I have here to meet you two well-informed men who look at weights and measures from opposing angles. The first is Mr. Charles Jenkinson, who has been an official handicapper for several years." Mr. Jenkinson's self-conscious face appeared briefly on the screen. "And the other is the well-known trainer, Corin Kellar." Corin's thin face glowed with satisfaction. We'll never hear the last of this, I thought: and then with a stab remembered that I wouldn't be there to hear any of it.

"Mr. Jenkinson," said Maurice, "will explain how he builds a handicap. And Mr. Kellar will tell you how he tries to avoid having his horses defeated by their weights. The battle between handicappers and trainers is none the less fierce for being conducted in gentlemanly and largely uncomplaining reticence, and perhaps tonight you will capture a whiff of that unrelenting struggle." He smiled engagingly. "A handicapper's pinnacle of success is for every single runner in a race to pass the winning post in a straight line abreast—a multiple dead-heat—since it is his aim to give each horse an exactly equal chance. It never actually happens, but handicappers dream about it in their softer moments." He grinned sideways in a friendly fashion toward his guest, and when Mr. Jenkinson appeared on the screen one could almost see the self-confidence begin to flow in him as he started to talk about his job.

I listened with only half my mind, the rest being submerged in persistent misery, and Corin had been speaking for some moments before I paid much attention to him. He was being of necessity less than frank, since the bald truth would have lost him his license very smartly. In practice he felt no qualms at all when giving his jockey orders to start at the back and stay there, but in theory, I was sardonically amused to see, he was righteously on the side of the angels.

"Horses from my stable are always doing their best to win," he said, lying without a tremor.

"But surely you don't insist on them being ridden hard at the end when they've no chance at all?" said Maurice reasonably.

"As hard as necessary, yes," Corin asserted. "I hate to see jockeys easing up too soon, even if they are beaten. I dismissed a jockey a short while ago for not riding hard enough at the end. He could have come third if he had ridden the horse out . . ." His voice droned on, pious and petulant, and I thought of Tick-Tock, thrown to the Stewards for obeying his orders too conscientiously and now having trouble getting other trainers to trust him. I thought of Art, nagged and contradicted and driven to death; and the active dislike I already felt for Corin Kellar sharpened in that dim pub corner into hatred.

Maurice dragged him back to handicapping and finally wrung from him a grudging admission that from the point of view of the weight he would be allotted in future, it was better for a horse to win by one length than by ten. Maurice would have done better, I thought, to have chosen almost anyone else to show how to dodge the handicapper; or perhaps he did not know Corin well enough to expect him hypocritically to deny in public what he had said in private. Every jockey who had ridden the Kellar horses had learned it the hard way.

"One is always in the hands of one's jockey," Corin was saying.

"Go on," said Maurice encouragingly, leaning forward. A light somewhere in the studio lent his eyes a momentary shimmer as he moved.

Corin said, "You can slave away for weeks preparing a horse for a race and then a jockey can undo it all with one stupid mistake."

"It does the handicap good though," Maurice interrupted, laughing. The pub audience laughed too.

"Well . . ." agreed Corin, nonplused.

"If you look at it that way," Maurice continued, "there is always some compensation for a jockey's not getting the most out of a horse. Whatever the reason; trivial, like a mistake, or more serious, like a failure of resolution at a crucial point—"

"No guts, you mean?" said Corin flatly. "I'd say that that would be as obvious to a handicapper as to everyone else, and that he'd take it into account. There's a case in point now . . ." he hesitated, but Maurice did not try to stop him, so he went on more boldly, "a case now where everything a certain jockey rides goes round at the back of the field. He is afraid of falling, you see. Well, you can't tell me any handicapper thinks those particular horses are not as good as they were. Of course they are. It's just the rider who's going downhill."

I could feel the blood rush to my head and begin to pulse there. I leaned my elbows on the table and bit my knuckles. Hard.

The voices went on inexorably.

Maurice said, "What are your views on that, Mr. Jenkinson?"

And the handicapper, looking embarrassed, murmured that "Of course . . . er . . . in certain circumstances, one would er . . . overlook the occasional result."

"Occasional!" said Corin. "I wouldn't call nearly thirty races in a row occasional. Are you going to overlook them all?"

"I can't answer that," protested Jenkinson.

"What do you usually do in these cases?" Maurice asked.

"I . . . that is . . . they aren't usually as blatant as this. I may have to consult . . . er, others, before coming to a decision. But it really isn't a thing I can discuss here."

"Where better?" said Maurice persuasively. "We all know that this poor chap took a toss three weeks ago and has ridden . . . ineffectively . . . ever since. Surely you'd have to take that into account when you are handicapping those horses?"

While the camera focused on Jenkinson hesitating over his answer, Corin's voice said, "I'll be interested to know what you decide. One of those horses was mine, you know. It was a shocking exhibition. Finn won't be riding for me again, or for anyone else either, I shouldn't wonder."

Jenkinson said uneasily, "I don't think we should mention names," and Maurice cut in quickly, saying, "No, no. I agree. Better not." But the damage was done.

"Well, thank you both very much for giving up your time this evening.

I am sorry to say we have come nearly to the end once again . . ." He slid expertly into his minute of chitchat and his closing sentences, but I was no longer listening. Between them he and Corin had hammered in the nails on the ruins of my brief career, and watching them at it on the glaring little screen had given me a blinding headache.

I stood up stiffly as the chatter broke out again in the crowded pub and threaded my way a little unsteadily to the door. The bunch of racing enthusiasts were downing their pints and I caught a scrap of their conversation as I squeezed round them.

"Laid it on a bit thick, I thought," one of them said.

"Not thick enough," contradicted another. "I lost a quid on Finn on Tuesday. He deserves all he gets, if you ask me, the windy bastard."

I stumbled out into the street, breathing in great gulps of cold air and making a conscious effort to stand up straight. It was no use sitting down and weeping in the gutter, which would have been easy enough to do. I walked slowly back to the dark empty flat, and without switching on any lights lay down fully dressed on my bed.

The glow from the street below dimly lit the small room, the window frame throwing an angular distorted shadow on the ceiling. My head throbbed. I remembered lying there like that before, the day Grant's fist pulped my nose. I remembered pitying him, and pitying Art. It had been so easy. I groaned aloud, and the sound shocked me.

It was a long way down from my window to the street. Five stories. A long, quick way down. I thought about it.

There was a chiming clock in the flat below ours, counting away the quarter hours, and in the quiet house I could hear it clearly. It struck ten, eleven, twelve, one, two.

The window threw its shadow steadily on the ceiling. I stared up at it. Five stories down. But however bad things were I couldn't take that way, either. It wasn't for me. I shut my eyes and lay still, and finally after the long despairing hours drifted into an exhausted, uneasy, dream-filled sleep.

I WOKE LESS than two hours later, and heard the clock strike four. My headache had gone, and my mind felt as clear and sharp as the starry sky outside: washed and shining. It was like coming out of a thick fog into sunshine. Like coolness after fever. Like being reborn.

Somewhere between sleeping and waking I found I had regained myself, come back to the life-saving certainty that I was the person I thought I was, and not the cracked-up mess that everyone else believed.

And that being so, I thought in puzzlement, there must be some other explanation of my troubles. All—*all* I had to do was find it. Looking back unsympathetically on the appalling desolation in which I had so recently allowed myself to flounder, I began at last, at long last, to use my brain.

Half an hour later it was clear that my stomach was awake too, and it was so insistent to be filled that I couldn't concentrate. I got up and fetched the tins of cheese straws and marrons glacés from the kitchen, but not the snails. How hungry would one have to be, I wondered idly, to face those mollusks cold and butterless at five o'clock in the morning?

I opened the tins and lay down again, and crunched up all the cheese straws while I thought, and then I chewed half the syrupy weight-producing chestnuts. My stomach quieted, like a dragon fed its daily maiden, and outside the stars faded into the wan London dawn.

In the morning I took the advice I had given to Grant, and went to see a psychiatrist.

CHAPTER 9

I HAD KNOWN the psychiatrist all my life as he was a friend of my father's and, I hoped, I knew him well enough to ring him up for help on a morning that he always reserved for golf. At eight o'clock I telephoned to his house in Wimpole Street, where he lived in a flat above his consulting rooms.

He asked after my father. He sounded in a hurry.

"Can I come and see you, sir?" I said.

"Now? No. Saturday. Golf," he said economically.

"Please . . . it won't take long."

There was a brief pause.

"Urgent?" A professional note to his question.

"Yes," I said.

"Come at once, then. I'm due at Wentworth at ten."

"I haven't shaved . . ." I said, catching sight of myself in the looking glass and realizing what a wreck I looked.

"Do you want to shave or do you want to talk?" he said, exasperated.

"Talk," I said.

"Then arrive," he said, and put down his receiver.

I took a taxi, and he opened the door to me with a corner of toast and marmalade in his hand. The eminent Mr. Claudius Mellit, whose patients usually saw him in striped trousers and black jacket, was sensibly attired for winter golf in waterproof trousers and a comfortably sloppy Norwegian sweater. He gave me a piercing preliminary glance and gestured, "Upstairs."

I followed him up. He finished his breakfast on the way. We went into his dining room, where he gave me a seat at the oval mahogany table, and some lukewarm coffee in a gold-rimmed cup.

"Now," he said, sitting down opposite me.

"Suppose . . ." I began, and stopped. It didn't seem so easy, now that I was there. What had seemed obvious and manifest at five in the morning was now tinged with doubt. The dawn hours had shown me a pattern I believed in, but in the full light of day I felt sure it was going to sound preposterous.

"Look," he said, "if you really need help, my golf can go hang. When I said on the telephone that I was in a hurry I hadn't seen the state you are in . . . and if you will excuse me saying so, your suit looks as if you had slept in it."

"Well, yes, I did," I said, surprised.

"Relax then, and tell me all." He grinned, a big bear of a man, fifty years old and formidably wise.

"I'm sorry I look so untidy and unshaved," I began.

"And sunken-eyed and hollow-cheeked," he murmured, smiling.

"But I don't feel as bad as I suppose I look. Not any more. I won't keep you away from your golf if you'll just tell me . . .".

"Yes?" He waited for me calmly.

"Suppose I had a sister," I said, "who was as good a musician as Mother and Father, and I was the only one in the entire family to lack their talent— as you know I am—and I felt they despised me for lacking it, how would you expect me to act?"

"They don't despise you," he protested.

"No . . . but if they did, would there be any way in which I could persuade them—and myself—that I had a very good excuse for not being a musician?"

"Oh, yes," he said instantly, "I'd expect you to do exactly what you have done. Find something you can do, and pursue it fanatically until in your own sphere you reach the standard of your family in theirs."

I felt as if I'd been hit in the solar plexus. So simple an explanation of my compulsion to race had never occurred to me.

"That . . . that isn't what I meant," I said helplessly. "But when I come to think of it, I see it is true." I paused. "What I really meant to ask was, could I, when I was growing up, have developed a physical infirmity to explain away my failure? Paralysis, for instance, so that I simply couldn't play a violin or a piano or any musical instrument? An apparently honorable way out?"

He looked at me for a few moments, unsmiling and intent.

"If you were a certain type of person, yes, it's possible. But not in your case. You had better stop waltzing round it and ask me your question straight out. The real question. I am very well accustomed to hypothetical questions . . . I meet them every day . . . but if you want a trustable answer you'll have to ask the real question."

"There are two," I said. I still hesitated. So very much, my whole life, depended on his answers. He waited patiently.

I said at last, "Could a boy whose family were all terrific cross-country riders develop asthma to hide the fact that he was afraid of horses?" My mouth was dry.

He didn't answer at once. He said, "What is the other question?"

"Could that boy, as a man, develop such a loathing for steeplechase jockeys that he would try to smash their careers? Even if, as you said, he had found something else which he could do extremely well?"

"I suppose this man has that sister you mentioned?"

"Yes," I said. "She is getting to be the best girl point-to-point rider for a generation."

He slouched back in his chair.

"It obviously matters so desperately to you, Robert, that I can't give you an answer without knowing more about it. I'm not giving you a couple of casual yeses, and find afterward that I've let you stir up disastrous trouble for all sorts of people. You must tell me why you ask these questions."

"But your golf," I said.

"I'll go later," he said calmly. "Talk."

So I talked. I told him what had happened to Art, and to Grant, and to Peter Cloony, and to Tick-Tock, and to myself.

I told him about Maurice Kemp-Lore. "He comes from a family who ride as soon as walk; and he's the right build for steeplechasing. But horses give him asthma, and that, everyone knows, is why he doesn't race himself. Well, it's a good reason, isn't it? Of course there are asthmatics who do ride—asthma doesn't stop people who think that racing is worth the wheezing—but no one would dream of blaming a man who didn't."

I paused, but as he made no comment, I went on: "You can't help being drawn to him. You can't imagine the spell of his personality unless you've felt it. You can see people wake up and sparkle when he speaks to them. He has the ear of everyone from the Stewards down—and I think he uses his influence to sow seeds of doubt about jockeys' characters."

"Go on," Claudius said, his face showing nothing.

"The men who seem to be especially under his spell are Corin Kellar, a trainer, and John Ballerton, a member of the ruling body. Neither of them ever has a good word to say for jockeys. I think Kemp-Lore picked them out as friends solely because they had the right sort of mean-mindedness for broadcasting every damaging opinion he insinuated into their heads. I think all the ruinous rumors start with Kemp-Lore, and that even the substance behind the rumors is mostly his work. Why isn't he content with having so much? The jockeys he is hurting like him and are pleased when he talks to them. Why does he need to destroy them?"

He said, "If this were a hypothetical case I would tell you that such a man could both hate and envy his father—and his sister—and have felt both these emotions from early childhood. But because he knows these feelings are wrong he represses them, and the aggression is unfortunately transferred onto people who show the same qualities and abilities that he hates in his father. Such individuals can be helped. They can be understood and treated, and forgiven."

"I can't forgive him," I said. "And I'm going to stop him."

He considered me. "You must make sure of your facts," he said, stroking his thumbnail down his upper lip. "At present you are just guessing. And as I've had no opportunity to talk to him, you'll get no more from me than an admission that your suspicions of Kemp-Lore may be *possibly* correct. Not even probably correct. He is a public figure of some standing. You are making a very serious accusation. You need cast-iron facts. Until you have them, there is always the chance that you have interpreted what has happened to you as malice from outside in order to explain away your own inner failure. Asthma of the mind, in fact."

"Don't psychologists ever take a simple view?" I said, sighing.

He shook his head. "Few things are simple."

"I'll get the facts, starting today," I said. I stood up. "Thank you for seeing me, and being so patient, and I'm sincerely sorry about your golf."

"I won't be very late," he assured me, ambling down the stairs and opening his front door. On the doorstep, shaking hands, he said as if making up his mind, "Be careful, Robert. Go gently. If you are right about Kemp-Lore, and it is just possible that you are, you must deal with him thoughtfully. Persuade him to ask for treatment. Don't drive him too hard. His sanity may be in your hands."

I said flatly, "I can't look at it from your point of view. I don't think of Kemp-Lore as ill, but as wicked."

"Where illness ends and crime begins . . ." He shrugged. "It has been debated for centuries, and no two people agree. But take care, take care." He turned to go in. "Remember me to your parents." He smiled and shut the door.

Round a couple of corners, first during a luxurious shave at a fresh-smelling barber's and second over a triple order of eggs and bacon in the café next door, I bent my mind to the problem of how the cast-iron facts were to be dug up. On reflection, there seemed to be precious few of them to work on, and in the digging, to start with at least, I was going to come up against the barrier of pity and contempt which my recent performances had raised. Nasty medicine, but if I wanted a cure I'd have to take it.

Using the café's telephone, I rang up Tick-Tock.

"Are you riding this afternoon?" I asked.

He said, "Do me a favor, pal. No unkind questions so early in the day. In a word—negative." A pause. "And you?" Innocently, too innocently.

"You're a bastard," I said.

"So my best friends tell me."

"I want the car," I said.

"Not if you're thinking of driving it over Beachy Head."

"I'm not," I said.

"Well, I'm relieved to hear it. But if you change your mind, let me know and I'll join you." His voice was light and mocking; the desperate truth underneath needed no stating.

"I want to call at some stables," I began.

"Whose?" he interrupted.

"Several people's . . . about six altogether, I think, apart from Axminster's. And Kellar's. I'll have to go there as well."

"You've got a nerve," said Tick-Tock.

"Thank you," I said. "You're about the only person in the country who thinks so."

"Damn it . . . I didn't mean . . ."

I grinned into the telephone. "Save it. Where's the car now?"

"Outside the window."

"I'll come down to Newbury by train and pick it up, if you'll meet me at the station," I said.

"It's no use going to any stables today," he said. "The trainers will all be at the races."

"Yes, I sincerely hope so," I agreed.

"What are you up to?" he asked suspiciously.

"Retrieving the fallen fortune of the House of Finn," I said. "I'll catch the nine-twenty. You meet it, okay?" And I put the receiver down, hearing, and ignoring, a protesting "Hey" before I cut him off.

But when I stepped off the train at Newbury he was waiting, dressed in a dandyish-waisted riding jacket of almost eighteenth-century length on top of some unbelievably narrow cavalry cord trousers. He enjoyed his moment ironically while I looked him up and down.

"Where's the cravat, the ruffles and the sword?" I asked.

He said, "You don't get the message. I'm tomorrow's man. My sword will be a do-it-yourself instant antiradiation kit. You must fit your defense to the danger you meet." He grinned.

Young Tick-Tock, I reflected, not for the first time, took an uncompromisingly realistic view of the world.

He opened the car door and settled himself behind the wheel.

"Where to?" he said.

"You're not coming," I said.

"I certainly am. This car is half mine. Where it goes, I go." He was clearly determined. "Where to?"

"Well . . ." I got in beside him, fished out of my pocket a list I had made on the train, and showed it to him. "These are the stables I want to go to. I've tried to arrange them in order so that there isn't too much backtracking, but even so it means a lot of driving."

"Phew!" he said. "There's a lot of them. Hampshire, Sussex, Kent, Oxford, Leicester and Yorkshire. How long will you be staying in each place?
We'll never cover this lot in one day. Especially as you look tired already."

I glanced at him, but he was looking down at the paper. It was true that
I felt tired, but disconcerted that it should be so obvious. I had thought that
the shave and breakfast and the return of self-confidence would have wiped
away the ravages of the previous day and night.

"You needn't come," I began.

"We've been through all that," he interrupted. "We'll start by going to
your digs and mine for overnight things, and then make for Kent. And on the
way you can tell me why we're going." He calmly let in the clutch and drove
off: and truth to tell I was very glad of his company.

We collected our things, and Tick-Tock pointed the Mini-Cooper's blunt
nose toward the first stable on the list, Corin Kellar's, in Hampshire.

"Now," he said. "The works."

"No," I said. "I'm not going to tell you why we're going. Listen and watch,
and then you tell me."

"You're a cagey blighter," he said, without arguing. He added, "I suppose
you've taken into account all that about saps rushing in where angels wouldn't
plonk their holy feet? I mean, to put it mildly, neither of us is in the red-
carpet bracket just now. Strictly doomsville, us."

"You are so right," I said, smiling.

Tick-Tock turned his head and gave me a surprised stare.

"Keep your eyes on the road," I said mildly.

"I'll never know you," he said. "I'd have thought you'd take it very
hard . . . what has happened . . . but since I picked you up at the station I've
felt more cheerful than I have for weeks." His foot went down on the accelerator and he began to whistle.

We arrived at Corin's extensive, well-groomed stable while the lads were
doing up the horses after the second morning exercise. Arthur, the head lad,
was crossing the yard with a bucket of oats when we climbed out of the little
car, and the crinkling smile with which he usually greeted me got halfway to
his eyes before he remembered. I saw the embarrassment take over and the
welcome fade away.

"The governor isn't here," he said awkwardly. "He's gone to the races."

"I know," I said. "Can I speak to Davey?"

Davey was the lad who looked after Shantytown.

"I suppose so," said Arthur doubtfully, "but you won't make no trouble?"

"No," I said. "No trouble. Where is he?"

"Fourth box from the end over that side," he said, pointing. Tick-Tock and I walked over, and found Davey tossing and tidying the straw bed round a big chestnut. Shantytown. We leaned over the bottom half of the door, and watched Davey's expression, too, change from warmth to disgust. He was a short, tough, sixteen-year-old boy with flaming red hair and an intolerant mouth. He turned his back on us and ran his hand down the horse's neck. Then he spat into the straw. Tick-Tock took a sharp breath and his hands clenched into fists.

I said quickly, "Davey, there's a quid for you if you feel like talking a bit."

"What about?" he said, without turning round.

"About the day I rode Shantytown at Dunstable," I said. "Three weeks ago. Do you remember?"

"I'll say I remember," he said offensively.

I ignored his tone. "Well, tell me what happened from the moment you arrived on the course until I got up on Shantytown in the parade ring."

"What the hell do you mean?" he said, wheeling round and coming over to the door. "Nothing happened. What should happen?"

I took a pound note out of my wallet and gave it to him. He looked at it for a second or two, then shrugged, and thrust it into his pocket.

"Start when you set off from here. Don't leave anything out," I said.

"Are you off your nut?" he said.

"No," I said, "and I want my quid's worth."

He shrugged again, but said, "We went in the horse box from here to Dunstable, and—"

"Did you stop on the way?" I asked.

"Yes, Joe's Caff, same as always when we go to Dunstable."

"Did you see anyone there you knew?"

"Well, Joe, and the girl who pours out the char."

"No one you wouldn't expect?" I pressed.

"No, of course not. Like I said, we got to the course and unloaded the horses, two of them, in the stables there, and went and got another cuppa and a wad in the canteen, and then I went round the bookies, like, and put ten bob on Bloggs in the first, and went up on the stands, and watched it get stuffed—sodding animal didn't try a yard—and then I went back to the stables and got Shantytown and put on his paddock clothing and led him out into the paddock . . ." His voice was bored as he recited the everyday racing routine of his job.

"Could anyone have given Shantytown anything to eat or drink in the stables, say a bucket of water just before the race?" I asked.

"Don't be so ruddy stupid. Of course not. Whoever heard of giving a horse anything to eat or drink before a race? A mouthful of water, I dare say, a couple of hours beforehand, but a bucketful . . ." The scorn in his voice suddenly changed to anger, "Here, you're not suggesting I gave him a drink, are you? Oh, no, mate, you're not putting the blame on me for the balls you made of it."

"No," I said, "no, Davey. Clam down. How tight is the security on the Dunstable stables? Would anyone but a lad or a trainer get in there?"

"No," he said, more moderately, "it's as tight as a drum. The last gateman got sacked for letting an owner in alone without a trainer, and the new man's as pernickety as they come."

"Go on, then," I said. "We've got you as far as the paddock."

"Well, I walked the horse round the assembly ring for a bit, waiting for the governor to bring the saddle up from the weighing room—" he smiled suddenly, as at some pleasant memory—"and then when he came I took Shanty into one of the saddling boxes and the governor saddled up, and then I took Shanty down into the parade ring and walked him round until they called me over and you got up on him." He stopped. "I can't see what you wanted to hear all that for."

"What happened while you were walking round the assembly ring?" I asked. "Something you enjoyed? Something you smile about when you re-member it?"

He sniffed. "It's nothing you'd want to know."

I said, "The quid was for telling everything."

"Oh, very well then, but it's nothing to do with racing. It was that chap on the telly, Maurice Kemp-Lore, he came over and spoke to me and admired the horse. He said he was a friend of the owner, old man Ballerton. He patted Shanty and gave him a couple of sugar lumps, which I wasn't too keen on, mind, but you can't be narky with a chap like him, somehow, and he asked me what his chances were, and I said pretty good—more fool me—and then he went away again. That's all. I told you it wasn't anything to do with racing."

"No," I said. "Well, never mind. Thanks for trying."

I straightened up and turned away from the door, and Tick-Tock had taken a step or two toward the car when Davey said under his breath behind me, "Trying . . . you two could both do a bit more of that yourselves, if you ask me." But Tick-Tock fortunately didn't hear, and we folded ourselves back into the Mini-Cooper and drove unmourned out of the yard.

Tick-Tock exploded. "Anyone would think you'd killed your mother and robbed your grandmother, the way they look at you. Losing your nerve isn't a crime."

"Unless you can put up with a few harmless sneers you'd better get out at the next railway station," I said cheerfully, having blessedly discovered in the past half hour that they no longer hurt. "And I haven't lost my nerve. Not yet, anyway."

He opened his mouth and shut it again and flicked a glance at me, and drove another twenty miles without speaking.

We reached the next yard on my list shortly before one o'clock, and disturbed the well-to-do farmer, who trained his own horses, just as he was about to sit down to his lunch. When he opened the door to us a warm smell of stew and cabbage edged past him, and we could hear a clatter of saucepans in the kitchen. I had ridden several winners for him in the past two years before disgracing his best horse the previous week, and after he had got over the unpleasant shock of finding me on his doorstep, he asked us, in a friendly enough fashion, to go in for a drink. But I thanked him and refused, and asked where I could find the lad who looked after the horse in question. He came out to the gate with us and pointed to a house down the road.

We talked the lad out of his digs and into the car, where I gave him a pound and invited him to describe in detail what had happened on the day I had ridden his horse. He was older, less intelligent and less truculent than Davey, but not much more willing. He didn't see no sense in it, he didn't. He said so several times. Eventually I got him started, and then there was no stopping him. Detail I had asked for, and detail I got, solidly, for close on half an hour.

Sandwiched between stripping off the paddock clothing and buckling up the saddle came the news that Maurice Kemp-Lore had lounged into the saddling box, said some complimentary things to the farmer-owner about his horse, meanwhile feeding the animal some lumps of sugar, and had drifted away again leaving behind him the usual feeling of friendliness and pleasure.

"A proper corker, ain't he?" was how the lad put it.

I waited until he had reached the point when the farmer had given me a leg up onto the horse, and then stopped him and thanked him for his efforts. We left him muttering that we were welcome, but he still didn't see the point.

"How odd," said Tick-Tock pensively as we sped along the road to the next stable, eighty miles away. "How odd that Maurice Kemp-Lore . . ." He didn't finish the sentence; nor did I.

Two hours later, in Kent, we listened, for another pound, to a gaunt boy of twenty telling us what a smashing fellow Maurice Kemp-Lore was, how interested he'd been in the horse, how kind to give him some sugar, though it wasn't really allowed in his stables, but how could you tell a man like that not to when he was being so friendly? The lad also treated us with a rather offensive superiority, but even Tick-Tock by now had become too interested to care.

"He drugged them," he said flatly, after a long silence, turning on to the Maidstone bypass. "He drugged them to make it look as if you couldn't ride them . . . to make everyone believe you'd lost your nerve."

"Yes," I agreed.

"But it's impossible," he protested vehemently. "Why on earth should he? It can't be right. It must be a coincidence that he gave sugar to three horses you rode."

"Maybe. We'll see," I said.

And we did see. We went to the stables of every horse (other than James's) that I had ridden since Shantytown, talking to every lad concerned. And in every single case we heard that Maurice Kemp-Lore had made memorable the lad's afternoon (before I had blighted it) by admiring the way the lad had looked after his horse, and by offering those tempting lumps of sugar. It took us the whole of Saturday, and all Sunday morning, and we finished the last stable on my list on the edge of the Yorkshire moors at two o'clock in the afternoon. Only because I wanted my facts to be as cast-iron as possible had we gone so far north. Tick-Tock had become convinced in Northamptonshire.

I drove us back to our respective digs in Berkshire, and the following morning, Monday, I walked up to the Axminster stables to see James.

He had just come in from supervising the morning exercise, and the cold downland air had numbed his toes and fingers.

"Come into the office," he said when he saw me waiting. His tone was neutral, but his protruding lower jaw was unrelenting. I followed him in, and he turned on an electric heater to warm his hands.

"I can't give you much to ride," he said, with his back to me. "All the owners have cried off, except one. You'd better look at this; it came this morning." He stretched out his hand, picked up a paper from his desk, and held it out to me.

I took it. It was a letter from Lord Tirrold.

Dear James,

Since our telephone conversation I have been thinking over our decision to replace Finn on Template next Saturday, and I now consider that we should reverse this and allow him to ride as originally planned. It is, I confess, at least as much for our sake as for his, since I do not want it said that I hurried to throw him out at the first possible moment, showing heartless ingratitude after his many wins on my horses. I am prepared for the disappointment of not winning the Midwinter and I apologize to you for robbing you of the chance of adding this prize to your total, but I would rather lose the race than the respect of the racing fraternity.

Yours ever,
George

I put the letter back on the desk.

"He doesn't need to worry," I said thickly. "Template will win."

"Do you mean you aren't going to ride it?" said James, turning round quickly. There was a damaging note of eagerness in his voice, and he saw that I had heard it. "I . . . I mean . . ." He trailed off.

"James," I said, sitting down unasked in one of the battered armchairs. "There are a few things I'd like you to know. First, however bad it looks, and whatever you believe, I have not lost my nerve. Second, every single horse I have ridden since that fall three weeks ago has been doped. Not enough to be very noticeable, just enough to make it run like a slug. Third, the dope has been given to all the horses by the same man. Fourth, the dope has been given to the horses in sugar lumps. I should think it was some form of sleeping draught, but I've no way of knowing for sure." I stopped abruptly.

James stood looking at me with his mouth open, the prominent lower teeth bared to the gums as his lip dropped in shocked disbelief.

I said, "Before you conclude that I am out of my mind, do me the one favor of calling in one of the lads, and listening to what he has to say."

James shut his mouth with a snap. "Which lad?"

"It doesn't really matter. Any of them whose horse I have ridden in the past three weeks."

He paused dubiously, but finally went to the door and shouted for someone to find Eddie, the lad who looked after Hugo's big chestnut. In less than a minute the boy arrived, out of breath, and with his curly fair hair sticking up in an uncombed halo.

James gave me no chance to do the questioning. He said brusquely to Eddie, "When did you last talk to Rob?"

The boy looked scared and began to stutter. "N-not since l-l-last week."

"Since last Friday?" That was the day James himself had last seen me.

"No, sir."

"Very well, then. You remember the big chestnut running badly last Wednesday?"

"Yes, sir." Eddie treated me to a scornful glance.

"Did anyone give the chestnut a lump of sugar before the race?" There was now only interest to be heard in James's voice; the severity was masked.

"Yes, sir," said Eddie eagerly. The familiar remembering smile appeared on his grubby face, and I breathed an inward sigh of bottomless relief.

"Who was it?"

"Maurice Kemp-Lore, sir. He said how splendidly I looked after my horses, sir. He was leaning over the rails of the assembly ring and he spoke to me as I was going past. So I stopped, and he was ever so nice. He gave the chestnut some sugar, sir, but I didn't think it would matter as Mr. Hugo is always sending sugar for him anyway."

"Thank you, Eddie," said James, rather faintly. "No matter about the sugar. Run along now."

Eddie went. James looked at me blankly. The loud clock ticked.

Presently I said, "I've spent the past two days talking to the lads of all the horses I've ridden for other stables since I had that fall. Every one of them told me that Maurice Kemp-Lore gave each horse some lumps of sugar before I rode it. Ingersoll came with me. He heard them too. You've only to ask him if you can't believe it from me."

"Maurice never goes near horses at the races," James protested, "or anywhere else for that matter."

"That's precisely what helped me to understand what was happening," I said. "I talked to Kemp-Lore on the stands at Dunstable just after Shantytown and two other horses had run hopelessly for me, and he was wheezing quite audibly. He had asthma, which meant that he had recently been very close to horses. I didn't give it a thought at the time, but it means a packet to me now."

"But Maurice . . ." he repeated, unbelievingly. "It's just not possible."

"It is however possible," I said, more coldly than I had any right to, having believed it myself for twelve awful hours, "for me to fall apart from a small spot of concussion?"

"I don't know what to think," he said uncomfortably. There was a pause. There were two things I wanted James to do to help me; but in view of his ingrained disinclination to do favors for anyone, I did not think my requests would be very enthusiastically received. However, if I didn't ask I wouldn't get.

I spoke slowly, persuasively, as if the thought had just occurred to me. "Let me ride a horse for you . . . one of your own, if the owners won't have me . . . and see for yourself if Kemp-Lore tries to give it sugar. Perhaps you could stick with the horse yourself all the time? And if he comes up with his sugar lumps, maybe you could manage to knock them out of his hand before the horse eats them. Perhaps you could pick them up yourself and put them in your pocket, and give the horse some sugar lumps of your own instead? Then we would see how the horse runs."

It was too much trouble; his face showed it. He said, "That's too fantastic. I can't do things like that."

"It's simple," I said mildly; "you've only to bump his arm."

"No," he said, but not obstinately. A hopeful no, to my ears. I didn't press him, knowing from experience that he would irrevocably stick in his toes if urged too vehemently to do anything he did not want to.

I said instead, "Aren't you friendly with that man who arranges the regular dope tests at the races?" Three or four spot checks were taken at every meeting, mainly to deter trainers of doubtful reputation from pepping up or slowing down their horses with drugs. At the beginning of each afternoon the Stewards decided which horses to test—for example, the winner of the second race, the favorite in the fourth race (especially if he was beaten), and all runners in the fifth. No one, not even the Stewards, always knew in advance exactly which horses would have their saliva taken, and the value of the whole system lay in this uncertainty.

James followed my thoughts. "You mean, will I ask him if any of the horses you have ridden since your fall have been tested for dope in the normal course of events?"

"Yes," I agreed. "Could you possibly do that?"

"Yes, I'll do that," he said. "I will ring him up. But if any of them have been tested and proved negative, you do realize that it will dispose of your wild accusations absolutely?"

"I do," I agreed. "Actually, I've ridden so many beaten favorites that I can't think why such systematic doping has not already been discovered."

"You really do believe it, don't you?" said James wonderingly.

"Yes," I said, getting up and going to the door. "Yes, I believe it. And so will you, James."

But he shook his head, and I left him staring frozen-faced out the window, the incredible nature of what I had said to him still losing the battle against his own personal knowledge of Kemp-Lore. James liked the man.

CHAPTER 10

LATE THAT MONDAY evening James rang me up and told me that I could ride his own horse, Turniptop, which was due to run in the novice chase at Stratford-upon-Avon on the following Thursday. I began to thank him, but he interrupted, "I'm doing you no favor. You know it won't win. He's never been over fences, only hurdles, and all I want is for you to give him an easy race round, getting used to the bigger obstacles. All right?"

"Yes," I said. "All right." And he rang off. There was no mention of whether he would or would not contemplate juggling with sugar lumps.

I was tired. I had spent the whole day driving to Devon and back to visit Art Mathews's beautiful widow, the ice maiden. A fruitless journey. She had been as chilly as ever. Widowhood had warmed her no more than wifehood had done. Blonde, well-bred and cold, she had answered my questions calmly and incuriously and with a complete lack of interest. Art had been dead four months. She spoke of him as though she could hardly remember what he had looked like.

No, she did not know exactly why Art had quarreled so continuously with Corin. No, she did not know why Art had thought fit to shoot himself. No, Art had not got on well with Mr. John Ballerton, but she did not know why. Yes, Art had once appeared on television on *Turf Talk*. It had not been a success, she said, the shadow of an old grievance sharpening her voice. Art had been made to look a fool. Art, whose meticulous sense of honor and order had earned him only respect on the racecourse, had been made to look a cantankerous, mean-minded fool. No, she could not remember exactly how it had been done, but she did remember, only too well, the effect it had had on her own family and friends. They had, it appeared, loudly pitied her on her choice of husband.

But I, listening to her, inwardly pitied poor dead Art on his choice of wife.

On the following day, Tuesday, I again appropriated the Mini-Cooper, much to Tick-Tock's disgust. This time I went toward Cheltenham, and called at Peter Cloony's neat, new bungalow, turning down the narrow, winding lane from the high main road to the village in the hollow.

Peter's wife opened the door to me and asked me in with a strained smile. She no longer looked happy and rosily content. She was too thin, and her hair hung straight and wispy round her neck. It was very nearly as cold inside the house as it was outside, and she wore some tattered fur boots, thick stockings, bulky clothes, and gloves. With no lipstick and no life in her eyes, she was almost unrecognizable as the loving girl who had put me up for the night four months before.

"Come in," she said, "but I'm afraid Peter isn't here. He was given a lift to Birmingham races . . . perhaps he'll get a spare ride." She spoke without hope.

"Of course he will," I said. "He's a good jockey."

"The trainers don't seem to think so," she said despairingly. "Ever since he lost his regular job, he's barely had one ride a week. We can't live on it, how could we? If things don't change very soon, he's going to give up racing and try something else. But he only cares for horses and racing—it will break his heart if he has to leave it."

She had taken me into the sitting room. It was as bare as before. Barer. The rented television set had gone. In its place stood a baby's cot, a wickerwork basket affair on a metal stand. I went over and looked down at the tiny baby, only a small bump under the mound of blankets. He was asleep. I made admiring remarks about what I could see of him, and his mother's face momentarily livened up with pleasure.

She insisted on making us a cup of tea, and I had to wait until the questions of no milk, no sugar, no biscuits had all been settled before asking her what I really wanted to know.

I said, "That Jaguar—the one which blocked the lane and made Peter late—who did it belong to?"

"We don't know," she said. "It was very old. No one came to move it away and it stayed across the lane all that morning. In the end the police arranged for it to be towed away. I know Peter asked the police who owned it, because he wanted to tell the man just what his filthy Jaguar had cost him, but they said they hadn't yet traced him."

"You don't happen to know where the Jaguar is now?" I asked.

"I don't know if it is still there," she said, "but it used to be outside the big garage beside Timberley Station. They're the only garage round here with a breakdown truck, and they were the ones who towed it away."

I thanked her and stood up, and she came out to the car with me to say good-by. I had spent some time going through the form book, adding up the number of races Peter had ridden during the past few weeks, and I knew how little he had earned. I had brought with me a big box of groceries, butter, eggs, cheese, and so on, and a stack of tins, and also a string of plastic ducks for the baby. This collection I carried back into the bungalow and dumped on the kitchen table, ignoring her surprised protest as she followed me in.

I grinned. "They are too heavy to take back. You'll have to make the best of it."

She began to cry.

"Cheer up," I said, "things will get better soon. But, meanwhile, don't you think the bungalow is too cold for a baby? I read somewhere that some babies die every winter from breathing freezing air, even though they may be as warmly wrapped up as yours is."

She looked at me aghast, tears trickling down her cheeks.

"You ought to heat that room a little, and especially keep it warm all night, too, if he sleeps in there," I said.

"But I can't," she said jerkily, "the payments on the bungalow take nearly all we have. We can't afford a fire, except just in the evenings. Is it really true about babies dying?"

She was frightened.

"Yes, quite true," I said. I took a sealed envelope out of my pocket and gave it to her. "This is a present for the baby. Warmth. It's not a fortune, but it will pay your electricity bills for a while, and buy some coal if you want it. There's likely to be a lot of cold weather coming, so you must promise to spend most of it on keeping warm."

"I promise," she said faintly.

"Good." I smiled at her as she wiped her eyes, and then I went back to the car and drove away up the lane.

The garage at Timberley Station was a modernized affair with the front all snowy plaster and the back, when I walked round there, of badly pointed cheap brickwork. The elderly abandoned Jaguar stood there, tucked away between the burned-out remains of a Standard 8 and a pile of old tires. I went round to the front of the garage to talk to the man in charge, and I asked him if I could buy the car.

"Sorry, sir, no can do," he said breezily. He was a dapper, thirtyish man with no oil on his hands.

"Why not?" I said. "It doesn't look good for anything but the scrap heap."

"I can't sell it to you because I don't know who it belongs to," he said regretfully, "but," he brightened, "it's been here so long now that it might be mine after all . . . like unclaimed lost property. I'll ask the police."

With a bit of prompting he told me all about the Jaguar's being stuck across the lane and how his firm had fetched it.

I said, "But someone must have seen the driver after he left the car?"

"The police think he must have got a lift, and then decided the car wasn't worth coming back for. But it's in good enough order. And it wasn't hot . . . stolen, I mean."

"What's it worth?" I asked.

"To you, sir," he smiled glossily, "I'd have let it go for a hundred."

A hundred. I parted from him and strolled out onto the forecourt. Was it worth a hundred to Kemp-Lore, I wondered, to ruin Peter Cloony? Was his obsessive hatred of jockeys so fierce? But then a hundred to Kemp-Lore, I reflected, was probably a lot less than a hundred to me.

Timberley railway station (six stopping trains a day and twenty-two expresses) lay on my left. I stood and considered it. The station was nearly four miles from the top of the lane leading to Peter's village; say an hour's quick walk. Peter had found the Jaguar across the lane at eleven o'clock, and it had to have been jammed in position only seconds before he came up the hill, as his had been the first car to be obstructed. I had a vivid mental picture of Kemp-Lore parked in the gateway where the lane began to curve downward, watching Peter's house through binoculars, seeing him go out and get into his car and start on his way to the races. There wouldn't have been much time to force the Jaguar into position, lock its door, and disappear before Peter got there. Not much time; but enough.

And then? The one tremendous disadvantage Kemp-Lore had to overcome, I thought, was his own fame. His face was so well known to almost the entire British population that he could not hope to move about the country inconspicuously, and wherever he went he would be noticed and remembered. Surely, I thought, in this sparsely populated area it should be possible to find someone who had seen him.

As I was there anyway, I started with the station. Outside, I looked up the times of the stopping trains. There was, I found, a down train at 12:30, but no up train until five o'clock. The only other trains ran early in the morning and later in the evening. The booking office was shut. I found the clerk/ticket collector/porter nodding over a hot stove and a racing paper in the parcels office. A large basket of hens squawked noisily in a corner as I walked in, and he woke with a jerk and told me the next train was due in one hour and ten minutes.

I got him talking via the racing news, but there was nothing to learn. Maurice Kemp-Lore had never (more's the pity, he said) caught a train at Timberley. If it had happened when he was off duty, he'd have heard about it all right. And yes, he said, he'd been on duty the day they'd fetched the Jaguar down to the garage. Disgusting that. Shouldn't be allowed, people being rich enough to chuck their old cars in the ditch like cigarette ends.

I asked him if the station had been busy that day; if there had been a lot of passengers catching the midday train.

"A lot of passengers?" he repeated scornfully. "Never more than three or four, excepting Cheltenham race days."

"I was just wondering," I said idly, "whether the chap who left his Jaguar behind could have caught a train from here that morning."

"Not from here, he didn't," the railway man said positively. "Because, same as usual, all the people who caught the train were ladies."

"Ladies?"

"Yeah, women. Shopping in Cheltenham. We haven't had a man catch the midday—excepting race days, of course—since young Simpkins from the garage got sent home with chickenpox last summer. Bit of a joke it is round here, see, the midday."

I gave him a hot tip for Birmingham that afternoon (which won, I was glad to see later) and left him busily putting a call through to his bookmaker on the government's telephone bill.

Timberley village pub, nearly empty, had never been stirred, they told me regretfully, by the flashing presence of Maurice Kemp-Lore.

The two transport cafés along the main road hadn't heard of any of their chaps giving him a lift.

None of the garages within ten miles had seen him, ever.

The local taxi service had never driven him. He had never caught a bus on the country route.

It wasn't hard at each place to work conversation round to Kemp-Lore, but it was never quick. By the time a friendly bus conductor had told me, over a cigarette at the Cheltenham terminus, that none of his mates had ever had such a famous man on board because they'd never have kept quiet about it (look how Bill went on for days and days when Dennis Compton took a ten-penny single), it was seven o'clock in the evening.

If I hadn't been so utterly, unreasonably sure that it was Kemp-Lore who had abandoned the Jaguar, I would have admitted that, if no one had seen him, then he hadn't been there. As it was, I was depressed by the failure of my search, but not convinced that there was nothing to search for.

The army tank carrier that had blocked Peter's and my way to Cheltenham was there accidentally: that much was clear. But Peter had got into such trouble for being late that a weapon was put straight into the hand of his enemy. He had only had to make Peter late again, and to spread his little rumors, and the deed was done. No confidence, no rides, no career for Cloony.

I found I still hoped by perseverance to dig something up, so I booked a room in a hotel in Cheltenham and spent the evening in a cinema to take my mind off food. On the telephone Tick-Tock sounded more resigned than angry to hear that he would be carless yet again. He asked how I was getting on, and when I reported no progress, he said, "If you're right about our friend, he's as sly and cunning as all get-out. You won't find his tracks too easily."

Without much hope I went down in the morning to the Cheltenham railway station and sorted out, after a little difficulty with old time sheets and the passing of a pound note, the man who had collected the tickets from the passengers on the stopping train from Timberley on the day the Jaguar was abandoned.

He was willing enough, but he too had never seen Kemp-Lore, except on television; though he hesitated while he said so.

"What is it?" I asked.

"Well, sir, I've never seen him, but I think I've seen his sister."

"What was she like?" I asked.

"Very like him, of course, sir, or I wouldn't have known who she was. And she had riding clothes on. You know—jodhpurs, I think they're called. And a scarf over her head. Pretty she looked, very pretty. I couldn't think who she was for a bit, and then it came to me, afterwards like. I didn't talk to her, see? I just took her ticket when she went through the barrier, that's all. I remember taking her ticket."

"When was it that you saw her?" I asked.

"Oh, I couldn't say. I don't rightly know when it was. Before Christmas though, sometime before Christmas, I'm certain of that."

He flipped the pound I gave him expertly into an inner pocket. "Thank you, sir, thank you indeed," he said.

I DRESSED AND shaved with particular care on the Thursday morning as, I supposed, a sort of barrier against the reception I knew I was going to meet. It was six days since I had been racing, six days in which my shortcomings and the shreds of my riding reputation would have been brought up, pawed over and discarded. Life moved fast in the changing room; today was important, tomorrow more so; but yesterday was dead. I belonged to yesterday. I was ancient news.

Even my valet was surprised to see me, although I had written to say I was coming.

"You are riding today, then?" he said. "I was wondering if you wanted to sell your saddle; there's a boy just starting who needs one."

"I'll keep it a bit longer," I said. "I'm riding Turniptop in the fourth. Mr. Axminster's colors."

It was a strange day. As I no longer felt that I deserved the pitying glances to which I was treated, I found that they had, to a great extent, ceased to trouble me, and I even watched with fair equanimity the success of two of my ex-mounts in the first two races. The only thing I worried about was whether or not James would have both sugar lumps in his pocket and willingness in his heart.

He was so busy with his other runners that I did not exchange more than a few words with him during the first part of the afternoon, and when I went out into the parade ring to join him for Turniptop's race, he was standing alone, thoughtfully gazing into the distance.

"Maurice Kemp-Lore's here," he said abruptly.

"Yes, I know," I said. "I saw him."

"He has given sugar to several horses already."

"What?" I exclaimed.

"I have asked quite a few people . . . Maurice has been feeding sugar to any number of horses during the past few weeks, not only to the ones you have ridden."

"Oh," I said weakly. Cunning as all get-out, Tick-Tock had said.

"None of the horses you rode were picked for the regulation dope test," said James, "but some of the other horses Maurice gave sugar to were tested. All negative."

"He gave doped sugar only to my mounts. The rest were camouflage," I said. It sounded improbable, but I was sure of it.

James shook his head.

"Did you . . . ?" I began without much hope. "Did he . . . Kemp-Lore . . . try to give Turniptop any sugar?"

James compressed his lips and stared into the middle distance. I positively held my breath.

"He did come into the saddling box," he said grudgingly. "He admired the horse's coat."

Turniptop ambled past glowing with good health, but before James could say any more one of the Stewards came over to talk to him, and I had no chance to find out about the sugar before it was time to mount and go out for the race.

I knew by the second fence that whether Kemp-Lore had fed him sugar or not, Turniptop was not doped. The leaden sluggishness which had afflicted my last twenty-eight mounts, and which I had been forced to believe was due to my own deficiency, had lifted like a spent thundercloud.

Turniptop leapt and sprang and surged, pulling like a train and doing his damnedest to run away with me. I could have shouted aloud with relief. He was an untidy jumper with more enthusiasm than judgment, a style which had brought him no especial grief over hurdles; but now, in his first steeple-chase, he showed signs of treating fences with the same disrespect. It wouldn't really do; there's a world of difference between a single-thickness, easily knocked down hurdle and a three-foot-wide fence, solidly built of birch twigs, particularly when an open ditch lies in front of it. But Turniptop did not want to be steadied. He was eager. He was rash.

With things as they were, and with James to be convinced, I must admit that my mood matched Turniptop's exactly. We infected each other with recklessness. We took indefensible risks, and got away with them.

I kept him continually on the rails, squeezing forward into tiny openings and letting him take all the bumps that came his way. When he met a fence dead right he gained lengths over it, and when he met one wrong he scrambled through and found a foot to land on somehow. It was more like a roller-coaster ride than the sensible, well-judged race James had indicated, but it taught the tough-minded Turniptop just as much about getting himself out of trouble as going round quietly on the outside would have done.

Coming into the second to last fence, I was afraid we would win. Afraid, because I knew James wanted to sell the horse, and if he had already won a novice chase he would be less valuable than if he had not. An apparent paradox; but Turniptop, young and still green, showed great promise. Too early a win would disqualify him from entering a string of good novice chases in the following season.

It would be far, far better, I knew, to come second. To have shown what he could do but not actually to have won would have put hundreds on his value. But we had run too close a race, and at the second last the disaster of winning seemed unavoidable. There was only one other tiring horse alongside, and I could hear no others on my tail.

Turniptop rose, or rather fell, to the occasion. In spite of my urging him to put in another stride, he took off far too soon and landed with his hind feet tangled hopelessly in the birch. His forelegs buckled under the strain and he went down onto his knees, with my chin resting on his right ear and my hands touching each other round his throat. Even then his indomitable sense of balance rescued him, and he staggered back onto his feet with a terrific up-thrust of his shoulders, tipping me back into the saddle, and tossing his head as if in disgust he set off again toward the winning post. The horse which had been alongside was now safely ahead, and two that had been behind me had jumped past, so that we came into the last fence in fourth position.

I had lost my irons in the debacle and couldn't get my feet into them again in time to jump, so we went over the last with them dangling and clanking in the air. I gathered him together and squeezed my legs, and Turniptop, game to the end, accelerated past two of the horses ahead and flashed into second place four strides from the post.

James waited for me to dismount in the unsaddling enclosure with a face from which all expression had studiously been wiped. Poker-faced to match, I slid from the saddle.

"Don't ever ride a race like that for me again," he said.

"No," I agreed. I undid the girth buckles and took my saddle over my arm, and at last looked into his eyes.

They gleamed, narrowed and inscrutable. He said, "You proved your point. But you could have killed my horse doing it."

I said nothing.

"And yourself," he added, implying that that was less important.

I shook my head, smiling faintly. "Not a chance," I said.

"Hm." He gave me a hard stare. "You'd better come up to the stable this evening," he said. "We can't talk about . . . what we have to talk about . . . here. There are too many people about."

As if to punctuate this remark the owner of the winner leaned over the dividing rails to admire Turniptop and I had to loop up the girths and go and weigh in, still without knowing exactly what had happened in the saddling box before the race.

Tick-Tock was standing by my peg in the changing room, one smoothly shod foot up on the bench and the Tyrolean hat pushed back on his head.

"Before you ride like that again, you might make a will leaving me your half of the car," he said. "It would solve so many legal complications."

"Oh, shut up," I said, peeling off first the crimson and white sweater, James's colors, and then the thin brown jersey underneath. I took a towel from the valet and went along to the washbasin.

"A lot of people," said Tick-Tock in a loud voice across the room, "are going to have a fine old time eating their words, and I hope it gives them indigestion." He followed me along and watched me wash, leaning languidly against the wall. "I suppose you realize that your exploits this afternoon were clearly visible to several million assorted housewives, invalids, babes in arms, and people hanging about on the pavement outside electric shops?"

"What?" I exclaimed.

"It's a fact. Didn't you really know? The last three races are filling up the spare time between *Six for Sixth Forms* and *Goggle with Granny.* Universal T. C. Maurice's lot. I wonder," he finished more soberly, "what he'll do when he knows you've rumbled the sugar bit?"

"He may not know," I said, toweling my chest and shoulders. "He may think it was accidental. . . . I haven't heard yet from James what happened before the race."

"Anyway," said Tick-Tock confidently, "his campaign against you is over. He won't risk going on with it after today."

I agreed with him. It just shows how little either of us understood about obsession.

JAMES WAS WAITING for me in the office, busy with papers at his big desk. The fire blazed hotly and the light winked on the glasses standing ready beside the whisky bottle.

He stopped writing when I came in, and got up and poured out drinks, and stood towering above me as I sat in the battered armchair by the fire. His strong heavy face looked worried.

"I apologize," he said abruptly.

"Don't." I said. "No need."

"I very nearly let Maurice give Turniptop that damned sugar," he said. "I couldn't believe him capable of a scheme as fantastic as doping every horse you ride. I mean, it's . . . it's ridiculous."

"What happened in the saddling box?" I asked.

He took a sip from his glass. "I gave Sid instructions that no one, absolutely no one, however important he was, was to give Turniptop anything to eat or drink before the race. When I reached the box with your saddle, Maurice was in the box next door and I watched him giving the horse there some sugar. Sid said no one had given Turniptop anything." He paused and drank again. "I put on your number cloth, weight pad and saddle, and began to do up with girths. Maurice came round the partition from the next box and said hello. That infectious smile of his . . . I found myself smiling back and thinking you were mad. He was wheezing a bit with asthma . . . and he put his hand in his pocket and brought out two lumps of sugar. He did it naturally, casually, and held them out to Turniptop. I had my hands full of girths and I thought you were wrong . . . but . . . I don't know . . . there was something in the way he was standing, with his arm stretched out rather stiffly and the sugar flat on the palm of his hand, that didn't look right. People who are fond of horses stroke their muzzles when they give them sugar, they don't stand as far away as possible. And if Maurice wasn't fond of horses, why was he giving them sugar? Anyway, I did decide suddenly that there would be no harm done if Turniptop didn't eat that sugar, so I dropped the girths and pretended to trip, and grabbed Maurice's arm to steady myself. The sugar fell off his hand onto the straw on the ground and I stepped on it as if by accident while I was recovering my balance."

"What did he say?" I asked, fascinated.

"Nothing," said James. "I apologized for bumping into him, but he didn't answer. Just for a second he looked absolutely furious. Then he smiled again and"—James's eyes glinted—"he said how much he admired me for giving poor Finn this one last chance."

"Dear of him," I murmured.

"I told him it wasn't exactly your last chance. I said you would be riding Template on Saturday as well. He just said, 'Oh, really?' and wished me luck and walked away."

"So the sugar was crunched up and swept out with the dirty straw," I said.

"Yes," he agreed.

"Nothing to analyze. No evidence." A nuisance.

"If I hadn't stepped on it, Maurice could have picked it up and offered it to Turniptop again. I hadn't taken any sugar with me . . . I hadn't any lumps to substitute . . . I didn't believe I would need them."

He hadn't intended to bother, I knew. But he had bothered. I would never stop feeling grateful.

We drank our whisky. James said suddenly, "Why? I don't understand why he should have gone to such lengths to discredit you. What has he got against you?"

"I am a jockey, and he is not," I said flatly. "That's all." I told him about my visit to Claudius Mellit and the answers he had given me. "It's no coincidence that you and most other trainers have had trouble finding and keeping a jockey. You've all been swayed by Kemp-Lore, either by him directly or through those two shadows of his, Ballerton and Corin Kellar, who soak up his poison like sponges and drip it out into every receptive ear. They've said it all to you. You repeated it to me yourself, not so long ago. Peter Cloony is always late, Tick-Tock doesn't try, Danny Higgs bets too heavily, Grant sold information, Finn has lost his nerve."

He stared at me, appalled.

I said, "You believed it all, James, didn't you? Even you? And so did
everyone else. Why shouldn't they, with so much evident foundation for
the rumors? It doesn't take much for an owner or a trainer to lose confidence
in a jockey. The thought has only to be insinuated, however fleetingly, that
a jockey is habitually late, or dishonest, or afraid, and very soon, very soon
indeed, he is on his way out. Art. Art killed himself because Corin sacked
him. Grant had a mental breakdown. Peter Cloony is so broke his wife
was starving herself in a freezing-cold house. Tick-Tock makes jokes like
Pagliacci."

"And you?" asked James.

"I? Well, I haven't exactly enjoyed the past three weeks."

"No," he said, as if thinking about it from my point of view for the first
time. "No, I don't suppose you have."

"It's been so calculated, this destruction of jockeys," I said. "Every week
on *Turf Talk*, looking back on it, there has been some damaging reference to
one jockey or another. When he had me on the program, he introduced me as
an unsuccessful rider, and he meant me to stay that way. Do you remember
that ghastly bit of film he showed of me? You'd never have taken me on if
you'd seen that before I'd ridden for you, would you?"

He shook his head, very troubled.

I went on: "On every occasion—when Template won the King Chase, for
instance—he has reminded everyone watching on television that I am only
substituting for Pip and that I'll be out on my ear as soon as that broken leg
is strong again. Fair enough, it's Pip's job and he should have it back, but that
patronizing note in Kemp-Lore's voice was calculated to make everyone take
it for granted that my brief spell in the limelight was thoroughly undeserved.
I dare say it was, too. But I think a lot of your owners would have been read-
ier to trust your judgment in engaging me, and less quick to chuck me overboard at the first sign of trouble, if it hadn't been for the continual deflating
pinpricks Kemp-Lore had dealt out all round. And last Friday . . ." I tried,
not too successfully, to keep my voice evenly conversational. "Last Friday he
led Corin and that handicapper on until they said straight out that I was finished. Were you watching?"

James nodded, and poured us another drink.

"It's a matter for the National Hunt Committee," he said firmly.

"No," I said. "His father is a member of it."

James gasped sharply. "I had forgotten."

I said, "The whole Committee's a stronghold of pro-Kemp-Lore feeling. They're all sold on Maurice. Most of them wear the same old school tie." I grinned. James wore it too. "I would be very glad if you would say nothing to any of them just yet. They would take even more convincing than you did, and there aren't any facts that Kemp-Lore couldn't explain away. But I'm digging." I drank. "The day will come."

"You sound unexpectedly cheerful," he said.

"Oh, God, James." I stood up abruptly. "I wanted to kill myself last week. I'm glad I didn't. It makes me cheerful."

He looked so startled that I relaxed and laughed, and put down my glass. "Never mind," I said. "But you must understand, I don't think the National Hunt Committee meets the case at the moment. Too gentlemanly. I favor something more in the bitter-bit line for dear Maurice."

But I had as yet no useful plan, and dear Maurice still had his teeth; and they were sharp.

CHAPTER 11

ALTHOUGH NEITHER TICK-TOCK nor I had any rides the next day, I pinched the car from him to go to the meeting at Ascot, and walked round the course to get the feel of the turf. There was a bitterly cold northeast wind blowing across the Heath and the ground was hard with a touch of frost in the more exposed patches. It had been a surprisingly mild winter so far, but the high clear sky spoke ominously of ice to come. One more day, that was all I asked; only one more day. But prodding the earth on the landing side of the water jump with my heel I felt it jar instead of give.

I finished the circuit, planning the race in my mind as I went. If the ground remained firm, it would be a fast-run affair, but that suited Template well, especially with top weight to carry. Lugging packets of lead around in the mud was not what his lean streamlined frame was best fitted for.

Outside the weighing room Peter Cloony stopped me. His face was white and thin and mournful, and lines were developing on his forehead.

"I'll pay you back," he said, almost belligerently. He seemed prepared to argue about it.

"All right. One day. No hurry," I said mildly.

"You shouldn't have gone behind my back and given my wife that money and the food. I wanted to send it back at once, but she wouldn't let me. We don't need charity. I don't approve of it."

"You're a fool, Peter," I said. "Your wife was right to accept what I gave her, and I'd have thought her a stubborn ass if she hadn't. And you'd better get used to the idea: a box of groceries will be delivered to your house every week until you're earning a decent screw again."

"No!" he almost shouted. "I won't have it."

"I don't see why your wife and baby should suffer because of your misplaced pride," I said. "But if it will ease your conscience, I'll tell you why I'm doing it. You'll never get much work as long as you go around with that hangdog expression. Looking weak and miserable isn't going to persuade anyone to employ you. You need to cheer up, get fit again, and prove you're worth having. Well, all I'm doing is removing one of your worries so that you can think a bit more about racing and a bit less about your cold house and empty larder. So now you can get on with it—it's all up to you. And don't ever even risk being late."

I walked off and left Peter standing with his mouth open and his eyebrows halfway to his hair.

What Kemp-Lore had pulled down I could try to rebuild, I thought. When I had arrived I had seen him in the distance, talking animatedly to one of the Stewards, who was laughing. Slim, vital, and wholesome-looking, he seemed to attract the light of the day onto his fair head.

In the weighing room after the fourth race I was handed a telegram. It said: "Pick me up White Bear, Uxbridge, 6:30 P.M. Important. Ingersoll." I felt like cursing Tick-Tock soundly because Uxbridge was in the opposite direction from home. But the car was half his, after all, and I'd had more than my fair share of it during the past week.

The afternoon dragged. I hated having to watch, hated it even more after my reassuring ride on Turniptop, but I tried to take my own advice to Peter and look cheerful: and I was rewarded, as time went on, with a definitive thawing of the cold shoulder. It made life much easier not finding everyone too embarrassed to speak to me; but I was also left in no doubt that most final judgments were being reserved until after Template's race. I didn't mind that. I was confident that he was the fastest chaser in training and I had James's promise that he would be guarded every second against being doped.

I dawdled after racing ended, with two hours to kill before turning up to collect Tick-Tock. I watched the men from Universal Telecast erecting their scaffolding towers, ready to televise the Midwinter the next day. I recognized the man directing them as Gordon Kildare, still in navy-blue pin-stripe suiting and still looking like a rising young executive who knew the score. He passed me with the practiced half-smile which from a man of his sort always means that he doesn't know whom he's smiling at, but smiles all the same in case he should later find out it was someone important. However, he had gone only two steps past me when he turned and came back.

"We've had you on the program," he said pleasantly. "No, don't tell me . . ." His brow furrowed; then he snapped his fingers. "Finn, that's it, Finn." But his smile at the triumph of his memory began to slip, and I knew he was also remembering what had been said about me on his program a week ago.

"Yes, Finn," I said, taking no notice. "All set for tomorrow?"

"Er, oh, yes. Busy day. Well, now, I'm sorry to have to rush off, but you know how it is—we've got the program to put out tonight and I'm due back in the studios. Maurice went ages ago."

He looked at his watch, gave me a noncommittal smile, and gracefully retreated.

I watched him drive off in the latest streamlined Ford, picturing the studio he was going to; the ranks of cameras, the dazzling lights, the plates of sandwiches; they would all be the same. And who, I wondered, was to be Kemp-Lore's victim this evening? For whom was the chopper poised, the false charm ready?

There was so little I could do against him. Pick up some of the pieces, start some counterrumors. Try to undermine his influence. All that, yes. But I didn't have his sparkle, nor his prestige, nor yet his ruthlessness. I thrust my hands into my pockets, went out to the Mini-Cooper, and drove off to fetch Tick-Tock.

Mine was only the second car in the dark park beside the White Bear. It was one of those disappointing pubs built of tidy pinkish bricks with cold lighting inside and no atmosphere. The saloon bar was empty. The public bar held only a droopy-mustached old man pursing his lips to the evening's first half-pint. I went back to the saloon bar and ordered a whisky. No Tick-Tock. I looked at my watch. Twenty to seven.

The green plastic seats round the walls were so inhospitable that I didn't wonder the pub was empty. The dark-green curtains didn't help. Nor the fluorescent strip lights on the ceiling.

I looked at my watch again.

"Are you by any chance waiting for someone, sir?" asked the characterless barman.

"Yes, I am," I said.

"You wouldn't be a Mr. Finn?"

"Yes."

"Then I've a message for you, sir. A Mr. Ingersoll telephoned just now and said he couldn't get here to meet you, sir, and he was very sorry but could you go and pick him up from the station at six-fifty-five. The station is just down the road, first turning left and straight on for half a mile."

Finishing my drink, I thanked the barman and went out to the car. I climbed into the driving seat and stretched my hand out to turn on the lights and the ignition. I stretched out my hand . . . but I didn't reach the lights.

My neck was gripped violently from behind.

There was movement then in the back of the car as the arms shifted to get a better leverage, a rustling of clothes and the scrape of a shoe across the thin carpet.

I flung up my hands and clawed but I couldn't reach the face of whoever was behind me, and my nails were useless against his gloves. Thick leather gloves. The fingers inside them were strong, and what was worse, they knew exactly where to dig in and press, each side of the neck, just above the collarbone, where the carotid arteries branch upward. Pressure on one carotid, I remembered wildly from some distant first-aid course, stops arterial bleeding from the head, but pressure on both at once blocks all blood supplies to the brain.

I hadn't a chance. My struggles were hampered by the steering wheel and gained me nothing. In the few seconds before a roaring blackness took me off, I had time for only two more thoughts. First that I should have known that Tick-Tock would never meet me in a dreary pub like that. Second, angrily, that I was dead.

I COULDN'T HAVE been out very long, but it was long enough. When consciousness slowly and fuzzily returned, I found I could open neither my eyes nor my mouth. Both were covered with sticking plaster. My wrists were tied together, and my ankles, when I tried to move them, would part only a foot or two: they were hobbled together, like a gypsy pony's.

I was lying on my side, awkwardly doubled up, on the floor in the back of a car which, from the size and smell and feel, I knew to be the Mini-Cooper. It was very cold, and after a while I realized that this was because I was no longer wearing either a jacket or an overcoat. My shirt-sleeved arms were dragged forward between the two front seats so that I couldn't reach the sticking plaster to rip it off, and I was extremely, horribly uncomfortable. I tried once as hard as I could to free my arms, lifting and jerking at the same time, but they were securely fastened, and a fist—I supposed—crashed down on them so brutally that I didn't attempt it again.

I couldn't see who was driving the car, and driving it fast, but I didn't need to. There was only one person in the world who would have set such a trap; complicated but effective, like the Jaguar in the lane. Only one person who had any reason to abduct me, however mad that reason might be. I had no illusions. Maurice Kemp-Lore did not intend that I should win the Mid-winter Cup and was taking steps to prevent it.

Did he know, I wondered helplessly, that it was no accident that Turniptop had not eaten the doped sugar? Did he guess that I knew all about his anti-jockey activities? Had he heard about my trek round the stables or my inquiries about the Jaguar? If he did know these things, what was he going to do with me? To this last rather bleak question I was in no hurry to discover the answer.

When the journey had been going on for some time, the car swung suddenly to the left and bumped onto an unevenly surfaced side road, increasing my discomfort. After a while it slowed, turned again, and rolled to a stop.

Kemp-Lore got out of the car, tipped forward the driver's seat, and tugged me out after him by the wrists. I couldn't get my feet under me because of the hobble, and I fell out onto the back of my shoulders. The ground was hard and gravelly. My shirt tore, and the sharp stones scraped into my skin.

He pulled me to my feet, and I stood there swaying, blinded by the plaster on my eyes and unable to run even if I could have wrenched myself from his grasp. He had some sort of lead fixed to my tied wrists, and he began to pull me forward by it. The ground was uneven and the rope joining my ankles was very short. I kept stumbling, and twice fell down.

It was very unpleasant, falling when I couldn't see, but I managed somehow to twist before hitting the ground, landing on my shoulders instead of my face. Always he pulled my hands so far in front of me that I couldn't reach the sticking plaster: the second time I fell I made a great effort to get it off, but he wrenched my arms roughly over my head and dragged me along the ground on my back for a long way. I very painfully lost a good deal more skin.

At length he paused and let me stand up again. He still didn't speak. Not a word. And I couldn't. There was only the sound of our footsteps on the stony ground and the faint sigh of the sharp northeaster in some nearby trees. My tattered shirt was no shield against that wind, and I began to shiver.

He stopped, and there was the sound of a door being opened, and I was tugged on. This time there was a step up, as I realized a fraction too late to prevent myself falling again. I hadn't time to twist, either. I fell flat on my stomach, elbows and chest. It knocked the wind out of me and made me dizzy.

It was a wooden floor, I thought, with my cheek on it. It smelled strongly of dust, and faintly of horses. He pulled me to my feet again and I felt my wrists being hauled upward and fastened to something just above my head. When he had finished and stepped away I explored with my fingers to find out what it was; and as soon as I felt the smooth metal hooks I knew exactly the sort of place I was in.

It was a tack room. Every stable has one. It is the place where the saddles and bridles are kept, along with all the brushes and straps and bandages and rugs that horses need. From the ceiling of every tack room hangs a harness hook, a gadget something like a three-pronged anchor, which is used for hanging bridles on while they are being cleaned. There were no bridles hanging from these particular hooks. Only me. I was securely fastened at the point where they branched off their stem.

Most tack rooms are warm, heated by a stove which dries damp rugs and prevents leather from getting mildewed. This tack room was very cold indeed, and in the air the ingrained smells of leather and saddle soap were overlaid by a dead sort of mustiness. It was an unused room: an empty room. The silence took on a new meaning. There were no horses moving in the boxes. It was an empty stable. I shivered from something more than cold.

I heard him step out into the gritty yard, and presently there was a familiar rattle of bolts and the clang of a stable door being opened. After a few seconds it was shut again, and another one was opened. This again was shut, and another opened. He went on down the row, opening six doors. I thought he must be looking for something, and numbly wondered what it was, and began to hope very much that he wouldn't find it.

After the sixth stable door shut he was gone for some time, and I couldn't hear what he was doing. But the car had not been started, so I knew he must still be there. I could make no impression at all on the strands of rope twined round my wrists. They were narrow and slippery to touch, and felt like nylon, and I couldn't even find a knot, much less undo one.

Eventually he came back, and dumped down outside the door something that clattered. A bucket.

He stepped into the room and walked softly on the wooden floor. He stopped in front of me. It was very quiet everywhere. I could hear a new sound, the high faint asthmatic wheeze of the air going into his lungs. Even an empty stable, it seemed, could start him off.

Nothing happened for a while. He walked all round me, slowly, and stopped again. Walked and stopped. Making up his mind, I thought. But to do what?

He touched me once, dragging his gloved hand across my raw shoulders. I flinched, and his breath hissed sharply. He began to cough, the dry difficult asthmatic's cough. And may you choke, I thought.

He went outside, still coughing, and picked up the bucket and walked away across the yard. I heard the bucket clatter down and a tap being turned on. The water splashed into the bucket, echoing in the stillness.

Jack and Jill went up the hill, said my brain ridiculously, to fetch a pail of water. Jack fell down and broke his crown and Jill threw the water all over him.

Oh, no, I thought, oh, no, I'm so cold already.

Part of my mind said I wouldn't mind what he did to me if only he'd let me go in time to ride Template, and the rest said don't be a fool, that's the whole point, he won't let you go, and anyway if you do get away you'll be so cold and stiff after this you won't be able to ride a donkey.

He turned off the tap and came back across the yard, the water splashing slightly as he walked. He brought the bucket with him into the tack room and stopped behind me. The handle of the bucket clanked. I ground my teeth and took a deep breath, and waited.

He threw the water. It hit me squarely between the shoulder blades and soaked me from head to foot. It was bitterly, icy cold, and it stung like murder on the skinned patches.

After a short pause he went across the yard again and refilled the bucket. I thought I was almost past caring about that. You can't be wetter than wet and you can't be colder than freezing. And my arms, with being hauled up higher than my head, were already beginning to feel heavy and to ache. I began to worry less about the immediate future and more about how long he intended to leave me where I was.

He came back with the bucket, and this time he threw the water in my face. I had been wrong about not caring. It was at least as bad as the first time, mostly because too much of it went up my nose. Couldn't he see, I thought desperately, that he was drowning me? My chest hurt. I couldn't get my breath. Surely he would pull the plaster off my mouth, surely . . . surely . . .

He didn't.

By the time a reasonable amount of air was finding its way into my heaving lungs he was across the yard again, with more water splashing into the bucket. In due course he turned the tap off, and his feet began once more to crunch methodically in my direction. Up the step and across the wooden floor. There wasn't anything I could do to stop him. My thoughts were unprintable.

He came round in front of me again. I twisted my face sideways and buried my nose against my upper arm. He poured the whole arctic bucketful over my head. After this, I thought, I am going to have more sympathy for those clowns in circuses. I hoped the poor blighters used warm water, anyway.

It seemed that he now thought I was wet enough. In any case he dumped the bucket down outside the door instead of going to fill it again, and came back and stood close beside me. His asthma was worse.

He put his hand in my hair and pulled my head back, and spoke for the first time.

He said in a low voice, with obvious satisfaction, "That should fix *you*."

He let go of my hair and went out of the room, and I heard him walk away across the yard. His footsteps faded into the distance and after a while there was the distant slam of the Mini-Cooper's door. The engine started, the car drove off, and soon I could hear it no more.

It wasn't very funny being abandoned in a trussed condition soaking wet on a cold night. I knew he wouldn't be back for hours, because it was Friday. From eight o'clock until at least 9:30 he would be occupied with his program; and I wondered in passing what effect his recent capers would have on his performance.

One thing was clear, I could not meekly stand still and wait to be released. The first necessity was obviously to get some of the sticking plaster off. I thought that as it was wet it would come away fairly easily, but it was very adhesive, and after a good deal of rubbing my mouth against my arm I only succeeded in peeling back one corner of it. It was enough to let in a precious extra trickle of air, but no good for shouting for help.

The cold was a serious problem. My wet trousers clung clammily to my legs, my shoes were full of water, and my shirt, what was left of it, was plastered against my arms and chest. Already my fingers were completely numb, and my feet were going through the stage that precedes loss of feeling. He had left the door open on purpose, I knew, and although the biting wind was not blowing straight in, there were enough eddies swirling off the walls outside for me to be in a considerable draft. I shivered from head to foot.

Harness hooks. I considered their anatomy. A stem with three upward curving branches at the bottom. At the top a ring, and attached to the ring a chain. The length of the chain depended on the height of the ceiling. At the top of the chain, a staple driven into a beam. As the whole thing was solidly constructed to resist years of vigorous stablemen putting their weight on bridles while they cleaned them, it was absolutely hopeless to try to tug it straight out of the ceiling.

I had seen harness hooks which were only hitched onto their chains and would detach easily if lifted up instead of being pulled down, but after some fruitless and tiring maneuvering I knew the one I was attached to was not so obliging.

But somewhere, I thought, there must be a weak link. Literally a weak link. When they were bought, harness hooks didn't have chains on them. Chain was cut to the length needed and added when the hook was installed in the tack room. Therefore somewhere there was a join.

The bottom curve of the hooks brushed my hair, and my wrists were tied some three inches above that. It gave me very little leverage, but it was the only hope I had. I started pivoting, leaning my forearms on the hooks and twisting the chain, putting a strain on it and hearing the links rub hollowly together. In two and a half full turns, as nearly as I could judge, it locked solid. If I could turn it farther, the weak link would snap.

The theory was simple. Putting it into operation was different. For one thing, twisting the chain had shortened it, so that my arms were stretched higher above my head and gave me less leverage than ever. And for another, they had begun to ache in earnest.

I pressed round as hard as I could. Nothing happened. I unwound the chain a fraction, and forcibly jerked it tight again. The jolt ran right down my body and threw me off my feet.

I stumbled miserably upright again, and with my legs braced repeated the process. This time the jolt shook only the top part of my body. I did it again. The chain didn't break.

After that, as a respite from rattling my arms in their sockets, I got back to work on the sticking plaster and a while later dislodged the piece over my lips. It meant that at last I could open my mouth and yell.

I yelled.

No one came. My voice echoed round the tack room and sounded loud in my ears, but I feared that outside the wind would sweep it away. I shouted, on and off, for a long while. No results.

It was at this point, perhaps an hour after Kemp-Lore had gone, that I became both very frightened and very angry.

I was frightened for my hands, which I could no longer feel. I was now not only shivering but shuddering with cold, and the blood supply to my hands was having, to put it literally, an uphill job; and with the weight of my aching arms to support, the rope tying my wrists was viciously tight.

The dismal fact had to be faced that if I had to stay where I was all night, my hands might be dead in the morning. My imagination trotted on unasked with scarifying pictures. Dead. Gangrenous. Amputated.

He can't have meant that, I thought suddenly. Surely he hadn't meant that all along. No one could be so savagely cruel. I remembered the satisfaction in his voice, "That will fix *you*," he had said. But I'd thought he meant for the next day only. Not for life.

Being angry gave me both strength and resolution. I would not, I absolutely would not let him get away with it. The chain had to be broken.

I wound it up tight again and jerked. It took my breath away. I told myself not to be a baby. I loosened and jerked, loosened and jerked, pushing against the hooks, trying to twist them round with all my strength. The chain rattled, and held.

I started doing it rhythmically. Six jerks and a rest. Six jerks and a rest. On and on, six jerks and a rest, until I was sobbing.

At least, I thought, with a last flicker of humor, the exercise is making me warmer. But it was little consolation for the cracking pain in my arms and shoulders, or the red-hot pincers which seemed to have attached themselves to the back of my neck, or the bite of the rope into my wrists as the friction rubbed away the skin.

Six jerks and a rest. Six jerks and a rest. The rests got longer. Anyone who has tried crying with sticking plaster over his eyes will know that the tears run down inside the nose. When I sniffed, they came into my mouth. Salty. I got tired of the taste.

Six jerks and a rest. I wouldn't stop. I refused to stop. Six jerks. Rest. Six. Rest.

After a while I unwound the chain by turning round and round where I stood and wound it up again in the opposite direction. I thought that jolting it the other way might both snap it more quickly and be easier on my protesting muscles; but I was wrong on both counts. Eventually, I wound back again.

Time passed. Because I couldn't see I became giddy as I grew tired. I began to sway and buckle at the knees if I didn't concentrate, and neither of these things did my arms any good.

Why—jerk—wouldn't—jerk—the ruddy chain—jerk—jerk—break? I wasn't going to admit it was too much for me without struggling to the end, though the disgusting temptation gradually grew to give up the excruciating wrenching and just hang and faint away and get some peace. A temporary, deceptive, useless, dangerous peace.

I went on jerking for what seemed like hours, sometimes sobbing, sometimes cursing, sometimes maybe praying as well.

I was quite unprepared for it, when it happened. One minute I was screwing up the dregs of willpower for another series of jerks and the next, after a convulsive, despairing heave, I was collapsing in a tumbling heap on the floor with the harness hook clattering down on top of me, still tied to my wrists.

For a moment or two I could hardly believe it. My head was whirling, all sense of direction gone. But the floor was hard beneath my body, dusty smelling and real, damp and reassuring.

After a while, when my head cleared, I rolled into a kneeling position so that the blood was flowing down my arms at last, and put my hands between my thighs to try to warm them. They felt like lumps of frozen meat, with no sensation and no movement. The rope round my wrists didn't cut so much now that it had no weight to support, and there was room for the blood to get back into my hands, I thought, if only it would.

The unimaginable relief of having my arms down made me forget for some time how cold I was, and how wet, and how far still from getting warm and dry. I felt almost cheerful, as if I had won a major battle; and indeed, looking back on it, I know I had.

CHAPTER 12

KNEELING VERY SOON became uncomfortable, so I shuffled across the floor until I came to a wall, and sat with the bottom of my spine propped against it and my knees bent up.

The plaster on my eyes was still stuck tight. I tried to scrape it off by rubbing it against the rope on my wrists, but made no headway. The hooks hindered me and bumped into my face, and in the end I gave it up and concentrated again on warming my hands, alternately cradling them between my thighs and thumping them against my knees to restore the circulation.

After a time I found I could move my fingers. I still couldn't feel them at all, but movement was a tremendous step forward, and I remember smiling about it for at least ten minutes.

I put my hands up to my face and tried to scrape the plaster off with my thumbnail. My thumb slid across my cheek, checked on the edge of the plaster and, when I pushed from the elbow, bent uselessly and slithered away. I tried again. It had to be done, because until I could see where I was going I couldn't leave the tack room. It was colder outside, and my ankles were still hobbled, and wandering about blind in those conditions did not appeal to me.

I bent my head down and put my right thumb in my mouth, to warm it. Every few minutes I tested the results on the edge of the plaster and at last got to the stage where the thumb would push without bending. I needed only to prize a corner up, but even that took a long time. Eventually, however, my nail had pushed unstuck a flap big enough for me to grip between my wrists, and with several false starts and a fair selection of oaths, I managed in the end to pull the obstinate thing off.

Dazzling moonlight poured through the open door and through a window beside it. I was sitting against the end wall with the door away on my left. Above my head and all round the room there were empty wooden supports for saddles and bridles, and bare shelves and a cupboard on the wall facing me.

An efficient-looking stove occupied the corner on my right, with a few dead cinders still scattered on the floor beside it.

From the center of the ceiling, pale in the moonlight, hung twenty inches of sturdy galvanized chain.

I looked down at my hands. The harness hook glinted with reflected light. No wonder it had been so difficult to break, I thought. The chain and the hook were almost new. Not the dark old rusty things I had been imagining all along. I swallowed, really shattered. It was just as well I hadn't known.

My hands themselves, including the thumb I had tried to warm, were white. Almost as white as my shirtsleeves. Almost as white as the nylon rope which wound round the hooks. Only my wrists were dark.

I stretched my feet out. More nylon rope ran from one ankle to the other; about fifteen inches of it.

My fingers wouldn't undo the knots. My pockets had been emptied; no knife, no matches. There was nothing in the tack room to cut with. I stood up stiffly, leaning against the wall, and slowly, carefully, shuffled over to the door. My foot kicked against something, and I looked down. On the edge of a patch of moonlight lay the broken link. It was a grotesquely buckled piece of silver metal. It had given me a lot of trouble.

I went on to the door and negotiated the step. The bucket stood there, dully gray. I looked round the moonlit L-shaped yard. Four boxes stretched away to my right, and at right angles to them were two more, on the short arm of the L. Over there, too, was the tap; and beside the tap, on the ground, an object I was very glad to see. A bootscraper made of a thin metal plate bedded in concrete.

With small careful steps I made my way to it across the hard-packed gravel, the cutting wind ripping the last remnants of warmth from my body.

Leaning against the wall, and with one foot on the round, I stretched the rope tautly over the bootscraper and began to rub it to and fro, using the other foot as a pendulum. The blade of the scraper was far from sharp and the rope was new, and it took a long time to fray it through, but it parted in the end. I knelt down and tried to do the same with the strands round my wrists, but the harness hook kept getting in the way again and I couldn't get anything like the same purchase. I stood up wearily. It looked as though I'd have to lug that tiresome piece of iron-mongery around with me a while longer.

Being able to move my legs, however, gave me a marvelous sense of freedom. Stiffly, shaking with cold, I walked out of the yard and round to the house looming darkly behind it. There were no lights, and on looking closer I found the downstairs windows were all shuttered. It was as empty as the stable; an unwelcome but not unexpected discovery.

I waked a bit unsteadily past the house and down the drive. It was a long drive with no lodge at the gate, only an estate agent's board announcing that this desirable country gentleman's residence was for sale, together with some modern stabling, forty acres of arable land, and an apple orchard.

A country lane ran past the end of the drive, giving no indication as to which way lay civilization. I tried to remember from which direction the Mini-Cooper had come, but I couldn't. It seemed a very long time ago. I glanced automatically at my left wrist but there was only rope there, no watch. Since it had to be one thing or the other, I turned right. It was a deserted road with open fields on the far sides of its low hedges. No cars passed, and nowhere could I see a light. Cursing the wind and aching all over I stumbled on, hanging on to the fact that if I went far enough I was bound to come to a house in the end.

What I came to first was not a house but something much better. A telephone box. It stood alone, brightly lit inside, square and beckoning, on the corner where the lane turned into a more main road, and it solved the embarrassing problem of presenting myself at some stranger's door looking like a scarecrow and having to explain how I got into such a state.

There were a lot of people I could have called. Police, ambulance or the fire brigade, for a start; but by the time I had forced my still nearly useless hands to pull open the door far enough for me to get my foot in, I had had time to think. Once I called in authority in any form there would be unending questions to answer and statements to make, and like as not I'd end up for the night in the local cottage hospital. I hated being in hospitals.

Also, although I felt so bone-cold, it was not, I thought, actually freezing. The puddles at the side of the road had no ice on them. They would be racing at Ascot the next day. Template would turn up for the Midwinter, and James didn't know his jockey was wandering around unfit to ride.

Unfit . . . Between seeing the telephone box and clumsily picking up the receiver I came to the conclusion that the only satisfactory way to cheat Kemp-Lore of his victory was to go and ride the race, and win it if I could, and pretend that tonight's misfortunes had not happened. He had had things his own way for far too long. He was not, he was positively not, I vowed, going to get the better of me any more.

I dialed O with an effort, gave the operator my credit card number, and asked to be connected to the one person in the world who would give me the help I needed and keep quiet about it afterward, and not try to argue me out of what I intended to do.

Her voice sounded sleepy. She said, "Hello?"

"Joanna, are you busy?" I asked.

"Busy? At this hour?" she said. "Is that you, Rob?"

"Yes."

"Well, go back to bed and ring me in the morning," she said. "I was asleep. Don't you know what time it is?" I heard her yawn.

"No," I said.

"Well, it's . . . er . . . twenty to one. Good night."

"Joanna, don't go," I said urgently. "I need your help. I really do. Please don't ring off."

"What's the matter?" She yawned again.

"I . . . I . . . Joanna, come and help me. Please."

There was a little silence and she said in a more awake voice, "You've never said 'please' like that to me before. Not for anything."

"Will you come?"

"Where to?"

"I don't really know," I said despairingly. "I'm in a telephone box on a country road miles from anywhere. The telephone exchange is Hampden Row." I spelled it out for her. "I don't think it's very far from London, and somewhere on the West, probably."

"You can't come back on your own?" she asked.

"No," I said. "I've no money and my clothes are wet."

"Oh." A pause. "All right, then. I'll find out where you are and come in a taxi. Anything else?"

"Bring a sweater," I said, "I'm cold. And some dry socks, if you have any. And some gloves. Don't forget the gloves. And a pair of scissors."

"Sweater, socks, gloves, scissors. Okay. You'll have to wait while I get dressed again, but I'll come as soon as I can. Stay by the telephone box."

"Yes," I said.

"I'll hurry, don't worry," she said. "Good-by."

"Good-by." I fumbled the receiver back onto its rest. However quick she was, she wouldn't arrive for an hour. Well, what was one hour more after so many? I had had no idea it was so late: the evening had certainly seemed to have been going on for an eternity, but I had lost all sense of actual time. And Kemp-Lore hadn't come back. His show had been over for hours, and he hadn't come back. The bloody, murdering bastard, I thought.

I sat down on the floor of the box and leaned gingerly against the wall beside the telephone, with my head resting on the coin box. Exercise and the bitter wind outside, inactivity and shelter inside; one looked as cold a prospect as the other. But I was too tired to walk any more if I didn't have to, so the choice was easy.

I put my hands up to my face and one by one bit my fingers. They were icy cold and yellowish white, and none of them had any feeling. They would curl and uncurl, but slowly and weakly, and that was all. I got to work on them seriously then, rubbing them up and down against my legs, bumping them on my knees, forcing them open and shut, but it seemed to make little difference. I persevered from fear that they should get worse if I didn't, and paid for it in various creaks from my sore and sorely misused shoulders.

There was a good deal to think about to take my mind off my woes. That sticking plaster, for instance. Why had he used it? The strip over my mouth, I had assumed, had been to stop me shouting for help; but when I got it off at last and shouted, there was no one to hear. No one could have heard however loud I yelled, because the stable was so far from the lane.

The strip over my eyes should have been to prevent my seeing where I was going, but why did it matter if I saw an empty yard and a deserted tack room? What would have happened differently, I wondered, if I had been able to see and talk?

To see . . . I would have seen Kemp-Lore's expression while he went about putting me out of action. I would have seen Kemp-Lore . . . that was it! It was himself he had not wanted me to see, not the place.

If that was so, it was conceivable that he had prevented me from talking simply so that he should not be trapped into answering. He had spoken only once, and that in a low, unrecognizable tone. I became convinced that he had not wanted me to hear and recognize his voice.

In that case he must have believed I did not know who had abducted me, that I didn't know who he was. He must still believe it. Which meant that he thought James had knocked Turniptop's doped sugar out of his hand by accident, that he hadn't heard about Tick-Tock and me going round all the stables, and that he didn't know I had been asking about the Jaguar. It gave me, I thought, a fractional advantage for the future. If he had left any tracks any where, he would not see any vital, immediate need to obliterate them. If he didn't know he was due for destruction himself, he would not be excessively on his guard.

Looking at my bloodless hands and knowing that on top of everything else I still had to face the pain of their return to life, I was aware that all the civilized brakes were off in my conscience. Helping to build up what he had broken was not enough. He himself had hammered into me the inner implacability I had lacked to avenge myself and all the others thoroughly, and do it physically and finally and without compunction.

JOANNA CAME, IN the end.

I heard a car draw up and a door slam, and her quick tread on the road. The door of the telephone box opened, letting in an icy blast, and there she was, dressed in trousers and woolly boots and a warm padded jacket, with the light falling on her dark hair and making hollows of her eyes.

I was infinitely glad to see her. I looked up at her and did my best at a big smile of welcome, but it didn't come off very well. I was shivering too much.

She knelt down and took a closer look at me. Her face went stiff with shock.

"Your hands," she said.

"Yes. Did you bring the scissors?"

Without a word she opened her handbag, took out a sensible-sized pair, and cut me free. She did it gently. She took the harness hook from between my knees and laid it on the floor, and carefully peeled from my wrists the cut pieces of rope. They were all more brown than white, stained with my blood, and where they had been there were big corrugated raw patches, dark and deep. She stared at them.

"More bits of rope down there," I said, nodding toward my feet.

She cut the pieces round my ankles, and I saw her rubbing my trouser leg between her fingers. The air had been too cold to dry them and my body had not generated enough heat, so they were still very damp.

"Been swimming?" she said flippantly. Her voice cracked.

There was a step on the road outside and a man's shape loomed up behind Joanna.

"Are you all right, miss?" he said in a reliable-sounding Cockney voice.

"Yes, thank you," she said. "Do you think you could help me get my cousin into the taxi?"

He stepped into the doorway and looked down at me, his eyes on my wrists and my hands.

"Christ!" he said.

"Very aptly put," I said.

He looked at my face. He was a big sturdy man of about fifty, weather-beaten like a sailor, with eyes that looked as if they had seen everything and found most of it disappointing.

"You've been done proper, haven't you?" he said.

"Proper," I agreed.

He smiled faintly. "Come on then. No sense in hanging about here."

I stood up clumsily and lurched against Joanna, and put my arms round her neck to save myself from falling; and as I was there it seemed a shame to miss the opportunity, so I kissed her. On the eyebrow, as it happened.

"Did you say 'cousin'?" said the taxi driver.

"Cousin," said Joanna firmly. Much too firmly.

The driver held the door open. "We'd better take him to a doctor," he said.

"No," I said. "No doctor."

Joanna said, "You need one."

"No."

"That's frostbite," said the driver, pointing to my hands.

"No," I said. "It isn't freezing. No ice on the puddles. Just cold. Not frost-bite." My teeth were chattering and I could only speak in short sentences.

"What happened to your back?" asked the driver, looking at the tattered bits of shirt sticking to me.

"I . . . fell over," I said. "On some gravel."

He looked skeptical.

"It's a terrible mess, and there's a lot of dirt in it," said Joanna, peering round me and sounding worried.

"You wash it," I said. "At home."

"You need a doctor," said the driver again.

I shook my head. "I need disinfectant, aspirins and sleep."

"I hope you know what you're doing," said Joanna. "What else?"

"Sweater," I said.

"It's in the taxi," she said. "And some other clothes. You can change as we go along. The sooner you get into a hot bath the better."

"I'd be careful about that, miss," said the driver. "Don't go warming those hands up too fast or the fingers will drop off." A comforting chap. Inaccurate too, I trusted. Joanna looked more worried than ever.

We walked from the telephone box to the taxi. It was an ordinary black London taxi. I wondered what charm Joanna had used to get it so far out into the country in the middle of the night; and also, more practically, whether the meter was still ticking away. It was.

"Get in, out of the wind," she said, opening the taxi door.

I did as I was told. She had brought a suitcase, from which she now produced a thin pale-blue cardigan of her own and a padded man-sized olive-colored parka which zipped up the front. She looked at me judiciously, and out came the scissors. Some quick snips and the ruins of my shirt lay on the seat beside me. She cut two long strips off it and wound them carefully round my wrists. The taxi driver watched.

"This is a police job," he suggested.

I shook my head. "Private fight."

He held the harness hook, which he had brought across from the telephone box.

"What sort of thing is this?" he asked.

"Throw it in the ditch," I said, averting my eyes.

"You'll be needing it for the police," he insisted.

"I told you," I said wearily, "no police."

His disillusioned face showed that he knew all about people who got themselves beaten up but wouldn't report it. He shrugged and went off into the darkness, and came back without the hook.

"It's in the ditch just behind the telephone box, if you change your mind," he said.

"Thanks," I said.

Joanna finished the bandages and helped my arms into both the garments she had brought, and fastened the fronts. The next thing the suitcase produced was a pair of fur-lined mittens, which went on without too much trouble, and after that a thermos flask full of hot soup, and some cups.

I looked into Joanna's black eyes as she held the cup to my mouth. I loved her. Who wouldn't love a girl who thought of hot soup at a time like that?

The driver accepted some soup too, and stamped his feet on the ground and remarked that it was getting chilly. Joanna gave him a pained look, and I laughed.

He glanced at me appraisingly and said, "Maybe you can do without a doctor, at that." He thanked Joanna for the soup, gave her back the cup, settled himself in the driver's seat and, switching off the light inside the taxi, started to drive us back to London.

"Who did it?" said Joanna.

"Tell you later."

"All right." She didn't press. She bent down to the case and brought out some fleecy slippers, thick socks, and a pair of her own stretch pants. "Take your trousers off."

I said ironically, "I can't undo the zip."

"I forgot."

"Anyway," I said, "I'll settle for the socks; can't manage the trousers." Even I could hear the exhaustion in my voice, and Joanna without arguing got down on her knees in the swaying cab and changed my wet socks and shoes for dry ones.

"Your feet are freezing," she said.

"I can't feel them," I said. The moon shone clearly through the window and I looked at the slippers. They were too large for me; much too large for Joanna.

"Have I stepped into Brian's shoes?" I asked.

After a pause she said neutrally, "They are Brian's, yes."

"And the jacket?"

"I bought it for him for Christmas."

So that was that. It wasn't the best moment to find out.

"I didn't give it to him," she said after a moment, as if she had made up her mind about something.

"Why not?"

"It didn't seem to suit a respectable life in the outer suburbs. I gave him a gold tiepin instead."

"Very suitable," I said dryly.

"A farewell present," she said quietly.

I said sincerely, "I'm sorry." I knew it hadn't been easy for her.

She drew in a breath sharply. "Are you made of iron, Rob?"

"Iron filings," I said.

The taxi sped on.

"We had a job finding you," she said. "I'm sorry we were so long. It was such a big area, you see."

"You came, though."

"Yes."

I found sitting in the swaying taxi very uncomfortable. My arms and shoulders ached unceasingly and if I leaned back too heavily the raw bits didn't like it. After a while I gave it up, and finished the journey sitting on the floor with my head and my hands in Joanna's lap.

I WAS OF course quite used to being knocked about. I followed, after all, an occupation in which physical damage was a fairly frequent though unimportant factor; and especially during my first season, when I was a less efficient jockey and most of the horses I rode were the worst to be had, there was rarely a time when some area of my body was not black and blue. I had broken several of the smaller bones, been kicked in tender places, and dislocated one or two joints. But none of these things had made the slightest dent on my general sense of well being, and on my optimism that I wouldn't crash unmendably. It seemed that in common with most other jockeys I had been born with the sort of resilient constitution that could take a bang and be ready for business, if not the following day, at least a good deal quicker than the medical profession considered normal.

Practice had given me a certain routine for dealing with discomfort, which was mainly to ignore it and concentrate on something else: but this system had not operated very well that evening. It didn't work, for instance, when I sat for a while in a light armchair in Joanna's warm room with my elbows on my knees, watching my fingers gradually change color from yellowy white to smudgy charcoal, to patchy purple, and finally to red.

It began as a tingle, faint and welcome, soon after we had got back and Joanna had turned on both her powerful heaters. She had insisted at once on removing my clammy trousers and also my underpants, and on my donning her black pants, which were warm but not long enough by several inches. It was odd, in a way, letting her undress me, which she did matter-of-factly and without remark; but in another way it seemed completely natural, a throwback to our childhood, when we had been bathed together on our visits to each other's houses.

She dug out some rather powdery-looking aspirins in a bottle. There were only three of them left, which I swallowed. Then she made some black coffee and held it for me to drink. It was stiff with brandy.

"Warming," she said laconically. "Anyway, you've stopped shivering at last."

It was then that my fingers tingled, and I told her.

"Will it be bad?" she said prosaically, putting down the empty coffee mug.

"Possibly."

"You won't want me to sit and watch you, then."

I shook my head. She took the empty mug into the kitchen and was several minutes coming back with a full one for herself.

The tingle increased first to a burning sensation and then to a feeling of being squeezed in a vise, tighter and tighter, getting more and more agonizing until it felt that at any minute my fingers would disintegrate under the pressure. But there they were, harmlessly hanging in the warm air, with nothing to show for it except that they were slowly turning puce.

Joanna came back from the kitchen and wiped the sweat off my forehead.

"Are you all right?" she asked.

"Yes," I said.

She nodded, and gave me a faint edition of the smile which had my heart doing flipflaps from boyhood, and drank her coffee.

When the pulse got going it felt as though my hands had been taken out of the vise, laid on a bench, and were being rhythmically hammered. It was terrible. And it went on too long. My head drooped.

When I looked up she was standing in front of me, watching me with an expression which I couldn't read. There were tears in her eyes.

"Is it over?" she said, blinking to disguise them.

"More or less."

We both looked at my hands, which were now a fierce red all over.

"And your feet?" she asked.

"They're fine," I said. Their awakening had been nothing.

"I'd better wash those grazes on your back" she said.

"No. In the morning."

"There's a lot of dirt in them," she protested.

"It's been there so long already that a few more hours won't hurt," I said. "I've had four anti-tetanus injections in the last two years, and there's always penicillin . . . and I'm too tired."

She didn't argue. She unzipped and helped me take off the parka, and made me get into her bed, still incongruously dressed in her black pants and blue cardigan and looking like a second-rate ballet dancer with a hangover. The sheets were rumpled from her lying in them before I had wakened her, and there was still a dent in her pillow where her head had been. I put mine there too, with an odd feeling of delight. She saw me grin, and correctly read my mind.

"It's the first time you've got into my bed," she said. "And it'll be the last."

"Have a heart, Joanna," I said.

She perched herself on the edge of the mattress and looked down at me.

"It's no good for cousins," she said.

"And if we weren't cousins?"

"I don't know . . ." She sighed. "But we are."

She bent down to kiss me good night on the forehead.

I couldn't help it; I put my arms up round her shoulders and pulled her down onto my chest and kissed her properly, mouth to mouth. It was the first time I had ever done it, and into it went all the pent-up and suppressed desire I had ever felt for her. It was too hungry, too passionate, much too desperate. I knew it, but I couldn't stop it. For a moment she seemed to relax and melt and kiss me back, but it was so brief and passing that I thought I had imagined it, and afterward her body grew rigid.

I let her go. She stood up abruptly and stared at me, her face scrubbed of any emotion. No anger, no disgust; and no love. She turned away without speaking and went across the room to the sofa, where she twisted a blanket around herself and lay down. She stretched out her hand to the table light and switched it off.

Her voice reached me across the dark room, calm, self-controlled. "Good night, Rob."

"Good night, Joanna," I said politely.

There was dead silence.

I rolled over onto my stomach and put my face in her pillow.

CHAPTER 13

I DON'T KNOW whether Joanna slept or not during the next four hours. The room was quiet. The time passed slowly.

The pulse in my hands went on throbbing violently for a while; but who cared? It was comforting, even if it hurt. I thought about all the fat red corpuscles forcing their way through the shrunken capillaries like water gushing along dry irrigation ditches after a drought. Very nice. Very life-giving. By tomorrow afternoon, I thought—correction, this afternoon—they might be fit for work. They'd got to be, that was all there was about it.

Some time after it was light I heard Joanna go into her narrow bathroom-kitchen where she brushed her teeth and made some fresh coffee. The warm roasted smell floated across to me. Saturday morning, I thought. Midwinter Cup day. I didn't leap out of bed eagerly to greet it; I turned over slowly from my stomach onto my side, shutting my eyes against the stiffness, which afflicted every muscle from neck to waist, and the sharp soreness of my back and wrists. I really didn't feel very well.

She came across the room with a mug of steaming coffee and put it on the bedside table. Her face was pale and expressionless.

"Coffee," she said unnecessarily.

"Thank you."

"How do you feel?" she asked, a little too clinically.

"Alive," I said.

There was a pause.

"Oh, go on," I said. "Either slosh me one or smile . . . one or the other. But don't stand there looking tragic, as if the Albert Hall had burned down on the first night of the Proms."

"Damn it, Rob," she said, her face crinkling into a laugh.

"Truce?" I asked.

"Truce," she agreed, still smiling. She even sat down again on the edge of the bed. I shoved myself up into a sitting position, wincing somewhat from various aches, and brought a hand out from under the bedclothes to reach for the coffee.

As a hand it closely resembled a bunch of beef sausages. I produced the other one. It also was swollen. The skin on both felt very tender and they were still unnaturally red.

"Blast," I said. "What's the time?"

"About eight o'clock," she said. "Why?"

Eight o'clock. The race was at 2:30. I began counting backward. I would have to be at Ascot by at the latest 1:30, preferably earlier, and the journey down, going by taxi, would take about fifty minutes. Allow an hour for holdups. That left me precisely four and a half hours in which to get fit enough to ride, and the way I felt it was a tall order.

I began to consider ways and means. There were the Turkish baths, with heat and massage; but I had lost too much skin for that to be an attractive idea. There was a workout in a gym; a possibility, but rough. There was a canter in the Park—a good solution on any day except Saturday, when the Row would be packed with little girls on leading reins; or better still a gallop on a racehorse at Epsom, but there was neither time to arrange it nor a good excuse to be found for needing it.

"What's the matter?" asked Joanna.

I told her.

"You don't mean it?" she said. "You aren't seriously thinking of racing today?"

"I seriously am."

"You're not fit to."

"That's the point. That's what we are discussing, how best to get fit."

"That isn't what I mean," she protested. "You look ill. You need a long quiet day in bed."

"I'll have it tomorrow," I said. "Today I am riding Template in the Midwinter Cup."

She began more forcefully to try to dissuade me, so I told her why I was going to ride. I told her everything, all about Kemp-Lore's anti-jockey obsession and all that had happened on the previous evening before she found me in the telephone box. It took quite a time. I didn't look at her while I told her about the tack-room episode, because for some reason it embarrassed me to describe it, even to her, and I knew then quite certainly that I was not going to repeat it to anyone else.

When I had finished she looked at me without speaking for half a minute—thirty solid seconds—and then she cleared her throat and said, "Yes, I see. We'd better get you fit, then."

I smiled at her.

"What first?" she said.

"Hot bath and breakfast," I said. "And can we have the weather forecast on?" I listened to it every morning, as a matter of routine.

She switched on the radio, which was busy with some sickening matinee music, and started tidying up the room, folding the blanket she had slept in and shaking the sofa cushions. Before she had finished the music stopped, and we heard the 8:30 news headlines, followed by the forecast.

"There was a slight frost in many parts of the country last night," said the announcer smoothly, "and more is expected tonight, especially in exposed areas. Temperatures today will reach five degrees centigrade, forty-one Fahrenheit, in most places, and the northeasterly wind will moderate slightly. It will be bright and sunny in the south. Further outlook: colder weather is expected in the next few days. And here is an announcement: The Stewards at Ascot inspected the course at eight o'clock this morning and have issued the following statement: 'Two or three degrees of frost were recorded on the racecourse last night, but the ground on both sides of the fences was protected by straw, and unless there is a sudden severe frost during the morning, racing is certain.'"

Joanna switched off. She said, "Are you absolutely determined to go?"

"Absolutely," I said.

"Well, I'd better tell you. I watched that program on television last night. *Turf Talk.*"

"Did you now!" I said, surprised.

"I sometimes do, since you were on it. If I'm in. Anyway I watched last night."

"And?" I prompted.

"He," she said, neither of us needing help to know whom she meant, "talked about the Midwinter Cup nearly all the time; canned biographies of the horses and trainers, and so on. I was waiting to hear him mention you, but he didn't. He just went on and on about how superb Template is; not a word about you. But what I thought you'd like to know is that he said that as it was such an important race he personally would be commentating the finish today, and that he personally would interview the winning jockey afterward. If only you can win, he'll have to describe your doing it, which would be a bitter enough pill, and then, congratulate you publicly in full view of several million people."

I gazed at her awestruck.

"That's a great thought," I said.

"Like he interviewed you after that race on Boxing Day," she added.

"That was the race that sealed my fate with him, I imagine," I said. "And you seem to have done some fairly extensive viewing, if I may say so."

She looked taken aback. "Well, didn't I see you sitting unobtrusively at the back of a concert I gave in Birmingham one night last summer?"

"I thought those lights were supposed to dazzle you," I said.

"You'd be surprised," she said.

I pushed back the bedclothes. The black pants looked even more incongruous in the daylight.

"I'd better get going," I said. "What do you have in the way of disinfectant and bandages, and a razor?"

"Only a few bits of elastic bandage," she said apologetically, "and the razor I defuzz my legs with. There's a chemist two roads away, though, who will be open by now. I'll make a list." She wrote it on an old envelope.

"And A.P.C. tablets," I said. "They are better than just aspirins."

"Right," she said. "I won't be long."

When she had gone I got out of bed and went into the bathroom. It's easy enough to say, but it wasn't all that easy to do, since I felt as if some overzealous laundress had fed me several times through a mangle. It was exasperating, I thought bitterly, how much havoc Kemp-Lore had worked on my body by such simple means. I turned on the taps, took off the pants and socks and stepped into the bath. The blue cardigan had stuck to my back and the shirt bandages to my wrists, so I lay down in the hot water without tugging at them and waited for them to soak off.

Gradually the heat did its customary work of unlocking the worst of the cramps, until I could rotate my shoulders and turn my head from side to side without feeling that I was tearing something adrift. Every few minutes I added more hot water, so that by the time Joanna came back I was up to my throat in it and steaming nicely, warm to the backbone and beyond.

She had dried my trousers and underpants overnight, and she pressed them for me while I eased myself out of the blue cardigan and reluctantly got out of the bath. I put on the trousers and watched her setting out her purchases on the kitchen table, a dark lock of hair falling forward into her eyes and a look of concentration firming her mouth. Quite a girl.

I sat down at the table and she bathed the abrasions with disinfectant, dried them, and covered them with large pieces of lint spread with zinc-and-castor-oil ointment which she stuck on with adhesive tape. She was neat and quick, and her touch was light.

"Most of the dirt came out in the bath luckily," she observed, busy with the scissors. "You've got quite an impressive set of muscles, haven't you? You must be strong. I didn't realize."

"At the moment I've got an impressive set of jellies." I sighed. "Very wobbly, very weak." And aching steadily, though there wasn't any point in saying so.

She went into the other room, rummaged in a drawer, and came back with another cardigan. Pale green, this time; the color suited my state of health rather well, I thought.

"I'll buy you some new ones," I said, stretching it across my chest to do up the fancy buttons.

"Don't bother," she said, "I loathe both of them."

"Thanks," I said, and she laughed.

I put the parka on again on top of the jersey and pushed the knitted cuffs up my forearms. Joanna slowly unwound the bloodstained bandages on my wrists. They still stuck a bit in spite of the soaking, and what lay underneath was a pretty disturbing sight, even to me, now that we could see it in daylight.

"I can't deal with this," she said positively. "You must go to a doctor."

"This evening," I said. "Put some more bandages on, for now."

"It's too deep," she said. "It's too easy to get it infected. You can't ride like this, Rob, really you can't."

"I can," I said. "I'll dunk them in a bowl of disinfectant for a while, and then you can wrap them up again. Nice and flat, so they won't show."

"Don't they hurt?" she said.

I didn't answer.

"Yes," she said. "Silly question." She sighed, and fetched a bowl full of warm water, pouring in solution so that it turned a milky white, and I soaked my wrists in it for ten minutes.

"That's fixed the infection," I said. "Now . . . nice and flat."

She did as I asked, fastening the ends of the bandages down with little gold safety pins. When she had finished the white cuffs looked tidy and nar-row, and I knew they would be unnoticeable under racing colors.

"Perfect," I said appreciatively, pulling down the parka sleeves to cover them. "Thank you, Florence."

"And Nightingale to you, too," she said, making a face at me. "When are you going to the police?"

"I'm not. I told you," I said. "I'm not going at all. I meant what I said last night."

"But why not? Why not?" She didn't understand. "You could get him prosecuted for assault or for causing grievous bodily harm, or whatever the technical term is."

I said, "I'd rather fight my own battles. And anyway, I can't face the thought of telling the police what happened last night, or being examined by their doctors, and photographed; or standing up in court, if it came to that, and answering questions about it in public, and having the whole rotten lot printed in gory detail in the papers. I just can't face it, that's all."

"Oh," she said slowly. "I suppose it would be a bit of an ordeal, if you look at it like that. Perhaps you feel humiliated. Is that it?"

"You may be rather bruisingly right," I admitted grudgingly, thinking about it. "And I'll keep my humiliation to myself, if you don't mind."

She laughed. "You don't need to feel any," she said. "Men are funny creatures."

The pity about hot baths is that, although they loosen one up beautifully for the time being, the effect does not last; one has to consolidate the position by exercise. And exercise, my battered muscles protested, was just what they would least enjoy; all the same I did a few rather halfhearted bend-stretch arm movements while Joanna scrambled some eggs, and after we had eaten and I had shaved I went back to it with more resolution, knowing that if I didn't get onto Template's back in a reasonably supple condition he had no chance of winning. It wouldn't help anyone if I fell off at the first fence.

After an hour's work, though I couldn't screw myself up to swinging my arms round in complete circles, I did get to the stage where I could lift them above shoulder height without wanting to cry out.

Joanna washed up and tidied the flat, and soon after ten o'clock, while I was taking a breather, she said, "Are you going on with this health and beauty kick until you leave for Ascot?"

"Yes."

"Well," she said, "it's only a suggestion, but why don't we go skating instead?"

"All that ice," I said, shuddering.

She smiled. "I thought you had to remount at once, after a fall?"

I saw the point.

"Anyway," she said, "it's good, warming exercise, and far more interesting than what you've been doing."

"You're a blooming genius, my darling Joanna," I said fervently.

"Er . . . maybe," she said. "I still think you ought to be in bed."

When she was ready we went along to my family's flat where I borrowed one of my father's shirts and a tie and also his skates, which represented his only interest outside music. Then we called at the bank, since the taxi ride the night before had taken nearly all Joanna's cash, and apart from needing money myself I wanted to repay her. Lastly, we stopped at a shop to buy me a pair of brown, silk-lined leather gloves, which I put on, and finally we reached the ice rink in Queensway where we had both been members from the days when we were taken there as toddlers on afternoons too rainy for playing in the Park.

We had not skated together since we were sixteen, and it was fascinating to see how quickly we fell back into the same dancing techniques that we had practiced as children.

She was right about the exercise. After an hour of it I had loosened up from head to foot, with hardly a muscle that wasn't moving reasonably freely. She herself, sliding over the ice beside me, had color in her cheeks and a dazzling sparkle in her eyes. She looked young and vivid.

At twelve o'clock, Cinderella-like, we slid off the rink.

"All right?" she asked, smiling.

"Gorgeous," I said, admiring the clear, intelligent face turned up to mine.

She didn't know whether I meant her or the skating, which was perhaps just as well.

"I mean, how are the aches and pains?"

"Gone," I said.

"You're a liar," she said, "but at least you don't look as gray as you did."

We went to change, which for me simply meant substituting my father's shirt and tie for the pale-green cardigan, and putting back the parka on top, and the gloves. Necessary, the gloves. Although my fingers were less swollen, less red, and no longer throbbed, the skin in places was beginning to split in short thread-thin cracks.

In the foyer Joanna put the cardigan and my father's skates into her bag and zipped it up, and we went into the street. She had already told me that she would not come to Ascot with me, but would watch on television. "And mind you win," she said. "After all this."

"Can I come back to your place afterward?" I said.

"Why, yes . . . yes," she said, as if surprised that I had asked.

"Fine," I said. "Well, good-by."

"Good luck, Rob," she said seriously.

CHAPTER 14

THE THIRD CRUISING taxi that I stopped just round the corner in Bayswater Road agreed to take me all the way to Ascot. During the journey, which was quick and skillfully driven, I kept the warmth and flexibility going in my arms by some minor exercises and imaginary piano playing, and if the driver saw me at it in his mirror he probably imagined I was suffering from a sad sort of St. Vitus's dance.

When I paid him at the gate, he announced that as it was his own cab he might as well stay and have a flutter on the races himself, so I arranged for him to drive me back to London at the end of the afternoon.

"Got any tips?" he said, counting my change.

"How about Template, in the big race?" I said.

"I dunno." He pursed his lips. "I dunno as I fancy that Finn. They say he's all washed."

"Don't believe all you hear," I said, smiling. "See you later."

"Right."

I went through the gate and along to the weighing room. The hands of the clock on the tower pointed to 1:05. Sid, James's head traveling lad, was standing outside the weighing-room door when I got there, and as soon as he saw me he came to meet me, and said, "You're here then."

"Yes," I said. "Why not?"

"The governor posted me here to wait for you. I had to go and tell him at once if you came. He's having lunch. There's a rumor going round that you weren't going to turn up, see?" He bustled off.

I went through the weighing room into the changing room.

"Hello," said my valet. "I thought you'd cried off."

"So you came after all," said Peter Cloony.

Tick-Tock said, "Where in hell have you been?"

"Why did everyone believe I wouldn't get here?" I asked.

"I don't know. Some rumor or other. Everyone's been saying you frightened yourself again on Thursday and you'd chucked up the idea of riding any more."

"How very interesting," I said grimly.

"Never mind that now," said Tick-Tock. "You're here, and that's that. I rang your pad this morning, but your landlady said you hadn't been back all night. I wanted to see if it was okay for me to have the car after racing today and for you to get a lift back with Mr. Axminster. I have met," he finished gaily, "a smashing girl. She's here at the races and she's coming out with me afterward."

"The car?" I said. "Oh, yes. Certainly. Meet me outside the weighing room after the last, and I'll show you where it is."

"Super," he said. "I say, are you all right?"

"Yes, of course."

"You look a bit night-afterish, to my hawk eyes," he said. "Anyway the best of luck on Template, and all that rot."

An official peered into the changing room and called me out. James was waiting in the weighing room outside.

"Where have you been?" he said.

"In London," I said. "What's this rumor about me not turning up?"

"God knows." He shrugged. "I was sure you wouldn't have stayed away without letting me know, but . . ."

"No," I said, "of course not." Not unless, I thought, I had still been hanging in a deserted tack room in the process of being crippled for life.

He dismissed the subject and began to talk about the race. "There's a touch of frost in the ground still," he said, "but that's really to our advantage." I told him I had walked round the course the day before, and knew which parts were best avoided.

"Good," he said.

I could see that for once he was excited. There was a sort of uncharacteristic shyness about his eyes, and the lower teeth gleamed in an almost perpetual half-smile. Anticipation of victory, that's what it is, I thought. And if I hadn't spent such a taxing night and morning I would have been feeling the same. As it was, I looked forward to the race without much joy, knowing from past experience that riding with injuries never made them better. Even so, I wouldn't have given up my place on Template for anything I could think of.

When I went back into the changing room to put on breeches and colors, the jockeys riding in the first race had gone out, leaving a lot of space and quiet behind them. I went along to my peg, where all my kit was out ready, and sat down for a while on the bench. My conscience ought to have been troubling me. James and Lord Tirrold had a right to expect their jockey to be in tiptop physical condition for so important a race, and, to put it mildly, he wasn't. However, I reflected wryly, looking down at my gloved hands, if we all owned up to every spot of damage we'd spend far too much time on the stands watching others win on our mounts. It wasn't the first time I had deceived an owner and trainer in this way and yet won a race, and I fervently hoped it wouldn't be the last.

I thought about the Midwinter. Much depended on how it developed, but basically I intended to start on the rails, sit tight in about fourth place all the way round, and sprint the last three furlongs. There was a new Irish mare, Emerald, that had come over with a terrific reputation and might take a lot of beating, especially as her jockey was a wily character, very clever at riding near the front and slipping the field by a hard-to-peg-back ten lengths round the last bend. If Emerald led into the last bend, I decided, Template would have to be close to her, not still waiting in fourth place. Fast though he was, it would be senseless to leave him too much to do up the straight.

It is not customary for jockeys to stay in the changing room while a race is on, and I saw the valets looking surprised that I had not gone out to watch it. I stood up, picked up the underjersey and Lord Tirrold's colors and went to change into them in the washroom. Let the valets think what they like, I thought. I wanted to change out of sight, partly because I had to do it more slowly than usual but mostly so that they shouldn't see the bandages. I pulled down the sleeves of the finely knitted green and black jersey until they hid those on my wrists.

The first race was over and the jockeys were beginning to stream into the changing room when I went back to my peg. I finished changing into breeches, nylons and boots and took my saddle and weight-cloth along to the trial scales for Mike to adjust the amount of lead needed to bring me to twelve stone.

"You've got gloves on," he pointed out.

"Yes," I said mildly, "it's a cold day. I'd better have some silk ones for riding in, though."

"Okay," he said. He produced from a hamper a bundle of whitish gloves and pulled out a pair for me.

I went along to the main scales to weigh out, and gave my saddle to Sid, who was standing there waiting for it.

He said, "The governor says I'm to saddle Template in the stable, and bring him straight down into the parade ring when it's time, and not go into the saddling boxes at all."

"Good," I said emphatically.

"We've had two private dicks and a bloody great dog patrolling the yard all night," he went on. "And another dick came with us in the horse box, and he's sitting in Template's box at this very minute. You never saw such a circus."

"How's the horse?" I asked, smiling. Evidently James was splendidly keeping his word that Template would not be doped.

"He'll eat 'em," Sid said simply. "The Irish won't know what hit them. All the lads have got their wages on him. Yeah, I know they've been a bit fed up that you were going to ride him, but I saw you turn that Turniptop inside out on Thursday and I told 'em they've nothing to worry about."

"Thanks," I said, sincerely enough: but it was just one more ounce on a load of responsibility.

The time dragged. My shoulders ached. To take my mind off that I spent time imagining the expression on Kemp-Lore's face when he saw my name up in the number frame. He would think at first it was a mistake. He would wait for it to be changed. And at any moment now, I thought maliciously, he will begin to realize that I am indeed here.

The second race was run with me still sitting in the changing room, the object of now frankly curious looks from the valets. I took the brown gloves off and put on the grayish ones. They had originally been really white, but nothing could entirely wash out a season's accumulated stains of mud and leather. I flexed my fingers. Most of the swelling had gone, and they seemed to be getting fairly strong again in spite of the cracked and tender skin.

Back came the other jockeys, talking, laughing, swearing, dealing out friendly and not so friendly abuse, yelling to the valets, dumping down their kit—the ordinary, comradely, noisy changing-room mixture—and I felt apart from it, as if I were living in a different dimension. Another slow quarter of an hour crawled by. Then an official put his head in and shouted, "Jockeys out, hurry up there, please."

I stood up, put on the parka, fastened my helmet, picked up my whip, and followed the general drift to the door. The feeling of unreality persisted.

Down in the paddock, where in June the chiffons and ribbons fluttered in the heat, stood cold little bunches of owners and trainers, most of them muffled to the eyes against the wind. It seared through the bare branches of the trees beside the parade ring, leaving a uniformity of pinched faces among the people lining the rails. The bright winter sunshine gave an illusion of warmth, which blue noses and runny eyes belied. But the parka, as I had been pleased to discover, was windproof.

Lord Tirrold wore on his fine-boned face the same look of excited anticipation that I could still see on James's. They are both so sure, I thought uneasily, that Template will win. Their very confidence weakened mine.

"Well, Rob," said Lord Tirrold, shaking me too firmly by the hand, "this is it."

"Yes, sir," I agreed, "this is it."

"What do you think of Emerald?" he asked.

We watched her shamble round the parade ring with the sloppy walk and low-carried head that so often denotes a champion.

"They say she's another Kerstin," said James, referring to the best steeplechasing mare of the century.

"It's too soon to say that," said Lord Tirrold; and I wondered if the same thought sprang into his mind as into mine, that after the Midwinter it might not be too soon, after all. But he added, as if to bury the possibility, "Template will beat her."

"I think so," James agreed.

I swallowed. They were too sure. If he won, they would expect it. If he lost, they would blame me; and probably with good cause.

Template himself stalked round the parade ring in his navy-blue rug, playing up each time as he came face on to the wind, trying to turn round so that it blew on his quarters, with his lad hanging onto his leading rein like a small child on a large kite.

A bell rang, indicating that it was time for the jockeys to mount. James beckoned to the boy, who brought Template across to us and took off his rug.

"Everything all right?" James asked.

"Yes, sir."

Template's eyes were liquid clear, his ears were pricked, his muscles quivering to be off: a picture of a taut, tuned racing machine eager to get on with the job he was born for. He was not a kind horse: there was no sweetness in his makeup and he inspired admiration rather than affection; but I liked him for his fire and his aggressiveness and his unswerving will to win.

"You've admired him long enough, Rob," said James teasingly. "Get up on him."

I took off the parka and dropped it on the rug. James gave me a leg up into the saddle and I gathered the reins and put my feet into the irons.

What he read in my face I don't know, but he said suddenly, anxiously, "Is anything wrong?"

"No," I said, "everything's fine." I smiled down at him, reassuring myself as much as him.

Lord Tirrold said, "Good luck," as if he didn't think I needed it, and I touched my cap to him and turned Template away to take his place in the parade down the course.

There was a television camera on a tower not far down the course from the starting gate, and I found the thought of Kemp-Lore raging at the sight of me on his monitor set a most effective antidote to the freezing wind. We circled round for five minutes, eleven of us, while the assistant starter tightened girths and complained that anyone would think we were in perishing Siberia.

I remembered that Tick-Tock, the last time we had ridden together on the course on a cold day, had murmured, "Ascot's blasted heath. Where are the witches?" And I thought of him now, putting a brave face on his inactivity in the stands. I thought briefly of Grant, probably hating my guts while he watched the race on television, and of Peter Cloony's wife, with no set to watch on at all, and of the jockeys who had given up and gone into factories, and of Art, under the sod.

"Line up," called the starter, and we straightened into a ragged row across the course, with Template firmly on the inside, hugging the rails.

I thought of myself driven to distraction by having it drummed into me that I had lost my nerve, and I thought of myself dragged over flinty ground and tied to a piece of galvanized chain; and I didn't need any more good reasons why I had to win the Midwinter Cup.

I watched the starter's hand. He had a habit of stretching his fingers just before he pulled the lever to let the tapes up, and I had no intention of letting anyone get away before me and cut me out of the position I had acquired on the rails.

The starter stretched his fingers. I kicked Template's flanks. He was moving quite fast when we went under the rising tapes, with me lying flat along his withers to avoid being swept off like other riders who had jumped the start too effectively in the past.

The tapes whistled over my head and we were away securely on the rails and on the inside curve for at least the next two miles.

The first three fences were the worst, as far as my comfort was concerned. By the time we had jumped the fourth—the water—I had felt the thinly healed crusts on my back tear open, had thought my arms and shoulders would split apart with the strain of controlling Template's eagerness, and had found just how much my wrists and hands had to stand from the tug of the reins.

My chief feeling, as we landed over the water, was one of relief. It was all bearable; I could contain it and ignore it, and get on with the job.

The pattern of the race was simple from my point of view, because from start to finish I saw only three other horses, Emerald and the two lightly weighted animals whom I had allowed to go on and set the pace. The jockeys of this pair, racing ahead of me nose for nose, consistently left a two-foot gap between themselves and the rails, and I reckoned that if they were still there by the time we reached the second-last fence in the straight, they would veer very slightly toward the stands, as horses usually do at Ascot, and widen the gap enough for me to get through.

My main task until then was keeping Emerald from cutting across to the rails in front of me and being able to take the opening instead of Template. I left just too little room between me and the front pair for Emerald to get in, forcing the mare to race all the way on my outside. It didn't matter that she was two or three feet in front: I could see her better there, and Template was too clever a jumper to be brought down by the half-length trick—riding into a fence half a length in front of an opponent, causing him to take off at the same moment as oneself and land on top of the fence instead of safely on the ground on the other side.

With the order unchanged we completed the whole of the first circuit

and swept out to the country again. Template jumped the four fences down
to Swinley Bottom so brilliantly that I kept finding myself crowding the tails
of the pacemakers as we landed, and had to ease him back on the flat each
time to avoid taking the lead too soon, and yet not ease him so much that
Emerald could squeeze into the space between us.

From time to time I caught a glimpse of the grimness on Emerald's
jockey's face. He knew perfectly well what I was doing to him, and if I hadn't
beaten him to the rails and made a flying start, he would have done the same
to me. Perhaps I had Kemp-Lore to thank that he hadn't even tried, I thought
fleetingly; if the bonfire Kemp-Lore had made of my reputation had led the
Irishman to misjudge what I would do, so much the better.

For another half mile the two horses in front kept going splendidly, but
one of the jockeys picked up his whip at the third-last fence, and the other
was already busy with his hands. They were dead ducks, and because of that
they swung a little wide going round the last bend into the straight. The
Irishman must have had his usual bend tactics too firmly fixed in his mind,
for he chose that exact moment to go to the front. It was not a good occasion
for that maneuver. I saw him spurt forward from beside me and accelerate,
but he had to go round on the outside of the two front horses, who were
themselves swinging wide, and he was wasting lengths in the process. The
mare carried seven pounds less weight than Template, and on that bend she
lost the advantage they should have given her.

After the bend, tackling the straight for the last time, with the second-
last fence just ahead, Emerald was in the lead on the outside, then the two tiring horses, then me.

There was a three-foot gap then between the innermost pacemaker and
the rails. I squeezed Template. He pricked his ears and bunched his colossal
muscles and thrust himself forward into the narrow opening. He took off at
the second-last fence half a length behind and landed a length in front of the
tiring horse, jumping so close to him on one side and to the wings on the
other that I heard the other jockey cry out in surprise as I passed.

One of Template's great advantages was his speed away from a fence.
With no check in his stride he sped smoothly on, still hugging the rails, with
Emerald only a length in front on our left. I urged him a fraction forward to
prevent the mare from swinging over to the rails and blocking me at the last
fence. She needed a two-length lead to do it safely, and I had no intention of
letting her have it.

The utter joy of riding Template lay in the feeling of immense power which he generated. There was no need to make the best of things, on his back; to fiddle and scramble, and hope for others to blunder, and find nothing to spare for a finish. He had enough reserve strength for his jockey to be able to carve up the race as he wished, and there was nothing in racing, I thought, more ecstatic than that.

As we galloped toward the last fence, I knew that Template would beat Emerald if he jumped it in anything like his usual style. She was a length ahead and showing no sign of flagging, but I was still holding Template on a tight rein. Ten yards from the fence I let him go. I kicked his flanks and squeezed with the calves of my legs, and he went over the birch like an angel, smooth, surging, the nearest to flying one can get.

He gained nearly half a length on the mare, but she didn't give up easily. I sat down and rode Template for my life, and he stretched himself willingly into his flat-looking stride. He came level with Emerald halfway along the run in. She hung on grimly for a short distance, but Template would have none of it. He floated past her with an incredible increase of speed, and he won, in the end, by two clear lengths.

There are times beyond words, and that was one of them. I patted Template's sweating neck over and over. I could have kissed him. I would have given him anything. But how does one thank a horse? How could one ever repay him, in terms he would understand, for giving one such a victory?

The two tall men were pleased all right. They stood side by side, waiting for us in the unsaddling enclosure, the same elated expression on both their faces. I smiled at them, and shook my feet out of the irons and slid onto the ground. Onto the ground: down to earth. The end of an unforgettable experience.

"Rob," said James, shaking his big head. "Rob." He slapped Template's steaming shoulder and watched me struggle to undo the girth buckles with fingers shaking from both weakness and excitement.

"I knew he'd do it," Lord Tirrold said. "What a horse! What a race!"

I had got the buckles undone at last and had pulled the saddle off over my arm when an official came over and asked Lord Tirrold not to go away, as the Cup was to be presented to him in a few minutes. To me he said, "Will you come straight out again after you have weighed in? There's a trophy for the winning jockey as well."

I nodded, and went in to sit on the scales. Now that the concentration of the race was over, I began to be aware of the extra damage it had done. Across the back of my shoulders and down my arms to the fingertips every muscle felt like lead, draggingly heavy, shot with stabbing and burning sensations. I was appallingly weak and tired, and the pain in my wrists had increased to the point where I was finding it very difficult to keep it all out of my face. A quick look revealed that the bandages were red again, and so were the cuffs of the silk gloves and parts of the fawn underjersey. But if the blood had soaked through the black jersey as well, at least it didn't show.

With a broad smile Mike took my saddle from me in the changing room and unbuckled my helmet and pulled it off my head.

"They are wanting you outside, did you know?" he said.

I nodded. He held out a comb. "Better smarten your hair a bit. You can't let the side down."

I obediently took the comb and tidied my hair, and went back outside.

The horses had been led away and in their place stood a table bearing the Midwinter Cup and other trophies, with a bunch of racecourse directors and Stewards beside it.

And Maurice Kemp-Lore as well.

It was lucky I saw him before he saw me. I felt my scalp contract at the sight of him and an unexpectedly strong shock of revulsion ran right down my body. He couldn't have failed to understand it if he had seen it.

I found James at my elbow. He followed my gaze.

"Why are you looking so grim?" he said. "He didn't even try to dope Template."

"No," I agreed. "I expect he was too tied up with his television work to be sure of having time to do it."

"He has given up the whole idea," said James confidently. "He must have seen there was no chance any more of persuading anyone you had lost your nerve. Not after the way you rode on Thursday."

It was the reckless way I had ridden on Thursday that had infuriated Kemp-Lore into delivering the packet I had taken on Friday. I understood that very well.

"Have you told anyone about the sugar?" I asked James.

"No, since you asked me not to. But I think something must be done. Slander or no slander, evidence or not—"

"Will you wait," I asked, "until next Saturday? A week today? Then you can tell whomever you like."

"Very well," he said slowly. "But I still think——"

He was interrupted by the arrival at the trophy table of the day's V.I.P., a pretty Duchess, who with a few well-chosen words and a genuinely friendly smile presented the Midwinter Cup to Lord Tirrold, a silver tray to James, and a cigarette box to me. An enterprising press photographer let off a flash bulb as the three of us stood together admiring our prizes, and after that we gave them back again to the Clerk of the Course, for him to have them engraved with Template's name and our own.

I heard Kemp-Lore's voice behind me as I handed over the cigarette box, and it gave me time to arrange my face into a mildly smiling blankness before turning round. Even so, I was afraid that I wouldn't be able to look at him without showing my feelings.

I pivoted slowly on my heels and met his eyes. They were piercingly blue and very cold, and they didn't blink or alter in any way as I looked back at them. I relaxed a little, inwardly, thankful that the first difficult hurdle had been crossed. He had searched but had not read in my face that I knew it was he who had abducted me the evening before.

"Rob Finn," he said in his charming television voice, "is the jockey you just watched being carried to victory by this wonder horse, Template." He was speaking into a hand microphone from which trailed yards of black cord, and looking alternately at me and at a camera on a scaffolding tower nearby. The camera's red eye glowed. I mentally girded up my loins and prepared to forestall every disparaging opinion he might utter.

He said, "I expect you enjoyed being his passenger?"

"It was marvelous," I said emphatically, smiling a smile to outdazzle his. "It is a great thrill for any jockey to ride a horse as superb as Template. Of course," I went on amiably, before he had time to speak, "I am lucky to have had the opportunity. As you know, I have been taking Pip Pankhurst's place all these months, while his leg has been mending, and today's win should have been his. He is much better now, I'm glad to say, and we are all delighted that it won't be long before he is riding again." I spoke truthfully: whatever it meant to me in fewer rides, it would benefit the sport as a whole to have its champion back in action.

A slight chill crept into the corner of Kemp-Lore's mouth.

"You haven't been doing as well, lately——" he began.

"No," I interrupted warmly. "Aren't they extraordinary, those runs of atrocious luck in racing? Did you know that Doug Smith once rode ninety-nine losers in succession? How terrible he must have felt. It makes my twenty or so seem quite paltry."

"You weren't worried, then, by . . . er . . . by such a bad patch as you've been going through?" His smile was slipping.

"Worried?" I repeated lightheartedly. "Well, naturally I wasn't exactly delighted, but these runs of bad luck happen to everyone in racing, once in a while, and one just has to live through them until another winner comes along. Like today's," I finished with a grin at the camera.

"Most people understood it was more than bad luck," he said sharply. There was a definite crack in his jolly-chums manner, and for an instant I saw in his eyes a flash of the fury he was controlling. It gave me great satisfaction, and because of it I smiled at him more vividly.

I said, "People will believe anything when their pockets are touched. I'm afraid a lot of people lost their money backing my mounts. It's only natural to blame the jockey—nearly everyone does when they lose."

He listened to me mending the holes he had torn in my life and he couldn't stop me without giving an impression of being a bad sport: and nothing kills the popularity of a television commentator quicker than obvious bad-sportsmanship.

He had been standing at right angles to me with his profile to the camera, but now he took a step toward me and turned so that he stood beside me on my left side. As he moved there was a fleeting set to his mouth that looked like cruelty to me, and it prepared me in some measure for what he did next.

With a large gesture which must have appeared as genuine friendship on the television screen, he dropped his right arm heavily across my shoulders, with his right thumb lying forward on my collarbone and his fingers spread out on my back.

I stood still, and turned my head slowly toward him, and smiled sweetly. Few things have ever cost me more effort.

"Tell us a bit about the race, then, Rob," he said, advancing the microphone in his left hand. "When did you begin to think you might win?"

His arm felt like a ton weight, an almost unsupportable burden on my aching muscles. I gathered my straying wits. "Oh, I thought, coming into the last fence," I said, "that Template might have the speed to beat Emerald on the flat. He can produce such a sprint at the end, you know."

"Yes, of course." He pressed his fingers more firmly into the back of my shoulder and gave what passed for a friendly shake. My head began to spin. Everything on the edge of my vision became blurred. I went on smiling, concentrating desperately on the fair, good-looking face so close to mine, and was rewarded by the expression of puzzlement and disappointment in his eyes. He knew that under his fingers, beneath two thin jerseys, were patches which must be sore if touched, but he didn't know how much or how little trouble I had had in freeing myself in the tack room. I wanted him to believe it had been none at all, that the ropes had slipped undone or the hook fallen easily out of the ceiling. I wanted to deny him even the consolation of knowing how nearly he had succeeded in preventing me from riding Template.

"And what are Template's plans for the future?" He strove to be conversational, normal. The television interview was progressing along well-trodden ways.

"There's the Gold Cup at Cheltenham," I said. I was past telling whether I sounded equally unruffled, but there was still no leap of triumph in his face, so I went on. "I expect he will run there, in three weeks' time. All being well, of course."

"And do you hope to ride him again in that?" he asked. There was an edge to his voice which stopped just short of offensiveness. He was finding it as nearly impossible to put on an appearance of affection for me as I for him.

"It depends," I said, "on whether or not Pip is fit in time . . . and on whether Lord Tirrold and Mr. Axminster want me to, if he isn't. But of course I'd like to, if I get the chance."

"You've never yet managed to ride in the Gold Cup, I believe?" He made it sound as if I had been trying unsuccessfully for years to beg a mount.

"No," I agreed. "But it has only been run twice since I came into racing, so if I get a ride in it so soon in my career I'll count myself very lucky."

His nostrils flared, and I thought in satisfaction, That got you squarely in the guts, my friend. You'd forgotten how short a time I've been a jockey.

He turned his head away from me toward the camera and I saw the rigidity in his neck and jaw and the pulse that beat visibly in his temple. I imagined he would willingly have seen me dead; yet he was enough in command of himself to realize that if he pressed my shoulder any harder I would be likely to guess it was not accidental.

Perhaps if he had been less controlled at that moment I would have been more merciful to him later. If his professionally pleasant expression had exploded into the rage he was feeling, or if he had openly dug his nails with ungovernable vindictiveness into my back, I could perhaps have believed him more mad than wicked, after all. But he knew too well where to stop; and since I could not equate madness with such self-discipline, by my standards he was sane; sane and controlled, and therefore unlikely to destroy himself from within. I threw Claudius Mellit's plea for kid gloves finally overboard.

Kemp-Lore was speaking calmly toward the camera, finishing off his broadcast. He gave me a last, natural-looking little squeezing shake, and let his arm drop away from my shoulders. Slowly and methodically I silently repeated to myself the ten most obscene words I knew, and after that Ascot racecourse stopped attempting to whirl round and settled down again into bricks and mortar and grass and people, all sharp and perpendicular.

The man behind the camera on the tower held up his thumb and the red eye blinked out.

Kemp-Lore turned directly to me again and said, "Well, that's it. We're off the air now."

"Thank you, Maurice," I said, carefully constructing one last warm smile. "That was just what I needed to set me back on top of the world. A big-race win and a television interview with you to clinch it. Thank you very much." I could rub my fingers in his wounds, too.

He gave me a look in which the cultivated habit of charm struggled for supremacy over spite, and still won. Then he turned on his heel and walked away, pulling his black microphone cord along the ground after him.

It is impossible to say which of us loathed the other more.

CHAPTER 15

I SPENT MOST of the next day in Joanna's bed. Alone, unfortunately.

She gave me a cup of coffee for breakfast, a cozy grin, and instructions to sleep. So I lazily went on snoozing in the pajamas she had bought me, dreaming about her on her own pillow, doing nothing more energetic than occasionally raising my blood pressure by thinking about Kemp-Lore.

I had arrived on her doorstep in a shaky condition the evening before, having first taken Tick-Tock and his space-age girlfriend by taxi to the boring White Bear at Uxbridge, where, as I had imagined, the Mini-Cooper stood abandoned in the car park. It had seemed to me certain that Kemp-Lore had driven to the White Bear in his own car, had used the Mini-Cooper for his excursion to the abandoned stables, and had changed back again to his own car on the return journey. His route, checked on the map, was simple: direct almost. All the same, I was relieved to find the little Mini safe and sound.

Tick-Tock's remarks about my carelessness with communal property trickled to a stop when he found my wrist watch and wallet and other things out of my pockets on the glove shelf, and my jacket and overcoat and a length of white nylon rope on the back seat.

"Why the blazes," he said slowly, "did you leave your watch and your money and your coats here? It's a wonder they weren't pinched. And the car too."

"It's the northeast wind," I said solemnly. "Like the moon, you know. I always do mad things when there's a northeast wind."

"Northeast my aunt Fanny." He grinned, picked up the coats, and transferred them to the waiting taxi. Then he surprisingly shoveled all my small belongings into my trousers pockets and put my watch into my gloved hand.

"You may have fooled everyone else, mate," he said lightly, "but to me you have looked like death inefficiently warmed up all day, and it's something to do with your maulers. The gloves are new . . . you don't usually wear any. What happened?"

"You work on it," I said amiably, getting back into the taxi. "If you haven't anything better to do." I glanced across at his little hepcat, and he laughed and flipped his hand, and went to help her into the Mini-Cooper.

The taxi driver, in a good mood because he had backed three winners, drove me back to Joanna's mews without a single complaint about the roundabout journey. When I paid him and added a fat tip on top he said, "Were you on a winner too, then?"

"Yes," I said. "Template."

"Funny thing that," he said. "I backed him myself, after what you said about not believing all you hear. You were quite right, weren't you? That fellow Finn's not washed up at all, not by a long chalk. He rode a hell of a race. I reckon he can carry my money again, any day." He shifted his gears gently, and drove off.

Watching his taillight bump away down the cobbled mews, I felt ridiculously happy and very much at peace. Winning the race had already been infinitely worth the cost, and the taxi driver, not knowing whom he was speaking to, had presented me with the bonus of learning that, as far as the British racing public was concerned, I was back in business.

I leaned wearily but contentedly against Joanna's doorpost and rang her bell.

That wasn't quite the end of the most exhausting twenty-four hours of my life, however. My thoughtful cousin, anticipating correctly that I would refuse to turn out again to see a doctor, had imported one of her own. He was waiting there when I arrived, a blunt no-bedside-manner Scot with busy eyebrows and three warts on his chin.

To my urgent protests that I was in no state to withstand his ministrations, both he and Joanna turned deaf ears. They put me into a chair, and off came my clothes again, the leather gloves and the silk racing ones I had not removed after riding, then the parka, my father's shirt and the underjersey, also not returned to Mike, then the bits of lint Joanna had stuck on in the morning, and finally the blood-soaked bandages round my wrists. Toward the end of all this rather ruthless undressing the room began spinning as Ascot had done, and I regrettably rolled off the chair onto the floor, closer to fainting than I had been the whole time.

The Scotsman picked me up and put me back on the chair and told me to pull myself together and be a man.

"You've only lost a wee bit of skin," he said sternly.

I began to laugh weakly, which didn't go down well either. He was a joyless fellow. He compressed his mouth until the warts quivered when I shook my head to his inquiries and would not tell him what had happened. But he bound me up again comfortably enough and gave me some painkilling pills which turned out to be very effective; and when he had gone I got into Joanna's bed and sank thankfully into oblivion.

Joanna worked at her painting most of the next day, and when I surfaced finally at about four o'clock in the afternoon she was singing quietly at her easel. Not the angular, spiky songs she specialized in, but a Gaelic ballad in a minor key, soft and sad. I lay and listened with my eyes shut because I knew she would stop if she found me awake. Her voice was true even at a level not much above a whisper, the result of well-exercised vocal cords and terrific breath control. A proper Finn, she is, I thought wryly. Nothing done by halves.

She came to the end of the ballad, and afterward began another. "I know where I'm going, and I know who's going with me. I know who I love, but the dear knows who I'll marry. Some say he's black, but I say he's bonny—" She stopped abruptly and said quietly but forcefully, "Damn, damn and blast." I heard her throw down her palette and brushes and go into the kitchen.

After a minute I sat up in bed and called to her.

"Yes?" she shouted, without reappearing.

"I'm starving," I said.

"Oh." She gave a laugh which ended in a choke, and called out, "All right. I'll cook."

And cook she did; fried chicken with sweet corn and pineapple and bacon. While the preliminary smells wafted tantalizingly out of the kitchen I got up and put my clothes on, and stripped her bed. There were clean sheets in the drawer beneath, and I made it up again fresh and neat for her to get into.

She carried a tray of plates and cutlery in from the kitchen and saw the bundle of dirty sheets and the smooth bed.

"What are you doing?"

"The sofa isn't good for you," I said. "You obviously haven't slept well . . . and your eyes are red."

"That isn't . . ." she began, and thought better of it.

"It isn't lack of sleep?" I finished.

She shook her head. "Let's eat."

"Then what's the matter?" I said.

"Nothing. Nothing. Shut up and eat."

I did as I was told. I was hungry.

She watched me finish every morsel. "You're feeling better," she stated.

"Oh, yes. Much. Thanks to you."

"And you are not sleeping here tonight?"

"No."

"You can try the sofa," she said mildly. "You might as well find out what I have endured for your sake." I didn't answer at once, and she added compulsively, "I'd like you to stay, Rob. Stay."

I looked at her carefully. Was there the slightest chance, I wondered, that her gentle songs and her tears in the kitchen and now her reluctance to have me leave meant that she was at last finding the fact of our cousinship more troublesome than she was prepared for? I had always known that if she ever came to love me as I wanted and also was not able to abandon her rigid prejudice against our blood relationship it would very likely break her up. If that was what was happening to her, it was definitely not the time to walk out.

"All right," I said, smiling. "Thank you. I'll stay. On the sofa."

She became suddenly animated and talkative, and told me in great detail how the race and the interview afterward had appeared on television. Her voice was quick and light. "At the beginning of the program he said he thought your name was a mistake on the number boards, because he had heard you weren't there, and I began to worry that you had broken down on the way and hadn't got there after all. But of course you had. And afterward you looked like lifelong buddies standing there with his arm round your shoulders and you smiling at him as if the sun shone out of his eyes. How did you manage it? But he was trying to needle you, wasn't he? It seemed like it to me, but then that was perhaps because I knew—" She stopped in mid-flow, and in an entirely different, sober tone of voice she said, "What are you going to do about him?"

I told her. It took some time.

She was shaken. "You can't," she said.

I smiled at her, but didn't answer.

She shivered. "He didn't know what he was up against when he picked on you."

"Will you help?" I asked. Her help was essential.

"Won't you change your mind and go to the police?" she asked seriously.

"No."

"But what you are planning . . . it's cruel."

"Yes," I agreed.

"And complicated, and a lot of work, and expensive."

"Yes. Will you make that one telephone call for me?"

She sighed and said, "You don't think you'll relent once everything has stopped hurting?"

"I'm quite certain," I said.

"I'll think about it," she said, standing up and collecting the dishes. She wouldn't let me help her wash up, so I went over to the easel to see what she had been working on all day: and I was vaguely disturbed to find it was a portrait of my mother sitting at her piano.

I was still looking at the picture when she came back.

"It's not very good, I'm afraid," she said, standing beside me. "Something seems to have gone wrong with the perspective of the piano."

"Does Mother know you are doing it?" I asked.

"Oh, no," she said.

"When did you start it?"

"Yesterday afternoon," she said.

There was a pause. Then I said, "It won't do you any good to try to convince yourself your feelings for me are maternal."

She jerked in surprise.

"I don't want mothering," I said. "I want a wife."

"I can't . . ." she said, with a tight throat.

I turned away from the picture feeling that I had pressed her too far, too soon. Joanna abruptly picked up a turpentine-soaked rag and scrubbed at the still wet oils, wiping out all her work.

"You see too much," she said. "More than I understood myself."

I grinned at her and after a moment, with an effort, she smiled back. She wiped her fingers on the rag, and hung it on the easel.

"I'll make that telephone call," she said. "You can go ahead with . . . with what you plan to do."

ON THE FOLLOWING morning, Monday, I hired a drive-yourself car and went to see Grant Oldfield.

The hard overnight frost, which had caused the day's racing to be canceled, had covered the hedges and trees with sparkling rime, and I enjoyed the journey even though at the end of it I expected a reception as cold as the day.

I stopped outside the gate, walked up the short path through the desolate garden, and rang the bell.

It had only just struck me that the brass bell push was brightly polished when the door opened and a neat dark-haired young woman in a green wool dress looked at me inquiringly.

"I came . . ." I said. "I wanted to see . . . er . . . I wonder if you could tell me where I could find Grant Oldfield?"

"Indoors," she said. "He lives here; I'm his wife. Just a minute, and I'll get him. What name shall I say?"

"Rob Finn," I said.

"Oh," she said in surprise; and she smiled warmly. "Do come in. Grant will be so pleased to see you."

I doubted it, but I stepped into the narrow hall and she shut the door behind me. Everything was spotless and shining; it looked a different house from the one I remembered. She led the way to the kitchen and opened the door onto another area of dazzling cleanliness.

Grant was sitting at a table, reading a newspaper. He glanced up as his wife came in, and when he saw me his face too creased into a smile of surprised welcome. He stood up. He was much thinner and older looking, and shrunken in some indefinable inner way; but he was, or he was going to be soon, a whole man again.

"How are you, Grant?" I said inadequately, not understanding their friendliness.

"I'm much better, thanks," he said. "I've been home a fortnight now."

"He was in hospital," his wife explained. "They took him there the day after you brought him home. Dr. Parnell wrote to me and told me Grant was ill and couldn't help being how he was. So I came back." She smiled at Grant. "And everything's going to be all right now. Grant's got a job lined up too. He starts in two weeks, selling toys."

"Toys?" I exclaimed. Of all the incongruous things, I thought.

"Yes," she said, "they thought it would be better for him to do something which had nothing to do with horses, so that he wouldn't start brooding again."

"We've a lot to thank you for, Rob," Grant said.

"Dr. Parnell told me," his wife said, seeing my surprise, "that you would have been well within your rights if you had handed him over to the police instead of bringing him here."

"I tried to kill you," Grant said in a wondering voice, as if he could no longer understand how he had felt. "I really tried to kill you, you know."

"Dr. Parnell said if you had been a different sort of person Grant could have ended up in a criminal lunatic asylum."

I said uncomfortably, "Dr. Parnell appears to have been doing too much talking altogether."

"He wanted me to understand," she said, smiling, "that you had given Grant another chance, so I ought to give him another chance too."

"Would it bother you," I said to Grant, "if I asked you a question about how you lost your job with Axminster?"

Mrs. Oldfield moved protectively to his side. "Don't bring it all back," she said anxiously, "all that resentment."

"It's all right, love," Grant said, putting his arm round her waist. "Go ahead."

"I believe you were telling the truth when you told Axminster you had not sold information to that professional punter, Lubbock," I said. "But Lubbock did get information, and did pay for it. The question is, whom was he actually handing over the money to, if he thought he was paying it to you?"

"You've got it wrong, Rob," Grant said. "I went over and over it at the time, and went to see Lubbock and got pretty angry with him." He smiled ruefully. "And Lubbock said that until James Axminster tackled him about it he hadn't known for sure who he was buying information from. He had guessed it was me, he said. But he said I had given him the information over the telephone and he had sent the payments to me in the name of Robinson, care of a post office in London. He didn't believe I knew nothing about it, of course. He just thought I hadn't covered myself well enough and was trying to wriggle out of trouble." There was a remarkable lack of bitterness in his voice; his spell in a mental hospital, or his illness itself, seemed to have changed his personality to the roots.

"Can you give me Lubbock's address?" I asked.

"He lives in Solihull," he said slowly. "I might know the house again, but I can't remember the name of it, or the road."

"I'll find it," I said.

"Why do you want to?" he asked.

"Would it mean anything to you if I happened to prove that you were telling the truth all along?"

His face came suddenly alive from within. "I'll say it would. You can't imagine what it was like, losing that job for something I didn't do, and having no one believe me any more."

I didn't tell him that I knew exactly what it was like, only too well. I said, "I'll do my best, then."

"But you won't go back to racing?" his wife said to him anxiously. "You won't start all over again?"

"No, love. Don't worry," he said calmly. "I'm going to enjoy selling toys. You never know, we might start a toy shop of our own, next year, when I've learned the business."

I DROVE THE thirty miles to Solihull, looked up Lubbock in the telephone directory, and rang his number. A woman answered. She told me that he was not in, but if I wanted him urgently I would probably get hold of him at the Queen's Hotel in Birmingham, as he was lunching there.

Having lost my way twice on the one-way streets I miraculously found a place to park outside the Queen's, and went in. I wrote a note on the hotel paper, asking Mr. Lubbock, whom I did not know even by sight, if he would be so very kind as to give me a few minutes of his time. Sealing the note in an envelope I asked the head porter if he would have one of the page boys find Mr. Lubbock and give it to him.

"He went into the dining room with another gentleman a few minutes ago," he said. "Here, Dickie, take this note in to Mr. Lubbock."

Dickie returned with an answer on the back of the note: Mr. Lubbock would meet me in the lounge at 2:15.

Mr. Lubbock proved to be a plumpish, middle-aged man with a gingery mustache and a thin section of lank hair brushed across a balding skull. He accepted from me a large brandy and a fat cigar with such an air of surprised irony that I was in no doubt that he was used to buying these things for jockeys, and not the other way about.

"I want to know about Grant Oldfield," I said, coming straight to the point.

"Oldfield?" he murmured, sucking flame down the cigar. "Oh, yes, I remember, Oldfield." He gave me a sharp upward glance. "You . . . er . . . you still work for the same firm, don't you? Do you want a deal, is that it? Well, I don't see why not. I'll give you the odds to a pony for every winner you put me on to. No one could say fairer than that."

"Is that what you paid Oldfield?" I said.

"Yes," he said.

"Did you give it to him personally?" I asked.

"No," he said. "But then he didn't ask me personally. He fixed it up on the telephone. He was very secretive: said his name was Robinson, and asked me to pay him in uncrossed money orders, and to send them to a post office for him to collect."

"Which one?" I asked.

He took a swig at the brandy and gave me an assessing look. "Why do you want to know?"

"It sounds a good idea," I said casually.

He shrugged. "I can't remember," he said. "Surely it's unimportant which post office it was? Somewhere in a London suburb, I know, but I can't remember where after all this time. N.E.7? N.12? Something like that?"

"You wouldn't have a record of it?"

"No," he said decisively. "Why don't you ask Oldfield himself if you need to know."

I sighed. "How many times did he give you information?" I asked.

"He told me the names of about five horses altogether, I should think. Three of them won, and I sent him the money on those occasions."

"You didn't know it was Oldfield selling you tips, did you?" I said.

"It depends what you mean by 'know,'" he said. "I had a pretty good idea. Who else could it have been? But I suppose I didn't actually 'know' until Axminster said, 'I hear you have been buying information from my jockey,' and I agreed that I had."

"So you wouldn't have told anyone before that that it was Oldfield who was selling you tips?"

"Of course not."

"No one at all?" I pressed.

"No, certainly not." He gave me a hard stare. "You don't broadcast things like that, not in my business, and especially if you aren't dead sure of your facts. Just what is all this about?"

"Well . . ." I said. "I'm very sorry to have misled you, Mr. Lubbock, but I am not really in the market for information. I'm just trying to unstick a bit of the mud that was thrown at Grant Oldfield."

To my surprise he gave a fat chuckle and knocked half an inch of ash off the cigar.

"Do you know," he said, "if you'd agreed to tip me off I'd have been looking for the catch? There's some jockeys you can square, and some you can't, and in my line you get an instinct for which are which. Now you"—he jabbed the cigar in my direction—"you aren't the type."

"Thanks," I murmured.

"And more fool you," he said, nodding. "It's not illegal."

I grinned.

"Mr. Lubbock," I said, "Oldfield was not Robinson, but his career and his health were broken up because you and Mr. Axminster were led to believe that he was."

He stroked his mustache with the thumb and forefinger of his left hand, pondering.

I went on: "Oldfield has now given up all thought of riding again, but it would still mean a great deal to him to have his name cleared. Will you help to do it?"

"How?" he said.

"Would you just write a statement to the effect that you saw no evidence at any time to support your guess that in paying Robinson you were really paying Oldfield, and that at no time before James Axminster approached you did you speak of your suspicions of Robinson's identity?"

"Is that all?" he said.

"Yes."

"All right," he said. "It can't do any harm. But I think you're barking up the wrong tree. No one but a jockey would go to all that trouble to hide his identity. No one would bother if his job didn't depend on not being found out. Still, I'll write what you ask."

He unscrewed a pen, took a sheet of hotel writing paper, and in a decisive hand wrote the statement I had suggested. He signed it, and added the date and read it through.

"There you are," he said. "Though I can't see what good it will do."

I read what he had written, and folded the paper, and put it in my wallet.

"Someone told Mr. Axminster that Oldfield was selling you information," I said. "If you hadn't told anyone at all—who knew?"

"Oh." His eyes opened. "I see, yes, I see. Robinson knew. But Oldfield would never have let on . . . so Oldfield was not Robinson."

"That's about it," I agreed, standing up. "Thank you very much, Mr. Lubbock, for your help."

"Any time." He waved the diminishing cigar, smiling broadly. "See you at the races."

CHAPTER 16

ON TUESDAY MORNING I bought a copy of the *Horse and Hound* and spent a good while telephoning to a few of the people who had advertised their hunters for sale. With three of them I made appointments to view the animal in question in two days' time.

Next I rang up one of the farmers I rode for and persuaded him to lend me his Land Rover and trailer on Thursday afternoon.

Then, having borrowed a tape measure out of Joanna's workbox—she was out at a rehearsal—I drove the hired car down to James's stables. I found him sitting in his office dealing with his paperwork. The fire, newly lit in the grate, was making little headway against the raw chill in the air, and outside in the yard the lads looked frozen as they scurried about doing their horses after the second morning exercise.

"No racing again today," James remarked. "Still, we've been extraordinarily lucky this winter up to now."

He stood up and rubbed his hands, and held them out to the inadequate fire. "Some of the owners have telephoned," he said. "They're willing to have you back. I told them"—he looked at me from his eyebrows—"that I was satisfied with your riding and that you would be on Template in the Gold Cup."

"What!" I exclaimed. "Do you mean it?"

"Yes." The glimmer deepened in his eyes.

"But . . . Pip . . ." I said.

"I've explained to Pip," he said, "that I can't take you off the horse when you've won both the King Chase and the Midwinter on him. And Pip agrees. I have arranged with him that he start again the week after Cheltenham, which will give him time to get a few races in before the Grand National. He'll be riding my runner in that—the horse he rode last year."

"It finished sixth," I said, remembering.

"Yes, that's right. Now, I've enough horses to keep both Pip and you fairly busy, and no doubt you'll get outside rides as well. It should work out all right for both of you."

"I don't know how to thank you," I said.

"Thank yourself," he said sardonically. "You earned it." He bent down and put another lump of coal on the fire.

"James," I said, "will you write something down for me?"

"Write? Oh, you'll get a contract for next season, the same as Pip."

"I didn't mean that," I said awkwardly. "It's quite different. Would you just write down that it was Maurice Kemp-Lore who told you that Oldfield was selling information about your horses, and that he said he had learned it from Lubbock?"

"Write it down?"

"Yes, please," I said.

"I don't see . . ." He gave an intent look and shrugged. "Oh, very well then." He sat down at his desk, took a sheet of paper headed with his name and address, and wrote what I asked.

"Signature and date?" he said.

"Yes, please."

He blotted the page. "What good will that do?" he said, handing it to me.

I took Mr. Lubbock's paper out of my wallet and showed it to him. He read it through three times.

"My God," he said. "It's incredible. Suppose I had checked carefully with Lubbock? What a risk Maurice took."

"It wasn't so big a risk," I said. "You wouldn't have thought of questioning what he put forward as a friendly warning. Anyway it worked. Grant got the sack."

"I'm sorry for that," James said slowly. "I wish there was something I could do about it."

"Write to Grant and explain," I suggested. "He would appreciate it more than anything in the world."

"I'll do that," he agreed, making a note.

"On Saturday morning," I said, taking back Lubbock's statement and putting it with his in my wallet, "these little documents will arrive with a plop on the Senior Steward's doormat. Of course they aren't conclusive enough to base any legal proceedings on, but they should be enough to kick friend Kemp-Lore off his pedestal."

"I should say you were right." He looked at me gravely, and then said, "Why wait until Saturday?"

"I . . . er . . . I won't be ready until then," I said evasively.

He didn't pursue it. We walked out into the yard together and looked in on some of the horses, James giving instructions, criticism and praise—in that order—to the hurrying lads. I realized how used I had grown to the efficiency and prosperity of his organization, and how much it meant to me to be a part of it.

We walked slowly along one row of boxes, and James went into the tack room at the end to talk to Sid about the cancellation of the following day's racing. Unexpectedly I stopped dead on the threshold. I didn't want to go in. I knew it was stupid, but it made no difference. Parts of me were still too sore.

The harness hook hung from the center of the ceiling, with a couple of dirty bridles swinging harmlessly on two of its curving arms. I turned my back on it and looked out across the tidy yard, and wondered if I would ever again see one without remembering.

UP IN THE rolling, grassy hills a mile or so away from his stable, James owned an old deserted keeper's cottage. In the past it had been the home of the man who looked after the gallops, James had told me once on a journey to the races, but as it had no electricity, no piped water and no sanitation, the new groundsman preferred, not unnaturally, to live in comfort in the village below and go up the hill to work on a motorbike.

The old cottage lay down an overgrown lane leading off a public but little-used secondary road which led nowhere except up and along the side of the hill and down again to join the main road four miles farther on. It served only two farms and one private house, and because of its quietness it was a regular route for the Axminster horses on roadwork days.

After leaving James I drove up to the cottage. I had not seen it at close quarters before, only a glimpse of its blank wall from the end of the lane as I rode by. I now found it was a four-roomed bungalow, set in a small fenced garden with a narrow path leading from the gate to the front door. There was one window to each room, two facing the front and two the back.

Getting in without a key presented no difficulty, as most of the glass in the windows was broken. I opened one and climbed in. The whole place smelled of fungus and rot, though faintly, as if the decay were only warming up for future onslaught. The walls and floorboards were still in good condition, and only one of the rooms was damp. I found that all four rooms opened onto a small central hall inside the front entrance; and as I made my tour I reflected that it could not have been more convenient if I had designed it myself.

I let myself out the front door, and walking round to the back I took out Joanna's tape and measured the window frame: three feet high, four feet wide. Then I returned to the front, counted the number of broken panes of glass, and measured one of them. That done, I returned to James and asked him to lend me the cottage for a few days to store some things for which there was no room at my digs.

"As long as you like," he agreed absently, busy with paperwork.

"May I mend some of the windows, and put on a new lock to make it more secure?" I asked.

"Help yourself," he said. "Do what you like."

I thanked him and drove into Newbury, and at a builders' merchant's waited while they made me up an order of ten panes of glass, enough putty to put them in with, several pieces of water pipe cut to a specified length, a bucket, some screws, a stout padlock, a bag of cement, a pot of green paint, a putty knife, a screwdriver, a cement trowel, and a paintbrush. Loaded to the axles with that lot I returned to the cottage.

I painted the weather-beaten front door and left it open to dry, reflecting that no one could blame a keeper—or his wife for that matter—for not wanting to live in that lonely, inconvenient cul de sac.

I went into one of the back rooms and knocked out all the panes of glass, which still remained in their little oblong frames. Then, outside in the garden, I mixed a good quantity of cement, using water from the rain butt, and fixed six three-foot lengths of water pipe upright in a row across the window. That done, I went round into the hall, and on the doorpost and door of the same room screwed firmly home the fittings for the padlock. On the inside of the door I unscrewed the handle and removed it.

The final job was replacing the glass in the front windows, and it took me longest to do, chipping out all the old putty and squeezing on the new; but at last it was done, and with its whole windows and fresh green door the cottage already looked more cheerful and welcoming.

I smiled to myself. I retrieved the car from where I had parked it inconspicuously behind some bushes and drove back to London.

THE SCOTS DOCTOR was drinking gin with Joanna when I let myself in.

"Oh, no," I said unceremoniously.

"Oh, yes, laddie," he said. "You were supposed to come and see me yesterday, remember."

"I was busy," I said.

"I'll just take a look at those wrists, if you don't mind," he said, putting down the gin and standing up purposefully.

I sighed and sat down at the table, and he unwrapped the bandages. There was blood on them again.

"I thought I told you to take it easy," he said sternly. "How do you expect them to heal? What have you been doing?"

I could have said, Screwing in screws, chipping out putty and mixing cement, but instead I rather uncooperatively muttered, "Nothing."

Irritated, he slapped on a new dressing with unnecessary force, and I winced. He snorted; but he was gentler with the second one.

"All right," he said, finishing them off. "Now, rest them a bit this time. And come and see me on Friday."

"Saturday," I said. "I won't be in London on Friday."

"Saturday morning, then. And mind you, come." He picked up his glass, tossed off the gin, and said a friendly good night exclusively to Joanna.

She came back laughing from seeing him out.

"He isn't usually so unsympathetic," she said. "But I think he suspects you were engaged in some sort of sadistic disgusting orgy last week, as you wouldn't tell him how you got like that."

"And he's dead right," I said morosely. He had stirred up my wrists properly, and they hadn't been too good to start with after my labors at the cottage.

For the third night I went to bed on the sofa and lay awake in the darkness, listening to Joanna's soft sleeping breath. Every day she hesitantly asked me if I would like to stay another night in her flat, and as I had no intention of leaving while there was any chance of thawing her resistance, I accepted promptly each time, even though I was progressively finding that no bread would have been more restful. Half a loaf, in the shape of Joanna padding in and out of the bathroom in a pretty dressing gown and going to bed five yards away, was decidedly unsatisfying. But I could easily have escaped and gone to a nontantalizing sleep in my own bed in my family's flat half a mile away; if I didn't, it was my own fault, and I pointed this out to her when every morning she remorsefully apologized for being unfair.

ON WEDNESDAY MORNING I went to a large photographic agency and asked to see a picture of Maurice Kemp-Lore's sister Alice. I was given a bundle of photographs to choose from, varying from Alice front-view in spotted organza at a Hunt Ball to Alice back-view winning over the last fence in a point-to-point. Alice was a striking girl with dark hair, high cheekbones, small fierce eyes, and a tight aggressive mouth. A girl to avoid, as far as I was concerned. I bought a copy of a waist-length photograph that showed her watching some hunter trials, dressed in a hacking jacket and headscarf.

On leaving the agency I went to the city offices of my parents' accountants and talked "our Mr. Stuart" in the records department into letting me use first a typewriter and then his photocopying machine.

On plain typing paper I wrote a bald account of Kemp-Lore's actions against Grant Oldfield, remarking that as a result of Axminster's relying on the apparent disinterestedness of Kemp-Lore's accusation, Oldfield had lost his job, had subsequently suffered great distress of mind, and had undergone three months' treatment in a mental hospital. I made ten copies of this statement and then on the photocopier printed ten copies each of the statements from Lubbock and James. I thanked "our Mr. Stuart" profusely and returned to Joanna's mews.

When I got back I showed Joanna the photograph of Alice Kemp-Lore, and explained who she was.

"But," said Joanna, "she isn't a bit like her brother. It can't have been her that the ticket collector saw at Cheltenham."

"No," I said. "It was Kemp-Lore himself. Could you draw me a picture of him wearing a headscarf?"

She found a piece of cartridge paper and with concentration made a reasonable likeness in charcoal of the face I now unwillingly saw in dreams.

"I've only seen him on television," she said. "It isn't very good."

She began to sketch in a headscarf, adding with a few strokes an impression of a curl over the forehead. Then putting her head on one side and considering her work, she emphasized the lips so that they looked dark and full.

"Lipstick," she murmured, explaining. "How about clothes?" Her charcoal hovered over the neck.

"Jodhpurs and hacking jacket," I said. "The only clothes which look equally right on men and women."

"Crumbs," she said, staring at me. "It was easy, wasn't it? On with the headscarf and lipstick and exit the immediately recognizable Kemp-Lore."

I nodded. "Except that he still reminded people of himself."

She drew a collar and tie and the shoulders of a jacket with revers. The portrait grew into a likeness of a pretty young woman dressed for riding. It make my skin crawl.

I found Joanna regarding me with sympathetic eyes.

"You can hardly bear to look at him, can you?" she said. "And you talk in your sleep."

I rolled up the picture, bounced it on top of her head, and said lightly, "Then I'll buy you some earplugs."

"He was taking a big risk, all the same, pretending to be a girl," she said, smiling.

"I don't suppose he did it a minute longer than he had to," I agreed. "Just long enough to get from Timberley to Cheltenham."

I filled ten long envelopes with the various statements, and sealed them. I addressed one to the Senior Steward and four others to influential people on the National Hunt Committee. One to the Chairman of Universal Telecast, one to John Ballerton, and one to Corin Kellar, to show them their idol's clay feet. One to James. And one to Maurice Kemp-Lore.

"Can't he get you for libel?" asked Joanna, looking over my shoulder.

"Not a chance," I said. "There's a defense in libel actions called justification, which roughly means that if a man has done something dishonest you are justified in disclosing it. You have to prove that it is true, that's all."

"I hope you are right," she said dubiously, sticking on some stamps.

"Don't worry. He won't sue me," I said positively.

I stacked nine of the envelopes into a neat pile on the bookshelf and propped the tenth, the unstamped one for Kemp-Lore, up on end behind them.

"We'll post that lot on Friday," I said. "And I'll deliver the other one myself."

AT 8:30 ON Thursday morning Joanna made the telephone call upon which so much depended.

I dialed the number of Kemp-Lore's London flat. There was a click as soon as the bell started ringing, and an automatic answering device invited us to leave a recorded message. Joanna raised her eyebrows: I shook my head, and she put down the receiver without saying anything.

"Out," I said unnecessarily. "Damn."

I gave her the number of Kemp-Lore's father's house in Essex and she was soon connected and talking to someone there. She nodded to me and put her hand over the mouthpiece, and said, "He's there. They've gone to fetch him I . . . I hope I don't mess it up."

I shook my head encouragingly. We had rehearsed pretty thoroughly what she was going to say. She licked her lips and looked at me with anxious eyes.

"Oh? Mr. Kemp-Lore?" She could do a beautiful Cockney-suburban accent, not exaggerated and very convincing. "You don't know me, but I wondered if I could tell you something that you could use on your program in the newsy bits at the end? I do admire your program, I do really. It's ever so good, I always think——"

His voice clacked, interrupting the flow.

"What information?" repeated Joanna. "Oh, well you know all the talk there's been about athletes using them pep pills and injections and things, well, I wondered if you wanted to know about jockeys doing it too. . . . One jockey, actually that I know of, but I expect they all do it if the truth were known. . . . Which jockey? . . . Oh . . . er, Robbie Finn, you know, the one you talked to on the telly on Saturday after he won that race. Pepped to the eyebrows as usual he was, didn't you guess? You was that close to him I thought you must have. . . . How I know? Well, I do know. . . . You want to know how I know. . . . Well, it's a bit dodgy, like, but it was me got some stuff for him once. I work in a doctor's dispensary—cleaning, you see—and he told me what to take and I got it for him. But now look here, I don't want to get into trouble, I didn't mean to let on about that. . . . I think I'd better ring off. . . . Don't ring off? You won't say nothing about it then, you know, me pinching the stuff?

"Why am I telling you? . . . Well, he don't come to see me no more, that's why." Her voice was superbly loaded with jealous spite. "After all I've done for him. I did think of telling one of the newspapers, but I thought I'd see if you was interested first. I can tell them if you'd rather . . . Check, what do you mean check? . . . You can't take my word for it on the telephone? Well, yes, you can come and see me if you want to . . . No, not today. I'm at work all day. Yes, all right, tomorrow morning then.

"How do you get there? . . . Well, you go to Newbury and then out toward Hungerford . . ." She went on with the directions slowly while he wrote them down. "And it's the only cottage along there, you can't miss it. Yes, I'll wait in for you, about eleven o'clock, all right then. What's my name? . . . Doris Jones. Yes, that's right. Mrs. Doris Jones. Well, ta-ta then." The telephone clicked and buzzed as he disconnected.

She put the receiver down slowly, looking at me with a serious face.

"Hook, line and sinker," she said.

WHEN THE BANKS opened I went along and drew out one hundred and fifty pounds. As Joanna had said, what I was doing was complicated and expensive; but complications and expense had achieved top-grade results for Kemp-Lore, and at least I was paying him the compliment of copying his methods. I grudged the money not at all: what is money for, if not to get what you want? What I wanted, admirable or not, was to pay him in his own coin.

I drove off to the Bedfordshire farmer who promised to lend me his Land Rover and trailer. It was standing ready in the yard when I arrived at noon, and before I left I bought from the farmer two bales of straw and one of hay, which we stowed in the back of the Land Rover. Then, promising to return that evening, I started away to the first of my appointments with the *Horse and Hound* advertisers.

The first hunter, an old gray gelding in Northamptonshire, was so lame that he could hardly walk out of his box and he was no bargain even at the fifty pounds they were asking for him. I shook my head, and pressed on into Leicestershire.

The second appointment proved to be with a brown mare, sound in limb but noisy in wind, as I discovered when I cantered her across a field. She was big, about twelve years old and gawky, but quiet to handle and not too bad to look at, and she was for sale only because she could not go as fast as her ambitious owner liked. I haggled him from the hundred he had advertised her for down to eighty-five pounds, and clinched the deal. Then I loaded the mare, whose name, her ex-owner said, was Buttonhook, into the trailer and turned my face south again to Berkshire.

Three hours later, at half past five in the afternoon, I turned the Land Rover into the lane to the cottage, and bumped Buttonhook to a standstill on the rough ground behind the bushes beyond the building. She had to wait in the trailer while I got the straw and spread it thickly over the floorboards in the room with the water pipes cemented over the window, and again while I filled her a bucket of water out of the rain butt and carried an armful of hay into the room and put it in the corner behind the door.

She was an affectionate old thing, I found. She came docilely out of the trailer and made no fuss when I led her up the little garden path and in through the front door of the cottage and across the little hall into the room prepared for her. I gave her some sugar and rubbed her ears, and she butted her head playfully against my chest. After a while, as she seemed quite content in her unusual and not very spacious box, I went out into the hall, shut the door, and padlocked her in. Then I walked round the outside of the cottage and shook the water pipe bars to see if they were secure, as the frosty night air might have prevented the cement from setting properly. But they were immovably fixed.

The mare came to the window and tried to poke her muzzle through the glassless squares of the window frame and through the bars outside them, but the maze defeated her. I put my hand through and fondled her muzzle, and she blew contentedly down her nostrils. Then she turned and went over to the corner where her hay was, and quietly and trustfully put her head down to eat.

I dumped the rest of the straw and hay in one of the front rooms of the cottage, shut the front door, maneuvered the trailer round with some difficulty into the lane again, and set off back to Bedfordshire. In due course I delivered the Land Rover and trailer to their owner, thanked him, and drove the hired car back to Joanna's mews.

When I went in, she kissed me. She sprang up from the sofa where she had been sitting reading, and kissed me lightly on the mouth. It was utterly spontaneous; without thought: and it was a great surprise to both of us. I put my hands on her arms and smiled incredulously down into her black eyes, and watched the surprise there turn to confusion and the confusion to panic. I took my hands away and turned my back on her to give her time, taking off the parka and saying casually over my shoulder, "The lodger is installed in the cottage. A big brown mare with a nice nature."

I hung up the parka in the closet.

"I was just . . . glad to see you back," she said in a high voice.

"That's fine," I said lightly. "Can I rustle up an egg, do you think?"

"There are some mushrooms for an omelette," she said, more normally.

"Terrific," I said, going into the kitchen. "Not peeled, by any chance?"

"Damn it, no," she said, following me and beginning to smile. She made the omelette for me and I told her about Buttonhook, and the difficult moment passed.

Later she announced that she was coming down to the cottage with me when I went in the morning.

"No," I said.

"Yes." She nodded. "He is expecting Mrs. Doris Jones to open the door to him. It will be much better if she does."

I couldn't budge her.

"And," she said, "I don't suppose you've thought of putting curtains in the windows? If you want him to walk into your parlor you'll have to make it look normal. He probably has a keen nose for rats." She fished some printed cotton material out of a drawer and held it up. "I've never used this. We can pin it up to look like curtains."

She busily collected some drawing pins and scissors, and then rolled up the big rag rug which the easel stood on and took a flower picture off the wall.

"What are those for?" I said.

"To furnish the hall, of course. It's got to look right."

"Okay, genius," I said, giving in. "You can come."

We put all the things she had gathered into a tidy pile by the door, and I added two boxes of cubed sugar from her cupboard, the big electric torch she kept in case of power cuts, and a broom.

AFTER THAT SPRINGING kiss, the sofa was more of a wasteland than ever.

CHAPTER 17

WE SET OFF early and got down to the cottage before nine, because there was a good deal to be done before Kemp-Lore arrived.

I hid the car behind the bushes again, and we carried the rug and the other things indoors. Buttonhook was safe and sound in her room, and was delighted to see us, neighing purringly in her throat when we opened the door. While I tossed her straw and fetched her some more hay and water, Joanna said she would clean the windows at the front of the cottage, and presently I heard her humming softly as she wiped away the grime of years.

The putty round the new panes had hardened well, and after I had finished Buttonhook, and Joanna was stepping back admiring the sparkle of the glass, I fetched the paint and began the tedious job of covering the patchwork of old decayed black paint and pale new putty with a bright green skin. Joanna watched me for a while and then went indoors. She put down the rug in the little hall, and I heard her banging a nail into the wall to hang up the picture just inside the front door where no visitor could fail to see it. After that she worked on the inside of the windows while I painted their outsides. She cut the flowery material into lengths and pinned it so that it hung like curtains at the sides.

When we had both finished we stood at the gate in front of the cottage admiring our handiwork. With its fresh paint, pretty curtains and the rug and picture showing through the half-open door, it looked well cared for and homely.

"Has it got a name?" Joanna asked.

"I don't think so. It's always called the keeper's cottage, as far as I know," I said.

"We should name it Sundew," she said.

"After the Grand National winner?" I said, puzzled.

"No," she said soberly, "the carnivorous plant."

I put my arm round her waist. She didn't stir.

"You will be careful, won't you?" she said.

"Yes, I will," I assured her. I looked at my watch. It was twenty minutes to eleven. "We'd better go indoors in case he comes early."

We went in and shut the front door and sat on the remains of the hay bale in the front room, giving ourselves a clear view of the front gate.

A minute or two ticked by in silence. Joanna shivered.

"Are you too cold?" I said with concern. There had been another frost during the night and there was of course no heating in the cottage. "We should have brought a stove."

"It's nerves as much as cold," she said, shivering again.

I put my arm round her shoulders. She leaned comfortably against me, and I kissed her cheek. Her black eyes looked gravely, warily into mine.

"It isn't incest," I said.

Her eyelids flickered in shock, but she didn't move.

"Our fathers may be brothers," I said, "but our mothers are not related to them or to each other."

She said nothing. I had a sudden feeling that if I lost this time I had lost forever, and a leaden chill of despair settled in my stomach.

"No one forbids marriage between cousins," I said slowly. "The law allows it and the Church allows it, and you can be sure they wouldn't if there were anything immoral in it. And in a case like ours, the medical profession raises no objection either. If there were a good genetic reason why we shouldn't marry, it would be different. But you know there isn't." I paused, but she still looked at me gravely and said nothing. Without much hope I said, "I don't really understand why you feel the way you do."

"It's instinct," she said. "I don't understand it myself. It's just that I have always thought of it as wrong—and impossible."

There was a little silence.

I said, "I think I'll sleep in my digs down here in the village tonight, and ride out at exercise with the horses tomorrow morning. I've been neglecting my job this week."

She sat up straight, pulling free of my arm.

"No," she said abruptly. "Come back to the flat."

"I can't. I can't anymore," I said.

She stood up and went over to the window and looked out. Minutes passed. Then she turned round and perched on the windowsill with her back to the light, and I couldn't see her expression.

"It's an ultimatum, isn't it?" she said shakily. "Either I marry you or you clear out altogether? No more having it both ways, like you've given me this past week."

"It isn't a deliberate ultimatum," I protested. "But we can't go on like this forever. At least, I can't. Not if you know beyond any doubt that you'll never change your mind."

"Before last weekend there wasn't any problem as far as I was concerned," she said. "You were just something I couldn't have—like oysters, which give me indigestion—something nice, but out of bounds. And now—" she tried to laugh—"now it's as if I've developed a craving for oysters. And I'm in a thorough muddle."

"Come here," I said persuasively. She walked across and sat down again beside me on the hay bale. I took her hand.

"If we weren't cousins, would you marry me?" I held my breath.

"Yes," she said simply. No reservations, no hesitation anymore.

I turned toward her and put my hands on the sides of her head and tilted her face up. There wasn't any panic this time. I kissed her; gently, and with love.

Her lips trembled, but there was no rigidity in her body, no blind instinctive retreat as there had been a week ago. I thought, If seven days can work such a change, what could happen in seven weeks?

I hadn't lost after all. The chill in my stomach melted away. I sat back on the bale, holding Joanna's hand again and smiling at her.

"It will be all right," I said. "Our being cousins won't worry you in a little while."

She looked at me wonderingly for a moment and then unexpectedly her lips twitched at the corners.

"I believe you," she said, "because I've never known anyone more determined in all my life. You've always been like that. You don't care what trouble you put yourself to to get what you want—like riding in that race last Saturday, and fixing up this fly trap of a cottage, and living with me how you have this week—so my instinct against blood relatives marrying, wherever it is seated, will have to start getting used to the idea that it is wrong, I suppose, otherwise I'll find myself being dragged by you along to Claudius Mellit to be psychoanalyzed or brainwashed, or something. I will try," she finished, sighing, "not to keep you waiting very long."

"In that case," I said, matching her lightheartedness, "I'll go on sleeping on your sofa as often as possible, so as to be handy when the breakthrough occurs."

She laughed without strain. "Starting tonight?" she asked.

"I guess so," I said, smiling. "I never did like my digs much."

"Ouch," she said.

"But I'll have to come back here on Sunday evening in any case. As James has given me my job back, the least I can do is show some interest in his horses."

We went on sitting on the hay bale, talking calmly as if nothing had happened; and nothing had, I thought, except a miracle that one could reliably build a future on, the miracle that Joanna's hand now lay intimately curled in mine without her wanting to remove it.

The minutes ticked away toward eleven o'clock.

"Suppose he doesn't come?" she said.

"He will."

"I almost hope he doesn't," she said. "Those letters would be enough by themselves."

"You won't forget to post them when you get back, will you?" I said.

"Of course not," she said. "But I wish you'd let me stay."

I shook my head. We sat on, watching the gate. The minute hand crept round to twelve on my watch, and passed it.

"He's late," she said.

Five past eleven. Ten past eleven.

"He isn't coming," Joanna murmured.

"He'll come," I said.

"Perhaps he got suspicious and checked up and found there wasn't any Mrs. Doris Jones living in the keeper's cottage," she said.

"There shouldn't be any reason for him to be suspicious," I pointed out. "He clearly didn't know at the end of that television interview with me last Saturday that I was on to him, and nothing I've done since should have got back to him, and James and Tick-Tock promised to say nothing to anyone about the doped sugar. As far as Kemp-Lore should know, he is unsuspected and undiscovered. If he feels as secure as I am sure he does, he'll never pass up an opportunity to learn about something as damaging as pep pills. So he'll come."

A quarter past eleven.

He had to come. I found that all my muscles were tense as if I were listening for him with my whole body, not only my ears. I flexed my toes inside my shoes and tried to relax. There were traffic jams, breakdowns, detours, any number of things to delay him. It was a long way, and he could easily have misjudged the time it would take.

Twenty past eleven.

Joanna sighed and stirred. Neither of us spoke for ten minutes. At 11:30 she said again, "He isn't coming."

I didn't answer.

At 11:33 the sleek cream nose of an Aston Martin slid to a stop at the gate and Maurice Kemp-Lore stepped out. He stretched himself, stiff from driving, and glanced over the front of the cottage. He wore a beautifully cut hacking jacket and cavalry twill trousers, and there were poise and grace in his every movement.

"Glory, he's handsome," breathed Joanna in my ear. "What features! What coloring! Television doesn't do him justice. It's difficult to think of anyone who looks so young and noble doing any harm."

"He's thirty-three," I said, "and Nero died at twenty-nine."

"You know the oddest things," she murmured.

Kemp-Lore unlatched the garden gate, walked up the short path, and banged the knocker on the front door.

We stood up. Joanna picked a piece of hay off her skirt, swallowed, gave me a half-smile, and walked unhurriedly into the hall. I followed her and stood against the wall where I would be hidden when the front door opened.

Joanna licked her lips.

"Go on," I whispered.

She put her hand on the latch, and opened the door.

"Mrs. Jones?" the honey voice said. "I'm so sorry I'm a little late."

"Won't you come in, Mr. Kemp-Lore," said Joanna in her Cockney-suburban accent. "It's ever so nice to see you."

"Thank you," he said, stepping over the threshold. Joanna took two paces backward and Kemp-Lore followed her into the hall.

Slamming the front door with my foot, I seized Kemp-Lore from behind by both elbows, pulling them backward and forcing him forward at the same time. Joanna opened the door of Buttonhook's room and I brought my foot into the small of Kemp-Lore's back and gave him an almighty push. He staggered forward through the door and I had a glimpse of him falling face downward in the straw before I had the door shut again and the padlock firmly clicking into place.

"That was easy enough," I said with satisfaction. "Thanks to your help."
Kemp-Lore began kicking the door.

"Let me out!" he shouted. "What do you think you're doing?"

"He didn't see you," said Joanna softly.

"No," I agreed. "I think we'll leave him in ignorance while I take you
into Newbury to catch the train."

"Is it safe?" she said, looking worried.

"I won't be away long," I promised. "Come on."

Before driving her down to Newbury I moved Kemp-Lore's car along and
off the lane until it was hidden in the bushes. The last thing I wanted was
some stray inquisitive local inhabitant going along to the cottage to investigate. Then I took Joanna to the station and drove straight back again, a matter of twenty minutes each way, and parked in the bushes as usual.

Walking quietly I went along the side of the cottage and round to
the back.

Kemp-Lore's hands stuck out through the glassless window frames, gripping the water pipe bars and shaking them vigorously. They had not budged
in their cement.

He stopped abruptly when he saw me and I watched the anger in his face
change to black surprise.

"Who did you expect?" I said.

"I don't know what's going on," he said. "Some damn fool of a woman
locked me in here nearly an hour ago and went away and left me. You can let
me out. Quickly." His breath wheezed sharply in his throat. "There's a horse
in here," he said, looking over his shoulder, "and they give me asthma."

"Yes," I said steadily, without moving. "Yes, I know."

It hit him then. His eyes widened.

"It was you . . . who pushed me . . ."

"Yes," I said.

He stood staring at me through the crisscross of window frames and bars.

"You did it on purpose? You put me in here with a horse on purpose?"
His voice rose.

"Yes," I agreed.

"Why?" he cried. He must have known the answer already, but when I
didn't reply he said again, almost in a whisper, "Why?"

"I'll give you half an hour to think about it," I said, turning to walk away.

"No!" he exclaimed. "My asthma's bad. Let me out at once." I turned back and stood close to the window. His breath whistled fiercely, but he had not even loosened his collar and tie. He was in no danger.

"Don't you have some pills?" I said.

"Of course. I've taken them. But they won't work with a horse so close. Let me out."

"Stand by the window," I said, "and breathe the fresh air."

"It's cold," he objected. "This place is like an ice-house."

I smiled. "Maybe it is," I said. "But then you are fortunate. You can move about to keep warm, and you have your jacket on—and I have not poured three bucketfuls of cold water over your head."

He gasped sharply, and it was then, I think, that he began to realize that he was not going to escape lightly or easily from his prison.

Certainly, when I returned to him after sitting on the hay bale for half an hour listening to him alternately kicking the door and yelling for help out the window, he was no longer assuming that I had lured him all the way from London and gone to the trouble of converting a cottage room into a loose box merely to set him free again at his first squawk.

When I walked round to the window I found him fending off Button-hook, who was putting her muzzle affectionately over his shoulder. I laughed callously, and he nearly choked with rage.

"Get her away from me!" he screamed. "She won't leave me alone. I can't breathe."

He clung onto a bar with one hand, and chopped at Buttonhook with the other.

"If you don't make so much noise she'll go back to her hay," I observed.

He glared at me through the bars, his face distorted with rage and hate and fright. His asthma was much worse. He had unbuttoned his shirt collar and pulled down his tie, and I could see his throat heaving.

I put the box of sugar cubes I was carrying on the inner window sill, withdrawing my hand quickly as he made a grab at it.

"Put some sugar on her hay," I said. "Go on," I added, as he hesitated. "This lot isn't doped."

His head jerked up. I looked bitterly into his staring eyes.

"Twenty-eight horses," I said, "starting with Shantytown. Twenty-eight sleepy horses who all ate some sugar from your hand before they raced."

Savagely he picked up the box of sugar, tore it open, and sprinkled the cubes on the pile of hay at the other end of the room. Buttonhook, following him, put her head down and began to crunch. He came back to the window, wheezing laboriously.

"You won't get away with this," he said. "You'll go to jail for this. I'll see you pilloried for this."

"Save your breath," I said brusquely. "I've a good deal to say to you. After that, if you want to complain to the police about the way I've treated you, you're welcome."

"You'll be in jail so fast you won't know what hit you," he said, the breath hissing through his teeth. "Now, hurry up and say whatever it is you want to say."

"Hurry?" I said slowly. "Well, now, it's going to take some time."

"You'll have to let me out by two-thirty at the latest," he said unguardedly. "I've got rehearsals at five today."

I smiled at him. I could feel it wasn't a pleasant smile.

I said, "It isn't an accident that you are here on a Friday."

His jaw literally dropped. "The program . . ." he said.

"Will have to go on without you," I agreed.

"But you can't," he shouted, gasping for enough breath, "you can't do that!"

"Why not?" I said mildly.

"It's . . . it's television!" he shouted, as if I didn't know. "Millions of people are expecting to see the program."

"Then millions of people are going to be disappointed," I said.

He stopped shouting and took three gulping, wheezing breaths.

"I know," he said, with a visible effort at moderation and at getting back to normal, "that you don't really mean to keep me here so long that I can't get to the studio in time for the program. All right, then." He paused for a couple of wheezes. "If you let me go in good time for the rehearsals, I won't report you to the police as I threatened. I'll overlook all this."

"I think you had better keep quiet and listen," I said. "I suppose you'll find it hard to realize, but I don't give a damn for your influence, or for the pinnacle the British public have seen fit to put you on, or for your dazzling synthetic personality. They are a fraud. Underneath there is only a sick mess of envy and frustration and spite. But I wouldn't have found you out if you hadn't doped twenty-eight horses I rode and told everyone I lost my nerve. And you can spend this afternoon reflecting that you wouldn't be missing your program tonight if you hadn't tried to stop me from riding Template."

He stood stock-still, his face pallid and suddenly sweating.

"You mean it," he whispered.

"Indeed I do," I said.

"No," he said. A muscle in his cheek started twitching. "No. You can't. You did ride Template. You must let me do the program."

"You won't be doing any more programs," I said. "Not tonight or any night. I didn't bring you here just for a personal revenge, though I don't deny I felt like killing you last Friday night. I brought you here on behalf of Art Mathews and Peter Cloony and Grant Oldfield. I brought you because of Danny Higgs and Ingersoll, and every other jockey you have hit where it hurts. In various ways you saw to it that they lost their jobs; so now you are going to lose yours."

For the first time he was speechless. His lips moved but no sound came out except the high asthmatic whine of his breathing. His eyes seemed to fall back in their sockets and his lower jaw hung slack, making hollows of his cheeks. He looked like a death's-head caricature of the handsome charmer he had been.

I took out of my pocket the long envelope addressed to him and held it to him through the bars. He took it mechanically, with slack fingers.

"Open it," I said.

He pulled out the sheets of paper and read them. He read them through twice, though his face showed from the first that he understood the extent of the disaster. The haggard hollows deepened.

"As you will see," I said, "those are photostat copies. More like them are in the post to the Senior Steward and to your boss at Universal Telecast, and to several other people as well. They will get them tomorrow morning. And they will no longer wonder why you failed to turn up for your program tonight."

He still seemed unable to speak, and his hands shook convulsively. I passed to him through the bars the rolled-up portrait Joanna had drawn of him. He opened it, and it was clearly another blow.

"I brought it to show you," I said, "so that you would realize beyond any doubt that I know exactly what you have been doing. All along you have found that having an instantly recognizable face was a big handicap when it came to doing things you couldn't explain away, like ramming an old Jaguar across Peter Cloony's lane."

His head jerked back, as if it still surprised him that I knew so much.

I said calmly, "A ticket collector at Cheltenham said you were pretty."

I smiled faintly. He looked very far from pretty at that moment.

"As for that Jaguar," I said, "I haven't had time yet to find out where it came from, but it can be done. It's only a question of asking. Advertising its number in the trade papers, tracing its former owner—that sort of thing. Tedious, I dare say, but definitely possible, and if necessary I will do it. No one would forget having you for a customer.

"You must have bought it in the week after the tank carrier blocked Cloony's lane, because that is what gave you the idea. Do you think you can explain away the time sequence of acquiring the Jaguar and abandoning it exactly where and when and how you did? And disappearing from the scene immediately afterward?"

His mouth hung open and the muscle twitched in his cheek.

"Most of your vicious rumors," I said, changing tack, "were spread for you by Corin Kellar and John Ballerton, who you found would foolishly repeat every thought that you put into their heads. I hope you know Corin well enough to realize that he never stands by his friends. When the contents of the letter he will receive in the morning sink into that rat brain of his, and he finds that other people have had letters like it, there won't be anyone spewing out more damaging truth about you than him. He will start telling everyone, for instance, that it was you who set him at loggerheads with Art Mathews. There won't be any stopping him.

"You see," I finished after a pause, "I think it is only justice that as far as possible you should suffer exactly what you inflicted on other people."

He spoke at last. The words came out in a wheezing croak, and he was past caring what admissions he made. "How did you find it out?" he said disbelievingly. "You didn't know last Friday, you couldn't see . . ."

"I did know last Friday," I said. "I knew just how far you had gone to smash Peter Cloony, and I knew you hated me enough to give yourself asthma doping my mounts. I knew the dope business had gone sour on you when it came to Turniptop at Stratford. And you may care to learn that it was no accident that James Axminster jogged your arm and stepped on the sugar lumps; I asked him to, and told him what you were doing. I knew all about your curdled, obsessive jealousy of jockeys. I didn't need to see you last Friday to know you. There wasn't anyone else with any reason to want me out of action."

"You can't have known all that," he said obstinately, clinging to it as if it mattered. "You didn't know the next day when I interviewed you after the race . . ." His voice trailed off into a wheeze and he stared at me hopelessly through the bars.

"You aren't the only one who can smile and hate at the same time," I said neutrally. "I learned it from you."

He made a sound like a high-pitched moan, and turned his back toward me with his arms bent upward and folded over his head in an attitude of utmost misery and despair. It may be regrettable, but I felt no pity for him at all.

I walked away from his window, round the cottage and in at the front door, and sat down again on the hay in the front room. I looked at my watch. It was a quarter to two. The afternoon stretched lengthily ahead.

Kemp-Lore had another spell of screaming for help through the window, but no one came; then he tried the door again, but there was no handle on his side of it for him to pull, and it was too solidly constructed for him to kick his way through. Buttonhook grew restive again from the noise and started pawing the ground, and Kemp-Lore shouted to me furiously to let him out, let him out, let him out.

Joanna's great fear had been that his asthma would make him seriously ill, and she had repeatedly warned me to be careful; but I judged that while he had enough breath for so much yelling he was in no real danger, and I sat and listened to him without relenting. The slow hours passed, punctuated only by the bursts of fury from the back room, while I stretched myself comfortably across the hay and daydreamed about marriage to my cousin.

At about five o'clock he was quiet for a long time. I got up and walked round the outside of the cottage and looked in through the window. He was lying face down in the straw near the door, not moving at all.

I watched him for a few minutes and called his name, but as he still did not stir I began to be alarmed, and decided I would have to make sure he was all right. I returned to the hall, and having shut the front door firmly behind me, I unlocked the padlock on the back room. The door swung inward, and Buttonhook, lifting her head, greeted me with a soft whinny.

Kemp-Lore was alive, that at least was plain. The sound of his high, squeezed breath rose unmistakably from his still form. I bent down beside him to see into just how bad a spasm he had been driven, but I never did get around to turning him over or feeling his pulse. As soon as I was down on one knee beside him he heaved himself up and into me, knocking me sprawling off balance, and sprang like lightning for the door.

I caught his shoe as it zipped across three inches from my face and yanked him back. He fell heavily on top of me and we rolled toward Buttonhook, with me trying to pin him down on the floor and he fighting like a tiger to get free. The mare was frightened. She cowered back against the wall to get out of our way, but it was a small room and our struggling took us among Buttonhook's feet and under her belly. She stepped gingerly over us and made cautiously for the open door.

Kemp-Lore's left hand was clamped round my right wrist, a circumstance which hindered me considerably. If he'd been clairvoyant he couldn't have struck on anything better calculated to cause me inconvenience. I hit him in the face and neck with my left hand, but I was too close to get any weight behind it and was also fairly occupied dodging the blows he aimed at me in return.

After he had lost the advantage of surprise, he seemed to decide he could only get free of me by lacing his fingers in my hair and banging my head against the wall, and this he tried repeatedly to do. He was staggeringly strong, more than I would have believed possible in view of his asthma, and the fury and desperation which fired him blazed in his blue eyes like a furnace.

If my hair hadn't been so short he would probably have succeeded in knocking me out, but his fingers kept slipping when I twisted my head violently in his grasp, and the third time my ear grazed the plaster I managed at last to wrench my right hand free as well.

After that, hauling off a fraction, I landed a socking right jab in his short ribs, and the air whistled out of his lungs screeching like an express train. He went a sick gray-green color and fell slackly off me, gasping and retching and clawing his throat for air.

I got to my feet and hauled him up, and staggered with him over to the window, holding him where the fresh cold air blew into his face. After three or four minutes his color improved and the terrifying heaving lessened, and some strength flowed back into his sagging legs.

I clamped his fingers round the window frames and let go of him. He swayed a bit, but his hands held, and after a moment I walked dizzily out of the room and padlocked the door behind me.

Buttonhook had found her way into the front room and was placidly eating the hay. I leaned weakly against the wall and watched her for a while, cursing myself for the foolish way I had nearly got myself locked into my own prison. I was badly shaken, not only by the fight itself but by the strength with which Kemp-Lore had fought and by the shocking effect my last blow had had on him. I ought to have had more sense, I knew, than to hit an asthmatic with that particular punch.

There was no sound from the back room. I straightened up and walked round to the window. He was standing there, holding onto the frames where I had put him, and there were tears running down his cheeks.

He was breathing safely enough, the asthma reduced to a more manageable wheeze, and I imagined it would not get any worse from then on, as Buttonhook was no longer in the room with him.

"Damn you," he said. Another tear spilled over. "Damn you. Damn you."

There wasn't anything to say.

I went back to Buttonhook, and put on her halter. I had meant to deal with her later, after I had let Kemp-Lore go, but in the changed circumstances I decided to do it straightaway, while it was still light. Leading her out the front door and through the gate, I jumped on to her back and rode her away up past the two cars hidden in the bushes and along the ridge of the hill.

A mile farther on I struck the lane which led up to the Downs, and turning down that came soon to a gate into a field owned by a farmer I had often ridden for. Slipping off Buttonhook I opened the gate, led her through, and turned her loose.

She was so amiable that I was sorry to part with her, but I couldn't keep her in the cottage, I couldn't stable an elderly hunter in James's yard and expect his lads to look after her, I couldn't find a snap buyer for her at six o'clock in the evening; and I frankly didn't know what else to do with her. I fondled her muzzle and patted her neck and fed her a handful of sugar. Then I slapped her on the rump and watched my eighty-five quid kick up her heels and canter down the field like a two-year-old. The farmer would no doubt be surprised to find an unclaimed brown mare on his land, but it would not be the first time a horse had been abandoned in that way, and I hadn't any doubt that he would give her a good home.

I turned away and walked back along the hill to the cottage. It was beginning to get dark, and the little building lay like a shadow in the hollow as I went down to it through the trees and bushes. All was very quiet, and I walked softly through the garden to the back window.

He was still standing there. When he saw me he said quite quietly, "Let me out."

I shook my head.

"Well, at least go and telephone the company, and tell them I'm ill. You can't let them all wait and wait for me to come, right up to the last minute."

I didn't answer.

"Go and telephone," he said again.

I shook my head.

He seemed to crumple inside. He stretched his hands through the bars and rested his head against the window frames.

"Let me out."

I said nothing.

"For pity's sake," he said, "let me out."

For pity's sake.

I said, "How long did you intend to leave me in that tack room?"

His head snapped up as if I'd hit him. He drew his hands back and gripped the bars.

"I went back to untie you," he said, speaking quickly, wanting to convince me. "I went back straight after the program was over, but you'd gone. Someone found you and set you free pretty soon, I suppose, since you were able to ride the next day."

"And you went back to find the tack room empty?" I said. "So you knew I had come to no harm?"

"Yes," he said eagerly. "Yes, that's what happened. I wouldn't have left you there very long, because of the rope stopping your circulation."

"You did think there was some danger of that, then?" I said innocently.

"Yes, of course there was, and that's why I wouldn't have left you there too long. If someone hadn't freed you first, I'd have let you go in good time. I only wanted to hurt you enough to stop you from riding." His voice was disgustingly persuasive, as if what he was saying were not abnormal.

"You're a liar," I said calmly. "You didn't go back to untie me after the show. You would have found me still there if you had. In fact it took me until midnight to get free, because no one came. Then I found a telephone and rang up for a car to fetch me, but by the time it reached me, which was roughly two o'clock, you had still not returned. When I got to Ascot the following day everyone was surprised to see me. There was a rumor, they said, that I wouldn't turn up. You even mentioned on television that my name in the number frames was a mistake. Well, no one but you had any reason to believe that I wouldn't arrive at the races: so when I heard that rumor I knew that you had not gone back to untie me, not even in the morning. You thought I was still swinging from that hook, in God knows what state. And, as I understand it, you intended to leave me there indefinitely, until someone found me by accident . . . or until I was dead."

"No," he said faintly.

I looked at him without speaking for a moment, and then turned to walk away.

"All right!" he screamed suddenly, banging on the bars with his fists. "All right! I didn't care whether you lived or died. Do you like that? Is that what you want to hear? I didn't care if you died. I thought of you hanging there with your arms going black . . . with the agony going on and on . . . and I didn't care. I didn't care enough to stay awake. I went to bed. I went to sleep. I didn't care. I didn't care. And I hope you like it."

His voice cracked, and he sank down inside the room so that all I could see in the gathering dusk was the top of his fair head and the hands gripping the bars with the knuckles showing white through the skin.

"I hope you like it," he said brokenly.

I didn't like it. Not one little bit. It made me feel distinctly sick.

I went slowly round into the front room and sat down again on the hay. I looked at my watch. It was a quarter past six. Still three hours to wait: three hours in which the awful truth would dawn on Kemp-Lore's colleagues in the television studio, three hours of anxious speculation and stopgap planning, culminating in the digging out of a bit of old film to fill in the empty fifteen minutes and the smooth announcement: "We regret that owing to the er— illness of Maurice Kemp-Lore there will be no *Turf Talk* tonight."

Or ever again, mates, I thought, if you did but know it.

As it grew dark, the air got colder. It had been frosty all day, but with the disappearance of the sun the evening developed a subzero bite, and the walls of the unlived-in cottage seemed to soak it up. Kemp-Lore began kicking the door again.

"I'm cold," he shouted. "It's too cold."

"Too bad," I said under my breath.

"Let me out!" he yelled.

I lay on the hay without moving. The wrist which he had latched onto while we fought was uncomfortably sore, and blood seeped through the bandage again. What the Scots doctor would have to say when he saw it I hated to think. The three warts would no doubt quiver with disapproval. I smiled at the picture.

Kemp-Lore kicked the door for a long time, trying to break through it, but he didn't succeed. At the same time he wasted a good deal of breath yelling that he was cold and hungry and that I was to let him out. I made no reply to him at all, and after about an hour of it the kicking and shouting stopped, and I heard him slither down the door as if exhausted and begin sobbing with frustration.

I stayed where I was and listened while he went on and on moaning and weeping in desolation. I listened to him without emotion; for I had cried, too, in the tack room.

The hands crawled round the face of my watch.

At a quarter to nine, when nothing could any longer save his program and even a message explaining his absence could scarcely be telephoned through in time, Kemp-Lore's decreasing sobs faded away altogether, and the cottage was quiet.

I got stiffly to my feet and went out into the front garden, breathing deeply in the clear air with an easing sense of release. The difficult day was over, and the stars were bright in the frosty sky. It was a lovely night.

I walked along to the bushes and started Kemp-Lore's car, turning it and driving it back to the gate. Then for the last time I walked round the cottage to talk to him through the window, and he was standing there already, his face a pale blur behind the window frames.

"My car," he said hysterically. "I heard the engine. You're going to drive away in my car and leave me."

I laughed. "No. You are going to drive it away yourself. As fast and as far as you like. If I were you, I'd drive to the nearest airport and fly off. No one is going to like you very much when they've read those letters in the morning, and it will be only a day or two before the newspapers get on to it. As far as racing goes, you will certainly be warned off. Your face is too well known in Britain for you to hide or change your name or get another job. And as you've got all night and probably most of tomorrow before the storm breaks and people start eyeing you with sneers and contempt, you can pack up and skip the country quite easily, without any fuss."

"You mean . . . I can go? Just go?" He sounded astounded.

"Just go," I said, nodding. "If you go quickly enough, you'll avoid the inquiry the Stewards are bound to hold and you'll avoid any charge they might think of slapping on you. You can get away to some helpful distant country where they don't know you, and you can start again from scratch."

"I suppose I haven't much choice," he muttered. His asthma was almost unnoticeable.

"And find a country where they don't have steeplechasing," I finished.

He moaned sharply, and crashed his fists down on the window frame.

I went round into the cottage and in the light of Joanna's big torch unlocked the padlock and pushed open the door. He turned from the window and walked unsteadily toward me across the straw, shielding his ravaged face from the light. He went through the door, passed me without a glance, and stumbled down the path to his car; and I walked down the path behind him, shining the torch ahead. I propped the torch on top of the gatepost so as to leave my hands free in case I needed to use them, but there didn't seem to be much fight left in him.

He paused when he was sitting in his car, and with the door still wide open looked out at me.

"You don't understand," he said, his voice shaking. "When I was a boy I wanted to be a jockey. I wanted to ride in the Grand National, like my father. And then there was this thing about falling off: I'd see the ground rushing past under my horse and there would be this terrible sort of pain in my guts, and I sweated until I could pull up and get off. And then I'd be sick."

He made a moaning noise and clutched his stomach at the memory. His face twisted. Then he said suddenly, fiercely, "It made me feel good to see jockeys looking worried. I broke them up, all right. It made me feel warm inside. Big."

He looked up at me with renewed rage, and his voice thickened venomously.

"I hated you more than all the others. You rode too well for a new jockey and you were getting on too quickly. Everyone was saying, 'Give Finn the bad horses to ride, he doesn't know what fear is.' It made me furious when I heard that. So I had you on my program, remember? I meant to make you look like a fool. It worked with Mathews, why not with you? But Axminster took you up and then Pankhurst broke his leg. . . . I wanted to smash you so much that it gave me headaches. You walked about with that easy confidence of yours as if you took your strength for granted, and too many people were getting to say you'd be champion one day. . . .

"I waited for you to have a fall that looked fairly bad, and then I used the sugar. It worked. You know it worked. I felt ten feet tall, looking at your white face and listening to everyone sniggering about you. I watched you find out how it felt. I wanted to see you writhe when everyone you cared for said—as my father said to all his friends—that it was a pity about you . . . a pity you were a sniveling little coward, a pity you had no nerve . . . no nerve . . ."

His voice died away, and his hollowed eyes were wide, unfocused, as if he were staring back into an unbearable past.

I stood looking down at the wreck of what could have been a great man. All that vitality, I thought; all that splendid talent wasted for the sake of hurting people who had not hurt him.

Such individuals could be understood, Claudius Mellit had said. Understood, and treated, and forgiven.

I could understand him in a way, I supposed, because I was myself the changeling in a family. But my father had rejected me kindly, and I felt no need to watch musicians suffer.

Treated . . . The treatment I had given him that day might not have cured the patient, but he would no longer spread his disease, and that was all I cared about.

Without another word I shut the car door on him and gestured him to drive away. He gave me one more incredulous glance as if he still found it impossible that I should let him go, and began to fumble with the light switches, the ignition, and the gears.

I hoped he was going to drive carefully. I wanted him to live. I wanted him to live for years, thinking about what he had thrown away. Anything else would be too easy, I thought.

The car began to roll, and I caught a last glimpse of the famous profile, the eclipsed, exiled profile, as he slid away into the dark. The brake lights flashed red as he paused at the end of the lane, then he turned out into the road and was gone. The sound of his engine died away.

I took the torch from the gatepost and walked up the path to the quiet cottage, to sweep it clean.

Forgiveness, I thought. That was something else again.

It would take a long time to forgive.

FOR KICKS

CHAPTER 1

THE EARL OF October drove into my life in a pale-blue Holden which had seen better days.

I noticed the car turn in through the gateposts as I walked across the little paddock toward the house, and I watched its progress up our short private road with a jaundiced eye. Salesmen, I thought, I can do without. The blue car rolled to a gentle halt between me and my own front door.

The man who climbed out looked about forty-five and was of medium height and solid build, with a large, well-shaped head and smoothly brushed brown hair. He wore gray trousers, a fine wool shirt, and a dark, discreet tie, and he carried the inevitable briefcase. I sighed, bent through the paddock rails, and went over to send him packing.

"Where can I find Mr. Daniel Roke?" he asked. An English voice, which even to my untuned ear evoked expensive public schools; and he had a subtle air of authority inconsistent with the opening patter of representatives. I looked at him more attentively, and decided after all not to say I was out. He might even, in spite of the car, be a prospective customer.

"I," I said, without too much joy in the announcement, "am Daniel Roke."

His eyelids flickered in surprise.

"Oh," he said blankly.

I was used to this reaction. I was no one's idea of the owner of a prosperous stud farm. I looked, for a start, too young, though I didn't feel it; and my sister Belinda says you don't often meet a businessman you can mistake for an Italian peasant. Sweet girl, my sister. It is only that my skin is sallow and tans easily, and I have black hair and brown eyes. Also I was that day wearing the oldest, most tattered pair of jeans I possessed, with unpolished jodhpur boots, and nothing else.

I had been helping a mare who always had difficulty in foaling: a messy job, and I had dressed for it. The result of my—and the mare's—labors was a weedy filly with a contracted tendon in the near fore and a suspicion of one in the off fore, too, which meant an operation, and more expense than she was likely to be worth.

My visitor stood for a while looking about him at the neat white-railed paddocks, the L-shaped stable yard away ahead, and the row of cedar-shingled foaling boxes off to the right, where my poor little newcomer lay in the straw. The whole spread looked substantial and well-maintained, which it was; I worked very hard to keep it that way, so that I could reasonably ask good prices for my horses.

The visitor turned to gaze at the big blue-green lagoon to the left, with the snow-capped mountains rising steeply in rocky beauty along the far side of it. Puffs of cloud like plumes crowned the peaks. Grand and glorious scenery it was, to his fresh eyes.

But to me, walls.

"Breathtaking," he said appreciatively. Then turning to me briskly, but with some hesitation in his speech, he said, "I . . . er . . . I heard in Perlooma that you have . . . er . . . an English stable hand who . . . er . . . wants to go back home. . . ." He broke off, started again. "I suppose it may sound surprising, but in certain circumstances, and if he is suitable, I am willing to pay his fare and give him a job at the other end. . . ." He trailed off again.

There couldn't, I thought, be such an acute shortage of stableboys in England that they needed to be recruited from Australia.

"Will you come into the house?" I said. "And explain?"

I led the way into the living room, and heard his exclamation as he stepped behind me. All our visitors were impressed by that room. Across the far end a great expanse of window framed the most spectacular part of the lagoon and mountains, making them seem even closer and, to me, more overwhelming than ever. I sat down in an old bentwood rocker with my back to them, and gestured him into a comfortable armchair facing the view.

"Now, Mr. . . . er . . . ?" I began.

"October," he said easily. "Not Mr.—Earl."

"October . . . as the month?" It was October at the time.

"As the month," he assented.

I looked at him curiously. He was not my idea of an earl. He looked like a hardheaded company chairman on holiday. Then it occurred to me that there was no bar to an earl's being a company chairman as well, and that quite probably some of them needed to be.

"I have acted on impulse, coming here," he said more coherently. "And I am not sure that it is ever a good thing to do." He paused, took out a machine-turned gold cigarette case, and gained time for thought while he flicked his lighter. I waited.

He smiled briefly. "Perhaps I had better start by saying that I am in Australia on business—I have interests in Sydney—but that I came down here to the Snowies as the last part of a private tour I have been making of your main racing and breeding centers. I am a member of the body which governs National Hunt racing—that is to say, steeplechasing, jump racing—in England, and naturally your horses interest me enormously. . . . Well, I was lunching in Perlooma," he went on, referring to our nearest township, fifteen miles away, "and I got talking to a man who remarked on my English accent and said the only other pommy he knew was a stable hand here who was fool enough to want to go back home."

"Yes," I agreed. "Simmons."

"Arthur Simmons," he said, nodding. "What sort of man is he?"

"Very good with horses," I said. "But he only wants to go back to England when he's drunk. And he only gets drunk in Perlooma. Never here."

"Oh," he said. "Then wouldn't he go, if he were given the chance?"

"I don't know. It depends what you want him for."

He drew on his cigarette, and tapped the ash off, and looked out of the window.

"A year or two ago we had a great deal of trouble with the doping of racehorses," he said abruptly. "A very great deal of trouble. There were trials and prison sentences, and stringent all-around tightening of stable security, and a stepping up of regular saliva and urine tests. We began to test the first four horses in many races, to stop doping-to-win, and we tested every suspiciously beaten favorite for doping-to-lose. Nearly all the results since the new regulations came into force have been negative."

"How satisfactory," I said, not desperately interested.

"No. It isn't. Someone has discovered a drug which our analysts cannot identify."

"That doesn't sound possible," I said politely. The afternoon was slipping away unprofitably, I felt, and I still had a lot to do.

He sensed my lack of enthusiasm. "There have been eleven cases, all winners. Ten that we are sure of. The horses apparently look conspicuously stimulated—I haven't myself actually seen one—but nothing shows up in the tests." He paused. "Doping is nearly always an inside job," he said, transferring his

gaze back to me. "That is to say, stable lads are nearly always involved somehow, even if it is only to point out to someone else which horse is in which
box." I nodded. Australia had had her troubles, too.

"We—that is to say, the other two Stewards of the National Hunt Committee and myself—have once or twice discussed trying to find out about the
doping from the inside, so to speak—"

"By getting a stable lad to spy for you?" I said.

He winced slightly. "You Australians are so direct," he murmured. "But
that was the general idea, yes. We didn't do anything more than talk about
it, though, because there are many difficulties to such a plan and frankly we
didn't see how we could positively guarantee that any lad we approached was
not already working for . . . er . . . the other side."

I grinned. "And Arthur Simmons has that guarantee?"

"Yes. And as he's English, he would fade indistinguishably into the racing scene. It occurred to me as I was paying my bill after lunch. So I asked the
way here and drove straight up, to see what he was like."

"You can talk to him, certainly," I said, standing up. "But I don't think
it will be any good."

"He would be paid far in excess of the normal rate," he said, misunder-
standing me.

"I didn't mean that he couldn't be tempted to go," I said, "but he just
hasn't the brain for anything like that."

He followed me back out into the spring sunshine. The air at that alti-
tude was still chilly and I saw him shiver as he left the warmth of the house.
He glanced appraisingly at my still bare chest.

"If you'll wait a moment, I'll fetch him," I said, and walking round the
corner of the house, whistled shrilly, with my fingers in my teeth, toward the
small bunkhouse across the yard. A head poked inquiringly out of a window
and I shouted, "I want Arthur."

The head nodded, withdrew, and presently Arthur Simmons, elderly,
small, bowlegged, and of an endearing simplicity of mind, made his crablike
way toward me. I left him and Lord October together, and went over to see if
the new filly had taken a firm hold on life. She had, though her efforts to
stand on her poor misshapen foreleg were pathetic to see.

I left her with her mother, and went back toward Lord October, watching him from a distance as he took a note from his wallet and offered it to
Arthur. Arthur wouldn't accept it, even though he was English. He's been

here so long, I thought, that he's as Australian as anyone. He'd hate to go back to Britain, whatever he says when he's drunk.

"You were right," October said. "He's a splendid chap, but no good for what I want. I didn't even suggest it."

"Isn't it expecting a great deal of any stable lad, however bright, to uncover something which has got men like you up a gum tree?"

He grimaced. "Yes. That is one of the difficulties I mentioned. We're scraping the bottom of the barrel, though. Any idea is worth trying. Any. You can't realize how serious the situation is."

We walked over to his car, and he opened the door.

"Well, thank you for your patience, Mr. Roke. As I said, it was an impulse, coming here. I hope I haven't wasted too much of your afternoon?" He smiled, still looking slightly hesitant and disconcerted.

I shook my head and smiled back and he started the car, turned it, and drove off down the road. He was out of my thoughts before he was through the gateposts.

HE CAME BACK again the next day at sundown. I found him sitting patiently smoking in the small blue car, having no doubt discovered that there was no one in the house. I walked back toward him from the stable block, where I had been doing my share of the evening's chores, and reflected idly that he had again caught me at my dirtiest.

He got out of the car when he saw me coming, and stamped out his cigarette.

"Mr. Roke." He held out his hand, and I shook it.

This time he made no attempt to rush into speech. This time he had not come on impulse. There was absolutely no hesitation in his manner; instead, his natural air of authority was much more pronounced, and it struck me that it was with this power that he set out to persuade a board room full of hard directors to agree to an unpopular proposal.

I knew instantly, then, why he had come back.

I looked at him warily for a moment, then gestured toward the house and led him again into the living room.

"A drink?" I asked. "Whiskey?"

"Thank you." He took the glass.

"If you don't mind," I said, "I will go and change." And think, I added privately.

I showered and put on some decent trousers, socks, and house shoes, and a white poplin shirt with a navy-blue silk tie. I brushed back my damp hair carefully in front of the mirror, and made sure my nails were clean. There was no point in entering an argument at a social disadvantage. Particularly with an earl as determined as this.

He stood up when I went back, and took in my changed appearance with one smooth glance.

I smiled fleetingly, and poured myself a drink, and another for him.

"I think," he said, "that you may have guessed why I am here."

"Perhaps."

"To persuade you to take the job I had in mind for Simmons," he said without preamble, and without haste.

"Yes," I said. I sipped my drink. "And I can't do it."

We stood there eyeing each other. I knew that what he was seeing was a good deal different from the Daniel Roke he had met before. More substantial. More the sort of person he would have expected to find, perhaps. Clothes maketh the man, I thought wryly.

The day was fading, and I switched on the lights. The mountains outside the window retreated into darkness; just as well, as I judged I would need all my resolution, and they were both literally and figuratively ranged behind October. The trouble was, of course, that with more than half my mind I wanted to take a crack at his fantastic job. And I knew it was madness. I couldn't afford it, for one thing.

"I've learned a good deal about you now," he said slowly. "On my way from here yesterday it crossed my mind that it was a pity you were not Arthur Simmons; you would have been perfect. You did, if you will forgive me saying so, look the part." He sounded apologetic.

"But not now?"

"You know you don't. You changed so that you wouldn't, I imagine. But you could again. Oh, I've no doubt that if I'd met you yesterday inside this house looking as civilized as you do at this moment, the thought would never have occurred to me. But when I saw you first, walking across the paddock very tattered and half bare and looking like a gypsy, I did in fact take you for the hired help. . . . I'm sorry."

I grinned faintly. "It happens often, and I don't mind."

"And there's your voice," he said. "That Australian accent of yours . . . I know it's not as strong as many I've heard, but it's as near to cockney as dammit, and I expect you could broaden it a bit. You see," he went on firmly, as he saw I was about to interrupt, "if you put an educated Englishman into a stable as a lad, the chances are the others would know at once by his voice that he wasn't genuine. But they couldn't tell, with you. You look right, and you sound right. You seem to me the perfect answer to all our problems. A better answer than I could have dreamed of finding."

"Physically," I commented dryly.

He drank, and looked at me thoughtfully.

"In every way. You forget, I told you I know a good deal about you now. By the time I reached Perlooma yesterday afternoon I had decided to . . . er . . . investigate you, one might say, to find out what sort of man you really were . . . to see if there was the slightest chance of your being attracted by such a . . . a job." He drank again, and paused, waiting.

"I can't take on anything like that," I said. "I have enough to do here." The understatement of the month, I thought.

"Could you take on twenty thousand pounds?" He said it casually, conversationally.

The short answer to that was "Yes"; but instead, after a moment's stillness, I said, "Australian, or English?"

His mouth curled down at the corners and his eyes narrowed. He was amused.

"English. Of course," he said ironically.

I said nothing. I simply looked at him. As if reading my thoughts, he sat down in an armchair, crossed his legs comfortably, and said, "I'll tell you what you would do with it, if you like. You would pay the fees of the medical school your sister Belinda has set her heart on. You would send your younger sister, Helen, to art school, as she wants. You would put enough aside for your thirteen-year-old brother, Philip, to become a lawyer, if he is still of the same mind when he grows up. You could employ more labor here, instead of working yourself into an early grave feeding, clothing, and paying school fees for your family."

I suppose I should have been prepared for him to be thorough, but I felt a surge of anger that he should have pried so very intimately into my affairs. However, since the time when an angry retort had cost me the sale of a yearling who broke his leg the following week, I had learned to keep my tongue still whatever the provocation.

"I also have had two girls and a boy to educate," he said. "I know what it is costing you. My elder daughter is at university, and the twin boy and girl have recently left school."

When I again said nothing, he continued. "You were born in England, and were brought to Australia when you were a child. Your father, Howard Roke, was a barrister, a good one. He and your mother were drowned together in a sailing accident when you were eighteen. Since then you have supported yourself and your sisters and brother by horse dealing and breeding. I understand that you had intended to follow your father into the law, but instead used the money he had left to set up business here, in what had been your holiday house. You have done well at it. The horses you sell have a reputation for being well broken in and beautifully mannered. You are thorough, and you are respected."

He looked up at me, smiling. I stood stiffly. I could see there was still more to come.

He said, "Your headmaster at Geelong says you had a brain and are wasting it. Your bank manager says you spend little on yourself. Your doctor says you haven't had a holiday since you settled here nine years ago except for a month you spent in hospital once with a broken leg. Your pastor says you never go to church, and he takes a poor view of it." He drank slowly.

Many doors, it seemed, were open to determined earls.

"And finally," he added, with a lopsided smile, "the barkeeper of the Golden Platypus in Perlooma says he'd trust you with his sister, in spite of your good looks."

"And what were your conclusions after all that?" I asked, my resentment a little better under control.

"That you are a dull, laborious prig," he said pleasantly.

I relaxed at that, and laughed, and sat down.

"Quite right," I agreed.

"On the other hand, everyone says you do keep on with something once you start it, and you are used to hard physical work. You know so much about horses that you could do a stable lad's job with your eyes shut standing on your head."

"The whole idea is screwy," I said, sighing. "It wouldn't work, not with me, or Arthur Simmons, or anybody. It just isn't feasible. There are hundreds of training stables in Britain, aren't there? You could live in them for months and hear nothing, while the dopers got strenuously to work all around you."

He shook his head. "I don't think so. There are surprisingly few dishonest lads, far fewer than you or most people would imagine. A lad known to be corruptible would attract all sorts of crooks like an unguarded gold mine. All our man would have to do would be to make sure that the word was well spread that he was open to offers. He'd get them, no doubt of it."

"But would he get the ones you want? I very much doubt it."

"To me it seems a good enough chance to be worth taking. Frankly, any chance is worth taking, the way things are. We have tried everything else. And we have failed. We have failed in spite of exhaustive questioning of everyone connected with the affected horses. The police say they cannot help us. As we cannot analyze the drug being used, we can give them nothing to work on. We employed a firm of private investigators. They got nowhere at all. Direct action has achieved absolutely nothing. Indirect action cannot achieve less. I am willing to gamble twenty thousand pounds that with you it can achieve more. Will you do it?"

"I don't know," I said, and cursed my weakness. I should have said, "No, certainly not."

He pounced on it, leaning forward and talking more rapidly, every word full of passionate conviction. "Can I make you understand how concerned my colleagues and I are over these undetectable cases of doping? I own several racehorses—mostly steeplechasers—and my family for generations have been lovers and supporters of racing. The health of the sport means more to me, and people like me, than I can possibly say . . . and for the second time in three years it is being seriously threatened. During the last big wave of doping there were satirical jokes in the papers and on television, and we simply cannot afford to have it happen again. So far we have been able to stifle comment because the cases are still fairly widely spaced—it is well over a year since the first—and if anyone inquires we merely report that the tests were negative. But we *must* identify this new dope before there is a widespread increase in its use. Otherwise it will become a worse menace to racing than anything which has happened before. If dozens of undetectably doped winners start turning up, public faith will be destroyed altogether, and steeplechasing will suffer damage which it will take years to recover from, if it ever does. There is much more at stake than a pleasant pastime. Racing is an industry employing thousands of people . . . and not the least of them are stud owners like you. The collapse of public support would mean a great deal of hardship.

"You may think that I have offered you an extraordinarily large sum of money to come over and see if you can help us, but I am a rich man, and, believe me, the continuance of racing is worth a great deal more than that to me. My horses won nearly that amount in prize money last season, and if it can buy a chance of wiping out this threat, I will spend it gladly."

"You are much more vehement today," I said slowly, "than you were yesterday."

He sat back. "Yesterday I didn't need to convince you. But I felt just the same."

"There must be someone in England who can dig out the information you want," I protested. "People who know the ins and outs of your racing. I know nothing at all. I left your country when I was nine. I'd be useless. It's impossible."

That's better, I approved myself. That's much firmer.

He looked down at his glass, and spoke as if with reluctance. "Well . . . we did approach someone in England . . . a racing journalist, actually. Very good nose for news; very discreet, too; we thought he was just the chap. Unfortunately he dug away without success for some weeks. And then he was killed in a car crash, poor fellow."

"Why not try someone else?" I persisted.

"It was only in June that he died, during steeplechasing's summer recess. The new season started in August, and it was not until after that that we thought of the stable lad idea, with all its difficulties."

"Try a farmer's son," I suggested. "Country accent, knowledge of horses . . . the lot."

He shook his head. "England is too small. Send a farmer's son to walk a horse around the parade ring at the races, and what he was doing would soon be no secret. Too many people would recognize him, and ask questions."

"A farmworker's son, then, with a high IQ."

"Do we hold an exam?" he said sourly.

There was a pause, and he looked up from his glass. His face was solemn, almost severe.

"Well?" he said.

I meant to say "No," firmly. What I actually said was again, "I don't know."

"What can I say to persuade you?"

"Nothing," I said. "I'll think about it. I'll let you know tomorrow."

"Very well." He stood up, declined my offer of a meal, and went away as he had come, the strength of his personality flowing out of him like heat. The house felt empty when I went back from seeing him off.

The full moon blazed in the black sky, and through a gap in the hills behind me Mount Kosciusko distantly stretched its blunt snow-capped summit into the light. I sat on a rock up on the mountain, looking down on my home.

There lay the lagoon, the big pasture paddocks stretching away to the bush, the tidy white-railed small paddocks near the house, the silvery roof of the foaling boxes, the solid bulk of the stable block, the bunkhouse, the long, low graceful shape of the dwelling house with a glitter of moonlight on the big window at the end.

There lay my prison.

It hadn't been bad at first. There were no relations to take care of us, and I had found it satisfying to disappoint the people who said I couldn't earn enough to keep three small children, Belinda and Helen and Philip, with me. I liked horses, I always had, and from the beginning the business went fairly well. We all ate, anyway, and I even convinced myself that the law was not really my vocation after all.

My parents had planned to send Belinda and Helen to Frensham, and when the time came, they went. I daresay I could have found a cheaper school, but I had to try to give them what I had had . . . and that was why Philip was away at Geelong. The business had grown progressively, but so had the school fees and the men's wages and the maintenance costs. I was caught in a sort of upward spiral, and too much depended on my being able to keep going. The leg I had broken in a steeplechase when I was twenty-two had caused the worst financial crisis of the whole nine years: and I had had no choice but to give up doing anything so risky.

I didn't grudge the unending labor. I was very fond of my sisters and brother. I had no regrets at all that I had done what I had. But the feeling that I had built a prosperous trap for myself had slowly eaten away the earlier contentment I had found in providing for them.

In another eight or ten years they would all be grown, educated, and married, and my job would be done. In another ten years I would be thirty-seven. Perhaps I, too, would be married by then, and have some children of my own, and send them to Frensham and Geelong. . . . For more than four years I had done my best to stifle a longing to escape. It was easier when they were at home in the holidays, with the house ringing with their noise and Philip's carpentry all over the place and the girls' frillies hanging to dry in the bathroom. In the summer we swam or rowed on the lagoon (the lake, as my English parents had called it) and in the winter we skied on the mountains. They were very good company and never took anything they had for granted.

Nor, now that they were growing up, did they seem to be suffering from any form of teen-age rebellions. They were, in fact, thoroughly rewarding.

It usually hit me about a week after they had gone back to school, this fierce aching desperation to be free. Free for a good long while: to go farther than the round of horse sales, farther than the occasional quick trip to Sydney or Melbourne or Cooma.

To have something else to remember but the procession of profitable days, something else to see besides the beauty with which I was surrounded. I had been so busy stuffing worms down my fellow nestlings' throats that I had never stretched my wings.

Telling myself that these thoughts were useless, that they were self-pity, that my unhappiness was unreasonable, did no good at all, I continued at night to sink into head-holding miseries of depression, and kept these moods out of my days—and balance sheets—only by working to my limit.

When Lord October came, the children had been back at school for eleven days, and I was sleeping badly. That may be why I was sitting on a mountainside at four o'clock in the morning trying to decide whether or not to take a peculiar job as a stable lad on the other side of the world. The door of the cage had been opened for me, all right. But the tidbit that had been dangled to tempt me out seemed suspiciously large.

Twenty thousand English pounds . . . a great deal of money. But then he couldn't know of my restless state of mind, and he might think that a smaller sum would make no impression. (What, I wondered, had he been prepared to pay Arthur?)

On the other hand, there was the racing journalist who had died in a car crash. . . . If October or his colleagues had the slightest doubt it was an accident, that too would explain the size of his offer, as conscience money. Throughout my youth, owing to my father's profession, I had learned a good deal about crime and criminals, and I knew too much to dismiss the idea of an organized accident as fantastic nonsense.

I had inherited my father's bent for orderliness and truth and had grown up appreciating the logic of his mind, though I had often thought him too ruthless with innocent witnesses in court. My own view had always been that justice should be done and that my father did the world no good by getting the guilty acquitted. I would never make a barrister, he said, if I thought like that. I'd better be a policeman instead.

England, I thought. Twenty thousand pounds. Detection. To be honest, the urgency with which October viewed the situation had not infected me. English racing was on the other side of the world. I knew no one engaged in it. I cared frankly little whether it had a good or a bad reputation. If I went, it would be no altruistic crusade: I would be going only because the adventure appealed to me, because it looked amusing and a challenge, because it beckoned me like a siren to fling responsibility to the wind and cut the self-imposed shackles off my wilting spirit.

Common sense said that the whole idea was crazy, that the Earl of October was an irresponsible nut, that I hadn't any right to leave my family to fend for themselves while I went gallivanting around the world, and that the only possible course open to me was to stay where I was, and learn to be content.

Common sense lost.

CHAPTER 2

NINE DAYS LATER I flew to England in a Boeing 707.

I slept soundly for most of the thirty-six hours from Sydney to Darwin, from Darwin to Singapore, Rangoon and Calcutta, from Calcutta to Karachi and Damascus, and from Damascus to Frankfurt and London Airport.

Behind me I left a crowded week into which I had packed months of paperwork and a host of practical arrangements. Part of the difficulty was that I didn't know how long I would be away, but I reckoned that if I hadn't done the job in six months, I wouldn't be able to do it at all, and made that a basis for my plans.

The head stud groom was to have full charge of the training and sale of the horses already on the place, but not to buy or breed any more. A firm of contractors agreed to see to the general maintenance of the land and buildings. The woman currently cooking for the lads who lived in the bunkhouse assured me that she would look after the family when they came back for the long Christmas summer holiday from December to February.

I arranged with the bank manager that I should send post-dated checks for the next term's school fees and for the fodder and tack for the horses, and

I wrote a pile for the head groom to cash one at a time for the men's food and wages. October assured me that my "fee" would be transferred to my account without delay.

"If I don't succeed, you shall have your money back, less what it has cost me to be away," I told him.

He shook his head, but I insisted; and in the end we compromised. I was to have ten thousand outright, and the other half if my mission was successful.

I took October to my solicitors and had the rather unusual appointment shaped into a dryly worded legal contract, to which, with a wry smile, he put his signature alongside mine.

His amusement, however, disappeared abruptly when, as we left, I asked him to insure my life.

"I don't think I can," he said, frowning.

"Because I would be . . . uninsurable?" I asked.

He didn't answer.

"I have signed a contract," I pointed out. "Do you think I did it with my eyes shut?"

"It was your idea." He looked troubled. "I won't hold you to it."

"What really happened to the journalist?" I asked.

He shook his head and didn't meet my eyes. "I don't know. It looked like an accident. It almost certainly *was* an accident. He went off the road at night on a bend on the Yorkshire moors. The car caught fire as it rolled down into the valley. He hadn't a hope. He was a nice chap. . . ."

"It won't deter me if you have any reason for thinking it was not an accident," I said seriously, "but you must be frank. If it was not an accident, he must have made a lot of progress . . . he must have found out something pretty vital. It would be important to me to know where he had gone and what he had been doing during the days before he died."

"Did you think about all this before you agreed to accept my proposition?"

"Yes, of course."

He smiled as if a load had been lifted from him. "By God, Mr. Roke, the more I see of you, the more thankful I am I stopped for lunch in Perlooma and went to look for Arthur Simmons. Well . . . Tommy Stapleton—the journalist—was a good driver, but I suppose accidents can happen to anyone. It was a Sunday early in June. Monday, really. He died about two o'clock at night. A local man said the road was normal in appearance at one-thirty, and at two-thirty a couple going home from a party saw the broken railings on the bend and stopped to look. The car was still smoldering; they could see the red glow of it in the valley, and they drove on into the nearest town to report it.

"The police think Stapleton went to sleep at the wheel. Easy enough to do. But they couldn't find out where he had been between leaving the house of some friends at five o'clock, and arriving on the Yorkshire moors. The journey would have taken him only an hour, which left eight hours unaccounted for. No one ever came forward to say he'd spent the evening with them, though the story was in most of the papers. I believe it was suggested he could have been with another man's wife . . . someone who had a good reason for keeping quiet. Anyway, the whole thing was treated as a straightforward accident.

"As to where he had been during the days before . . . we did find out, discreetly. He'd done nothing and been nowhere that he didn't normally go in the course of his job. He'd come up from the London offices of his newspaper on the Thursday, gone to Bogside races on the Friday and Saturday, stayed with friends near Hexham, Northumberland, over the weekend, and, as I said, left them at five on Sunday, to drive back to London. They said he had been his normal charming self the whole time.

"We—that is, the other two Stewards and I—asked the Yorkshire police to let us see anything they salvaged from the car, but there was nothing of any interest to us. His leather briefcase was found undamaged halfway down the hillside, near one of the rear doors which had been wrenched off during the somersaulting, but there was nothing in it besides the usual form books and racing papers. We looked carefully. He lived with his mother and sister—he was unmarried—and they let us search their house for anything he might have written down for us. There was nothing. We also contacted the sports editor of his paper and asked to see any possessions he had left in his office. There were only a few personal oddments and an envelope containing some press cuttings about doping. We kept that. You can see them when you get to England. But I'm afraid they will be no use to you. They were very fragmentary."

"I see," I said. We walked along the street to where our two cars were parked, his hired blue Holden, and my white utility. Standing beside the two dusty vehicles, I remarked, "You want to believe it was an accident . . . I think you want to believe it very much."

He nodded soberly. "It is appallingly disturbing to think anything else. If it weren't for those eight missing hours, one would have no doubt at all."

I shrugged. "He could have spent them in dozens of harmless ways. In a bar. Having dinner. In a cinema. Picking up a girl."

"Yes, he could," he said. But the doubt remained, both in his mind and mine.

He was to drive the hired Holden back to Sydney the following day and fly to England. He shook hands with me in the street and gave me his address in London, where I was to meet him again. With the door open and with one foot in the car, he said, "I suppose it would be part of your . . . er . . . procedure to appear as a slightly—shall we say—unreliable type of stable lad, so that the crooked element would take to you?"

"Definitely." I grinned.

"Then, if I might suggest it, it would be a good idea for you to grow a couple of sideburns. It's surprising what a lot of distrust can be caused by an inch of extra hair in front of the ears!"

I laughed. "A good idea."

"And don't bring many clothes," he added. "I'll fix you up with British stuff suitable for your new character."

"All right."

He slid down behind the wheel.

"Au revoir, then, Mr. Roke."

"Au revoir, Lord October," I said.

After he had gone, and without his persuasive force at my elbow, what I was planning to do seemed less sensible than ever. But then I was tired to death of being sensible. I went on working from dawn to midnight to clear the decks, and found myself waking each morning with impatience to be on my way.

Two days before I was due to leave, I flew down to Geelong to say good-bye to Philip and explain to his headmaster that I was going to Europe for a while; I didn't know exactly how long. I came back via Frensham to see my sisters, both of whom exclaimed at once over the dark patches of stubble which were already giving my face the required "unreliable" appearance.

"For heaven's sake shave them off," said Belinda. "They're far too sexy. Most of the seniors are crazy about you already and if they see you like that you'll be mobbed."

"That sounds delicious," I said, grinning at them affectionately.

Helen, nearly sixteen, was fair and gentle and as graceful as the flowers she liked to draw. She was the most dependent of the three, and had suffered worst from not having a mother.

"Do you mean," she said anxiously, "that you will be away the whole summer?" She looked as if Mount Kosciusko had crumbled.

"You'll be all right. You're nearly grown up now," I teased her.

"But the holidays will be so dull."

"Ask some friends to stay, then."

"Oh!" Her face cleared. "Can we? Yes. That would be fun."

She kissed me more happily good-bye, and went back to her lessons.

Belinda and I understood each other very well, and to her alone, knowing I owed it to her, I told the real purpose of my "holiday." She was upset, which I had not expected.

"Dearest Dan," she said, twining her arm in mine and sniffing to stop herself from crying. "I know that bringing us up has been a grind for you, and if for once you want to do something for your own sake, we ought to be glad. Only please do be careful. We do . . . we do want you back."

"I'll come back," I promised helplessly, lending her my handkerchief. "I'll come back."

THE TAXI FROM the air terminal brought me through a tree-filled square to the Earl of October's London house in a gray drizzle which in no way matched my spirits. Lighthearted, that was me. Springs in my heels.

In answer to my ring, the elegant black door was opened by a friendly-faced manservant, who took my grip from my hand and said that as his lordship was expecting me, he would take me up at once. "Up" turned out to be a crimson-walled drawing room on the first floor where round an electric heater in an Adam fireplace three men stood with glasses in their hands. Three men standing easily, their heads turned toward the opening door. Three men radiating as one the authority I had been aware of in October. They were the ruling triumvirate of National Hunt racing. Big guns. Established and entrenched behind a hundred years of traditional power. They weren't taking the affair as effervescently as I was.

"Mr. Roke, my lord," said the manservant, showing me in.

October came across the room to me and shook hands.

"Good trip?"

"Yes, thank you."

He turned toward the other men. "My two co-Stewards arranged to be here to welcome you."

"My name is Macclesfield," said the taller of them, an elderly, stooping man with riotous white hair. He leaned forward and held out a sinewy hand. "I am most interested to meet you, Mr. Roke." He had a hawk-eyed, piercing stare.

"And this is Colonel Beckett." October gestured to the third man, a slender, ill-looking person, who shook hands also, but with a weak, limp grasp. All three of them paused and looked at me as if I had come from outer space.

"I am at your disposal," I said politely.

"Yes . . . well, we may as well get straight down to business," said October, directing me to a hide-covered armchair. "But a drink first?"

"Thank you."

He gave me a glass of the smoothest whiskey I'd ever tasted, and they all sat down.

"My horses," October began, speaking easily, conversationally, "are trained in the stable block adjoining my house in Yorkshire. I do not train them myself, because I am away too often on business. A man named Inskip holds the license—a public license—and apart from my own horses, he trains several for my friends. At present there are about thirty-five horses in the yard, of which eleven are my own. We think it would be best if you started work as a lad in my stable, and then you can move on somewhere else when you think it is necessary. Clear so far?"

I nodded.

He went on. "Inskip is an honest man, but unfortunately he's also a bit of a talker, and we consider it essential for your success that he should not have any reason to chatter about the way you joined the stable. The hiring of the lads is always left to him, so it will have to be he, not I, who hires you.

"In order to make certain that we are shorthanded—so that your application for work will be immediately accepted—Colonel Beckett and Sir Stuart Macclesfield are each sending three young horses to the stables two days from now. The horses are no good, I may say, but they're the best we could do in the time."

They all smiled. And well they might. I began to admire their staff work.

"In four days, when everyone is beginning to feel overworked, you will arrive in the yard and offer your services. All right?"

"Yes."

"Here is a reference." He handed me an envelope. "It is from a woman cousin of mine in Cornwall who keeps a couple of hunters. I have arranged that if Inskip checks with her she will give you a clean bill. You can't appear too doubtful in character to begin with, you see, or Inskip will not employ you."

"I understand," I said.

"Inskip will ask you for your insurance card and an income tax form, which you would normally have brought on from your last job. Here they are." He gave them to me. "The insurance card is stamped up to date and is no problem, as it will not be queried in any way until next May, by which time we hope there will be no more need for it. The income tax situation is more difficult, but we have constructed the form so that the address on the part which Inskip has to send off to the Inland Revenue people when he engages you is illegible. Any amount of natural-looking confusion should arise from that; and the fact that you were not working in Cornwall should be safely concealed."

"I see," I said. And I was impressed, as well.

Sir Stuart Macclesfield cleared his throat and Colonel Beckett pinched the bridge of his nose between thumb and forefinger.

"About this dope," I said. "You told me your analysts couldn't identify it, but you didn't give me any details. What is it that makes you positive that it is being used?"

October glanced at Macclesfield, who said in his slow, rasping, elderly voice, "When a horse comes in from a race frothing at the mouth with his eyes popping out and his body drenched in sweat, one naturally suspects that he has been given a stimulant of some kind. Dopers usually run into trouble with stimulants, since it is difficult to judge the dosage needed to get a horse to win without arousing suspicion. If you had seen any of these particular horses we have tested, you would have sworn that they had been given a big overdose. But the test results were always negative."

"What do your pharmacists say?" I asked.

Beckett said sardonically, "Word for word? It's blasphemous."

I grinned. "The gist."

Beckett said, "They simply say there isn't a dope they can't identify."

"How about adrenalin?" I asked.

The Stewards exchanged glances, and Beckett said, "Most of the horses concerned did have a fairly high adrenalin count, but you can't tell from one analysis whether that is normal for that particular horse or not. Horses vary tremendously in the amount of adrenalin they produce naturally, and you would have to test them before and after several races to establish their normal output, and also at various stages of their training. Only when you know their normal levels could you say whether any extra had been pumped into them. From the practical point of view, adrenalin can't be given by mouth, as I expect you know. It has to be injected, and it works instantaneously. These horses were all calm and cool when they went to the starting gate. Horses which have been stimulated with adrenalin are pepped up at that point. In addition to that, a horse often shows at once that he has had a subcutaneous adrenalin injection because the hairs for some way round the site of the puncture stand up on end and give the game away. Only an injection straight into the jugular vein is really foolproof; but it is a very tricky process, and we are quite certain that it was not done in these cases."

"The lab chaps," said October, "told us to look for something mechanical. All sorts of things have been tried in the past, you see. Electric shocks, for instance. Jockeys used to have saddles or whips made with batteries concealed in them so that they could run bursts of current into the horses they were riding and galvanize them into winning. The horses' own sweat acted as a splendid conductor. We went into all that sort of thing very thoroughly indeed, and we are firmly of the opinion that none of the jockeys involved carried anything out of the ordinary in any of their equipment."

"We have collected all our notes, all the lab notes, dozens of press cuttings, and anything else we thought could be of the slightest help," said Macclesfield, pointing to three boxes of files which lay in a pile on a table by my elbow.

"And you have four days to read them and think about them," added October, smiling faintly. "There is a room ready for you here, and my man will look after you. I am sorry I cannot be with you, but I have to return to Yorkshire tonight."

Beckett looked at his watch and rose slowly. "I must be going, Edward." To me, with a glance as alive and shrewd as his physique was failing, he said, "You'll do. And make it fairly snappy, will you? Time's against us."

I thought October looked relieved. I was sure of it when Macclesfield shook my hand and rasped, "Now that you're actually here, the whole scheme suddenly seems more possible. . . . Mr. Roke, I sincerely wish you every success."

October went down to the street door with them, and came back and looked at me across the crimson room. "They are sold on you, Mr. Roke, I am glad to say."

UPSTAIRS IN THE luxurious deep-green-carpeted, brass-bedsteaded guest room where I slept for the next four nights, I found the manservant had unpacked the few clothes I had brought with me and put them tidily on the shelves of a heavy Edwardian wardrobe. On the floor beside my own canvas-and-leather grip stood a cheap fiber suitcase with rust-marked locks. Amused, I explored its contents. On top there was a thick sealed envelope with my name on it. I slit it open and found it was packed with five-pound notes, forty of them, and an accompanying slip which read "Bread for throwing on waters." I laughed aloud.

Under the envelope October had provided everything from underclothes to washing things, jodhpur boots to raincoat, jeans to pajamas.

Another note from him was tucked into the neck of a black leather jacket.

This jacket completes what sideburns begin. Wearing both, you won't have any character to speak of. They are regulation dress for delinquents! Good luck.

I eyed the jodhpur boots. They were second-hand and needed polishing, but to my surprise, when I slid my feet into them, they were a good fit. I took them off and tried on a violently pointed pair of black walking shoes. Horrible, but they fitted comfortably also, and I kept them on to get my feet (and eyes) used to them.

The three box files, which I had carried up with me after October had left for Yorkshire, were stacked on a low table next to a small armchair, and with a feeling that there was no more time to waste, I sat down, opened the first of them, and began to read.

Because I went painstakingly slowly through every word, it took me two days to finish all the papers in those boxes. And at the end of it I found myself staring at the carpet without a helpful idea in my head. There were accounts, some in typescript, some in longhand, of interviews the Stewards had held with the trainers, jockeys, head traveling lads, stable lads, blacksmiths, and veterinary surgeons connected with the eleven horses suspected of being doped. There was a lengthy report from a firm of private investigators who had interviewed dozens of stable lads in "places of refreshment," and got nowhere. A memo ten pages long from a bookmaker went into copious details of the market which had been made on the horses concerned; but the last sentence summed it up: "We can trace no one person or syndicate which has won consistently with these horses, and therefore conclude that if any one person or syndicate is involved, their betting was done on the Tote." Further down the box I found a letter from Tote Investors Ltd., saying that not one of their credit clients had backed all the horses concerned, but that of course they had no check on cash betting at racecourses.

The second box contained eleven laboratory reports of analyses made on urine and saliva samples. The first report referred to a horse called Charcoal and was dated eighteen months earlier. The last gave details of tests made on a horse called Rudyard as recently as September, when October was in Australia.

The word "negative" had been written in a neat hand at the end of each report.

The press had had a lot of trouble dodging the laws of libel. The clippings from daily papers in the third box contained such sentences as "Charcoal displayed a totally uncharacteristic turn of foot" and "In the unsaddling enclosure Rudyard appeared to be considerably excited by his success."

There were fewer references to Charcoal and the following three horses, but at that point someone had employed a news-gathering agency: the last seven cases were documented by clippings from several daily, evening, local, and sporting papers.

At the bottom of the clippings I came across a medium-size manila envelope. On it was written: "Received from Sports Editor, *Daily Scope*, June 10." This, I realized, was the packet of cuttings collected by Stapleton, the unfortunate journalist, and I opened the envelope with much curiosity. But to my great disappointment, because I badly needed some help, all the clippings except three were duplicates of those I had already read.

Of these three, one was a personality piece on the woman owner of Charcoal, one was an account of a horse (not one of the eleven) going berserk and killing a woman on June 3 in the paddock at Cartmel, Lancashire, and the third was a long article from a racing weekly discussing famous cases of doping, how they had been discovered, and how dealt with. I read this attentively, with minimum results.

After all this unfruitful concentration, I spent the whole of the next day wandering round London, breathing in the city's fumes with a heady feeling of liberation, asking the way frequently and listening carefully to the voices which replied.

In the matter of my accent I thought October had been too hopeful, because two people, before midday, commented on my being Australian. My parents had retained their Englishness until their death, but at nine I had found it prudent not to be "different" at school, and had adopted the speech of my new country from that age. I could no longer shed it, even if I wanted to, but if it was to sound like cockney English, it would clearly have to be modified.

I drifted eastward, walking, asking, listening. Gradually I came to the conclusion that if I knocked off the aitches and didn't clip the ends of my words, I might get by. I practiced all that afternoon, and finally managed to alter a few vowel sounds as well. No one asked me where I came from, which I took as a sign of success, and when I asked the last man, a barrow boy, where I could catch a bus back to the West, I could no longer detect much difference between my question and his answer.

On my way back I stopped at the Bank of Australia and made an arrangement about mail. I wanted to be able to write to my family sometimes and to receive letters from them, but I was afraid that the regular arrival of airmail from Australia would arouse comment. The Bank thought it decidedly odd, but agreed in the end to forward letters on to me in fresh (English) envelopes, adorned with English stamps.

I made one purchase, a zipper-pocketed money belt made of strong canvas webbing. It buckled flat around my waist under my shirt, and into it I packed the two hundred pounds: wherever I was going I thought I might be glad to have that money readily available.

In the evening, refreshed, I tried to approach the doping problem from another angle, by seeing if the horses had had anything in common.

Apparently they hadn't. All were trained by different trainers. All were owned by different owners; and all had been ridden by different jockeys. The only thing they had in common was that they had nothing in common.

I sighed, and went to bed.

TERENCE, THE MANSERVANT, with whom I had reached a reserved but definite friendship, woke me on the fourth morning by coming into my room with a laden breakfast tray.

"The condemned man ate hearty," he observed, lifting a silver cover and allowing me a glimpse and a sniff of a plateful of eggs and bacon.

"What do you mean?" I said, yawning contentedly.

"I don't know what you and his lordship are up to, sir, but wherever you are going, it is different from what you are used to. That suit of yours, for instance, didn't come from the same sort of place as this little lot."

He picked up the fiber suitcase, put it on a stool, and opened the locks. Carefully, as if they had been silk, he laid out on a chair some cotton underpants and a checked cotton shirt, followed by a tan ribbed pullover, some drainpipe charcoal trousers, and black socks. With a look of disgust, he picked up the black leather jacket and draped it over the chair back, and neatly arranged the pointed shoes.

"His lordship said I was to make certain that you left behind everything you came with, and took only these things with you," he said regretfully.

"Did you buy them?" I asked, amused, "or was it Lord October?"

"His lordship bought them." He smiled suddenly as he went over to the door. "I'd love to have seen him pushing around in that chain store among all those bustling women."

I finished my breakfast, bathed, shaved, and dressed from head to foot in the new clothes, putting the black jacket on top and zipping up the front. Then I brushed the hair on top of my head forward instead of back, so that the short black ends curved onto my forehead.

Terence came back for the empty tray and found me standing looking at myself in a full-length mirror. Instead of grinning at him as usual, I turned slowly around on my heel and treated him to a hard, narrow-eyed stare.

"Holy hell!" he said explosively.

"Good," I said cheerfully. "You wouldn't trust me, then?"

"Not as far as I could throw that wardrobe."

"What other impressions do I make on you? Would you give me a job?"

"You wouldn't get through the front door here, for a start. Basement entrance, if any. I'd check your references carefully before I took you on; and I don't think I'd have you at all if I wasn't desperate. You look shifty . . . and a bit . . . well . . . almost dangerous."

I unzipped the leather jacket and let it flap open, showing the checked shirt collar and tan pullover underneath. The effect was altogether sloppier.

"How about now?" I asked.

He put his head on one side, considering. "Yes, I might give you a job now. You look much more ordinary. Not much more honest, but less hard to handle."

"Thank you, Terence. That's exactly the note, I think. Ordinary but dishonest." I smiled with pleasure. "I'd better be on my way."

"You haven't got anything of your own with you?"

"Only my watch," I assured him.

"Fine," he said.

I noticed with interest that for the first time in four days he had failed to punctuate any sentence with any easy, automatic "sir," and when I picked up the cheap suitcase, he made no move to take it from me and carry it himself, as he had done with my grip when I arrived.

We went downstairs to the street door, where I shook hands with him and thanked him for looking after me so well, and gave him a five-pound note. One of October's. He took it with a smile and stood with it in his hand, looking at me in my new character.

I grinned at him widely.

"Good-bye, Terence."

"Good-bye, and thank you . . . sir," he said, and I walked off leaving him laughing.

The next intimation I had that my change of clothes meant a violent drop in status came from the taxi driver I hailed at the bottom of the square. He refused to take me to King's Cross Station until I had shown him that I had enough money to pay his fare. I caught the noon train to Harrogate and intercepted several disapproving glances from a prim middle-aged man with frayed cuffs sitting opposite me. This was all satisfactory, I thought, looking out at the damp autumn countryside flying past; this assures me that I do immediately make a dubious impression. It was rather a lopsided thing to be pleased about.

From Harrogate I caught a country bus to the small village of Slaw, and having asked the way, walked the last two miles to October's place, arriving just before six o'clock, the best time of day for seeking work in a stable.

Sure enough, they were rushed off their feet; I asked for the head lad, and he took me with him to Inskip, who was doing his evening round of inspection.

Inskip looked me over and pursed his lips. He was a stringy, youngish man with spectacles, sparse sandy hair, and a sloppy-looking mouth.

"References?" In contrast, his voice was sharp and authoritative.

I took the letter from October's Cornish cousin out of my pocket and gave it to him. He opened the letter, read it, and put it away in his own pocket.

"You haven't been with racehorses before, then?"

"No."

"When could you start?"

"Now." I indicated my suitcase.

He hesitated, but not for long. "As it happens, we are short-handed. We'll give you a try. Wally, arrange a bed for him with Mrs. Alnutt, and he can start in the morning. Usual wages," he added to me. "Eleven pounds a week, and three pounds of that goes to Mrs. Alnutt for your keep. You can give me your cards tomorrow. Right?"

"Yes," I said, and I was in.

CHAPTER 3

I EDGED GENTLY into the life of the yard like a heretic into heaven, trying not to be discovered and flung out before I became part of the scenery. On my first evening I spoke almost entirely in monosyllables, because I didn't trust my new accent, but I slowly found out that the lads talked with such a variety of regional accents themselves that my cockney-Australian passed without comment.

Wally, the head lad, a wiry, short man with ill-fitting dentures, said I was to sleep in the cottage where about a dozen unmarried lads lived, beside the gate into the yard. I was shown into a small, crowded upstairs room containing six beds, a wardrobe, two chests of drawers, and four bedside chairs; which left roughly two square yards of clear space in the center. Thin flowered curtains hung at the windows, and there was polished linoleum on the floor.

My bed proved to have developed a deep sag in the center over the years, but it was comfortable enough, and was made up freshly with white sheets and gray blankets. Mrs. Alnutt, who took me in without a second glance, was a round, cheerful little person with hair fastened in a twist on the top of her head. She kept the cottage spotless and stood over the lads to make sure they washed. She cooked well, and the food was plain but plentiful. All in all, it was a good billet.

I walked a bit warily to start with, but it was easier to be accepted and to fade into the background than I had imagined.

Once or twice during the first few days I stopped myself just in time from absentmindedly telling another lad what to do; nine years' habit died hard. And I was surprised, and a bit dismayed, by the subservient attitude everyone had to Inskip, at least to his face; my own men treated me at home with far more familiarity. The fact that I paid and they earned gave me no rights over them as men, and this we all clearly understood. But at Inskip's, and throughout all England, I gradually realized, there was far less of the almost aggressive egalitarianism of Australia. The lads, on the whole, seemed to accept that in the eyes of the world they were of secondary importance as human beings to Inskip and October. I thought this extraordinary, undignified, and shameful. And I kept my thoughts to myself.

Wally, scandalized by the casual way I had spoken on my arrival, told me to call Inskip "Sir"—and October "My Lord"—and said that if I was a ruddy communist I could clear off at once; so I quickly exhibited what he called a proper respect for my betters.

On the other hand, it was precisely because the relationship between me and my own men was so free and easy that I found no difficulty in becoming a lad among lads. I felt no constraint on their part and, once the matter of accents had been settled, no self-consciousness on mine. But I did come to realize that what October had implied was undoubtedly true: had I stayed in England and gone to Eton (instead of its equivalent, Geelong), I could not have fitted so readily into his stable.

Inskip allotted me to three newly arrived horses, which was not very good from my point of view as it meant that I could not expect to be sent to a race meeting with them. They were neither fit nor entered for races, and it would be weeks before they were ready to run, even if they proved to be good enough. I pondered the problem while I carried their hay and water and cleaned their boxes and rode them out at morning exercise with the string.

On my second evening October came around at six with a party of house guests. Inskip, knowing in advance, had had everyone running to be finished in good time and walked around himself first, to make sure that all was in order.

Each lad stood with whichever of his horses was nearest the end from which the inspection started. October and his friends, accompanied by Inskip and Wally, moved along from box to box, chatting, laughing, discussing each horse as they went.

When they came to me, October flicked me a glance and said, "You're new, aren't you?"

"Yes, my lord."

He took no further notice of me then, but when I had bolted the first horse in for the night and waited farther down the yard with the second one, he came over to pat my charge and feel his legs; and as he straightened up he gave me a mischievous wink. With difficulty, since I was facing the other men, I kept a deadpan face. He blew his nose to stop himself from laughing. We were neither of us very professional at this cloak-and-dagger stuff.

When they had gone, and after I had eaten the evening meal with the other lads, I walked down to the Slaw pub with two of them. Halfway through the first drinks, I left them and went and telephoned October.

"Who is speaking?" a man's voice inquired.

I was stumped for a second; then I said, "Perlooma," knowing that that would fetch him.

He came on the line. "Anything wrong?"

"No," I said. "Does anyone at the local exchange listen to your calls?"

"I wouldn't bet on it." He hesitated. "Where are you?"

"Slaw, in the phone booth at your end of the village."

"I have guests for dinner; will tomorrow do?"

"Yes."

He paused for thought. "Can you tell me what you want?"

"Yes," I said. "The form books for the last seven or eight seasons, and every scrap of information you can possibly dig up about the eleven . . . subjects."

"What are you looking for?"

"I don't know yet," I said.

"Do you want anything else?"

"Yes, but it needs discussion."

He thought. "Behind the stable yard there is a stream which comes down from the moors. Walk up beside it tomorrow, after lunch."

"Right."

I hung up, and went back to my interrupted drink in the pub.

"You've been a long time," said Paddy, one of the lads I had come with. "We're one ahead of you. What have you been doing—reading the walls in the Gents?"

"There's some remarks on them walls," mused the other lad, a gawky boy of eighteen, "that I haven't fathomed yet."

"Nor you don't want to," said Paddy approvingly. At forty he acted as unofficial father to many of the younger lads.

They slept one each side of me, Paddy and Grits, in the little dormitory. Paddy, as sharp as Grits was slow, was a tough little Irishman with eyes that never missed a trick. From the first minute I hoisted my suitcase onto the bed and unpacked my night things under his inquisitive gaze, I had been glad that October had been so insistent about a complete change of clothes.

"How about another drink?"

"One more, then," assented Paddy. "I can just about run to it, I reckon."

I took the glasses to the bar and bought refills; there was a pause while Paddy and Grits dug into their pockets and repaid me eleven pence each. The beer, which to me tasted strong and bitter, was not, I thought, worth four miles' walk, but many of the lads, it appeared, had bicycles or rickety cars and made the trek on several evenings each week.

"Nothing much doing tonight," observed Grits gloomily. He brightened. "Payday tomorrow."

"It'll be full here tomorrow, and that's a fact," agreed Paddy. "With Soupy and that lot from Granger's and all."

"Granger's?" I asked.

"Sure, don't you know nothing?" said Grits with mild contempt. "Granger's stable, over t'other side of the hill."

"Where have you been all your life?" said Paddy.

"He's new to racing, mind you," said Grits, being fair.

"Yes, but all the same!" Paddy drank past the halfway mark, and wiped his mouth on the back of his hand.

Grits finished his beer and sighed. "That's it, then. Better be getting back, I suppose."

We walked back to the stables, talking as always about horses.

The following afternoon I wandered casually out of the stables and started up the stream, picking up stones as I went and throwing them in, as if to enjoy the splash. Some of the lads were punting a football about in the paddock behind the yard, but none of them paid any attention to me. A good long way up the hill, where the stream ran through a steep, grass-sided gully, I came across October sitting on a boulder smoking a cigarette. He was accompanied by a black retriever, and a gun and a full game bag lay on the ground beside him.

"Doctor Livingstone, I presume," he said, smiling.

"Quite right, Mr. Stanley. How did you guess?" I perched on a boulder near him.

He kicked the game bag. "The form books are in here, and a notebook with all that Beckett and I could rake up at such short notice about those eleven horses. But surely the reports in the files you read would be of more use than the odd snippets we can supply?"

"Anything may be useful . . . you never know. There was one clipping in that packet of Stapleton's which was interesting. It was about historic dope cases. It said that certain horses apparently turned harmless food into something that showed a positive dope reaction, just through chemical changes in their bodies. I suppose it isn't possible that the reverse could occur? I mean, could some horses break down any sort of dope into harmless substances, so that no positive reaction showed in the test?"

"I'll find out."

"There's only one other thing," I said. "I have been assigned to three of those useless brutes you filled the yard up with, and that means no trips to racecourses. I was wondering if perhaps you could sell one of them again, and then I'd have a chance of mixing with lads from several stables at the sales. Three other men are doing three horses each here, so I shouldn't find myself redundant, and I might well be given a raceable horse to look after."

"I will sell one," he said, "but if it goes for auction it will take time. The application forms have to go to the auctioneer nearly a month before the sale date."

I nodded. "It's utterly frustrating. I wish I could think of a way of getting myself transferred to a horse which is due to race shortly. Preferably one going to a far distant course, because an overnight stop would be ideal."

"Lads don't change their horses midstream," he said, rubbing his chin.

"So I've been told. It's the luck of the draw. You get them when they come and you're stuck with them until they leave. If they turn out useless, it's just too bad."

We stood up. The retriever, who had lain quiet all this time with his muzzle resting on his paws, got to his feet also and stretched himself, and wagging his tail slowly from side to side, looked up trustingly at his master. October bent down, gave the dog an affectionate slap, and picked up the gun. I picked up the game bag and swung it over my shoulder.

We shook hands, and October said, smiling, "You may like to know that Inskip thinks you ride extraordinarily well for a stable lad. His exact words were that he didn't really trust men with your sort of looks, but that you'd the hands of an angel. You'd better watch that."

"Hell," I said, "I hadn't given it a thought."

He grinned and went off up the hill, and I turned downward along the stream, gradually becoming ruefully aware that however much of a lark I

might find it to put on wolf's clothing, it was going to hurt my pride if I had
to hash up my riding as well.

The pub in Slaw was crowded that evening and the pay envelope took a
hiding. About half the strength from October's stables was there—one of
them had given me a lift down in his car—and also a group of Granger's lads,
including three lasses, who took a good deal of doublemeaning teasing and
thoroughly enjoyed it. Most of the talk was friendly bragging that each lad's
horses were better than those of anyone else.

"My bugger'll beat yours with his eyes shut on Wednesday."

"You've got a ruddy hope . . ."

". . . Yours couldn't run a snail to a close finish."

". . . The jockey made a right muck of the start and never got in touch . . ."

". . . fat as a pig and bloody obstinate as well."

The easy chat ebbed and flowed while the room grew thick with cigarette
smoke and the warmth of too many lungs breathing the same box of air. A
game of darts between some inaccurate players was in progress in one corner,
and the balls of bar billiards clicked in another. I lolled on a hard chair with
my arm hooked over the back and watched Paddy and one of Granger's lads
engage in a needle match of dominoes. Horses, cars, football, boxing, films,
the last local dance, and back to horses, always back to horses: I listened to it
all and learned nothing except that these lads were mostly content with their
lives, mostly good natured, mostly observant, and mostly harmless.

"You're new, aren't you?" said a challenging voice in my ear.

I turned my head and looked up at him. "Yeah," I said languidly.

These were the only eyes I had seen in Yorkshire which held anything of
the sort of guile I was looking for. I gave him back his stare until his lips
curled in recognition that I was one of his kind.

"What's your name?"

"Dan," I said. "And yours?"

"Thomas Nathaniel Tarleton." He waited for some reaction, but I didn't
know what it ought to be.

"T.N.T.," said Paddy obligingly, looking up from his dominoes. "Soupy."
His quick gaze flickered over both of us.

"The high-explosive kid himself," I murmured.

Soupy Tarleton smiled a small, carefully dangerous smile—to impress
me, I gathered. He was about my own age and build, but much fairer,
with the reddish skin which I had noticed so many Englishmen had. His

light-hazel eyes protruded slightly in their sockets, and he had grown a narrow mustache on the upper lip of his full, moist-looking mouth. On the little finger of his right hand he wore a heavy gold ring, and on his left wrist, an expensive wristwatch. His clothes were of good material, though distinctly sharp in cut, and the enviable fleece-lined quilted jacket he carried over his arm would have cost him three weeks' pay.

He showed no signs of wanting to be friendly. After looking me over as thoroughly as I had him, he merely nodded, said, "See you," and detached himself to go over and watch the bar billiards.

Grits brought a fresh half pint from the bar and settled himself on the bench next to Paddy.

"You don't want to trust Soupy," he told me confidentially, his raw-boned, unintelligent face full of kindness.

Paddy put down a double three, and looking round at us, gave me a long, unsmiling scrutiny.

"There's no need to worry about Dan, Grits," he said. "He and Soupy, they're alike. They'd go well in double harness. Birds of a feather, that's what they are."

"But you said I wasn't to trust Soupy," objected Grits, looking from one to the other of us with troubled eyes.

"That's right," said Paddy flatly. He put down a three-four and concentrated on his game.

Grits shifted six inches toward Paddy and gave me one puzzled, embarrassed glance. Then he found the inside of his beer mug suddenly intensely interesting and didn't raise his eyes to mine again.

I think it was at that exact moment that the charade began to lose its light-heartedness. I liked Paddy and Grits, and for three days they had accepted me with casual good humor. I was not prepared for Paddy's instant recognition that it was with Soupy that my real interest lay, nor for his immediate rejection of me on that account. It was a shock which I ought to have foreseen, and hadn't; and it should have warned me what to expect in the future, but it didn't.

COLONEL BECKETT'S STAFF work continued to be of the highest possible kind. Having committed myself to the offensive, he was prepared to back the attack with massive and immediate reinforcements: which is to say that as soon as he had heard from October that I was immobilized in the stable with three useless horses, he set about liberating me.

On Tuesday afternoon, when I had been with the stable for a week, Wally, the head lad, stopped me as I carried two buckets full of water across the yard.

"That horse of yours in number seventeen is going tomorrow," he said. "You'll have to look sharp in the morning with your work, because you are to be ready to go with it at twelve-thirty. The horse box will take you to another racing stable, down near Nottingham. You are to leave this horse there and bring a new one back. Right?"

"Right," I said. Wally's manner was cool with me; but over the weekend I had made myself be reconciled to the knowledge that I had to go on inspiring a faint mistrust all around, even if I no longer much liked it when I succeeded.

Most of Sunday I had spent reading the form books, which the others in the cottage regarded as a perfectly natural activity; and in the evening, when they all went down to the pub, I did some pretty concentrated work with a pencil, making analyses of the eleven horses and their assisted wins. It was true, as I had discovered from the newspaper cuttings in London, that they all had different owners, trainers, and jockeys; but it was not true that they had absolutely nothing in common. By the time I had sealed my notes into an envelope and put it with October's notebook into the game bag under some form books, away from the inquiring gaze of the beer-happy returning lads, I was in possession of four unhelpful points of similarity.

First, the horses had all won selling chases—races where the winner was subsequently put up for auction. In the auction three horses had been bought back by their owners, and the rest had been sold for modest sums.

Second, in all their racing lives, all the horses had proved themselves to be capable of making a show in a race, but had either no strength or no guts when it came to a finish.

Third, none of them had won any races except the ones for which they were doped, though they had occasionally been placed on other occasions.

Fourth, none of them had won at odds of less than ten to one.

I learned both from October's notes and from the form books that several of the horses had changed trainers more than once, but they were such moderate, unrewarding animals that this was only to be expected. I was also in possession of the useless information that the horses were all by different sires out of different dams, that they varied in age from five to eleven, and that they were not all of the same color. Neither had they all won on the same course, though in this case they had not all won on different courses, either; and geographically I had a vague idea that the courses concerned were all in the northern half of the country—Kelso, Haydock, Sedgefield, Stafford, and Ludlow. I decided to check them on a map, to see if this was right, but there wasn't one to be found chez Mrs. Alnutt.

I went to bed in the crowded little dormitory with the other lads' beery breath gradually overwhelming the usual mixed clean smells of boot polish and hair oil, and lost an argument about having the small sash window open more than four inches at the top. The lads all seemed to take their cue from Paddy, who was undoubtedly the most aware of them, and if Paddy declined to treat me as a friend, so would they. I realized that if I had insisted on having the window shut tight they would probably have opened it wide and given me all the air I wanted. Grinning ruefully in the dark, I listened to the squeaking bedsprings and their sleepy, gossiping giggles as they thumbed over the evening's talk; and as I shifted to find a comfortable spot on the lumpy mattress, I began to wonder what life was really like from the inside for the hands who lived in my own bunkhouse, back home.

Wednesday morning gave me my first taste of the biting Yorkshire wind, and one of the lads, as we scurried around the yard with shaking hands and running noses, cheerfully assured me that it could blow for six months solid, if it tried. I did my three horses at the double, but by the time the horse box took me and one of them out of the yard at twelve-thirty, I had decided that if the gaps in my wardrobe were anything to go by, October's big square house up the drive must have very efficient central heating.

About four miles up the road, I pressed the bell which in most horse boxes connects the back compartment to the cab. The driver stopped obediently, and looked inquiringly at me when I walked along and climbed up into the cab beside him.

"The horse is quiet," I said, "and it's warmer here."

He grinned and started off again, shouting over the noise of the engine. "I didn't have you figured for the conscientious type, and I was damn right. That horse is going to be sold and has got to arrive in good condition. The boss would have a fit if he knew you were up front."

I had a pretty good idea the boss, meaning Inskip, wouldn't be at all surprised; bosses, judging by myself, weren't as naïve as all that.

"The boss can stuff himself," I said unpleasantly.

I got a sidelong glance for that, and reflected that it was dead easy to give oneself a bad character if one put one's mind to it. Horse-box drivers went to race meetings in droves, and had no duties when they got there. They had time to gossip in the canteen, time all afternoon to wander about and wag their tongues. There was no telling what ears might hear that there was a possible chink in the honesty of Inskip lads.

We stopped once on the way to eat in a transport café, and again a little farther on for me to buy myself a couple of woolen shirts, a black sweater, some thick socks, woolen gloves, and a knitted yachting cap like those the other lads had worn that bitter morning. The box driver, coming into the shop with me to buy some socks for himself, eyed my purchases and remarked that I seemed to have plenty of money. I grinned knowingly, and said it was easy to come by if you knew how; and I could see his doubts of me growing.

In midafternoon we rolled in to a racing stable in Leicestershire, and it was here that the scope of Beckett's staff work became apparent. The horse I was to take back and subsequently care for was a useful hurdler just about to start his career as a novice 'chaser, and he had been sold to Colonel Beckett complete with all engagements. This meant, I learned from his former lad, who handed him over to me with considerable bitterness, that he could run in all the races for which his ex-owner had already entered him.

"Where is he entered?" I asked.

"Oh, dozens of places, I think—Newbury, Cheltenham, Sandown, and so on—and he was going to start next week at Bristol." The lad's face twisted with regret as he passed the halter rope into my hand. "I can't think what on earth persuaded the Old Man to part with him. He's a real daisy, and if I ever see him at the races not looking as good and well cared for as he does now, I'll find you and beat the living daylights out of you, I will straight."

I had already discovered how deeply attached racing lads became to the horses they looked after, and I understood that he meant what he said.

"What's his name?" I asked.

"Sparking Plug . . . God-awful name, he's no plug . . . Hey, Sparks, old boy . . . hey, boy . . . hey, old fellow . . ." He fondled the horse's muzzle affectionately.

We loaded him into the horse box and this time I did stay where I ought to be, in the back, looking after him. If Beckett was prepared to give a fortune for the cause, as I guessed he must have done to get hold of such an ideal horse in so few days, I was going to take good care of it.

Before we started back, I took a look at the road map in the cab, and found to my satisfaction that all the racecourses in the country had been marked in on it in india ink. I borrowed it at once, and spent the journey

studying it. The courses where Sparking Plug's lad had said he was entered
were nearly all in the south. Overnight stops, as requested. I grinned.

The five racecourses where the eleven horses had won were not, I found,
all as far north as I had imagined. Ludlow and Stafford, in face, could almost
be considered southern, especially as I found I instinctively based my view of
the whole country from Harrogate. The five courses seemed to bear no relation to each other on the map: far from presenting a tidy circle from which a
center might be deduced, they were all more or less in a curve from northeast
to southwest, and I could find no significance in their location.

I spent the rest of the journey back as I spent most of my working hours,
letting my mind drift over what I knew of the eleven horses, waiting for an
idea to swim to the surface like a fish in a pool, waiting for the disconnected
facts to sort themselves into a pattern. But I didn't really expect this to happen yet, as I knew I had barely started, and even electronic computers won't
produce answers if they are not fed enough information.

ON FRIDAY NIGHT I went down to the pub in Slaw and beat Soupy at
darts. He grunted, gestured to the bar billiards, and took an easy revenge. We
then drank a half pint together, eyeing each other. Conversation between us
was almost nonexistent, nor was it necessary; and shortly I wandered back to
watch the dart players. They were no better than the week before.

"You beat Soupy, didn't you, Dan?" one of them said.

I nodded and immediately found a bunch of darts thrust into my hand.

"If you can beat Soupy you must be in the team."

"What team?" I asked.

"The stable darts team. We play other stables, and have sort of a Yorkshire League. Sometimes we go to Middleham or Wetherby or Richmond or
sometimes they come here. Soupy's the best player in Granger's team. Could
you beat him again, do you think, or was it a fluke?"

I threw three darts at the board. They all landed in the twenty. For some
unknown reason I had always been able to throw straight.

"Cor," said the lads. "Go on."

I threw three more: the twenty section got rather crowded.

"You're in the team, mate, and no nonsense," they said.

"When's the next match?" I asked.

"We had one here a fortnight ago. Next one's next Sunday at Burndale,
after the football. You can't play football as well as darts, I suppose?"

I shook my head. "Only darts."

I looked at the one dart still left in my hand. I could hit a scuttling rat with a stone; I had done it often when the men had found one around the corn bins and chased it out. I saw no reason why I couldn't hit a galloping horse with a dart: it was a much bigger target.

"Put that one in the bull," urged the lad beside me.

I put it in the bull. The lads yelled with glee.

"We'll win the league this season," they said, grinning. Grits grinned, too. But Paddy didn't.

CHAPTER 4

OCTOBER'S SON AND daughters came home for the weekend, the elder girl in a scarlet TR-4, which I grew to know well by sight as she drove in and out past the stables, and the twins more sedately, with their father. As all three were in the habit of riding out when they were at home, Wally told me to saddle up two of my horses to go out with the first string on Saturday, Sparking Plug for me and the other for Lady Patricia Tarren.

Lady Patricia Tarren, as I discovered when I led out the horse in the half light of early dawn and held it for her to mount, was a raving beauty with a pale-pink mouth and thick curly eyelashes which she knew very well how to use. She had tied a green head scarf over her chestnut hair, and she wore a black-and-white harlequin skiing jacket to keep out the cold. She was carrying some bright-green woolen gloves.

"You're new," she observed, looking up at me through the eyelashes. "What's your name?"

"Dan . . . miss," I said. I realized I hadn't the faintest idea what form of address an earl's daughter was accustomed to. Wally's instructions hadn't stretched that far.

"Well . . . give me a leg up, then."

I stood beside her obediently, but as I leaned forward to help her, she ran her bare hand over my head and around my neck, and took the lobe of my right ear between her fingers. She had sharp nails, and she dug them in. Her eyes were wide with challenge. I looked straight back. When I didn't move or say anything, she presently giggled and let go and calmly put on her gloves. I gave her a leg up into the saddle and she bent down to gather the reins, and fluttered the fluffy lashes close to my face.

"You're quite a dish, aren't you, Danny boy," she said, "with those goo-goo dark eyes."

I couldn't think of any answer to her which was at all consistent with my position. She laughed, nudged the horse's flanks, and walked off down the yard. Her sister, mounting a horse held by Grits, looked from twenty yards away in the dim light to be much fairer in coloring and very nearly as beautiful. Heaven help October, I thought, with two like that to keep an eye on.

I turned to go and fetch Sparking Plug and found October's eighteen-year-old son at my elbow. He was very like his father, but not yet as thick in body or as easily powerful in manner.

"I shouldn't pay too much attention to my twin sister," he said in a cool, bored voice, looking me up and down. "She is apt to tease." He nodded and strolled over to where his horse was waiting for him; and I gathered that what I had received was a warning off. If his sister behaved as provocatively with every male she met, he must have been used to delivering them.

Amused, I fetched Sparking Plug, mounted, and followed all the other horses out of the yard, up the lane, and on to the edge of the moor. As usual on a fine morning, the air and the view were exhilarating. The sun was no more than a promise on the far distant horizon and there was a beginning-of-the-world quality in the light. I watched the shadowy shapes of the horses ahead of me curving around the hill with white plumes streaming from their nostrils in the frosty air. As the glittering rim of the sun expanded into full light, the colors sprang out bright and clear, the browns of the jogging horses topped with the bright stripes of the lads' ear-warming knitted caps and the jolly garments of October's daughters.

October himself, accompanied by his retriever, came up onto the moor in a Land Rover to see the horses work. Saturday morning, I had found, was the busiest training day of the week as far as gallops were concerned, and as he was usually in Yorkshire at the weekend, he made a point of coming out to watch.

Inskip had us circling around at the top of the hill while he paired off the horses and told their riders what to do.

To me he said, "Dan . . . three-quarter-speed gallop. Your horse is running on Wednesday. Don't overdo him but we want to see how he goes." He directed one of the stable's most distinguished animals to accompany me.

When he had finished giving his orders, he cantered off along the broad sweep of green turf which stretched through the moorland scrub, and October drove slowly in his wake. We continued circling until the two men reached the other end of the gallop, about a mile and a half away up the gently curved, gently rising track.

"O.K.," said Wally to the first pair. "Off you go."

The two horses set off together, fairly steadily at first and then at an increasing pace until they had passed Inskip and October, when they slowed and pulled up.

"Next two," Wally called.

We were ready, and set off without more ado. I had bred, broken, and re-broken uncountable race horses in Australia, but Sparking Plug was the only good one I had so far ridden in England, and I was interested to see how he compared. Of course he was a hurdler, while I was more used to flat racers, but this made no difference, I found; and he had a bad mouth which I itched to do something about, but there was nothing wrong with his action. Balanced and collected, he sped smoothly up the gallop, keeping pace effortlessly with the star performer beside him, and though, as ordered, we went only three-quarters speed at our fastest, it was quite clear that Sparking Plug was fit and ready for his approaching race.

I was so interested in what I was doing that it was not until I had reined in—not too easy with that mouth—and began to walk back that I realized I had forgotten all about messing up the way I rode. I groaned inwardly, exasperated with myself; I would never do what I had come to England for if I could so little keep my mind on the job.

I stopped with the horse who had accompanied Sparking Plug in front of October and Inskip, for them to have a look at the horses and see how much they were blowing. Sparking Plug's ribs moved easily: he was scarcely out of breath. The two men nodded, and I and the other lad slid off the horses and began walking them around while they cooled down.

Up from the far end of the gallop came the other horses, pair by pair. One of the lads in the third pair lifted his whip and gave his horse two resounding lashes on the flanks. The animal burst forward and flashed past the Land Rover at sprinting pace, pulling up with a jolt as the lad jabbed him in the mouth twenty yards farther on.

October yelled at him to come back and gave him the completest dressing down I had ever heard. His voice carried clearly in the frosty air. His body shook with anger as he gesticulated with his arms to ram home his disapproval. The lads leading their horses around with me grinned slyly at each other and winked.

One, coming alongside for a moment, said reflectively, "Always like that, his lordship is, if you touch one of his horses unnecessary like. You wouldn't think it, would you? I shouldn't give any of his horses a clout, if I was you."

"I won't," I said.

"Got a temper like a volcano, he has, if you hurt one of his horses."

"I'll remember that," I said. "Thanks for telling me."

He nodded and walked on. October finished his tirade and the dejected lad began to walk alone back to the stable, leading his horse. The show was over. The paired gallops went on as before, finishing with a bunch who weren't ready for anything faster than a canter.

When everyone had worked, most of the lads remounted and we all began to walk back down the gallop toward the track to the stable. Leading my horse on foot, I set off last in the string, with October's elder daughter riding immediately in front of me and effectively cutting me off from the chat of the lads ahead. She was looking about her at the rolling vistas of moor, and not bothering to keep her animals close on the heels of the one in front, so that by the time we entered the track, there was a ten-yard gap ahead of her.

As she passed a scrubby gorse bush, a bird flew out of it with a squawk and flapping wings, and the girl's horse whipped around and up in alarm. She stayed on with a remarkable effort of balance, pulling herself back up into the saddle from somewhere below the horse's right ear, but under her thrust the stirrup leather broke apart at the bottom, and the stirrup iron itself clanged to the ground.

I stopped and picked up the iron, but it was impossible to put it back on the broken leather.

"Thank you," she said. "What a nuisance."

She slid off her horse. "I might as well walk the rest of the way."

I took her rein and began to lead both of the horses, but she stopped me, and took her own back again.

"It's very kind of you," she said, "but I can quite well lead him myself." The track was wide at that point, and she began to walk down the hill beside me.

On closer inspection she was not a bit like her sister, Patricia. She had smooth silver-blond hair under a blue head scarf, fair eyelashes, direct gray eyes, a firm, friendly mouth, and a composure which gave her an air of graceful reserve. We walked in easy silence for some way.

"Isn't it a gorgeous morning," she said eventually.

"Gorgeous," I agreed, "but cold." The English always talk about the weather, I thought; and a fine day in November is so rare as to be remarked on. It would be hotting up for summer, at home. . . .

"Have you been with the stable long?" she asked, a little farther on.

"Only about ten days."

"And do you like it here?"

"Oh, yes. It's a well-run stable."

"Mr. Inskip would be delighted to hear you say so," she said in a dry voice.

I glanced at her, but she was looking ahead down the track, and smiling.

After another hundred yards she said, "What horse is that that you were riding? I don't think that I have seen him before, either."

"He only came on Wednesday. . . ." I told her the little I knew about Sparking Plug's history, capabilities, and prospects.

She nodded. "It will be nice for you if he can win some races. Rewarding, after your work for him here."

"Yes," I agreed, surprised that she should think like that.

We reached the last stretch to the stable.

"I am so sorry," she said pleasantly, "but I don't know your name."

"Daniel Roke," I said; and I wondered why to her alone of all the people who had asked me that question in the last ten days it had seemed proper to give a whole answer.

"Thank you." She paused; then, having thought, continued in a calm voice which I realized with wry pleasure was designed to put me at my ease. "Lord October is my father. I'm Elinor Tarren."

We had reached the stable gate. I stood back to let her go in first, which she acknowledged with a friendly but impersonal smile, and she led her horse away across the yard toward its own box. A thoroughly nice girl, I thought briefly, buckling down to the task of brushing the sweat off Sparking Plug, washing his feet, brushing out his mane and tail, sponging out his eyes and mouth, putting his straw bed straight, fetching his hay and water, and then repeating the whole process with the horse that Patricia had ridden. Patricia, I thought, grinning, was not a nice girl at all.

When I went in to breakfast in the cottage, Mrs. Alnutt gave me a letter which had just arrived for me. The envelope, postmarked London the day before, contained a sheet of plain paper with a single sentence typed on it:

Mr. Stanley will be at Victoria Falls 3 P.M. Sunday.

I stuffed the letter into my pocket, laughing into my porridge.

THERE WAS A heavy drizzle falling when I walked up beside the stream the following afternoon. I reached the gully before October, and waited for him with the raindrops finding ways to trickle down my neck. He came down the hill with his dog as before, telling me that his car was parked above us on the little-used road.

"But we'd better talk here, if you can stand the wet," he finished, "in case anyone saw us together in the car, and wondered."

"I can stand the wet," I assured him, smiling.

"Good . . . Well, how have you been getting on?"

I told him how well I thought of Beckett's new horse and the opportunities it would give me.

He nodded. "Roddy Beckett was famous in the war for the speed and accuracy with which he got supplies moved about. No one ever got the wrong ammunition or all left boots when he was in charge."

I said, "I've sown a few seeds of doubt about my honesty, here and there, but I'll be able to do more of that this week at Bristol, and also next weekend, at Burndale. I'm going there on Sunday to play in a darts match."

"They've had several cases of doping in that village in the past," he said thoughtfully. "You might get a nibble there."

"It would be useful . . ."

"Have you found the form books helpful?" he asked. "Have you given those eleven horses any more thought?"

"I've thought of little else," I said, "and it seems just possible . . . perhaps it's only a slight chance, but it does seem possible that you might be able to make a dope test on the next horse in the sequence *before* he runs in a race. That is to say, always providing that there is going to be another horse in the sequence . . . and I don't see why not, as the people responsible have got away with it for so long."

He looped at me with some excitement, the rain dripping off the overturned brim of his hat.

"You've found something?"

"No, not really. It's only a statistical indication. But it's more than even money, I think, that the next horse will win a selling chase at Kelso, Sedgefield, Ludlow, Stafford, or Haydock." I explained my reasons for expecting this, and went on, "It should be possible to arrange for wholesale saliva samples to be taken before all the selling chases on those particular tracks—it can't be more than one race at each two-day meeting—and they can throw the samples away without going to the expense of testing them if no . . . er . . . joker turns up in the pack."

"It's a tall order," he said slowly, "but I don't see why it shouldn't be done, if it will prove anything."

"The analysts might find something useful in the results."

"Yes. And I suppose even if they didn't, it would be a great step forward for us to be able to be on the lookout for a joker, instead of just being mystified when one appeared. Why on earth"—he shook his head in exasperation—"didn't we think of this months ago? It seems such an obvious way to approach the problem, now that you have done it."

"I expect it is because I am the first person really to be given all the collected information all at once, and deliberately search for a connecting factor. All the other investigations seemed to have been done from the other end, so to speak, by trying to find out in each case separately who had access to the horse, who fed him, who saddled him, and so on."

He nodded gloomily.

"There's one other thing," I said. "The lab chaps told you that since they couldn't find dope you should look for something mechanical. . . . Do you know whether the horses' skins were investigated as closely as the jockeys and their kit? It occurred to me the other evening that I could throw a dart with an absolute certainty of hitting a horse's flank, and any good shot could plant a pellet in the same place. Things like that would sting like a hornet . . . enough to make any horse shift along faster."

"As far as I know, none of the horses showed any signs of that sort of thing, but I'll make sure. And by the way, I asked the analysts whether horses' bodies could break drugs down into harmless substances, and they said it was impossible."

"Well, that clears the decks a bit, if nothing else."

"Yes." He whistled to his dog, who was quartering the far side of the gully. "After next week, when you'll be away at Burndale, we had better meet here at this time every Sunday afternoon to discuss progress. You will know if I'm away, because I won't be here for the Saturday gallops. Incidentally, your horsemanship stuck out a mile on Sparking Plug yesterday. And I thought we agreed that you had better not make too good an impression. On top of which," he added, smiling faintly, "Inskip says you are a quick and conscientious worker."

"Heck . . . I'll be getting a good reference if I don't watch out."

"Too right you will," he agreed, copying my accent sardonically. "How do you like being a stable lad?"

"It has its moments. . . . Your daughters are very beautiful."

He grinned. "Yes; and thank you for helping Elinor. She told me you were most obliging."

"I did nothing."

"Patty is a bit of a handful," he said reflectively. "I wish she'd decide what sort of job she'd like to do. She knows I don't want her to go on as she has during her season, never-ending parties and staying out till dawn . . . Well, that's not your worry, Mr. Roke."

We shook hands as usual, and he trudged off up the hill. It was still drizzling mournfully as I went down.

Sparking Plug duly made the 250-mile journey south to Bristol, and I went with him. The racecourse was some way out of the city, and the horse-box driver told me, when we stopped for a meal on the way, that the whole of the stable block had been newly rebuilt there after a fire had gutted it.

Certainly the loose boxes were clean and snug, but it was the new sleeping quarters that the lads were in ecstasies about. The hostel was a surprise to me, too. It consisted mainly of a recreation room and two long dormitories with about thirty beds in each, made up with clean sheets and fluffy blue blankets. There was a wall light over each bed, vinyl-tile flooring, under-floor heating, modern showers in the washroom, and a hot room for drying wet clothes. The whole place was warm and light, with color schemes which were clearly the work of a professional.

"Ye gods, we're in the ruddy Hilton," said one cheerful boy, coming to a halt beside me just through the dormitory door and slinging his canvas grip onto an unoccupied bed.

"You haven't seen the half of it," said a bony, long-wristed boy in a shrunken blue jersey. "Up that end of the passage there's a ruddy great canteen with decent chairs and a telly and a Ping-Pong table and all."

Other voices joined in.

"It's as good as Newbury."

"Easily."

"Better than Ascot, I'd say."

Heads nodded.

"They have bunk beds at Ascot, not singles, like this."

The hostels at Newbury and Ascot were, it appeared, the most comfortable in the country.

"Anyone would think the bosses had suddenly cottoned on to the fact that we're human," said a sharp-faced lad, in a belligerent, rabble-rousing voice.

"It's a far cry from the bug-ridden doss houses of the old days," nodded a desiccated, elderly little man with a face like a shrunken apple. "But a fellow told me the lads have it good like this in America all the time."

"They know if they don't start treating us decent they soon won't get anyone to do the dirty work," said the rabble-rouser. "Things are changing."

"They treat us decent enough where I come from," I said, putting my things on an empty bed next to his and nerving myself to be natural, casual, unremarkable. I felt much more self-conscious than I had at Slaw, where at least I knew the job inside out and had been able to feel my way cautiously into a normal relationship with the other lads. But here I had only two nights, and if I was to do any good at all, I had to direct the talk toward what I wanted to hear.

The form books were by now as clear to me as a primer, and for a fortnight I had listened acutely and concentrated on soaking in as much racing jargon as I could, but I was still doubtful whether I would understand everything I heard at Bristol and also afraid that I would make some utterly incongruous, impossible mistake in what I said myself.

"And where do you come from?" asked the cheerful boy, giving me a cursory looking over.

"Lord October's," I said.

"Oh, yes . . . Inskip's, you mean? You're a long way from home."

"Inskip's may be all right," said the rabble-rouser, as if he regretted it. "But there are some places where they still treat us like mats to wipe their feet on, and don't reckon that we've got a right to a bit of sun, same as everyone else."

"Yeah," said the rawboned boy seriously. "I heard that at one place they practically starve the lads and knock them about if they don't work hard enough, and they all have to do about four or five horses each because they can't keep anyone in the yard for more than five minutes!"

I said idly, "Where's that? Just so I know where to avoid, if I ever move on from Inskip's."

"Up your part of the country," he said doubtfully, "I think."

"No, farther north, in Durham," another boy chimed in, a slender pretty boy with a soft down still growing on his cheeks.

"You know about it, too, then?"

He nodded. "Not that it matters; only a raving nit would take a job there. It's a blooming sweatshop, a hundred years out of date. All they get are riffraff that no one else will have."

"It wants exposing," said the rabble-rouser belligerently. "Who runs the place?"

"Bloke called Humber," said the pretty boy. "He couldn't train ivy up a wall . . . and he has about as many winners as tits on a billiard ball. You see his head traveling lad at the meetings sometimes, trying to press-gang people to go and work there, and getting the brush-off, right and proper."

"Someone ought to do something," said the rabble-rouser automatically; and I guessed that was his usual refrain: "Someone ought to do something"; but not, when it came to the point, himself.

There was a general drift into the canteen, where the food proved to be good, unlimited, and free. A proposal to move on to a pub came to nothing when it was discovered both that the nearest was nearly two (busless) miles away and that the bright, warm canteen had some crates of beer under its counter.

It was easy enough to get the lads started on the subject of doping, and they seemed prepared to discuss it endlessly. None of the twenty-odd there had ever, as far as they would admit, given "anything" to a horse, but they all knew someone who knew someone who had. I drank my beer and listened and looked interested, which I was.

". . . nobbled him with a squirt of acid as he walked out of the bleeding paddock . . ."

". . . gave it such a whacking dollop of stopping powder that it died in its box in the morning . . ."

"Seven rubber bands came out in the droppings . . ."

". . . overdosed him so much that he never even tried to jump the first fence: blind, he was, stone blind . . ."

". . . gave him a bloody great bucketful of water half an hour before the race, and didn't need any dope to stop him with all that sloshing about inside his gut."

". . . poured half a bottle of whiskey down his throat . . ."

". . . used to tube horses that couldn't breathe properly on the morning of the race until they found it wasn't the extra fresh air that was making the horses win but the cocaine they stuffed them full of for the operation . . ."

"They caught him with a hollow apple packed with sleeping pills . . ."

". . . dropped a syringe right in front of an effing steward."

"I wonder if there's anything which hasn't been tried yet," I said.

"Black magic. Not much else left," said the pretty boy.

They all laughed.

"Someone might find something so good," I pointed out casually, "that it couldn't be detected, so the people who thought of it could go on with it forever and never be found out."

"Blimy," exclaimed the cheerful lad, "you're a comfort, aren't you? God help racing, if that happened. You'd never know where you were. The bookies would all be climbing the walls." He grinned hugely.

The elderly little man was not so amused.

"It's been going on for years and years," he said, nodding solemnly. "Some trainers have got it to a fine art, you mark my words. Some trainers have been doping their horses regular, for years and years."

But the other lads didn't agree. The dope tests had done for the dope-minded trainers of the past; they had lost their license, and gone out of racing. The old rule had been a bit unfair on some, they allowed, when a trainer had been automatically disqualified if one of his horses had been doped. It wasn't always the trainer's fault, especially if the horse had been doped to lose. What trainer, they asked, would nobble a horse he'd spent months training to win? But they thought there was probably *more* doping since that rule was changed, not less.

Stands to reason, a doper knows now he isn't ruining the trainer for life, just one horse for one race. Makes it sort of easier on his conscience, see? More lads, maybe, would take fifty quid for popping the odd aspirin into the feed if they knew the stable wouldn't be shut down and their jobs gone for a burton very soon afterward.

They talked on, thoughtful and ribald; but it was clear that they didn't know anything about the eleven horses I was concerned with. None of them, I knew, came from any of the stables involved, and obviously they had not

read the speculative reports in the papers, or if they had, had read them separately over a period of eighteen months, and not in one solid, collected, intense bunch, as I had done.

The talk faltered and died into yawns, and we went chatting to bed, I
sighing to myself with relief that I had gone through the evening without
much notice having been taken of me.

By watching carefully what the other lads did, I survived the next day
also without any curious stares. In the early afternoon I took Sparking Plug
from the stables into the paddock, walked him around the parade ring, stood
holding his head while he was saddled, led him around the parade ring again,
held him while the jockey mounted, led him out on to the course, and went
up into the little stand by the gate with the other lads to watch the race.

Sparking Plug won. I was delighted. I met him again at the gate and led
him into the spacious winner's unsaddling enclosure.

Colonel Beckett was there, waiting, leaning on a stick. He patted the
horse and congratulated the jockey, who unbuckled his saddle and departed
into the weighing room. Beckett said to me sardonically, "That's a fraction of
his purchase price back, anyway."

"He's a good horse, and absolutely perfect for his purpose."

"Good. Do you need anything else?"

"Yes. A lot more details about those eleven horses . . . where they were
bred, what they ate, whether they had had any illnesses, what cafés their box
drivers used, who made their bridles, whether they had racing plates fitted at
meetings, and by which blacksmiths . . . anything and everything."

"Are you serious?"

"Yes."

"But they had nothing in common except that they were doped."

"As I see it, the question really is what was it that they had in common
that made it *possible* for them to be doped." I smoothed Sparking Plug's nose.
He was restive and excited after his victory. Colonel Beckett looked at me
with sober eyes.

"Mr. Roke, you shall have your information."

I grinned at him. "Thank you; and I'll take good care of Sparking
Plug. . . . He'll win you all the purchase price, before he's finished."

"Horses away," called an official; and with a weak-looking gesture of a
farewell from Colonel Beckett's limp hand, I took Sparking Plug back to the
racecourse stables and walked him around until he had cooled off.

There were far more lads in the hostel that evening, as it was the middle night of the two-day meeting, and this time, besides getting talk around again to doping and listening attentively to everything that was said, I also tried to give the impression that I didn't think taking fifty quid to point out a certain horse's box in his home stable to anyone prepared to pay that much for the information was a proposition I could be relied on to turn down. I earned a good few disapproving looks for this, and also one sharply interested glance from a very short lad whose outsize nose sniffed monotonously.

In the washroom in the morning, he used the basin next to me, and said out of the side of his mouth, "Did you mean it, last night, that you'd take fifty quid to point out a box?"

I shrugged. "I don't see why not."

He looked around furtively. It made me want to laugh. "I might be able to put you in touch with someone who'd be interested to hear that—for a fifty-percent cut."

"You've got another thing coming," I said offensively. "Fifty percent . . . what the hell do you think I am?"

"Well . . . a fiver, then," he sniffed, climbing down.

"I dunno . . ."

"I can't say fairer than that," he muttered.

"It's a wicked thing, to point out a box," I said virtuously, drying my face on a towel.

He stared at me in astonishment.

"And I couldn't do it for less than sixty, if you are taking a fiver out of it."

He didn't know whether to laugh or spit. I left him to his indecision, and went off grinning to escort Sparking Plug back to Yorkshire.

CHAPTER 5

AGAIN ON FRIDAY evening I went down to the Slaw pub and ex-changed bug-eyed looks with Soupy across the room.

On the Sunday, half the lads had the afternoon off to go to Burndale for the football and darts matches, and we won both, which made for a certain amount of back slapping and beer drinking. But beyond remarking that I was new, and a blight on their chances in the dart league, the Burndale lads paid me little attention. There was no one like Soupy among them in spite of what October had said about the cases of doping in the village, and no one, as far as I could see, who cared if I were as crooked as a corkscrew.

During the next week I did my three horses, and read the form books, and thought . . . and got nowhere. Paddy remained cool and so did Wally, to whom Paddy had obviously reported my affinity with Soupy. Wally showed his disapproval by giving me more than my share of the afternoon jobs, so that every day, instead of relaxing in the usual free time between lunch and evening stables at four o'clock, I found myself bidden to sweep the yard, clean the tack, crush the oats, cut the chaff, wash Inskip's car, or clean the windows of the loose boxes. I did it all without comment, reflecting that if I needed an excuse for a quick row and walked out later on, I could reasonably, at eleven hours a day, complain of overwork.

However, at Friday midday I set off again with Sparking Plug, this time to Cheltenham, and this time accompanied not only by the box driver but by Grits and his horse, and the head traveling lad as well.

Once in the racecourse stables, I learned that this was the night of the dinner given to the previous season's champion jockey, and all the lads who were staying there overnight proposed to celebrate by attending a dance in the town. Grits and I, therefore, having bedded down our horses, eaten our meal, and smartened ourselves up, caught a bus down the hill and paid our entrance money to the hop. It was a big hall and the band was loud and hot, but not many people were dancing. The girls were standing about in little groups eyeing larger groups of young men, and I bit back just in time a remark on how odd I found it; Grits would expect me to think it normal. I took him off into the bar, where there were already groups of lads from the racecourse mingled with the local inhabitants, and bought him a beer, regretting that he was with me to see what use I intended to make of the evening. Poor Grits: he was torn between loyalty to Paddy and an apparent liking for me, and I was about to disillusion him thoroughly. I wished I could explain. I was tempted to spend the evening harmlessly. But how could I justify passing over an unrepeatable opportunity just to keep temporarily the regard of one slow-witted stable lad, however much I might like him? I was committed to earning ten thousand pounds.

"Grits, go and find a girl to dance with."

He gave me a slow grin. "I don't know any."

"It doesn't matter. Any of them would be glad to dance with a nice chap like you. Go and ask one."

"No. I'd rather stay with you."

"All right, then. Have another drink."

"I haven't finished this."

I turned around to the bar, which we had been leaning against, and banged my barely touched half pint down on the counter. "I'm fed up with this pap," I said violently. "Hey, you, barman, give me a double whiskey."

"Dan!" Grits was upset by my tone, which was a measure of its success. The barman poured the whiskey and took my money.

"Don't go away," I said to him in a loud voice. "Give me another while you're at it."

I felt rather than saw the group of lads farther up the bar turn around and take a look, so I picked up the glass and swallowed all the whiskey in two gulps and wiped my mouth on the back of my hand. I pushed the empty glass across to the barman and paid for the second drink.

"Dan." Grits tugged my sleeve. "Do you think you should?"

"Yes," I said, scowling. "Go and find a girl to dance with."

But he didn't go. He watched me drink the second whiskey and order a third. His eyes were troubled.

The bunch of lads edged toward us along the bar.

"Hey, fella, you're knocking it back a bit," observed one, a tallish man of my own age in a flashy bright-blue suit.

"Mind your own ruddy business," I said rudely.

"Aren't you from Inskip's?" he asked.

"Yeah . . . Inskip's . . . bloody Inskip's . . ." I picked up the third glass. I had a hard head for whiskey, which was going down on top of a deliberately heavy meal. I reckoned I could stay sober a long time after I would be expected to be drunk; but the act had to be put on early, while the audience were still sober enough themselves to remember it clearly afterward.

"Eleven sodding quid," I told them savagely. "That's all you get for sweating your guts out seven days a week."

It struck a note with some of them, but Blue Suit said, "Then why spend it on whiskey?"

"Why bloody not? It's great stuff—gives you a kick. And, by God, you need something in this job."

Blue Suit said to Grits, "Your mate's got an outsized gripe."

"Well . . ." said Grits, his face anxious, "I suppose he has had a lot of extra jobs this week, come to think—"

"You're looking after horses they pay thousands for and you know damn well that the way you ride and groom them and look after them makes a hell of a lot of difference to whether they win or not, and they grudge you a decent wage. . . ." I finished the third whiskey, hiccuped, and said, "It's bloody unfair."

The bar was filling up, and from the sight of them and from what I could catch of their greetings to each other, at least half the customers were in some way connected with racing. Bookmakers' clerks and touts as well as stable lads—the town was stuffed with them, and the dance had been put on to attract them. A large amount of liquor began disappearing down their collective throats, and I had to catch the barman on the wing to serve my fourth double whiskey in fifteen minutes.

I stood facing a widening circle with the glass in my hand, and rocked slightly on my feet.

"I want . . ." I began. What on earth did I want? I searched for the right phrases. "I want . . . a motor bike. I want to show a bird a good time. And go abroad for a holiday . . . and stay in a swank hotel and have them running about at my beck and call . . . and drink what I like . . . and maybe one day put a deposit on a house—and what chance do I have of any of these? I'll tell you. Not a snowball's hope in hell. You know what I got in my pay envelope this morning? Seven pounds and four pence . . ."

I went on and on, grousing and complaining, and the evening wore slowly away. The audience drifted and changed, and I kept it up until I was fairly sure that all the racing people there knew there was a lad of Inskip's who yearned for more money, preferably in large amounts. But even Grits, who hovered about with an unhappy air throughout it all and remained cold sober himself, didn't seem to notice that I got progressively drunker in my actions while making each drink last longer than the one before.

Eventually, after I had achieved an artistic lurch and clutch at one of the pillars, Grits said loudly in my ear, "Dan, I'm going now and you'd better go, too, or you'll miss the last bus, and I shouldn't think you could walk back, like you are."

"Huh?" I squinted at him. Blue Suit had come back and was standing just behind him.

"Want any help getting him out?" he asked Grits.

Grits looked at me disgustedly, and I fell against him, putting my arm around his shoulders. I definitely did not want the sort of help Blue Suit looked as though he might give.

"Grits, me old pal, if you say go, we go."

We set off for the door, followed by Blue Suit, me staggering so heavily that I pushed Grits sideways. There were by this time, I noticed, a lot of others having difficulty in walking a straight line, and the queue of lads that waited at the bus stop undulated slightly like an ocean swell on a calm day. I grinned in the safe darkness and looked up at the sky, and thought that if the seeds I had sown in all directions bore no fruit, there was little doping going on in British racing.

I MAY NOT have been drunk, but I woke the next morning with a shattering headache, just the same: all in a good cause, I thought, trying to ignore the blacksmith behind my eyes.

Sparking Plug ran in his race and lost by half a length. I took the opportunity of saying aloud on the lads' stand that there was the rest of my week's pay gone down the bloody drain.

Colonel Beckett patted his horse's neck in the cramped unsaddling enclosure and said casually to me, "Better luck next time, eh? I've sent you what you wanted, in a parcel." He turned away and resumed talking to Inskip and his jockey about the race.

We went all the way back to Yorkshire that night, with Grits and me sleeping most of the way on the benches in the back of the horse box.

He said reproachfully, as he lay down, "I didn't know you hated it at Inskip's . . . and I haven't seen you drunk before, either."

"It isn't the work, Grits, it's the pay." I had to keep it up.

"Still there are some who are married and have kids to keep on what you were bleating about." He sounded disapproving, and indeed my behavior must have affected him deeply, because he seldom spoke to me after that night.

There was nothing of interest to report to October the following afternoon, and our meeting in the gully was brief. He told me, however, that the information then in the mail from Beckett had been collected by eleven keen young officer cadets from Aldershot who had been given the task as an initiative exercise and told they were in competition with each other to see which of them could produce the most comprehensive report of the life of his allotted horse. A certain number of questions—those I had suggested—were outlined for them. The rest had been left to their own imagination and detective ability, and October said Beckett had told him they had used them to the full.

I returned down the hill more impressed than ever with the colonel's staff work, but not as staggered as when the parcel arrived the following day. Wally again found some wretched job for me to do in the afternoon, so that it was not until after the evening meal, when half the lads had gone down to Slaw, that I had an opportunity of taking the package up to the dormitory and opening it. It contained 237 numbered typewritten pages bound into a cardboard folder, like the manuscript of a book, and its production in the space of one week must have meant a prodigious effort not only from the young men themselves, but from the typists as well. The information was given in note form for the most part, and no space had anywhere been wasted in flowing prose: it was solid detail from cover to cover.

Mrs. Alnutt's voice floated up the stairs. "Dan, come down and fetch me a bucket of coal, will you, please?"

I thrust the typescript down inside my bed between the sheets, and went back to the warm communal kitchen—living room where we ate and spent most of our spare time. It was impossible to read anything private there, and my life was very much supervised from dawn to bedtime; and the only place I could think of where I could concentrate uninterruptedly on the typescript was the bathroom. Accordingly that night I waited until all the lads were asleep, and then went along the passage and locked myself in, ready to report an upset stomach if anyone should be curious.

It was slow going: after four hours I had read only half. I got up stiffly, stretched, yawned, and went back to bed. Nobody stirred. The following night, as I lay waiting for the others to go to sleep so that I could get back at my task, I listened to them discussing the evening that four of them had spent in Slaw.

"Who's that fellow who was with Soupy?" asked Grits. "I haven't seen him around before."

"He was there last night, too," said one of the others. "Queer sort of bloke."

"What was queer about him?" asked the boy who had stayed behind, watching television while I in an armchair caught up on some sleep.

"I dunno," said Grits. "His eyes didn't stay still, like."

"Sort of as if he was looking for someone," added another voice.

Paddy said firmly from the wall on my right, "You just all keep clear of that chap, and Soupy, too. I'm telling you. People like them are no good."

"But that chap, the one with that smashing gold tie, he bought us a round, you know he did. He can't be too bad if he bought us a round. . . ."

Paddy sighed with exasperation that anyone could be so simple. "If you'd have been Eve, you'd have eaten the apple as soon as look at it. You wouldn't have needed a serpent."

"Oh, well," yawned Grits. "I don't suppose he'll be there tomorrow. I heard him say something to Soupy about time getting short."

They muttered and murmured and went to sleep, and I lay awake in the dark thinking that perhaps I had just heard something very interesting indeed. Certainly a trip down to the pub was indicated for the following evening.

With a wrench I stopped my eyes from shutting, got out of my warm bed, repaired again to the bathroom, and read for another four hours until I had finished the typescript. I sat on the bathroom floor with my back against the wall and stared sightlessly at the fixtures and fittings. There was nothing, not one single factor, that occurred in the life histories of all of the eleven microscopically investigated horses. No common denominator at all. There were quite a few things that were common to four or five—but not often the same four or five—like the make of saddle their jockeys used, the horse cube nuts they were fed with, or the auction rings they had been sold in; but the hopes I had had of finding a sizable clue in those packages had altogether evaporated. Cold, stiff, and depressed, I crept back to bed.

The next evening at eight I walked alone down to Slaw, all the other lads saying they were skint until payday and that in any case they wanted to watch *Z Cars* on television.

"I thought you lost all your cash on Sparks at Cheltenham," observed Grits.

"I've about two bob left," I said, producing some pennies. "Enough for a pint."

The pub, as often on Wednesdays, was empty. There was no sign of Soupy or his mysterious friend, and having bought some beer, I amused myself at the dart board, throwing one-to-twenty sequences, and trying to make a complete ring in the trebles. Eventually I pulled the darts out of the board, looked at my watch, and decided I had wasted the walk; and it was at that moment that a man appeared in the doorway, not from the street but from the saloon bar next door. He held a glass of gently fizzling amber liquid and a slim cigar in his left hand and pushed open the door with his right. Looking me up and down, he said, "Are you a stable lad?"

"Yes."

"Granger's or Inskip's?"

"Inskip's."

"Hmmm." He came farther into the room and let the door swing shut behind him. "There's ten bob for you if you can get one of your lads down here tomorrow night . . . and as much beer as you can both drink."

I looked interested. "Which lad?" I asked. "Any special one? Lots of them will be down here on Friday."

"Well, now, it had better be tomorrow, I think. Sooner the better, I always say. And as for which lad . . . er . . . you tell me their names and I'll pick one of them—how's that?"

I thought it was damn stupid, and also that he wished to avoid asking too directly, too memorably for . . . well . . . for me?

"O.K. Paddy, Grits, Wally, Steve, Ron . . ." I paused.

"Go on," he said.

"Reg, Norman, Dave, Jeff, Dan, Mike . . ."

His eyes brightened. "Dan," he said. "That's a sensible sort of name. Bring Dan."

"I am Dan," I said.

There was an instant in which his balding scalp contracted and his eyes narrowed in annoyance.

"Stop playing games," he said sharply.

"It was you," I pointed out gently, "who began it."

He sat down on one of the benches and carefully put his drink down on the table in front of him.

"Why did you come here tonight, alone?" he asked.

"I was thirsty."

There was a brief silence while he mentally drew up a plan of campaign. He was a short, stocky man in a dark suit a size too small, the jacket hanging open to reveal a monogrammed cream shirt and golden silk tie. His fingers were fat and short, and a roll of flesh overhung his coat collar at the back, but there was nothing soft in the way he looked at me.

At length he said, "I believe there is a horse in your stable called Sparking Plug?"

"Yes."

"And he runs at Leicester on Monday?"

"As far as I know."

"What do you think his chances are?" he asked.

"Look, do you want a tip, mister, is that what it is? Well, I do Sparking Plug myself and I'm telling you there isn't an animal in next Monday's race to touch him."

"So you expect him to win?"

"Yeah, I told you."

"And you'll bet on him, I suppose."

"Of course."

"With half your pay? Four pounds, perhaps?"

"Maybe."

"But he'll be favorite. Sure to be. And at best you'll probably only get even money. Another four quid. That doesn't sound like much, does it, when I could perhaps put you in the way of winning . . . a hundred?"

"You're barmy," I said, but with a sideways leer that told him that I wanted to hear more.

He leaned forward with confidence. "Now, you can say no if you want to. You can say no, and I'll go away, and no one will be any the wiser, but if you play your cards right, I could do you a good turn."

"What would I have to do for a hundred quid?" I asked flatly.

He looked around cautiously, and lowered his voice still further. "Just add a little something to Sparking Plug's feed on Sunday night. Nothing to it, you see? Dead easy."

"Dead easy," I repeated; and so it was.

"You're on, then?" He looked eager.

"I don't know your name," I said.

"Never you mind." He shook his head with finality.

"Are you a bookmaker?"

"No," he said. "I'm not. And that's enough with the questions. Are you on?"

"If you're not a bookmaker," I said slowly, thinking my way, "and you are willing to pay a hundred pounds to make sure a certain favorite doesn't win, I'd guess that you didn't want just to make money backing all the other runners, but that you intend to tip off a few bookmakers that the race is fixed, and they'll be so grateful they'll pay you say, fifty quid each, at the very least.

There are about eleven thousand bookmakers in Britain. A nice big market. But I expect you go to the same ones over and over again. Sure of your welcome, I should think."

His face was a study of consternation and disbelief, and I realized I had hit the target, bang on.

"Who told you . . ." he began weakly.

"I wasn't born yesterday," I said with a nasty grin. "Relax. No one told me." I paused. "I'll give Sparking Plug his extra nosh, but I want more for it. Two hundred."

"No. The deal's off." He mopped his forehead.

"All right." I shrugged.

"A hundred and fifty then," he said grudgingly.

"A hundred and fifty," I agreed. "Before I do it."

"Half before, half after," he said automatically. It was by no means the first time he had done this sort of deal.

I agreed to that. He said if I came down to the pub on Saturday evening I would be given a packet for Sparking Plug and seventy-five pounds for myself, and I nodded and went away, leaving him staring moodily into his glass.

On my way back up the hill I crossed Soupy off my list of potentially useful contacts. Certainly he had procured me for a doping job, but I had been asked to stop a favorite in a novice 'chase, not to accelerate a dim long-priced selling plater. It was extremely unlikely that both types of fraud were the work of one set of people.

Unwilling to abandon Colonel Beckett's typescript, I spent chunks of that night and the following two nights in the bathroom, carefully rereading it. The only noticeable result was that during the day I found the endless stable work irksome because for five nights in a row I had had only three hours' sleep. But I frankly dreaded having to tell October on Sunday that the eleven young men had made their mammoth investigation to no avail, and I had an unreasonable feeling that if I hammered away long enough, I could still wring some useful message from those densely packed pages.

On Saturday morning, though it was bleak, bitter, and windy, October's daughters rode out with the first string. Elinor only came near enough to exchange polite good mornings, but Patty, who was again riding one of my horses, made my giving her a leg up a moment of eyelash-fluttering intimacy, deliberately and unnecessarily rubbing her body against mine.

"You weren't here last week, Danny boy," she said, putting her feet in the irons. "Where were you?"

"At Cheltenham . . . miss."

"Oh. And next Saturday?"

"I'll be here."

She said, with intentional insolence, "Then kindly remember next Saturday to shorten the leathers on the saddle before I mount. These are far too long."

She made no move to shorten them herself, but gestured for me to do it for her. She watched me steadily, enjoying herself. While I was fastening the second buckle, she rubbed her knee forward over my hands and kicked me none too gently in the ribs.

"I wonder you stand me teasing you, Danny boy," she said softly, bending down. "A dishy guy like you should answer back more. Why don't you?"

"I don't want the sack," I said, with a dead straight face.

"A coward, too," she said sardonically, and twitched her horse away.

And she'll get into bad trouble one day, if she keeps on like that, I thought. She was too provocative. Stunningly pretty, of course, but that was only the beginning; and her hurtful little tricks were merely annoying. It was the latent invitation which disturbed and aroused.

I shrugged her out of my mind, fetched Sparking Plug, sprang up onto his back, and moved out of the yard and up to the moor for the routine working gallops.

The weather that day was steadily worse until while we were out with the second string it began to rain heavily in fierce splashing gusts, and we struggled miserably back against it with stinging faces and sodden clothes. Perhaps because it went on raining, or possibly because it was, after all, Saturday, Wally for once refrained from making me work all afternoon, and I spent the three hours sitting with about nine other lads in the kitchen of the cottage, listening to the wind shrieking around the corners outside and watching Chepstow races on television, while our damp jerseys, breeches, and socks steamed gently around the fire.

I put the previous season's form book on the kitchen table and sat over it with my head propped on the knuckles of my left hand, idly turning the pages with my right. Depressed by my utter lack of success with the eleven horses' dossiers, by the antipathy I had to arouse in the lads, and also, I think, by the absence of the hot sunshine I usually live in at that time of year, I began to feel that the whole masquerade had been from the start a ghastly mistake. And the trouble was that having taken October's money, I couldn't back out; not for months. This thought depressed me further still. I sat slumped in unrelieved gloom, wasting my much-needed free time.

I think now that it must have been the sense that I was failing in what I had set out to do, more than mere tiredness, which beset me that afternoon, because although later on I encountered worse things, it was only for that short while that I ever truly regretted having listened to October, and unreservedly wished myself back in my comfortable Australian cage.

The lads watching the television were making disparaging remarks about the jockeys and striking private bets against each other on the outcome of the races.

"The uphill finish will sort 'em out as usual," Paddy was saying. "It's a long way from the end . . . Aladin's the only one who's got the stamina for the job."

"No," contradicted Grits. "Lobster Cocktail's a flier . . ."

Morosely I rifled the pages of the form book, aimlessly looking through them for the hundredth time, and came by chance on the map of Chepstow racecourse in the general-information section at the beginning of the book. There were diagrammatic maps of all the main courses, showing the shape of the tracks and the positioning of the fences, stands, starting gates, and winning posts, and I had looked before at those for Ludlow, Stafford, and Haydock, without results. There was no map of Kelso or Sedgefield. Next to the map section were a few pages of information about the courses, the lengths of their circuits, the names and addresses of the officials, the record times for the races, and so on.

For something to do, I turned to Chepstow's paragraph. Paddy's "long way from the end" was detailed there: 250 yards. I looked up Kelso, Sedgefield, Ludlow, Stafford, and Haydock. They had much longer run-ins than Chepstow. I looked up the run-ins of all the courses in the book. The Aintree Grand National run-in was the second longest. The longest of all was Sedgefield, and in third, fourth, fifth, and sixth positions came Ludlow, Haydock, Kelso, and Stafford. All had run-ins of over four hundred yards.

Geography had nothing to do with it: those five courses had almost certainly been chosen by the dopers because in each case it was about a quarter of a mile from the last fence to the winning post.

It was an advance, even if a small one, to have made at least some pattern out of the chaos. In a slightly less abysmal frame of mind, I shut the form book and at four o'clock followed the other lads out into the unwelcome rain-swept yard to spend an hour with each of my three charges, grooming them thoroughly to give their coats a clean, healthy shine, tossing and tidying their straw beds, fetching their water, holding their heads while Inskip walked around, rugging them up comfortably for the night, and finally fetching their evening feed. As usual it was seven before we had all finished, and eight before we had eaten and changed and were bumping down the hill to Slaw, seven of us sardined into a rickety old Austin.

Bar billiards, darts, dominoes, the endless friendly bragging, the ingredients as before. Patiently I sat and waited. It was nearly ten, the hour when the lads began to empty their glasses and think about having to get up the next morning, when Soupy strolled across the room toward the door and, seeing my eyes on him, jerked his head for me to follow him. I got up and went out after him, and found him in the lavatories.

"This is for you. The rest on Tuesday," he said economically; and treating me to a curled lip and stony stare to impress me with his toughness, he handed me a thick brown envelope. I put it in the inside pocket of my black leather jacket, and nodded to him. Still without speaking, without smiling, hard-eyed to match, I turned on my heel and went back into the bar; and after a while, casually, he followed.

So I crammed into the Austin and was driven up the hill, back to bed in the little dormitory, with seventy-five pounds and a packet of white powder sitting snugly over my heart.

CHAPTER 6

OCTOBER DIPPED HIS finger in the powder and tasted it.

"I don't know what it is either," he said, shaking his head. "I'll get it analyzed."

I bent down and patted his dog, and fondled its ears.

He said, "You do realize what a risk you'll be running if you take his money and don't give the dope to the horse?"

I grinned up at him.

"It's no laughing matter," he said seriously. "They can be pretty free with their boots, these people, and it would be no help to us if you get your ribs kicked in. . . ."

"Actually," I said, straightening up, "I do think it might be best if Sparking Plug didn't win. . . . I could hardly hope to attract custom from the dopers we are really after if they heard I had double-crossed anyone before."

"You're quite right." He sounded relieved. "Sparking Plug must lose; but Inskip . . . how on earth can I tell him that the jockey must put back?"

"You can't," I said. "You don't want them getting into trouble. But it won't matter much if I do. The horse won't win if I keep him thirsty tomorrow morning and give him a bucketful of water just before the race."

He looked at me with amusement. "I see you've learned a thing or two."

"It'd make your hair stand on end, what I've learned."

He smiled back. "All right then. I suppose it's the only thing to do. I wonder what the National Hunt Committee would think of a Steward conspiring with one of his own stable lads to stop a favorite?" He laughed. "I'll tell Roddy Beckett what to expect . . . though it won't be so funny for Inskip, nor for the lads here, if they back the horse, nor for the general public, who'll lose their money."

"No," I agreed.

He folded the packet of white powder and tucked it back into the envelope with the money. The seventy-five pounds had foolishly been paid in a bundle of new fivers with consecutive numbers; and we had agreed that October would take them and try to discover to whom they had been issued.

I told him about the long run-ins on all of the courses where the eleven horses had won.

"It almost sounds as if they might have been using vitamins after all," he said thoughtfully. "You can't detect them in dope tests because technically they are not dope at all, but food. The whole question of vitamins is very difficult."

"They increase stamina?" I asked.

"Yes, quite considerably. Horses that 'die' in the last half mile—and as you pointed out, all eleven are that type—would be ideal subjects. But vitamins were among the first things we considered, and we had to eliminate them. They can help horses to win, if they are injected in massive doses into the bloodstream, and they are undetectable in analysis because they are used up in the winning, but they are undetectable in other ways, too. They don't excite, they don't bring a horse back from a race looking as though Benzedrine were coming out of his ears." He sighed. "I don't know. . . ."

With regret I made my confession that I had learned nothing from Beckett's typescript.

"Neither Beckett nor I expected as much from it as you did," he said. "I've been talking to him a lot this week, and we think that although all those extensive inquiries were made at the time, you might find something that was overlooked if you moved to one of the stables where those eleven horses were trained when they were doped. Of course, eight of the horses were sold and have changed stables, which is a pity, but three are still with their original trainers, and it might be best if you could get a job with one of those."

"Yes," I said. "All right. I'll try all three trainers and see if one of them will take me on. But the trail is very cold by now . . . and joker number twelve will turn up in a different stable altogether. There was nothing, I suppose, at Haydock this week?"

"No. Saliva samples were taken from all the runners before the selling chase, but the favorite won quite normally, and we didn't have the samples analyzed. But now that you've spotted that those five courses must have been chosen deliberately for their long finishing straights, we will keep stricter watches there than ever. Especially if one of those eleven horses runs there again."

"You could check with the racing calendar to see if any have been entered," I agreed. "But so far none of them has been doped twice, and I can't see why the pattern should change."

A gust of bitter wind blew down the gully, and he shivered. The little stream, swollen with yesterday's rains, tumbled busily over its rocky bed. October whistled to his dog, who was sniffing along its banks.

"By the way," he said, shaking hands, "the vets are of the opinion that the horses were not helped on their way by pellets or darts, or anything shot or thrown. But they can't be a hundred percent certain. They didn't at the time examine all the horses very closely. But if we get another one, I'll see they go over every inch looking for punctures."

"Fine." We smiled at each other and turned away. I liked him. He was imaginative and had a sense of humor to leaven the formidable big-business-

executive power of his speech and manner. A tough man, I thought appreciatively; tough in mind, muscular in body, unswerving in purpose: a man of the
kind to have earned an earldom, if he hadn't inherited it.

Sparking Plug had to do without his bucket of water that night and
again the following morning. The box driver set off to Leicester with a pock-
etful of hard-earned money from the lads and their instructions to back the
horse to win; and I felt a traitor.

Inskip's other horse, which had come in the box, too, was engaged in the
third race, but the novice 'chase was not until the fifth race on the card, which
left me free to watch the first two races as well as Sparks' own. I bought a race
card and found a space on the parade-ring rails, and watched the horses for
the first race being led around. Although from the form books I knew the
names of a great many trainers, they were still unknown to me by sight; and
accordingly, when they stood chatting with their jockeys in the ring, I tried,
for interest, to identify some of them. There were only seven of them engaged
in the first race: Owen, Cundell, Beeby, Cazalet, Humber. . . . Humber?
What was it that I had heard about Humber? I couldn't remember. Nothing
very important, I thought.

Humber's horse looked the least well of the lot, and the lad leading him
around wore unpolished shoes, a dirty raincoat, and an air of not caring to im-
prove matters. The jockey's jersey, when he took his coat off, could be seen to
be still grubby with mud from a former outing, and the trainer who had
failed to provide clean colors or to care about stable smartness was a large,
bad-tempered-looking man leaning on a thick, knobbed walking stick.

As it happened, Humber's lad stood beside me on the stand to watch
the race.

"Got much chance?" I asked idly.

"Waste of time running him," he said, his lip curling. "I'm fed to the
back molars with the sod."

"Oh. Perhaps your other horse is better, though?" I murmured, watching
the runners line up for the start.

"My other horse?" He laughed without mirth. "Three others, would you
believe it? I'm fed up with the whole sodding setup. I'm packing it in at the
end of the week, pay or no pay."

I suddenly remembered what I had heard about Humber. The worst stable
in the country to work for, the boy in the Bristol hostel had said; they starved
the lads and knocked them about and could only get riffraff to work there.

"How do you mean, pay or no pay?" I asked.

"Humber pays sixteen quid a week, instead of eleven," he said, "but it's not bloody worth it. I've had a bellyful of bloody Humber. I'm getting out."

The race started, and we watched Humber's horse finish last. The lad disappeared, muttering, to lead it away.

I smiled, followed him down the stairs, and forgot him, because waiting near the bottom step was a seedy, black-mustached man whom I instantly recognized as having been in the bar at the Cheltenham dance.

I walked slowly away to lean over the parade-ring rail, and he inconspicuously followed. He stopped beside me, and with his eyes on the one horse already in the ring, he said, "I hear that you are hard up."

"Not after today, I'm not," I said, looking him up and down.

He glanced at me briefly. "Oh. Are you so sure of Sparking Plug?"

"Yeah," I said with an unpleasant smirk. "Certain." Someone, I reflected, had been kind enough to tell him which horse I looked after; which meant he had been checking up on me. I trusted he had learned nothing to my advantage.

"Hmm."

A whole minute passed. Then he said casually, "Have you ever thought of changing your job . . . going to another stable?"

"I've thought of it," I admitted, shrugging. "Who hasn't?"

"There's always a market for good lads," he pointed out, "and I've heard you're a dab hand at the mucking out. With a reference from Inskip you could get in anywhere, if you told them you were prepared to wait for a vacancy."

"Where?" I asked; but he wasn't to be hurried. After another minute he said, still conversationally, "It can be very . . . er . . . lucrative . . . working for some stables."

"Oh?"

"That is"—he coughed discreetly—"if you are ready to do a bit more than the stable tells you to."

"Such as?"

"Oh . . . general duties," he said vaguely. "It varies. Anything helpful to . . . er . . . the person who is prepared to supplement your income."

"And who's that?"

He smiled thinly. "Look upon me as his agent. How about it? His terms are a regular fiver a week for information about the results of training gallops and things like that, and a good bonus for occasional special jobs of a more . . . er . . . risky nature."

"It don't sound bad," I said slowly, sucking in my lower lip. "Can't I do it at Inskip's?"

"Inskip's is not a betting stable," he said. "The horses always run to win. We do not need a permanent employee in that sort of place. There are, however, at present two betting stables without a man of ours in them, and you would be useful in either."

He named two leading trainers, neither of whom was one of the three people I had already planned to apply to. I would have to decide whether it would not be more useful to join what was clearly a well-organized spy system than to work with a once-doped horse who would almost certainly not be doped again.

"I'll think it over," I said. "Where can I get in touch with you?"

"Until you're on the payroll, you can't," he said simply. "Sparking Plug's in the fifth, I see. Well, you can give me your answer after that race. I'll be somewhere on your way back to the stables. Just nod if you agree, and shake your head if you don't. But I can't see you passing up a chance like this, not one of your sort." There was a sly contempt in the smile he gave me that made me unexpectedly wince inwardly.

He turned away and walked a few steps, and then came back.

"Should I have a big bet on Sparking Plug, then?" he asked.

"Oh . . . er . . . well . . . if I were you, I'd save your money."

He looked surprised, and then suspicious, and then knowing. "So that's how the land lies," he said. "Well, well, well." He laughed, looking at me as if I'd crawled out from under a stone. He was a man who despised his tools. "I can see you're going to be very useful to us. Very useful indeed."

I watched him go. It wasn't from kindheartedness that I had stopped him from backing Sparking Plug, but because it was the only way to retain and strengthen his confidence. When he was fifty yards away, I followed him. He made straight for the bookmakers in Tattersall's and strolled along the rows, looking at the odds displayed by each firm; but as far as I could see, he was in fact innocently planning to bet on the next race, and not reporting to anyone the outcome of his talk with me. Sighing, I put ten shillings on an outsider and went back to watch the horses go out for the race.

Sparking Plug thirstily drank two full buckets of water, stumbled over the second from the last fence, and cantered tiredly in behind the other seven runners to the accompaniment of boos from the cheaper enclosure. I watched him with regret. It was a thankless way to treat a greathearted horse.

The seedy, black-mustached man was waiting when I led the horse away to the stables. I nodded to him, and he sneered knowingly back.

"You'll hear from us," he said.

There was gloom in the box going home and in the yard the next day over Sparking Plug's unexplainable defeat, and I went alone to Slaw on Tuesday evening, when Soupy handed over another seventy-five pounds. I checked it. Another fifteen new fivers, consecutive to the first fifteen.

"Ta," I said. "What do you get out of this yourself?"

Soupy's full mouth curled. "I do all right. You mugs take the risks, I get a cut for setting you up. Fair enough, eh?"

"Fair enough. How often do you do this sort of thing?" I tucked the envelope of money into my pocket.

He shrugged, looking pleased with himself. "I can spot blokes like you a mile off. Inskip must be slipping, though. First time I've known him to pick a bent penny, like. But those dart matches come in very handy. . . . I'm good, see. I'm always in the team. And there's a lot of stables in Yorkshire . . . with a lot of beaten favorites for people to scratch their heads over."

"You're very clever," I said.

He smirked. He agreed.

I walked up the hill planning to light a fuse under T.N.T., the high-explosive kid.

IN VIEW OF the black-mustached man's offer, I decided to read through Beckett's typescript yet again, to see if the eleven dopings could have been the result of systematic spying. Looking at things from a fresh angle might produce results, I thought, and also might help me make up my mind whether or not to back out of the spying job and go to one of the doped horses' yards as arranged.

Locked in the bathroom, I began again at page one. On page sixty-seven, fairly early in the life history of the fifth of the horses, I read: "Bough at Ascot Sales, by D. L. Mentiff, Esq., of York for 420 guineas, passed on for 500 pounds to H. Humber of Posset, County Durham, remained three months, ran twice unplaced in maiden hurdles, subsequently sold again, at Doncaster, being bought for 600 guineas by N. W. Davies, Esq., of Leeds. Sent by him to L. Peterson's training stables at Mars Edge, Staffs, remained eighteen months, ran in four maiden hurdles, five novice chases, all without being placed. Races listed below." Three months at Humber's. I smiled. It appeared that horses didn't stay with him any longer than lads. I plowed on through the details, page after solid page.

On page ninety-four I came across the following: "Alamo was then offered for public auction at Kelso, and a Mr. John Arbuthnot, living in Berwickshire, paid 300 guineas for him. He sent him to be trained by H. Humber at Posset, County Durham, but he was not entered for any races, and Mr. Arbuthnot sold him to Humber for the same sum. A few weeks later he was sent for resale at Kelso. This time Alamo was bought for 375 guineas by a Mr. Clement Smithson, living at Nantwick, Cheshire, who kept him at home for the summer and then sent him to a trainer called Samuel Martin at Malton, Yorkshire, where he ran unplaced in four maiden hurdles before Christmas (see list attached)."

I massaged my stiff neck. Humber again.

I read on.

On page 180, I read: "Ridgeway was then acquired as a yearling by a farmer, James Green, of Home Farm, Crayford, Surrey, in settlement of a bad debt. Mr. Green put him out to grass for two years, and had him broken in, hoping he would be a good hunter. However, a Mr. Taplow of Pusey, Wilts, said he would like to buy him and put him in training for racing. Ridgeway was trained for flat races by Ronald Streat of Pusey, but was unplaced in all his four races that summer. Mr. Taplow then sold Ridgeway privately to Albert George, farmer of Bridge Lewes, Shropshire, who tried to train him himself but said he found he didn't have time to do it properly, so he sold him to a man a cousin of his knew near Durham, a trainer called Hedley Humber. Humber apparently thought the horse was no good, and Ridgeway went up for auction at Newmarket in November, fetching 290 guineas and being bought by Mr. P. J. Brewer, of the Manor, Witherby, Lancs. . . ."

I plowed right on to the end of the typescript, threading my way through the welter of names, but Humber was not mentioned anywhere again.

Three of the eleven horses had been in Humber's yard for a brief spell at some distant time in their careers. That was all it amounted to.

I rubbed my eyes, which were gritty from lack of sleep, and an alarm clock rang suddenly, clamorously, in the silent cottage. I looked at my watch in surprise. It was already half-past six. Standing up and stretching, I made use of the bathroom facilities, thrust the typescript up under my pajama jacket and the jersey I wore on top, and shuffled back yawning to the dormitory, where the others were already up and struggling puffy-eyed into their clothes.

Down in the yard it was so cold that everything one touched seemed to suck the heat out of one's fingers, leaving them numb and fumbling, and the air was as intense an internal shaft to the chest as iced coffee sliding down the esophagus. Muck out the boxes, saddle up, ride up to the moor, canter, walk, ride down again, brush the sweat off, make the horse comfortable, give it food and water, and go in to breakfast. Repeat for the second horse, repeat for the third, and go into lunch.

While we were eating, Wally came in and told two others and me to go and clean the tack, and when we had finished our canned plums and custard, we went along to the tack room and started on the saddles and bridles. It was warm there from the stove, and I put my head back on a saddle and fell solidly asleep.

One of the others jogged my legs and said, "Wake up, Dan, there's a lot to do," and I drifted to the surface again. But before I opened my eyes the other lad said, "Oh, leave him, he does his share," and with blessings on his head, I sank back into blackness. Four o'clock came too soon, and with it the three hours of evening stables: then supper at seven and another day nearly done.

For most of the time I thought about Humber's name cropping up three times in the typescript. I couldn't really see that it was of more significance than that four of the eleven horses had been fed on horse cubes at the time of their doping. What was disturbing was that I should have missed it entirely on my first two readings. I realized that I had had no reason to notice the name Humber before seeing him and his horse and talking to his lad at Leicester, but if I had missed one name occurring three times, I could have missed others as well. The thing to do would be to make lists of every single name mentioned in the typescript, and see if any other turned up in association with several of the horses. An electric computer could have done it in seconds. For me, it looked like another night in the bathroom.

There were more than a thousand names in the typescript. I listed half of them on Wednesday night, and slept a bit, and finished them on Thursday night, and slept some more.

On Friday the sun shone for a change, and the morning was beautiful on the moor. I trotted Sparking Plug along the track somewhere in the middle of the string and thought about the lists. No names except Humber's and one other occurred in connection with more than two of the horses. But the one other was a certain Paul J. Adams, and he had at one time or another owned six of them. Six out of eleven. It couldn't be a coincidence. The odds against it were phenomenal. I was certain I had made my first really useful discovery, yet I couldn't see why the fact that P. J. Adams, Esq., had owned a horse for a few months once should enable it to be doped a year or two later. I puzzled over it all morning without a vestige of understanding.

As it was a fine day, Wally said, it was a good time for me to scrub some rugs. This meant laying the rugs the horses wore to keep them warm in their boxes flat on the concrete in the yard, soaking them with the aid of a hose pipe, scrubbing them with a long-handled broom and detergent, hosing them off again, and hanging the wet rugs on the fence to drip before they were trans-ferred to the warm tack room to finish drying thoroughly. It was an unpopu-lar job, and Wally, who had treated me even more coldly since Sparking Plug's disgrace (though he had not gone so far as to accuse me of engineering it), could hardly conceal his dislike when he told me that it was my turn to do it.

However, I reflected, as I laid out five rugs after lunch and thoroughly soaked them with water, I had two hours to be alone and think. And as so of-ten happens, I was wrong.

At three o'clock, when the horses were dozing and the lads were either copying them or had made quick trips to Harrogate with their new pay en-velopes; when stable life was at its siesta and only I with my broom showed signs of reluctant activity, Patty Tarren walked in through the gate, across the tarmac, and slowed to a halt a few feet away.

She was wearing a straightish dress of soft-looking knobbly green tweed with a row of silver buttons from throat to hem. Her chestnut hair hung in a clean shining bob on her shoulders and was held back from her forehead by a wide green band, and with her fluffy eyelashes and pale-pink mouth, she looked about as enticing an interruption as a hard-worked stable hand could ask for.

"Hullo, Danny boy," she said.

"Good afternoon, miss."

"I saw you from my window," she said.

I turned in surprise, because I had thought October's house entirely hid-den by trees, but sure enough, up the slope, one stone corner and window could be seen through a gap in the leafless boughs. It was, however, a long way off. If Patty recognized me from that distance, she had been using binoculars.

"You looked a bit lonely, so I came down to talk to you."

"Thank you, miss."

"As a matter of fact," she said, lowering her eyelashes, "the rest of the family don't get here until this evening, and I had nothing to do in that barn of a place all by myself, and I was bored. So I thought I'd come down and talk to you."

"I see." I leaned on the broom, looking at her lovely face and thinking that there was an expression in her eyes too old for her years.

"It's rather cold out here, don't you think? I want to talk to you about something. . . . Don't you think we could stand in the shelter of that doorway?" Without waiting for an answer, she walked toward the doorway in question, which was that of the hay barn, and went inside. I followed her, resting the broom against the doorpost on the way.

"Yes, miss?" I said. The light was dim in the barn.

It appeared that talking was not her main object after all.

She put her hands around the back of my neck and offered her mouth for a kiss. I bent my head and kissed her. She was no virgin, October's daughter. She kissed with her tongue and with her teeth, and she moved her stomach rhythmically against mine. My muscles turned to knots. She smelled sweetly fresh of soap, more innocent than her behavior.

"Well . . . that's all right, then," she said with a giggle, disengaging herself and heading for the bulk of the bales of hay which half filled the barn.

"Come on," she said over her shoulder, and climbed up the bales to the flat level at the top. I followed her slowly. When I got to the top, I sat looking down at the hay-barn floor with the broom, the bucket, and the rug touched with sunshine through the doorway. On top of the hay had been Philip's favorite play place for years when he was little . . . and this is a fine time to think of my family, I thought.

Patty was lying on her back three feet away from me. Her eyes were wide and glistening, and her mouth curved open in an odd little smile. Slowly, holding my gaze, she undid all the silver buttons down the front of her dress to a point well below her waist. Then she gave a little shake so that the edges of the dress fell apart.

She had absolutely nothing on underneath.

I looked at her body, which was pearl pink and slender, and very desirable; and she gave a little rippling shiver of anticipation.

I looked back at her face. Her eyes were big and dark, and the odd way in which she was smiling suddenly struck me as being half furtive, half greedy;

and wholly sinful. I had an abrupt vision of myself as she must see me, as I had seen myself in the long mirror in October's London house, a dark, flashy-looking stableboy with an air of deceitfulness and an acquaintance with dirt.

I understood her smile then.

I turned around where I sat until I had my back to her, and felt a flush of anger and shame spread all over my body.

"Do your dress up," I said.

"Why? Are you impotent after all, Danny boy?"

"Do your dress up," I repeated. "The party's over."

I slid down the hay, walked across the floor and out of the door without looking back. Twitching up the broom and cursing under my breath, I let out my fury against myself by scrubbing the rug until my arms ached.

After a while I saw her—her dress rebuttoned—come slowly out of the hay barn, look around her, and go across to a muddy puddle on the edge of the tarmac. She dirtied her shoes thoroughly in it, then childishly walked onto the rug I had just cleaned, and wiped all the mud off carefully in the center.

Her eyes were wide and her face expressionless as she looked at me.

"You'll be sorry, Danny boy," she said, and without haste strolled away down the yard, the chestnut hair swinging gently on the green tweed dress.

I scrubbed the rug again. Why had I kissed her? Why, after knowing about her from that kiss, had I followed her up into the hay? Why had I been such a stupid, easily roused, lusting fool? I was filled with useless dismay.

One didn't have to accept an invitation to dinner, even if the appetizer made one hungry. But having accepted, one should not so brutally reject what was offered. She had every right to be angry.

And I had every reason to be confused. I had been for nine years a father of two girls, one of whom was nearly Patty's age. I had taught them when they were little not to take lifts from strangers and when they were bigger how to avoid more subtle snares. And here I was, indisputably on the other side of the parental fence.

I felt an atrocious sense of guilt toward October, for I had had the intention, and there was no denying it, of doing what Patty wanted.

CHAPTER 7

IT WAS ELINOR who rode out on my horse the following morning, and Patty, having obviously got her to change mounts, studiously refused to look at me at all.

Elinor, a dark scarf protecting most of the silver-blond hair, accepted a leg up with impersonal grace, gave me a warm smile of thanks, and rode away at the head of the string with her sister. When we got back after the gallops, however, she led the horse into its box and did half of the jobs for it while I was attending to Sparking Plug. I didn't know what she was doing until I walked down the yard, and was surprised to find her there, having grown used to Patty's habit of bolting the horse into the box still complete with saddle, bridle, and mud.

"You go and get the hay and water," she said. "I'll finish getting the dirt off, now I've started."

I carried away the saddle and bridle to the tack room, and took back the hay and water. Elinor gave the horse's mane a few final strokes with the brush, and I put on his rug and buckled the roller around his belly. She watched while I tossed the straw over the floor to make a comfortable bed, and waited until I had bolted the door.

"Thank you," I said. "Thank you very much."

She smiled faintly. "It's a pleasure. It really is. I like horses. Especially racehorses. Lean and fast and exciting."

"Yes," I agreed. We walked down the yard together, she to go to the gate and I to the cottage which stood beside it.

"They are so different from what I do all the week," she said.

"What do you do all week?"

"Oh . . . study. I'm at Durham University." There was a sudden, private, recollecting grin. Not for me. On level terms, I thought, one might find more in Elinor than good manners.

"It's really extraordinary how well you ride," she said suddenly. "I heard

Mr. Inskip telling Father this morning that it would be worth getting a license for you. Have you ever thought of racing?"

"I wish I could," I said fervently, without thinking.

"Well, why not?"

"Oh . . . I might be leaving soon."

"What a pity." It was polite; nothing more.

We reached the cottage. She gave me a friendly smile and walked straight on, out of the yard, out of sight. I may not ever see her again, I thought; and was mildly sorry.

WHEN THE HORSE box came back from a day's racing (with a winner, a third, and an also-ran), I climbed up into the cab and borrowed the map again. I wanted to discover the location of the village where Mr. Paul Adams lived, and after some searching I found it. As its significance sank in, I began to smile with astonishment. There was, it seemed, yet another place where I could apply for a job.

I went back into the cottage, into Mrs. Alnutt's cosy kitchen, and ate Mrs. Alnutt's delicious eggs and chips and bread and butter and fruitcake, and later slept dreamlessly on Mrs. Alnutt's lumpy mattress, and in the morning bathed luxuriously in Mrs. Alnutt's shining bathroom. And in the afternoon I went up beside the stream with at last something worthwhile to tell October.

He met me with a face of granite, and before I could say a word he hit me hard and squarely across the mouth. It was a backhanded expert blow which started from the waist, and I didn't see it coming until far too late.

"What the hell's that for?" I said, running my tongue around my teeth and being pleased to find that none of them were broken off.

He glared at me. "Patty told me . . ." He stopped as if it was too difficult to go on.

"Oh," I said blankly.

"Yes, oh," he mimicked savagely. He was breathing deeply and I thought he was going to hit me again. I thrust my hands into my pockets and his stayed where they were, down by his sides, clenching and unclenching.

"What did Patty tell you?"

"She told me everything." His anger was almost tangible. "She came to me this morning in tears . . . she told me how you made her go into the hay barn . . . and held her there until she was worn out with struggling to get away . . . She told the . . . the disgusting things you did to her with your hands . . . and then how you forced her . . . forced her to . . ." He couldn't say it.

I was appalled. "I didn't," I said vehemently. "I didn't do anything like that. I kissed her . . . and that's all. She's making it up."

"She couldn't possibly have made it up. It was too detailed. . . . She couldn't know such things unless they had happened to her."

I opened my mouth and shut it again. They had happened to her, right enough; somewhere, with someone else, more than once, and certainly also with her willing cooperation. And I could see that to some extent at least she was going to get away with her horrible revenge, because there are some things you can't say about a girl to her father, especially if you like him.

October said scathingly, "I have never been so mistaken in a man before. I thought you were responsible . . . or at least able to control yourself. Not a cheap lecherous jackanapes who would take my money—and my regard— and amuse yourself behind my back, debauching my daughter."

There was enough truth in that to hurt, but the guilt I felt over my stupid behavior didn't help. But I had to put up some kind of defense, because I would never have harmed Patty in any way and there was still the investigation into the doping to be carried on. Now that I had got so far, I did not want to be packed off home in disgrace.

I said slowly, "I did go with Patty into the hay barn. I did kiss her. Once. Only once. After that I didn't touch her. I literally didn't touch any part of her, not her hand, not her dress . . . nothing."

He looked at me steadily for a long time while the fury slowly died out of him and a sort of weariness took its place.

At length he said, almost calmly, "One of you is lying. And I have to believe my daughter." There was an unexpected flicker of entreaty in his voice.

"Yes," I said. I looked away, up the gully. "Well . . . this solves one problem, anyway."

"What problem?"

"How to leave here with the ignominious sack and without a reference."

It was so far away from what he was thinking about that it was several moments before he showed any reaction at all, and then he gave me an attentive, narrow-eyed stare which I did not try to avoid.

"You intend to go on with the investigation, then?"

"If you are willing."

"Yes," he said heavily, at length. "Especially as you are moving on and will have no more opportunities of seeing Patty. In spite of what I personally think of you, you do still represent our best hope of success, and I suppose I must put the good of racing first."

He fell silent. I contemplated the rather grim prospect of continuing to do that sort of work for a man who hated me. Yet the thought of giving up was worse. And that was odd.

Eventually he said, "Why do you want to leave without a reference? You won't get a job in any of these three·stables without a reference."

"The only reference I need to get a job in the stable I am going to is no reference at all."

"Whose stable?"

"Hedley Humber's."

"Humber!" He was somberly incredulous. "But why? He's a very poor trainer and he didn't train any of the doped horses. What's the point of going there?"

"He didn't train any of the horses when they won," I agreed, "but he had three of them through his hands earlier in their careers. There is also a man called P. J. Adams who at one time or another owned six more of them. Adams lives, according to the map, less than ten miles from Humber. Humber lives at Posset, in Durham, and Adams at Tellbridge, just over the Northumberland border. That means that nine of the eleven horses spent some time in that one small area of the British Isles. None of them stayed long. The dossiers of Transistor and Rudyard are much less detailed than the others on the subject of their earlier life, and I have now no doubt that check- ing would show that they, too, for a short while, came under the care of either Adams or Humber."

"But how could the horses' having spent some time with Adams or Humber possibly affect their speeds months or years later?"

"I don't know," I said. "But I'll go and find out."

There was a pause.

"Very well," he said heavily. "I'll tell Inskip that you are to be dismissed. And I'll tell him it is because you pestered Patricia."

"Right."

He looked at me coldly. "You can write me reports. I don't want to see you again."

I watched him walk away strongly up the gully. I didn't know whether or not he really believed any more that I had done what Patty said; but I did know that he needed to believe it. The alternative, the truth, was so much worse. What father wants to discover that his beautiful eighteen-year-old daughter is a lying slut?

And as for me, I thought that on the whole I had got off lightly; if I had found that anyone had assaulted Belinda or Helen, I'd have half killed him.

AFTER THE SECOND exercise the following day, Inskip told me exactly what he thought of me, and I didn't particularly enjoy it.

After giving me a public dressing-down in the center of the tarmac (with the lads grinning in sly amusement as they carried their buckets and hay nets, with both ears flapping), he handed back the insurance card and income tax form—there was still a useful muddle going on over the illegible Cornish address on the one October had originally provided me with—and told me to pack my bags and get out of the yard at once. It would be no use giving his name as a reference, he said, because Lord October had expressly forbidden him to vouch for my character, and it was a decision with which he thoroughly agreed. He gave me a week's wages in lieu of notice, less Mrs. Alnutt's share, and that was that.

I packed my things in the little dormitory, patted good-bye to the bed I had slept in for six weeks, and went down to the kitchen, where the lads were having their midday meal. Eleven pairs of eyes swiveled in my direction. Some were contemptuous, some were surprised, one or two thought it funny. None of them looked sorry to see me go. Mrs. Alnutt gave me a thick cheese sandwich, and I ate it walking down the hill to Slaw to catch the two-o'clock bus to Harrogate.

And from Harrogate, where?

No lad in his senses would go straight from a prosperous place like Inskip's to ask for a job at Humber's, however abruptly he had been thrown out; there had to be a period of some gentle sliding downhill if it was to look unsuspicious. In fact, I decided, it would be altogether much better if it was Humber's head traveling lad who offered me work, and not I who asked for it. It should not be too difficult. I could turn up at every course where Humber had a runner, looking seedier and seedier and more and more ready to take any job at all, and one day the lad-hungry stable would take the bait.

Meanwhile I needed somewhere to live. The bus trundled down to Harrogate while I thought it out. Somewhere in the northeast, to be near Humber's local meetings. A big town, so that I could be anonymous in it. An alive town, so that I could find ways of passing the time between race meetings. With the help of maps and guidebooks in Harrogate public library, I settled on Newcastle, and with the help of a couple of tolerant truck drivers, I arrived there late that afternoon and found myself a room in a backstreet hotel.

It was a terrible room with peeling, coffee-colored walls, tatty printed linoleum wearing out on the floor, a narrow, hard divan bed, and some scratched furniture made out of stained plywood. Only its unexpected cleanliness and a shiny new washbasin in one corner made it bearable, but it did, I had to admit, suit my appearance and purpose admirably.

I dined in a fish-and-chip shop for three and six, and went to a cinema, and enjoyed not having to groom three horses or think twice about every word I said. My spirits rose several points at being free again and I succeeded in forgetting the trouble I was in with October.

In the morning I sent off to him in a registered package the second seventy-five pounds, which I had not given him in the gully on Sunday, together with a short formal note explaining why there would have to be a delay before I engaged myself to Humber.

From the post office I went to a betting shop and from their calendar copied down all the racing fixtures for the next month. It was the beginning of December, and I found there were very few meetings in the north before the first week in January; which was, from my point of view, a waste of time and a nuisance. After the following Saturday's program at Newcastle itself there was no racing north of Nottinghamshire until Boxing Day, more than a fortnight later.

Pondering this setback, I next went in search of a serviceable secondhand motorcycle. It took me until late afternoon to find exactly what I wanted, a souped-up 500-cc Norton, four years old and the ex-property of a now one-legged young man who had done the ton once too often on the Great North Road. The salesman gave me these details with relish as he took my money and assured me that the bike would still do a hundred at a push. I thanked him politely and left the machine with him to have a new silencer fitted, along with some new hand grips, brake cables, and tires.

Lack of private transport at Slaw had not been a tremendous drawback, and I would not have been concerned about my mobility at Posset were it not for the one obtrusive thought that I might at some time find it advisable to depart in a hurry. I could not forget the journalist, Tommy Stapleton. Between Hexham and Yorkshire he had lost eight hours, and turned up dead. Between Hexham and Yorkshire lay Posset.

THE FIRST PERSON I saw at Newcastle races four days later was the man with the black mustache who had offered me steady employment as a stable spy. He was standing in an unobtrusive corner near the entrance, talking to a big-eared boy whom I later saw leading around a horse from one of the best-known gambling stables in the country.

From some distance away I watched him pass to the boy a white envelope and receive a brown envelope in return. Money for information, I thought, and so openly done as to appear innocent.

I strolled along behind Black Mustache when he finished his transaction and made his way to the bookmakers' stands in Tattersall's. As before, he appeared to be doing nothing but examining the prices offered on the first race; and as before I staked a few shillings on the favorite in case I should be seen to be following him. In spite of his survey, he placed no bets at all, but strolled down to the rails that separated the enclosure from the course itself. There he came to an unplanned-looking halt beside an artificial redhead wearing a yellowish leopard-skin jacket over a dark-gray skirt.

She turned her head toward him, and they spoke. Presently he took the brown envelope from his breast pocket and slipped it into his race card; and after a few moments he and the woman unobtrusively exchanged race cards. He wandered away from the rails, while she put the card containing the envelope into a large, shiny black handbag and snapped it shut. From the shelter of the last row of bookies I watched her walk to the entrance into the club and pass through onto the members' lawn. I could not follow her there, but I went up onto the stands and watched her walk across the next-door enclosure. She appeared to be well known. She stopped and spoke to several people—a bent old man with a big floppy hat, an obese young man who patted her arm repeatedly, a pair of women in mink cocoons, a group of three men who laughed loudly and hid her from my view so I could not see if she had given any of them the envelope from her handbag.

The horses cantered down the course and the crowds moved up onto the stands to watch the race. The redhead disappeared among the throng on the members' stand, leaving me frustrated at losing her. The race was run, and the favorite cantered in by ten lengths. The crowd roared with approval.

While people around me flowed down from the stands, I stood where I was, waiting without too much hope to see if the leopard-skin redhead would reappear.

Obligingly, she did. She was carrying her handbag in one hand, her race card in the other. Pausing to talk again, this time to a very short fat man, she eventually made her way over to the bookmakers who stood along the rails separating Tattersall's from the club and stopped in front of one nearest the stands, and nearest to me. For the first time I could see her face clearly: she was younger than I had thought and plainer of feature, with gaps between her top teeth.

She said in a piercing, tinny voice, "I'll settle my account, Bimmo dear," and opening her handbag, took out a brown envelope and gave it to a small man in spectacles, who stood on a box beside a board bearing the words: BIMMO BOGNOR (EST. 1920), MANCHESTER AND LONDON.

Mr. Bimmo Bognor took the envelope and put it in his jacket pocket, and his hearty "Ta, love" floated up to my attentive ears.

I went down from the stands and collected my small winnings, thinking that while the brown envelope that the redhead had given to Bimmo Bognor *looked* like the envelope that the big-eared lad had given to Black Mustache, I could not be a hundred percent sure of it. She might have given the lad's envelope to any one of the people I had watched her talk to, or to anyone on the stands while she was out of my sight; and she might then have gone quite honestly to pay her bookmaker.

If I wanted to be certain of the chain, perhaps I could send an urgent message along it, a message so urgent that there would be no wandering among the crowds, but an unconcealed direct line between a and b, and b and c. The urgent message, since Sparking Plug was a runner in the fifth race, presented no difficulty at all; but being able to locate Black Mustache at exactly the right moment entailed keeping him in sight all the afternoon.

He was a creature of habit, which helped. He always watched the races from the same corner of the stand, patronized the same bar between times, and stood inconspicuously near the gate onto the course when the horses were led out of the parade ring. He did not bet.

Humber had two horses at the meeting, one in the third race and one in the last; and although it meant leaving my main purpose untouched until late in the afternoon, I let the third race go by without making any attempt to find his head traveling lad. I padded slowly along behind Black Mustache instead.

After the fourth race I followed him into the bar and jogged his arm violently as he began to drink. Half of his beer splashed over his hand and ran down his sleeve, and he swung around cursing, to find my face nine inches from his own.

"Sorry," I said. "Oh, it's you." I put as much surprise into my voice as I could.

His eyes narrowed. "What are you doing here? Sparking Plug runs in this race."

I scowled. "I've left Inskip's."

"Have you got one of the jobs I suggested? Good."

"Not yet. There might be a bit of a delay there, like."

"Why? No vacancies?"

"They don't seem all that keen to have me since I got chucked out of Inskip's."

"You got what?" he said sharply.

"Chucked out of Inskip's," I repeated.

"Why?"

"They said something about Sparking Plug losing last week on the day you spoke to me . . . said they could prove nothing but they didn't want me around no more, and to get out."

"That's too bad," he said, edging away.

"But I got the last laugh," I said, sniggering and holding on to his arm. "I'll tell you straight, I got the bloody last laugh."

"What do you mean?" He didn't try to keep the contempt out of his voice, but there was interest in his eyes.

"Sparking Plug won't win today neither," I stated. "He won't win because he'll feel bad in his stomach."

"How do you know?"

"I soaked his salt lick with liquid paraffin," I said. "Every day since I left on Monday he's been rubbing his tongue on a laxative. He won't be feeling like racing. He won't bloody win, he won't." I laughed.

Black Mustache gave me a sickened look, pried my fingers off his arm, and hurried out of the bar. I followed him carefully. He almost ran down into Tattersall's, and began frantically looking around. The redheaded woman was nowhere to be seen, but she must have been watching, because presently I saw her walking briskly down the rails, to the same spot where they had met before. And there, with a rush, she was joined by Black Mustache. He talked vehemently. She listened and nodded. He then turned away more calmly, and walked away out of Tattersall's and back to the parade ring. The woman waited until he was out of sight; then she walked firmly into the members' enclosure and along the rails until she came to Bimmo Bognor. The little man leaned forward over the rails as she spoke earnestly into his ear. He nodded several times and she began to smile, and when he turned around to talk to his clerks, I saw that he was smiling broadly, too.

Unhurriedly I walked along the rows of bookmakers, studying the odds they offered. Sparking Plug was not favorite, owing to his waterlogged defeat last time out, but no one would chance more than five to one. At that price I staked forty pounds—my entire earnings at Inskip's—on my old charge, choosing a prosperous, jolly-looking bookmaker in the back row.

Hovering within earshot of Mr. Bimmo Bognor a few minutes later, I heard him offer seven to one against Sparking Plug to a stream of clients, and watched him rake in their money, confident that he would not have to pay them out.

Smiling contentedly, I climbed to the top of the stands and watched Sparking Plug make mincemeat of his opponents over the fences and streak insultingly home by twenty lengths. It was a pity, I reflected, that I was too far away to hear Mr. Bognor's opinion of the result.

My jolly bookmaker handed me 240 pounds in fivers without a second glance. To avoid Black Mustache and any reprisals he might be thinking of organizing, I then went over to the cheap enclosure in the center of the course for twenty boring minutes; returning through the horse gate when the runners were down at the start for the last race, and slipping up the stairs to the stand used by the lads.

Humber's head traveling lad was standing near the top of the stands. I pushed roughly past him and tripped heavily over his feet.

"Look where you're bloody going," he said crossly, focusing a pair of shoebutton eyes on my face.

"Sorry, mate. Got corns, have you?"

"None of your bloody business," he said, looking at me sourly. He would know me again, I thought.

I bit my thumbnail. "Do you know which of this lot is Martin Davies' head traveling lad?" I asked.

He said, "That chap over there with the red scarf. Why?"

"I need a job," I said, and before he could say anything, I left him and pushed along the row to the man in the red scarf. His stable had one horse in the race; I asked him quietly if they ran two, and he shook his head and said no.

Out of the corner of my eye I noticed that this negative answer had not been wasted on Humber's head lad. He probably thought, or so I hoped, that I had asked for work, and had been refused. Satisfied that the seed was planted, I watched the race (Humber's horse finished last) and slipped quietly away from the racecourse via the paddock rails and the members' car park, without any interception of Black Mustache or a vengeful Bimmo Bognor.

A SUNDAY ENDURED half in my dreary room and half walking around the empty streets was enough to convince me that I could not drag through the next fortnight in Newcastle doing nothing, and the thought of a solitary Christmas spent staring at coffee-colored peeling paint was unattractive. Moreover, I had two hundred pounds of bookmakers' money packed into my belt alongside what was left of October's; and Humber had no horses entered before the Stafford meeting on Boxing Day. It took me only ten minutes to decide what to do with the time between.

On Sunday evening I wrote to October a report on Bimmo Bognor's intelligence service, and at one in the morning I caught the express to London.

Monday I spent shopping. I sent off gifts to Belinda and Helen and Philip and wrote to them apologizing in advance for the very few letters they would receive from me during the next weeks. I called at the Bank of Australia and asked them to keep all incoming mail for me until I collected it personally. News from home had been a slight risk and slow. At Posset it would be a dangerous luxury I would have to do without.

On Tuesday evening, looking civilized in some decent new clothes and equipped with an extravagant pair of Kastle skis, I signed the register of a comfortable, bright little hotel in a snow-covered village in the Dolomites.

The fortnight I spent in Italy made no difference one way or another to the result of my work for October, but it made a great deal of difference to me. It was the first real holiday I had had since my parents died, the first utterly carefree, purposeless, self-indulgent break for nine years.

I grew younger. Fast, strenuous days on the snow slopes and a succession of evenings dancing with my skiing companions peeled away the years of responsibility like skins, until at last I felt twenty-seven instead of fifty, a young man instead of a father; until the unburdening process, begun when I left Australia and slowly fermenting through the weeks at Inskip's, suddenly seemed complete.

There was also a bonus in the shape of one of the receptionists, a rounded, glowing girl whose dark eyes lit up the minute she saw me and who, after a minimum of persuasion, uninhibitedly spent a proportion of her nights in my bed. She called me her Christmas box of chocolates. She said I was the happiest lover she had had for a long time, and that I pleased her. She was probably doubly as promiscuous as Patty but she was much more wholesome; and she made me feel terrific instead of ashamed.

On the day I left, when I gave her a gold bracelet, she kissed me and told me not to come back, as things were never as good the second time. She was God's gift to bachelors, that girl.

I flew back to England on Christmas night feeling as physically and mentally fit as I had ever been in my life, and ready to take on the worst that Humber could dish out. Which, as it happened, was just as well.

CHAPTER 8

AT STAFFORD ON Boxing Day one of the runners in the first race, the selling chase, threw off his jockey a stride after landing in fourth place over the last fence, crashed through the rails, and bolted away across the rough grass in the center of the course.

A lad standing near me on the drafty steps behind the weighing room ran off cursing to catch him; but as the horse galloped crazily from one end of the course to the other, it took the lad, the trainer, and about ten assorted helpers a quarter of an hour to lay their hands on his bridle. I watched them as with worried faces they led the horse, an undistinguished bay, off the course and past me toward the racecourse stables.

The wretched animal was white and dripping with sweat and in obvious distress; foam covered his nostrils and muzzle, his eyes rolled wildly in their sockets. His flesh was quivering, his ears lay flat back on his head, and he was inclined to lash out at anyone who came near him.

His name, I saw from the race card, was Superman. He was not one of the eleven horses I had been investigating: but his hotted-up appearance and frantic behavior, coupled with the fact that he had met trouble at Stafford in a selling chase, convinced me that he was the twelfth of the series. The twelfth; and he had come unstuck. There was, as Beckett had said, no mistaking the effect of whatever had pepped him up. I had never before seen a horse in such a state, which seemed to me much worse than the descriptions of "excited winners" I had read in the press cuttings; and I came to the conclusion that Superman was either suffering from an overdose, or had reacted excessively to whatever the others had been given.

Neither October nor Beckett nor Macclesfield had come to Stafford. I could only hope that the precautions October had promised had been put into operation in spite of its being Boxing Day, because I could not, without blowing open my role, ask any of the officials if the pre-race dope tests had been made or other precautions taken, nor insist that the jockey be asked at once for his impressions, that unusual bets should be investigated, and that the horse be thoroughly examined for punctures.

The fact that Superman had safely negotiated all the fences inclined me more and more to believe that he could not have been affected by the stimulant until he was approaching, crossing, or landing over the last. It was there that he had gone wild and, instead of winning, thrown his jockey and decamped. It was there that he had been given the power to sprint the four hundred yards, that long run-in which gave him the time and room to overhaul the leading horses.

The only person on the racecourse to whom I could safely talk was Superman's lad, but because of the state of his horse it was bound to be some time before he came out of the stables. Meanwhile there were more steps to be taken toward getting myself a job with Humber.

I had gone to the meeting with my hair unbrushed, pointed shoes unpolished, leather collar turned up, hands in pockets, sullen expression in place. I looked, and felt, a disgrace.

Changing back that morning into stable-lad clothes had not been a pleasant experience. The sweaters stank of horses, the narrow, cheap trousers looked scruffy, the underclothes were gray from insufficient washing, and the jeans were still filthy with mud and muck. Because of the difficulty of getting them back on Christmas night, I had decided against sending the whole lot to the laundry while I was away, and in spite of my distaste in putting them on again, I didn't regret it. I looked all the more on the way to being down and out.

I had changed and shaved in the cloakroom at the West Kensington Air Terminal, parked my skis and grip of ski clothes in the Left Luggage department of Euston Station, slept uneasily on a hard seat for an hour or two, breakfasted on sandwiches and coffee from the cafeteria, and caught the race train to Stafford. At this rate, I thought wryly, I would have bundles of belongings scattered all over London; because neither on the outward nor on the return journeys had I cared to go to October's London house to make use of the clothes I had left with Terence. I did not want to meet October. I liked him, and saw no joy in facing his bitter resentment again unless I absolutely had to.

Humber had only one runner on Boxing Day, a weedy-looking hurdler in the fourth race. I hung over the rails by the saddling boxes and watched his head traveling lad saddle up, while Humber himself leaned on his knobbed walking stick and gave directions. I had come for a good close look at him, and what I saw was both encouraging from the angle that one could believe him capable of any evil, and discouraging from the angle that I was going to have to obey him.

His large body was encased in a beautifully cut short camel's hair overcoat, below which protruded dark trousers and impeccable shoes. On his head he wore a bowler, set very straight, and on his hands some pale unsoiled pigskin gloves. His face was large, not fat, but hard. Unsmiling eyes, a grim trap of a mouth, and deep lines running from the corners of his nose to his chin gave his expression a look of cold willfulness.

He stood quite still, making no unnecessary fussy movements, the complete opposite of Inskip, who was forever walking busily from side to side of his horse, checking straps and buckles, patting and pulling at the saddle, running his hand down legs, nervously making sure over and over that everything was in order.

In Humber's case it was the boy who held the horse's head who was nervous. Frightened, I thought, was hardly too strong a word for it. He kept giving wary, startled-animal glances at Humber, and staying out of his sight on the far side of the horse as much as possible. He was a thin, ragged-looking boy of about sixteen, and not far, I judged, from being mentally deficient.

The head traveling lad, middle-aged, with a big nose and an unfriendly air, unhurriedly adjusted the saddle and nodded to the lad to lead the horse off into the parade ring. Humber followed. He walked with a slight limp, more or less disguised by the use of the walking stick, and he proceeded in a straight line like a tank, expecting everyone else to get out of his way.

I transferred myself to the parade-ring rails in his wake and watched him give instructions to his jockey, an allowance-claimer who regarded his mount with justified disillusion. It was the head traveling lad, not Humber, who gave the jockey a leg up, and who picked up and carried off with him the horse's rug.

Around the lads' stand, I carefully stood directly in front of the head traveling lad, and in the lull before the race started, I turned sideways and tried to borrow some money from the lad standing next to me, whom I didn't know. Not unexpectedly, but to my relief, the lad refused indignantly and more than loudly enough for Humber's head lad to hear. I hunched my shoulders and resisted the temptation to look around and see if the message had reached its destination.

Humber's horse ran out of energy in the straight and finished second to last. No one was surprised.

After that I stationed myself outside the stable gate to wait for Superman's lad, but he didn't come out for another half hour, until after the fifth race. I fell into step beside him as if by accident, saying, "Rather you than me, chum, with one like that to look after." He asked me who I worked for; I said Inskip, and he loosened up and agreed that a cup of char and a wad would go down a treat, after all that caper.

"Is he always that het up after a race?" I said, halfway through the cheese sandwiches.

"No. Usually he's dog tired. There's been all hell breaking loose this time, I can tell you."

"How do you mean?"

"Well, first they came and took some tests on all the runners before the race. Now I ask you, why before? It's not the thing, is it? Not before. You ever had one done before?"

I shook my head.

"Then, see, old Super, he was putting up the same sort of job he always does, looking as if he is going to come on to a place at least and then packing it in and going into the last. Stupid basket. No guts, I reckon. They had his heart tested, but it ticks O.K. So it's no guts, sure enough. Anyway, then at the last he suddenly kicks up his heels and bolts off as if the devil was after him. I don't suppose you saw him? He's a nervy customer always, really, but he was climbing the wall when we finally caught him. The old man was dead worried. Well, the horse looked as though he had been got at, and he wanted to stick his oar in first and get a dope test done so that the Stewards shouldn't accuse him of using a booster and take away his ruddy license. They had a couple of vets fussing over him taking things to be analyzed—dead funny it was, because old Super was trying to pitch them over the stable walls—and in the end they gave him a jab of something to quieten him down. But how we're going to get him home I don't know."

"Have you looked after him long?" I asked sympathetically.

"Since the beginning of the season. About four months, I suppose. He's a jumpy customer, as I said, but before this I had just about got him to like me. Gawd, I hope he calms down proper before the jab wears off, I do straight."

"Who had him before you?" I asked casually.

"Last year he was in a little stable in Devon with a private trainer called Beaney, I think. Yes, Beaney, that's where he started, but he didn't do any good there."

"I expect they made him nervous there, breaking him in," I said.

"No, now that's a funny thing. I said to one of Beaney's lads when we were down in Devon for one of the August meetings, and he said I must be talking about the wrong horse because Superman was a placid old thing and no trouble. He said if Superman was nervous, it must have been on account of something that had happened during the summer after he left their place and before he came to us."

"Where did he go for the summer?" I asked, picking up the cup of orange-colored tea.

"Search me. The old man bought him at Ascot sales, I think, for a cheap horse. I should think he will shuffle him off again after this if he can get more than knacker's price for him. Poor old Super. Silly nit." The lad stared gloomily into his tea.

"You don't think he went off his rocker today because he was doped, then?"

"I think he just went bonkers," he said. "Stark, staring, raving bonkers. I mean, no one had a chance to dope him, except me and the old man and Chalky, and I didn't, and the old man didn't, because he's not that sort, and you wouldn't think Chalky would either, he's so darn proud being promoted head traveling lad only last month . . ."

We finished our tea and went around to watch the sixth race, still talking about Superman, but his lad knew nothing else which was of help to me.

After the race I walked the half mile into the center of Stafford, and from a telephone booth sent two identical telegrams to October, one to London and one to Slaw, as I did not know where he was. They read: "Request urgent information re Superman, specifically where did he go from Beaney, permit holder, Devon, last May approximately. Answer care Post Restante, Newcastle on Tyne."

I spent the evening, incredibly distant from the gaiety of the day before, watching a dreary musical in a three-quarters-empty cinema, and slept that night in a dingy bed-and-breakfast hotel where they looked me up and down and asked for their money in advance. I paid, wondering if I would ever get used to being treated like dirt. I felt a fresh shock every time. I suppose I had been too accustomed to the respect I was offered in Australia even to notice it, far less appreciate it. I would appreciate some of it now, I ruefully thought, following the landlady into an unwelcoming little room and listening to her suspicious lectures on no cooking, no hot water after eleven, and no girls.

The following afternoon I conspicuously mooched around the front of Humber's head traveling lad with a hangdog and worried expression, and after the races went back by bus and train to Newcastle for the night. In the morning I collected the motorcycle, fitted with the new silencer and other parts, and called at the post office to see if there was a reply from October.

The clerk handed me a letter. Inside, without salutation or signature, there was a single sheet of typescript, which read:

Superman was born and bred in Ireland. Changed hands twice before reaching John Beaney in Devon. He was then sold by Beaney to H. Humber, Esq., of Posset, Co. Durham, on May 3. Humber sent him to Ascot sales in July, where he was bought by his present trainer for 260 guineas.

Investigations re Superman at Stafford yesterday are all so far uninformative; dope analyses have still to be completed but there is little hope they will show anything. The veterinary surgeon at the course was as convinced as you apparently were that this is another "joker," and made a thorough examination of the horse's skin. There were no visible punctures except the ones he made himself giving the horse sedation.

Superman was apparently in a normal condition before the race. His jockey reports all normal until the last fence, when the horse seemed to suffer a sort of convulsion, and ejected him from the saddle.

Further inquiries re Rudyard revealed he was bought four winters ago by P. J. Adams of Tellbridge, Northumberland, and sold again within a short time at Ascot. Transistor was bought by Adams at Doncaster three years ago, sold Newmarket Dispersal Sales three months later.

Inquiries re thirty consecutive five-pound notes reveal they were issued by Barclays Bank, Birmingham New Street branch, to a man called Lewis Greenfield, who corresponds exactly to your description of the man who approached you in Slaw. Proceedings against Greenfield and T. N. Tarleton are in hand, but will be held in abeyance until after your main task is completed.

Your report on Bimmo Bognor is noted, but as you say, the buying of stable information is not a punishable offense in law. No proceedings are at present contemplated, but warning that a spy system is in operation will be given privately to certain trainers.

I tore the page up and scattered it in the litter basket, then went back to the motorcycle and put it through its paces down the A1 to Catterick. It handled well, and I enjoyed the speed and found it quite true that it would still do a hundred.

At Catterick that Saturday Humber's head traveling lad rose like a trout to the fly.

Inskip had sent two runners, one of which was looked after by Paddy; and up on the lads' stand before the second race I saw the sharp little Irishman and Humber's head lad talking earnestly together. I was afraid that Paddy might relent toward me enough to say something in my favor, but I needn't have worried. He put my mind at rest himself.

"You're a bloody young fool," he said, looking me over from my unkempt head to my grubby toes. "And you've only got what you deserve. That man of Humber's was asking me about you, why you got the kick from Inskip's, and I told him the real reason, not all that eyewash about messing about with his nibs' daughter."

"What real reason?" I asked, surprised.

His mouth twisted in contempt. "People talk, you know. You don't think they keep their traps shut, when there's a good bit of gossip going around? You don't think that Grits didn't tell me how you got drunk at Cheltenham and blew your mouth off about Inskip's? And what you said at Bristol about being willing to put the finger on the horse's box in the yard . . . well, that got around to me, too. And thick as thieves with that crook Soupy you were, as well. And there was that time when we all put our wages on Sparking Plug and he didn't go a yard . . . I'd lay any money that was your doing. So I told Humber's man he would be a fool to take you on. You're poison, Dan, and I reckon any stable is better off without you, and I told him so."

"Thanks."

"You can ride," said Paddy disgustedly, "I'll say that for you. And it's an utter bloody waste. You'll never get a job with a decent stable again. It would be like putting a rotten apple into a box of good ones."

"Did you say all that to Humber's man?"

"I told him no decent stable would take you on," he said, nodding. "And if you ask me, it bloody well serves you right." He turned his back on me and walked away.

I sighed, and told myself I should be pleased that Paddy believed me such a black character.

Humber's head traveling lad spoke to me in the paddock between the last two races.

"Hey, you," he said, catching my arm. "I hear you're looking for a job."

"That's right."

"I might be able to put you in the way of something. Good pay, better than most."

"Whose stable?" I asked. "And how much?"

"Sixteen quid a week."

"Sounds good," I admitted. "Where?"

"Where I work. For Mr. Humber. Up in Durham."

"Humber," I repeated sourly.

"Well, you want a job, don't you? Of course, if you are so well off you can do without a job, that's different." He sneered at my unprosperous appearance.

"I need a job," I muttered.

"Well, then?"

"He might not have me," I said bitterly. "Like some others I could mention."

"He will if I put in a word for you. We're short a lad just now. There's another meeting here next Wednesday. I'll put in a word for you before that and if it is O.K., you can see Mr. Humber on Wednesday and he'll tell you whether he'll have you or not."

"Why not ask him now?" I said.

"No. You wait till Wednesday."

"All right," I said grudgingly. "If I've got to."

I could almost see him thinking that by Wednesday I would be just that much hungrier, just that much more anxious to take any job that was offered, and less likely to be frightened off by rumors of bad conditions.

I had spent all the bookmaker's two hundred, as well as half of the money I had earned at Inskip's, on my Italian jaunt (of which I regretted not one penny), and after paying for the motorcycle and the succession of dingy lodgings, I had almost nothing left of October's original two hundred. He had not suggested giving me any more for expenses, and I was not going to ask him for any; but I judged that the other half of my Inskip pay could be spent how I liked, and I dispatched nearly all of it in the following three days on a motorcycle trip to Edinburgh, walking around and enjoying the city and thinking myself the oddest tourist in Scotland.

On Tuesday evening, when hogmanay was in full swing, I braved the head-waiter of L'Aperitif, who to his eternal credit treated me with beautifully self-controlled politeness, but quite reasonably checked, before he gave me a little table in a corner, that I had enough money to pay the bill. Impervious to scandalized looks from better dressed diners, I slowly ate, with Humber's establishment in mind, a perfect and enormous dinner of lobster, duck bigarade, lemon soufflé, and Brie, and drank most of a bottle of Chateau Leoville Lescases 1959.

With which extravagant farewell to being my own master, I rode down the A1 to Catterick on New Year's Day and in good spirits engaged myself to the worst stable in the country.

CHAPTER 9

RUMOR HAD HARDLY done Hedley Humber justice. The discomfort in which the lads were expected to live was so methodically devised that I had been there only one day before I came to the conclusion that its sole purpose was to discourage anyone from staying too long. I discovered that only the head lad and the head traveling lad, who both lived out in Posset, had worked in the yard for more than three months, and that the average time it took for an ordinary lad to decide that sixteen pounds a week was not enough was eight to ten weeks.

This meant that none of the stable hands except the two head lads knew what had happened to Superman the previous summer, because none of them had been there at the time. And caution told me that the only reason the two top men stayed was because they knew what was going on, and that if I asked *them* about Superman, I might find myself following smartly in Tommy Stapleton's footsteps.

I had heard all about the squalor of the living quarters at some stables, and I was aware also that some lads deserved no better—some I knew of had broken up and burned their chairs rather than go outside and fetch coal, and others had stacked their dirty dishes in the lavatory and pulled the chain to do the washing up. But even granted that Humber only employed the dregs, his arrangements were very nearly inhuman.

The dormitory was a narrow hayloft over the horses. One could hear every bang of their hoofs and the rattle of chains, and through the cracks in the plank floor one could see straight down into the boxes. Upward through the cracks rose a smell of dirty straw and an icy draft. There was no ceiling in the hayloft except the rafters and the tiles of the roof, and no way up into it except a ladder through a hole in the floor. In the one small window a broken pane of glass had been pasted over with brown paper, which shut out the light and let in the cold.

The seven beds, which were all the hayloft held in the way of furniture, were stark, basic affairs made of a piece of canvas stretched tautly onto a tubular metal frame. On each bed there were supposed to be one pillow and two gray blankets, but I had to struggle to get mine back because they had been appropriated by others as soon as my predecessor left. The pillow had no cover, there were no sheets, and there were no mattresses. Everyone went to bed fully dressed to keep warm, and on my third day there it started snowing.

The kitchen at the bottom of the ladder, the only other room available to the lads, was nothing more than the last loose box along one side of the yard. So little had been done to make it habitable as to leave a powerful suggestion that its inmates were to be thought of, and treated, as animals. The bars were still in place over the small window, and there were still bolts on the outside of the split stable door. The floor was still of bare concrete crisscrossed with drainage grooves; one side wall was of rough boards with kick marks still in them and the other three were of bare bricks. The room was chronically cold and damp and dirty; and although it may have been big enough as a home for one horse, it was uncomfortably cramped for seven men.

The mimimal furniture consisted of rough benches around two walls, a wooden table, a badly chipped electric cooker, a shelf for crockery, and an old marble washstand bearing a metal jug and a metal basin, which was all there was in the way of a bathroom. Other needs were catered to in a wooden hut beside the muck heap.

The food, prepared by a slatternly woman perpetually in curlers, was not up to the standard of the accommodation.

Humber, who had engaged me with an indifferent glance and a nod, directed me with equal lack of interest, when I arrived in the yard, to look after four horses, and told me the numbers of their boxes. Neither he nor anyone else told me their names. The head lad, who did one horse himself, appeared to have very little authority, contrary to the practice in most other training stables, and it was Humber himself who gave the orders and who made sure they were carried out.

He was a tyrant, not so much in the quality of the work he demanded as in the quantity. There were some thirty horses in the yard. The head lad cared for one horse, and the head traveling lad, who also drove the horse box, did none at all. That left twenty-nine horses for seven lads, who were also expected to keep the gallops in order and do all the cleaning and maintenance work of the whole place. On racing days, when one or two lads were away, those remaining often had six horses to see to. It made my stint at Inskip's seem like a rest cure.

At the slightest sign of shirking, Humber would dish out irritating little punishments and roar in an acid voice that he paid extra wages for extra work, and anyone who didn't like it could leave. As everyone was there because better stables would not risk employing them, leaving Humber's automatically meant leaving racing altogether. And taking whatever they knew about the place with them. It was very, very neat.

My companions in this hellhole were neither friendly nor likable. The best of them was the nearly half-witted boy I had seen at Stafford on Boxing Day. His name was Jerry, and he came in for a lot of physical abuse because he was slower and more stupid than anyone else.

Two of the others had been to prison and their outlook on life made Soupy Tarleton look like a Sunday-school favorite. It was from one of these, Jimmy, that I had had to wrench my blanket, and from the other, a thickset tough called Charlie, my pillow. They were the two bullies of the bunch, and in addition to the free use they made of their boots, they could always be relied upon to tell lying tales and wriggle themselves out of trouble, seeing to it that someone else was punished in their stead.

Reggie was a food stealer. Thin, white faced, and with a twitch in his left eyelid, he had long prehensile hands which could whisk the bread off your plate faster than the eye could follow. I lost a lot of my meager rations to him before I caught him at it, and it always remained a mystery why, when he managed to eat more than anyone else, he stayed the thinnest.

One of the lads was deaf. He told me phlegmatically in a toneless mumble that his dad had done it when he was little, giving him a few clips too many over the ear holes. His name was Bert, and as he occasionally wet himself in bed, he smelled appalling.

The seventh, Geoff, had been there longest, and even after ten weeks never spoke of leaving. He had a habit of looking furtively over his shoulder, and any mention by Jimmy or Charlie about their prison experiences brought him close to tears, so that I came to the conclusion that he had committed some crime and was terrified of being found out. I supposed ten weeks at Humber's might be preferable to jail, but it was debatable.

They knew all about me from the head traveling lad, Jud Wilson. My general dishonesty they took entirely for granted, but they thought I was lucky to have got off without going inside if it was true about October's daughter, and they sniggered about it unendingly, and made merciless obscene jibes that hit their target all too often.

I found their constant closeness a trial, the food disgusting, the work exhausting, the beds relentless, and the cold unspeakable. All of which rather roughly taught me that my life in Australia had been soft and easy, even when I thought it most demanding.

Before I went to Humber's I had wondered why anyone should be foolish enough to pay training fees to a patently unsuccessful trainer, but I gradually found out. The yard itself, for one thing, was a surprise. From the appearance of the horses at race meetings one would have expected their home surroundings to be weedy gravel, broken-hinged boxes, and flaked-off paint; but in fact the yard was trim and prosperous looking, and was kept that way by the lads, who never had time off in the afternoons. This glossy window dressing cost Humber nothing but an occasional gallon of paint and a certain amount of slave driving.

His manner with the owners who sometimes arrived for a look around was authoritative and persuasive, and his fees, I later discovered, were lower than anyone else's, which attracted more custom than he would otherwise have had. In addition, some of the horses in the yard were not racehorses at all, but hunters at livery, for whose board, lodging, and exercise he received substantial sums without the responsibility of having to train them.

I learned from the other lads that only seven of the stable's inmates had raced at all that season, but that those seven had been hard worked, with an average of a race each every ten days. There had been one winner, two seconds, and a third among them.

None of those seven was in my care. I had been allotted a quartet consisting of two racehorses that belonged, as far as I could make out, to Humber himself, and two hunters. The two racehorses were bays, about seven years old; one of them had a sweet mouth and no speed and the other a useful sprint over schooling fences but a churlish nature. I pressed Cass, the head lad, to tell me their names, and he said they were Dobbin and Sooty. These unraceman-like names were not to be found in the form book, nor in Humber's list in *Horses in Training*; but it seemed to me highly probable that Rudyard, Superman, Charcoal, and the rest had all spent their short periods in the yard under similar uninformative pseudonyms.

A lad who had gone out of racing would never connect the Dobbin or Sooty he had once looked after with the Rudyard who won a race for another trainer two years later.

But why, *why* did he win two years later? About that I was as ignorant as ever.

The cold weather came and gripped, and stayed. But nothing, the other lads said, could be as bad as the fearsome winter before; and I reflected that in that January and February I had been sweltering under the midsummer sun. I wondered how Belinda and Helen and Philip were enjoying their long vacation, and what they would think if they could see me in my dirty, downtrodden sub-existence, and what the men would think, to see their employer brought so low. It amused me a good deal to imagine it; and it not only helped the tedious hours to pass more quickly, but kept me from losing my own inner identity.

As the days of drudgery mounted up, I began to wonder if anyone who embarked on so radical a masquerade really knew what he was doing.

Expression, speech, and movement had to be unremittingly schooled into a convincing show of uncouth dullness. I worked in a slovenly fashion and rode, with a pang, like a mutton-fisted clod; but as time passed all these deceptions became easier. If one pretended long enough to be a wreck, did one finally become one? I wondered. And if one stripped oneself continuously of all human dignity, would one in the end be unaware of its absence? I hoped the question would remain academic; and as long as I could have a quiet laugh at myself now and then, I supposed I was safe enough.

My belief that after three months in the yard a lad was given every encouragement to leave was amply borne out by what happened to Geoff Smith.

Humber never rode out to exercise with his horses, but drove in a van to the gallops to watch them work, and returned to the yard while they were still walking back to have a poke around to see what had been done and not done.

One morning, when we went in with the second lot, Humber was standing in the center of the yard radiating his frequent displeasure.

"You, Smith, and you, Roke, put those horses in their boxes and come here."

We did so.

"Roke."

"Sir?"

"The mangers of all your four horses are in a disgusting state. Clean them up."

"Yes, sir."

"And to teach you to be more thorough in future, you will get up at five-thirty for the next week."

"Sir."

I sighed inwardly, but this was to me one of his more acceptable forms of pinprick punishment, since I didn't particularly mind getting up early. It entailed merely standing in the middle of the yard for over an hour, doing nothing. Dark, cold, and boring. I don't think he slept much himself. His bedroom window faced down the yard, and he always knew if one was not standing outside by twenty to six, and shining a torch to prove it.

"And as for you." He looked at Geoff with calculation. "The floor of number seven is caked with dirt. You'll clean out the straw and scrub the floor with disinfectant before you get your dinner."

"But, sir," protested Geoff incautiously, "if I don't go in for dinner with the others, they won't leave me any."

"You should have thought of that before, and done your work properly in the first place. I pay half as much again as any other trainer would, and I expect value for it. You will do as you are told."

"But, sir," whined Geoff, knowing that if he missed his main meal he would go very hungry, "can't I do it this afternoon?"

Humber casually slid his walking stick through his hand until he was holding it at the bottom. Then he swung his arm and savagely cracked the knobbled handle across Geoff's thigh.

Geoff yelped and rubbed his leg.

"Before dinner," remarked Humber, and walked away, leaning on his stick.

Geoff missed his share of the watery, half-stewed lumps of mutton, and came in panting to see the last of the bread-and-suet pudding spooned into Charlie's traplike mouth.

"You bloody sods," he yelled miserably. "You bloody lot of sods!"

He stuck it for a whole week. He stood six more heavy blows on various parts of his body, and missed his dinner three more times, and his breakfast twice, and his supper once. Long before the end of it he was in tears, but he didn't want to leave.

After five days Cass came into the kitchen at breakfast and told Geoff, "The boss has taken against you, I'm afraid. You won't ever do anything right for him again from now on. Best thing you can do—and I'm telling you for your own good, mind—is to find a job somewhere else. The boss gets these fits now and then when one of the lads can't do anything right, and no one can change him when he gets going. You can work until you're blue in the face, but he won't take to you anymore. You don't want to get yourself bashed up anymore, now, do you? All I'm telling you is that if you stay here you'll find that what has happened so far is only the beginning. See? I'm only telling you for your own good."

Even so, it was two more days before Geoff painfully packed his old army kit bag and sniffed his way off the premises.

A weedy boy arrived the next morning as a replacement, but he only stayed three days, as Jimmy stole his blankets before he came and he was not strong enough to get them back. He moaned piteously through two freezing nights, and was gone before the third.

The next morning, before breakfast, it was Jimmy himself who collected a crack from the stick.

He came in late and cursing and snatched a chunk of bread out of Jerry's hand.

"Where's my bloody breakfast?"

We had eaten it, of course.

"Well," he said, glaring at us, "you can do my ruddy horses, as well. I'm off. I'm not bloody well staying here. This is worse than doing bird. You won't catch me staying here to be swiped at, I'll tell you that."

Reggie said, "Why don't you complain?"

"Who to?"

"Well . . . the bluebottles."

"Are you out of your mind?" said Jimmy in amazement. "You're a bloody nit, that's what you are. Can you see me with my form, going into the cop house and saying I got a complaint to make about my employer, he hit me with his walking stick? For a start, they'd laugh. They'd laugh their bleeding heads off. And then what? Supposing they come here and asked Cass if he's seen anyone getting the rough end of it? Well, I'll tell you, that Cass wants to keep his cushy job. Oh, no, he'd say, I ain't seen nothing. Mr. Humber, he's a nice, kind gentleman with a heart of gold, and what can you expect from an ex-con but a pack of bull? Don't ruddy well make me laugh, I'm off, and if the rest of you've got any sense, you'll be out of it, too."

No one, however, took his advice.

I found out from Charlie that Jimmy had been there two weeks longer than he, which made it, he thought, about eleven weeks.

As Jimmy strode defiantly out of the yard, I went rather thoughtfully about my business. Eleven weeks, twelve at the most, before Humber's arm started swinging. I had already been there three, which left me a maximum of nine more in which to discover how he managed the doping. It wasn't that I couldn't probably last out as long as Geoff if it came to the point, but that if I hadn't uncovered Humber's method before he focused his attention on getting rid of me, I had very little chance of doing it afterward.

Three weeks, I thought, and I had found out nothing at all except that I wanted to leave as soon as possible.

Two lads came to take Geoff's and Jimmy's places, a tall boy called Lenny, who had been to Borstal and was proud of it, and Cecil, a far-gone alcoholic of about thirty-five. He had, he told me, been kicked out of half the stables in England because he couldn't keep his hands off the bottle. I don't know where he got the liquor from or how he managed to hide it, but he was certainly three parts drunk every day by four o'clock, and snored in a paralytic stupor every night.

Life, if you could call it that, went on.

All the lads seemed to have a good reason for having to earn the extra

wages Humber paid. Lenny was repaying some money he had stolen from another employer, Charlie had a wife somewhere drawing maintenance, Cecil
drank, Reggie was a compulsive saver, and Humber sent Jerry's money
straight off to his parents. Jerry was proud of being able to help them.

I had let Jud Wilson and Cass know that I badly needed to earn sixteen
pounds a week because I had fallen behind on installment payments on the
motorcycle, and this also gave me an obvious reason for needing to spend
some time in the Posset post office on Saturday afternoons.

Public transport from the stables to Posset, a large village a mile and a
half away, did not exist. Cass and Jud Wilson both had cars, but would give
no lifts. My motorcycle was the only other transport available, but to the lads'
fluently expressed disgust, I refused to use it on the frosty, snow-strewn roads
for trips down to the pub in the evenings. As a result, we hardly ever went to
Posset except on the two hours we had off on Saturday afternoons, and also on
Sunday evenings, when after a slightly less relentless day's work everyone had
enough energy left to walk for their beer.

On Saturdays I unwrapped the motorcycle from its thick plastic cocoon
and set off to Posset with Jerry perched ecstatically on the pillion. I always took
poor simpleminded Jerry because he got the worst of everything throughout
the week; and we quickly fell into routine. First we went to the post office for
me to mail my imaginary installment. Instead, leaning on the shelf among the
telegram forms and scraps of pink blotting paper, I wrote each week a report to
October, making sure that no one from the stables looked over my shoulder.
Replies, if any, I collected, read, and tore up over the litter basket.

Jerry accepted without question that I would be at least a quarter of an
hour in the post office, and spent the time unsuspiciously at the other end of
the shop inspecting the stock in the toy department. Twice he bought a big
friction drive car and played with it, until it broke, on the dormitory floor;
and every week he bought a children's four penny comic, over whose picture
strips he giggled contentedly for the next few days. He couldn't read a word,
and often asked me to explain the captions, so that I became intimately ac-
quainted with the doings of Mickey the Monkey and Flip McCoy.

Leaving the post office, we climbed back onto the motorcycle and rode
two hundred yards down the street to have tea. This ritual took place in a
square, bare café with margarine-colored walls, cold lighting, and messy
tabletops. For decoration there were Pepsi-Cola advertisements, and for ser-

vice a bored-looking girl with no stockings and mousy hair piled into a matted, wispy mountain on top of her head.

None of this mattered. Jerry and I ordered and ate with indescribable enjoyment a heap of lamb chops, fried eggs, flabby chips, and bright-green peas. Charlie and the others were to be seen doing the same at adjoining tables. The girl knew where we came from, and looked down on us, as her father owned the café.

On our way out, Jerry and I packed our pockets with bars of chocolate to supplement Humber's food, a hoard which lasted each week exactly as long as it took Reggie to find it.

By four o'clock we were back in the yard, the motorcycle wrapped up again, the week's highlight nothing but a memory and a belch, the next seven days stretching drearily ahead.

There were hours, in that life, in which to think. Hours of trotting the horses around and around a straw track in a frozen field, hours of brushing the dust out of their coats, hours of cleaning the muck out of their boxes and carrying their water and hay, hours of lying awake at night listening to the stamp of the horses below and the snores and mumblings from the row of beds.

Over and over again I thought my way through all I had seen or read or heard since I came to England; and what emerged as most significant was the performance of Superman at Stafford. He had been doped; he was the twelfth of the series; but he had not won.

Eventually I changed the order of these thoughts. He had been doped, and he had not won; but was he, after all, the twelfth of the series? He might be the thirteenth, the fourteenth; there might have been others who had come to grief.

On my third Saturday, when I had been at Humber's just over a fortnight, I wrote asking October to look up the newspaper cutting which Tommy Stapleton had kept, about a horse going berserk and killing a woman in the paddock at Cartmel races. I asked him to check the horse's history.

A week later I read his typewritten reply.

Old Etonian, destroyed at Cartmel, Lancashire, at Whitsun this year, spent the previous November and December in Humber's yard. Humber claimed him in a selling race, and sold him again at Leicester sales seven weeks later.

But: *Old Etonian went berserk in the parade ring* before *the race; he was due to run in a handicap, not a seller; and the run-in at Cartmel is short. None of these facts conform to the pattern of the others.*
Dope tests were made on Old Etonian, but proved negative.
No one could explain why he behaved as he did.

Tommy Stapleton, I thought, must have had an idea, or he would not have cut out the report, yet he could not have been sure enough to act on it without checking up. And checking up had killed him. There could be no more doubt of it.

I tore up the paper and took Jerry along to the café, more conscious than usual of the danger breathing down my neck. It didn't, however, spoil my appetite for the only edible meal of the week.

At supper a few days later, in the lull before Charlie turned on his transistor radio for the usual evening of pops from Luxembourg (which I had grown to enjoy), I steered the conversation around to Cartmel races. What, I wanted to know, were they like?

Only Cecil, the drunk, had ever been there.

"It's not like it used to be in the old days," he said owlishly, not noticing Reggie filch a hunk of his bread and margarine.

Cecil's eyes had a glazed, liquid look, but I had luckily asked my question at exactly the right moment, in the loquacious half hour between the silent bleariness of the afternoon's liquor and his disappearance to tank up for the night.

"What was it like in the old days?" I prompted.

"They had a fair there." He hiccuped. "A fair with roundabouts and swings and sideshows and all. Bank holidays, see? Whitsun and all that. Only place outside the Derby you could go on the swings at the races. Course, they stopped it now. Don't like no one to have a good time, they don't. It weren't doing no harm, it weren't, the fair."

"Fairs," said Reggie scornfully, his eyes flicking to the crust Jerry held loosely in his hand.

"Good for dipping," commented Lenny, with superiority.

"Yeah," agreed Charlie, who hadn't yet decided if Borstal qualified Lenny as a fit companion for one from the higher school.

"Eh?" said Cecil, lost.

"Dipping. Working the pockets," Lenny said.

"Oh. Well, it can't have been that with the hound trails, and they stopped them, too. They were good sport, they were. Bloody good day out, it used to be, at Cartmel, but now it's the same as any other ruddy place. You might as well be at Newton Abbot or somewhere. Nothing but ordinary racing like any other day of the week." He belched.

"What were the hound trails?" I asked.

"Dog races," he said, smiling foolishly. "Bloody dog races. They used to have one before the horse races, and one afterward, but they've ruddy well stopped it now. Bloody killjoys, that's all they are. Still"—he leered triumphantly—"if you know what's what you can still have a bet on the dogs. They have a hound trail in the morning now, on the other side of the village from the racetrack, but if you get your horse bedded down quick enough you can get there in time for a bet."

"Dog races?" said Lenny disbelievingly. "Dogs won't race around no horse track. There ain't no bloody electric hare, for a start."

Cecil swiveled his head unsteadily in Lenny's direction.

"You don't have a track for hound trails," he said earnestly, in his slurred voice. "It's a *trail*, see? Some bloke sets off with a bagful of aniseed and paraffin, or something like that, and drags it for miles and miles around the hills and such. Then they let all the dogs loose and the first one to follow all around the trail and get back quickest is the winner. Year before last, someone shot at the bloody favorite half a mile from home and there was a bleeding riot. They missed him, though. They hit the one just behind, some ruddy outsider with no chance."

"Reggie's ate my crust," said Jerry sadly.

"Did you go to Cartmel this year, too?" I asked.

"No," Cecil said regretfully. "Can't say I did. A woman got killed there, and all."

"How?" asked Lenny, looking avid.

"Some bloody horse bolted in the paddock, and jumped the rails of the parade ring and landed on some poor bloody woman who was just having a nice day out. She backed a loser all right, she did that day. I heard she was cut to bits, time that crazy animal trampled all over her trying to get out through the crowd. He didn't get far, but he kicked out all over the place and broke another man's leg before they got the vet to him and shot him. Mad, they said he was. A mate of mine was there, see, leading one around in the same race, and he said it was something awful, that poor woman all cut up and bleeding to death in front of his eyes."

The others looked suitably impressed at this horrific story, all except
Bert, who couldn't hear it.

"Well," said Cecil, getting up, "it's time for my little walk."

He went out for his little walk, which was presumably to wherever he
had hidden his alcohol, because as usual he came reeling back less than an
hour later and stumbled up the ladder to his customary oblivion.

CHAPTER 10

TOWARD THE END of my fourth week Reggie left (complaining of
hunger) and in a day or two was duly replaced by a boy with a soft face who
said in a high-pitched voice that his name was Kenneth.

To Humber I clearly remained one insignificant face in this endless procession of human flotsam; and as I could safely operate only as long as that
state of affairs continued, I did as little as possible to attract his attention. He
gave me orders, and I obeyed them; and he cursed me and punished me—but
not more than anyone else—for the things I left undone.

I grew to recognize his moods at a glance. There were days when he glowered silently all through first and second exercise and turned out again to make
sure that no one skimped the third, and on these occasions even Cass walked
warily and only spoke if he was spoken to. There were days when he talked a
great deal but always in sarcasm, and his tongue was so rough that everyone
preferred the silence. There were occasional days when he wore an abstract air
and overlooked our faults, and even rarer days when he looked fairly pleased
with life.

At all times he was impeccably turned out, as if to emphasize the difference between his state and ours. His clothes, I judged, were his main personal
vanity, but his wealth was also evident in his car, the latest type of Cunard-
size Bentley. It was fitted with back-seat television, plush carpets, radio-
telephone, fur rugs, air-conditioning, and a built-in drinks cabinet holding
in racks six bottles, twelve glasses, and a glittering array of chromiumed
corkscrews, ice picks, and miscellaneous objects like swizzle sticks.

I knew the car well, because I had to clean it every Monday afternoon. Bert had to clean it on Fridays. Humber was proud of his car.

He was chauffeured on long journeys in this above-his-status symbol by Jud Wilson's sister Grace, a hard-faced amazon of a woman who handled the huge car with practiced ease but was not expected to maintain it. I never once spoke to her; she bicycled in from wherever she lived, drove as necessary, and bicycled away again. Frequently the car had not been cleaned to her satisfaction, but her remarks were relayed to Bert and me by Jud.

I looked into every cranny every time while cleaning the inside, but Humber was neither so obliging nor so careless as to leave hypodermic syringes or phials of stimulants lying about in the glove compartments.

All through my first month there, the freezing weather was not only a discomfort but also a tiresome delay. While racing was suspended, Humber could dope no horses, and there was no opportunity for me to see what difference it made to his routine when the racing was scheduled for any of the five courses with long run-ins.

On top of that, he and Jud Wilson and Cass were always about in the stables. I wanted to have a look around inside Humber's office, a brick hut standing across the top end of the yard, but I could not risk a search when any one of them might come in and find me at it. With Humber and Jud Wilson away at the races, though, and with Cass gone home to his midday meal, I reckoned I could go into the office to search while the rest of the lads were eating.

Cass had a key to the office, and it was he who unlocked the door in the morning and locked it again at night. As far as I could see, he did not bother to lock up when he went home for lunch, and the office was normally left open all day, except on Sunday. This might mean, I thought, that Humber kept nothing there which could possibly be incriminating; but on the other hand, he could perhaps keep something there which was apparently innocent but would be incriminating if one understood its significance.

However, the likelihood of solving the whole mystery by a quick look around in an unlocked stable office was so doubtful that it was not worth risking discovery, and I judged it better to wait with what patience I could until the odds were in my favor.

There was also Humber's house, a whitewashed converted farmhouse adjoining the yard. A couple of stealthy surveys, made on afternoons when I was bidden to sweep snow from his garden path, showed that this was an ultra-neat soulless establishment like a series of rooms in shop windows, impersonal and unlived in. Humber was not married, and downstairs at least there seemed to be nowhere at all snug for him to spend his evenings.

Through the windows I saw no desk to investigate and no safe in which to lock away secrets; all the same I decided it would be less than fair to ignore his home, and if I both drew a blank and got away with an entry into the office, I would pay the house a visit at the first opportunity.

At last it began to thaw on a Wednesday night and continued fast all day Thursday and Friday, so that by Saturday morning the thin slush was disintegrating into puddles, and the stables stirred with the reawakening of hunting and racing.

Cass told me on Friday night that the man who owned the hunters I looked after required them both to be ready for him on Saturday, and after second exercise I led them out and loaded them into the horse box which had come for them.

Their owner stood leaning against the front wing of a well-polished Jaguar. His hunting boots shone like glass, his cream breeches were perfection, his pink coat fitted without a wrinkle, his stock was smooth and snowy. He held a sensible leather-covered riding stick in his hand and snapped it against his boot. He was tall, broad, and bareheaded, about forty years old, and, from across the yard, handsome. It was only when one was close to him that one could see the dissatisfied look on his face and the evidences of dissipation on his skin.

"You," he said, pointing at me with his stick. "Come here."

I went. He had heavy-lidded eyes and a few purple thread veins on his nose and cheeks. He looked at me with superior bored disdain. I am five feet nine inches tall; he was four inches taller, and he made the most of it.

"You'll pay for it if those horses of mine don't last the day. I ride them hard. They need to be fit."

His voice had the same expensive timbre as October's.

"They're as fit as the snow would allow," I said calmly.

He raised his eyebrows.

"Sir," I added.

"Insolence," he said, "will get you nowhere."

"I am sorry, sir. I didn't mean to be insolent."

He laughed unpleasantly. "I'll bet you didn't. It's not so easy to get another job, is it? You'll watch your tongue when you speak to me in the future, if you know what's good for you."

"Yes, sir."

"And if those horses of mine aren't fit, you'll wish you'd never been born."

Cass appeared at my left elbow, looking anxious.

"Is everything all right, sir?" he asked. "Has Roke done anything wrong, Mr. Adams?"

How I managed not to jump out of my skin I am not quite sure. Mr. Adams. Paul James Adams, sometime owner of seven subsequently doped horses?

"Is this bloody gypsy doing my horses any good?" said Adams offensively.

"He's not worse than any of the other lads," said Cass soothingly.

"And that's saying precious little." He gave me a mean stare. "You've had it easy during the freeze. Too damned easy. You'll have to wake your ideas up now hunting has started again. You won't find me as soft as your master, I can tell you that."

I said nothing. He slapped his stick sharply against his boot.

"Do you hear what I say? You'll find me harder to please."

"Yes, sir," I muttered.

He opened his fingers and let the stick fall at his feet.

"Pick it up," he said.

As I bent to pick it up, he put his booted foot on my shoulder and gave me a heavy, overbalancing shove, so that I fell sprawling onto the soaking, muddy ground.

He smiled with malicious enjoyment.

"Get up, you clumsy lout, and do as you are told. Pick up my stick."

I got to my feet, picked up his stick, and held it out to him. He twitched it out of my hand, and looking at Cass, said, "You've got to show them you won't stand any nonsense. Stamp on them whenever you can. This one"—he looked me coldly up and down—"needs to be taught a lesson. What do you suggest?"

Cass looked at me doubtfully. I glanced at Adams. This, I thought, was not funny. His grayish-blue eyes were curiously opaque, as if he were drunk; but he was plainly sober. I had seen that look before, in the eyes of a stable hand I had once for a short time employed, and I knew what it could mean. I had to guess at once, and guess right, whether he preferred bullying the weak or the strong. From instinct, perhaps because of his size and evident worldliness, I guessed that crushing the weak would be too tame for him. In which case it was definitely not the moment for any show of strength. I drooped in as cowed and unresisting a manner as I could devise.

"God," said Adams in disgust. "Just look at him. Scared out of his bloody wits." He shrugged impatiently. "Well, Cass, just find him some stinking useless occupation like scrubbing the paths and put him to work. There's no sport for me here. No backbone for me to break. Give me a fox any day; at least they've got some cunning and some guts."

His gaze strayed sideways to where Humber was crossing the far end of the yard. He said to Cass, "Tell Mr. Humber I'd like to have a word with him," and when Cass had gone he turned back to me.

"Where did you work before this?"

"At Mr. Inskip's, sir."

"And he kicked you out?"

"Yes, sir."

"Why?"

"I . . . er . . ." I stuck. It was incredibly galling to have to lay oneself open to such a man; but if I gave him answers he could check in small things, he might believe the whopping lies without question.

"When I ask a question, you will answer it," said Adams coldly. "Why did Mr. Inskip get rid of you?"

I swallowed. "I got the sack for . . . er . . . for messing about with the boss's daughter."

"For messing about . . ." he repeated. "Good God." With lewd pleasure he said something which was utterly obscene. He saw me wince and laughed at my discomfiture. Cass and Humber returned. Adams turned to Humber, still laughing, and said, "Do you know why this cockerel got chucked out of Inskip's?"

"Yes," said Humber flatly. "He seduced October's daughter." He wasn't interested. "And there was also the matter of a favorite that came in last. He looked after it."

"October's daughter!" said Adams, surprised, his eyes narrowing. "I thought he meant Inskip's daughter." He casually dealt me a sharp clip on the ear. "Don't try lying to me."

"Mr. Inskip hasn't got a daughter," I protested.

"And don't answer back." His hand flicked out again. He was rather adept at it. He must have indulged in a lot of practice.

"Hedley," he said to Humber, who had impassively watched this one-sided exchange, "I'll give you a lift to Nottingham races on Monday if you like. I'll pick you up at ten."

"Right," agreed Humber.

Adams turned to Cass. "Don't forget that lesson for this lily-livered Romeo. Cool his ardor a bit."

Cass sniggered sycophantically and raised goose pimples on my neck.

Adams climbed coolly into his Jaguar, started it up, and followed the horse box containing his two hunters out of the yard.

Humber said, "I don't want Roke out of action, Cass. You've got to leave him fit to work. Use some sense this time." He limped away to continue his inspection of the boxes.

Cass looked at me, and I looked steadily down at my damp, muddy clothes, very conscious that the head lad counted among the enemy, and not wanting to risk his seeing that there was anything but submissiveness in my face.

He said, "Mr. Adams don't like to be crossed."

"I didn't cross him."

"Nor he don't like to be answered back to. You mind your lip."

"Has he any more horses here?" I asked.

"Yes," said Cass, "and it's none of your business. Now he told me to punish you, and he won't forget. He'll check up later."

"I've done nothing wrong," I said sullenly, still looking down. What on earth would my foreman say about this, I thought; and nearly smiled at the picture.

"You don't need to have done nothing wrong," said Cass. "With Mr. Adams it's a case of punish first so that you won't do nothing wrong after. Sense, in a way." He gave a snort of laughter. "Saves trouble, see?"

"Are his horses all hunters?" I asked.

"No," said Cass, "but the two you've got are, and don't you forget it. He rides those himself, and he'll notice how you look after every hair on their hides."

"Does he treat the lads who look after his other horses so shocking unfair?"

"I never heard Jerry complaining. Mr. Adams won't treat you too bad if you mind you p's and q's. Now that lesson he suggested . . ."

I had hoped he had forgotten it.

"You can get down on your knees and scrub the concrete paths around the yard. Start now. You can break for dinner, and then go on until evening stables."

I went on standing in a rag-doll attitude of dejectedness, looking at the ground, but fighting an unexpectedly strong feeling of rebellion. What the hell, I thought, did October expect of me? Just how much was I to take? Was there any point at which, if he went there, he would say, "Stop; all right; that's enough. That's too much. Give it up"? But remembering how he felt about me, I supposed not.

Cass said, "There's a scrubbing brush in the cupboard in the tack room. Get on with it." He walked away.

The concrete paths were six feet wide and ran around all sides of the yard in front of the boxes. They had been scraped clear of snow throughout the month I had been there so that the feed trolley could make its usual smooth journey from horse to horse, and as in most modern stables, including Inskip's and my own, they would always be kept clean of straw and excessive dust. But scrubbing them on one's knees for nearly four hours on a slushy day at the end of January was a miserable, back-breaking, insane waste of time. Ludicrous besides, and unheroic.

I had a clear choice of scrubbing the paths or getting on the motorcycle and going. Thinking firmly that I was being paid at least ten thousand pounds for doing it, I scrubbed; and Cass hung around the yard all day to watch that I didn't rest.

The lads, who had spent much of the afternoon amusing themselves by jeering at my plight as they set off for and returned from the café in Posset, made quite sure during evening stables that the concrete paths ended the day even dirtier than they had begun. I didn't care a damn about that; but Adams had sent his hunters back caked with mud and sweat and it took me two hours to clean them, because by the end of that day many of my muscles were trembling with fatigue.

Then, to crown it all, Adams came back. He drove his Jaguar into the yard, climbed out, and after having talked to Cass, who nodded and gestured around the paths, he walked without haste toward the box where I was still struggling with his black horse.

He stood in the doorway and looked down his nose at me; and I looked back. He was superbly elegant in a dark-blue pin-striped suit with a white shirt and a silver-gray tie. His skin looked fresh, his hair well brushed, his hands clean and pale. I imagined he had gone home after hunting and enjoyed a deep hot bath, a change of clothes, a drink. . . . I hadn't had a bath for a month and was unlikely to get one as long as I stayed at Humber's. I was filthy and hungry and extremely tired. I wished he would go away and leave me alone.

No such luck.

He took a step into the box and surveyed the mud still caked solid on the horse's hind legs.

"You're slow," he remarked.

"Sorry, sir."

"This horse must have been back here three hours ago. What have you been doing?"

"My three other horses, sir."

"You should do mine first."

"I had to wait for the mud to dry, sir. You can't brush it out while it's still wet."

"I told you this morning not to answer back." His hand lashed out across the ear he had hit before. He was smiling slightly. Enjoying himself. Which was more than could be said for me.

Having, so to speak, tasted blood, he suddenly took hold of the front of my jersey, pushed me back against the wall, and slapped me twice in the face, forehand and backhand. Still smiling.

What I wanted to do was to jab my knee into his groin and my fist into his stomach; and refraining wasn't easy. For the sake of realism I knew I should have cried out loudly and begged him to stop, but when it came to the point I couldn't do it. However, one could act what one couldn't say, so I lifted both arms and folded them defensively around my head.

He laughed and let go, and I slid down onto one knee and cowered against the wall.

"You're a proper little rabbit, aren't you, for all your fancy looks."

I stayed where I was, in silence. As suddenly as he had begun, he lost interest in ill-treating me.

"Get up, get up," he said irritably. "I didn't hurt you. You're not worth hurting. Get up and finish this horse. And make sure it is done properly or you'll find yourself scrubbing again."

He walked out of the box and away across the yard. I stood up, leaned against the doorpost, and with uncharitable feelings watched him go up the path to Humber's house. To a good dinner, no doubt. An armchair. A fire. A glass of brandy. A friend to talk to. Sighing in depression, I went back to the tiresome job of brushing off the mud.

Shortly after a supper of dry bread and cheese, eaten to the accompaniment of crude jokes about my day's occupation and detailed descriptions of the meals which had been enjoyed in Posset, I had had quite enough of my fellow workers. I climbed the ladder and sat on my bed. It was cold upstairs. I had had quite enough of Humber's yard. I had had more than enough of being kicked around. All I had to do, as I had been tempted to do that morning, was to go outside, unwrap the motorcycle, and make tracks for civilization. I could stifle my conscience by paying most of the money back to October and pointing out that I had done at least half of the job.

I went on sitting on the bed and thinking about riding away on the motor bike. I went on sitting on the bed. And not riding away on the motor bike.

Presently I found myself sighing. I knew very well I had never had any real doubts about staying, even if it meant scrubbing those dreadful paths every day of the week. Quite apart from not finding myself good company in future if I ran away because of a little bit of eccentric charring, there was the certainty that it was specifically in Mr. P. J. Adams' ruthless hands that the good repute of British racing was in danger of being cracked to bits. It was him that I had come to defeat. It was no good decamping because the first taste of him was unpleasant.

His named typed on paper had come alive as a worse menace than Humber himself had ever seemed. Humber was merely harsh, greedy, bad-tempered, and vain, and he beat his lads for the sole purpose of making them leave. But Adams seemed to enjoy hurting for its own sake. Beneath that glossy crust of sophistication, and not far beneath, one glimpsed an irresponsible savage. Humber was forceful; but Adams, it now seemed to me, was the brains of the partnership. He was a more complex man and far more fearsome adversary. I had felt equal to Humber. Adams dismayed me.

Someone started to come up the ladder. I thought it would be Cecil, reeling from his Saturday-night orgy, but it was Jerry. He came and sat on the bed next to mine. He looked downcast.

"Dan?"

"Yes."

"It weren't . . . it weren't no good in Posset today, without you being there."

"Wasn't it?"

"No." He brightened. "I bought my comic, though. Will you read it to me?"

"Tomorrow," I said tiredly.

There was a short silence while he struggled to organize his thoughts.

"Dan."

"Mm?"

"I'm sorry, like."

"What for?"

"Well, for laughing at you, like, this afternoon. It wasn't right . . . not when you've took me on your motor bike and all. I do ever so like going on your bike."

"It's all right, Jerry."

"The others were ribbing you, see, and it seemed the thing, like, to do what they done. So they would . . . would let me go with them, see?"

"Yes, Jerry, I see. It doesn't matter, really it doesn't."

"You never ribbed me when I done wrong."

"Forget it."

"I've been thinking," he said, wrinkling his forehead, "about me mam. She tried scrubbing some floors once. In some offices, it was. She came home fair whacked, she did. She said scrubbing floors was wicked. It made your back ache something chronic, she said, as I remember."

"Did she?"

"Does your back ache, Dan?"

"Yes, a bit."

He nodded, pleased. "She knows a thing or two, does my mam." He lapsed into one of his mindless silences, rocking himself gently backward and forward on the creaking bed.

I was touched by his apology.

"I'll read your comic for you," I said.

"You ain't too whacked?" he asked eagerly.

I shook my head.

He fetched the comic from the cardboard box in which he kept his few belongings and sat beside me while I read him the captions of Mickey the Monkey, Beryl and Peril, Julius Cheeser, The Bustom Boys, and all the rest. We went through the whole thing at least twice, with him laughing contentedly and repeating the words after me. By the end of the week he would know most of them by heart.

At length I took the comic out of his hands and put it down on the bed.

"Jerry," I said, "which of the horses you look after belongs to Mr. Adams?"

"Mr. Adams?"

"The man whose hunters I've got. The man who was here this morning, with a gray Jaguar, and a scarlet coat."

"Oh, that Mr. Adams."

"Why, is there another one?"

"No, that's Mr. Adams, all right." Jerry shuddered.

"What do you know about him?" I asked.

"The chap what was here before you came—Dennis, his name was—Mr. Adams didn't like him, see? He cheeked Mr. Adams, he did."

"Oh," I said. I wasn't sure I wanted to hear what had happened to Dennis.

"He weren't here above three weeks," said Jerry reflectively. "The last couple of days, he kept on falling down. Funny, it was, really."

I cut him short. "Which of your horses belongs to Mr. Adams?" I repeated.

"None of them do," he said positively.

"Cass said so."

He looked surprised, and also scared. "No, Dan, I don't want none of Mr. Adams' horses."

"Well, who do your horses belong to?"

"I don't rightly know. Except of course Pageant. He belongs to Mr. Byrd."

"That's the one you take to the races?"

"Uh huh, that's the one."

"How about the others?"

"Well, Mickey . . ." His brow furrowed.

"Mickey is the horse in the box next to Mr. Adams' black hunter, which I do?"

"Yeah." He smiled brilliantly, as if I had made a point.

"Who does Mickey belong to?"

"I dunno."

"Hasn't his owner ever been to see him?"

He shook his head doubtfully. I wasn't sure whether or not he would remember if an owner had in fact called.

"How about your other horse?" Jerry had only three horses to do, as he was slower than everyone else.

"That's Champ," said Jerry triumphantly.

"Who owns him?"

"He's a hunter."

"Yes, but who owns him?"

"Some fellow." He was trying hard. "A fat fellow. With sort of sticking-out ears." He pulled his own ears forward to show me.

"You know him well?"

He smiled widely. "He gave me ten bob for Christmas."

So it was Mickey, I thought, who belonged to Adams, but neither Adams nor Humber nor Cass had let Jerry know it. It looked as though Cass had let it slip out by mistake.

I said, "How long have you worked here, Jerry?"

"How long?" he echoed vaguely.

"How many weeks were you here before Christmas?"

He put his head on one side and thought. He brightened. "I came on the day after the Rovers beat the Gunners. My Dad took me to the match, see? Near our house, the Rovers' ground is."

I asked him more questions, but he had no clearer idea than that about when he had come to Humber's.

"Well," I said, "was Mickey here already, when you came?"

"I've never done no other horses since I've been here," he said. When I asked him no more questions, he placidly picked up the comic again and began to look at the pictures. Watching him, I wondered what it was like to have a mind like his, a brain like cotton wool upon which the accumulated learning of the work could make no dent, in which reason, memory, and awareness were blanketed almost out of existence.

He smiled happily at the comic strips. He was, I reflected, none the worse off for being simpleminded. He was good at heart, and what he did not understand could not hurt him. There was a lot to be said for life on that level. If one didn't realize one was the object of calculated humiliations, there would be no need to try to make oneself be insensitive to them. If I had his simplicity, I thought, I would find life at Humber's very much easier.

He looked up suddenly and saw me watching him, and gave me a warm, contented, trusting smile.

"I like you," he said, and turned his attention back to the paper.

There was a raucous noise from downstairs and the other lads erupted up the ladder, pushing Cecil among them, as he was practically unable to walk. Jerry scuttled back to his own bed and put his comic away carefully; and I, like all the rest, wrapped myself in two gray blankets and lay down, boots and all, on the inhospitable canvas. I tried to find a comfortable position for my excessively weary limbs, but unfortunately failed.

CHAPTER 11

THE OFFICE WAS as cold and unwelcoming as Humber's personality, with none of the ostentation of his car. It consisted of a long, narrow room with the door and the single smallish window both in the long wall facing down the yard. At the far end, away to the left as one entered, there was a door which opened into a washroom; this was whitewashed and lit by three slitlike frosted-glass windows, and led through an inner door into a lavatory. In the washroom itself there was a sink, a plastic-top table, a refrigerator, and two wall cupboards. The first of these on investigation proved to hold all the bandages, liniments, and medicines in common use with horses.

Careful not to move anything from its original position, I looked at every bottle, packet, and tin. As far as I could see, there was nothing of a stimulating nature among them.

The second cupboard, however, held plenty of stimulant in the shape of alcohol for human consumption, an impressive collection of bottles with a well-stocked shelf of glasses above them. For the entertainment of owners, not the quickening of their horses. I shut the door.

There was nothing in the refrigerator except four bottles of beer, some milk, and a couple of trays of ice cubes.

I went back into the office.

Humber's desk stood under the window, so that when he was sitting at it he could look straight out down the yard. It was a heavy, flat-topped kneehole desk with drawers at each side, and it was almost aggressively tidy. Granted Humber was away at Nottingham races and had not spent long in the office in the morning, but the tidiness was basic, not temporary. None of the drawers was locked, and their contents (stationery, tax tables, and so on) could be seen at a glance. On top of the desk there was only a telephone, an adjustable reading lamp, a tray of pens and pencils, and a green glass paperweight the size of a cricket ball. Trapped air bubbles rose in a frozen spray in its depths.

The single sheet of paper which it held down bore only a list of duties for the day and had clearly been drawn up for Cass to work from. I saw disconsolately that I would be cleaning tack that afternoon with baby-voiced Kenneth, who never stopped talking, and doing five horses at evening stables, this last because the horses normally done by Bert, who had gone racing, had to be shared out among those left behind.

Apart from the desk, the office contained a large floor-to-ceiling cupboard in which form books and racing colors were kept; too few of those for the space available. Three dark-green filing cabinets, two leather armchairs, and an upright wooden chair with a leather seat stood around the walls.

I opened the unlocked drawers of the filing cabinets one by one and searched quickly through the contents. They contained racing calendars, old accounts, receipts, press cuttings, photographs, papers to do with the horses currently in training, analyses of form, letters from owners, records of saddlery and fodder transactions; everything that could be found in the office of nearly every trainer in the country.

I looked at my watch. Cass usually took an hour off for lunch. I had waited five minutes after he had driven out of the yard, and I intended to be out of the office ten minutes before he could be expected back. This had given me a working time of three-quarters of an hour, of which nearly half had already gone.

Borrowing a pencil from the desk and taking a sheet of writing paper from a drawer, I applied myself to the drawer full of current accounts. For each of seventeen racehorses there was a separate hard-covered blue ledger, in which was listed every major and minor expense incurred in its training. I wrote a list of their names, few of which were familiar to me, together with their owners and the dates when they had come into the yard. Some had been there for years, but three had arrived during the past three months, and it was only these, I thought, which were of any real interest. None of the horses which had been doped had stayed at Humber's longer than four months.

The names of the three newest horses were Chin-Chin, Kandersteg, and Starlamp. The first was owned by Humber himself and the other two by Adams.

I put the account books back where I had found them and looked at my watch. Seventeen minutes left. Putting the pencil back on the desk, I folded the list of horses and stowed it away in my money belt. The webbing pockets were filling up again with fivers, as I had spent little of my pay, but the belt still lay flat and invisible below my waist under my jeans; and I had been careful not to let any of the lads know it was there, so as not to be robbed.

I riffled quickly through the drawers of press cuttings and photographs, but found no reference to the eleven horses or their successes. The racing calendars bore more fruit in the shape of a penciled cross against the name of Superman in the Boxing Day selling chase, but there was no mark against the selling chase scheduled for the coming meeting at Sedgefield.

It was at the back of the receipts drawer that I struck most gold. There was another blue accounts ledger there, with a double page devoted to each of the eleven horses. Among these eleven were interspersed nine others who had in various ways failed in their purpose. One of these was Superman and another Old Etonian.

On the left-hand page of each double spread had been recorded the entire racing career of the horse in question, and on the right-hand pages of my eleven old friends were details of the race they each won with assistance. Beneath were sums of money which I judged must be Humber's winnings on them. His winnings had run into thousands on every successful race. On Superman's page he had written: "Lost: three hundred pounds." On Old Etonian's right-hand page there was no race record: only the single word "Destroyed."

A crossing-out line had been drawn diagonally across all the pages except those concerning a horse called Six-Ply; and two new double pages had been prepared at the end, one for Kandersteg, and one for Starlamp. The left-hand pages for these three horses were written up: the right-hand pages were blank.

I shut the book and put it back. It was high time to go, and with a last look around to make sure that everything was exactly as it had been when I came in, I let myself quietly, unnoticed, out of the door, and went back to the kitchen to see if by some miracle the lads had left me any crumbs of lunch. Naturally, they had not.

THE NEXT MORNING Jerry's horse Mickey disappeared from the yard while we were out at second exercise, but Cass told him Jud had run him down to a friend of Humber's on the coast, for Mickey to paddle in the sea water to strengthen his legs, and that he would be back that evening. But the evening came, and Mickey did not.

On Wednesday Humber ran another horse, and I missed my lunch to have a look inside his house while he was away. Entry was easy through an open ventilator, but I could find nothing whatever to give me any clue as to how the doping was carried out.

All day Thursday I fretted about Mickey being still away at the coast. It sounded perfectly reasonable. It was what a trainer about twelve miles from the sea could be expected to arrange. Sea water was good for horses' legs. But something happened to horses sometimes at Humber's which made it possible for them to be doped later, and I had a deeply disturbing suspicion that whatever it was was happening to Mickey at this moment, and that I was missing my only chance of finding it out.

According to the accounts books, Adams owned four of the racehorses in the yard, in addition to his two hunters. None of his racehorses was known in the yard by its real name: therefore Mickey could be any one of the four. He could in fact be Kandersteg or Starlamp. It was an even chance that he was one or the other, and was due to follow in Superman's footsteps. So I fretted.

On Friday morning a hired box took the stable runner to Haydock races, and Jud and Humber's own box remained in the yard until lunchtime. This was a definite departure from normal; and I took the opportunity of noting the mileage on the speedometer.

Jud drove the box out of the yard while we were still eating midday sludge, and we didn't see him come back, as we were all out on the gallop farthest away from the stables sticking back into place the divots kicked out of the soft earth that week by the various training activities; but when we returned for evening stables at four, Mickey was back in his own quarters.

I climbed up into the cab of the horse box and looked at the mileage indicator. Jud had driven exactly sixteen and a half miles. He had not, in fact, been as far as the coast. I thought some very bitter thoughts.

When I had finished doing my two racehorses, I carried the brushes and pitchforks along to see to Adams' black hunter, and found Jerry leaning against the wall outside Mickey's next-door box with tears running down his cheeks.

"What's the matter?" I said, putting down my stuff.

"Mickey . . . bit me," he said. He was shaking with pain and fright.

"Let's see."

I helped him slide his left arm out of his jersey, and took a look at the damage. There was a fierce red-and-purple circular weal on the fleshy part of his upper arm near the shoulder. It had been a hard, savage bite.

Cass came over.

"What's going on here?"

But he saw Jerry's arm, and didn't need to be told. He looked over the bottom half of the door into Mickey's box, then turned to Jerry and said, "His legs were too far gone for the sea water to cure them. The vet said he would have to put on a blister, and he did it this afternoon when Mickey got back. That's what's the matter with him. Feels a bit off color, he does, and so would you if someone slapped a flaming plaster on your legs. Now you just stop this stupid blubbering and get right back in there and see to him. And you, Dan, get on with that hunter and mind your own bloody business." He went off along the row.

"I can't," whispered Jerry, more to himself than to me.

"You'll manage it," I said cheerfully.

He turned to me a stricken face. "He'll bite me again."

"I'm sure he won't."

"He tried lots of times. And he's kicking out something terrible. I daren't go into his box. . . ." He stood stiffly, shivering with fright, and I realized that it really was beyond him to go back.

"All right," I said, "I'll do Mickey and you do my hunter. Only do him well, Jerry, very well. Mr. Adams is coming to ride him again tomorrow and I don't want to spend another Saturday on my knees."

He looked dazed. "Ain't no one done nothing like that for me before."

"It's a swap," I said brusquely. "You mess up my hunter and I'll bite you worse than Mickey did."

He stopped shivering and began to grin, which I had intended, and slipping his arm painfully back inside his jersey, he picked up my brushes and opened the hunter's door.

"You won't tell Cass?" he asked anxiously.

"No," I reassured him, and unbolted Mickey's box door.

The horse was tied up safely enough, and wore on his neck a long wooden barred collar called a cradle which prevented his bending his head down to bite the bandages off his forelegs. Under the bandages, according to Cass, Mickey's legs were plastered with "blister," a sort of caustic paste used to contract and strengthen the tendons. Blistering was a normal treatment for dickey tendons. The only trouble was that Mickey's legs had not needed treatment. They had been, to my eyes, as sound as rocks. But now, however, they were definitely paining him; at least as much as with a blister, and possibly more.

As Jerry had indicated, Mickey was distinctly upset. He could not be soothed by hand or voice, but lashed forward with his hind feet whenever he thought I was in range, and made equal use of his teeth. I was careful not to walk behind him, though he did his best to turn his quarters in my direction while I was banking up his straw bed around the back of the box. I fetched him hay and water, but he was not interested, and changed his rug, as the one he wore was soaked with sweat and would give him a chill during the night. Changing his rug was a bit of an obstacle race, but by warding off his attacks with a pitchfork, I got it done unscathed.

I took Jerry with me to the feed bins, where Cass was doling out the right food for each horse, and when we got back to the boxes we solemnly exchanged bowls. Jerry grinned happily. It was infectious. I grinned back.

Mickey didn't want food either, not, that is, except lumps of me. He didn't get any. I left him tied up for the night and took myself and Jerry's sack of brushes to safety on the far side of the door. Mickey would, I hoped, have calmed down considerably by the morning.

Jerry was grooming the black hunter practically hair by hair, humming tonelessly under his breath.

"Are you done?" I said.

"Is he all right?" he asked anxiously.

I went in to have a look.

"Perfect," I said truthfully. Jerry was better at strapping a horse than at most things; and the next day, to my considerable relief, Adams passed both hunters without remark and spoke hardly a word to me. He was in a hurry to be off to a distant meet, but all the same it seemed I had succeeded in appearing too spineless to be worth tormenting.

MICKEY WAS A good deal worse that morning. When Adams had gone, I stood with Jerry looking over the half door of Mickey's box. The poor animal had managed to rip one of the bandages off in spite of the cradle, and we could see a big raw area over his tendon.

Mickey looked around at us with baleful eyes and flat ears, his neck stretched forward aggressively. Muscles quivered violently in his shoulders and hindquarters. I had never seen a horse behave like that except when fighting; and he was, I thought, dangerous.

"He's off his head," whispered Jerry, awestruck.

"Poor thing."

"You ain't going in?" he said. "He looks like he'd kill you."

"Go and get Cass," I said. "No, I'm not going in, not without Cass knowing how things are, and Humber, too. You go and tell Cass that Mickey's gone mad; that ought to fetch him to have a look."

Jerry trotted off and returned with Cass, who seemed to be alternating between anxiety and scorn as he came within earshot. At the sight of Mickey, anxiety abruptly took over, and he went to fetch Humber, telling Jerry on no account to open Mickey's door.

Humber came unhurriedly across the yard leaning on his stick, with Cass, who was a short man, trotting along at his side. Humber looked at Mickey for a good long time. Then he shifted his gaze to Jerry, who was standing there shaking again at the thought of having to deal with a horse in such a state, and then farther along to me, where I stood at the door of the next box.

"That's Mr. Adams' hunter's box," he said to me.

"Yes, sir; he went with Mr. Adams just now, sir."

He looked me up and down, and then Jerry the same, and finally said to Cass, "Roke and Webber had better change horses. I know they haven't an ounce of guts between them, but Roke is much bigger, stronger, and older." And also, I thought with a flash of insight, Jerry has a father and mother to make a fuss if he gets hurt, whereas against Roke in the next-of-kin file was the single word "None."

"I'm not going in there alone, sir," I said. "Cass will have to hold off with a pitchfork while I muck him out." And even then, I thought, we'd both be lucky to get out without being kicked.

Cass, to my amusement, hurriedly started telling Humber that if I was too scared to do it on my own, he would get one of the other lads to help me. Humber, however, took no notice of either of us, but went back to staring somberly at Mickey.

Finally he turned to me and said, "Fetch a bucket and come over to the office."

"An empty bucket, sir?"

"Yes," he said impatiently, "an empty bucket." He turned and gently limped over to the long brick hut. I took the bucket out of the hunter's box, followed him, and waited by the door.

He came out with a small labeled glass-stoppered chemist's jar in one hand and a teaspoon in the other. The jar was three-quarters full of white powder. He gestured to me to hold out the bucket, then he put half a teaspoonful of the powder into it.

"Fill the bucket only a third full of water," he said. "And put it in Mickey's manger, so that he can't kick it over. It will quieten him down, once he drinks it."

He took the jar and spoon back inside the office, and I picked a good pinch of the white powder out of the bottom of the bucket and dropped it down inside the lists of Humber's horses in my money belt. I licked my fingers and thumb afterward; the particles of powder clinging there had a faintly bitter taste. The jar, which I had seen in the cupboard in the washroom, was labeled "Soluble Phenobarbitone," and the only surprising factor was the amount of it that Humber kept available.

I ran water into the bucket, stirred it with my hand, and went back to Mickey's box. Cass had vanished. Jerry was across the yard seeing to his third horse. I looked around for someone to ask for help, but everyone was carefully keeping out of sight. I cursed. I was not going in to Mickey alone; it was just plain stupid to try it.

Humber came back across the yard.

"Get on in," he said.

"I'd spill the water dodging him, sir."

"Huh."

Mickey's hoofs thudded viciously against the wall.

"You mean you haven't got the guts."

"You'd need to be a bloody fool to go in there alone, sir," I said sullenly.

He glared at me, but he must have seen it was no use insisting. He suddenly picked up the pitchfork from where it stood against the wall and transferred it to his right hand and the walking stick to his left.

"Get on with it then," he said harshly. "And don't waste time."

He looked incongruous, brandishing his two unconventional weapons while dressed like an advertisement for *Country Life*. I hoped he was going to be as resolute as he sounded.

I unbolted Mickey's door and we went in. It had been an injustice to think Humber might turn tail and leave me there alone: he behaved as coldly as ever, as if fear was quite beyond his imagination. Efficiently he kept Mickey penned first to one side of the box and then to the other while I mucked out and put down fresh straw; he remained steadfastly at his post while I cleaned the uneaten food out of the manger and wedged the bucket of doped water in place. Mickey didn't make it easy for him, either. The teeth and hoofs were busier and more dangerous than the night before.

It was especially aggravating in the face of Humber's coolness to have to remember to behave like a bit of a coward myself, though I minded less than if he had been Adams.

When I had finished the jobs, Humber told me to go out first, and he retreated in good order after me, his well-pressed suit scarcely rumpled from his exertions.

I shut the door and bolted it, and did my best to look thoroughly frightened. Humber looked me over with disgust.

"Roke," he said sarcastically, "I hope you will feel capable of dealing with Mickey when he is half asleep with drugs?"

"Yes, sir," I muttered.

"Then in order not to strain your feeble stock of courage, I suggest we keep him drugged for some days. Every time you fetch him a bucket of water, you can get Cass or me to put some sedative in it. Understand?"

"Yes, sir."

"Right." He dismissed me with a chop of his hand.

I carried the sack of dirty straw around to the muck heap, and there took a close look at the bandage which Mickey had dislodged. Blister is a red paste. I had looked in vain for red paste on Mickey's raw leg; and there was not a smear of it on the bandage. Yet from the size and severity of the wound, there should have been half a cupful.

I TOOK JERRY down to Posset on the motorcycle again that afternoon and watched him start to browse contentedly in the toy department of the post office.

There was a letter for me from October.

> *Why did we receive no report from you last week? It is your duty to keep us informed of the position.*

I tore the page up, my mouth twisting. Duty. That was just about enough to make me lose my temper. It was not from any sense of duty that I stayed at Humber's to endure a minor version of slavery. It was because I was obstinate, and liked to finish what I started, and although it sounded a bit grandiose, it was because I really wanted, if I could, to remove British steeplechasing from Adams' clutches. If it had been only a matter of duty I would have repaid October his money and cleared out.

"It is your duty to keep us informed of the position."

He was still angry with me about Patty, I thought morosely, and he wrote that sentence only because he knew I wouldn't like it.

I composed my report.

Your humble and obedient servant regrets that he was unable to carry out his duty last week by keeping you informed of the position.

The position is still far from clear, but a useful fact has been ascertained. None of the original eleven horses will be doped again; but a horse called Six-Ply is lined up to be the next winner. He is now owned by a Mr. Henry Waddington, of Lewes, Sussex.

May I please have the answers to the following questions:

1. Is the powder in the enclosed twist of paper soluble Phenobarbitone?

2. What are in detail the registered physical characteristics of the racehorses Chin-Chin, Kandersteg, and Starlamp?

3. On what date did Blackburn, playing at home, beat Arsenal?

And that, I thought, sticking down the envelope and grinning to myself, that will fix him and his duty.

Jerry and I gorged ourselves at the café. I had been at Humber's for five weeks and two days, and my clothes were getting looser.

When we could eat no more, I went back to the post office and bought a large-scale hiker's map of the surrounding district, and a cheap pair of compasses. Jerry spent fifteen shillings on a toy tank which he had resisted before, and after checking to see if my goodwill extended so far, a second comic for me to read to him. And we went back to Humber's.

Days passed. Mickey's drugged water acted satisfactorily, and I was able to clean his box and look after him without much trouble. Cass took the second bandage off, revealing an equal absence of red paste. However, the wounds gradually started healing.

As Mickey could not be ridden and showed great distress if one tried to lead him out along the road, he had to be walked around the yard for an hour each day, which exercised me more than him, but gave me time to think some very fruitful thoughts.

Humber's stick landed with a resounding thump across Charlie's shoulders on Tuesday morning, and for a second it looked as though Charlie would hit him back. But Humber coldly stared him down, and the next morning, delivered an even harder blow in the same place. Charlie's bed was empty that night.

He was the fourth lad to leave in the six weeks I had been there (not counting the boy who stayed only three days) and of my original half-dozen dormitory companions, only Bert and Jerry remained. The time was getting perceptibly closer when I would find myself at the top of the queue for walking the plank.

Adams came with Humber when he made his usual rounds on Thursday evening. They stopped outside Mickey's box but contented themselves with looking over the half door.

"Don't go in, Paul," said Humber warningly. "He's still very unpredictable, in spite of the drugs."

Adams looked at me where I stood by Mickey's head.

"Why is that gypsy doing this horse? I thought it was the moron's job." He sounded angry and alarmed.

Humber explained that as Mickey had bitten Jerry, he had made me change places with him. Adams still didn't like it, but looked as if he would save his comments until he wouldn't be overheard.

He said, "What is the gypsy's name?"

"Roke," said Humber.

"Well, Roke, come here, out of that box."

Humber said anxiously, "Paul, don't forget we're one lad short already."

These were not particularly reassuring words to hear. I walked across the box, keeping a wary eye on Mickey, let myself out through the door, and stood beside it, drooping and looking at the ground.

"Roke," said Adams in a pleasant-sounding voice, "what do you spend your wages on?"

"The never-never on my motor bike, sir."

"The never-never? Oh, yes. And how many installments have you still to pay?"

"About . . . er . . . fifteen, sir."

"And you don't want to leave here until you've finished paying them off."

"No, sir."

"Will they take your motorcycle away if you stop paying?"

"Yes, sir, they might do."

"So Mr. Humber doesn't need to worry about you leaving him?"

I said slowly, unwillingly, but as it happened truthfully, "No, sir."

"Good," he said briskly. "Then that clears the air, doesn't it? And now you can tell me where you find the guts to deal with an unstable, half-mad horse?"

"He's drugged, sir."

"You and I both know, Roke, that a drugged horse is not necessarily a safe horse."

I said nothing. If there was ever a time when I needed an inspiration, this was it; and my mind was a blank.

"I don't think, Roke," he said softly, "that you are as feeble as you make out. I think there is a lot more stuffing in you than you would have us believe."

"No, sir," I said helplessly.

"Let's find out, shall we?"

He stretched out his hand to Humber, and Humber gave him his walking stick. Adams drew back his arm and hit me fairly smartly across the thigh.

If I was to stay in the yard, I had to stop him. This time the begging simply had to be done. I slid down the door, gasping, and sat on the ground.

"No, sir, don't," I shouted. "I got some pills. I was dead scared of Mickey, and I asked the chemist in Posset on Saturday if he had any pills to make me brave, and he sold me some, and I've been taking them regular ever since."

"What pills?" said Adams disbelievingly.

"Tranquil-something, he said. I didn't rightly catch the word."

"Tranquilizers."

"Yes, that's it, tranquilizers. Don't hit me anymore, sir, please, sir. It was just that I was so dead scared of Mickey. Don't hit me anymore, sir."

"Well, I'm damned." Adams began to laugh. "Well, I'm damned. What will they think of next?" He gave the stick back to Humber, and the two of them walked casually away along to the next box.

"Take tranquilizers to help you out of a blue funk. Well, why not?" Still laughing, they went in to see the next horse.

I got up slowly and brushed the dirt off the seat of my pants. Damn it, I thought miserably, what else could I have done? Why was pride so important, and abandoning it so bitter?

It was more clear than ever that weakness was my only asset. Adams had this fearful kink of seeing any show of spirit as a personal challenge to his ability to crush it. He dominated Humber, and exacted instant obedience from Cass, and they were his allies. If I stood up to him even mildly, I would get nothing but a lot of bruises and he would start wondering why I stayed to collect still more. The more tenaciously I stayed, the more incredible he would find it. Hire purchase on the motor bike wouldn't convince him for long. He was quick. He knew, if he began to think about it, that I had come from October's stables. He must know that October was a Steward and therefore his natural enemy. He would remember Tommy Stapleton. The hypersensitivity of the hunted to danger would stir the roots of his hair. He could check and find out from the post office that I did not send money away each week, and discover that the chemist had sold me no tranquilizers. He was in too deep to risk my being a follow-up to Stapleton; and at the very least, once he was suspicious of me, my detecting days would be over.

Whereas if he continued to be sure of my utter spinelessness, he wouldn't bother about me, and I could if necessary stay in the yard up to five or six weeks more. And heaven forbid, I thought, that I would have to.

Adams, although it had been instinct with him, not reason, was quite right to be alarmed that it was I and not Jerry who was now looking after Mickey.

In the hours I had spent close to the horse, I had come to understand what was really the matter with him, and all my accumulated knowledge about the affected horses, and about all horses in general, had gradually shaken into place. I did by that day know in outline how Adams and Humber had made their winners win.

I knew in outline, but not in detail. A theory, but no proof. For detail and proof I still needed more time, and if the only way I could buy time was to sit on the ground and implore Adams not to beat me, then it had to be done. But it was pretty awful, just the same.

CHAPTER 12

OCTOBER'S REPLY WAS unrelenting.

Six-Ply, according to his present owner, is not going to be entered in any selling races. Does this mean that he will not be doped?

The answers to your questions are as follows:

1. The powder is soluble Phenobarbitone.

2. The physical characteristics of Chin-chin are: bay gelding, white blaze down nose, white sock, off fore. Kandersteg: gelding, washy chestnut,

*three white socks, both forelegs and near hind. Starlamp: brown gelding, left
hind white heel.*

   3. Blackburn beat Arsenal on November 30.

   *I do not appreciate your flippancy. Does your irresponsibility now extend
to the investigation?*

Irresponsibility. Duty. He could really pick his words.

I read the descriptions of the horses again. They told me that Starlamp
was Mickey. Chin-Chin was Dobbin, one of the two racehorses I did which
belonged to Humber. Kandersteg was a pale, shambling creature looked after by Bert, and known in the yard as Flash.

If Blackburn beat Arsenal on November 30, Jerry had been at Humber's
eleven weeks already.

I tore up October's letter and wrote back:

   *Six-Ply may now be vulnerable whatever race he runs in, as he is
the only shot left in the locker since Old Etonian and Superman both
misfired.*

   *In case I fall on my nut out riding, or get knocked over by a passing car,
I think I had better tell you that I had this week realized how the scheme
works, even though I am as yet ignorant of most of the details.*

I told October that the stimulant Adams and Humber used was in fact
adrenalin; and I told him how I believed it was introduced into the bloodstream.

   *As you can see, there are two prime facts which must be established before
Adams and Humber can be prosecuted. I will do my best to finish the job properly, but I can't guarantee it, as the time factor is a nuisance.*

Then, because I felt very alone, I added impulsively, jerkily, as a postscript:

   Believe me. Please believe me. I did nothing to Patty.

When I had written it, I looked at this *cri de coeur* in disgust. I am getting
as soft as I pretend, I thought. I tore the bottom off the sheet of paper and
threw the pitiful words away, and posted my letter in the box.

Thinking it wise actually to buy some tranquilizers in case anyone checked, I stopped at the chemist's and asked for some. The chemist absolutely refused to sell me any, as they could only be had on a doctor's or dentist's prescription. How long would it be, I wondered ruefully, before Adams or Humber discovered this awkward fact.

Jerry was disappointed when I ate my meal in the café very fast, and left him alone to finish and walk back from Posset, but I assured him that I had jobs to do. It was high time I took a look at the surrounding countryside.

I rode out of Posset and, stopping the motorcycle in a lay-by, got out the map over which I had pored intermittently during the week. I had drawn on it with pencil and compasses two concentric circles: the outer circle had a radius of eight miles from Humber's stables, and the inner circle a radius of five miles. If Jud had driven straight there and back when he had gone to fetch Mickey, the place he had fetched him from would lie in the area between the circles.

Some directions from Humber's were unsuitable because of open-cast coal mines; and eight miles to the southeast lay the outskirts of the sprawling mining town called Clavering. All around the north and west sides, however, there was little but moorland interspersed with small valleys like the one in which Humber's stable lay, small fertile pockets in miles and miles of stark, windswept heath.

Tellbridge, the village where Adams lived, lay outside the outer circle by two miles, and because of this I did not think Mickey could have been lodged there during his absence from Humber's. But all the same, the area on a line from Humber's yard to Adams' village seemed the most sensible to take a look at first.

As I did not wish Adams to find me spying out the land around his house, I fastened on my crash helmet, which I had not worn since the trip to Edinburgh, and pulled up over my eyes a large pair of goggles, under which even my sisters wouldn't have recognized me. I didn't, as it happened, see Adams on my travels; but I did see his house, which was a square, cream-colored Georgian pile with gargoyle heads adorning the gateposts. It was the largest, most imposing building in the tiny group of a church, a shop, two pubs, and a gaggle of cottages which made up Tellbridge.

I talked about Adams to the boy who filled my petrol tank in the Tellbridge garage.

"Mr. Adams? Yes, he bought old Sir Lucas' place three, four years ago. After the old man died. There weren't no family to keep it on."

"And Mrs. Adams?" I suggested.

"Blimy, there isn't any Mrs. Adams," he said, laughing and pushing his fair hair out of his eyes with the back of his wrist. "But a lot of birds he has there sometimes. Often got a houseful there, he has. Nobs, now, don't get me wrong—never has anyone but nobs in his house, doesn't Mr. Adams. And anything he wants, he gets, and quick. Never mind anyone else. He woke the whole village up at two in the morning last Friday because he got into his head that he'd like to ring the church bells. He smashed a window to get in. . . . I ask you! Of course, no one says much, because he spends such a lot of money in the village. Food and drink and wages, and so on. Everyone's better off since he came."

"Does he often do things like that—ringing the church bells?"

"Well, not that exactly, but other things, yes. I shouldn't think you could believe all you hear. But they say he pays up handsome if he does any damage, and everyone just puts up with it. High spirits, that's what they say it is."

"Does he buy his petrol here?" I asked idly, fishing in my pocket for some money.

"Not often he doesn't; he has his own tank." The smile died out of the boy's open face. "In fact, I only served him once when his supplies had run out."

"What happened?"

"Well, he trod on my foot. In his hunting boots, too. I couldn't make out if he did it on purpose, because it seemed like that really, but why would he do something like that?"

"I can't imagine."

He shook his head, wondering. "He must have thought I'd moved out of his way, I suppose. Put his heel right on top of my foot, he did, and leaned back. I only had sneakers on. Darn nearly broke my bones, he did. He must weigh getting on for sixteen stone, I shouldn't wonder." He sighed and counted my change into my palm, and I thanked him and went on my way, thinking that it was extraordinary how much a psychopath could get away with if he was big enough and clever and well born.

It was a cold afternoon, and cloudy, but I enjoyed it. Stopping on the highest point of a shoulder of moorland, I sat straddling the bike and looking around at rolling distances of bare, bleak hills and at the tall chimneys of Clavering pointing up on the horizon. I took off my helmet and goggles and pushed my fingers through my hair to let the cold wind into my scalp. It was invigorating.

There was almost no chance, I knew, of my finding where Mickey had been kept. It could be anywhere, in any barn, outhouse, or shed. It didn't have to be a stable, and quite likely was not a stable; and indeed, all I was sure of was that it would be somewhere tucked away out of sight and sound of any neighbors. The trouble was that in that part of Durham, with its widely scattered villages, its sudden valleys, and its miles of open heath, I found there were dozens of places tucked away out of sight and sound of neighbors.

Shrugging, I put my helmet and goggles on again, and spent what little was left of my free time finding two vantage points on high ground, from one of which one could see straight down the valley into Humber's yard, and from the other a main crossroad on the way from Humber's to Tellbridge, together with good stretches of road in all directions from it.

Kandersteg's name being entered in Humber's special hidden ledger, it was all Durham to a doughnut that one day he would take the same trail that Mickey-Starlamp had done. It was quite likely that I would still be unable to find out where he went, but there was no harm in getting the lie of the land clear in my head.

At four o'clock, I rolled back into Humber's yard with the usual lack of enthusiasm, and began my evening's work.

Sunday passed, and Monday. Mickey got no better; the wounds on his legs were healing but he was still a risky prospect, in spite of the drugs, and he was beginning to lose flesh. Although I had never seen or had to deal with a horse in this state before, I gradually grew certain that he would not recover, and that Adams and Humber had another misfire on their hands.

Neither Humber nor Cass liked the look of him, either, though Humber seemed more annoyed than anxious, as time went on. Adams came one morning, and from across the yard in Dobbin's box I watched the three of them standing looking in at Mickey. Presently Cass went into the box for a moment or two, and came out shaking his head. Adams looked furious. He took Humber by the arm and the two of them walked across to the office in what looked like an argument. I would have given much to have overheard them. A pity I couldn't lip-read, I thought, and that I hadn't come equipped with one of those long-range listening devices. As a spy, I was really a dead loss.

On Tuesday morning at breakfast there was a letter for me, postmarked Durham, and I looked at it curiously because there were so few people who either knew where I was or would bother to write to me. I put it in my pocket until I could open it in private and I was glad I had, for to my astonishment it was from October's elder daughter.

She had written from her university address, and said briefly:

Dear Daniel Roke,

I would be glad if you could call to see me for a few moments sometime this week. There is a matter I must discuss with you.

Yours sincerely,
Elinor Tarren

October, I thought, must have given her a message for me, or something he wanted me to see, or perhaps he intended to be there to meet me himself, and had not risked writing to me direct. Puzzled, I asked Cass for an afternoon off, and was refused. Only Saturday, he said, and Saturday only if I behaved myself.

I thought Saturday might be too late, or that she would have gone to Yorkshire for the weekend, but I wrote to her that I could come only on that day, and walked into Posset after the evening meal on Tuesday to post the letter.

Her reply came on Friday, brief again and to the point, with still no hint of why I was to go.

Saturday afternoon will do very well. I will tell the porter you are coming. Go to the side door of the College (this is the door used by students and their visitors) and ask to be shown to my room.

She enclosed a penciled sketch to show me where to find the College, and that was all.

On Saturday morning I had six horses to do, because there was still no replacement for Charlie, and Jerry had gone with Pageant to the races. Adams came as usual to talk to Humber and to supervise the loading up of his hunters, but wasted no attention or energy on me, for which I was thankful. He spent half of the twenty minutes he was in the yard looking into Mickey's box with a scowl on his handsome face.

Cass himself was not always unkind, and because he knew I particularly wanted the afternoon free, he even went so far as to help me get finished before the midday meal. I thanked him, surprised, and he remarked that he knew there had been a lot of extra for everyone (except himself, incidentally) to do, as we were still a lad short, and that I hadn't complained about it as much as most of the others. And that, I thought, was a mistake I would not have to make too often.

I washed as well as the conditions would allow; one had to heat all washing water in a kettle on the stove and pour it into the basin on the marble washstand; and shaved more carefully than usual, looking into the six-by-eight-inch fly-blown bit of looking glass, jostled by the other lads who wanted to be on their way to Posset.

None of the clothes I had were fit for visiting a woman's college. With a sigh I settled for the black sweater, which had a high collar, the charcoal drainpipe trousers, and the black leather jacket. No shirt, because I had no tie. I eyed the sharp-pointed shoes, but I had not been able to overcome my loathing for them, so I scrubbed my jodhpur boots under the tap in the yard, and wore those. Everything else I was wearing needed cleaning, and I supposed I smelled of horses, though I was too used to it to notice.

I shrugged. There was nothing to be done about it. I unwrapped the motor bike and made tracks for Durham.

CHAPTER 13

ELINOR'S COLLEGE STOOD in a tree-lined road along with other sturdy and learned-looking buildings. It had an imposing front entrance and a less imposing tarmacked drive entrance along to the right. I wheeled the motorcycle down there and parked it beside a long row of bicycles. Beyond the bicycles stood six or seven small cars, one of which was Elinor's little scarlet two-seater.

Two steps led up to a large oak door embellished with the single word

"Students." I went in. There was a porter's desk just inside on the right, with a mournful-looking middle-aged man sitting behind it, looking at a list.

"Excuse me," I said. "Could you tell me where to find Lady Elinor Tarren?"

He looked up and said. "You visiting? You expected?"

"I think so," I said.

He asked my name, and thumbed down the list painstakingly. "Daniel Roke to visit Miss Tarren, please show him her room. Yes, that's right. Come on, then." He got down off his stool, came around from behind his desk, and breathing noisily, began to lead me deeper into the building.

There were several twists in the corridors and I could see why it was necessary to have a guide. On every hand were doors with their occupant or purpose written up on small cards set into metal slots. After going up two flights of stairs and around a few more corners, the porter halted outside one more door just like the rest.

"Here you are," he said unemotionally. "This is Miss Tarren's room." He turned away and started to shuffle back to his post.

The card on the door said Miss E. C. Tarren. I knocked. Miss E. C. Tarren opened it.

"Come in," she said. No smile.

I went in. She shut the door behind me. I stood still, looking at her room. I was so accustomed to the starkness of the accommodation at Humber's that it was an odd, strange sensation to find myself again in a room with curtains, carpet, sprung chairs, cushions, and flowers. The colors were mostly blues and greens, mixed and blending, with a bowl of daffodils and red tulips blazing against them.

There was a big desk with books and papers scattered on it; a bookshelf, a bed with a blue cover, a wardrobe, a tall built-in cupboard, and two easy chairs. It looked warm and friendly. A very good room for working in. If I had more than a moment to stand and think about it, I knew I would be envious; this was what my father's and mother's death had robbed me of, the time and liberty to study.

"Please sit down." She indicated one of the easy chairs.

"Thank you." I sat, and she sat down opposite me, but looking at the floor, not at me. She was solemn and frowning, and I rather gloomily wondered if what October wanted her to say to me meant more trouble.

"I asked you to come here . . ." she started. "I asked you to come here because . . ." She stopped and stood up abruptly, and walked around behind me and tried again.

"I asked you to come," she said to the back of my head, "because I have got to apologize to you, and I'm not finding it very easy."

"Apologize?" I said, astonished. "What for?"

"For my sister."

I stood up and turned toward her. "Don't," I said vehemently. I had been too much humbled myself in the past weeks to want to see anyone else in the same position.

She shook her head. "I'm afraid"—she swallowed—"I'm afraid that my family has treated you very badly."

The silver-blond hair shimmered like a halo against the pale sunshine which slanted sideways through the window behind her. She was wearing a scarlet jersey under a sleeveless dark-green dress. The whole effect was colorful and gorgeous, but it was clearly not going to help her if I went on looking at her. I sat down again in the chair and said with some lightheartedness, as it appeared October had not after all dispatched a dressing-down, "Please don't worry about it."

"Worry!" she exclaimed. "What else can I do? I knew, of course, why you were dismissed, and I've said several times to Father that he ought to have had you sent to prison, and now I find none of it is true at all. How can you say there is nothing to worry about when everyone thinks you are guilty of some dreadful crime, and you aren't?"

Her voice was full of concern. She really minded that anyone in her family should have behaved as unfairly as Patty had. She felt guilty just because she was her sister. I liked her for it; but then I already knew she was a thoroughly nice girl.

"How did you find out?" I asked.

"Patty told me last weekend. We were just gossiping together, as we often do. She had always refused to talk about you, but this time she laughed, and told me quite casually, as if it didn't matter anymore. Of course I know she's . . . well . . . used to men. She's just built that way. But this . . . I was so shocked. I couldn't believe her at first."

"What exactly did she tell you?"

There was a pause behind me, then her voice went on, a little shakily. "She said she tried to make you make love to her, but you wouldn't. She said . . . she said she showed you her body, and all you did was to tell her to cover herself up. She said she was so flamingly angry about that that she thought all next day about what revenge she would have on you, and on Sunday morning she worked herself up into floods of tears, and went and told Father . . . told Father . . ."

"Well," I said good-humoredly, "yes, that is, I suppose, a slightly more accurate picture of what took place." I laughed.

"It isn't funny," she protested.

"No. It's a relief."

She came around in front of me and sat down and looked at me.

"You did mind, then, didn't you?"

My distaste must have shown. "Yes. I minded."

"I told Father she had lied about you. I've never told him before about her love affairs, but this was different. . . . Anyway, I told him on Sunday after lunch." She stopped, hesitating. I waited. At last she went on, "It was very odd. He didn't seem surprised, really. Not utterly overthrown, like I was. He just seemed to get very tired, suddenly, as if he had heard bad news. As if a friend had died after a long illness, that sort of sadness. I didn't understand it. And when I said that of course the only fair thing to do would be to offer you your job back, he utterly refused. I argued, but I'm afraid he is adamant. He also refuses to tell Mr. Inskip that you shouldn't have had to leave, and he made me promise not to repeat to him or anyone what Patty had said. It is so unfair," she concludes passionately, "and I felt that even if no one else is to know, at least you should. I don't suppose it makes it any better for you that my father and I have at last found out what really happened, but I wanted you to know that I am sorry, very, very sorry for what my sister did."

I smiled at her. It wasn't difficult. Her coloring was so blazingly fair that it didn't matter if her nose wasn't entirely straight. Her direct gray eyes were full of genuine, earnest regret, and I knew she felt Patty's misbehavior all the more keenly because she thought it had affected a stable lad who had no means of defending himself. This also made it difficult to know what to say in reply.

I understood, of course, that October couldn't declare me an injured innocent, even if he wanted to, which I doubted, without a risk of its reaching Humber's ears, and that the last thing that either of us wanted was for him to have to offer to take me back at Inskip's.

No one in his right mind would stay at Humber's if he could go to Inskip's.

"If you knew," I said slowly, "how much I have wanted your father to believe that I didn't harm your sister, you would realize that what you have just said is worth a dozen jobs to me. I like your father. I respect him. And he is quite right. He cannot possibly give me my old job back, because it would be as good as saying publicly that his daughter is at least a liar, if not more. You can't ask him to do that. You can't expect it. I don't. Things are best left as they are."

She looked at me for some time without speaking. It seemed to me that there was relief in her expression, and surprise, and finally puzzlement.

"Don't you want *any* compensation?"

"No."

"I don't understand you."

"Look," I said, getting up, away from her inquiring gaze. "I'm not as blameless as the snow. I did kiss your sister. I suppose I led her on a bit. And then I was ashamed of myself and backed out, and that's the truth of it. It wasn't her fault. I did behave very badly. So please . . . please don't feel so much guilt on my account." I reached the window and looked out.

"People shouldn't be hung for murders they decide not to commit," she said dryly. "You are being very generous, and I didn't expect it."

"Then you shouldn't have asked me here," I said idly. "You were taking too big a risk." The window looked down onto a quadrangle, a neat square of grass surrounded by broad paths, peaceful and empty in the pale winter sunshine.

"Risk . . . of what?" she said.

"Risk that I would raise a stink. Dishonor to the family. Tarnish to the Tarrens. That sort of thing. Lots of dirty linen and Sunday newspapers and your father losing face among his business associates."

She looked startled, but also determined. "All the same, a wrong had been done, and it had to be put right."

"And damn the consequences?"

"And damn the consequences," she repeated faintly.

I grinned. She was a girl after my own heart. I had been damning a few consequences, too.

"Well," I said reluctantly, "I'd better be off. Thank you for asking me to come. I do understand that you have had a horrible week screwing yourself up for this, and I appreciate it more than I can possibly say."

She looked at her watch, and hesitated. "I know it's an odd time of day, but would you like some coffee? I mean, you've come quite a long way . . ."

"I'd like some very much," I said.

"Well . . . sit down, and I'll get it."

I sat down. She opened the built-in cupboard, which proved to hold a washbasin and mirror on one side and a gas ring and shelves for crockery on the other. She filled a kettle, lit the gas, and put some cups and saucers on the low table between the two chairs, moving economically and gracefully. Unself-conscious, I thought. Sure enough of herself to drop her title where brains mattered more than birth. Sure enough of herself to have a man who looked like I did brought to her bed-sitting room, and to ask him to stay for coffee when it was not necessary, but only polite.

I asked her what subject she was studying, and she said English. She assembled some milk, sugar, and biscuits on the table.

"May I look at your books?" I asked.

"Go ahead," she said amiably.

I got up and looked along her bookshelves. There were the language textbooks—Ancient Icelandic, Anglo-Saxon, and Middle English—and a comprehensive sweep of English writings from Alfred the Great's *Chronicles* to John Betjeman's unattainable amazons.

"What do you think of my books?" she asked curiously.

I didn't know how to answer. The masquerade was damnably unfair to her.

"Very learned," I said lamely.

I turned away from the bookshelves, and came suddenly face to face with my full-length reflection in the mirror door of her wardrobe.

I looked at myself moodily. It was the first comprehensive view of Roke the stable lad that I had had since leaving October's London house months before, and time had not improved things.

My hair was too long, and the sideburns flourished nearly down to the lobes of my ears. My skin was a sort of pale yellow now that the suntan had all faded. There was a tautness in the face and a wary expression in the eyes which had not been there before; and in my black clothes I looked disreputable and a menace to society.

Her reflection moved behind me in the mirror, and I met her eyes and found her watching me.

"You look as if you don't like what you see," she said.

I turned around. "No," I said wryly. "Would anyone?"

"Well . . ." Incredibly she smiled mischievously. "I wouldn't like to set you loose in this college, for instance. If you don't realize, though, the effect which you . . . You may have a few rough edges, but I do now see why Patty tried . . . er . . . I mean . . ." Her voice trailed off in the first confusion she had shown.

"The kettle's boiling," I said helpfully.

Relieved, she turned her back on me and made the coffee. I went to the window and looked down into the deserted quad, resting my forehead on the cold glass.

It still happened, I thought. In spite of those terrible clothes, in spite of the aura of shadiness, it could still happen. What accident, I wondered for the thousandth time in my life, decided that one should be born with bones of a certain design? I couldn't help the shape of my face and head. They were a legacy from a pair of neat-featured parents: their doing, not mine. Like Elinor's hair, I thought. Born in you. Nothing to be proud of. An accident, like a birthmark or a squint. Something I habitually forgot, and found disconcerting when anyone mentioned it. And it had been expensive, moreover. I had lost at least two prospective customers because they hadn't liked the way their wives looked at me instead of my horses.

With Elinor, I thought, it was a momentary attraction which wouldn't last. She was surely too sensible to allow herself to get tangled up with one of her father's ex-stable lads. And as for me, it was strictly hands off the Tarren sisters, both of them. If I was out of the frying pan with one, I was not jumping into the fire with the other. It was a pity, all the same. I liked Elinor rather a lot.

"The coffee's ready," she said.

I turned and went back to the table. She had herself very well controlled again. There was no mischievous revealing light in her face anymore, and she looked almost severe, as if she very much regretted what she had said and was going to make quite certain I didn't take advantage of it.

She handed me a cup and offered the biscuits, which I ate because the lunch at Humber's had consisted of bread, margarine, and hard, tasteless cheese, and the supper would be the same. It nearly always was, on Saturdays, because Humber knew we ate in Posset.

We talked sedately about her father's horses. I asked how Sparking Plug was getting on, and she told me, "Very well, thank you. I've a newspaper clipping about him, if you'd like to see it?" she said.

"Yes, I'd like to."

I followed her to the desk while she looked for it. She shifted some papers to search underneath, and the top one fell onto the floor. I picked it up, put it back on the desk, and looked down at it. It seemed to be some sort of quiz.

"Thank you," she said. "I mustn't lose that, it's the Literary Society's competition, and I've only one more answer to find. Now where did I put that clipping?"

The competition consisted of a number of quotations to which one had to ascribe the author. I picked up the paper and began reading.

"That top one's a brute," she said over her shoulder. "No one's got it yet, I don't think."

"How do you win the competition?" I asked.

"Get a complete, correct set of answers in first."

"And what's the prize?"

"A book. But prestige, mostly. We only have one competition a term, and it's difficult." She opened a drawer full of papers and oddments. "I know I put that clipping somewhere." She began shoveling things out onto the top of the desk.

"Please don't bother anymore," I said politely.

"No, I want to find it." A handful of small objects clattered onto the desk.

Among them was a small chromium-plated tube about three inches long with a loop of chain running from one end to the other. I had seen something like it before, I thought idly. I had seen it quite often. It had something to do with drinks.

"What's that?" I asked, pointing.

"That? Oh, that's a silent whistle." She went on rummaging. "For dogs," she explained.

I picked it up. A silent dog whistle. Why then did I think it was connected with bottle and glasses and—The world stopped.

With an almost physical sensation, my mind leaped toward its prey. I held Adams and Humber in my hand at last. I could feel my pulse racing.

So simple. So very simple. The tube pulled apart in the middle to reveal that one end was a thin whistle, and the other its cap. A whistle joined to its cap by a little length of chain. I put the tiny mouthpiece to my lips and blew. Only a thread of sound came out.

"You can't hear it very well," Elinor said, "but of course a dog can. And you can adjust the whistle to make it sound louder to human ears, too." She took it out of my hand and unscrewed part of the whistle itself. "Now blow." She gave it back.

I blew again. It sounded much more like an ordinary whistle.

"Do you think I could possibly borrow this for a little while?" I asked. "If you're not using it? I . . . I want to try an experiment."

"Yes, I should think so. My dear old sheepdog had to be put down last spring, and I haven't used it since. But you will let me have it back? I am getting a puppy in the long vac, and I want to use it for his training."

"Yes, of course."

"All right, then. Oh, here's that clipping, at last."

I took the strip of newsprint, but I couldn't concentrate on it. All I could see was the drinks compartment in Humber's monster car, with the racks of ice picks, tongs, and little miscellaneous chromium-plated objects. I had never given them more than a cursory glance; but one of them was a small tube with a loop of chain from end to end. One of them was a silent whistle for dogs.

I made an effort, and read about Sparking Plug, and thanked her for finding the clipping.

I stowed her whistle in my money belt and looked at my watch. It was already after half-past three. I was going to be somewhat late back at work.

She had cleared me with October and shown me the whistle: two enormous favors. I wanted to repay her, and could think of only one way of doing it.

"'Nowhere either with more quiet or more freedom from trouble does a man retire than to his own soul. . . .'" I quoted.

She looked up at me, startled. "That's the beginning of the competition."

"Yes. Are you allowed help?"

"Yes. Anything. But . . ."

"It's Marcus Aurelius."

"*Who?*" She was staggered.

"Marcus Aurelius Antonius. Roman emperor, 121 to 180 A.D."

"The *Meditations?*"

I nodded.

"What language was it originally written in? We have to put that, too. Latin, I suppose."

"Greek."

"This is fantastic. . . . Just where did you go to school?"

"I went to a village school in Oxfordshire." So I had, for two years, until I was eight. "And we had a master who perpetually crammed Marcus Aurelius down our throats." But that master had been at Geelong.

I had been tempted to tell her the truth about myself all afternoon, but never more than at that moment. I found it impossible to be anything but my own self in her company, and even at Slaw I had spoken to her more or less in my natural accent. I hated having to pretend to her at all. But I didn't tell her where I had come from and why, because October hadn't, and I thought he ought to know his daughter better than I did. There were her cozy chats with Patty . . . whose tongue could not be relied on; and perhaps he thought it was a risk to his investigations. I didn't know. And I didn't tell her.

"Are you really sure it's Marcus Aurelius?" she said doubtfully. "We only get one shot. If it's wrong, you don't get another."

"I should check it then. It comes in a section about learning to be content with your lot. I suppose I remember it because it is good advice and I've seldom been able to follow it." I grinned.

"You know," she said tentatively, "it's none of my business, but I would have thought you could have got on a bit in the world. You seem . . . you seem decidedly intelligent. Why do you work in a stable?"

"I work in a stable," I told her with perfect, ironic truth, "because it's the only thing I know how to do."

"Will you do it for the rest of your life?"

"I expect so."

"And will it content you?"

"It will have to."

"I didn't expect this afternoon to turn out like this at all," she said. "To be frank, I was dreading it. And you have made it easy."

"That's all right, then," I said cheerfully.

She smiled. I went to the door and opened it, and she said, "I'd better see you out. This building must have been the work of a maze-crazy architect. Visitors have been found wandering about the upper reaches dying of thirst days after they were supposed to have left."

I laughed. She walked beside me back along the twisting corridors, down the stairs, and right back to the outside door, talking easily about her life in college, talking to me freely, as an equal. She told me that Durham was the oldest English university after Oxford and Cambridge, and that it was the only place in Britain which offered a course in geophysics. She was, indeed, a very nice girl.

She shook hands with me on the step.

"Good-bye," she said. "I'm sorry Patty was so beastly."

"I'm not. If she hadn't been, I wouldn't have been here this afternoon."

She laughed. "But what a price to pay."

"Worth it."

Her gray eyes had darker gray flecks in them, I noticed. She watched me go over and sit on the motorcycle and fasten on the helmet. Then she waved her hand briefly, and went back through the door. It closed with finality behind her.

CHAPTER 14

I STOPPED IN Posset on the return journey to see if there was any comment from October on the theory I had sent him the previous week, but there was no letter for me at all.

Although I was already late for evening stables, I stopped longer to write to him. I couldn't get Tommy Stapleton out of my head; he had died without passing on what he knew. I didn't want to make the same mistake. Or to die, either, if it came to that. I scribbled fast.

> *I think the trigger is a silent whistle, the sort used for dogs. Humber keeps one in the drinks compartment of his car. Remember Old Etonian? They hold hound trails at Cartmel, on the morning of the races.*

Having posted that, I bought a large slab of chocolate for food, and also Jerry's comic, and slid as quietly as I could back into the yard. Cass caught me, however, and said sourly that I'd be lucky to get Saturday off next week, as he would be reporting me to Humber. I sighed resignedly, started the load of evening chores, and felt the cold, dingy, subviolent atmosphere of the place seep back into my bones.

But there was a difference now. The whistle lay like a bomb in my money belt. A death sentence, if they found me with it. Or so I believed. There remained the matter of making sure I had not leaped to the wrong conclusion.

Tommy Stapleton had probably suspected what was going on and had walked straight into Humber's yard to tax him with it. He couldn't have known that the men he was dealing with were prepared to kill. But because he had died, I did know. I had lived under their noses for seven weeks, and I had been careful; and because I intended to remain undetected to the end, I spent a long time on Sunday wondering how I could conduct my experiment and get away with it.

On Sunday evening, at about five o'clock, Adams drove into the yard in his shining gray Jaguar. As usual at the sight of him, my heart sank. He walked around the yard with Humber when he made his normal tour of inspection, and stopped for a long time looking over the door at Mickey. Neither he nor Humber came in. Humber had been into Mickey's box several times since the day he helped me take in the first lot of drugged water, but Adams had not been in at all.

Adams said, "What do you think, Hedley?"

Humber shrugged. "There's no change."

"Write him off?"

"I suppose so." Humber sounded depressed.

"It's a bloody nuisance," said Adams violently. He looked at me. "Still bolstering yourself up with tranquilizers?"

"Yes, sir."

He laughed rudely. He thought it very funny. Then his face changed to a scowl, and he said savagely to Humber, "It's useless, I can see that. Give him the chop, then."

Humber turned away, said, "Right, I'll get it done tomorrow."

Their footsteps moved off to the next box. I looked at Mickey. I had done my best for him, but he was too far gone, and had been from the beginning. After a fortnight, what with his mental chaos, his continual state of druggedness, and his persistent refusal to eat, Mickey's condition was pitiable, and anyone less stony than Humber would have had him put down long ago.

I made him comfortable for his last night and evaded yet another slash from his teeth. I couldn't say I was sorry not to have to deal with him anymore, as a fortnight of looking after an unhinged horse would be enough for anyone; but the fact that he was to be put down the next day meant that I would have to perform my experiment without delay.

I didn't feel ready to do it. Thinking about it, as I put away my brushes for the night and walked across the yard toward the kitchen, I tried to find one good reason for putting it off.

The alacrity with which a good excuse for not doing it presented itself led me to the unwelcome, overwhelming realization that for the first time since my childhood, I was thoroughly afraid.

I could get October to make the experiment, I thought, on Six-Ply. Or on any of the other horses. I didn't have to do it myself. It would definitely be more prudent not to do it myself. October could do it with absolute safety, but if Humber found me out, I was as good as dead; therefore I should leave it to October.

It was then that I knew I was afraid, and I didn't like it.

It took me most of the evening to decide to do the experiment myself. On Mickey. The next morning. Shuffling it off onto October doubtless would have been more prudent, but I had myself to live with afterward. What had I really wanted to leave home for, if not to find out what I could or couldn't do?

When I took the bucket to the office door in the morning for Mickey's last dose of Phenobarbitone, there was only a little left in the jar. Cass tipped the glass container upside down and tapped it on the bucket so that the last grains of white powder should not be wasted.

"That's his lot, poor bastard," he observed, putting the stopper back in the empty jar. "Pity there isn't a bit more left; we could have given him a double dose, just this once. Well, get on with it," he added sharply. "Don't hang about looking mournful. It's not you that's going to be shot this afternoon."

Well, I hoped not.

I turned away, went along to the tap, splashed in a little water, swilled around in it the instantly dissolved Phenobarbitone, and poured it away down the drain. Then I filled the bucket with clean water and took it along for Mickey to drink.

He was dying on his feet. The bones stuck out more sharply under his skin and his head hung down below his shoulders. There was still a disorientated wildness in his eye, but he was going downhill so fast that he had little strength left for attacking anyone. For once he made no attempt to bite me when I put the bucket down at his head, but lowered his mouth into it and took a few half-hearted swallows.

Leaving him, I went along to the tack room and took a new head collar out of the basket of stores. This was strictly against the rules: only Cass was supposed to issue new tack. I took the head collar along to Mickey's box and fitted it onto him, removing the one he had weakened by constant fretting during his fortnight's illness, and hiding it under a pile of straw. I unclipped the tethering chain from the old collar and clipped it onto the ring of the new one. I patted Mickey's neck, which he didn't like, walked out of his box, and shut and bolted only the bottom half of the door.

We rode our first lot, and second lot; and by then, I judged, Mickey's brain, without its morning dose, would be coming out of its sedation.

Leading Dobbin, the horse I had just returned on, I went to look at Mickey over the stable door. His head was weaving weakly from side to side, and he seemed very restless. Poor creature, I thought. Poor creature. And for a few seconds I was going to make him suffer more.

Humber stood at his office door, talking to Cass. The lads were bustling in and out looking after their horses, buckets were clattering, voices calling to each other: routine stable noise. I was never going to have a better opportunity.

I began to lead Dobbin across the yard to his box. Halfway there I took the whistle out of my belt and pulled off its cap; then, looking around to make sure that no one was watching, I turned my head over my shoulder, put the tiny mouthpiece to my lips, and blew hard. Only a thread of sound came out, so high that I could hardly hear it above the clatter of Dobbin's feet on the ground.

The result was instantaneous and hideous.

Mickey screamed with terror.

His hoofs threshed wildly against the floor and walls, and the chain that held him rattled as he jerked against it.

I walked Dobbin quickly the few remaining yards into his stall, clipped his chain on, zipped the whistle back into my belt, and ran across toward Mickey's box. Everyone else was doing the same. Humber was limping swiftly down the yard.

Mickey was still screaming and crashing his hoofs against the wall as I looked into his box over the shoulders of Cecil and Lenny. The poor animal was on his hind legs, seemingly trying to beat his way through the bricks in front of him. Then, suddenly, with all his ebbing strength, he dropped his forelegs to the ground and charged backward.

"Look out," shouted Cecil, instinctively retreating from the frantically bunching hindquarters, although he was safely outside a solid door.

Mickey's tethering chain was not very long. There was a sickening snap as he reached the end of it and his backward momentum was joltingly, appallingly stopped. His hind legs slid forward under his belly and he fell with a crash onto his side. His legs jerked stiffly. His head, still secured in the strong new head collar, was held awkwardly off the ground by the taut chain, and by it unnatural angle told its own tale. He had broken his neck. As indeed, to put him quickly out of his frenzy, I had hoped he might.

Everyone in the yard had gathered outside Mickey's box. Humber, having glanced perfunctorily over the door at the dead horse, turned and looked broodingly at his six ragged stable lads. The narrow-eyed harshness of his expression stopped anyone from asking him questions. There was a short silence.

"Stand in a line," he said suddenly.

The lads looked surprised, but did as he said.

"Turn out your pockets," said Humber.

Mystified, the lads obeyed. Cass went down the line looking at what was produced and pulling the pockets out like wings to make sure they were empty. When he came to me I showed him a dirty handkerchief, a penknife, a few coins, and pulled my pockets inside out. He took the handkerchief from my hand, shook it out, and gave it back. The whistle at my waist was only an inch from his fingers.

I felt Humber's searching gaze on me from six feet away, but as I studied to keep my face vacantly relaxed and vaguely puzzled, I was astonished to find that I was neither sweating nor tensing my muscles to make a run for it. In an odd way the nearness of the danger made me cool and clearheaded. I didn't understand it, but it certainly helped.

"Back pocket?" asked Cass.

"Nothing in it," I said casually, turning half around to show him.

"All right. Now you, Kenneth."

I pushed my pockets in again, and replaced their contents. My hands were steady. Extraordinary, I thought.

Humber watched and waited until Kenneth's pockets had been innocently emptied; then he looked at Cass and jerked his head toward the loose boxes. Cass rooted around in the boxes of the horses we had just exercised. He finished the last, came back, and shook his head. Humber pointed silently toward the garage which sheltered the Bentley. Cass disappeared, reappeared, and again unexcitedly shook his head. In silence Humber limped away to his office, leaning on his heavy stick.

He couldn't have heard the whistle, and he didn't suspect that any of us had blown one for the sole purpose of watching its effect on Mickey, because if he had, he would have had us stripped and searched from head to foot. He was still thinking along the lines of Mickey's death being an accident; and having found no whistle in any of the lads' pockets or in their horses' boxes, he would conclude, I hoped, that it was none of that downtrodden bunch who had caused Mickey's brainstorm. If only Adams would agree with him, I was clear.

It was my afternoon for washing the car. Humber's own whistle was still there, tucked neatly into a leather retaining strap between a corkscrew and a pair of ice tongs. I looked, and left it where it was.

ADAMS CAME THE next day.

Mickey had gone to the dog-meat man, who had grumbled about his thinness, and I had unobtrusively returned the new head collar to the store basket, leaving the old one dangling as usual from the tethering chain. Even Cass had not noticed the substitution.

Adams and Humber strolled along to Mickey's empty box and leaned on the half door, talking. Jerry poked his head out of the box next door, saw them standing there, and hurriedly disappeared again. I went normally about my business, fetching hay and water for Dobbin and carting away the muck sack.

"Roke," shouted Humber, "come here. At the double."

I hurried over. "Sir?"

"You haven't cleaned out this box."

"I'm sorry, sir. I'll do it this afternoon."

"You will do it," he said deliberately, "before you have your dinner."

He knew very well that this meant having no dinner at all. I glanced at his face. He was looking at me with calculation, his eyes narrowed and his lips pursed.

I looked down. "Yes, sir," I said meekly. Damn it, I thought furiously; this was too soon. I had been there not quite eight weeks, and I ought to have been able to count on at least three more. If he was already intent on making me leave, I was not going to be able to finish the job.

"For a start," said Adams, "you can fetch out that bucket and put it away."

I looked into the box. Mickey's bucket still stood by the manger. I opened the door, walked over, picked it up, turned around to go back, and stopped dead.

Adams had come into the box after me. He held Humber's walking stick in his hand, and he was smiling.

I dropped the bucket and backed into a corner. He laughed.

"No tranquilizers today, eh, Roke?"

I didn't answer.

He swung his arm and the knobbed end of the stick landed on my ribs. It was hard enough, in all conscience. When he lifted his arm again, I ducked under it and bolted out through the door. His roar of laughter floated after me.

I went on running until I was out of sight, and then walked and rubbed my chest. It was going to be a fair-sized bruise, and I wasn't too keen on collecting many more. I supposed I should be thankful at least that they proposed to rid themselves of me in the ordinary way, and not over a hillside in a burning car.

All through that long, hungry afternoon I tried to decide what was best to do. To go at once, resigned to the fact that I couldn't finish the job, or to stay the few days I safely could without arousing Adams' suspicions. But what, I depressedly wondered, could I discover in three or four days that I had been unable to discover in eight weeks.

It was Jerry, of all people, who decided for me.

After supper (baked beans on bread, but not enough of it) we sat at the table with Jerry's comic spread open. Since Charlie had left, no one had a radio, and the evenings were more boring than ever. Lenny and Kenneth were playing dice on the floor. Cecil was out getting drunk. Bert sat in his silent world on the bench on the other side of Jerry, watching the dice roll across the concrete.

The oven door was open, and all the switches on the electric stove were turned on as high as they would go. This was Lenny's bright idea for supplementing the small heat thrown out by the paraffin stove Humber had grudgingly provided. It wouldn't last longer than the arrival of the electricity bill, but it was warm meanwhile.

The dirty dishes were stacked in the sink. Cobwebs hung like a cornice where the walls met the ceiling. A naked light bulb lit the brick-walled room. Someone had spilled tea on the table, and the corner of Jerry's comic had soaked it up.

I sighed. To think that I wasn't happy to be about to leave this squalid existence, now that I was being given no choice!

Jerry looked up from his comic, keeping his place with his finger.

"Dan?"

"Mmm?"

"Did Mr. Adams bash you?"

"Yes."

"I thought he did." He nodded several times, and went back to his comic.

I suddenly remembered his having looked out of the box next to Mickey's before Adams and Humber had called me over.

"Jerry," I said slowly, "did you hear Mr. Adams and Mr. Humber talking, while you were in the box with Mr. Adams' black hunter?"

"Yes," he said, without looking up.

"What did they say?"

"When you ran away, Mr. Adams laughed and told the boss you wouldn't stand it long. Stand it long," he repeated vaguely, like a refrain, "stand it long."

"Did you hear what they said before that? When they first got there, and you looked out and saw them?"

This troubled him. He sat up and forgot to keep his place.

"I didn't want the boss to know I was still there, see? I ought to have to finished that hunter a good bit before then."

"Yes. Well, you're all right. They didn't catch you."

He grinned and shook his head.

"What did they say?" I prompted.

"They were cross about Mickey. They said they would get on with the next one at once."

"The next what?"

"I don't know."

"Did they say anything else?"

He screwed up his thin little face. He wanted to please me, and I knew this expression meant he was thinking his hardest.

"Mr. Adams said you had been with Mickey too long, and the boss said yes, it was a bad . . . a bad . . . um . . . oh, yes . . . risk, and you had better leave, and Mr. Adams said yes, get on with that as quick as you can and we'll do the next one as soon as he's gone." He opened his eyes wide in triumph at this sustained effort.

"Say that again," I said. "The last bit, that's all."

One thing Jerry could do, from long practice with the comics, was to learn by heart through his ears.

Obediently he repeated, "Mr. Adams said get on with that as quick as you can and we'll do the next one as soon as he's gone."

"What do you want most on earth?" I asked.

He looked surprised and then thoughtful, and finally a dreamy look spread over his face.

"Well?"

"A train," he said. "One you wind up. You know. And rails and things. And a signal." He fell silent in rapture.

"You shall have them," I said. "As soon as I can get them."

His mouth opened.

I said, "Jerry, I'm leaving here. You can't stay when Mr. Adams starts bashing you, can you? So I'll have to go. But I'll send you the train. I won't forget, I promise."

The evening dragged away as so many others had done, and we climbed the ladder to our unyielding beds, where I lay on my back in the dark with my hands laced behind my head and thought about Humber's stick crashing down somewhere on my body in the morning. Rather like going to the dentist for a drilling, I thought ruefully: the anticipation was worse than the event. I sighed, and went to sleep.

Operation Eviction continued much as expected the next day.

When I was unsaddling Dobbin after the second exercise, Humber walked into the box behind me and his stick landed with a thud across my back.

I let go of the saddle—which fell on a pile of fresh droppings—and swung around.

"What did I do wrong, sir?" I said, in an aggrieved voice. I thought I might as well make it difficult for him, but he had an answer ready.

"Cass tells me you were late back at work last Saturday afternoon. And pick up that saddle. What do you think you're doing, dropping it in that dirt?"

He stood with his legs planted firmly apart, his eyes judging his distance.

Well, all right, I thought. One more, and that's enough.

I turned around and picked up the saddle. I already had it in my arms and was straightening up when he hit me again, more or less in the same place, but much harder. The breath hissed through my teeth.

I threw the saddle down again in the dirt and shouted at him. "I'm leaving. I'm off. Right now."

"Very well," he said coldly, with perceptible satisfaction. "Go and pack. Your cards will be waiting for you in the office." He turned on his heel and slowly limped away, his purpose successfully concluded.

How frigid he was, I thought. Unemotional, sexless, and calculating. Impossible to think of him loving, or being loved, or feeling pity, or grief, or any sort of fear.

I arched my back, grimacing, and decided to leave Dobbin's saddle where it was, in the dirt. A nice touch, I thought. In character, to the bitter end.

CHAPTER 15

I TOOK THE polythene sheeting off the motorcycle and coasted gently out of the yard. All the lads were out exercising the third lot, with yet more to be ridden when they got back; and even while I was wondering how five of them were possibly going to cope with thirty horses, I met a shifty-looking boy trudging slowly up the road to Humber's with a kit bag slung over his shoulder. More flotsam. If he had known what he was going to, he would have walked more slowly still.

I biked to Clavering, a dreary mining town of mean back-to-back ter-raced streets jazzed up with chromium and glass in the shopping center, and telephoned to October's London house.

Terence answered. Lord October, he said, was in Germany, where his firm was opening a new factory.

"When will he be back?"

"Saturday morning, I think. He went last Sunday, for a week."

"Is he going to Slaw for the weekend?"

"I think so. He said something about flying back to Manchester, and he's given me no instructions for anything here."

"Can you find the addresses and telephone numbers of Colonel Beckett and Sir Stuart Macclesfield for me?"

"Hang on a moment." There was a fluttering of pages, and Terence told me the numbers and addresses. I wrote them down and thanked him.

"Your clothes are still here, sir," he said.

"I know." I grinned. "I'll be along to fetch them quite soon, I think."

We rang off, and I tried Beckett's number. A dry, precise voice told me that Colonel Beckett was out, but that he would be dining at his club at nine, and could be reached then. Sir Stuart Macclesfield, it transpired, was in a nursing home recovering from pneumonia. I had hoped to be able to summon some help in keeping a watch on Humber's yard so that when the horse box left with Kandersteg on board it could be followed. It looked, however, as though I would have to do it myself, as I could visualize the local police neither believing my story nor providing anyone to assist me.

Armed with a rug and a pair of good binoculars bought in a pawnshop, and also with a pork pie, slabs of nut chocolate, a bottle of Vichy water, and some sheets of foolscap paper, I rode the motorcycle back through Posset and out along the road that crossed the top of the valley in which Humber's stables lay. Stopping at the point I had marked on my previous excursion, I wheeled the cycle a few yards down into the scrubby heathland, and found a position where I was off the skyline, more or less out of sight from passing cars, and also able to look down into Humber's yard through the binoculars. It was one o'clock, and there was nothing happening there.

I unbuckled the suitcase from the carrier and used it as a seat, settling myself to stay there for a long time. Even if I could reach Beckett on the telephone at nine, he wouldn't be able to rustle up reinforcements much before the next morning.

There was, meanwhile, a report to make, a fuller, more formal, more explanatory affair than the notes scribbled in Posset's post office. I took out the foolscap paper and wrote, on and off, for most of the afternoon, punctuating my work by frequent glances through the binoculars. But nothing took place down at Humber's except the normal routine of the stable.

I began:

To The Earl of October
Sir Stuart Macclesfield
Colonel Roderick Beckett

Sirs,
    The following is a summary of the facts which have so far come to light during my investigations on your behalf, together with some deductions which it seems reasonable to make from them.
    Paul James Adams and Hedley Humber started collaborating in a

scheme for ensuring winners about four years ago, when Adams bought the
Manor House and came to live at Tellbridge, Northumberland.

Adams (in my admittedly untrained opinion) has a psychopathic personality, in that he impulsively gives himself pleasure and pursues his own
ends without any consideration for other people or much apparent anxiety
about the consequences to himself. His intelligence seems to be above average,
and it is he who gives the orders. I believe it is fairly common for psychopaths
to be aggressive swindlers; it might be enlightening to dig up his life history.

Humber, though dominated by Adams, is not as irresponsible. He is cold
and controlled at all times. I have never seen him genuinely angry (he uses
anger as a weapon) and everything he does seems to be thought out and calculated. Whereas Adams may be mentally abnormal, Humber seems to be simply wicked. His comparative sanity may act as a brake on Adams, and have
prevented their discovery before this.

Jud Wilson, the head traveling lad, and Cass, the head lad, are both involved, but only to the extent of being hired subordinates. Neither of them does
as much stable work as their jobs would normally entail, but they are well
paid. Both own big cars of less than a year old.

Adams' and Humber's scheme is based on the fact that horses learn by association and connect noises to events. Like Pavlov's dogs who would come to
the sound of a bell because they had been taught it meant feeding time, horses
hearing the feed trolley rattling across the stable yard know very well that
their food is on the way.

If the horse is accustomed to a certain consequence following closely upon
a certain noise, he automatically expects the consequence whenever he hears the
noise. He reacts to the noise in anticipation of what is to come.

If something frightening were substituted—if, for instance, the rattle of
the feed trolley were followed always by a thrashing and no food—the horse
would soon begin to fear the noise, because of what it portended.

Fear is the stimulant which Adams and Humber have used. The appearance of all the apparently "doped" horses after they had won—the staring, rolling eyes and the heavy sweat—was consistent with their having been
in a state of terror.

Fear strongly stimulates the adrenal glands, so that they flood the bloodstream with adrenalin; and the effect of extra adrenalin, as of course you
know, is to release the upsurge of energy needed to deal with the situation,

either by fighting back or by running away. Running, in this case. At top speed, in panic.

The laboratory reports stated that the samples taken from all the original eleven horses showed a high adrenalin content, but that this was not significant because horses vary enormously, some always producing more adrenalin than others. I, however, think that it was significant that the adrenalin counts of those eleven horses were uniformly higher than average.

The noise which triggered off their fear is the high note of the sort of silent whistle normally used for training dogs. Horses can hear it well, though to human ears it is faint; this fact makes it ideal for the purpose, as a more obtrusive sound (a football rattle, for instance) would soon have been spotted. Humber keeps a dog whistle in the drinks compartment of his Bentley.

I do not yet know for sure how Adams and Humber frighten the horses, but I can make a guess.

For a fortnight I looked after a horse known in the yard as Mickey (registered name, Starlamp), who had been given the treatment. In Mickey's case, it was a disaster. He returned from three days' absence with large raw patches on his forelegs and in a completely unhinged mental state.

The wounds on his legs were explained by the head lad as having been caused by the application of a blister. But there was no blister paste to be seen, and I think they were ordinary burns caused by some sort of naked flame. Horses are more afraid of fire than of anything else, and it seems probable to me that it is expectation of being burnt that Adams and Humber have harnessed to the sound of a dog whistle.

I blew a dog whistle to discover its effect on Mickey. It was less than three weeks after the association had been planted, and he reacted violently and unmistakably. If you care to, you can repeat this trial on Six-Ply; but give him room to bolt in safety.

Adams and Humber chose horses that looked promising throughout their racing careers but had never won on account of running out of steam or guts at the last fence; and there are of course any number of horses like this. They bought them cheaply one at a time from auction sales or out of selling races, instilled into them a noise-fear association, and quietly sold them again. Often, far from losing on the deal, they made a profit (cf. past histories of horses collected by officer cadets).

Having sold a horse with such a built-in accelerator, Adams and Humber then waited for it to run in a selling chase at one of five courses: Sedgefield,

Haydock, Ludlow, Kelso, and Stafford. They seem to have been prepared to wait indefinitely for this combination of place and event to occur, and in fact it has only occurred twelve times (eleven winners and Superman) since the first case twenty months ago.

These courses were chosen, I imagine, because their extra-long run-in gave the most room for the panic to take effect. The horses were often lying fourth or fifth when landing over the last fence, and needed time to overhaul the leaders. If a horse was too hopelessly behind, Adams and Humber could just have left the whistle unblown, forfeited their stake money, and waited for another day.

Selling chases were preferred, I think, because horses are less likely to fall in them, and because of the good possibility of the winners changing hands yet again immediately afterward.

At first sight it looks as if it would have been safer to have applied this scheme to flat racing; but flat racers do not seem to change hands so often, which would lessen the confusion. Then again, Humber has never held a flat license, and probably can't get one.

None of the horses has been galvanized twice, the reason probably being that having once discovered they were not burned after hearing the whistle, they would be less likely to expect to be again. Their reaction would no longer be reliable enough to gamble on.

All the eleven horses won at very long odds, varying from 10-1 to 50-1, and Adams and Humber must have spread their bets thinly enough to raise no comment. I do not know how much Adams won on each race, but the least Humber made was 1,700 pounds, and the most was 4,500.

Details of all the processed horses, successful and unsuccessful, are recorded in a blue ledger at present to be found at the back of the third drawer down in the center one of three green filing cabinets in Humber's stable office.

Basically, as you see, it is a simple plan. All they do is make a horse associate fire with a dog whistle, and then blow a whistle as he lands over the last fence.

No drugs, no mechanical contrivances, no help needed from owner, trainer, or jockey. There was only a slight risk of Adams and Humber being found out, because their connection with the horses was so obscure and distant.

Stapleton, however, suspected them and I am certain in my own mind that they killed him, although there is no supporting evidence.

They believe now that they are safe and undetected; and they intend during the next few days to plant fear in a horse called Kandersteg. I have left

Humber's employ, and am writing this while keeping a watch on the yard. I propose to follow the horse box when Kandersteg leaves in it, and discover where and how the heat is applied.

I stopped writing and picked up the binoculars. The lads were bustling about doing evening stables and I stretched myself luxuriously and enjoyed not being down there among them.

It was too soon, I thought, to expect Humber to start on Kandersteg, however much of a hurry he and Adams were in. They couldn't have known for certain that I would depart before lunch, or even that day, and they were bound to let my dust settle before making a move. On the other hand, I couldn't risk missing them. Even the two miles to the telephone in Posset made ringing up Beckett a worrying prospect. It would take no longer for Kandersteg to be loaded up and carted off than for me to locate Beckett in his club. Mickey-Starlamp had been both removed and brought back in daylight, and it might be that Humber never moved any horses about by night. But I couldn't be sure. I bit the end of my pen in indecision. Finally, deciding not to telephone, I added a postscript to the report.

I would very much appreciate some help in this watch, because if it continues for several days I could easily miss the horse box through falling asleep. I can be found two miles out of Posset on the Hexham road, at the head of the valley which Humber's stables lie in.

I added the time, the date, and signed my name. Then I folded the report into an envelope, and addressed it to Colonel Beckett.

I raced down to Posset to put the letter in the box outside the post office. Four miles. I was away for just under six minutes. It was lucky, I think, that I met no traffic on either part of the trip. I skidded to a worried halt at the top of the hill, but all appeared normal down in the stables. I wheeled the motorcycle off the road again, down to where I had been before, and took a long look through the binoculars.

It was beginning to get dark and lights were on in nearly all the boxes, shining out into the yard. The dark, looming bulk of Humber's house, which lay nearest to me, shut off from my sight his brick office and all the top end of the yard, but I had a sideways view of the closed doors of the horse-box garage, and I could see straight into the far-end row of boxes, of which the fourth from the left was occupied by Kandersteg.

And there he was, a pale, washy chestnut, moving across and catching the light as Bert tossed his straw to make him comfortable for the night. I sighed with relief, and sat down again to watch.

The routine work went on, untroubled, unchanged. I watched Humber, leaning on his stick, make his slow inspection around the yard, and absent-mindedly rubbed the bruises he had given me that morning. One by one the doors were shut and the lights went out until only a single window glowed yellow, the last window along the righthand row of boxes, and window of the lads' kitchen. I put down the binoculars, and got to my feet and stretched.

As always on the moors, the air was on the move. It wasn't a wind, scarcely a breeze, more like cold current flowing around whatever it found in its path. To break its chilling persistence on my back I constructed a rough barricade of the motorcycle with a bank of brushwood on its roadward, moorward side. In the lee of this shelter I sat on the suitcase, wrapped myself in the rug, and was tolerably warm and comfortable.

I looked at my watch. Almost eight o'clock. It was a fine, clear night, and the sky was luminous with the white blaze of the stars. I still hadn't learned the northern-hemisphere patterns except for the Great Bear and Pole Star. And there was Venus dazzling away to the west-southwest. A pity that I hadn't thought of buying an astral map to pass the time.

Down in the yard the kitchen door opened, spilling out an oblong of light. Cecil's figure stayed there for a few seconds silhouetted; then he came out and shut the door, and I couldn't see him in the dark. Off to his bottle, no doubt.

I ate some pie, and a while later, a bar of chocolate.

Time passed. Nothing happened down in Humber's yard. Occasionally a car sped along the road behind me, but none stopped. Nine o'clock came and went. Colonel Beckett would be dining at his club, and I could after all have gone safely down to ring him up. I shrugged in the darkness. He would get my letter in the morning, anyway.

The kitchen door opened again, and two or three lads came out, picking their way with a torch around to the elementary sanitation. Upstairs in the hayloft a light showed dimly through that half of the window not pasted over with brown paper. Bedtime. Cecil reeled in, clutching the doorpost to stop himself from falling. The downstairs light went out, and finally the upper one as well.

The night deepened. The hours passed. The moon rose and shone brightly. I gazed out over the primeval rolling moors and thought some unoriginal thought, such as how beautiful the earth was, and how vicious the ape creature who inhabited it. Greedy, destructive, unkind, power-hungry old homo sapiens. Sapiens, meaning wise, discreet, judicious. What a laugh. So fair a planet should have evolved a sweeter-natured, saner race. Nothing that produced people like Adams and Humber could be termed a roaring success.

At four o'clock I ate some more chocolate and drank some water, and for some time thought about my stud farm sweltering in the afternoon sun twelve thousand miles away. A sensible, orderly life waiting for me when I had finished sitting on wintry hillsides in the middle of the night.

Cold crept through the blanket as time wore on, but it was no worse than the temperature in Humber's dormitory. I yawned and rubbed my eyes, and began to work out how many seconds had to pass before dawn. If the sun rose (as expected) at ten to seven, that would be a hundred and thirteen times sixty seconds, which made it 6,780 ticks to Thursday. And how many to Friday? I gave up. It was quite likely I would still be sitting on the hillside, but with a little luck, there would be a Beckett-sent companion to give me a pinch when things started moving.

At six-fifteen the light went on again in the lads' quarters, and the stable woke up. Half an hour later, the first string of six horses wound its way out of the yard and down the road to Posset. No gallops on the moors on Thursday. Road-work day.

Almost before they were out of sight, Jud Wilson drove into the yard in his substantial Ford and parked it beside the horse-box shed. Cass walked across the yard to meet him, and the two of them stood talking together for a few minutes. Then through the binoculars I watched Jud Wilson go back to the shed and open its big double doors, while Cass made straight for Kandersteg's box, the fourth door from the end.

They were off.

And they were off very slickly. Jud Wilson backed the box into the center of the yard and let down the ramp. Cass led the horse straight across and into the horse box, and within a minute was out helping to raise and fasten the ramp again. There was then a fractional pause while they stood looking toward the house, from where almost instantly the limping back view of Humber appeared.

Cass stood watching while Humber and Jud Wilson climbed up into the cab. The horse box rolled forward out of the yard. The loading-up had taken barely five minutes from start to finish.

During this time I dropped the rug over the suitcase and kicked the brushwood away from the bike. The binoculars I slung around my neck and zipped inside the leather jacket. I put on my crash helmet, goggles, and gloves.

In spite of my belief that it would be to the north or the west that Kandersteg would be taken, I was relieved when this proved to be the case. The horse box turned sharply west and trundled up the far side of the valley along the road which crossed the one I was stationed on.

I wheeled the bike onto the road, started it, and abandoning (this time with pleasure) my third clump of clothes, rode with some dispatch toward the crossroads. There, from a safe quarter of a mile away, I watched the horse box slow down, turn right, northward, and accelerate.

CHAPTER 16

I CROUCHED IN a ditch all day and watched Adams, Humber, and Jud Wilson scare Kandersteg into a lathering frenzy.

It was wicked.

The means they used were as simple in essence as the scheme, and consisted mainly in the special layout of a small, two-acre field.

The thin, high hedge around the whole field was laced with wire to about shoulder height, strong but without barbs. About fifteen feet inside this there was a second fence, solidly made of posts and rails which had weathered to a pleasant grayish brown.

At first glance it looked like the arrangement found at many studs farms, where young stock are kept from damaging themselves on wire by a wooden protective inner fence. But the corners of this inner ring had been rounded, so that what in effect had been formed was a miniature race track between the outer and inner fences.

It all looked harmless. A field for young stock, a training place for race-horses, a show ring—take your pick. With a shed for storing equipment, just outside the gate at one corner. Sensible. Ordinary.

I half-knelt, half-lay in the drainage ditch which ran along behind the hedge, near the end of one long side of the field, with the shed little more than a hundred yards away in the far opposite corner, to my left. The bottom of the hedge had been cut and laid, which afforded good camouflage for my head, but from about a foot above the ground the leafless hawthorn grew straight up, tall and weedy; as concealing as a sieve. But as long as I kept absolutely still, I judged I was unlikely to be spotted. At any rate, although I was really too close for safety, too close even to need to use the binoculars, there was nowhere else that gave much cover at all.

Bare hillsides sloped up beyond the far fence and along the end of the field to my right; behind me lay a large open pasture of at least thirty acres; and the top end, which was screened from the road by a wedge of conifers, was directly under Adams' and Humber's eyes.

Getting to the ditch had entailed leaving the inadequate shelter of the last flattening shoulder of hillside and crossing fifteen yards of bare turf when none of the men was in sight. But retreating was going to be less pulse-quickening, since I had only to wait for the dark.

The horse box was parked beside the shed, and almost as soon as I had worked my way around the hill to my present position, there was a clattering of hoofs on the ramp as Kandersteg was unloaded. Jud Wilson led him around through the gate and onto the grassy track. Adams, following, shut the gate and then unlatched a swinging section of the inner fence and fastened it across the track, making a barrier. Walking past Jud and the horse, he did the same with another section a few yards farther on, with the result that Jud and Kandersteg were now standing in a small pen in the corner. A pen with three ways out: the gate out of the field, and the rails which swung across like level crossing gates on either side.

Jud let go of the horse, which quietly began to eat the grass, and he and Adams let themselves out and disappeared into the shed to join Humber. The shed, made of weathered wood, was built like a single loose box, with a window and a split door, and I imagined it was there that Mickey had spent much of the three days he had been away.

There was a certain amount of clattering and banging in the shed, which went on for some time, but as I had only a sideways view of the door, I could see nothing of what was happening.

Presently all three of them came out. Adams walked around behind the shed and reappeared beyond the field, walking up the hillside. He went at a good pace right to the top, and stood gazing about him at the countryside.

Humber and Wilson came through the gate into the field, carrying between them an apparatus which looked like a vacuum cleaner, a cylindrical tank with a hose attached to one end. They put the tank down in the corner, and Wilson held the hose. Kandersteg, quietly cropping the grass close beside them, lifted his head and looked at them, incurious and trusting. He bent down again to eat.

Humber walked the few steps along to where the swinging rail was fastened to the hedge, seemed to be checking something, and then went back to stand beside Wilson, who was looking up toward Adams.

On top of the hill, Adams casually waved his hand.

Down in the corner of the field, Humber had his hand to his mouth; I was too far away to see with the naked eye if what he held there was a whistle, and too close to risk getting out the glasses for a better look. But even though, try as I might, I could hear no noise, there wasn't much room for doubt. Kandersteg raised his head, pricked his ears, and looked at Humber.

Flame suddenly roared from the hose in Wilson's hand. It was directed behind the horse, but it frightened him badly, all the same. He sat back on his haunches, his ears flattening. Then Humber's arm moved, and the swinging barrier, released by some sort of catch, sprang back to let the horse out onto the track. He needed no telling.

He stampeded around the field, skidding at the corners, lurching against the inner wooden rail, thundering past ten feet from my head. Wilson opened the second barrier, and he and Humber retired through the gate. Kandersteg made two complete circuits at high speed before his stretched neck relaxed to a more normal angle and his wildly thrusting hindquarters settled down to a more natural gallop.

Humber and Wilson stood and watched him, and Adams strolled down the hill to join them at the gate.

They let the horse slow down and stop of his own accord, which he did away to my right, after about three and a half circuits. Then Jud Wilson unhurriedly swung one of the barriers back across the track, and waving a stick in one hand and a hunting whip in the other, began to walk around to drive the horse in front of him along into the corner. Kandersteg trotted warily ahead, unsettled, sweating, not wanting to be caught.

Jud Wilson swung his stick and his whip and trudged steadily on. Kandersteg trotted softly past where I lay, his hoofs swishing through the short grass; but I was no longer watching. My face was buried in the roots of the hedge, and I ached with the effort of keeping still. Seconds passed like hours.

There was a rustle of trouser leg brushing against trouser leg, a faint clump of boots on turf, a crack of the long thong of the whip . . . and no outraged yell of discovery. He went past, and on up the field.

The muscles that had been ready to expel me out of the ditch and away toward the hidden motorcycle gradually relaxed. I opened my eyes and looked at leaf mold close to my face, and worked some saliva into my mouth. Cautiously, inch by inch, I raised my head and looked across the field.

The horse had reached the barrier and Wilson was unhooking and swinging the other one shut behind him, so that he was again penned into the small enclosure. There, for about half an hour, the three men left him. They themselves walked back into the shed, where I could do nothing but wait for them to appear again.

It was a fine, clear, quiet morning, but a bit cold for lying in ditches, especially damp ones. Exercise, however, beyond curling and uncurling my toes and fingers, was a bigger risk than pneumonia; so I lay still, taking heart from the thought that I was dressed from head to foot in black, and had a mop of black hair as well, and was crouched in blackish-brown rotting dead leaves. It was because of the protective coloring it offered that I had chosen the ditch in preference to a shallow dip in the hillside, and I was glad I had, because it was fairly certain that Adams from his lookout point would at once have spotted a dark intruder on the pale-green hill.

I didn't notice Jud Wilson walk out of the shed, but I heard the click of the gate, and there he was, going into the little enclosure and laying his hand on Kandersteg's bridle, for all the world as if he was consoling him. But how could anyone who liked horses set about them with a flame-thrower? And Jud, it was clear, was going to do it again. He left the horse, went over to the corner, picked up the hose, and stood adjusting its nozzle.

Presently Adams appeared and climbed the hill, and then Humber, limping on his stick, joined Jud in the field.

There was a long wait before Adams waved his hand, during which three cars passed along the lonely moorland road. Eventually Adams was satisfied. His arm languidly rose and fell.

Humber's hand went immediately to his mouth.

Kandersteg already knew what it meant. He was running back on his haunches in fear before the flame shot out behind him and stopped him dead.

This time there was a fiercer, longer, closer burst to fire, and Kandersteg erupted in greater terror. He came scorching around the track . . . and around again; it was like waiting for the ball to settle in roulette with too much staked. But he stopped this time at the top end of the field, well away from my hiding place.

Jud walked across the middle of the field to come up behind him, not around the whole track. I sighed deeply with heartfelt relief.

I had folded my limbs originally into comfortable angles, but they were beginning to ache with inactivity, and I had a cramp in the calf of my right leg, but I still didn't dare move while all three men were in my sight and I in theirs.

They shut Kandersteg into his little pen and strolled away into the shed, and cautiously, as quietly as I could in the rotting leaves, I flexed my arms and legs, got rid of the cramp, and discovered pins and needles instead. Ah, well . . . it couldn't go on forever.

They were, however, plainly going to repeat the process yet again. The flamethrower still lay by the hedge.

The sun was high in the sky by this time, and I looked at the gleam it raised on the leather sleeve of my left arm, close to my head. It was too shiny. Hedges and ditches held nothing as light-reflecting as black leather. Could Wilson possibly, *possibly* walk a second time within feet of me without coming close enough to the hedge to see a shimmer which shouldn't be there?

Adams and Humber came out of the shed and leaned over the gate, looking at Kandersteg. Presently they lit cigarettes and were clearly talking. They were in no hurry. They finished the cigarettes, threw them away, and stayed where they were for another ten minutes. Then Adams walked over to his car and returned with a bottle and some glasses. Wilson came out of the shed to join them and the three of them stood there in the sun, quietly drinking and gossiping in the most commonplace way.

What they were doing was, of course, routine to them. They had done it at least twenty times before. Their latest victim stood warily in his pen, unmoving, frightened, far too upset to eat.

Watching them drink made me thirsty, but that was among the least of my troubles. Staying still was becoming more and more difficult. Painful, almost.

At long last they broke it up. Adams put the bottle and glasses away and strolled off up the hill, Humber checked the quick release on the swinging barrier, and Jud adjusted the nozzle of the hose.

Adams waved. Humber blew.

This time the figure of Kandersteg was sharply, terrifyingly silhouetted against a sheet of flame. Wilson swayed his body, and the brilliant, spreading jet flattened and momentarily swept under the horse's belly and among his legs.

I nearly cried out, as if it were I that was being burned, not the horse. And for one sickening moment it looked as if Kandersteg was too terrified to escape.

Then squealing, he was down the track like a meteor, fleeing from fire, from pain, from the dog whistle. . . .

He was going too fast to turn the corner. He crashed into the hedge, bounced off, stumbled and fell. Eyes starting out of his head, lips retracted from his teeth, he scrambled frantically to his feet and bolted on, past my head, up the field, around again and around again.

He came to a jolting halt barely twenty yards away from me. He stood stock still with sweat dripping from his neck and down his legs. His flesh quivered convulsively.

Jud Wilson, whip and stick in hand, started on his walk around the track. Slowly I put my face down among the roots and tried to draw some comfort from the fact that if he saw me there was still a heavily wired fence between us, and I should get some sort of start in running away. But the motorcycle was hidden on rough ground two hundred yards behind me, and the curving road lay at least as far beyond that again, and Adams' gray Jaguar was parked on the far side of the horse box. Successful flight wasn't something I'd have liked to bet on.

Kandersteg was too frightened to move. I heard Wilson shouting at him and cracking the whip, but it was a full minute before the hoofs came stumbling jerkily, in bursts and stamps, past my head.

In spite of the cold, I was sweating. Dear heavens, I thought, there was as much adrenalin pouring into my bloodstream as into the horse's; and I realized that from the time Wilson started his methodical walk around the track, I had been able to hear my own heart thudding.

Jud Wilson yelled at Kandersteg so close to my ear that it felt like a blow. The whip cracked.

"Get on, get on, get on there."

He was standing within feet of my head. Kandersteg wouldn't move. The whip cracked again. Jud shouted at the horse, stamping his boot on the ground in encouragement. The faint tremor came to me through the earth. He was a yard away, perhaps, with his eyes on the horse. He had only to turn his head . . . I began to think that anything, even discovery, was preferable to the terrible strain of keeping still.

Then, suddenly, it was over.

Kandersteg skittered away and bumped into the rails, and took a few more uneven steps back toward the top of the field. Jud Wilson moved away after him.

I continued to behave like a log, feeling exhausted. Slowly my heart subsided. I started breathing again . . . and unclamped my fingers from handfuls of leaf mold.

Step by reluctant step Jud forced Kandersteg around to the corner enclosure, where he swung the rails across and penned the horse in again. Then he picked up the flame-thrower and took it with him through the gate. The job was done. Adams, Humber, and Wilson stood in a row and contemplated their handiwork.

The pale coat of the horse was blotted with huge dark patches where the sweat had broken out, and he stood stiff legged, stiff necked, in the center of the small enclosure. Whenever any of the three men moved, he jumped nervously and then stood rigidly still again; and it was clearly going to be some long time before he had unwound enough to be loaded up and taken back to Posset.

Mickey had been away three days, but that, I judged, was only because his legs had been badly burned by mistake. As Kandersteg's indoctrination appeared to have gone without a hitch, he should be back in his own stable fairly soon.

I couldn't be too soon for me and my static joints. I watched the three men potter about in the sunlight, wandering between car and shed, shed and horse box, aimlessly passing the morning and managing never to be all safely out of sight at the same time. I cursed under my breath and resisted a temptation to scratch my nose.

At long last they made a move. Adams and Humber folded themselves into the Jaguar and drove off in the direction of Tellbridge. But Jud Wilson reached into the cab of the horse box, pulled out a paper bag, and proceeded to eat his lunch sitting on the gate. Kandersteg remained immobile in his little enclosure, and I did the same in my ditch.

Jud Wilson finished his lunch, rolled the paper bag into a ball, yawned, and lit a cigarette. Kandersteg continued to sweat, and I to ache. Everything was very quiet. Time passed.

Jud Wilson finished his cigarette, threw the stub away, and yawned again. Then slowly, slowly, he climbed down from the gate, picked up the flamethrower, and took it into the shed.

He was scarcely through the door before I was slithering down into the shallow ditch, lying full length along it on my side, not caring about the dampness but thankfully, slowly, painfully straightening one by one my cramped arms and legs.

The time, when I looked at my watch, was two o'clock. I felt hungry, and regretted that I hadn't had enough sense to bring some of the chocolate.

I lay in the ditch all afternoon, hearing nothing, but waiting for the horse box to start up and drive away. After a while, in spite of the cold and the presence of Jud Wilson, I had great difficulty in keeping awake; a ridiculous state of affairs which could only be remedied by action. Accordingly I rolled over onto my stomach and inch by careful inch raised my head high enough to see across to Kandersteg and the shed.

Jud Wilson was again sitting on the gate. He must have seen my movements out of the corner of his eye, because he looked away from Kandersteg, who stood in front of him, and turned his head in my direction. For a fleeting second it seemed that he was looking straight into my eyes; then his gaze swept past me, and presently, unsuspiciously, returned to Kandersteg.

I let my held breath trickle out slowly, fighting down a cough.

The horse was still sweating, the dark patches showing up starkly, but there was a less fixed look about him, and while I watched, he swished his tail and restlessly shook his neck. He was over the hump.

More cautiously still, I lowered my head and chest down again onto my folded arms, and waited some more.

Soon after four, Adams and Hunter came back in the Jaguar, and again, like a rabbit out of its burrow, I edged up for a look.

They decided to take the horse home. Jud Wilson backed the horse box to the gate and let down the ramp, and Kandersteg, sticking in his feet at every step, was eventually pulled and prodded into it. The poor beast's distress was all too evident, even from across the field. I liked horses. I found I was wholly satisfied that because of me, Adams and Humber and Wilson were going to be out of business.

Gently I lay down again, and after a short while I heard both the engines—first the Jaguar's and then the horse box's—start up and drive off, back toward Posset.

When every sound of them had died away, I stood up—stretched, brushed the leaf mold from my clothes, and walked around the field to look at the shed.

It was fastened shut with a complicated-looking padlock, but through the window I could see it held little besides the flamethrower, some cans presumably holding fuel, a large tin funnel, and three garden chairs folded and stacked against one wall. There seemed little point in breaking in, though it would have been simple enough since the padlock fittings had been screwed straight onto the surface of the door and its frame. The screwdriver blade of my penknife could have removed the whole thing, fussy padlock intact. Crooks, I reflected, could be as fantastically dim in some ways as they were imaginative in others.

I went through the gate into Kandersteg's little enclosure. The grass where he had stood was scorched. The inside surfaces of the rails had been painted white, so that they resembled racecourse rails. I stood for a while looking at them, feeling a secondhand echo of the misery the horse had endured in that harmless-looking place, and then let myself out and walked away, around past my hiding place in the ditch and off toward the motorcycle. I picked it up, hooked the crash helmet onto the handlebars, and started the engine.

So that was the lot, I thought. My job was done. Safely, quietly, satisfactorily done. As it should be. Nothing remained but to complete yesterday's report and put the final facts at the Stewards' disposal.

I coasted back to the place from where I had kept a watch on Humber's yard, but there was no one there. Either Beckett had not got my letter or he had not been able to send any help, or the help, if it had arrived, had got tired of waiting and departed. The rug, suitcase, and remains of food lay where I had left them, undisturbed.

On an impulse, before packing up and leaving the area, I unzipped my jacket and took out the binoculars to have a last look down into the yard.

What I saw demolished in one second flat my complacent feeling of safety and completion.

A scarlet sports car was turning into the yard. It stopped beside Adams' gray Jaguar, a door opened, and a girl got out. I was too far away to distinguish her features but there was no mistaking that familiar car and that dazzling silver-blond hair. She slammed the car door and walked hesitantly toward the office, out of my sight.

I swore aloud. Of all damnable, unforeseeable, dangerous things to happen! I hadn't told Elinor anything. She thought I was an ordinary stable lad. I had borrowed a dog whistle from her. And she was October's daughter. What were the chances, I wondered numbly, of her keeping quiet on the last two counts and not giving Adams the idea that she was a threat to him.

She ought to be safe enough, I thought. Reasonably, she ought to be safe as long as she made it clear that it was I who knew the significance of dog whistles, and not she.

But supposing she didn't make it clear? Adams never behaved reasonably, to start with. His standards were not normal. He was psychopathic. He could impulsively kill a journalist who seemed to be getting too nosy. What was to stop him from killing again, if he got it into his head that it was necessary?

I would give her three minutes, I thought. If she asked for me, and was told I had left, and went straight away again, everything would be all right.

I willed her to return from the office and drive away in her car. I doubted whether in any case, if Adams was planning to harm her, I could get her out safely, since the odds against, in the shape of Adams, Humber, Wilson, and Cass, were too great for common sense. I wasn't too keen on having to try. But the three minutes went past, and the red car stood empty in the yard.

She had stayed to talk and she had no notion that there was anything that should not be said. If I had done as I had wanted and told her why I was at Humber's, she would not have come at all. It was my fault she was there. I clearly had to do my best to see she left again in mint condition. There was no choice.

I put the binoculars in the suitcase and left it and the rug where they were. Then, zipping up the jacket and fastening on the crash helmet, I restarted the bike and rode it down and around and in through Humber's gate.

I left the bike near the gate and walked across toward the yard, passing the shed where the horse box was kept. The doors were shut, and there was no sign of Jud Wilson. Perhaps he had already gone home, and I hoped so. I went into the yard at the top end beside the wall of the office, and saw Cass at the opposite end looking over the door of the fourth box from the left. Kandersteg was home.

Adams' Jaguar and Elinor's TR-4 stood side by side in the center of the yard. Lads were hustling over their evening jobs, and everything looked normal and quiet.

I opened the office door, and walked in.

CHAPTER 17

SO MUCH FOR my fears, I thought. So much for my melodramatic imagination. She was perfectly safe. She held a half-empty glass of pink liquid in her hand, having a friendly drink with Adams and Humber, and she was smiling.

Humber's heavy face looked anxious, but Adams was laughing and enjoying himself. It was a picture which printed itself clearly on my mind before they all three turned and looked at me.

"Daniel!" Elinor exclaimed. "Mr. Adams said you had gone."

"Yes. I left something behind. I came back for it."

"Lady Elinor Tarren," said Adams with deliberation, coming around behind me, closing the door and leaning against it, "came to see if you had conducted the experiment she lent you her dog whistle for."

It was just as well, after all, that I had gone back.

"Oh, surely I didn't say that," she protested. "I just came to get the whistle, if Daniel had finished with it. I mean, I was passing, and I thought I could save him the trouble of sending it . . ."

I turned to him. "Lady Elinor Tarren," I said with equal deliberation, "does not know what I borrowed her whistle for. I didn't tell her. She knows nothing about it."

His eyes narrowed and then opened into a fixed stare. His jaw bunched. He took in the way I had spoken to him, the way I looked at him. It was not what he was used to from me. He transferred his stare to Elinor.

"Leave her alone," I said. "She doesn't know."

"What on earth are you talking about?" said Elinor, smiling. "What was this mysterious experiment, anyway?"

"It wasn't important," I said. "There's . . . er . . . there's a deaf lad here, and we wanted to know if he could hear high-pitched noises, that's all."

"Oh," she said. "And could he?"

I shook my head. "I'm afraid not."

"What a pity." She took a drink, and ice tinkled against the glass. "Well, if you've no more use for it, do you think I could have my whistle back?"

"Of course." I dug into my money belt, brought out the whistle, and gave it to her. I saw Humber's astonishment and Adams' spasm of fury that Humber's search had missed so elementary a hiding place.

"Thank you," she said, putting the whistle in her pocket. "What are your plans now? Another stable job? You know," she said to Humber, smiling. "I'm surprised you let him go. He rode better than any lad we've ever had in Father's stables. You were lucky to have him."

I had not ridden well for Humber. He began to say heavily, "He's not at all good . . ." when Adams smoothly interrupted him.

"I think we have underestimated Roke, Hedley. Lady Elinor, I am sure Mr. Humber will take him back on your recommendation, and never let him go again."

"Splendid," she said warmly.

Adams was looking at me with his hooded gaze to make sure I had appreciated his little joke. I didn't think it very funny.

"Take your helmet off," he said. "You're indoors and in front of a lady. Take if off."

"I think I'll keep it on," I said equably. And I could have done with a full suit of armor to go with it. Adams was not used to my contradicting him, and he shut his mouth with a snap.

Humber said, puzzled, "I don't understand why you bother with Roke, Lady Elinor. I thought your father got rid of him for . . . well . . . molesting you."

"Oh, no." She laughed. "That was my sister. But it wasn't true, you know. It was all made up." She swallowed the last of her drink and with the best will in the world put the finishing touches to throwing me to the wolves. "Father made me promise not to tell anyone that it was all a story, but as you're Daniel's employer, you really ought to know that he isn't anything like as bad as he lets everyone believe."

There was a short, deep silence. Then I said, smiling, "That's the nicest reference I've ever had. . . . You're very kind."

"Oh, dear," she said, laughing. "You know what I mean . . . and I can't think why you don't stick up for yourself more."

"It isn't always advisable," I said, and raised an eyebrow at Adams. He showed signs of not appreciating my jokes either. He took Elinor's empty glass.

"Another gin and Campari?" he suggested.

"No, thank you. I must be going."

He put her glass down on the desk with his own, and said, "Do you think Roke would be the sort of man who'd need to swallow tranquilizers before he found the nerve to look after a difficult horse?"

"Tranquilizers? *Tranquilizers?* Of course not. I shouldn't think he ever took a tranquilizer in his life. Did you?" she said, turning to me and beginning to look puzzled.

"No," I said. I was very anxious for her to be on her way before her puzzlement grew any deeper. Only while she suspected nothing and learned nothing was she safe enough.

"But you said . . ." began Humber, who was still unenlightened.

"It was a joke. Only a joke," I told him. "Mr. Adams laughed about it quite a lot, if you remember."

"That's true. I laughed," said Adams somberly. At least he seemed willing for her ignorance to remain undisturbed, and to let her go.

"Oh." Elinor's face cleared. "Well . . . I suppose I'd better be getting back to college. I'm going to Slaw tomorrow for the weekend. . . . Do you have any message for my father, Daniel?"

It was a casual, social remark, but I saw Adams stiffen.

I shook my head.

"Well . . . it's been very pleasant, Mr. Humber. Thank you so much for the drink. I hope I haven't taken too much of your time."

She shook Humber's hand, and Adams', and finally mine.

"How lucky you came back for something. I thought I'd missed you . . . and that I could whistle for my whistle." She grinned.

I laughed. "Yes, it was lucky."

"Good-bye then. Good-bye, Mr. Humber," she said, as Adams opened the door for her. She said good-bye to him on the doorstep, where he remained, and over Humber's shoulder I watched through the window as she walked across to her car. She climbed in, started the engine, waved gaily to Adams, and drove out of the yard. My relief at seeing her go was even greater than my anxiety about getting out myself.

Adams stepped inside, shut the door, locked it, and put the key in his pocket. Humber was surprised. He still did not understand.

He said, staring at me, "You know, Roke doesn't seem the same. And his voice is different."

"Roke, damn him to hell, is God knows what."

The only good thing in the situation that I could see was that I no longer had to cringe when he spoke to me. It was quite a relief to be able to stand up straight for a change. Even if it didn't last long.

"Do you mean it is Roke, and not Elinor Tarren, after all, who knows about the whistle?"

"Of course," said Adams impatiently. "For Christ's sake, don't you understand anything? It looks as though October planted him on us, though how in hell he knew . . ."

"But Roke is only a stable lad."

"Only," said Adams savagely. "But that doesn't make it any better. Stable lads have tongues, don't they? And eyes? And look at him. He's not the stupid worm he's always seemed."

He picked up one of the glasses and smashed it violently against the wall.

"No one would take his word against yours," said Humber.

"No one is going to take his word at all."

"What do you mean?"

"I'm going to kill him," said Adams.

"I suppose that might be more satisfactory." Humber sounded as if he were discussing putting down a horse.

"It won't help you," I said. "I've already sent a report to the Stewards."

"We were told that once before," said Humber, "but it wasn't true."

"It is, this time."

Adams said violently, "Report or no report, I'm going to kill him. There are other reasons. . . ." He broke off, glared at me, and said, "You fooled me. *Me.* How?"

I didn't reply. It hardly seemed a good time for light conversation.

"This one," said Humber reflectively, "has a motorcycle."

I remembered that the windows in the office's washroom were all too small to escape through. The door to the yard was locked, and Humber stood in front of his desk, between me and the window. Yelling could only bring Cass, not the poor rabble of lads, who didn't even know I was there, and wouldn't bother to help me in any case. Both Adams and Humber were taller and heavier than I was, Adams a good deal so. Humber had his stick and I didn't know what weapon Adams proposed to use; and I had never been in a serious fight in my life. The next few minutes were not too delightful a prospect.

On the other hand I was younger than they and, thanks to the hard work they had exacted, as fit as an athlete. Also I had the crash helmet. And I could throw things . . . Perhaps the odds weren't impossible after all.

A polished wooden chair with a leather seat stood by the wall near the door. Adams picked it up and walked toward me. Humber, remaining still, slid his stick through his hands and held it ready.

I felt appallingly vulnerable.

Adams' eyes were more opaque than I had ever seen them, and the smile which was growing on his mouth didn't reach them. He said loudly, "We might as well enjoy it. They won't look too closely at a burned-out smash."

He swung the chair. I dodged it all right but in doing so got within range of Humber, whose stick landed heavily on top of my shoulder, an inch from my ear. I stumbled and fell, and rolled; and stood up just in time to avoid the chair as Adams crashed it down. One of the legs broke off as it hit the floor, and Adams bent down and picked it up. A solid, straight, square-edged chair leg with a nasty sharp point where it had broken from the seat.

Adams smiled more, and kicked the remains of the chair into a corner.

"Now," he said, "we'll have some sport."

If you could call it sport, I suppose they had it.

Certainly after a short space of time they were still relatively unscathed, while I had added some more bruises to my collection, together with a fast-bleeding cut on the forehead from the sharp end of Adams' chair leg. But the crash helmet hampered their style considerably, and I discovered a useful talent for dodging. I also kicked.

Humber, being a slow mover, stayed at his post guarding the window and slashed at me whenever I came within his reach. As the office was not large, this happened too often. I tried from the beginning either to catch hold of one of the sticks, or to pick up the broken chair, or to find something to throw, but all that happened was that my hands fared badly, and Adams guessed my intentions regarding the chair and made sure I couldn't get hold of it. As for throwing things, the only suitable objects in that bare office were on Humber's desk, behind Humber.

Because of the cold night on the hillside, I was wearing two jerseys under my jacket, and they did act as some sort of cushion; but Adams particularly hit very hard, and I literally shuddered whenever he managed to connect. I had had some idea of crashing out through the window, glass and all, but they gave me no chance to get there, and there was a limit to the time I could spend trying.

In desperation I stopped dodging and flung myself at Humber. Ignoring Adams, who promptly scored two fearful direct hits, I grasped my ex-employer by the lapels, and with one foot on the desk for leverage, swung him around and threw him across the narrow room. He landed with a crash against the filing cabinets.

There on the desk was the green glass paperweight. The size of a cricket ball. It slid smoothly into my hand, and in one unbroken movement I picked it up, pivoted on my toes, and flung it straight at Humber where he sprawled off balance barely ten feet away.

It took him centrally between the eyes. A sweet shot. It knocked him unconscious. He fell without a sound.

I was across the room before he hit the floor, my hand stretching out for the green glass ball, which was a better weapon to me than any stick or broken chair. But Adams understood too quickly. His arm went up.

I made the mistake of thinking one more blow would make no real difference and didn't draw back from trying to reach the paperweight even when I knew Adams' chair leg was on its way down. But this time, because I had my head down, the crash helmet didn't save me. Adams hit me below the rim of the helmet, behind the ear.

Dizzily twisting, I fell against the wall and ended up lying with my shoulders propped against it and one leg doubled underneath me. I tried to stand up, but there seemed to be no strength left in me anywhere. My head was floating. I couldn't see very well. There was a noise inside my ears.

Adams leaned over me, unsnapped the strap of my crash helmet, and pulled it off my head. That meant something, I thought groggily. I looked up. He was standing there smiling, swinging the chair leg. Enjoying himself.

In the last possible second my brain cleared a little and I knew that if I didn't do something about it, this blow was going to be the last. There was no time to dodge. I flung up my right arm to shield my undefended head, and the savagely descending piece of wood crashed into it.

It felt like an explosion. My hand felt numb and useless by my side.

What was left? Ten seconds. Perhaps less. I was furious. I particularly didn't want Adams to have the pleasure of killing me. He was still smiling. Watching to see how I would take it, he slowly raised his arm for the coup de grace.

No, I thought, no. There was nothing wrong with my legs. What on earth was I thinking of, lying there waiting to be blacked out when I still had two good legs? He was standing on my right. My left leg was bent under me and he took no special notice when I disentangled it and crossed it over in front of him. I lifted both my legs off the ground, one in front and one behind his ankles, then I kicked across with my right leg, locked my feet tight together, and rolled my whole body over as suddenly and strongly as I could.

Adams was taken completely by surprise. He overbalanced with wildly swinging arms and fell with a crash on his back. His own weight made the fall more effective from my point of view, because he was winded and slow to get up. I couldn't throw any longer with my numb right hand. Staggering to my feet, I picked the green glass ball up in my left hand and smashed it against Adams' head while he was still on his knees. It seemed to have no effect. He continued to get up. He was grunting.

Desperately I swung my arm and hit him again, low down on the back of his head. And this time he did go down; and stayed down.

I half fell beside him, dizzy and feeling sick, with pain waking up viciously all over my body and blood from the cut on my forehead dripping slowly onto the floor.

I don't know how long I stayed like that, gasping to get some breath back, trying to find the strength to get up and leave the place, but it can't really have been very long. And it was the thought of Cass, in the end, which got me to my feet. By that stage I would have been a pushover for a toddler, let alone the wiry little head lad.

Both of the men were lying in heaps on the ground, not stirring. Adams was breathing very heavily; snoring, almost. Humber's chest scarcely moved.

I passed my left hand over my face and it came away covered with blood. There must be blood all over my face, I thought. I couldn't go riding along the road covered in blood. I staggered into the washroom to rinse it off.

There were some half-melted ice cubes in the sink. Ice. I looked at it dizzily. Ice in the refrigerator. Ice clicking in the drinks. Ice in the sink. Good for stopping bleeding. I picked up a lump of it and looked in the mirror. A gory sight. I held the lump of ice on the cut and tried, in the classic phrase, to pull myself together. With little success.

After a while I splashed some water into the sink and rinsed all the blood off my face. The cut was then revealed as being only a couple of inches long and not serious, though still obstinately oozing. I looked around vaguely for a towel.

On the table by the medicine cupboard stood a glass jar with the stopper off and a teaspoon beside it. My glance flickered over it, looking for a towel, and then back, puzzled. I took three shaky steps across the room. There was something the jar should be telling me, I thought, but I wasn't grasping things very clearly.

A bottle of Phenobarbitone, in powder form, like the stuff I'd given Mickey every day for a fortnight. Only Phenobarbitone, that was all. I sighed.

Then it struck me that Mickey had had the last dose in the bottle. The bottle should be empty. Tipped out. Not full. Not a new bottle full to the bottom of the neck, with the pieces of wax from the seal still lying in crumbs on the table beside it. Someone had just opened a new bottle of soluble Phenobarbitone and used a couple of spoonfuls.

Of course. For Kandersteg.

I found a towel and wiped my face. Then I went back into the office and knelt down beside Adams to get the door key out of his pocket. He had stopped snoring.

I rolled him over.

There isn't a pretty way of saying it. He was dead.

Small trickles of blood had seeped out of his ears, eyes, nose, and mouth. I felt his head where I had hit him, and the dented bones moved under my fingers.

Aghast and shaking, I searched in his pockets and found the key. Then I stood up and went slowly over to the desk to telephone to the police.

The telephone had been knocked onto the floor, where it lay with the receiver off. I bent down and picked it up, clumsily left-handed, and my head swam with dizziness. I wished I didn't feel so ill. Straightening up with an effort, I put the telephone back on the desk. Blood started trickling down past my elbow. I hadn't the energy to wash it off again.

Out in the yard one or two lights were on, including the one in Kandersteg's box. His door was wide open and the horse himself, tied up by the head, was lashing out furiously in a series of kicks. He didn't look in the least sedated.

I stopped with my finger in the dial of the telephone, and felt myself go cold. My brain cleared with a click.

Kandersteg was not sedated. They wouldn't want his memory lulled. The opposite, in fact. Mickey had not been given any Phenobarbitone until he was clearly deranged.

I didn't want to believe what my mind told me: that one or more teaspoonfuls of soluble Phenobarbitone in a large gin and Campari would be almost certainly fatal.

Sharply I remembered the scene I had found in the office, the drinks, the anxiety on Humber's face, the enjoyment on Adams'. It matched the enjoyment I had seen when he thought he was killing me. He enjoyed killing. He had thought from what she had said that Elinor had guessed the purpose of the whistle, and he had wasted no time in getting rid of her.

No wonder he had raised no objections to her leaving. She would drive back to college and die in her room miles away, a silly girl who had taken an overdose. No possible connection with Adams or Humber.

And no wonder he had been so determined to kill me: not only because of what I knew about his horses, or because I had fooled him, but because I had seen Elinor drink her gin.

I didn't need too much imagination to picture the scene before I had arrived. Adams saying smoothly, "So you came to see if Roke had used the whistle?"

"Yes."

"And does your father know you're here? Does he know about the whistle?"

"Oh, no, I only came on impulse. Of course he doesn't know."

He must have thought her a fool, blundering in like that; but probably he was the sort of man who thought all women were fools, anyway.

"You'd like some ice in your drink? I'll get some. No bother. Just next door. Here you are, my dear, a strong gin and Phenobarbitone and a quick trip to heaven."

He had taken the same reckless risk of killing Stapleton, and it had worked. And who was to say that if I had been found in the next county over some precipice, smashed up in the ruins of a motor bike, and Elinor died in her college, he wouldn't have gotten away with two more murders?

If Elinor died.

My finger was still in the telephone dial. I turned it three times—nine, nine, nine. There was no answer. I rattled the button, and tried again. Nothing. It was dead, the whole telephone was dead. Everything was dead. Mickey was dead, Stapleton was dead, Adams was dead, Elinor . . . Stop it, stop it. I dragged my scattering wits together. If the telephone wouldn't work, someone would have to go to Elinor's college and prevent her from dying.

My first thought was that I couldn't do it. But who else? If I was right, she needed a doctor urgently, and any time I wasted on bumbling about finding another telephone or another person to go in my stead was just diminishing her chances. I could reach her in less than twenty minutes. By telephoning in Posset I could hardly get help for her any quicker.

It took me three shots to get the key in the keyhole. I couldn't hold the key at all in my right hand, and the left one was shaking. I took a deep breath, unlocked the door, walked out, and shut it behind me.

No one noticed me as I went out of the yard the way I had come and went back to the motor bike. But it didn't fire properly the first time I kicked the starter, and Cass came around the end of the row of boxes to investigate.

"Who's that?" he called. "Is that you, Dan? What are you doing back here?" He began to come toward me.

I stamped on the starter fiercely. The engine sputtered, coughed, and roared. I squeezed the clutch and kicked the bike into gear.

"Come back," yelled Cass. But I turned away from his hurrying figure, out of the gate and down the road to Posset, with gravel spurting under the tires.

The throttle was incorporated into the hand grip of the right-hand handlebar. One merely twisted it toward one to accelerate and away to slow down. Twisting the hand grip was normally easy. It was not easy that evening because once I had managed to grip it hard enough to turn it, the numbness disappeared from my arm with a vengeance. I damned nearly fell off before I was through the gate.

It was ten miles northeast to Durham. One and a half downhill to Posset, seven and a half across the moors on a fairly straight and unfrequented secondary road, one mile through the outskirts of the city. The last part, with turns and traffic and too much change of pace, would be the most difficult.

Only the knowledge that Elinor would probably die if I came off kept me on the motor bike at all, and altogether it was a ride I would not care to repeat.

I didn't know how many times I had been hit, but I didn't think a carpet had too much to tell me. I tried to ignore it and concentrate on the matter in hand.

Elinor, if she had driven straight back to college, could not have been there long before she began to feel sleepy. As far as I could remember, never having taken much notice, barbiturates took anything up to an hour to work. But barbiturate dissolved in alcohol was a different matter. Quicker. Twenty minutes to a half hour, perhaps. I didn't know. Twenty minutes from the time she had left the yard was easily enough for her to drive back safely. Then what? She would go up to her room; feel tired; lie down; and go to sleep.

During the time I had been fighting with Adams and Humber, she had been on her way to Durham. I wasn't sure how long I had wasted dithering about in the washroom in a daze, but she couldn't have been back in college much before I started after her. I wondered whether she would have felt ill enough to tell a friend, to ask for help; but even if she had, neither she nor anyone else would know what was the matter with her.

I reached Durham; made the turns; even stopped briefly for a red traffic light in a busy street; and fought down an inclination to go the last half mile at walking pace in order to avoid having to hold the throttle anymore. But my ignorance of the time it would take the poison to do irreparable damage added wings to my anxiety.

CHAPTER 18

IT WAS GETTING dark when I swung into the College entrance, switched off the engine, and hurried up the steps to the door. There was no one at the porter's desk and the whole place was very quiet. I ran down the corridors, trying to remember the turns, found the stairs, went up two flights. And it was then that I got lost. I had suddenly no idea which way to turn to find Elinor's room.

A thin, elderly woman with pince-nez was walking toward me carrying a sheaf of papers and a thick book on her arm. One of the staff, I thought.

"Please," I said, "which is Miss Tarren's room?"

She came close to me and looked at me. She did not approve of what she saw. What would I give, I thought, for a respectable appearance at this moment.

"Please," I repeated. "She may be ill. Which is her room?"

"You have blood on your face," she observed.

"It's only a cut . . . please tell me . . ." I gripped her arm. "Look, show me her room, then if she's all right and perfectly healthy I will go away without any trouble. But I think she may need help very badly. Please believe me . . ."

"Very well," she said reluctantly. "We will go and see. It is just around here . . . and around here."

We arrived at Elinor's door. I knocked hard. There was no answer. I bent down low to the keyhole. They key was in the lock on her side, and I could not see in

"Open it," I urged the woman, who was still eyeing me dubiously. "Open it, and see if she's all right."

She put her hand on the knob and turned it. But the door didn't budge. It was locked.

I banged on the door again. There was no reply.

"Now please listen," I said urgently. "As the door is locked on the inside, Elinor Tarren is in there. She doesn't answer because she can't. She needs a doctor very urgently indeed. Can you get hold of one at once?"

The woman nodded, looking at me gravely through the pince-nez. I wasn't sure that she believed me, but apparently she did.

"Tell the doctor she has been poisoned with Phenobarbitone and gin. About forty minutes ago. And please, please hurry. Are there any more keys to this door?"

"You can't push out the key that's already there. We've tried on other doors, on other occasions. You will have to break the lock. I will go and telephone." She retreated sedately along the corridor, still breathtakingly calm in the face of a wild-looking man with blood on his forehead and the news that one of her students was halfway to the coroner. A tough-minded university lecturer.

The Victorians who had built the place had not intended importunate men friends to batter down the girls' doors. They were a solid job. But in view of the thin woman's calm assumption that breaking in was within my powers, I didn't care to fail. I broke the lock with my heel, in the end. The wood gave way on the jamb inside the room, and the door opened with a crash.

In spite of the noise I had made, no students had appeared in the corridor. There was still no one about. I went into Elinor's room, switched on the light, and swung the door back into its frame behind me.

She was lying sprawled on top of her blue bedspread fast asleep, the silver hair falling in a smooth swath beside her head. She looked peaceful and beautiful. She had begun to undress, which was why, I supposed, she had locked her door, and she was wearing only a bra and briefs under a simple slip. All these garments were white with pink rosebuds and ribbons. Pretty. Belinda would have liked them. But in these circumstances they were too poignant, too defenseless. They increased my grinding worry.

The suit that Elinor had worn at Humber's had been dropped in two places on the floor. One stocking hung over the back of a chair; the other was on the floor just beneath her slack hand. A clean pair of stockings lay on the dressing table, and a blue woolen dress on a hanger was hooked onto the outside of the wardrobe. She had been changing for the evening.

If she hadn't heard me kicking the door in, she wouldn't wake by being touched, but I tried. I shook her arm. She didn't stir. Her pulse was normal, her breathing regular, her face as delicately colored as normal. Nothing looked wrong with her. I found it frightening.

How much longer, I wondered anxiously, was the doctor going to be? The door had been stubborn—or I had been weak, whichever way you looked at it—and it must have been more than ten minutes since the thin woman had gone to telephone.

As if on cue, the door swung open and a tidy, solid-looking middle-aged man in a gray suit stood there taking in the scene. He was alone. He carried a suitcase in one hand and a fire hatchet in the other. Coming in, he looked at the splintered wood, pushed the door shut, and put the ax down on Elinor's desk.

"That saved time, anyway," he said briskly. He looked me up and down without enthusiasm and gestured to me to get out of the way. Then he cast a closer glance at Elinor with her rucked-up slip and her long, bare legs, and said to me sharply, suspiciously, "Did you touch her clothes?"

"No," I said bitterly. "I shook her arm. And felt her pulse. She was lying like that when I came in."

Something, perhaps it was only my obvious weariness, made him give me a suddenly professional, impartial survey. "All right," he said, and bent down to Elinor.

I waited behind him while he examined her, and when he turned around

I noticed he had decorously pulled down her rumpled slip so that it reached smoothly to her knees.

"Phenobarbitone and gin," he said. "Are you sure?"

"Yes."

"Self-administered?" He started opening his case.

"No. Definitely not."

"This place is usually teeming with women," he said inconsequentially. "But apparently they're all at some meeting or another." He gave me another intent look. "Are you fit to help?"

"Yes."

He hesitated. "Are you sure?"

"Tell me what to do."

"Very well. Find me a good-sized jug and a bucket or large basin. I'll get her started first, and you can tell me how this happened later."

He took a hypodermic syringe from his case, filled it, and gave Elinor an injection into the vein on the inside of the elbow. I found a jug and a basin in the built-in cupboard.

"You've been here before," he observed, eyes again suspicious.

"Once," I said; and for Elinor's sake added, "I am employed by her father. It's nothing personal."

"Oh. All right, then." He withdrew the needle, dismantled the syringe, and quickly washed his hands.

"How many tablets did she take, do you know?"

"It wasn't tablets. Powder. A teaspoonful, at least. Maybe more."

He looked alarmed, but said, "That much would be bitter. She'd taste it."

"Gin and Campari . . . it's bitter anyway."

"Yes. All right. I'm going to wash out her stomach. Most of the drug must have been absorbed already, but if she had as much as that . . . well, it's still worth trying."

He directed me to fill the jug with tepid water, while he carefully slid a thickish tube down inside Elinor's throat. He surprised me by putting his ear to the long protruding end of it when it was in position, and he explained briefly that with an unconscious patient who couldn't swallow, one had to make sure the tube had gone into the stomach and not into the lungs. "If you can hear them breathe, you're in the wrong place," he said.

He put a funnel into the end of the tube, held out his hand for the jug, and carefully poured in the water. When what seemed to me a fantastic amount had disappeared down the tube, he stopped pouring, passed me the jug to put down, and directed me to push the basin near his foot. Then, removing the funnel, he suddenly lowered the end of the tube over the side of the bed and into the basin. The water flowed out again, together with all the contents of Elinor's stomach.

"Hm," he said calmly. "She had something to eat first. Cake, I should say. That helps."

I couldn't match his detachment.

"Will she be all right?" My voice sounded strained.

He looked at me briefly and slid the tube out.

"She drank the stuff less than an hour before I got here?"

"About fifty minutes, I think."

"And she'd eaten. . . . Yes, she'll be all right. Healthy girl. The injection I gave her—Megimide—is an effective antidote. She'll probably wake up in an hour or so. A night in the hospital, and it will be out of her system. She'll be as good as new."

I rubbed my hand over my face.

"Time makes a lot of difference," he said calmly. "If she'd lain here many hours . . . A teaspoonful; that must be twelve grains or more." He shook his head. "She would have died."

He took a sample of the contents of the basin for analysis, and covered the rest with a hand towel.

"How did you cut your head?" he said suddenly.

"In a fight."

"It needs stitching. Do you want me to do it?"

"Yes. Thank you."

"I'll do it after Miss Tarren has gone to the hospital. Dr. Pritchard said she would ring for an ambulance. They should be here soon."

"Dr. Pritchard?"

"The lecturer who fetched me in. My office is only around the corner. She telephoned and said a violent, blood-stained youth was insisting that Miss Tarren was poisoned, and that I'd better come and see." He smiled briefly. "You haven't told me how all this happened."

"Oh . . . it's such a long story," I said tiredly.

"You'll have to tell the police," he pointed out.

I nodded. There was too much I would have to tell the police. I wasn't looking forward to it. The doctor took out pen and paper and wrote a letter to go with Elinor to the hospital.

There was a sudden eruption of girls' voices down the passage, and a tramp of many scholarly feet, and the opening and shutting of doors. The students were back from their meeting; from Elinor's point of view, too soon, as they would now see her being carried out.

Heavier footsteps came right up to her room and knuckles rapped. Two men in ambulance uniform had arrived with a stretcher, and with economy of movement and time, they lifted Elinor between them, tucked her into blankets, and bore her away. She left a wake of pretty voices raised in sympathy and speculation.

The doctor swung the door shut behind the ambulance men and without more ado, took from his case a needle and thread to sew up my forehead. I sat on Elinor's bed while he fiddled around with disinfectant and the stitching.

"What did you fight about?" he asked, tying knots.

"Because I was attacked," I said.

"Oh?" He shifted his feet to sew from a different angle, and put his hand on my shoulder to steady himself. He felt me withdraw from the pressure and looked at me quizzically.

"So you got the worst of it?"

"No," I said slowly. "I won."

He finished the stitching and gave a final snip with the scissors.

"There you are, then. It won't leave much of a scar."

"Thank you." It sounded a bit weak.

"Do you feel all right?' he said abruptly. "Or is pale fawn tinged with gray your normal coloring?"

"Pale fawn is normal. Gray just about describes how I feel." I smiled faintly. "I got a bang on the back of the head, too."

He explored the bump behind my ear and said I would live. He was asking me how many other tender spots I had about me, when another heavy tramp of footsteps could be heard coming up the corridor, and presently the door was pushed open with a crash.

Two broad-shouldered, businesslike policemen stepped into the room.

They knew the doctor. It appeared that he did a good deal of police work in Durham. They greeted each other politely and the doctor started to say that Miss Tarren was on her way to the hospital. They interrupted him.

"We've come for him, sir," said the taller of them, pointing at me. "Stable lad, name of Daniel Roke."

"Yes, he reported Miss Tarren's illness . . ."

"No, sir, it's nothing to do with a Miss Tarren or her illness. We want him for questioning on another matter."

The doctor said, "He's not in very good shape. I think you had better go easy. Can't you leave it until later?"

"I'm afraid that's impossible, sir."

They both came purposefully over to where I sat. The one who had done the talking was a redheaded man about my own age with an unsmiling, wary face. His companion was slightly shorter, brown eyed, and just as much on guard. They looked as if they were afraid I was going to leap up and strangle them.

With precision, they leaned down and clamped hard hands around my forearms. The redhead, who was on my right, dragged a pair of handcuffs from his pocket, and between them they fastened them on my wrists.

"Better take it quietly, chum," advised the redhead, evidently mistaking my attempt to wrench my arm free of his agonizing grip as a desire to escape in general.

"Let . . . go," I said. "I'm not . . . running anywhere."

They did let go, and stepped back a pace, looking down at me. Most of the wariness had faded from their faces, and I gathered that they really had been afraid I would attack them. It was unnerving. I took two deep breaths to control the soreness of my arm.

"He won't give us much trouble," said the dark one. "He looks like death."

"He was in a fight," remarked the doctor.

"Is that what he told you, sir?" The dark one laughed.

I looked down at the handcuffs locked around my wrists; they were, I discovered, as uncomfortable as they were humiliating.

"What did he do?" asked the doctor.

The redhead answered. "He . . . er . . . he'll be helping in inquiries into an attack on a racehorse trainer he worked for and who is still unconscious, and on another man who had his skull bust right in."

"Dead?"

"So we are told, sir. We haven't actually been to the stables, though they say it's a shambles. We two were sent up from Clavering to fetch him, and that's where we're taking him back to, the stables being in our area, you see."

"You caught up with him very quickly," commented the doctor.

"Yes," said the redhead with satisfaction. "It was a nice bit of work by some of the lads. A lady here telephoned to the police in Durham about half an hour ago and described *him*, and when they got the general call from Clavering about the job at the stables, someone connected the two descriptions and told us about it. So we were sent up to see, and bingo . . . there was his motor bike, right number plate and all, standing outside the College door."

I lifted my head. The doctor looked down at me. He was disillusioned, disenchanted. He shrugged his shoulders and said in a tired voice, "You never know with them, do you? He seemed . . . well . . . not quite the usual sort of tearaway. And now this." He turned away and picked up his bag.

It was suddenly too much. I had let too many people despise me and done nothing about it. This was one too many.

"I fought because they attacked me," I said.

The doctor half turned around. I didn't know why I thought it was important to convince him, but it seemed so at the time.

The dark policeman raised an eyebrow and said to the doctor, "The trainer was his employer, sir, and I understand the man who died is a rich gentleman whose horses were trained there. The head lad reported the killing. He saw Roke belting off on his motor bike and thought it was strange, because Roke had been sacked the day before, and he went to tell the trainer about it, and found him unconscious and the other man dead."

The doctor had heard enough. He walked out of the room without looking back. What was the use of trying? Better just do what the redhead said, and take it quietly, bitterness and all.

"Let's be going, chum," said the dark one. They stood there, tense again, with watchful eyes and hostile faces.

I got slowly to my feet. Slowly, because I was perilously near to not being able to stand up at all, and I didn't want to seem to be asking for a sympathy I was clearly not going to get. But it was all right; once upright I felt better, which was psychological as much as physical, because they were then not two huge threatening policemen but two quite ordinary young men of my own height doing their duty, and very concerned not to make any mistakes.

It worked the other way with them, of course. I think they had subconsciously expected a stable lad to be very short, and they were taken aback to discover I wasn't. They became visibly more aggressive; and I realized that in the circumstances, and in those black clothes, I probably seemed to them, as Terence had once put it, a bit dangerous and hard to handle.

I didn't see any sense in getting roughed up anymore, especially by the law, if it could be avoided.

"Look," I sighed. "Like you said, I won't give you any trouble."

But I supposed they had been told to bring in someone who had gone berserk and smashed a man's head in, and they were taking no chances. Redhead took a fierce grip of my right arm above the elbow and shoved me over to the door, and once outside the passage, the dark one took a similar grip on the left.

The corridor was lined with girls standing in little gossiping groups. I stopped dead. The two policemen pushed me on. And the girls stared.

That old saying about wishing the floor would open and swallow one up suddenly took on a fresh personal meaning. What little was left of my sense of dignity revolted totally against being exhibited as a prisoner in front of so many intelligent and personable young women. They were the wrong age. The wrong sex. I could have stood it better if they had been men.

But there was no easy exit. It was a good long way from Elinor's room to the outside door, along those twisting corridors and down two flights of stairs, and every single step was watched by interested female eyes.

This was the sort of thing one wouldn't be able to forget. It went too deep. Or perhaps, I thought miserably, one could even get accustomed to being hauled around in handcuffs if it happened often enough. If one were used to it, perhaps one wouldn't care . . . which would be peaceful.

I did at least manage not to stumble, not even on the stairs, so to that extent something was saved from the wreck. The police car, however, into which I was presently thrust seemed a perfect haven in contrast.

I sat in front, between them. The dark one drove.

"Phew," he said, pushing his cap back an inch. "All those girls." He had blushed under their scrutiny and there was a dew of sweat on his forehead.

"He's a tough boy, is this," said Redhead, mopping his neck with a white handkerchief as he sat sideways against the door and stared at me. "He didn't turn a hair."

I looked straight ahead through the windshield as the lights of Durham began to slide past, and thought how little could be told from a face. That walk had been a torture. If I hadn't shown it, it was probably only because I had by then had months of practice of hiding my feelings and thoughts, and the habit was strong. I guessed—correctly—that it was a habit I would find strength in clinging to for some time to come.

I spent the rest of the journey reflecting that I had got myself into a proper mess and that I was going to have a very unpleasant time getting out. I had indeed killed Adams. There was no denying or ducking that. And I was not going to be listened to as a respectable solid citizen but as a murdering villain trying every dodge to escape the consequences. I was going to be taken at face value, which was very low indeed. That couldn't be helped. I had, after all, survived eight weeks at Humber's only because I looked like dregs. The appearance which had deceived Adams was going to be just as convincing to the police, and proof that in fact it already was sat on either side of me in the car, watchful and antagonistic.

Redhead's eyes never left my face.

"He doesn't talk much," he observed, after a long silence.

"Got a lot on his mind," agreed the dark one, with sarcasm.

The damage Adams and Humber had done gave me no respite. I shifted uncomfortably in my seat, and the handcuffs clinked. The lightheartedness with which I had gone in my new clothes to Slaw seemed a long, long time ago.

The lights of Clavering lay ahead. The dark one gave me a look of subtle enjoyment. A capture made. His purpose fulfilled. Redhead broke another long silence, his voice full of the same sort of satisfaction.

"He'll be a lot older when he gets out," he said.

I emphatically hoped not; but I was all too aware that the length of time I remained in custody depended solely on how conclusively I could show that I had killed in self-defense. I wasn't a lawyer's son for nothing.

The next hours were abysmal. The Clavering police force were collectively a hardened, cynical bunch suppressing as best they could a vigorous crime wave in a mining area with a high unemployment percentage. Kid gloves did not figure in their book. Individually they may have loved their wives and been nice to their children, but if so, they kept their humor and humanity strictly for leisure.

They were busy. The building was full of bustle and hurrying voices. They shoved me, still handcuffed, from room to room under escort and barked out intermittent questions. "Later," they said. "Deal with that one later. We've got all night for him."

I thought with longing of a hot bath, a soft bed, and a handful of aspirins. I didn't get any of them.

At some point late in the evening they gave me a chair in a bare, brightly lit little room, and I told them what I had been doing at Humber's and how I had come to kill Adams. I told them everything that had happened that day. They didn't believe me, for which one couldn't blame them. They immediately, as a matter of form, charged me with murder. I protested. Uselessly.

They asked me a lot of questions. I answered them. They asked them again. I answered. They asked the questions like a relay team, one of them taking over presently from another, so that they all appeared to remain full of fresh energy while I grew more and more tired. I was glad I did not have to maintain a series of lies in that state of continuing discomfort and growing fatigue, as it was hard to keep a clear head, even for the truth, and they were waiting for me to make a mistake.

"Now tell us what really happened."

"I've told you."

"Not all that cloak-and-dagger stuff."

"Cable to Australia for a copy of the contract I signed when I took on the job." For the fourth time I repeated my solicitor's address, and for the fourth time they didn't write it down.

"Who did you say engaged you?"

"The Earl of October."

"And no doubt we can check with him, too?"

"He's in Germany until Sunday."

"Too bad." They smiled nastily. They knew from Cass that I worked in October's stable. Cass had told them I was a slovenly stable lad, dishonest, easily frightened, and not very bright. As he had believed what he said, he had carried conviction.

"You got into trouble with his lordship's daughter, didn't you?"

Damn Cass, I thought bitterly, damn Cass and his chattering tongue.

"Getting your own back on him for sacking you, aren't you, by dragging his name into this?"

"Like you got your own back on Mr. Humber for sacking you yesterday."

"No. I left because I had finished my job there."

"For beating you, then?"

"No."

"The head lad said you deserved it."

"Adams and Humber were running a crooked racing scheme. I found them out, and they tried to kill me." It seemed to me it was the tenth time that I had said that without making the slightest impression.

"You resented being beaten. You went back to get even . . . It's a common enough pattern."

"No."

"You brooded over it and went back and attacked them. It was a shambles. Blood all over the place."

"It was my blood."

"We can group it."

"Do that. It's my blood."

"From that little cut? Don't be so stupid."

"It's been stitched."

"Ah, yes, that brings us back to Lady Elinor Tarren. Lord October's daughter. Got her into trouble, did you?"

"No."

"In the family way . . ."

"No. Check with the doctor."

"So she took sleeping pills . . ."

"No. Adams poisoned her." I had told them twice about the bottle of Phenobarbitone, and they must have found it when they had been at the stables, but they wouldn't admit it.

"You got the sack from her father for seducing her. She couldn't stand the disgrace. She took sleeping pills."

"She had no reason to feel disgraced. It was not she, but her sister, Patricia, who accused me of seducing her. Adams poisoned Elinor in gin and Campari. There are gin and Campari and Phenobarbitone in the office and also in the sample from her stomach."

They took no notice. "She found you had deserted her on top of everything else. Mr. Humber consoled her with a drink, but she went back to college and took sleeping pills."

"No."

They were skeptical, to put it mildly, about Adams' use of the flamethrower.

"You'll find it in the shed."

"This shed, yes. Where did you say it was?"

I told them again, exactly. "The field probably belongs to Adams. You could find out."

"It only exists in your imagination."

"Look and you'll find it, and the flamethrower."

"That's likely to be used for burning off the heath. Lots of farmers have them, around here."

They had let me make two telephone calls to try to find Colonel Beckett. His manservant in London said he had gone to stay with friends in Berkshire for Newbury races. The little local exchange in Berkshire was out of action, the operator said, because a water main had burst and flooded a cable. Engineers were working on it.

Didn't my wanting to talk to one of the top brass of steeplechasing convince them, I wanted to know?

"Remember that chap we had in here once who'd strangled his wife? Nutty as a fruitcake. Insisted on ringing up Lord Bertrand Russell, didn't he, to tell him he'd struck a blow for peace."

At around midnight one of them pointed out that even if—and, mind you, he didn't himself believe it—even if all I had said about being employed to find out about Adams and Humber was, against all probability, true, that still didn't give me the right to kill them.

"Humber isn't dead," I said.

"Not yet."

My heart lurched. Dear God, I thought, not Humber, too. Not Humber, too.

"You clubbed Adams with the walking stick, then?"

"No, I told you, with a green glass ball. I had it in my left hand and I hit him as hard as I could. I didn't mean to kill him, just to knock him out. I'm right-handed . . . I couldn't judge very well how hard I was hitting with my left."

"Why did you use your left hand, then?"

"I told you."

"Tell us again."

I told them again.

"And after your right arm was put out of action, you got on a motorcycle and rode ten miles to Durham? What sort of fools do you take us for?"

"The fingerprints of both my hands are on that paperweight. The right ones from when I threw it at Humber, and the left ones on top, from where I hit Adams. You have only to check."

"Fingerprints now," they said sarcastically.

"And while you're on the subject, you'll also find the fingerprints of my left hand on the telephone. I tried to call you from the office. My left-hand prints are on the top in the washroom . . . and on the key, and on the door handle, both inside and out. Or at least, they were. . . ."

"All the same, you rode that motor bike."

"The numbness had gone by then."

"And now?"

"It isn't numb now, either."

One of them came around beside me, picked up my right wrist, and pulled my arm up high. The handcuffs jerked and lifted my left arm as well. The bruises had all stiffened and were very sore. The policeman put my arm down again. There was a short silence.

"That hurt," one of them said at last, grudgingly.

"He's putting it on."

"Maybe . . ."

They had been drinking endless cups of tea all evening and had not given me any. I asked if I could have some then, and got it; only to find that the difficulty I had in lifting the cup was hardly worth it.

They began again.

"Granted Adams struck your arm, but he did it in self-defense. He saw you throw the paperweight at your employer and realized you were going to attack him next. He was warding you off."

"He had already cut my forehead open . . . and hit me several times on the body, and once on the head."

"Most of that was yesterday, according to the head lad. That's why you went back and attacked Mr. Humber."

"Humber hit me only twice yesterday. I didn't particularly resent it. The rest was today, and it was mostly done by Adams." I remembered something. "He took my crash helmet off when he had knocked me dizzy. His fingerprints must be on it."

"Fingerprints again."

"They spell it out," I said.

"Let's begin again at the beginning. How can we believe a yob like you?"

Yob. One of the leather boys. Tearaway. Rocker. I knew all the words. I knew what I looked like. What a millstone of a handicap.

I said despairingly, "There's no point in pretending to be a disreputable, dishonest stable lad if you don't look the part."

"You look the part all right," they said offensively. "Born to it, you were."

I looked at their stony faces, their hard, unimpressed eyes. Tough, efficient policemen who were not going to be conned. I could read their thoughts like glass: if I convinced them and they later found out it was all a pack of lies, they'd never live it down. Their instincts were all dead against having to believe. My bad luck.

The room grew stuffy and full of cigarette smoke and I became too hot in my jerseys and jacket. I knew they took the sweat on my forehead to be guilt, not heat, not pain.

I went an answering all their questions. They covered the ground twice more with undiminished zeal, setting traps, sometimes shouting, walking around me, never touching me again, but springing the questions from all directions. I was really much too tired for that sort of thing, because apart from the wearing-out effect of the injuries, I had not slept for the while of the previous night. Toward two o'clock I could hardly speak from exhaustion, and after they had woken me from a sort of dazed sleep three times in half an hour, they gave it up.

From the beginning I had known that there was only one logical end to that evening, and I had tried to shut it out of my mind, because I dreaded it. But there you are . . . you set off on a primrose path and if it leads to hell that's just too bad.

Two uniformed policemen, a sergeant and a constable, were detailed to put me away for the night, which I found involved a form of accommodation to make Humber's dormitory seem a paradise.

The cell was cubic, eight feet by eight, built of glazed bricks, brown to shoulder height and white above that. There was a small barred window too high to see out of, a narrow slab of concrete for a bed, a bucket with a lid on it in a corner, and a printed list of regulations on one wall. Nothing else. Bleak enough to shrink the guts; and I had never much cared for small enclosed spaces.

The two policemen brusquely told me to sit on the concrete. They removed my boots and the belt from my jeans, and also found and unbuckled the money belt underneath. They took off the handcuffs. Then they went out, shut the door with a clang, and locked me in.

The rest of that night was in every way rock bottom.

CHAPTER 19

IT WAS COOL and quiet in the corridors of Whitehall. A superbly mannered young man deferentially showed me the way and opened a mahogany door into an empty office.

"Colonel Beckett will not be long, sir. He has just gone to consult a colleague. He said I was to apologize if you arrived before he came back, and to ask if you would like a drink. And cigarettes are in the box, sir."

"Thank you." I smiled. "Would coffee be a nuisance?"

"By no means. I'll have some sent in straight away. If you'll excuse me?" He went out and quietly closed the door.

It rather amused me to be called "sir" again, especially by smooth civil servants barely younger than myself. Grinning, I sat down in the leather chair facing Beckett's desk, crossed my elegantly trousered legs, and lazily settled to wait for him.

I was in no hurry. It was eleven o'clock on Tuesday morning, and I had all day and nothing to do but buy a clockwise train for Jerry and book an air ticket back to Australia.

No noise filtered into Beckett's office. The room was square and high, and was painted a restful pale-greenish-gray color, walls, door, and ceiling alike. I supposed that here the furnishings went with rank; but if one were an outsider, one would not know how much to be impressed by a large but threadbare carpet, an obviously personal lampshade, or leather, brass-studded chairs. One had to belong, for these things to matter.

I wondered about Colonel Beckett's job. He had given me the impression that he was retired, probably on a full disability pension since he looked so frail in health, yet here he was with a well-established niche at the Ministry of Defense.

October had told me that in the war Beckett had been the sort of supply officer who never sent all left boots or the wrong ammunition. Supply officer. He had supplied me with Sparking Plug and the raw material containing the pointers to Adams and Humber. He'd had enough pull with the Army to dispatch in a hurry eleven young officer cadets to dig up the past history to obscure steeplechasers. What, I wondered, did he supply nowadays, in the normal course of events?

I suddenly remembered October's saying, "We thought of planting a stable lad. . . ." Not "I thought," but "We." And for some reason I was now sure that it had been Beckett, not October, who had originally suggested the plan; and that explained why October had been relieved when Beckett approved me at our first meeting.

Unexcitedly turning these random thoughts over in my mind, I watched two pigeons fluttering around the windowsill and tranquilly waited to say good-bye to the man whose staff work had ensured the success of the idea.

A pretty young woman knocked and came in with a tray on which stood a coffeepot, cream jug, and pale-green cup and saucer. She smiled, asked if I needed anything else, and when I said no, gracefully went away.

I was getting quite good at left-handedness. I poured the coffee and drank it black, and enjoyed the taste.

Snatches of the past few days drifted idly in and out of my thoughts. . . .

Four nights and three days in a police cell trying to come to terms with the fact that I had killed Adams. It was odd, but although I had often considered the possibility of being killed, I had never once thought that I myself might kill. For that, as for so much else, I had been utterly unprepared; and to have caused another man's death, however much he might have asked for it, needed a bit of getting over.

Four nights and three days of gradually finding that even the various ignominies of being locked up were bearable if one took them quietly, and feeling almost like thanking Redhead for his advice.

On the first morning, after a magistrate had agreed that I should stay where I was for seven days, a police doctor came and told me to strip. I couldn't, and he had to help. He looked impassively at Adams' and Humber's widespread handiwork, asked a few questions, and examined my right arm, which was black from the wrist to well above the elbow. In spite of the protection of two jerseys and a leather jacket the skin was broken where the chair leg had landed. The doctor helped me dress again and impersonally departed. I didn't ask him for his opinion, and he didn't give it.

For most of the four nights and three days I just waited, hour after silent hour. Thinking about Adams: Adams alive and Adams dead. Worrying about

Humber. Thinking of how I could have done things differently. Facing the thought that I might not get out without a trial . . . or not get out at all. Waiting for the soreness to fade from the bruises and failing to find a comfortable way of sleeping on concrete. Counting the number of bricks from the floor to the ceiling and multiplying by the length of the walls (subtract the door and window). Thinking about my stud farm and my sisters and brother, and about the rest of my life.

On Monday morning there was the by then familiar scrape of the door being unlocked, but when it opened it was not as usual a policeman in uniform, but October.

I was standing up, leaning against the wall. I had not seen him for three months. He stared at me for a long minute, taking in with obvious shock my extremely disheveled appearance.

"Daniel," he said. His voice was low and thick.

I didn't think I needed any sympathy. I hooked my left thumb into my pocket, struck a faint attitude, and raised a grin.

"Hullo, Edward."

His face lightened, and he laughed.

"You're so bloody tough," he said. Well . . . let him think so.

I said, "Could you possibly use your influence to get me a bath?"

"You can have whatever you like as soon as you are out."

"Out? For good?"

"For good." He nodded. "They are dropping the charge."

I couldn't disguise my relief.

He smiled sardonically. "They don't think it would be worth wasting public funds on trying you. You'd be certain of getting an absolute discharge. Justifiable homicide, quite legitimate."

"I didn't think they believed me."

"They've done a lot of checking up. Everything you told them on Thursday is now the official version."

"Is Humber . . . all right?"

"He regained consciousness yesterday, I believe. But I understand he isn't lucid enough yet to answer questions. Didn't the police tell you that he was out of danger?"

I shook my head. "They aren't a very chatty lot here. How is Elinor?"

"She's well. A bit weak, that's all."

"I'm sorry she got caught up in things. It was my fault."

"My dear chap, it was her own," he protested. "And Daniel . . . about Patty . . . and the things I said . . ."

"Oh, nuts to that," I interrupted. "It was a long time ago. When you said 'Out,' did you mean out now, this minute?"

He nodded. "That's right."

"Then let's not hang around in here anymore, shall we? If you don't mind?"

He looked about him and involuntarily shivered. Meeting my eyes, he said apologetically, "I didn't foresee anything like this."

I grinned faintly. "Nor did I."

We went to London, by car up to Newcastle and then by train. Owing to some delay at the police station discussing the details of my return to attend Adams' inquest, any cleaning-up processes would have meant our missing the seats October had reserved on the nonstop Flying Scotsman, so I caught it as I was.

October led the way into the dining car, but as I was about to sit down opposite him, a waiter caught hold of my elbow.

"Here, you," he said roughly. "Clear out. This is first class only."

"I've got a first-class ticket," I said mildly.

"Oh, yes? Let's see it, then."

I produced from my pocket the piece of white cardboard.

H sniffed and gestured with his head toward the seat opposite October. "All right, then." To October he said, "If he makes a nuisance of himself, just tell me, sir, and I'll have him chucked out, ticket or no ticket." He went off, swaying to the motion of the accelerating train.

Needless to say, everyone in the dining car had turned around to have a good view of the rumpus.

Grinning, I sat down opposite October. He looked exceedingly embarrassed.

"Don't worry on my account," I said. "I'm used to it." And I realized that I was indeed used to it at last and that no amount of such treatment would ever trouble me again. "But if you would rather pretend you don't know me, go ahead." I picked up the menu.

"You are insulting."

I smiled at him over the menu. "Good."

"For deviousness, Daniel, you are unsurpassed. Except possibly by Roddy Beckett."

"My dear Edward . . . have some bread."

He laughed, and we traveled amicably to London together, as ill-assorted-looking a pair as ever rested heads on British Railways' starched white antimacassars.

I POURED SOME more coffee and looked at my watch. Colonel Beckett was twenty minutes late. The pigeons sat peacefully on the windowsill and I shifted gently in my chair, but with patience, not boredom, and thought about my visit to October's barber, and the pleasure with which I had had my hair cut short and sideburns shaved off. The barber himself (who had asked me to pay in advance) was surprised, he said, at the results.

"We look a lot more like a gentleman, don't we? But might I suggest . . . a shampoo?"

Grinning, I agreed to the shampoo, which left a high-water mark of cleanliness about midway down my neck. Then, at October's house, there was the fantastic luxury of stepping out of my filthy disguise into a deep hot bath, and the strangeness with which I afterward put on my own clothes. When I had finished dressing, I took another look in the same long mirror. There was the man who had come from Australia four months ago, a man in a good dark-gray suit, a white shirt, and a navy-blue silk tie; there was his shell, anyway. Inside I wasn't the same man, nor ever would be again.

I went down to the crimson drawing room, where October walked solemnly all around me, gave me a glass of bone-dry sherry, and said, "It is utterly unbelievable that you are the young tyke who just came down with me on the train."

"I am," I said dryly, and he laughed.

He gave me a chair with its back to the door, where I drank some sherry and listened to him making social chitchat about his horses. He was hovering around the fireplace, not entirely at ease, and I wondered what he was up to.

I soon found out. The door opened and he looked over my shoulder and smiled.

"I want you both to meet someone," he said.

I stood up and turned around.

Patty and Elinor were there, side by side.

They didn't know me at first. Patty held out her hand politely and said, "How do you do?" clearly waiting for her father to introduce us.

I took her hand in my left one and guided her to a chair.

"Sit down," I suggested. "You're in for a shock."

She hadn't seen me for three months, but it was only four days since Elinor had made her disastrous visit to Humber's. She said hesitantly, "You don't look the same . . . but you're Daniel." I nodded, and she blushed painfully.

Patty's bright eyes looked straight into mine, and her pink mouth parted. "You . . . are you really? Danny boy?"

"Yes."

"Oh." A blush as deep as her sister's spread up from her neck, and for Patty that was shame indeed.

October watched their discomfiture. "It serves them right," he said, "for all the trouble they have caused."

"Oh, no," I exclaimed. "It's too hard on them . . . and you still haven't told them anything about me, have you?"

"No," he agreed uncertainly, beginning to suspect there was more for his daughters to blush over than he knew, and that his surprise meeting was not an unqualified success.

"Then tell them now, while I go and talk to Terence . . . and Patty . . . Elinor. . . ." They looked surprised at my use of their first names and I smiled briefly. "I have a very short and defective memory."

They both looked subdued when I went back, and October was watching them uneasily. Fathers, I reflected, could be very unkind to their daughters without intending it.

"Cheer up," I said. "I'd have had a dull time in England without you two."

"You were a beast," said Patty emphatically, sticking to her guns.

"Yes . . . I'm sorry."

"You might have told us," said Elinor in a low voice.

"Nonsense," said October. "He couldn't trust Patty's tongue."

"I see," said Elinor slowly. She looked at me tentatively. "I haven't thanked you for . . . for saving me. The doctor told me . . . all about it." She blushed again.

"Sleeping beauty." I smiled. "You looked like my sister."

"You have a sister?"

"Two," I said. "Sixteen and seventeen."

"Oh," she said, and looked comforted.

October flicked me a glance. "You are far too kind to them, Daniel. One of them made me loathe you and the other nearly killed you, and you don't seem to care."

I smiled at him. "No. I don't. I really don't. Let's just forget it."

So in spite of a most unpromising start, it developed into a good evening, the girls gradually losing their embarrassment and even, by the end, being able to meet my eyes without blushing.

When they had gone to bed, October put two fingers into an inner pocket, drew out a slip of paper, and handed it to me without a word. I unfolded it. It was a check for ten thousand pounds. A lot of noughts. I looked at them in silence. Then, slowly, I tore the fortune in half and put the pieces in the ashtray.

"Thank you very much," I said. "But I can't take it."

"You did the job. Why not accept the pay?"

"Because . . ." I stopped. Because what? I was not sure I could put it into words. It had something to do with having learned more than I had bargained for. With diving too deep. With having killed. All I was sure of was that I could no longer bear the thought of receiving money for it.

"You must have a reason," said October, with a touch of irritation.

"Well, I didn't really do it for the money, to start with, and I can't take that sort of sum from you. In fact, when I get back I am going to repay you all that is left of the first ten thousand."

"No," he protested. "You've earned it. Keep it. You need it for your family."

"What I need for my family, I'll earn by selling horses."

He stubbed out his cigar. "You're so infuriatingly independent that I don't know now how you could face being a stable lad. If it wasn't for the money, why did you do it?"

I moved in my chair. The bruises still felt like bruises. I smiled faintly, enjoying the pun.

"For kicks, I suppose."

THE DOOR OF the office opened, and Beckett unhurriedly came in. I stood up. He held out his hand, and remembering the weakness of his grasp, I put out my own. He squeezed gently and let go.

"It's been a long time, Mr. Roke."

"More than three months," I agreed.

"And you completed the course."

I shook my head, smiling. "Fell at the last fence, I'm afraid."

He took off his overcoat and hung it on a knobbed hat rack, and unwound a gray woolen scarf from his neck. His suit was nearly black, a color which only enhanced his extreme pallor and emphasized his thinness; but his eyes were as alive as ever in the gaunt, shadowed sockets. He gave me a long, observant scrutiny.

"Sit down," he said. "I am sorry to have kept you waiting. I see they've looked after you all right."

"Yes, thank you." I sat down again in the leather chair, and he walked around and sank carefully into the one behind his desk. His chair had a high back and arms, and he used them to support his head and elbows.

"I didn't get your report until I came back to London from Newbury on Sunday morning," he said. "It took two days to come from Posset and didn't reach my house until Friday. When I had read it, I telephoned to Edward at Slaw and found he had just been rung up by the police at Clavering. I then telephoned to Clavering myself. I spent a good chunk of Sunday hurrying things up for you in various conversations with ever higher ranks, and early on Monday it was decided finally in the office of the Director of Public Prosecutions that there was no charge for you to answer."

"Thank you very much," I said.

He paused, considering me. "You did more toward extricating yourself than Edward or I did. We only confirmed what you had said and had you freed a day or two sooner than you might have been. But it appeared that the Clavering police had already discovered from a thorough examination of the stable office that everything you had told them was borne out by the facts. They had also talked to the doctor who had attended Elinor, and to Elinor herself, and taken a look at the shed with the flamethrower, and cabled to your solicitor for a summary of the contract you signed with Edward. By the time I spoke with them, they were taking the truth of your story for granted, and were agreeing that you had undoubtedly killed Adams in self-defense.

"Their own doctor—the one who examined you—had told them straight away that the amount of crushing your right forearm had sustained was entirely consistent with it having been struck by a force strong enough to have smashed in your skull. He was of the opinion that the blow had landed more or less along the inside of your arm, not straight across it, thus causing extensive damage to muscles and blood vessels, but no bone fracture; and he told them that it was perfectly possible for you to have ridden a motor bike a quarter of an hour later if you had wanted to enough."

"You know," I said, "I didn't think they had taken any notice of a single word I said."

"Mmm. Well, I spoke to one of the C.I.D. men who questioned you last Thursday evening. He said they brought you in as a foregone conclusion, and that you looked terrible. You told them a rigmarole which they thought was nonsense, so they asked a lot of questions to trip you up. They thought it would be easy. The C.I.D. man said it was like trying to dig a hole in a rock with your fingernails. They all ended up by believing you, much to their own surprise."

"I wish they'd told me," I sighed.

"Not their way. They sounded a tough bunch."

"They seemed it, too."

"However, you survived."

"Oh, yes."

Beckett looked at his watch. "Are you in a hurry?"

"No." I shook my head.

"Good . . . I've rather a lot to say to you. Can you lunch?"

"Yes. I'd like to."

"Fine. Now, this report of yours." He dug the handwritten foolscap pages out of his inside breast pocket and laid them on the table. "What I'd like you to do now is to lop off the bit asking for reinforcements and substitute a description of the flamethrower operation. Right? There's a table and chair over there. Get to work, and when it's done I'll have it typed."

When I had finished the report, he spent some time outlining and discussing the proceedings which were to be taken against Humber, Cass, and Jud Wilson, and also against Soupy Tarleton and his friend Lewis Greenfield. He then looked at his watch again and decided it was time to go out for lunch. He took me to his club, which seemed to me to be dark brown throughout, and we ate steak, kidney, and mushroom pie, which I chose because I could manage it unobtrusively with a fork. He noticed, though.

"That arm still troubling you?"

"It's much better."

He nodded and made no further comment. Instead he told me of a visit he had paid the day before to an elderly uncle of Adams', whom he had discovered living in bachelor splendor in Piccadilly.

"Young Paul Adams, according to his uncle, was the sort of child who would have been sent to reform school if he hadn't had rich parents. He was sacked from Eton for forging checks and from his next school for persistent gambling. His parents bought him out of scrape after scrape and were told by a psychiatrist that he would never change, or at least not until late middle age. He was their only child. It must have been terrible for them. The father died when Adams was twenty-five, and his mother struggled on, trying to keep him out of too disastrous trouble. About five years ago she had to pay out a fortune to hush up a scandal in which Adams had apparently broken a youth's arm for no reason at all, and she threatened to have him certified if he did anything like that again. And a few days later she fell out of her bedroom window and died. The uncle, her brother, says he has always thought that Adams pushed her."

"Very likely, I should think," I agreed.

"So you were right about his being psychopathic."

"Well, it was pretty obvious."

"From the way he behaved to you personally?"

"Yes."

We had finished the pie and were on to cheese. Beckett looked at me curiously and said, "What sort of life did you really have at Humber's stable?"

"Oh"—I grinned—"you could hardly call it a holiday camp."

He waited for me to go on and when I didn't, he said, "Is that all you've got to say about it?"

"Yes, I think so. This is very good cheese."

We drank coffee and a glass of brandy out of a bottle with Beckett's name on it, and eventually walked back slowly to his office.

As before, he sank gratefully into his chair and rested his head and arms, and I as before sat down opposite him on the other side of his desk.

"You are going back to Australia soon, I believe?" he said.

"Yes."

"I expect you are looking forward to getting back into harness."

I looked at him. His eyes stared straight back, steady and grave. He waited for an answer.

"Not altogether."

"Why not?"

I shrugged, grinned. "Who likes harness?"

There was no point, I thought, in making too much of it.

"You are going back to prosperity, good food, sunshine, your family, a beautiful house, and a job you do well . . . isn't that right?"

I nodded. It wasn't reasonable not to want to go to all that.

"Tell me the truth," he said abruptly. "The unvarnished, honest truth. What is wrong?"

"I'm a discontented idiot, that's all," I said lightly.

"Mr. Roke." He sat up slightly in the chair. "I have a good reason for asking these questions. Please give me truthful answers. What is wrong with your life in Australia?"

There was a pause, while I thought and he waited. When at last I answered, I was aware that whatever his good reason was, it would do no harm to speak plainly.

"I do a job which I ought to find satisfying, and it leaves me bored and empty."

"A diet of milk and honey, when you have teeth," he observed.

I laughed. "A taste for salt, perhaps."

"What would you have been had your parents not died and left you with three children to bring up?"

"A lawyer, I think, though possibly . . ." I hesitated.

"Possibly what?"

"Well . . . it sounds a bit odd, especially after the last few days . . . A policeman."

"Ah," he said softly. "That figures." He leaned his head back again and smiled.

"Marriage might help you feel more settled," he suggested.

"More ties," I said. "Another family to provide for. The rut forever."

"So that's how you look at it. How about Elinor?"

"She's a nice girl."

"But not for keeps?"

I shook my head.

"You went to a great deal of trouble to save her life," he pointed out.

"It was only because of me that she got into danger at all."

"You couldn't know that she would be so strongly attracted to you and find you so . . . er . . . irresistible that she would drive out to take another look at you. When you went back to Humber's to extricate her, you had already finished the investigation, tidily, quietly, and undiscovered. Isn't that right?"

"I suppose so. Yes."

"Did you enjoy it?"

"Enjoy it?" I repeated, surprised.

"Oh, I don't mean the fracas at the end, or the hours of honest toil you had to put in." He smiled briefly. "But the . . . shall we say, the chase?"

"Am I, in fact, a hunter by nature?"

"Are you?"

"Yes."

There was a silence. My unadorned affirmative hung in the air, bald and revealing.

"Were you afraid at all?" His voice was matter-of-fact.

"Yes."

"To the point of incapacity?"

I shook my head.

"You knew Adams and Humber would kill you if they found you out. What effect did living in perpetual danger have on you?" His voice was so clinical that I answered with similar detachment.

"It made me careful."

"Is that all?"

"Well, if you mean was I in a constant state of nervous tension, then no, I wasn't."

"I see." Another of his small pauses. Then he said, "What did you find hardest to do?"

I blinked, grinned, and lied. "Wearing those loathsome pointed shoes."

He nodded as if I had told him a satisfying truth. I probably had. The pointed shoes had hurt my pride, not my toes.

And pride had got the better of me properly when I visited Elinor in her college and hadn't been strong enough to play an oaf in her company. All the stuff about Marcus Aurelius was sheer showing off, and the consequences had been appalling. It didn't bear thinking of, let alone confessing.

Beckett said idly, "Would you ever consider doing something similar again?"

"I should think so. Yes. But not like that."

"How do you mean?"

"Well . . . I didn't know enough, for one thing. For example, it was just luck that Humber always left his office unlocked, because I couldn't have got in if he hadn't. I don't know how to open doors without keys. I would have found a camera useful; I could have taken films of the blue ledger in Humber's office, and so on, but my knowledge of photography is almost nil. I'd have got the exposures wrong. Then I had never fought anyone in my life before. If I'd known anything at all about unarmed combat, I probably wouldn't have

killed Adams or been so much battered myself. Apart from all that, there was
nowhere where I could send you or Edward a message and be sure you would
receive it quickly. Communications, in fact, were pretty hopeless."

"Yes. I see. All the same, you did finish the job in spite of those disad-
vantages."

"It was luck. You couldn't count on being lucky twice."

"I suppose not." He smiled. "What do you plan to do with your twenty
thousand pounds?"

"I . . . er . . . plan to let Edward keep most of it."

"What do you mean?"

"I can't take that sort of money. All I ever wanted was to get away for a
bit. It was he who suggested such a large sum, not me. I don't think he
thought I would take on the job for less, but he was wrong. . . . I'd have done
it for nothing if I could. All I'll accept is the amount it has cost for me to be
away. He knows; I told him last night."

There was a long pause. Finally Beckett sat up and picked up the telephone. He dialed and waited.

"This is Beckett," he said. "It's about Daniel Roke. . . . Yes, he's here."
He took a postcard out of an inner pocket. "Those points we were discussing
this morning . . . I have had a talk with him. You have your card?"

He listened for a moment, and leaned back again in his chair. His eyes
were steady on my face.

"Right?" He spoke into the telephone. "Numbers one to four can all have
an affirmative. Number five is satisfactory. Number six, his weakest spot . . .
he didn't maintain his role in front of Elinor Tarren. She said he was good
mannered and intelligent. No one else thought so. . . . Yes, I should say so,
sexual pride . . . apparently only because Elinor is clever as well as pretty,
since he kept it up all right with her younger sister. . . . Yes . . . oh, undoubtedly it was his intellect as much as his physical appearance which attracted her. . . . Yes, very good-looking; I believe you sometimes find that
useful. . . . No, he doesn't. He didn't look in the mirror in the washroom at
the club or in the one on the wall here. . . . No, he didn't admit it today, but
I'd say he is well aware he failed on that point. . . . Yes, rather a harsh lesson.
It may still be a risk, or it may have been sheer unprofessionalism. . . . Your
Miss Jones could find out, yes."

I didn't particularly care for this dispassionate vivisection, but short of walking out, there seemed to be no way of avoiding it. His eyes still looked at me expressionlessly.

"Number seven . . . normal reaction. Eight, slightly obsessive, but that's all the better from your point of view." He glanced momentarily down at the card he held in his hand. "Nine . . . well, although he is British by birth and spent his childhood here, he is Australian by inclination, and I doubt whether subservience comes easily. . . . I don't know, he wouldn't talk about it. . . . No, I wouldn't say he had a vestige of a martyr complex, he's clear on that. . . . Of course you never get a perfect one. . . . It's entirely up to you. . . . Number ten? The three *b*'s. I should say definitely not to the first two, much too proud. As for the third, he's the type to shout for help. Yes, he's still here. Hasn't moved a muscle. . . . Yes, I do think so. . . . All right. . . . I'll ring you again later."

He put down the receiver. I waited. He took his time, and I refrained consciously from fidgeting under his gaze.

"Well?" he said at last.

"If you're going to ask what I think, the answer is no."

"Because you don't want to, or because of your sisters and brother?"

"Philip is still only thirteen."

"I see." He made a weak-looking gesture with his hand. "All the same, I'd better make sure you know what you are turning down. The colleague who kept me late this morning, and to whom I was talking just now, runs one of the counterespionage departments—not only political but scientific and industrial, and anything else which crops up. His section is rather good at doing what you have done—becoming an inconspicuous part of the background. It's amazing how little notice even agents take of servants and workmen . . . and his lot have had some spectacular results. They are often used to check on suspected immigrants and political refugees who may not be all they seem, not by watching from afar, but by working for or near them day by day. And recently, for instance, several of the section have been employed as laborers on top-secret construction sites. . . . There have been some disturbing leaks of security—complete site plans of secret installations have been sold abroad—and it was found that a commercial espionage firm was getting information through operatives actually putting brick on brick and photographing the building at each stage."

"Philip," I said, "is only thirteen."

"You wouldn't be expected to plunge straight into such a life. As you yourself pointed out, you are untrained. There would be at least a year's instruction in various techniques before you were given a job."

"I can't," I said.

"Between jobs all his people are given leave. If a job takes as long as four months, like the one you have just done, they get about six weeks off. They never work more than nine months in a year, if it can be helped. You could often be home in the school holidays."

"If I am not there all the time, there won't be enough money for fees and there won't be any home."

"It is true that the British Government wouldn't pay you as much as you earn now," he said mildly, "but there are such things as full-time stud managers."

I opened my mouth and shut it again.

"Think about it," he said gently. "I've another colleague to see. . . . I'll be back in an hour."

He levered himself out of the chair and slowly walked out of the room.

The pigeons fluttered peaceably on the windowsill. I thought of the years I had spent building up the stud farm, and what I had achieved there. In spite of my comparative youth, the business was a solid success, and by the time I was fifty, I could with a bit of luck put it among the top studs in Australia and enjoy a respected, comfortably off, influential middle age.

What Beckett was offering was a lonely life of unprivileged jobs and dreary lodgings, a life of perpetual risk which could very well end with a bullet in the head.

Rationally there was no choice. Belinda and Helen and Philip still needed a secure home with the best I could do for them as a father-substitute. And no sensible person would hand over to a manager a prosperous business and become instead a sort of sweeper-up of some of the world's smaller messes . . . one couldn't put the job any higher than that.

But irrationally . . . with very little persuasion I had already left my family to fend for themselves, for as Beckett said, I wasn't of the stuff of martyrs; and the prosperous business had already driven me once into a pit of depression.

I knew now clearly what I was, and what I could do.

I remembered the times when I had been tempted to give up, and hadn't. I remembered the moment when I held Elinor's dog whistle in my hand and my mind made an almost muscular leap at the truth. I remembered the satisfaction I felt in Kandersteg's scorched enclosure, knowing I had finally uncovered and defeated Adams and Humber. No sale of any horse had ever brought so quiet and complete a fulfillment.

The hour passed. The pigeons defecated on the window and flew away. Colonel Beckett came back.

"Well?" he said. "Yes or no?"

"Yes."

He laughed aloud. "Just like that? No questions or reservations?"

"No reservations. But I will need time to arrange things at home."

"Of course." He picked up the telephone receiver. "My colleague will wish you to see him before you go back." He rested his fingers on the dial. "I'll make an appointment."

"And one question."

"Yes?"

"What are the three b's of number ten?"

He smiled secretly, and I knew he had intended that I should ask: which meant that he wanted me to know the answer. Devious indeed. My nostrils twitched as if at the scent of a whole new world. A world where I belonged.

"Whether you could be bribed or bludgeoned or blackmailed," he said casually, "into changing sides."

He dialed the number, and altered my life.

See why Dick Francis was named
Grand Master by the Mystery Writers of America!

THE
DICK FRANCIS
COMPANION

Jean Swanson and Dean James

0-425-18187-1

The definitive source to the works of the
three-time Edgar Allan Poe Award-winning
New York Times bestselling author,
including book-by-book synopses,
little-known facts, and quotes.